No Man's Land

No Man's Land

A Novel

Simon Tolkien

NAN A. TALESE

Doubleday

NEW YORK   LONDON   TORONTO   SYDNEY   AUCKLAND

Copyright © 2016 by Simon Tolkien

All rights reserved. Published in the United States by Nan A. Talese/Doubleday, a division of Penguin Random House LLC, New York, and distributed in Canada by Random House of Canada, a division of Penguin Random House Canada Limited, Toronto. Originally published in hardcover in Great Britain by HarperCollins Publishers, London, in 2016.

www.nanatalese.com

DOUBLEDAY is a registered trademark of Penguin Random House LLC. Nan A. Talese and the colophon are trademarks of Penguin Random House LLC.

The extract on page 283 is copyright Siegfried Sassoon, by kind permission of the Estate of George Sassoon.

Book design by Maria Carella
Jacket design by Claire Ward © HCPL
Jacket images: (background) Shutterstock;
(poppy) Stephen Mulcahey / Arcangel Images;
(soldiers) The Art Archive / Alamy

Library of Congress Cataloging-in-Publication Data
Names: Tolkien, Simon, 1959– author.
Title: No man's land : a novel / Simon Tolkien.
Description: First American edition. | New York : Nan A. Talese/Doubleday, 2017.
Identifiers: LCCN 2016038311 (print) | LCCN 2016047163 (ebook) |
ISBN 9780385541978 (hardcover) | ISBN 9780385541985 (ebook)
Subjects: LCSH: England—Social life and customs—20th century—Fiction. | World War, 1914–1918—England—Fiction. | Social mobility—England—Fiction. | Social status—England—Fiction. | BISAC: FICTION / Historical. | FICTION / War & Military. | FICTION / Coming of Age. | GSAFD: Historical fiction.
Classification: LCC PR6120.O44 N6 2017 (print) | LCC PR6120.O44 (ebook) |
DDC 823/.92—dc23
LC record available at https://lccn.loc.gov/2016038311

MANUFACTURED IN THE UNITED STATES OF AMERICA

1 3 5 7 9 10 8 6 4 2

First American Edition

For my daughter,
Anna Tolkien

This book honours the memory of
my grandfather, J. R. R. Tolkien,
who fought on the Somme
between July and October 1916.

———•••———

Prologue

———

London

Unreal city,
Under the blue fog of a winter dawn,
A crowd flowed over London Bridge, so many,
I had not thought death had undone so many.

T. S. Eliot, *The Wasteland,* 1922

1900

The first world Adam knew was the street. It came to him through his senses without mental dilution, filling up his head with sounds and smells and images that he couldn't begin to unravel. Lying in bed at night with his eyes closed, he could see Punch and Judy bludgeoning each other with rolling pins, just as if they were right there in front of him. Down they went and up they came, again and again: gluttons for punishment. He knew that Benson, the rag-and-bone man with the blue scar across his chin, was pulling the strings behind the tattered red curtain, but that didn't make the garishly painted puppets any less real. Just thinking about them made him laugh until his insides hurt, in the same way that he laughed years later in the bioscope when he saw Charlie Chaplin with his bow legs and stick and black moustache, marching confidently up the road towards his next disaster.

For a long time there was no cinema in Islington where they lived. There didn't need to be—the street was a complete world, turning on its axis to the sound of the waltzes that flew up on a thousand notes out of the brightly painted barrel organ as the bald-headed grinder methodically turned the handle, looking neither to right nor left. He was solemn and sad and apparently unconnected to everything around him, even his monkey, which had a blue cap on its head with a tassel that bobbed up and down as it jumped around with the collection box. Sometimes the children danced to the music, weaving around each other in elaborate patterns, watching their feet to keep clear of the leaking tar and the horse manure. Some of them had no shoes and the tar was hard to get off the skin. You had to use margarine and even that didn't always work.

The street was familiar and exotic all at the same time: a maelstrom of life. The muffin man carried his wares in a tray balanced on the top of his head; it swayed as he walked but it never fell. The fishmonger wheeled a barrow and, if he dared to look inside, the dead black eyes of the cod staring up out of the white-crystal ice made Adam shiver. And the flycatcher wore a tall black hat with long strips of sticky paper fastened to it, all covered with dead insects, calling out dolefully as he passed: "Flies, flies, catch them alive!"

On Saturday nights in summer Adam could look out of his bedroom window and see Baxter, the fat butcher in his bloodstained greasy white apron, standing in the doorway of his shop, lit up by the flare of a paraffin lamp, shouting out to the worse-for-wear men leaving the Cricketers' Arms on the corner: "Buy me leg, buy me leg." It was because the poor man couldn't afford to keep the meat cold overnight, Adam's father told him; by morning it would be good for nothing.

And once a month two bent-over old men came slowly up the street, pushing a small cart with long handles, from which they sold solid blocks of salt. "Any salt please, lah-di?" they asked in their singsong foreign-sounding voices, holding up the white salt in their black fingerless gloves like an offering. Sometimes Adam's mother bought from them and sometimes she did not. It depended on whether there was any money in the house.

Adam's mother, Lilian, believed in God but Adam's father, Daniel Raine, did not. He believed in something else instead, called socialism, which Adam didn't understand until later, even though his father tried to explain it to him sometimes. Adam's mind wasn't yet ready for abstract concepts. God was different. He couldn't *see* God, of course, but he could feel his presence in the high fluted arches of the Holy Martyr Church with the soaring white spire that he went to with his mother on Sunday mornings. God—as Adam pictured him—had a huge head and a white snowy beard and he lived up above the grey London clouds, gazing down at his creation with big eagle eyes. He was surrounded by a throng of ancient saints who had slightly shorter beards and a lesser number of winged angels who did not. They were extra eyes in case God needed them.

And God was not happy. In fact he was angry, filled with "a righteous rage" according to Father Paul, an old priest with red mottled cheeks and thick grey bushy eyebrows that met in a wiry tangle in the middle of his wrinkled forehead, who was the rector of the Holy Martyr. God was incensed not by the poverty and injustice that Adam's father complained about, but by the wickedness and debauchery, the unbridled lechery and fornication, that was going on day and night down below. Adam wasn't clear what these sins were but he knew they were bad, very bad. "Repent; repent now before it is too late," the rector shouted at them all from the high, elaborately carved pulpit. Adam watched fascinated as beads of perspiration formed in the crevices of the old man's face and trickled down, dripping in globules on to his surplice. He sat very still, clutching his mother's hand, and wanted to urinate.

"Will Daddy go to hellfire?" he asked her as they crossed the park afterwards, going back home under a leaden November sky.

"No," Lilian said. "Definitely not. Your father is a good man."

"But he doesn't believe," said Adam. "And Father Paul says that if you don't believe, you can't be saved. That's what he said. I heard him."

"Jesus died for all of us," she said, squeezing her son's hand. "He loves us. You need to know that." And he was grateful to his mother for the reassurance, even though what she said didn't make much sense. Adam didn't like to think about Jesus if he could help it, bleeding to death on the big wooden cross, stuck up there under the hot sun in that horrible Golgotha place with all those Roman soldiers gawping at him; and he was secretly glad when his father said that the Bible was all lies, stories that the rich had made up to keep the poor in their place, doing the rich man's bidding.

" 'The opium of the people': that's what Karl Marx called religion and he was absolutely right," Daniel Raine shouted at his wife across the kitchen. "It's the promise of heaven to justify a hell while we're alive. The hell we're living in now," he added for good measure.

When his father raised his voice, Adam was frightened and slipped down under the table where he could push the black-and-silver-painted train with real tiny wheels that his father had made for him up and down the patterned lines on the oilcloth-covered floor. They were like the web of railway tracks he had seen at King's Cross Station when his mother had taken him there in the summer to see the steam trains coming and going in all their smoky glory.

He could still see her from where he was, standing at the range, stirring a pot with a big wooden spoon. There were onions in the soup she was preparing; he could smell them, and perhaps that was why there were tears in her eyes. Adam didn't know and he would have liked to run to her and put his arms around her thin waist, encircling her in a tight embrace, but he knew instinctively that he had to stay where he was; that he couldn't stop the trouble because the argument was about more than God and the man called Marx that his father so admired. It was about his father being out of work again and there not being enough money to pay for what they needed to buy.

The next day two men in brown overalls came with a horse cart and took away the piano that stood in pride of place in the front room of their small house. They brought a paper and said it was by order because Adam's father hadn't kept up with the payments. Adam knew what "by order" meant. It meant there was nothing you could do; it was the same as if God had ordered it as a punishment because you had sinned. There was no right of appeal.

Lilian had played the instrument sometimes in the evening, her long beautiful fingers caressing the keys, gliding in a space of their own. Her music was different from the barrel-organ waltzes the hurdy-gurdy man played—thinner and frailer and sadder, full of sweetness and loss, hinting at places far away that had vanished from the world. And Daniel would sit on an upright chair in the corner of the room, listening to his wife play with bowed head and folded hands, quite still; as though he was one of the devout worshippers in church on Sunday mornings, Adam thought, although he would never have dared say so.

Adam watched his father when the men came; watched the way

his hands balled up into useless fists, rocking from side to side as he shifted his weight from one foot to the other and back again; and watched as he beat his head uselessly against the frame of the front door after they had gone.

"It doesn't matter," Lilian said, laying her hand gently on the back of her husband's shoulder. "We don't need it, Daniel . . ."

"But we do," he shouted, refusing to turn around. "Life should be about more than grubbing around, trying to stay alive. We're not animals to be given just enough food and fuel to keep producing goods for the capitalists to sell until we get old and sick and are no more use to them any more. We're entitled to more than that; we must be."

It was as if he was asking a question but Lilian didn't have an answer, unless she told her husband to trust in the Lord, and she knew better than to do that. And he was wrong about the fuel. They had none, and that evening Daniel broke up the chairs and burnt them in the hearth. They ate bread and dripping in the light of the flames and later that night Adam heard his mother coughing on the other side of the thin wall, on and on into the small hours, making Adam's chest constrict in sympathy so he couldn't sleep and prayed instead to the big angry God in the clouds to give his father work.

God didn't answer at first. The building trade was always slow in winter and Daniel hadn't helped his prospects over the years by his largely fruitless efforts to persuade his fellow workers to stand up for themselves and join the union. What jobs there were came in dribs and drabs, and Adam's mother had to go out to work as a charwoman, bringing back scraps of meat to feed her family. "Leavings from the rich man's table," Daniel called them in disgust, but the family missed them when Lilian fell ill, and he had to go and ask for help from the thin-lipped, tight-fisted relieving officer known to everyone on the street as "Old Dry Bones."

Daniel came back furious. "Told me that I should put my new suit on next time I came," he said. "I told him that if I had a new suit I'd pawn it to get what I need rather than coming cap in hand to the likes of him. Like going in front of a judge and jury it was."

Adam's Sunday clothes had long ago been pawned. To begin

with, his mother would take them in on Monday morning and then queue up on Saturday night to redeem them for use the next day. And at church she told Adam not to kneel but just to sit on the edge of the bench and lean forward, as she was worried about him getting the trousers dirty. But when she got sick she stopped going to church and the pawn ticket stayed where it was, gathering dust on the front-room mantelpiece, across from the bare patch on the wall where the piano had once stood.

"God will understand," she told her son. But Adam wasn't sure she was right. He didn't miss his tight-fitting Sunday clothes or his visits to the church with the high arches, but he thought that their non-attendance would make God significantly less inclined to help his family in their hour of need.

That said it wasn't as if his father was being singled out for misfortune. Other families on the street were faring even worse. Some couldn't pay their rent and took off without warning, piling their belongings into over-laden donkey carts so that the bailiffs couldn't seize them when they came to levy distress. There was even a local barrow firm that advertised moves by moonlight. Friends that Adam made playing around the drinking fountain out in the street changed from day to day.

On Christmas Eve the gypsies set up a boxing ring in the marketplace and a tall black-eyed Romany in a frock coat, with red lapels buttoned over a dirty lace cravat, offered five shillings to anyone foolish enough to challenge his heavy, muscled champion; double if you managed to last a three-minute round; and a sovereign if you knocked him down. The man in the frock coat held up the gold coin, twirling it between his finger and thumb so that it glinted in the winter sunlight, attracting the attention of the crowd.

The gypsy fighter sat waiting on a folding stool in the corner of the ring, which seemed barely able to hold his weight. He was stripped to the waist in defiance of the cold and behind him an old grey-haired woman with long silver hoop rings in her ears stood with her legs akimbo, massaging oil into his broad back.

Adam was fascinated by the whole spectacle, although he didn't want to get too close. He remembered what the children sang on the street: "Take the earrings from your ears and put them through your nose and the gypsies'll take you." But from where he was, standing up on his tiptoes, he could see the coloured tattoos on the big fighter's biceps—a snake that writhed and a girl whose chest expanded each time he flexed his muscles. Thick black curly hair sprouted up on the top of the champion's flat-shaped head, and his tiny eyes set back under a domed forehead seemed to be focused on nothing at all.

Staring up at the gypsies, Adam only became aware of his father's decision to take the challenge when it was too late to try and stop him.

"Hold these for me," Daniel said, handing Adam his shirt and jacket. "And stay where you are. I'll be back in a minute, I promise," he added with a smile, seeing the look of panic on his son's face.

"Don't do it, Dad. He'll knock you out," Adam shouted, but his father had already climbed up into the ring and the gypsy man in the frock coat was leading him forward to introduce him to the crowd.

"Ladies and gentlemen, here's a brave volunteer. What's your name, mister?"

"Daniel. Daniel Raine," said Adam's father in a loud clear voice, and Adam felt a rush of pride springing up side by side with his fear. His father had to be scared—the gypsy fighter was built like a house—but he certainly wasn't showing it.

"And what do you do, Danny?" asked the man in the frock coat.

"I'm a builder when I have the work. But now I don't, which is why I'm up here. I sure as hell wouldn't be otherwise," said Adam's father, glancing over at his opponent. The crowd laughed and began to shout out words of encouragement.

"Well, good luck to you," said the man in the frock coat, beckoning his own fighter to approach. Standing, the man was even more formidable than he had looked sitting down. It was almost comical the way he towered over Adam's father, watching impassively as his opponent took off his shoes and pulled on a pair of old boxing gloves. Adam felt sick. He wished his mother was there because she would know what to do and for a moment he thought of running home to fetch her, but he knew that by the time he got back it would be too late and the fight would be over. His father had told him to stay where he was; he could always close his eyes if he couldn't bear to look.

At a signal from the man in the frock coat, the old woman in the corner rang a brass bell and the fight began. It was obvious from the start that Daniel had no chance of winning. He was a short, slightly built man and he didn't have the power in his arm to fell the ox-like strongman he was up against. But his focus on survival instead of victory seemed to help his cause. He was quick and courageous and he had the support of the crowd. Some of them seemed to know him and shouted out his name: "You can do it, Daniel. Don't let him get too close."

Time and again the huge gypsy swung his arms and missed as Daniel ducked or leant away, jabbing at his opponent's chest as he passed. Adam counted down the seconds. The round was supposed to last three minutes and it had surely been at least that already, and his father was still on his feet. But he was tiring. Adam could see that. And now the gypsy had him hemmed into the corner of the ropes, the same one where the old woman was still standing—Adam could see she had the bell in her hand but she wouldn't ring it. And his father couldn't stay where he was—he feinted to the left and spun away to the right and the gypsy almost missed with the haymaker punch he'd aimed at Daniel's nose. Instead he caught him on the side of the cheek and Adam's father fell down on the boards, momentarily stunned.

The man in the frock coat started to count to ten in a loud voice, hamming up the drama for the benefit of the crowd. Adam couldn't remember ever feeling more terrified. Everything seemed frozen, hanging suspended in the thin cold air. He stared at his father, focusing all his concentration on his prone figure, willing him to move. And, as if in response, he did. First with one arm and then with the other, Daniel hauled himself up on the ropes into a standing position. And behind him the gypsy woman rang the bell and the crowd roared their approval. The round was over. And he hadn't lost.

Walking home, Daniel made light of what had happened. He seemed pleased with himself, happy with the ten shillings that he had won, jingling the silver coins in his pocket.

"My winnings will pay for Christmas," he said. "Your mother will be pleased."

He looked over at his son and saw to his surprise that the boy was crying. "It's all right," he said, putting his arm round Adam's shoulder. "Nothing bad was going to happen. I knew what I was doing."

Suddenly something inside Adam snapped. "No, it's not all right," he shouted, the pent-up fear exploding out of him. "He could've killed you, but you didn't think. You never think." He didn't know he was beating on his father's chest with his fists until his father lifted him up and held him away.

He'd never shouted at his father like this and he expected him to be angry, but he wasn't. Instead he looked conscience-stricken, full of remorse.

"I'm sorry, son," he said, putting Adam down. "You're right. I didn't think, and I should have. It's in my nature, I suppose, to rush into things, to look for challenges wherever I can find them. Next time I'll try to be more sensible. Will that work for you?" he asked, squatting down and looking Adam in the eye.

Adam nodded, using his father's proffered handkerchief to dry his tears.

"Come on," said Daniel, looking across the street. "I know what we need." Weaving their way between horses, carts and bicycles, they crossed the road and went into a brightly lit confectioner's shop. It was a perfect heaven, but an earthly version, very different from the one they talked about in church. Row upon row of cylinder-shaped show-glasses were lined up on polished mahogany shelves containing liquorice shoestrings and peppermint drops and brandy balls and tiger eyes, and on the counter was a set of brass scales and weights for measuring out purchases. But Adam wanted none of them; before they had even entered the shop he had had his mind made up and his heart set on a perfectly sculpted brown toffee pig standing on its own in the window.

On the way home he clasped it tight to his chest, while his father clutched a hunk of ice to his bruised cheek. And at the door Daniel stuck out his hand for Adam to shake. "Quite a day we've had of it, haven't we, old man? Quite an adventure!" And Adam nodded: the pig was the best Christmas present he'd ever had.

The New Year brought fog: the kind of London fog that was like a moving creature, sucking at the air as it moved, enshrouding the people who had to endure its wet embrace. Dirty and acrid, it crept inside their clothes, clinging clammily to the skin, breeding sickness. The traffic slowed almost to a halt and men and horses reared up out of nowhere, suddenly illuminated by the gas-fired streetlights.

One evening Adam was out with his father and they bought two jacket potatoes at a stall, holding them in their palms to warm their ice-cold hands before they began to eat. After a few minutes the fog began to clear a little and they could see a large shed-like building on the other side of the road with "Salvation Army" emblazoned on a board above the main door.

"Come with me," said Daniel, suddenly excited. And taking his son's hand they went inside. For a moment Adam's eyes had to adjust to the light before he was able to take in the great size of the hall and the huge number of men inside it. They were sitting in rows on long benches all facing forward, and most of them were resting their heads on their folded arms, which were themselves supported by the backs of the benches in front of them.

"Listen," Daniel told his son, putting his finger to his lips to hush the questions about the place that the boy was clearly about to ask. And after a moment Adam could hear it—the deep rhythmic snoring emanating from hundreds of mouths and nostrils. Everyone was asleep, sitting down.

"They can't lie down. It's not allowed," Daniel said, pointing to a notice on the wall. "If they pay a penny they can sit here all night and keep warm but they've got to stay upright. "Penny sit-up": that's the name of this place, and it's better than the public library, where they have to sleep standing up, hanging on to the newspaper stands. And anyway the library's closed at night, like the parks. That's what the iron railings are for—to keep the paupers out," he added with a bitter laugh.

"But who are they? Where do they come from?" asked Adam, awed by this mass of sleeping humanity, the rows of destitute men stretching endlessly away as far as he could see.

"They're the poor of London. Men who have worked hard all their lives but have now outlived their purpose. Chewed up, spat out and left to die by the capitalists who've got no use for them any more. Look! They've got nothing to look forward to but their deaths, and that'll come soon enough."

Adam was frightened by the anger in his father's voice. He wanted to leave this terrible place behind. But Daniel hadn't finished.

"The strangest part is not that the poor suffer but that they accept their suffering," he went on, and it was almost as if he was talking to himself; as if he had forgotten his son standing beside him. "Ask them, and they'd say they are truly grateful for the crumbs that are thrown to them from the rich man's table and, if they had the vote, they'd vote without thinking for the perpetuation of the system that keeps them poor and cold, and will keep their children poor and cold when they are gone. But I won't accept that," he said passionately, turning back to his son. "I want a better world for you to live in: one where men are valued for who they are, not for what the rich can get out of them. It may never happen, but it's still worth fighting for. Can you understand that, Adam? I know it's hard, but it's important—what I'm trying to tell you."

The boy nodded slowly. His father had used a lot of long words that he hadn't heard before; and with his patched clothes and thin, unshaven face Daniel hardly looked convincing. In fact he looked almost as disreputable as the paupers sleeping on the benches in front of them. But the flame of his father's conviction burnt more strongly than ever in his bright blue eyes and Adam felt in that moment that he would follow his father into any danger, even that lion's den in Babylon that Father Paul had talked about in church, which had given him nightmares for days afterwards. It was a man called Daniel just like his father who had gone in there and come out unscathed, Adam remembered.

An attendant approached them, asking if they wanted to sit down, and his enquiry broke the spell.

"I'm sorry, Adam. I hope I didn't frighten you," Daniel said as they began to walk home through the gas-lit streets. "I forget how young you are sometimes."

"I'm not young. I'm old enough to go to school," said Adam.

"So you are. So you are," said Daniel with a smile, as if realizing the fact for the first time. "Well, we shall have to see about that, shan't we?"

School expanded Adam's horizons. Beyond his street, beyond his tiny terraced house with the small patch of ground at the back where his father dug at the hard sooty soil with a broken spade and tried to raise shrivelled vegetables under his mother's dripping washing line. Into a new world.

Lilian gave her son a St. Christopher medal to wear around his neck because he would be a traveller now, walking to school and back with his slate hung by a string over his shoulder. And she rubbed ointment into his head each morning to stop the lice coming. It smelt of sarsaparilla and Adam hated it, but it was better than being singled out and sent home when Matron ran her steel comb hard through the children's hair on her tours of inspection.

School was hot with combustion stoves where the children were allowed to warm their flasks of tea in the morning, and noisy with the sound of their coughing as they tried in vain to expel the coke fumes that they breathed down into their chests. All day the windows of the schoolroom were misted over with the humidity and the children drew faces in the fog. Some of them were unflattering pictures of Old Beaky, the first-form teacher, who was too short-sighted to see what they were doing. He had a tassel on his mortar board that reminded Adam of the organ grinder's monkey. It made Adam laugh, and, not for the first time or the last, his inability to control his mirth got him into trouble. Beaky needed to make an example and he punished Adam by shutting him up in the cellar. It was dark and wet and there was a creature, maybe a rat, rustling somewhere, and Adam was frightened. And when his father found out what had happened, he went with Adam to the school and shouted at Beaky who backed away into a corner of the classroom with his hat and tassel wobbling ridiculously on top of his old bald head.

After that school was better. Beaky taught his class about the Empire on which the sun never set and showed them a map of the world covered with pink. The pink was British and London where they were was the capital, the centre of everything. Sometimes the children sang "Rule Britannia" and threw their pens up into the air at the climax so that the nibs stuck in the ceiling.

Adam had boots too now, replacing the leaking, broken shoes that he had worn through the long winter. Just as in previous years, the building trade had picked up with the coming of warmer weather and his father was back in regular work. His mother coughed less and they had meat to eat on Sundays, and could go to the eel pie shop up on the High Street in the evenings where they wrapped the food in sheets from the penny newspapers which Adam read as he ate: accounts of stabbings and poisonings that made him shiver even as the hot food warmed his insides.

In the summer the travelling fair came to Islington and encamped on Highbury Fields. Adam went there every day, greedy to experience everything it had to offer. He rode swinging boats that went high up into the air, turning his stomach over when they fell, and the joy wheel that spun the riders round and round, whirling up their clothes so he could feast his eyes on the girls' white drawers and bare pink knees. He ate hot chestnuts and black peas and wiggle waggle, a toffee that blackened his face and lips; and gazed entranced at the strongest man on earth, who was twice the size of the champion his father had boxed in the market square, and at the human beast from the jungle who snarled and roared in his cage just like a wild animal. There were real beasts too—an elephant that stood on its hind legs and a lion on a steel chain that looked sad and dejected, not lion-like at all. At night Adam left his bedroom window open so that he could hear the roaring of the menagerie coming to him across the rooftops.

Beyond the fairground, beyond Islington, London went on forever, the roads and the rails and the tramlines snaking outward like the Gorgon's hair in the story his mother had told him about Perseus, the hero who had killed the monster by avoiding her eye, taking care only to look at her reflection in the face of his shining silver shield.

At weekends he helped the cabbies at Euston and King's Cross, loading and unloading bags, and used the pennies he earned to ride the brightly painted trams as they swayed through the city streets—he liked it best in the evenings when the flashes from their overhead cables lit up the darkness like blue lightning.

Or he would sit on the open upper deck of the new motor buses feeling the wind and the rain on his face as he looked down at the people in the streets—people everywhere, poor and rich, idle and hurrying, no end to them. He wondered where he fitted in amongst them all, what his place might be in this mad rushing world that stopped for no one.

He was getting older. He gambled with his school friends for cigarette cards on the canal towpath. If the policeman caught them, he passed his hat round for a bribe, the price of turning a blind eye, but often they just threw it in the water and then dived in themselves, surfacing on the other side, laughing. Always laughter surging up through Adam like life, making it possible to forget for a moment about his troubles: his mother's sickness, his father's anger, the endless need for money.

Everything changed when Halley's Comet came. That's how Adam remembered it afterwards. He was transfixed by its brightness—the flash of dazzling light drawn across the still night sky. He knew it was only gas and dust and rock held together by gravity, but he couldn't shake off the sense of foreboding that everyone seemed to feel as the comet approached its zenith. And when the King died it seemed as if the doomsayers might be right.

Adam went to Westminster with his parents to watch the funeral procession. Daniel had been going to stay at home but relented at the last moment. "I'm coming to watch, not to mourn," he said defiantly, refusing to put on his newly purchased best suit which Lilian had laid out for him, hoping for a change of mind. "He was king of his class, king of the one per cent who own half the wealth of this country and want to keep it that way," he added as he pulled on his working clothes and straightened his cloth cap.

"Daniel, please don't speak ill of the dead," said his long-suffering wife. She'd heard it all before—every statistic, every argument. Repeating them didn't change anything.

"He embodied them," Daniel went on, ignoring her. "I'll say that much for him. Gorging his way through four huge meals a day while the rest of us were left to starve; filling his fat stomach with disgusting rich food. I'm surprised the old devil lived as long as he did."

Something inside Lilian snapped. "Don't come if you don't want to. You're not doing me any favours. In fact, to tell you the truth, I'd prefer it if you didn't," she told her husband. She was soft-spoken by nature and her harsh tone startled him, making him look up. "You talk to me like I'm not here, like I don't exist except as an audience for your politics. But I do exist. I'm flesh and blood and tears and pain and—" She broke off, unable to go on as she strangled the cry in her throat, but the tears on her cheeks bore witness to the depth of her distress.

Out on the half-landing, Adam, uncomfortable in his tight Sunday suit, stood watching his parents' argument through the open door of their bedroom, the bed between them covered with a cheap eiderdown, the dust motes in the air illuminated by the morning sun coming in through the open window, a cheap wooden cross the only ornament on the mildew-stained wall. The moment burnt into his memory like an X-ray photograph.

Daniel was white-faced, standing up straight as if he had been struck, searching for words. He wanted to go to his wife, beg her forgiveness, but he couldn't, forced back by the intensity of her emotion.

"I'm sorry, Lil," he said, stumbling over his words. "You're right. I get carried away sometimes." He reached out his hand across the bed, but she ignored it, wiping her tears away instead with the back of her arm.

"It's for Adam's sake I want to go," she said. "It's history when the King of England dies and our son needs to see it. What you do is your own affair."

Daniel nodded, accepting the reproof. He picked up his best suit and began to change his clothes.

In the streets everyone was in black. The women seemed like giant crows behind heavy crape veils. Everywhere was closed up, silent, except for the muffled tolling of the church bells and the monotonous tread of the mourners walking from all directions towards Westminster.

It was still early when they reached Hyde Park and they were able to work their way to the front of the crowd by the time the draped gun carriage with the King's coffin came into view, followed immediately by a small dog, the King's fox terrier, Caesar, led by a kilted Highland soldier. But that was the last homely touch. The new king, George, rode behind his father's coffin at the front of a group of men dressed in wildly extravagant uniforms. The bright May sun reflected on their shining white-plumed helmets, half blinding Adam as they came abreast of where he was standing. And then for no apparent reason the cortège stopped—only for a moment or two but it was enough for the horseman closest to Adam to look down and catch the boy's eye. Immediately Adam recognized him. The huge absurd upturned moustache was unmistakable—it was the German Kaiser. It was only a few seconds at most, but Adam had time to sense the man's extraordinary rigidity—his frozen left arm, his chin thrust forward, his unblinking blue eyes; his concentration and self-absorption. He seemed mad somehow, capable of anything. And then, while Adam's impression was still forming, he was gone—a memory of scarlet and silver and gold. And the marching soldiers and sailors followed—thousands and thousands of them following their dead king down the road that led to Paddington Station, while the drums beat and the bagpipes wailed.

It was as if the old order had passed away into the mist, and now everything was changing. It was an age of wonders: a Frenchman had flown a monoplane across the Channel; there was newsreel of it at the Picture Palace where Adam also went to watch the official motion picture of the King's funeral, peering up at the grey-specked screen, hoping in vain to catch a glimpse of himself in the crowd, a participant in history.

The world seemed to be turning faster, rushing towards some invisible climax. Motor cars were everywhere, blowing their horns, whipping up clouds of dust from the poorly surfaced roads, running down people who left the safety of the pavements. And above the noise the newspaper boys cried out their violent headlines about a country torn apart by strife: suffragettes breaking windows in Whitehall; the need for more dreadnoughts; riots and mayhem.

And strikes—that word was on everyone's lips. Everywhere men were demanding better pay; better hours; better conditions. It was the time Daniel Raine had been waiting for: the dawn of a new age of social justice when workers would be fairly rewarded for their toil. He was the secretary of the local branch of the building workers' union, which met in a small private room at the Cricketers', the pub on the corner of his street. Membership was up and meetings went on late into the night, taking all his attention. But Adam's mother was unwell again and sometimes she sent Adam with messages to ask her husband to come home. Like other women on the street, she hated the pub, although in her case it was not for the usual reasons. Daniel had never been a drinker, wasting what little money they had on alcohol. Politics and the union were his addiction and the pub was where he was able to indulge his passion. Fired up with righteous zeal amid the dazzle of the gas lamps, he could forget about the rent arrears and the grocer's unpaid bill. But Lilian couldn't. She knew they couldn't afford a strike—not with the colder weather coming. The winter before had been bad enough; and everyone said that this one would be worse. But her husband wouldn't listen whenever she tried to talk to him about her worries: it was as if she didn't exist.

She felt as if there were taut strings inside her body that were being tightened like piano wire until they were almost at breaking point. When she tried to exert herself she coughed and coughed, and had to grope her way up the rickety stairs to her bedroom where she lay completely still, listening to the sounds of the street below coming up to her through the open window like the noise of the sea, receding away from her on an ebb tide.

In the end it was a safety issue that lit the fuse. Daniel and his crew had been refurbishing a department store on the north side of Oxford Street. It was a large job needing to be done quickly and the contractor had been cutting corners by using high ladders instead of scaffolding for painting the high ceilings. Some were so high that the painters had to work, balanced at ninety degrees almost on the top rung, and it wasn't long before a man fell, suffering appalling injuries when he hit the ground. The union demanded proper scaffolding be installed and refused to carry on working until it had been put in place, and the employers responded by bringing in new labour. They saw the strike as an opportunity: times were hard and the strike-breakers were prepared to work for lower wages.

Daniel was tireless, toiling day and night to organize the picket lines that the new workers had to cross to enter the building, but the strikers' shouts and curses didn't deter them. And as the refurbishment continued apace, the strikers' anger grew. Police were called in to keep the peace and stood in a solid blue line between the two sides, their truncheons at the ready. The rain ran down their capes into pools on the ground, but they stood motionless, ignoring the strikers' fury, indifferent to their frustration.

"How long will this go on?" Lilian asked her husband, confronting him in the hallway on one of his rare visits home.

"I don't know," he said. "As long as it takes. Until the owners see reason."

"And what if they don't? What do we live on?"

"The union will help."

"A few shillings," she said contemptuously. "That won't pay the rent."

"I don't know," he said wearily. He was dog-tired—all he wanted to do was sleep. "We'll have to do our best, make sacrifices. We have justice on our side—it's a cause worth fighting for."

"Worth starving for, worth dying for," she shot back, mimicking her husband's phrase, echoing it back to him, invested with all the despair she felt inside.

"It won't come to that, Lil," he said, moving past her to go up the stairs. "I promise you it won't."

Another week passed and she'd had enough. There was nothing to eat in the house and no money to pay the tradesmen who came knocking at the door. Next it would be the bailiffs. Daniel talked about justice but there was no justice in leaving her alone and abandoning his family. For Adam's sake he had to come home, give up the cause once and for all and start over; she would make him if she had to. Wrapping herself in her thin overcoat, she set out to find her husband.

It was getting towards evening and the strike-breakers were beginning to come out, keeping their heads down, hurrying between the lines of police to where the special buses provided by the employers were waiting to take them away. Another week's work done and Sunday, a day of rest, to look forward to, at home or in the public house with beer in their bellies and a warm fire in the hearth.

For the strikers it was too much. Enraged by their own impotence, hating the scabs who had stolen their jobs, imagining the pay jingling in the pockets of their enemies' overalls, they held up their banners and pressed forward against the phalanx of police, trying to find a way through the human barrier. And when it stayed firm, they began to throw stones. It was what the police had been waiting for. At a whistled command from behind, their front rank charged forward, laying about them indiscriminately with their truncheons and trampling the strikers, who fell down under their blows.

Daniel was hit on the side of the head and lost consciousness. When he came to, he was lying on his back in the gutter; he opened his eyes and then closed them immediately as the darkening sky came hurtling down towards him. His head ached and his shoulder hurt, and he swallowed back hard on the vomit that had risen up into his throat, mixing with the blood in his mouth. Slowly, very slowly, he pushed himself up on to his knees, looking back down the road to where his workmates were fighting a losing battle with the police. Everything was blurred and confused: a melee of movement; a cacophony of noise—cries and shouts and something else, a beating, and someone running towards him, calling out his name. Someone he recognized—Lilian, his wife, Lilian, with her beautiful blonde hair flying out behind her as it had when she was a girl and they had first met faraway by the sea—in another time, another century.

She was shouting: "No, no, no," running towards him and shouting: "No," and something else was running too—behind him where he could not see. The beating was the beating of hooves on the asphalt. In despair he held out his hands towards his wife—whether to stop her or to receive her he didn't know. His back contracted, shrinking up, anticipating its own destruction. But miraculously the horse passed over him, leaving him unscathed and able in the next instant to watch his wife being crushed to death only a few feet in front of where he knelt.

Afterwards he crawled forward, indifferent to the madness all around him, and covered her body with his, even though he knew that he had failed her and that it was too late to redeem his fault.

Daniel broke the news to his son in a flat, matter-of-fact way. He told him that he was responsible and that none of it would have happened if he'd been a better husband and a better father. And when Adam rushed away up the stairs he didn't follow him but just went out the back door and stood with his hands thrust deep into his pockets under the empty washing line, gazing up at the stars with dry, unblinking eyes.

Adam buried his face in his pillow, turning, winding the sheet around his body. And from outside he could hear a cry, human but inhuman, coming up from down below. Falling and rising on unconscious breath, it was the cry of a broken spirit, someone alive who could not bear to be alive. He heard it again five years later in the trenches in France on the night after battle and recognized it for what it was.

He slept, stupefied by exhaustion, and woke up in the early light and for a moment didn't know. And when he did, he pulled on his clothes quickly. He had to keep moving. Across the landing, his father was asleep, lying face down on the bed in all his clothes. His shoes hung over the edge and Adam thought of untying them, but he couldn't. It was his mother's bedroom too and he couldn't bear to go in there. In fact he couldn't bear to be in the house. Downstairs her sewing machine and her needlework, her spectacles and her apron, all spoke of her continuity, but her coat missing from the stand by the door told a different story. She was gone; she wasn't coming back. And each time he remembered, it was like the twist of a sharpened knife in a raw, open wound.

He went out into the street. But now he saw it with new eyes: it was a tawdry show, a mockery of life. Cabbage stalks and refuse in the gutter; horse manure; a dead cat. And the uncertain sympathy on people's faces made him remember when all he wanted to do was forget. He walked on quickly but aimlessly—anywhere to get away, and found himself outside the church his mother used to take him to. He gazed up at the high tapering spire pointing like a compass needle towards heaven and wondered if it was a meaningless gesture. Was there anyone up there? If there was, the God in the clouds wasn't a loving God as his mother had said. Adam knew better now: God was more cruel and vengeful than even Father Paul could imagine. Adam shook his fist at God and turned away.

He was hungry; famished. He wanted to die but he was desperate to eat. He had two pennies in his pocket and bought some fish and chips and ate them standing up, gulping down the food like an animal. Afterwards he felt sick, but he also felt as if he'd made a choice—to stay alive.

A day passed and then another and he went with his father to the inquest. He sat at the back, forgotten at the end of a long grey bench, while a police sergeant described in a monotonous voice what had happened to Adam's mother "on the fateful day," as he called it, cradling his helmet in his hands as he talked, as though it was a baby. The sergeant said he wasn't the horseman who had crushed the deceased, but that he'd had an excellent view of all that had occurred: the woman had run forward, giving the rider no chance to take evasive action. And then Adam's father spoke too, saying over and over again that it was his fault; that he was the one responsible: "If I'd been at home like Lilian wanted, then she'd be alive now and this would never have happened." But the coroner couldn't punish him; he didn't even want to. It was an accidental death, a tragedy, and he extended his sympathy to the family as he released the body to them for burial.

Daniel was a broken man but on one issue he was adamant: he wouldn't allow his wife's crushed and mutilated body to come home. There would be no wake, no laying out, no chance for Adam to see what had really happened to his mother. He rejected his neighbours' sympathy and their offers of help, and invited no one to the funeral, so that there was just Daniel and Adam and Father Paul's curate at the graveside as the undertakers' men dropped the small plain pine coffin down into the pit that the parish sexton had excavated out of the hard ground. Father Paul had made it quite clear that he considered himself far too grand for what was little better than a pauper's funeral.

Most of the other families on the street belonged to funeral clubs, contributing a penny or two a week to guarantee a proper send-off when their time came. And, left to her own devices, Lilian would have liked to have done the same, but Daniel had refused to allow it. He hated the idea that the only thing the poor saved for was their deaths, as if that was all they had to look forward to. He had wanted better for his family and now the cost of even the cheapest funeral that the undertaker had been able to offer had left him almost destitute.

Every day he walked the streets looking for work and came home in the evening empty-handed. The building trade was always slow in winter and his work with the union had marked him out as a troublemaker. He knew he was getting nowhere but being out was better than being at home, trapped inside with his memories, and he needed time to think, to come to terms with his grief.

He met Adam in the evenings, sharing inadequate meals beside the cold hearth. The silence between them had become tangible, almost developing into an estrangement. Daniel knew he was failing his son when the boy needed him most, but he also knew that he had nothing to give. Not yet, not until he had worked out what to do.

Each day he went farther, walking to forget his hunger, wearing out his boots as he tramped past miles and miles of windswept brick terraces until he reached unnamed places where tarred fences studded with nails and "No Trespass" boards stopped him from going on into wastelands strewn with broken glass, tin cans, and ash. And there, on the borders of nowhere, he finally made a decision and turned for home.

It was dark inside and Daniel wrote the letter to Edgar, the cousin he had not seen in fifteen years, by the light of a guttering candle, as there was no oil left for the lamp. It was harder than he had anticipated to find the right words and he abandoned his first draft after only a few sentences, screwing the paper up into a ball and throwing it into the empty fireplace. He got up from his chair and paced the room back and forth. He knew what was wrong. It was pride that was making him frame his sentences so carefully. And he had no right to pride: he'd left that behind forever in the Oxford Street gutter. All that he had left was a capacity for honesty and a love for his son that he had buried for too long underneath his grief. They were the emotions that should guide his pen.

Now the words came quickly and the scratching of Daniel's nib provided a counterpoint to the noise of a mouse burrowing in the shadowy wainscot on the other side of the room. He held nothing back and when he was done he folded the letter without reading over what he had written and sealed it in the envelope with wax from his candle, adding a penny stamp that he had bought on the way home.

He got up from the table and opened the front door and then paused on the threshold, looking up at the moon that seemed to be rushing across the sky as ragged clouds scurried across its face. The winter wind was gusting down the street and he held firmly onto the letter as if worried that it might be blown away out of his hand. It felt so light and inconsequential and yet it contained all his hope for the future. If his cousin couldn't help him, then no one could. The letter was his last throw of the dice.

At the corner, opposite the Cricketers', Daniel leant his head against the iron top of the mailbox after dropping the letter through the aperture. He was weak from lack of food and sleep and hardly aware that he was uttering a silent prayer to a God in whom he didn't believe until a tap on his shoulder brought him back to reality.

"'Ad one too many, 'ave we?" asked the constable, his fleshy face wrinkling in disapproval as he bent forward to sniff Daniel's breath.

"No, I was posting a letter. That's all. I'm going home now," said Daniel, retreating across the road as he spoke. He hurried on without looking back even though he thought he could hear the heavy footfalls of the policeman following behind him. And when he got back through his door, he stopped in the narrow hallway waiting for the knock. But none came and after a few moments he went up the stairs and lay down on his bed. The moon had emerged now from out of the clouds and its pale light illuminated the cheap wooden cross hanging slightly askew on the bedroom wall. But Daniel did nothing to straighten it; he just gazed up at it for a long time without stirring before his eyes finally closed and he fell asleep.

The reply came earlier than Daniel had expected, arriving at the same time as a peremptory letter from his landlord giving him notice to quit.

Edgar's handwriting was laboriously formed but easy to read, and it didn't take Daniel long to understand the purport of what his cousin was saying. He read the letter through twice and breathed hard, trying to control the sudden wild rush of elation that was shaking his thin body like a physical force.

He ran up the stairs and threw open the door of Adam's room but then stopped in his tracks, momentarily silenced by the look of settled hostility etched on his son's face.

"We have to go," he said.

"Go where?" asked Adam.

"North. There's a job. My cousin's found me one. And we can't stay here."

"Why not?"

"Because there's nothing for us here, Adam. Not unless you want to go to the workhouse."

Adam flinched at the word almost as if he had been struck. He was angry with his father and wanted to defy him, but the thought of the workhouse terrified him. He remembered what his father had said about the place in times gone by: it was where the poor were sent to die when they were no use to the rich any more; it was the house at the end of the world.

"I haven't got a bag," he said dully. "I'll need something to put my stuff in."

An hour later father and son left the house for the last time. Adam knew that he wouldn't be coming back, at least not for a long time, not until he'd become an older, different person revisiting childhood memories when they were no more than dust in the wind.

And as he followed his father down the street on that bright winter afternoon it all came back to him. The sepia lens through which he'd seen the world since his mother's death dropped away and he saw the barefoot children running behind the water cart soaking their legs and feet in the spray as it rattled over the cobblestones; saw them dancing round the horse trough where he'd spent a hundred Sundays; saw them stop and wave goodbye as he reached the Cricketers' on the corner and paused to look back one last time.

The golden rays of the sun glared back at Adam and his father from off the thick engraved glass in the pub's window panes, and from somewhere inside they could hear an invisible woman singing a popular song to the accompaniment of the pub's penny-in-the-slot piano:

"If I should plant a tiny seed of love
In the garden of your heart,

Would it grow to be a great big love some day?
Or would it die and fade away?"

She sang well, holding the melody, and Adam stopped to listen, but his father took his arm and pulled him forward. Away from everything that was familiar and into an unknown future.

Part One

———◆◆◆———

The Mine

Who made ten thousand people owners of the soil, and the rest of us
trespassers in the land of our birth? . . . Where did the table of that law
come from? Whose finger inscribed it?

David Lloyd George, Speech in Newcastle, 9 October 1909

Chapter One

The train left in the evening, and Adam and his father waited on the platform under the huge vaulted roof of the station as the day turned to dusk and everything around them dissolved into a blue and grey mist of vapour and smoke, pierced here and there by the pallid glow of the tall arc lights. Across from where they were sitting, they could see the rich coming and going through the door of the first-class restaurant: tall men in frock coats with hats and gloves escorting ladies in narrow-waisted hobble skirts who minced slowly along, their heads almost invisible under elaborate feathered hats. They reminded Adam of the flamingoes that he had seen at the zoo years before, inhabitants of an unknowable world operating on principles entirely outside his understanding.

As the departure time approached, the platform filled up and Adam felt his heart beating hard. He knew Euston from days spent in the shadow of the great arch, earning coppers loading and unloading luggage for cabbies at the roadside, but he had never been on a train. He had never been outside London.

He heard the locomotive before he saw it—the scream of its whistle, the screech of engaging brakes, the hiss of steam; and then emerging out of the great pall of smoke came the black-and-red engine, a breathing, snorting mammoth of incredible power. And suddenly there was a frenzy of activity: carriage doors opening and disgorging passengers all the way down the line; porters and guards shouting, holding back the pressing crowd.

"Come on," said Daniel, picking up his bag, and Adam almost lost his father in a sea of shabby jackets and cloth caps but caught sight of him at the last moment waving from the running board. He pushed forward and felt his father's hand on his, pulling him up into the train.

Inside the compartment they found seats, perched on the ends of two wooden benches, facing each other in the flickering gaslight. Doors slammed and the shouts of the people outside were stilled by the guard's whistle as the train spluttered back into life and began to pull away from the platform, picking up speed as it headed north, running smoothly along steel viaducts built high above the poor streets where Adam had grown up.

He closed his eyes and thought again of his mother: the leaving of London felt like a betrayal, as if he was leaving her behind too, somewhere back there in the smoky darkness, deliberately severing his last connection with her forever. He knew he was being irrational—that she was gone already—but that didn't help with the raw tearing emptiness he felt inside whenever he forgot she was dead and then suddenly remembered. He hated that he couldn't think of her without pain. It made him angry, and he realized that he was angry with her too—because she was supposed to explain these things to him and now she couldn't.

He shook his head hard as if to expel his thoughts and opened his eyes. His father was looking at him intently, as if he was trying to read his mind.

"I'm sorry, Adam. I know this is hard." Daniel spoke slowly, leaning forward towards his son. "It's hard for me too. But we've got no choice. London will chew us up and spit us out if we stay; it's a cruel town and it's hurt us enough already."

Adam nodded, not knowing how to respond. The death of his mother had set Adam against his father, but in spite of himself, he had begun to sense a change in Daniel in the last few days. His father seemed more thoughtful, less driven. Adam had seen how he had said nothing when they had sat watching the rich men and women coming and going at the station dressed in all their finery. In the past he wouldn't have been able to resist a political commentary accompanied by plentiful statistics about the unfair distribution of wealth in society, but today he had seemed hardly to notice. Adam wondered what the change meant for the future.

"What's this place where we're going?" he asked, looking out into the night. Surrounded by strangers in the spartan compartment, rushing forward on the express train towards a new unknown world, he felt apprehensive and hoped for reassurance.

"Scarsdale? It's a small coal-mining town not far from the sea. The north is full of places just like it. Everyone works at the mine, on the surface or down below. And it's hard work, harder than you can imagine, which makes the people hard—" Daniel stopped in mid-sentence, smiling at his inarticulacy. "But not mean, not cruel—miners stick together; by and large they're good people."

"How do you know?"

"I've worked with them. Not in Scarsdale but further south—in Nottinghamshire, where I grew up."

"You were a miner?" Adam asked, sounding surprised. He couldn't imagine his father as anything other than a builder. That's what he'd been all Adam's life.

"No, the firm I was apprenticed to specialized in putting up structures round pitheads to house the heavy machinery and to support it too. It meant I was working side by side with miners all the time so I got to know their ways."

"And is that what you're going to be doing now?" asked Adam. "Building things for them?"

"No, this is different—nothing to do with construction. I'm working with them—or rather for them, I suppose. I'm to be their checkweighman, which means I measure the weight of the coal in each tub they've mined to make sure they get paid the right amount for it."

"So you're down in the mine as well, with them?" asked Adam nervously. The thought alarmed him—it made him think of being buried, like his mother. He was brave by nature but the thought of being underground had always terrified him. He remembered the well at the back of the school in Islington that Old Beaky had told them was out of bounds. Adam had disobeyed at the first opportunity, using all his childish strength to push the thick wooden cover aside. And, if he shut his eyes, he could still relive the long wait after he threw in a stone, counting the seconds before he heard the faint splash deep down below. He'd had nightmares for weeks afterwards, dreaming of falling down into the thick darkness, his unheard cries echoing off the damp brick walls.

"No, don't worry. I'm up on the surface where the tubs of coal come out," said Daniel reassuringly. He knew all about his son's phobia—he'd never even been able to persuade Adam to set foot in the London Underground, let alone get on one of the trains. "The job's not dangerous," he went on, "but it's important, and the money will be better than what we've been used to, which will help."

Daniel's words were optimistic but Adam sensed an uncertainty lurking underneath and wondered if his father was feeling ashamed that he wouldn't be sharing the hardships of the men that he was working for. But Adam dismissed the thought: what mattered was that his father would be out of harm's way. He'd lost his mother and he didn't want to risk losing his father too.

"How did you get the job?" Adam asked. It made no sense that his father should have been able to walk into this cushy, well-paid job in this faraway place when by his own admission he'd never actually been a miner.

"I have a cousin who recommended me. He's a good man and he's worked in the Scarsdale pit most of his life so he has a lot of influence with the men. And it turned out they wanted me because of what I'd done down here with the builders' union—getting more members, getting organized. It's the miners' union that'll be paying me," said Daniel.

"Will you make them strike?" asked Adam anxiously. He knew what union work meant—poverty and violence and death. Was this what lay in store for them in the north? A second dose of what they were trying to leave behind?

"No, I hope it won't come to that," said Daniel, choosing his words carefully. "I do want to help, to make things better. But I hope I can achieve that by negotiating with the owner. I hope he'll listen to reason. I've learnt from what happened with your mother, Adam. It's changed me, you know, just like it's changed you."

Later, much later, they had to change trains. Crossing a foot-bridge in the rain, they looked across a moonlit landscape of ware-houses and factories to where the funnels and chimneys of a blast furnace were throwing columns of white fire and belching orange smoke up into the night sky.

Adam stopped, awestruck. He had never seen anything like it.

"The jaws of hell," said Daniel, clapping his son on the shoulder. "And inside it's hotter than hell; hot enough to make iron into steel, which is what the British Empire is built on. And the fires never stop. They can't because the demand never does. And the fires need coal, mountains of coal. Which is where we come in," he added with a smile.

They got to Scarsdale on the dawn train. And at first, as they approached, Adam could see nothing of the mine. Instead the view from the window was a vision of loveliness. Still-water lakes and green fields carpeted with the first wild flowers of spring, divided one from another by silvery white dry-stone walls; woods of beech and oak and quick-flowing streams, and up on the crest of a hill a pictur-esque village of thatched cottages surrounding the weathered tower of a mediaeval church. But the railway didn't go that way, curving round instead into the valley behind where all at once the landscape was utterly transformed. Down below in the valley bottom the mine was marked out by a line of wooden towers and tall red-brick chim-neys standing across from a huge man-made heap of slate-grey waste, and stretching up from it on all sides row upon row of squat grey houses, monotonous and monochrome, straddled the hillsides like an encamped army of insects. The change in the view shocked Adam. It was jarring—almost violent—to go from beauty to ugliness in a moment; from a world unchanged in centuries to this industrial out-crop of the new century, with both existing side by side in a bizarre juxtaposition.

As they got closer, Adam could see that the houses were built almost back-to-back along long, narrow streets, which all led down like the irregular hands of a giant clock towards the mine at the centre, surmounted by the high towers that dominated the landscape. They had huge wheels at their apex and Adam could see that one set was turning as they approached. The spokes of each one rotated in opposite directions and the sense of power they conveyed reminded Adam of the beast-like locomotive at the front of the train that had made such an impression on him at the station in London.

"What are they? What do they do?" Adam asked his father, pointing towards the towers.

"They're the headstocks—winding gear like I used to work on. The wheels draw the steel cables that raise and lower the cages up and down the mine shafts," said Daniel admiringly, looking at the structures with a craftsman's eye, taking pleasure in their design.

"How deep are they?" asked Adam.

"Different depths: I've heard the deepest is over five hundred feet," said Daniel.

Adam shivered. Again he remembered the well in the school yard, the stone falling and the splash far away down below. He'd been terrified but fascinated too, going back again and again for weeks afterwards, drawn to the well like a magnet, although he'd never removed the cover after that first time.

"Don't think about the shafts," said Daniel, sensing his son's anxiety. "I told you I'm going to be working at the pithead, not down below."

"What about me?" asked Adam.

"You?" said Daniel, sounding shocked. "I'd never let you work in a mine. You're my flesh and blood, all I've got left, and I'm going to look after you, keep you safe. You believe me, don't you?" he asked, looking hard at his son.

Adam nodded, grateful for the reassurance, although he wondered at his father's willingness to come to this place and represent the men when he was obviously so appalled at the idea of sending his own son underground to work with them.

"You're going to school," Daniel went on. "It's all arranged. You're a bright kid, brighter than I ever was, and you deserve a better life than I've had, one where you can use your talents and get on in the world. And that's what your mother would have wanted as well. I'm sure of that. Now come on," he added as the train came to a halt. "This is where we get off."

They had pulled into a small station halfway down the valley. From the platform Adam could see the railway line split in two with one set of tracks heading away over the far hill into the invisible land beyond and another continuing down to the pithead below where it wound around among the mismatched assortment of grey brick buildings surrounding the headstocks.

Shouldering their bags, Daniel and Adam walked out through an empty waiting room lined with posters advertising seaside holidays in Blackpool, Scarborough, Whitley Bay and other places Adam had never heard of. The world of brightly coloured deckchairs and bathing machines, pleasure boats and parasols under a hot sun, seemed a long way removed from this bleak mining town which was to be their new home.

Outside the station they had to pause for a minute as a column of cloth-capped miners came up the street from the direction of the mine, returning home from the night shift. Their faces were smeared black with coal dust and their iron-heeled clogs clattered on the roadway as they approached, setting off sparks on the cobbles. Some of them were singing. The tune reminded Adam of a hymn that the congregation used to sing at the church in Islington when he went there with his mother but he could not recognize any of the words. They seemed to be in another language.

The last of the group had almost gone past when a tall man stopped in mid-stride and rushed over to them. He had an open tool bag in his hand, which he dropped on the ground as he put his arms around Daniel, pulling him close in a bear hug. Something tin-like inside it clanged as it hit the pavement and Adam instinctively bent down and picked it up, holding it out to the stranger.

"So, this is thy boy, eh, Daniel?" said the stranger, releasing Daniel and looking Adam up and down with a broad smile. " 'E's the livin' image of thee, ain't 'e? An' good-mannered too, which I s'pose 'e gets from thee," he added, taking the bag. "Not like us miners. I'd shake thy hand, lad, but it needs washing first."

"Adam, this is your cousin, Edgar Tillett," said Daniel. "We're going to be staying with him and his family until we find our feet."

"Find thy feet," repeated Edgar with a laugh. "Thy feet're at the end of thy legs last time I looked so thou shouldna' be wastin' thy time tryin' to find 'em. An' you can stay wi' us as long as you need. You know that. Blood's thicker than water as they say, an' they say right." He clapped Daniel on the shoulder and Adam sensed his father's awkwardness in the face of his cousin's largesse as he smiled uncertainly in response.

The other miners had gone on ahead and now they began to follow them up the hill, walking towards the rising sun. Edgar walked in the centre with Daniel and Adam on either side.

"How was work?" asked Daniel.

"Tight," said the miner with a smile, pronouncing the word with relish as if pleased with the selection he'd made from a choice of other possible epithets. "That's the word for it, I'd say. We're workin' a plough seam jus' at present—that's a narrow 'un, no more'n two feet high—and so we 'ave to be on our 'ands an' knees most o' the time. Hurts the back and it hurts the 'ead too if thou doesna watch thyself," he said with a grin, stretching his arms out wide as if to release the tension. Adam could see that he was a powerfully built man, lean and strong with muscle.

"An' it hurts our pockets too when the owner won't pay us enough for all our hard work. Which is where you comes in," he said with a sideways look at Daniel. "You've come at the right time, Cousin, I can tell you that. I'm looking for'ards to seein' thee gangin' toe to toe with ol' Sir John and the managers," he added with a smile.

"Who's Sir John?" asked Adam, who'd been listening avidly to the conversation. The foreignness of everything in this new world had begun to excite him: the landscape, the way Edgar talked, the things he said. They made Adam want to understand, not to be left behind.

"Sir John? Why, 'e's the owner—o' the mine, an' o' nigh ivrything 'ereabouts," said Edgar with an expansive sweeping gesture of his hand that seemed to encompass everything in sight. " 'Cept me 'ouse o' course. I owns that, lock, stock an' barrel. I'm one of the few that do, so 'e canna evict me even if the notion takes 'im, which is nice to know."

They had followed the road up from the station without turning right or left and now came to a halt in front of the last house in the street. Beyond, a yellow cornfield ran up the rest of the hillside to a thick-limbed oak tree standing alone like a sentinel on the sharply etched skyline. The house was the same height as its neighbours but it had been extended out at least fifteen feet to the side where a vegetable and flower garden had been planted out in tidy rows behind a picket fence.

"Well, 'ere we are," said Edgar, pushing open the door and beckoning them to follow him inside. "Not exactly a stately 'ome but it'll do. Thomas, Ernest, say 'ow d'yer do to your cousins." This last was addressed to two young men sitting at a deal table on the other side of the large low room into which the entrance opened directly. There was no front parlour as Adam had been used to in London or, if there had been, the partition wall had been knocked down to increase the main living space, which was centred on a big fireplace with a bread oven set in its side. The fire was banked high with red coal and Adam could feel the thick heat radiating off it from the moment he came in.

Ernest, the younger of Edgar's two sons, came forward and shook Adam's hand. He was a few months older than Adam and seemed open and friendly like his father. His brother Thomas stood back. He appeared reserved, nodding his head rather than shaking hands. And behind him Adam could see a woman in a white apron and cap, evidently their mother, come bustling out from another room at the back of the house.

She didn't wait to be introduced but came straight over to Adam and kissed him on the cheek. "I'm Annie, Edgar's wife," she said. "And I'm glad you're here. Now, take your coat off and Ernest will show you your room. Edgar, you need to go in the back and wash yourself. You're black from the pit and you're not eating breakfast with the likes of us looking like that."

"Why do your parents talk different?" Adam asked as he followed Ernest up the stairs, and then immediately regretted the question. It was rude to ask about the way people spoke. His mother had told him that.

But Ernest didn't take offence. "She's had more schooling than our dad—he went down the pit when he was nine or ten. One of the two—sometimes he says eight but that's when he's had a few too many to drink on a Saturday night and he's trying to lay it on thick and make you feel sorry for him," he said with a laugh. "Schooling takes the Yorkshire out of thee, or at least that's what they say round here. And yes, I suppose it's done it to me too. That and my mother who'll clip me round the ear if I talk silly, as she calls it. But I don't know if it'll last: I'm working at the pithead now, on the screens, and it's hard not to talk like everyone else. We all end up down the pit sooner or later, you'll see. And now here's my room. And yours too— we'll be sharing if that's all right . . ."

Ernest threw open a door with a theatrical gesture and Adam found himself in a long thin room with two beds, each made up with a spotlessly white counterpane. A table with an oil lamp stood between them, facing a wide but low rectangular window with leaded panes from which he could see across to the oak tree at the top of the hill. They were clearly on the top floor of the side extension that he'd noticed earlier.

"Better than looking out the front," said Ernest, following Adam's gaze. "The houses here are all the same—it's easy enough to go in the wrong one if you aren't careful, coming home in the dark. It happens all the time. And you could end up in the wrong bed too, next to the wrong wife if you aren't careful. And I don't know what would happen then!"

Ernest laughed and Adam joined in, relaxing for the first time in as long as he could remember. Soon the laughter took him over and he had to sit down on the bed opposite Ernest, holding his sides. And that's how his father found them when he came upstairs with his bag.

"Good," he said. "You two'll be friends, I think, and I'm glad of that."

Chapter Two

January 1911

The next day, Daniel and Adam went on the bus to Gratton, the nearest town, to visit the board school. He sat in a room full of dusty books and completed an exam which he found easy—the standard here seemed lower than in London, and by the end of the day their business was done. There would be no fees to pay; all Adam had to do was buy his own textbooks and pay for the bus fares, and work hard.

"Your boy's got brains," said the headmaster, shaking Daniel's hand. He was an earnest-looking man with intense grey eyes and an evident sense of mission. "He'll go far if he stays the distance."

"Don't worry," said Daniel, looking pleased. "I'll make sure he does that."

"What does he mean—stay the distance?" asked Adam as they waited in the queue at the bus stop.

"Most children leave school even if they have the chance of staying on. Times are hard and there's pressure from their families to have the extra income, and then they want to have their own money too."

"Like Ernest?" said Adam.

"Yes. Edgar has bought his house and that means the family needs more. The rent we're paying will help too—my cousin's a generous man but he knows which side his bread's buttered."

"Don't you trust him, Dad?" asked Adam. There was something in his father's voice that he had picked up on—an anxiety, an uncertainty perhaps about the future. Adam couldn't put his finger on it but he knew it was there.

"I don't know," said Daniel meditatively. "Edgar's strong, and the other miners look up to him. I can tell that. And he wants to change their lives for them, just like he's changed his own. But he doesn't trust himself to be their leader; he thinks you need book learning for that, which is where I come in. I just hope he hasn't misjudged me."

It was dark when they got back to Scarsdale and rain was in the air, blown here and there by an indiscriminate wind that carried coal dust on its back up from the slag heap down below where a tangle of lights lit up the pithead. At the station Adam could see trucks on the sidings standing full of bright wet coal glistening in the moonlight, and by the doors of the miners' houses the rainwater was washing away the early shift times written in chalk on the knock-up slates. Daniel told him that they were there for the knocker-upper, an old man who rode round the streets of the town on a bicycle in the early mornings, waking up the miners by tapping on their windows, using a long pole with wires attached.

In the house at the end of Station Street it was bath night. The galvanized iron tub that Adam had noticed hanging on a hook outside the back door when he went out to use the privy in the morning had been dragged into the living room and filled with hot water which Edgar's wife had boiled up laboriously in the two kettles by the fire. And one by one the men of the family took turns bathing, scrubbing their pale bodies with Watson's Matchless Cleansing Carbolic, although it was Annie's job to wash their backs. Sitting out of the way in the corner of the room, Adam was touched to see how tenderly she ran the cloth across her husband's shoulder blades, dabbing at the multitude of pale blue scars like tattoo marks where the coal had lodged under his skin. And then at the end Adam and Ernest carried the bath outside to pour away the inky-black water and leave it ready for the laundry work to begin the next day.

Further at the back, beyond the privy and the ash pit, a pig grunted in its makeshift sty. Perhaps it didn't like the rain—Adam didn't know. There had been pigs in the back gardens in London too, fattened through the year for slaughter in the autumn, but Adam had avoided them, pained by the certainty of their coming death. He felt it an ill omen that there should be another here and hoped that he and his father would have "found their feet" and moved to their own house before killing time came round.

Back in the warmth of the house, Edgar, swathed in clean towels, was squatting in front of the fire, toasting brown sugar on a spoon until it turned black. Adam watched as he took a frying pan, added water and flour and mixed them with the burnt sugar for gravy. The movements of his big powerful hands were quick and fluid—hands that could make things but could unmake them too. He caught Adam's eye and smiled.

"Come over 'ere, lad. There's summat I wanna show thee."

He reached up above the mantelpiece and took down a small round tin box about two inches in diameter and six inches deep and turned it over in his fingers a moment before handing it to Adam.

"Hang on to that and I'll tell thee its story," he said. "Thy grand-uncle, thy father's uncle and my father, 'e made that. Forty year ago when 'e wor workin' in the Marley Main mine south o' here, and the pit went up wi' an explosion on account o' they was usin' matches to light their lamps—silly ignorant fools that they were—an' one caught the firedamp that they 'ave underground. Firedamp—it's a gas. Methane they calls it too," he added, catching the puzzled look on Adam's face. "Any road, a lot o' boys thy age lost their lives that day, but two 'o them survived by a miracle, trapped behind the fallen rock. An' my dad, 'e drilled a borehole through the stone so 'e could pass this 'ere tin through to 'em with food and water for 'em to 'ave while they were diggin' 'em out."

"And did they?" asked Adam, looking down at the old tin in his hand, wondering at how Edgar had transformed it from an apparently worthless object into something so precious in just a few sentences.

"Did they wot?"

"Dig them out. Did they survive—the two who were trapped?"

"One o' 'em did, t'other didn't. You takes your chances, but the point is that we stick together, us miners. We 'ave to," he added, glancing over at Daniel, who was sitting reading the newspaper at the table. And Adam sensed suddenly that Edgar had been telling the story to his father just as much as to him.

Ernest began his shift late on Monday and so there was time for him to walk with Adam to the bus. The stop was in a square across from the station where the village shop and pub and the Miners' Institute were also located. In the middle a set of rusty swings stood on an uneven patch of worn-out grass—the town's sole concession to the concept of small children's entertainment. On warmer days mothers sat on the wooden benches and gossiped, resting their legs before they walked home, and teenagers came here too when they weren't working, the girls watching the boys and the boys watching the girls and all of them pretending that they were doing nothing of the kind, gathered together in their separate self-conscious groups on opposite sides of the green.

The bus was late and some boys came over when they saw Ernest. One of them stood out from the rest. He was thin and wiry with short hair cropped tight to his skull, dressed in pit clothes that seemed too big for him, as if he was wearing his father's cast-offs, and he walked with an almost imperceptible limp, slightly favouring his left leg over his right. He was looking at Adam, not Ernest, and Adam sensed the boy's hostility. It seemed personal, as if he already knew who Adam was and didn't like what he knew.

"You're goin' up in the world, Ernest," he said. "Got a new pal wi' smart London clothes to wear. Wot's 'is name?"

The boy spoke with a strong local accent but Adam sensed that this was a choice, a deliberate statement of identity.

"My name's Adam," he said, stepping forward, putting out his hand. He refused to be cowed, not after all he had gone through.

The boy kept his hand in his pockets, looking at Adam's outstretched hand with contempt. "An' wot hast thou got in there?" he asked, nodding at Adam's bag

"School books," said Adam. "I'm going to the board school in Gratton."

"I knows where the board school is," said the boy. "I'm not stoopid, you know, even if I work for me livin'."

"I never said you were," said Adam, standing his ground.

The boy smiled coldly, apparently amused by Adam's boldness. "So let's see 'em," he demanded, pointing at the bag. "Show us what we're missin' while we're down mine, 'ackin' out the coal for thy fire."

"Leave him alone, Rawdon," said Ernest nervously. "He's done nothing to you."

" 'Done nothing to you,' " the boy repeated. He was a good mimic, catching the anxious defiance in Ernest's voice. "Aye, I s'pose 'e's done nowt, apart from 'is father comin' an' takin' me father's job," he said, switching his attention back to Adam. "An' 'im 'ere bein' too good for the pit an' the likes o' us. Now show us," he shouted, taking hold of Adam's bag and wrenching it out of his hand. "Show us what you've got!"

The bag opened and the textbooks fell out on to the muddy ground. Adam was horrified, momentarily lost for words. Less than two days previously he had felt such pride of ownership when his father had taken him to the bookshop in Gratton High Street and they'd selected the books from the densely packed shelves. His father had paid for them at the counter, and then made Adam a present of a pen with a fine silver nib with which to inscribe his name on the flyleaves. God knows how much they had all cost, and now here they were—covered in dirt, while this vile thug read out their titles in a clipped, mincing voice, a parody of his own. It was intolerable—a violation.

Adam grabbed at the mathematics book in Rawdon's hand but the boy was too quick for him, throwing it over Adam's head to one of his friends who caught it and threw it on to another. But Adam didn't turn round. He realized in that instant that there was no reasoning with his tormentors, that the only solution was to fight this boy, Rawdon, and to fight now while the anger was red hot inside him, giving him courage. He took a deep breath and charged forward. Perhaps Rawdon had underestimated his enemy, believed that he really was an effete southerner unable to stand up for himself, but he certainly wasn't ready for Adam's frontal attack. Their heads clashed and he fell to the ground winded, the spine of one of the textbooks cracking under his weight.

Immediately Adam got up, holding out his fists, and Rawdon's friends stepped back. "Fight, fight," one of them shouted and the rest took up the refrain. Adam glanced over at Ernest who nodded his understanding—Adam had at least succeeded in dividing Rawdon from his supporters. The fight would be between the two of them now—much better odds than they had been a moment before.

Slowly Rawdon got to his feet, his dark blue eyes fixed on Adam. He dropped his hands and then suddenly delivered a hooking punch up towards Adam's jaw. Instinctively Adam pulled out of the way, but he still felt the full force of Rawdon's follow-up blow, delivered hard to the chest with his other fist. He felt a dense pain followed immediately by a sharp nausea. But he refused to give into his hurt, remembering instead how his father had kept his head, fighting the huge gypsy in the Islington marketplace all those years before. Adam sensed he was his adversary's equal in strength, and, remembering Rawdon's limp, he knew he had an advantage in mobility if he could find a way to exploit it.

He moved back, shifting his weight from foot to foot, waiting for Rawdon's next move.

"What art thou then? Some sort o' prancin' ballet dancer?" sneered Rawdon. "Did you learn that down in London too?"

The other boys laughed but Adam didn't hear them. He had that rare ability to shut out all distraction when he wanted to, and to operate without emotion when the need arose. He was naturally brave and he had already put aside his anger. Fighting was about control—if he kept his self-control he sensed he could win.

He jabbed with his fist at Rawdon's face, cutting him under the eye, and then danced back, easily avoiding Rawdon's heavy-armed response. And then repeated the move again, aiming always at the same place, watching as the blood seeped out from under the skin and trickled down his enemy's cheek. Now it was Rawdon's turn to become enraged. He rushed at Adam, kicking out with his hard boots, reaching up to pull him to the ground. But Adam was too quick for him. He'd seen what was coming and stepped neatly out of the way, connecting with a hard punch to the side of Rawdon's head that sent him sprawling on the ground.

He lay face down in the dirt for a moment and then started to get up with his fists clenched.

"I'll 'ave thee," he shouted, his bleeding face twisted in rage, but Ernest stepped between him and Adam, pushing him back with his outstretched hands.

"That's enough, Rawdon," he said. "You lost the fight and that's an end of it. You must shake hands."

"I'll be damned if I will," Rawdon shouted. But he had lost the support of his friends.

"Ernie's right. Shake 'is 'and, Rawdon," said the tallest of them, a handsome boy with jet-black hair, putting his hand on Rawdon's shoulder.

Rawdon shook him off but, looking round, he knew the game was up, at least for now. Ernest gave him a searching look and stepped aside and Rawdon touched Adam's outstretched hand with his own and then turned away. "Some o' us 'round 'ere 'ave to go to work," he said, walking away towards the railway line. The rest of his friends followed him but the tall one stayed back, picking up the mathematics book from the ground and dusting off the dirt as best he could with his hand.

"You fought well," he said, handing the book to Adam. "You've nowt to be ashamed of."

"Who was that?" Adam asked, watching the boy walking quickly across the green to catch up with his friends.

"Luke Mason. He's all right. And the girls like him," said Ernest with a grin. "Most of the lads aren't so bad when you get to know them, but Rawdon's different. He's angry all the time—it'll be someone else's turn tomorrow, I'll be bound."

Adam smiled, grateful for his friend's attempt at reassurance, although he didn't believe it was genuine. Rawdon's antipathy had been deeply personal, not some offshoot of a general resentment against the world.

"What did he mean about my father taking his father's job?" he asked.

"Rawdon's father, Whalen, wanted to be the union secretary when old Harris retired. It goes with being checkweighman, which is a nice job—good pay and up on the pithead, not down below. Whalen's very political, very involved with the union, and he thought the job was his for the asking. But my dad wouldn't have it—he wanted your dad after what he read about him in the paper. And what my dad wants is pretty much law down the pit."

"What paper?"

"The *Herald*. They reported all about the strike your dad organized and about what happened to your mother . . ." Ernest stopped, clearly embarrassed at his casual mention of Adam's bereavement. "I'm sorry. I didn't mean . . ."

"It's all right," said Adam. "Thank you for helping me today. I won't forget it." The bus had arrived while they were talking and he reached over and shook Ernest's hand before he got on. He meant what he'd said—it was a long time since he'd felt he had a friend.

On Sunday Daniel took his son to church. Adam was surprised. He vividly remembered the division in the house in London between his mother's devout Christianity at one polar opposite and his father's outspoken atheism at the other. According to Daniel there couldn't be a God who would allow the world he'd created to be so unfair, so cruel to the vast majority of those who had the misfortune to be born into it. And since his mother's death Adam had been inclined to agree with his father. The God to whom he had once prayed to find his father work and watch over his family seemed like a foolish figment of his childhood imagination, a cardboard cut-out figure with his big white beard and all-seeing eyes.

"Why are we going, Dad?" he asked as they walked up the hill together in the cold bright morning, leaving the mine and the streets of grey terraced houses behind them.

"Because your mother would have wanted it," said Daniel. "It's one of the only ways we can honour her memory."

Adam nodded, accepting the explanation. "Does Edgar know we're going?" he asked. Like many of the miners, Daniel's cousin was not a religious man. Church for him was where the owners and the managers went: its doctrines of social respect and obedience were useful tools to buttress their control of the workforce.

"Yes, he knows. And he understands why," said Daniel. But Adam sensed an unease in his father's voice that belied the certainty of his response.

The church was beautiful. It was smaller and simpler in design than the church in Islington, made of an old silvery-grey stone that was cold to the touch. There was no stained glass and the morning light poured in through the high leaded windows of the clerestory. The brick floor of the nave was uneven, worn down by centuries of use, and the carvings on the oak-wood chancel screen were primitive and mysterious—flat ancient faces with thin mouths and opaque eyes. The building was timeless, far removed from the ugly excrescence of the mining town stretching out behind it down the hill.

It was a family church built and maintained through the centuries by the Scarsdale family. Their huge marble mausoleum surrounded by iron railings and encrusted with black names and dates dominated the churchyard; and inside, a baroque tomb of two seventeenth-century ancestors carved in relief, lying side by side on a stone bed in the south transept, struck the only unharmonious note in the church's architecture.

The empty front pew was reserved for the present occupants of Scarsdale Hall, who had not yet arrived when Daniel and Adam took their seats at the back of the church. They came in just before the service was about to start: the father, a straight-backed, thin-faced man in his fifties with a long aquiline nose and a short clipped grey beard and moustache, was dressed in the severe formal fashion of thirty years before, and had on his arm a younger wife, who moved slowly up the aisle, her movement sharply constricted by a wasp-waisted hobble skirt that reached narrowly down to her ankles. The wilting sleeves of her silk blouse dripped with expensive lace and a wide-brimmed hat covered with artificial flowers was perched on the front of her head at just the right angle to show off her conventionally pretty face.

They were an ill-assorted couple, Adam thought: the husband

making no effort at ostentation and the wife self-consciously fashionable and excessively over-dressed for the simple country setting. And behind them came their younger son, Brice, a boy of Adam's age in an expensive suit with a carnation in his buttonhole and a gold-topped walking cane and pearl-grey silk hat in his hand. He looked very like his mother and yet he hadn't inherited her good looks. The slightly drooping edges of her full mouth conveyed an impression of sensuality but the same feature on her son gave him a look of bored condescension, and while her dimpled chin was pretty, his small version made him seem weak and petulant.

Adam liked the parson, Mr. Vale. He seemed down-to-earth and preached an inclusive gospel based on the second commandment, although there were precious few miners there to hear him. They were either Methodists attending the chapel on the other side of the valley or non-believers like Edgar, who saw the sabbath as an opportunity to catch up on sleep after the heavy demands of the working week. None of the family had been out of bed when Daniel and Adam had left for church in the morning.

The parson was waiting at the lychgate in his surplice with his daughter beside him when the congregation came out after the service. She was the most beautiful girl Adam had ever seen; she stopped him in his tracks at the door of the church, staring at her wide-eyed over the gravestones. She was dressed in a plain black dress with lace-up Oxford shoes and a bonnet. Nothing special, nothing fancy—just dark liquid eyes and rich dark hair and skin like white honey and a way of looking about her that seemed shy and tender all the same time. Adam thought that if he had been asked to write down every feature of the perfect female face then each one would have been hers, and yet he had never imagined her face in any of his dreams.

He stayed just outside the porch feasting his eyes on her, memorizing her, and prayed that she wouldn't look back in his direction. He didn't want to embarrass her but he didn't want to stop watching her—the way she bent her slender neck forward to listen to her father, smiling in a way that lit up her face from inside as he spoke to the parishioners passing through the gate. And she didn't notice him, didn't feel his gaze. Someone else did instead—the owner's son, Brice Scarsdale, the boy with the gold-tipped cane and the weak chin. He'd been standing watching the girl too and now he realized suddenly that she had another admirer.

He left his parents and came over to Adam. "What's your name?" he asked angrily, twirling his stick.

"Adam Raine," said Adam evenly. "What's yours?"

"Never mind that. Don't you know it's rude to stare at a lady?" Brice demanded angrily.

"Yes," said Adam, looking him in the eye. "But you were doing the same."

"How dare you!" said Brice. "Why, I've half a mind to—" He raised the stick but then dropped it, remembering where he was. "You should learn some respect for your betters," he said and turned abruptly on his heel, walking quickly over to his parents, who were at that moment climbing into their chauffeur-driven motor car. And as they were driven away, Adam had the exquisite pleasure of being introduced to the parson's daughter. Miriam was her name and she smiled at him as he took her hand.

In the afternoon there was a visitor at the house in Station Street. Luke Mason, the boy who'd spoken to Adam after the fight, was at the door holding a football under his arm.

"Do you want to play, Ernest?" he asked. "It's a fine day. An' thy friend can come too if 'e wants," he added, nodding to Adam.

Adam did want to; he could think of nothing that he wanted to do more, in fact. Days sitting on the bus or in classrooms had left him pent up with nervous energy. And he liked football. It had been one of the street games he'd played growing up, although the make-shift balls they'd used had been nothing like the heavy dark brown leather object that Luke was carrying.

"What's it made of?" Adam asked.

"It's a rubber bladder inside an' then tanned leather on top, eighteen sections of it all stitched together. Look, you can see the seams: it's beautiful work," said Luke, holding the ball out for Adam to inspect. "Our team won it two year ago when we won the Mines Cup. Not the proper one, mind, but the one for kids our age. 'Twas the match ball an' we won in the last minute. It was a great day, weren't it, Ernest?" said Luke with a faraway look in his eye, remembering past glory.

"Yes, it was," said Ernest, smiling. "There's never been a better."

"Who scored the goal?" asked Adam.

"Rawdon. An' 'twas Ernest that gave 'im the cross," said Luke. Adam liked the way Luke wanted to tell everything correctly, to ensure that everyone got the credit he deserved.

"Will Rawdon be there today?" asked Adam.

"Yes, but there won't be any trouble. I can promise thee that. It's the game that matters," said Luke. And Adam believed him.

The football pitch was on the edge of the town. It was surprisingly well kept with nets behind the goals, benches for spectators, and a single-storey wooden pavilion for changing with a green and white scoreboard on the outside.

There were about fifteen boys already there when they arrived and they started playing almost straightaway. Adam was on Luke's team. He could see Rawdon down at the other end of the field, standing between the other side's goalposts.

"You look like a runner," said Luke. "So try it on the wing. See what you think."

The game was played at a frantic pace and the tackling was hard. Like the ball—when Adam headed it he felt as if he'd been hit with a lead weight, and Luke laughed. "Hurts the first time, don't it? But you'll get used to it."

Several times they had to stop to reinflate the ball's bladder and the boys drank water from the standpipe. Some of them had brought oranges and they ate them, leaning with their backs against the pavilion. Adam recognized several from the day of the fight but they were friendly now, united in their love of the game and the exhilaration of running in the open air after a week of working in the mine.

Near the end, when the score was tied at one apiece, Adam got the ball far out on the right and, instead of passing it as he had done up to then, he ran at the other side's full back, feinting to the outside and then cutting back in, leaving his opponent wrong-footed as he went past. He looked up but there was no one on his team nearby and so he ran on, heading towards the goal where Rawdon stood waiting for him, holding out his arms to make himself big and cut off the shot.

Adam could see that Rawdon had positioned himself well and that the angle was too tight to score. He'd taken one too many strides and his only hope was to go round the goalkeeper. And so at the last moment, just as he was about to collide with Rawdon, he twisted his body to the left, kicking the ball away from Rawdon's outstretched hand. Rawdon had already committed himself and, charging forward, he knocked Adam to the ground. It was a mirror image of what had happened on the day of the fight. One of the defenders rushing back was in time to kick the ball away and out of danger.

As Adam got to his feet, he found himself surrounded by the other players. They were arguing amongst themselves about what had happened; about whether Rawdon had committed a foul, whether there should be a penalty kick.

"'E ran into 'im. There wor nowt Rawdon could do about it," said one.

"Rawdon took 'is legs. The new kid would've scored if 'e 'adn't," said another.

There was no referee to make the decision and Adam couldn't see how they were going to resolve the dispute until Luke stepped in.

"What do you think, Rawdon?" he asked. "Was it a penalty?"

Rawdon hesitated, surprised to be asked. The rest of the players fell silent, waiting. Adam could see that it was a clever move by Luke. Would Rawdon take his own side or would he want to look fair? And the second choice also gave him a chance at glory if he could save the penalty kick.

He glanced at Adam, looking him up and down for a moment, and made his decision. "I reckon it was," he said. "But 'e's got to take it. Not thee, Luke. You know our rules."

"Good," said Luke. "I agree." And he handed the ball to Adam, pointing at the almost invisible white spot painted into the muddy grass twelve yards from the goal.

Adam took four steps back and braced himself, trying to concentrate on the ball and not look at Rawdon, who was staring at him from the goalmouth. He'd decided to go to the left. He didn't know why but he was certain of his decision, and yet the knowledge didn't stop his heart thumping in his chest. It felt like a hammer beat, but there was no time left to calm down. It was just a kick, he told himself as he got ready to run; just one stupid kick, and yet in that instant he wanted it to succeed more than he could ever remember wanting anything. Perhaps he wanted it too much, which was why he half slipped as he went forward, scuffing the shot so that it lost most of its power as it travelled towards the middle of the goal. It should have been easy to save but Rawdon had read Adam's intentions too well. He dived hard to his right and watched helplessly as the ball rolled past his feet into the net.

Adam's team cheered. They'd won the match and it didn't matter if the new boy had got lucky. He'd played well and he'd made the chance for himself. They laughed, clapping him on the back as they walked off, and even some of the other team's players joined in. But Rawdon stood watching him with a look of concentrated hostility. He waited, leaning against a goalpost, until they were alone, facing each other.

"It don't matter what 'appened," he said, looking Adam in the eye. "It don't matter how many goals you score. You don't belong here wi' us. An' you niver will."

He didn't wait for a response but walked quickly away, limping slightly as he went.

"What happened to Rawdon?" Adam asked Ernest as they began the walk home. "Luke said he used to score goals so why's he the goalkeeper now?"

"He hurt his leg down the mine," said Ernest. "The pony he was driving got scared of something and bolted. And then pulled up short and kicked back—britching, we call it. Rawdon caught his leg in the limmers—"

"Limmers? What are they?" asked Adam, interrupting.

"The shafts they put on the pony's harness to link him up to the tubs. You don't know anything, do you?" said Ernest, smiling. "Any road, Rawdon broke his leg in three places. He must've been in agony—he was white as a sheet when they brought him out but he didn't cry out at all. Rawdon's always been a brave lad, I'll say that for him. And then the hospital didn't do a good job with the operation, or at least that's what Rawdon's father, Whalen, said, although I reckon he was just after trying to duck out of the responsibility. He should have been watching out for his boy. Rawdon was only thirteen when it happened and maybe he wasn't ready for the tubs, although I suppose you've got to start somewhere. Except maybe with him it would have been different."

"What do you mean?" asked Adam, not understanding.

"Because of the football. Rawdon was really good, better than you can imagine. He could go round you before you knew what had happened, like he was picking your pocket," said Ernest, smiling at the memory. "And a lot of us thought he'd end up playing for one of the clubs, earning proper money, having a life that the likes of me can only dream about. But the mine's got a way of claiming you back when you're thinking of escaping it, and it's got Rawdon for life now, whether he likes it or not."

"I suppose it would've been different if he'd stayed at school," said Adam. "Then he wouldn't have got injured."

"I suppose," said Ernest. "But it's not the way here. I got good marks at school and my mother would have liked me to go on, but my dad wouldn't hear of it. Bought me a pair of moleskin trousers and a cloth cap for my fourteenth birthday and took me up to the manager's office to sign on the next day. And that was that."

"And you work while I sit in school," said Adam. "But it's not easy to be different, you know, Ernest. You don't belong anywhere. People resent you."

"Like Rawdon?"

"Yes."

"Well, you shouldn't worry about him. He resents everyone. Play football like you did today and you'll be all right," said Ernest, clapping Adam on the back.

But Adam did worry. Not just about Rawdon but about who he was, where he was going. He was an outsider, living in a town that he was striving to escape, learning Latin and Greek at the board school so he could move away and better himself, while everyone else in Scarsdale had their gaze fixed forever inwards, their lives dominated by the mine. It was like a magnet drawing men and boys down deeper and deeper into its black passages, while the women and girls slaved away in their mean box-like little houses to service their needs. Adam saw how Annie, Edgar's wife, toiled ceaselessly, washing clothes, baking bread, cooking meals, maintaining everything in a constant state of readiness for her menfolk, who often returned home at different hours of the day or night as their shift times changed from week to week. Sometimes she didn't go to bed at all but just dozed on a chair in front of the fire ready to jump up and wait on them when they came in. And perhaps the constant activity was a good thing, keeping her distracted from the gnawing fear that one day Edgar or Thomas or Ernest wouldn't come home at all, falling victim instead to one of the terrible underground accidents that seemed to happen almost every week.

The mine was cruel and the mine was king. And yet Adam had never once been inside it. He knew that he was frightened of it—terrified even. It was the embodiment of his worst childhood nightmares when he'd dreamed over and over again of being stuck fast in a narrow space in the pitch-black darkness unable to move, buried alive without hope of rescue. And yet he hated the fear too. Adam was brave by nature and his secret shamed him, becoming a challenge that he had to overcome. If he gave into it he wouldn't be able to hold up his head in front of the boys his age who worked down the mine every day. He needed to understand their experience; he needed to know what he was working so hard to try to get away from.

He waited a few days, screwing up his courage, and then asked his father to show him the mine. He had been anticipating opposition but instead Daniel seemed pleased by the request—once he had got over his initial surprise at being asked; he knew full well his son's fear of going underground.

"Come to the pithead tomorrow morning and I'll show you round," he said. "There's a lot to learn and it won't hurt you to miss one day of school."

Chapter Three

At first Adam was alone as he walked down the street from Edgar's house, but by the time he reached the station he had become part of a crowd of miners all heading the same way towards the valley bottom with their snap tins and drinking flasks dangling from their hands. The rising sun was shining on their backs and they seemed happy and carefree: laughing, smoking, jostling each other—a sea of cloth caps moving towards the headstocks whose wheels were running fast now, hauling the cages up and down the shafts. The men's mood increased Adam's sense of isolation—none of them could imagine the dread he was feeling in the pit of his stomach. He had to force himself to go on, placing one foot in front of the other.

Further down the road, they started to meet miners coming the other way, returning home from the night shift. They were black with coal, blinking bleary eyes in the sunlight as they shuffled wearily along. And now the road became a path, winding its way through a grey barren waste ground littered with the detritus of the mine—discarded feed sacks for the ponies, broken coal tubs and timber props, pieces of rusting machinery whose purpose Adam couldn't determine. Railway lines snaked here and there with the main line running on towards the screens area where Ernest worked.

Adam could see him with a group of other boys and men, standing on either side of a wide belt of moving coal, their hands in a constant flurry of motion as they pulled out stones and rubbish and threw them aside, although not fast enough to satisfy a corpulent red-faced man in a low round-crowned black hat who was standing on a gantry above the screens, shouting at the workers below, berating them for being too slow or too careless with a stream of profanity that never seemed to end.

It looked like terrible work, Adam thought. As fast as they worked, the coal kept on coming, tipped down a series of chutes on to the sorting belts by tippler machines. On and on, hour after hour, until it was time to go home and catch a few hours' sleep before beginning again. Adam wondered at his friend's patience and good humour. If he were in Ernest's shoes he thought he'd go mad within a week or at least throw a lump of coal at the slave-driving tyrant up above; anything to make him shut up if only for a moment.

"Not easy, is it?" said Daniel, who had been looking out for his son and now came up to him, observing the appalled look on his face. "But at least the screens are above ground—I suppose there's that much to be said for them."

"Why does he have to shout like that?" asked Adam, pointing up at the fat man, who was now threatening to dock the screen workers' wages if they got up to any more of their "damned dilly-dallying, playin' the fool on his lordship's time."

"Because that's the way he is," said Daniel with a smile. "Atkins's bark's worse than his bite but you're right—no one likes him much. Except the manager maybe—the cleaner the coal the more money it gets. And make no mistake—money's what this is all about. Sell the coal to the highest bidder and pay as little as you can to get it out of the ground, which is where I come in, of course—trying to make sure that the men get what they deserve, which isn't easy when you're dealing with people who worship profit margins like it's their religion. Come on. I'll show you where I work."

The weighing office was one of a group of mismatched buildings standing at different angles to each other around the base of the headstocks. Through an open door Adam glimpsed the blazing red fire of a blacksmith's forge and the acrid coal smoke mixed in his nostrils with the tarry, oily smell of the huge steam engine that was powering the headstock pulleys. Close up, the clank of the pistons, the hiss of expelled steam and the general roar of the machine made it hard for Adam to hear what his father was saying, and Daniel had to shout to make himself understood as he described how the tubs of coal came up out of the cage with the collier's motty tags attached, ready to be weighed.

"The owner's man weighs them and then I do the same so the colliers can be sure they're getting paid properly for the coal they've mined," said Daniel. "It's a big responsibility but I like that they trust me." The pride in his father's voice gave Adam pleasure. He had refused to buckle in the face of a terrible adversity and now here was his reward. But Adam sensed a new humility in his father too—it was as if suffering had added a new dimension to his personality, taught him that life was precarious and had to be treated carefully.

"So, are you ready?" asked Daniel, handing his son a lamp. Adam nodded, swallowing. He was sweating and his hands were shaking so he found it hard to attach the lamp to his belt as his father was doing.

"You don't have to do this, you know," said Daniel, looking hard at his son.

"Yes, I do," said Adam. He'd used up almost all his stock of bloody-minded determination to get this far and he didn't think he'd be able to try again if he turned back now. And he needed to be able to look at himself in the mirror without having to turn away—he couldn't bear to be less than he hoped he was. It was a virtue and a fault that he would carry with him all his life.

"Where do we light it?" he asked, pointing at his lamp.

"We don't—the overman does that down below. And if it goes out then we have to walk back to the lighting station to get it relit. You can't have any fire inside the mine—it's far too dangerous."

"Because of the gas?" Adam asked, shuddering as he remembered Edgar's account of the two boys trapped by fallen rock after an explosion.

"Yes. You can't smell it and you can't see it, but it'll explode if it gets near a flame. More miners have lost their lives from gas explosions than roof falls so we have to be careful all the time. Back when I was young miners used to take canaries down—once they stopped singing you knew it was time to go. But now they make the lamps so the light expands when there's gas about. They're ingenious these inventors—that's something I'd like to have been if I'd had the brains," Daniel said wistfully.

Adam was grateful to his father for his flow of chatter. Daniel wasn't talkative by nature and Adam knew that he was trying to keep him distracted from the ordeal ahead. But now there was no escaping it. Wreathed in jets of steam, they had joined a group of miners climbing up the wooden stairs leading to the cage platform; for Adam they were just like the steps going up to a monstrous gallows. He looked up as if expecting to find the noose, but instead saw the spokes of the great wheel flickering in the sunlight as it pulled the cage up to the top of the shaft.

The men inside walked out and the banksman beckoned them inside. Adam hesitated, looking wildly around. Away down below he could see bottles of tea left to warm beside the steam engine that was driving the mechanical screens. At that moment his life felt just as insignificant. He wanted to run back down the steps and up the hill away from the mine, putting it behind him forever, but he couldn't. He'd come too far to turn back. With a last despairing glance back at the sunlight, he took a deep breath and followed his father inside the cage and closed his eyes.

All around him the men were talking, without a care in the world. He could hear an electric bell ringing somewhere down below and one nearby answering it and then the clang of the gate as it slammed shut, and they were falling, slowly at first and then faster, faster than he would have thought possible. He was going to die—he was sure of it. He felt his stomach lifting up into his mouth and his feet coming up off the floor and someone—it had to be his father—holding him by the back of his collar, and then the brake kicked in and they were down below.

Adam opened his eyes. There was a little light coming down the shaft, and he could dimly see the faces of the miners queuing up at the lighting station. He was relieved to see that they paid him no attention—clearly no one except his father had noticed his distress in the cage on the way down. With their lamps lit, the miners walked away down one of the three sloping tunnels that radiated off the maingate, as the central area around the cage was called. Almost immediately they became no more than tiny points of light in the inky blackness before disappearing from view.

It was cold and Adam shivered, unprepared for the sudden change in temperature. The anxious sweat was now freezing on his skin. But he felt better—he'd overcome his fear, proved to himself that he was no coward. His overactive imagination had been the real enemy, he realized: the mine was never going to be as terrible as he'd built it up to be in his mind's eye.

They went first to the stables, which were still in the main landing area, not far from the cage. Daniel had made friends with the ostler and he took them from stall to stall, describing the merits and demerits of each pony. Some were hard workers; some liked to go on strike, refusing to move if you harnessed them up to too many tubs. And some could give you trouble, britching and kicking if you didn't get in there first and show them who was boss.

"Like the one that hurt Rawdon?" asked Adam.

"Whalen's boy? 'Twas 'is fault what 'appened to 'im," said the ostler, his face darkening. "Ridin' on the back o' the pony when 'e shouldna done. That's how accidents 'appen. An' then the pony 'ad to be put down when 'e didna need to be. Whalen made sure o' that, damn him."

The stables were clean and well kept and the ponies were clearly well looked after, but Adam still felt sorry for them, living their lives in the godforsaken darkness, hauling coal up and down through the dusty black tunnels until their strength gave out and they were put to merciful sleep. It seemed wrong, not what they had been born for, but that was true of the miners too, although at least they got to leave the pit at the end of the day when their work was done.

"Do they ever get out, have time up above?" Adam asked.

"Aye, they goes up once a year for respite. They 'ave races and the men bet on 'em. They're good days, they are. But it's hard to get 'em back down afterwards. Needs all thy strength to push 'em into their boxes."

"Perhaps it would be better if they didn't know," said Adam pensively.

"Know what?"

"About the sun and the wind and the rain. Then they wouldn't miss them."

"O' course they don't miss 'em. They're ponies, for Chrissake," said the ostler, sounding irritated. "He's a contrary lad, thy boy, ain't 'e?" he added, turning to Daniel.

"That he is, Joe. That he is," said Daniel, affecting a false jocularity that jarred on Adam. "But he doesn't mean any harm, do you, Adam?"

"No, I don't," said Adam uneasily. He was sorry that he'd got on the wrong side of the ostler, who seemed a good man, genuinely concerned for the welfare of the animals in his care. It wasn't the first time since he'd come to Scarsdale, Adam realized, that he'd put people's backs up just by being himself. His different voice, his book learning as they called it, made people suspicious of him or even dislike him—like Rawdon, who'd wasted no time becoming his sworn enemy for no reason at all except the spurious one that their fathers had been rivals for the same job. Adam wondered where Rawdon was now—he'd be working somewhere in the mine and Adam hoped that their paths wouldn't cross. He didn't want Rawdon to see him when he felt at such a disadvantage.

"Where's Edgar working?" Daniel asked the ostler, changing the subject.

"In Oakwell," said the ostler. "Same as before. 'E doesna stop carpin' about it, but 'es earnin' good money. There's good coal in there still even if you has to work hard to get it out."

"All right, Oakwell it is," said Daniel. "Thanks for showing my boy around, Joe."

The ostler nodded, but without looking at Adam. He was clearly still disgruntled by Adam's contrariness, but there was no time for Adam to attempt any further apology, as Daniel had already set off along one of the wide tunnels that led down into the mine.

"What's Oakwell?" Adam asked, catching him up.

"One of the districts."

"Districts?"

"Yes; they're the different seams in the mine. There are three active ones in the Scarsdale pit as well as several more that have been exhausted, and they call them after football grounds. Oakwell's where Barnsley play. I'm surprised you haven't found that out yet. People round here are mad about football."

"I know, Dad. I've been playing it, remember?"

"Yes, I do and I'm pleased you are," said Daniel warmly. "It'll help you make friends, get accepted. I know it's not easy—" He broke off, but Adam knew what his father had been going to say and he was right—it wasn't easy living in Scarsdale and not being a miner.

It was much darker now than it had been back in the white-washed stables: pitch-black outside the pools of light cast by their lamps. But the tunnel was still far less daunting than Adam had anticipated. A succession of curving steel supports holding up the roof gave him a sense of security and the generous height and width of the roadway were enough to keep his claustrophobia at bay. But it was still a ghostly place—water dripped continuously from a pipe running along the crown of the roof down into puddles on the ground in which Adam caught faint reflections of himself and his father in the lamplight.

The tunnel was empty except for two roadmen hard at work repairing the narrow railway that ran down the centre, constructed on top of wooden sleepers bolted together with fishplates. The noise of their claw hammers echoed off the walls—a clanging percussion that broke off suddenly when they got up and moved quickly to the sides of the roadway. Adam and Daniel followed suit, ducking into one of the manhole niches that were built at regular intervals along the sides of the tunnel. A pony was coming up the slope, hauling a line of coal tubs each full to the brim and marked with the iron motty tags that Daniel had told his son about earlier. As it came abreast of where they were standing, Adam saw that the pony had a rider. Rawdon was lying flat on the animal's back, his hands on its black ears, his head turned sideways in their direction. He caught Adam's eye as he passed and smiled—a cold, contemptuous smile that made Adam feel that Rawdon had seen right through him and felt the toxic fear that he was working so hard to keep under control.

"The boy's an idiot—that's how he hurt himself before," said Daniel, looking back at the train of tubs as it rounded a corner in the tunnel, its wheels rattling on the rails. "His father would be furious if he knew."

"Will you tell him?" asked Adam.

"No, Whalen wouldn't want to hear it from me," said Daniel, shaking his head. "And anyway today's about you, not Rawdon Dawes. We don't need to get distracted."

"About you"—once again Adam wondered why his father had been so quick to grant his request to see the mine. What was it he was hoping to achieve?

He wanted to follow his father's advice and put Rawdon's sudden apparition out of his mind, but it was hard—the encounter seemed like an ill omen, coming so soon on the heels of his wish that their paths shouldn't cross.

And it didn't help his peace of mind that the ceiling was getting lower now as they went further down into the mine so that they had begun to have to bend their necks forward as they walked to avoid hitting their heads on the overhead struts. Adam wasn't used to walking in a crouch and his back started to ache, but still his father pressed on.

And it was getting hotter too, so hot that Adam took off his shirt to better feel the soft breeze that the mine's ventilation system was blowing down the tunnel behind them. But even with the ventilation, he was starting to find it harder to breathe—the air was thick with dust and the stale sulphurous smell of the black powder used to blast the coal from the seam. Low stalls led off passages from the main tunnel in which Adam caught glimpses of miners working. They were down on their knees, stripped to the waist like him, and their torsos, black with coal dust and sweat, gleamed in the light from their lamps. On all sides there was a constant noise of hammering and hewing and breaking.

Adam felt his senses being overwhelmed as if by a raging tide. He wanted to scream out loud, but he doubted his father would have heard as he had hurried on ahead, looking for Edgar. All the time the tunnel was narrowing and the roof was getting lower. It was supported on timber props now, which left it sagging in places.

And then, just as Adam felt he had come to the limits of his endurance, just as he had decided to tell his father that he could go no further, Daniel stopped, standing at the entrance to a stall from which Adam could hear familiar voices coming.

Looking over his father's shoulder, Adam could see Edgar and his older son, Thomas, lying on their sides working at the face. Edgar was using a mandrel, a straight-bladed pick, to hack the coal from the seam and Thomas was shovelling it back into a waiting tub. Their lamps and most of their clothes were hanging from nails hammered into the wall and they both were naked apart from their underwear, boots and padded caps. Adam felt embarrassed, out of place. He wished he hadn't come and hung back behind his father, hoping that Edgar would not see him, which at first he didn't.

"Welcome, cousin, to my 'umble abode," said Edgar, doffing his cap and laughing at his affectation of a city voice. "What brings thee down 'ere out o' the sunshine?"

"To show his white-fingered son 'ow the other 'alf lives," said a caustic voice behind Adam, who turned round and came face to face with a thick-set, bald-headed man about his own height. He seemed to be about the same age as Edgar and like him was stripped to his underwear with his face and skin blackened with coal, but his outlandish appearance clearly had no effect on his confidence. The dirt was a badge of honour, an outward manifestation of his class credentials.

Because Whalen Dawes was a fanatic. Adam could tell that straightaway; it was clear to see in the hard chiselled set of his chin and in his unforgiving flinty grey eyes—different coloured eyes from his son, who was standing behind his father, watching with that same look of dry amusement that Adam had seen on his face before. After he had delivered the coal tubs, he must have ridden the pony straight back from the maingate to wherever his father worked in time to tell him about the visitors and give him the opportunity to intercept them.

Now Adam truly regretted asking his father to show him the mine. He'd hoped that the experience would bring him closer to the miners, help him to understand them better, but instead it was just going to make them see him as even more of an uppity outsider.

"Is this true, Daniel? Is that why you're here?" asked Edgar, who had now come forward and caught sight of Adam.

"No, of course it isn't," said Daniel. "Adam wanted to know what the mine was like, which is natural—he lives here after all, and so I agreed to show him."

"Agreed to show 'im cos you want to scare 'im, make sure 'e don't end up down 'ere, cos you thinks 'e's too good for the likes of us," said Whalen, pressing his advantage.

"No, that's not true," said Daniel angrily. But Adam knew that Rawdon's father was right—his father *had* been trying to scare him. He'd asked the ostler where Edgar worked but he hadn't needed to because he already knew. And he'd taken him to the Oakwell seam because it was the narrowest, lowest part of the mine, the place most likely to trigger his claustrophobia.

It made Adam angry to have been manipulated, and angry too that he had allowed it to happen. But there was nothing he could do. His father's plan had fully succeeded: panic was welling up inside him like a flooded dam about to burst its banks.

For a moment everyone was silent. It was as if they were all waiting on Edgar as he opened up his flask and took a long slow drink of the sweet milky tea that all the miners took with them into the pit.

"I don't know," said Edgar pensively. "Whalen likes nowt more'n to make trouble, I knows that . . ."

"I tells the truth," said Whalen vehemently. "If that makes trouble, then I makes no apology for it."

But Edgar held up his hand, insisting on finishing his thought. "As I says, I knows that. But that don't mean what 'e says ain't true, and I have to say, Daniel, that I doubt thee sometimes. I wish I didn't but I do."

There was an uneasy silence, broken when a pair of rats scurried across the floor of the tunnel, causing Adam to jump instinctively out of the way. Rawdon laughed. "You'll 'ave to get used to them if you're goin' to be makin' a habit of comin' down 'ere," he said. "We likes the rats, don't we, Dad—when they scurry about it gives us fair warnin' that the roof might be about to cave."

Whalen looked at his son and then over at Adam, seeing how he was swaying on his feet. Just a little push would send him over.

"You're right, Rawdon," he said. "Same as the timber props—we prefers 'em to the steel ones cos you can hear 'em creak and whine afore they go."

Adam didn't know if he could hear creaking or whining. But he could feel the millions of tons of earth and rock over his head bearing down on him, ready to bury him alive. It was intolerable, insupportable, more than he could stand. The tidal wave of his panic burst out, swamping his consciousness, and he fell to the ground in a dead faint.

Chapter Four

On an afternoon in the late summer Adam went for a walk with Ernest, who had the day off from the screens. Coming out of the house, turning away from the mine and into the light of the rising sun, they raced each other up the hill to the oak tree on the ridge. Adam was far ahead by the time they reached the top. He was a natural athlete and his growing prowess at football had helped him win friends in the town, even though there were still some who continued to give him the cold shoulder. Rawdon was their leader and he never tired of telling anyone who would listen how Adam had gone down the mine to "see 'ow the other 'alf live" and had had to be hauled out unconscious in an empty coal tub.

The shame of his misadventure gnawed at Adam far more than he was willing to admit. It wasn't just the humiliation—his struggles with adversity had given him a strong sense of his own worth and he was never going to be fatally undermined by jibes thrown at him in the street. It was his verdict on himself that made him suffer. He had set himself a challenge when he went down the mine and he had fallen short. And it was hard to look a miner in the eye when he knew and they knew that he could not last a single morning in the subterranean darkness where they laboured all their lives.

Adam wasn't used to failure. His instinct was always to try and try again until he had overcome the hurdle that had first defeated him, but this time there was no opportunity for redemption. He wouldn't be allowed back in the mine even if he asked to go. Not after what had happened. And so every day he was left to gaze over at the giant headstocks with their great spinning wheels and feel their reproach. Except that today they were standing motionless and from their vantage point at the crest of the hill Adam and Ernest could see lines of dejected men trooping home from the pit. They had been let off early for the third time that week. There was less demand for coal in the summer and so there would be less in the men's pay packets come Friday night.

"It's hard on my mother, hard on all the women," said Ernest, leaning back against the tree trunk with a sigh. "It's the old story: prices go up and wages go down. And when the women complain the men slink off out the back door to drown their troubles at the King's Head where they've got a nice fire and a smiling barmaid, and then there's no money left to pay the bills."

"It was like that in London too," said Adam. "Except that it was the other way round: the building trade was slack in the winter and picked up in the summer."

"Well, the answer's the minimum wage," said Ernest. "Everybody knows that. But the owners won't pay it so something'll have to give."

"There'll be a strike—is that what you mean?" asked Adam. Just saying the word made him nervous, bringing back those terrible last days in London and his mother's untimely, unnecessary death.

"Yes, I expect so. My dad wants to do something, I know that."

"And mine doesn't?" asked Adam.

"I don't know. My brother says he's trying to negotiate but there's a feeling that that's not going anywhere, that the owners are just playing him along."

"Taking him for a fool?"

"I didn't say that," said Ernest sharply. "Look, I don't know much more than you do. My dad doesn't say much and a lot of what I hear at the pithead is just rumour—men complaining, letting off steam."

Adam nodded, but he knew himself that all was not well between his father and Edgar. Ernest's father had gone out of his way to be kind to Adam after the debacle in the mine, telling him that a lot of "first-timers" found it hard to cope with the bad air and the noise in the deeper seams, but, as far as Adam was aware, there had been no rapprochement between the two cousins. They seemed ill at ease in each other's company and the atmosphere in the house was strained as a result. Adam remembered the rebuke that Edgar had administered to his father before he fainted away, and he wondered how much longer he and his father would be welcome under Edgar's roof.

But the ill feeling had certainly not affected his friendship with Ernest. As the months had gone by, he had grown to trust and admire his second cousin. He liked Ernest's lack of prejudice—the way he insisted on making up his own mind about issues even if the majority disagreed with him, and the way he never complained about his lot; this quality seemed even more impressive to Adam after he had seen at first hand the awful driving monotony involved in working on the pithead screens. If Ernest had a fault it was a lack of ambition. His world was what it was and he had no hope of changing it. He was stoic without being cynical, and his loyalty was absolute.

"Come on," he said, getting to his feet. "We're not here to talk about the mine, not on my day off. There's somewhere I want to show you."

They followed the path over the ridge and were suddenly in a new world. The mine and the grey monochrome houses of the town disappeared as if by magic, replaced in an instant by a pastoral landscape of woods and fields and streams unchanged in centuries. There was the sound of birdsong in the air and a red kite circled slowly overhead, allowing the fluctuating eddies of the faint breeze to direct its flight.

After a mile or so Ernest stopped, pointing down to his left, where they could see over a long grey brick wall to where the pale stucco exterior of a substantial country house glittered in the golden light of the afternoon against a background of thick-leaved elms and, closer in, rows of tall cypress trees, pointing like long dark green fingers up towards the sun. Between the two wings, the Palladian façade with elegant sash windows rising symmetrically on either side of the entrance portico was half reflected in the still surface of a lake, which abutted a wide manicured lawn that descended on a gentle slope from the quadrangular courtyard and ornamental stone terrace at the front of the house. Two regal swans were floating on the water, preening their long white necks.

"Scarsdale Hall," said Ernest, theatrically waving his hand. "Home of Sir John, who pays me a pittance for cleaning his coal."

"I've seen him," said Adam. "He comes to church sometimes with his wife wrapped up in furs and a son who doesn't like me."

"Why?"

"Because he doesn't think I've got the right to look at the parson's daughter."

"Miriam—she's pretty, isn't she?"

"Yes. How do you know? I thought your family never went near a church."

"We go there for funerals. Everyone does, whether they believe in it or not. A miner who's got blown to bits in a firedamp explosion deserves a good send-off; and it makes the family feel we care, which is what matters. The parson understands that—I'll say that for him. And Miriam looks beautiful in a black dress," said Ernest with a grin.

"You like her, don't you?" he added, laughing now at Adam's discomfort. He'd noticed how the colour had risen to his friend's cheeks each time he said her name. "Well, all I can say is: Don't let her mother know how you feel or she'll have you locked up. She's an invalid, never leaves the house, but that doesn't mean she's not the one who wears the trousers in the marriage. The parson's hard up and Mrs. Vale wants her daughter to marry money so I suppose Brice Scarsdale would fit the bill."

"Don't say that," said Adam fiercely. "She deserves better than him. He's the worst of his kind—stupid, selfish, arrogant—"

He broke off, suddenly self-conscious, and Ernest looked at him curiously. He was unused to his friend becoming so emotional, spitting out his words like venom.

"You're right," he said. "No one likes Brice and Miriam's a nice girl, but their lives aren't like ours. The Parsonage and the Hall are close to where we live but they might as well be on a different planet. See what it's like in church next time you go there: the poor and the miners at the back; the shopkeepers and the managers and the farmers in the middle; and Sir John up at the front. Everyone has their place in the world and you know where ours is."

"Well, I don't accept that," said Adam. "She shouldn't have to marry a worthless parasite like Brice just because her mother tells her to. She should be able to choose whom she wants when the time comes."

They relapsed into silence, each lost in their own thoughts, interrupted only when Ernest produced two slices of his mother's freshly baked fruit cake from his snap tin which they ate slowly, savouring the taste as they gazed down at the great house and the sun glinting on the golden weathervane up above the stone gables.

"It's beautiful, isn't it?" said Ernest.

"Yes."

"But paid for with so much suffering," he said thoughtfully. "Look down there, outside the wall—see the farmworkers' cottages all nicely thatched and weatherproof. Must make Sir John feel like he's a model landlord when he drives past them in his Rolls-Royce, but the truth is they're just a sideline. The real money comes from the mine and he never goes near that; leaves it instead to Atkins and the other managers to get their hands dirty. It's over the hill and out of sight. And what you don't see, you don't have to feel responsible for."

"And I suppose it's my dad's job to try to make him see," said Adam.

"Yes, that's right, and I don't envy him the task. With Whalen and my dad on one side and blind Sir John on the other, he's got to feel like he's being pulled apart by a couple of riled-up pit ponies," said Ernest, shaking his head.

"Do you know who Whalen reminds me of?" asked Adam, remembering his encounter with Rawdon's father in the mine—the hard unforgiving voice and the cruel flinty eyes.

Ernest shook his head.

"My dad—he used to be just like him. Any excuse to fight the oppressor and too bad if people got hurt in the process. He was a fanatic, a true believer, until my mother died. And then everything changed. He's a better man now, more sensible, more reasonable, but it's also like he's lost his spark, his passion—whatever you want to call it. It's like something in him died when she died. God knows how it'll all end," he finished sadly, sounding like an astrologer who'd lost his ability to read the stars.

"I'll tell you how it ends," said Ernest, looking hard at his friend. "No, better—I'll show you. Come on. It's not far."

They walked on quickly now with Ernest setting the pace. Over another hill and down into a valley where the path passed through the cool shadows of a beech wood, where bluebells grew in clusters beneath the gnarled mossy green trunks of the old trees. And then out into the open again as they climbed up the other side, walking between tall grasses under the cloudless azure sky.

"You're a liar," said Adam, stopping to wipe the sweat from his brow. "This is twice as far as we walked before."

"But worth it," said Ernest, beckoning to his friend to join him on the ridge. "Worth it to see what the end of the world looks like."

Adam stood stock still, staring down into a bowl-shaped valley similar to the one containing the Scarsdale pit but smaller and with just a single headstock at the bottom that had toppled over on to one side. Its wheels were brown with rust and the shack-like buildings around the pithead were in a state of pitiful disrepair, left to rot amid a sea of weeds and strangling vines. And the same was true of the miners' houses that stretched up the sides of the valley—the same mean streets as in the Scarsdale valley but built here of less durable materials which hadn't stood the test of time. A few of the windows still had broken glass but most were just holes in the walls—openings into black empty interiors, home to rats and spiders.

"What happened?" Adam asked.

"The seam was exhausted so they went down deeper; too deep, and the mine flooded. Some miners were drowned and the rest were laid off, so they moved to Scarsdale or other pits and the village died. Thorley it was called, and now the name means nothing."

"When did it happen?"

"Fifteen years ago—same year I was born. In another fifteen there probably won't be anything left and no one will even know that there was once a mine here and a village and a pub and a union.

And one day Scarsdale will go the same way and there's nothing my dad or your dad or Whalen Dawes can do to stop it."

They had gone down the hill a little way to where a street of tumbledown houses began. On a whim Adam pushed open the rotted door of the first one they came to. It creaked on its rusted hinges and immediately a pair of angry black birds—rooks or crows, it was too quick to know which they were—flew past him up into the air where they were joined by a flock of others, rising in a whirr of wings from the eaves of the other houses. They circled overhead, cawing angrily at the interlopers.

"Be careful," said Ernest, who had stayed back in the street. "The roof will cave in if you give it half a chance. A lot of them already have from the looks of it."

But Adam didn't respond. He had moved to the centre of the room, standing gingerly on the rotten joists that were all that was left of the floor as he listened intently to a sound of rocking that was coming from the upper floor. In the corner a rickety staircase was missing several of its steps. He didn't need Ernest to tell him that it would be stupid to climb it and yet he didn't think twice. He had to see who or what was making the noise above. He was halfway up when it stopped and the stairs began to give way beneath him. The nightmare memory of falling in the pit cage flashed across his mind and he reached out and grabbed the newel post at the top of the stairs and pulled himself up to safety just as the staircase collapsed behind him and the house seemed to tremble on its foundations.

He was in a square room, standing across from a small sash window that had long ago lost all its glass. Below the sill an emaciated black-and-white cat was standing, precariously keeping its balance on a rocking chair that was rocking violently to and fro again, responding to the shaking of the house. The animal was clearly enraged—its fur was standing on end, its back was arched and an angry snarl had exposed its teeth. Adam just had time to take a step back and put his hands up to protect his face before it sprang at him through the air, scratching his arms before it leapt down through the hole in the corner where the staircase had been and disappeared.

Adam looked down and inspected the damage: livid lacerations along the backs of both forearms that were starting to bleed. He took off his shirt and used the sleeves to staunch the blood. He felt faint and sat down on the cherry-wood chair, keeping his feet on the floor to stop it rocking. He could see it was handmade, each arm and leg lovingly carved and crafted to enable it to stand the test of time. The miner who had lived here had made it, Adam guessed, for his wife perhaps to sit at the window and look out at the sun rising over the hills.

He closed his eyes for a moment, imagining the past, and was startled by Ernest shouting his name from down below.

"I'm all right," he said, getting up and leaning out of the window. "I'll come down in a minute."

"How? You've broken the staircase, you idiot. I told you to be careful," said Ernest, laughing. "Wait there and I'll find something for you to jump down onto."

Adam turned to go back and sit in the chair but jumped, knocking it over, when a mouse scuttled under his feet, looking back at him for a moment before it vanished into a hole in the wainscot. And down next to the opening, he saw a toy train half hidden by some rags. He bent down and picked it up. It was made out of the same shining cherry wood as the rocking chair with each detail beautifully executed down to the wheels that slowly turned as he rolled it to and fro along a floor plank.

The chair for the wife and a toy for their child: Adam could see them in his mind's eye, looking out of the window at just this time of day, waiting for the miner to return home, putting their trust in a future which was about to be snatched away from them. Just like his own mother had in London. And thinking of her again, he suddenly saw her bedroom in the house in Islington as clearly as if he had been transported back in time and was standing on the half-landing looking in. There was the little desk in the corner where she did her accounts, there the cross on the mildew-stained wall, and there the empty bed covered with the cheap eiderdown to which she would never return. She had hoped and dreamed too, unaware of what lay in store for her just around the corner.

"Come on," shouted Ernest, his voice breaking in harshly on Adam's reverie. "Time to jump!"

Adam looked down and saw that Ernest had dragged an old mattress below the window.

"Better land on your feet," he said. "I wouldn't want to put my face in this fleabag."

Adam tried to lift the sash but it came away in his hands and so he knocked away the rest of the frame and laughed when he hit the ground amid an explosion of dust and feathers. He was young and the strong blood pumping through his veins wouldn't let him stay melancholy for very long.

Chapter Five

They had been at Scarsdale for almost a year and Adam had his own life now. He rose early to take the bus into Gratton and worked hard at his books all day and in the evening too, when he laboured over Latin and Greek translations, straining his eyes to read by the light of the dim oil lamp while Ernest snored in his bed on the other side of the room. Adam loved the ancient world. He'd first heard many of the stories from his mother. She'd begin by reading from books but would then put them down and carry on the narrative herself in her own words. She had a gift for painting word pictures and he could remember how as a child he'd seen in his mind's eye Odysseus and his comrades waiting nervously inside the wooden horse as the unsuspecting Trojans dragged it inside the gates of their city or Caesar stabbed to death on the ides of March. Listening to her, the heroes and villains of the past became more real than the people in his own life; and now, reading the ancient books, Adam felt the same thrill again.

He liked the school and he enjoyed being the headmaster's prize pupil. But in the house at the end of Station Street he was less happy. The atmosphere remained strained and he could see how his father was being eaten up with stress and anxiety. Daniel's proud receipt of the glowing reports that his son brought back from school seemed to be the only times when Adam saw his father happy. Otherwise he was a shadow of the man he'd been in London and it was hard for Adam to recognize him as the same happy-go-lucky person who had challenged the gypsy champion to a boxing match in the market square and come away with ten shillings jingling in his coat pocket.

It was Daniel's isolated position as negotiator between the union and the owners that was the source of the trouble. As he had promised Adam he would do in the train coming north, he had tried to negotiate solutions to disputes rather than use them as an excuse for escalating conflict. And in the process he had developed a good relationship with Sir John Scarsdale and the managers, but mutual respect had not brought with it significant concessions. The essence of the problem was that Scarsdale was an old pit. In its day it had filled the coffers of Sir John's father and financed handsome improvements at Scarsdale Hall, including the renovation of the agricultural cottages that Ernest had pointed out to Adam on their walk. But since the turn of the century productivity had steadily fallen. In response the miners had dug deeper and the narrow Oakwell seam had recently yielded good coal, but the greater depth brought more risks and the need for increased expenditure on safety.

Sometimes there were ad hoc union meetings on Friday evenings at Edgar's house after the week's money had been divvied up among the butty teams, and, from his bedroom up above, Adam would hear voices rising in anger and accusation. It was usually Whalen Dawes who took the lead. He had a way with words and knew how to play on his audience's fears, turning Daniel's long hours closeted with Sir John and the managers against him.

"You're cosyin' up with 'em," he'd say, taunting his enemy. "That's what you're doin'. Scarsdale gives thee a nice glass o' wine from one o' his deecanters an' calls thee a gen'l'man an' soon you're eatin' out o' 'is 'and like a pussycat, while the likes o' us are left to suffer, 'ackin out 'is coal in the dusty black darkness, earnin' next to nowt."

Daniel would deny the accusation but his words sounded empty and hollow when he had so little to show for his efforts. And when he was absent, Whalen would go further. " 'E's not one o' us; 'e's a southerner an' 'e doesna think like we do," he would say, watching Edgar all the time out of the corner of his eye to gauge his reaction while the other miners muttered amongst themselves. He was itching to have Daniel removed as checkweighman so that he could be appointed in his place and take control of the local union, but he could not move without Edgar's support and he wasn't sure of that yet.

He decided instead to act when the chance came to take on Sir John himself. The deaths of two Scarsdale miners gave him the opportunity. For whatever reason there had been a recent dramatic increase in the number of firedamp explosions in the mine. The cause was in dispute: the management blamed it on the growing depth of the seams being mined, but the men said that the deputies were not taking enough precautions to measure methane levels before work began each day.

This latest disaster had been particularly bad as the exploding gas ignited the coal dust on the walls of the main tunnel in the Hillsborough district, causing a flash fire which trapped a collier and his filler inside their gate, so that by the time the fire truck arrived they had burnt to death.

The whole town turned out for their funerals, walking up the hill to the church in a solemn black line behind the two widows and the men's brothers, who carried the Miners' Federation banner unfurled above their heads. The colliery brass band brought up the rear, playing the funeral march. Walking beside his father, Adam felt moved by the silent dignity of the mourners, their steps measured against the muffled beating of the bass drum.

But when they got inside the church they stopped in surprise. Whalen and Rawdon were sitting in Sir John Scarsdale's pew at the top of the nave, facing the parson in his black vestments, who was walking to and fro in front of the two coffins, which had been set up on trestles in front of the altar. He seemed agitated, apparently at a loss for what to do.

For several tense minutes there was a stand-off, broken only when Hardcastle, the mine manager, went up into the pew behind Whalen and leant forward, telling him in a loud whisper that he had to leave. But Whalen studiously ignored him, staring forward, waiting for the service to begin.

Hardcastle came back down the aisle and spoke to Daniel. "You've got to get him to move," he said.

"Why? Is Sir John coming?"

"Yes, he's outside now with Lady Scarsdale. I sent Atkins back to stop them coming in but I can't hold them much longer."

"I'll try," said Daniel, getting up. "But I doubt it'll do any good."

Adam watched as his father went up to Whalen in the front pew and tried to get his attention. This time Whalen reacted. "Get thy arm off me, you lackey," he snapped, shouting out the insult for everyone to hear as he pushed Daniel violently away, causing him to stumble back and half fall on to Miriam, the parson's daughter, who was sitting across the aisle.

Daniel picked himself up and pulled out his handkerchief to give to Miriam who was clearly distressed by what had happened. He hesitated and then beckoned to Adam to come forward from the back of the church.

"Can you take her home, Adam? I would but I'm needed here," Daniel asked. "I'm so sorry, Miss Vale. This was the last thing I intended."

Miriam nodded, accepting the apology, and instinctively Adam offered her his arm for support, flushing deeply when she accepted. As they walked back down the nave, he was intensely aware of her to the exclusion of everyone else around him. He felt the touch of her hand on his arm like electricity and could hear each rustle of her long black dress as they walked. He felt an exultation that made his heart pound, although it shamed him when he remembered it afterwards, thinking of the coffins behind him at the altar and the reason why they were all there. The raised voices and the confusion that had taken over the church were entirely outside his consciousness and he only came back to his senses when they got outside and saw Sir John standing with his wife and son and Atkins the under-manager over near the lychgate.

"You're Daniel Raine's son, aren't you?" said Sir John, coming up to them. He was clearly agitated, unable to stand still as he moved his weight from one foot to the other.

"Yes, I am," said Adam.

"Can you tell me what's happening in there?"

"Whalen, Mr. Dawes—"

"Was in our pew," said Sir John, interrupting. "Yes, I know that. But has he been removed?"

"No," said Adam. "My father was trying but it didn't work."

"Oh, this is so ridiculous," said Sir John. "I only came to show support because I thought it would give the families some comfort. If I had known—" He broke off, distracted by a sudden flurry of movement at the entrance to the church where several of the pit deputies had appeared, manhandling Whalen out into the churchyard where he stood, dusting himself off, looking delighted with the turn of events.

"You're a disgrace, sir," said Sir John, going up to him. "You should be ashamed of yourself."

"Nay, sir, it's thy treatment o' us miners that's the disgrace," said Whalen, looking Sir John squarely in the eye. "An' it's thee that should be ashamed. Come, Rawdon, it's time to go 'ome," he added, looking over at his son who had followed his father out of the church and was looking on with a shocked look on his face.

Adam watched the two of them walk away down the hill. He disliked them both cordially and was appalled by the father's behaviour and yet he couldn't help but admire his fearlessness. He turned back to Miriam, who had been standing beside him until a moment before, but found that she was gone and the feeling of disappointment struck him like a sudden and unexpected blow to the heart.

Feelings in the town ran high in the days that followed. The miners were angry with Whalen for using the funerals as a stage for his demonstration, but they also respected his pluck. There was a consensus that something needed to be done even if Whalen had gone the wrong way about it; that they couldn't allow Hardcastle and his lot to carry on taking advantage of them.

And they were quick to rally round Whalen when the manager announced that he had been suspended from work. Daniel's appeal to Hardcastle to think again fell on deaf ears and most of the miners downed tools and walked out of the mine when they heard the news.

They assembled in a crowd on the football ground, ignoring the steady drizzle as Whalen addressed them from a makeshift platform set up in front of the pavilion. The women were there too, standing further back but just as angry as the men.

"Thank ye for your support, comrades," Whalen shouted. "Solidarity's what's been missin' in our union up until now: leavin' our brethren in Wales to suffer alone while Churchill's thugs killed 'em with their batons and the black-'earted owners starved 'em to death. We need to stand up and be counted; we need to show Sir John Scarsdale and 'is like that they can't treat us like animals, payin' us next to nowt and not carin' tuppence about our safety, jus' so they can increase their profits. We've got to stop this lyin' down and lettin' 'em walk all over us; we've got to draw a line and say enough's enough. We're men too, just like them, entitled to the same respect as they get—more in fact, cos we work and they don't."

The men cheered and raised their hands in a unanimous show of support when Edgar proposed that they refuse to work until Whalen had been reinstated, and then walked back to the town over the muddy fields, sinking their hands deep in their pockets to keep them warm. It was the end of autumn and the last curled brown leaves were blowing down from the black trees, while behind them the wheels of the headstocks stood motionless, wreathed in the misty grey gloom of the early evening. The rain continued to fall steadily and they quickened their pace, needing the solace of alcohol and the warm fire at the King's Head if they were to maintain their spirit of defiance.

The streets were empty when Adam got off the bus and walked home. Everyone seemed to be inside the pub or the Miners' Institute on the other side of the green, talking about the strike and Whalen Dawes. And Edgar's house was deserted too, so Adam revived the fire and set the kettle to boil, lit the lamp, and sat down at the kitchen table with his books spread out in front of him.

The rain was coming down harder now, beating against the window panes so that at first he didn't hear the knock on the door. And when he opened it, he barely had time to take in the unexpected figure of Mr. Vale, the parson, standing on the doorstep before a sudden squall of rain-drenched wind blew them both back into the house. They clung to each other for support for a moment and then both started laughing.

"I'm sorry," Adam said, shutting the door. "Edgar's not here and nor is my father. I don't know which of them you came to see?" He was surprised by the parson's visit. Edgar and his family were non-believers and Adam's father had no contact with the church other than when he accompanied Adam to the service on Sunday mornings, and he hadn't even been doing that in recent months, excusing himself on the grounds that he had too much work. As far as Adam knew, Mr. Vale had never been to the house before.

"It was you I was looking for," said the parson, smiling as he bent to unfasten the bicycle clips from his trouser legs and took off his cape, which Adam hung on one of the hooks by the door.

"Me?"

"Yes, I wanted to thank you for helping my daughter at the funeral. She's a sensitive soul at the best of times and the occasion was always going to be difficult for her. Perhaps it would have been better if she hadn't come but she insisted. My wife is an invalid and so Miriam felt that she should come in her stead. And then the scuffle by the altar distressed her. As you may have heard, Mr. Dawes did not go willingly and so it would have been even worse for her if you hadn't come forward to rescue her from the mayhem."

"It was the least I could do," said Adam. "I was pleased to be able to help."

"And then she told me that she left without thanking you in person. It's perhaps understandable as she was frightened that there might be more violence when Mr. Dawes was thrown out of the church, but it must have seemed rude to you."

"No, not at all," said Adam awkwardly. The idea that he had been offended by Miriam when he remembered the few minutes that he had spent with her on his arm as being several of the most wonderful in his life was so absurd that it left him at a temporary loss for words. He covered up his confusion by offering the parson a seat at the table while he busied himself at the fire making tea.

"You're learning Latin," said the parson who'd been looking at Adam's books and now picked up his well-thumbed copy of Tacitus's *Annals*. "We have something in common—I was never happier than when I studied the classics at Oxford. Do you like it?"

"Yes, very much, although it seems a little useless sometimes—"

"Useless?" interrupted the parson sharply. "Why do you say that?"

"Because it was all so long ago; so far away from where we are now."

"Was it? I often think there are real parallels between the Roman Empire and our world. A ruling class that has become decadent, utterly given over to the pursuit of pointless pleasure, supported by a slave population—"

"We don't have slaves," Adam protested.

"Technically, no. I agree. But the conditions in which most of the population lives aren't much better than slavery. In fact I'd say the Roman slaves had a better diet than the poor do in this country."

"You sound like Whalen Dawes," said Adam and then immediately regretted his words, worrying that the parson would be offended by them, although he showed no signs of being so. In truth Adam was shocked: the parson preached the Christian virtues in his Sunday sermons, but he never talked like this. "I'm sorry," he said. "I shouldn't have said that."

"No, I understand what you mean. But I assure you I'm not like Dawes. I believe that society should be more just but that doesn't mean I believe in using violence to overthrow it as Dawes most certainly does. He wants to start a revolution and, like all revolutionaries, he doesn't care who gets hurt in the process."

"What do you think will happen?" asked Adam. He was enthralled by the conversation and didn't want it to stop. It was the first time in his life that a clever and educated man had spoken to him in this way, treating him as though he was an equal.

"I don't know," said the parson. "I have to say I fear the worst—

although whether it will be the Irish or the trades unions or the ridiculous German Kaiser with his dreadnoughts who pushes us over the edge I don't know."

"I saw him," said Adam.

"Did you? When?"

"At the old king's funeral. It was only for a minute."

"And what did you think?"

"I thought he seemed wound up, like he could get angry and make some terrible mistake," said Adam slowly, groping for the right words. He had thought of the encounter many times since it happened but he still remained unsure what to make of it.

"He wants every day to be his birthday. That's what Bismarck said about him and it's certainly a dangerous trait," said the parson, finishing his tea and getting up to go. "I've enjoyed our talk," he added. "Perhaps you would like to come to the Parsonage some time. I have some books about Rome that you might like to look at and it would do me good to discuss antiquity with a fellow enthusiast."

"I'd love to. I mean I'd like to very much," said Adam, trying not to sound too childishly enthusiastic. Not only would he be able to talk about Rome with the parson; he would also be able to see Miriam again and there was nothing he wanted more than that.

At the door they met Daniel coming in. He was excited, telling his news in a rush as he shook the parson's hand. "I persuaded Sir John to reinstate Whalen," he said. "And not only that—he'll invest more money in pit safety. There's new breathing apparatus and protective clothing Hardcastle can buy, and he's going to give instructions to water down the dust more between shifts. I must say he was very reasonable, although it was hard to get him to change his mind about Dawes . . ."

"I'm not surprised," said the parson. "Sir John's a good man at heart and he wants to do the right thing. But he's also a traditionalist, a dyed-in the-wool Tory, and property rights are a religion to him. And Dawes knows that. He's no fool. He knew exactly what he was doing when he sat in Sir John's pew—he couldn't have chosen a better symbol to attack."

"Yes, you're right," said Daniel. "Is that why you're here, Mr. Vale?

I don't think Dawes'll do it again, if that's what you're worried about. He's got what he wants from the church; the mine's where he'll be directing his attention from now on."

"No, I agree with you," said the parson. "I came to thank you for your help. I don't know how we would have managed without you. And I also wanted to thank your son for helping my daughter when she was distressed. He was very kind and considerate—you should be proud of him."

"I am," said Daniel warmly. "Sometimes I wonder about my future here—Dawes wants my job and he wants a strike and he may well end up getting both, the way we're going. But as soon as I'm about to get miserable I look at Adam and I feel better. I think he's going to go far, make a name for himself in this world."

The parson looked at Daniel carefully for a moment before he answered. "I think so too—Adam's a good lad and he certainly deserves to do well," he said. "But you must look after yourself as well, Mr. Raine. You look pale and careworn, if you don't mind me saying so. Adam needs you too—you should remember that. Come to church—I should like to see you there."

"I'll try," said Daniel, shaking the parson's hand and watching with Adam as Mr. Vale got on his bicycle and rode away up the hill. The rain had stopped but the wind was still blowing and the parson's billowing cape made him a strange, spectral figure in the twilight.

"He means well," said Daniel. "But he doesn't know what it's like for us. It's the same with all the gentlemen—none of them do."

Daniel's agreement with Sir John got the men back to work but it didn't stop the grumbling and it did little to enhance his standing with them either. Below ground, Whalen and his allies harped constantly on the checkweighman's close relationship with the owner. " 'E's spendin' too much time up at the Hall bein' wined and dined; 'e's gettin' a taste for the high life; 'e's sellin' us down the river." It didn't matter that none of this was true; the constant drip of innuendo had a cumulative effect which Daniel was powerless to counteract. And Whalen was preaching to an increasingly receptive audience.

All over the country there was a new mood of militancy among the miners. The talk everywhere was of the minimum wage, guaranteed to be paid regardless of fluctuations in profit. It was a principle that the employers could not or would not accept and as the year came to an end it became clear that a national strike was inevitable. The miners came out en masse on 26 February 1912—a date they soon had cause to regret as it was still cold in the north and they quickly began to miss their free ration of coal. In Scarsdale they took their children's prams up to the slag heap and picked through the shale in the rain, looking for lumps of coal in the grey waste to wheel home, and the more enterprising sank a pit outside the town, going down in turns to dig for coal by candlelight while the others used a pulley suspended from an old penny farthing bicycle wheel to bring what they could find up to the surface. By mid-March everyone was feeling the pinch and the union opened up a soup kitchen on the green.

But it was hard for Adam to share the general sense of despondency. Throughout the week he was away in Gratton where the school provided meals and the teachers lauded his academic prowess. And on Sundays after church he would go over to the Parsonage and drink a glass of sherry with the parson in his study. Soon this became the highlight of Adam's week. To begin with they talked about Greece and Rome, looking over the books that Mr. Vale had kept from his university days. Adam had always loved books, associating them with the magical childhood world that he had shared with his mother when she read to him in the house in Islington, and he was flattered by the way that the parson seemed genuinely interested in what he had to say when they sat talking on either side of the fire in Mr. Vale's study with the carefully tended lawn glistening silvery green in the winter sunlight outside the bow window.

And later, as they got to know each other better, the parson would talk to him about the present as well as the past. It was a frightening world that they lived in, he said. Everywhere there was conflict—not just between the miners and the mine owners but between all the workers and their employers. There was talk of the trades unions banding together to threaten a general strike, while in London the prison authorities were force-feeding the suffragettes through tubes thrust into their nostrils, and the Ulstermen in Ireland were openly preparing for rebellion. And beyond the shores of England the great powers jostled against each other, defining and redefining their competing spheres of influence.

"One spark could set it all off," said the parson. "And once a war has begun they won't be able to stop it even if they want to."

"Why?"

"Because the continent of Europe has become like a house of cards. Once one falls, they all do. The countries are prisoners of their alliances and the armies are too big to call back once they have begun to mobilize. And yet everywhere the rich and powerful go on as if they haven't a care in the world, spending money like water, living only for pleasure. Perhaps they sense the end is near. I fear for our future, Adam. Truly I do."

"What can we do?"

"We can pray. I don't think our country has ever stood in greater need of the good Lord and his teachings."

But these moments of gloom were few and far between at the Parsonage. Generally Adam found Mr. Vale to be good company, and there was also the exquisite pleasure of the time he was able to spend with Miriam. She would often come and sit in the corner of the study and listen to her father and Adam talk, supporting her pretty chin on the back of her hand as she stared at each of them in turn, absorbed in what they had to say. Adam wanted to include her in their conversations but she was naturally shy and he desisted when he saw how confused she became when he asked her opinion. But that was because she was in awe of her father; on the few times that they were left alone she was quick with her questions. And she asked them not for form's sake but because she wanted to know: about London, about the house in Station Street, about the strike and about his disastrous visit to the mine. She laughed when he told her about the ignominious way it had ended but that was because he had deliberately made his unconscious exit in the bottom of the coal tub appear comic, and indeed the experience seemed more absurd than terrible when he was in Miriam's company, and he laughed too at the memory.

But their laughter got them into trouble, leading as it did to

Adam's first encounter with Miriam's mother. Adam had never seen her in church for the very good reason that she never went there. As a self-declared permanent invalid, she never left the Parsonage, but she was nevertheless keenly interested in everything that went on in Scarsdale and at the Hall, relying on a network of contacts in both places to keep her informed, periodically rewarding them with small presents from her purse. She knew all about Adam's rescue of her daughter from the church on the day of Whalen Dawes's demonstration but she didn't feel grateful to him like her husband. On the contrary, she saw Adam as a possible emerging threat to her plan to marry Miriam off to a rich, well-connected man. Her own husband was respectable but he had no independent means, and she wished that she had detected his sad lack of worldly ambition before she made the mistake of marrying him. She was not one to waste time on past regrets, but she was determined to use the family's most precious asset, her daughter's beauty, to achieve financial security for her old age, and she was certainly not going to allow a penniless young man to get in her way.

"Miriam, where is your father?" she asked, not coming into the study, but standing in the doorway, looking at Adam with beady light grey eyes that were utterly unlike the beautiful heavy-lashed garnet-brown eyes of her daughter.

"He had to go over to the church. One of the bell-ringers needed him. He said he'd be back very soon," said Miriam, getting up nervously from her chair. Adam was struck by the dramatic effect that her mother's appearance had had on her. She was suddenly forced instead of natural, and she seemed to be making excuses when she hadn't yet been accused of anything. It was Miriam's curse that she could not be herself with either of her parents. With her father whom she loved she couldn't think of anything to say, whereas with her mother whom she feared she couldn't stop talking.

"This is Adam Raine," she said, pointing to Adam, who had also got to his feet. "His father works at the mine—"

"I know who he is," said Mrs. Vale, interrupting coldly. "And Mr. Raine's business is with your father, not you, as I'm sure you're well aware, Miriam."

It was part of the beauty of Miriam's face that it vividly reflected the changes in her emotions; she had no art of concealment, and the pain that she felt now in response to her mother's harsh reprimand and rudeness to their guest was plain to see. Adam was distressed by it; he wanted to ride to her defence but he was clear-headed enough to see that anything he said would only make things worse for Miriam.

"I am sorry that my husband has caused you this inconvenience," Mrs. Vale said, turning her attention back to Adam once her daughter had passed by her out of the door. "I will speak to him about it."

And clearly she did because Adam and Miriam were never left alone together after that. But the parson also went out of his way to encourage Adam to continue his Sunday visits and Miriam sometimes still joined them, although this occurred less frequently than before. From all of which Adam concluded that Ernest had been exaggerating a little when he said that it was the parson's wife who wore the trousers in the marriage, although he had a vested interest of course in wishing that not to be true.

Chapter Six

Early one Saturday morning Adam was shaken awake by Ernest, who was standing fully dressed by the side of the bed.

"Can you keep a secret?" he asked.

"What are you talking about? What kind of secret?" asked Adam. He was still bleary-eyed from sleep and he wondered if he was still dreaming. It was dark outside the window and the guttering candle in Ernest's hand was throwing weird shadows on the walls.

"No, that's not the way it works," said Ernest. "You've got to tell me you'll keep it first. You've got to promise."

"All right," said Adam doubtfully. "I promise. So what's the secret?"

"I'll tell you when we get there," said Ernest, laughing. "Now get dressed. We're supposed to be there in ten minutes."

Everyone in the house was still asleep and they crept down the stairs quietly and closed the door softly behind them. The sun was just beginning to rise in a pink mist over the far hills, dimly illuminating the silvery crystals of the hoar frost hanging on the trees and hedges, and their breath hung white between them in the cold air as they got on their bicycles and went freewheeling down the hill past the station, where they could see the silhouettes of the coal trucks that had been lined up empty and idle on the sidings since the strike began.

The mist was thicker, grey and fog-like in the valley bottom, and they could hardly see a yard in front of them when they dismounted, leaning their bicycles up against the side of the deputies' office.

Ernest whistled twice and waited a few seconds before whistling again and then after a minute the same signal was echoed back to them.

"Who is it?" Adam asked.

"Luke," said a familiar voice, close by but invisible. "An' 'Arry and Davy MacKenzie, an' I hope you can keep a secret, Adam Raine?"

"He will," said Ernest, answering for Adam. "I got him to promise before we left."

"Fair enough," said Luke, coming forward out of the mist and clapping Adam on the shoulder. He and the two boys with him were smoking cigarettes and the burning ends illuminated their faces. Adam knew them all from playing football.

"What's the secret?" he demanded. He'd been amused and irritated in equal measure by Ernest's refusal to tell him what was going on, but his frustration was getting the better of him now that he seemed to be the only one of the five of them who didn't know why they were there.

"Come on," said Luke. "You'll see."

The boys followed Luke as he led them over to the big shed-like building that housed the stores for the mine and produced two keys from his pocket.

"Where did you get them?" asked Adam, starting to feel worried.

"One of the deputies left 'em lying around an' Davy 'ere was sharp enough to nab 'em without anyone noticin'," said Luke, pointing to his friend, a boy of his age but of much smaller stature with curly sandy hair and a round cherub-like face that reminded Adam of the carvings in the church in Islington that he used to go to with his mother. Davy was constantly getting into trouble, letting off fireworks or pilfering from the village store, and relied on his false air of innocence to escape punishment. His twin brother, Harry, looked nothing like him. He was tall, dark-skinned and serious, and had a precocious talent for playing the violin that he had never been able to properly develop as he had been required, like his brother, to join their father and uncle down the mine on the day following their fourteenth birthday. The strike had given the boys their longest holiday since then even if it had also made them cold and hungry.

Luke fitted one of the keys into the lock on the door of the stores and they went inside, leaving Harry outside to stand lookout.

Luke and Davy lit candles and began to pick their way up and down the narrow lanes between the tall stacks of equipment piled up on all sides—ropes and rails and wheels and steel and timber roof props—before Luke gave a triumphant whistle as he halted in front of a tall cupboard at the far end of the shed which had the word "DANGER" painted in big red letters on the door under an image of a skull and crossbones.

The second key opened the padlock and the door swung open to reveal shelves of the various explosives used for shot firing in the mine. Luke carefully selected two sticks of dynamite.

"One should be enough; t'other one's just in case," he said as he relocked the door.

"What the hell are they for?" asked Adam, now feeling seriously alarmed. He was angry too. "You should have damned well told me, Ernest, that you were planning to blow up the mine before you hauled me out here," he told his friend, taking hold of his arm. "If I'd known, I wouldn't have come."

But Ernest shook him off and laughed. "Who said anything about blowing up the mine?" he said. "We're going fishing. That's what we're doing."

The roads were still deserted as they rode their bicycles out of the town, heading past the football pitch into the open countryside. Away from the valley bottom the early spring sunshine was burning off the mist and the clean cold air filling Adam's lungs gave him a sudden feeling of exhilaration as the boys increased their speed, weaving in and out of each other's paths but somehow never colliding. They halted at a crossroads a few miles from Scarsdale, arguing about which direction to take.

"It's up there," said Davy, pointing to the left where the road narrowed as it climbed up into a beech wood and disappeared. "I know cos this 'ere is the cross lanes where they 'ad the iron gibbet back in the olden days. They used to 'ang the 'ighwaymen up 'ere in chains after their executions as a warnin'. Pitch on their faces; tar on their bones. Imagine the wind blowing through the bars of the cage rattlin' their skeletons; imagine the sound o' it in the moonlight," he said, dropping his voice to an enthusiastic whisper.

"You're makin' it up," said Luke, pushing Davy playfully back with his hand. "I think you're maybe right about the lake, but the rest is nonsense, ain't it, 'Arry?"

"Nay, it's true," said Davy's brother. "Our granddad told us about the gibbet the year afore 'e died; 'e said 'e'd seen it 'ere when 'e was a kid."

"An' I s'pose you're sayin' that's what's we've got comin' to us for stealin' the dynamite?" said Luke, grinning.

"Nay, 'angin's too good for the likes o' us," said Davy, shaking his head in mock despair.

Laughing, they got back on their bicycles and pedalled hard to put the cross lanes behind them and reach their destination.

They slowed down once they reached the wood. They had to as the road quickly became no more than a dirt track and they bounced along in single file over the exposed tree roots until they reached a rise and stopped, looking out in wonder at the still waters of a semicircular lake ringed by weeping willow trees whose leafy branches were trailing down into the water.

The boys waited while Luke lit the fuse on the first stick of dynamite and threw it into the lake. Almost immediately a column of foaming water exploded upwards from the surface and with it came scores of fat fish glinting silver in the sunlight. They flew up through the air before cascading back to float stunned or dead on the surface, ready and waiting for the boys who were already wading out into the water with the nets that they had brought from home extended in front of them.

They sorted through their catch on the shore, looking for the green-scaled perch with black stripes down their flanks and a spiked dorsal fin on their backs. The rest they threw back. Adam was told off to gather twigs and branches for the fire while the other boys descaled and filleted the fish ready for cooking.

"Perch are the best to eat. And this lake's known for them. The carp taste of mud and the chub are full of forked bones and taste of mud too," said Ernest, grinning happily as he took the wood from Adam and built the fire.

Adam watched the quick way the boys worked together preparing the meal with a twinge of envy mixed with regret: there had been no opportunity for him to learn how to live outdoors back in London. Over the course of the last year he had come to love the countryside around Scarsdale, gazing out at it with pleasure every day from the window of the bus, but he still felt like an outsider looking in, utterly ignorant of how nature or agriculture actually worked.

But Adam's despondency was fleeting, chased away like a stray cloud by the delicious scent of the cooking mixed with the smell of smoke from the fire. Ernest had come equipped, producing a frying pan and flour and a bag of lemons from his knapsack, and the breakfast was the best and most satisfying meal Adam had eaten in as long as he could remember. The food prepared by Ernest's mother had always been bland, and quantity as well as quality had sharply deteriorated since the privations inflicted by the strike had begun to bite into the family's income.

Afterwards Adam lay back on the mossy bank with his eyes closed, using his rolled-up jacket as a makeshift pillow, and let the sunlight warm his face as it dappled down through the branches of the willow trees. He idly listened to the laughing voices of his friends, not taking in the words but letting them intermingle with the sound of birdsong and the tap-tap-tapping of a woodpecker further back inside the wood. The mine and the strike and the unresolved issues in his life seemed faraway and inconsequential, subsumed for now in a deep contentment. And later, in the midst of war and misfortune, he thought back on that moment lying beside the lake as the one where he had been most completely happy, wanting for nothing, at peace and in perfect harmony with the world around him.

In April the union voted to return to work. An Act rushed through Parliament by the Liberal government had appeared to answer the miners' demands. But it soon became apparent that they had achieved far less than they had hoped. The new law set up district boards made up of employers and employees to agree a minimum wage in each district, and when the Scarsdale Board failed to reach agreement, the Chairman, Sir John Scarsdale, used his power under the Act to set a five-shilling minimum.

At demonstrations all over the north the miners had chanted their slogan: "Eight hours' work, eight hours' play, eight hours' sleep and eight bob a day," and now they felt betrayed. The sacrifices they had made during the strike had been for nothing and they wanted someone to blame. Daniel Raine provided the obvious scapegoat.

Edgar had long ago come to regret bringing in his cousin to run the local branch of the union. It hadn't taken him long to realize that the cousin who had stepped off the train from London was not the same man as the firebrand strike leader that he had read about in the newspaper, and only a personal dislike of Whalen Dawes and a stubborn unwillingness to acknowledge his own mistake had kept him from switching his allegiance before now. Where Edgar led, the rest of the miners followed and in quick order at the next union meeting Daniel was removed as secretary and replaced by Whalen, who also took over as checkweighman. Not one miner spoke out in Daniel's support.

Returning to the house at the end of Station Street, Daniel told Adam to pack his bags as they were leaving the next morning. He'd seen what was coming and, knowing that they couldn't continue to live at Edgar's, he'd found them temporary lodgings in a widow's house close to the pithead. He'd also been to see Hardcastle, the pit manager, and got a job working as a tub-filler underground. Once he'd learnt the trade he could become a collier but until then money was going to be tight.

They left at sunrise, hoping to avoid awkward goodbyes, but Edgar was already downstairs, eating his breakfast at the table.

He got up and helped the carrier load their meagre belongings into the pony cart that Daniel had hired for the move, and then shook Daniel's hand.

"I wish thee the best o' luck," he said. "I know we 'aven't seen eye to eye recently, but that doesna mean we aren't still o' the same blood, an' if there's anythin' you need . . ."

"Thank you, Edgar," said Daniel. "You've been very good to us but it's time we stopped being a burden; we should have found our own place months ago but there was always something else to think of. You know how it is."

"Aye, I do," said Edgar warmly. "I do indeed. An' I wish thee luck too, young man," he said, turning to Adam and putting out his hand.

"Thank you," said Adam. But he wouldn't take Edgar's hand, acting as though he hadn't seen it as he climbed up beside the carrier. He was angry, and shaking hands would have meant condoning Edgar's treatment of his father. If Edgar was feeling guilty about what he'd done, then he would have to live with it; it wasn't Adam's responsibility to salve his conscience.

And Adam was frightened too: frightened for his father going down into the pit to work; frightened of what would become of them. If they couldn't live, they would have to go to the workhouse and Adam thought he would rather die than go there. He sat tense and unhappy as the pony trotted down the empty road in the grey early-morning light past the sleeping terraced houses, its hooves ringing out on the hard tarmac.

He looked over at his father, leaning forward on the box with his brow furrowed and his unseeing eyes focused on some inner struggle, and felt a sudden wave of protective love flood through him. They had drifted apart in the year since they had come north. It had not been Daniel's intention to allow his preoccupation with his work to create a gulf between him and his son, Adam realized that, but nevertheless that was what had happened. And as Daniel had withdrawn from his son's life, Adam had filled the space with new friends and interests which he did not share with his father. He felt guilty when he realized that he had begun to see the parson as a new father figure in his life. The comfort and softness of the Parsonage and the conversations about history and politics were experiences that Daniel could not provide. Adam had grown up and grown away and it was hard now for him to reach out across the emotional barrier, but he forced himself to try, laying his hand on top of his father's, causing Daniel to look up, called back for a moment from his own inner turmoil.

"It's not your fault, Dad," said Adam. "It was in London but not this time. You worked night and day for the men and they're plain ungrateful to throw it back in your face like they have. And Edgar's the worst of them," he went on, raising his voice as his anger got the better of him. "He's got a lot of nerve, pretending like everything's all right after what he's done."

"No, you shouldn't blame him," said Daniel quietly. "He thought that he was getting a class warrior when he brought me up here and he deserves credit for putting up with me for as long as he has once he realized I'd changed my spots. I've got a lot of sympathy for him, in fact. He wants the best for his people and God knows they're not getting the best now: they work in terrible conditions for far too little money. But the trouble is Sir John hasn't got enough to give them what they want. The mine's old and the coal's not good enough to fetch good prices and there's nothing anyone can do about it. Facts are facts. Of course Sir John should have offered the men more when they went back, but it was never going to be as much as they wanted. I'm glad I'm out of it, to be honest with you. Let someone else try their hand at making one and one add up to three."

They relapsed into an uneasy silence. Whatever the rights and wrongs of the past, it didn't change the fact that they would have far less money now. Adam didn't know if his father had any savings but they couldn't amount to much.

"I wish there was something I could do to help," he said. "Maybe if I got a job on the screens with Ernest? Then at least we'd have a bit more to go around."

"No," said Daniel, practically shouting the word. "The only thing that keeps me going is that you're doing so well at school and knowing that you're going to make a better life for yourself than I've had. Don't worry, Adam—we'll be all right. I'll make sure we are."

Adam saw no reason to believe his father, but he knew there was no point in arguing. The pony had halted in front of their new home, a small squat house in a dismal narrow street close to the mine.

Its peeling paint was blackened with soot and the grimy windows looked as though they had never been washed. Adam shivered as his father opened the door and they went inside.

The house belonged to a miner's widow whose husband had died from tuberculosis several years before. She still wore her widow's weeds and moved about the dimly lit rooms in a state of permanent misery, living as far as Adam could tell on an unchanging diet of cold tea and porridge. A sampler invoking the Lord to "Bless This House" gathered dust over the mantelpiece in the parlour above a faded photograph of the widow and her late husband on their wedding day. Even the aspidistra in the corner, the hardiest of indoor plants, wilted miserably, waiting to die.

Daniel and Adam had the upstairs rooms and shared use of the kitchen. There was a permanent smell of mouldy dampness in the air that fires could never quite chase away, but Daniel did his best to brighten the place up, pinning coloured pictures from penny magazines over the mildew stains on the walls and bringing home two matching armchairs to stand on either side of the fireplace—bargains bought from a family that was moving away and had no further use for them.

He never complained, although Adam guessed from the stiff way his father walked that he wasn't finding it easy to adapt to the hard manual labour and the cramped conditions inside the mine. And it was strange for Adam too seeing his father come back from work all black and dirty from the coal. He winced when he washed his father's back, seeing the cuts and abrasions—the physical toll exacted daily by the pit.

It was strange: adversity seemed to soften rather than harden Daniel, and in the evenings, father and son were often happy, sitting side by side in front of the fire, toasting bacon on a fork and catching the fat on their slices of bread. They played chess on a handmade board and Daniel listened while Adam told him about the heroes and villains of long ago, just as Adam had listened to his mother reading him the same stories when he was a boy, so that sometimes the dead world of the ancients seemed more real to them than the mining town lying quiet outside the window.

And when Adam had finished his storytelling, they talked about issues such as whether the senators had been right to assassinate Caesar—Daniel thought they were but Adam was less sure; and whether the Roman Empire had been doomed from the beginning. They argued sometimes until the candles had almost burnt away, and Adam smiled, thinking how unlikely such conversations were to be taking place in these shabby rooms in this shabby little house in the middle of nowhere, while the widow snored down below.

But later, lying in bed, Adam would see the lights sprawling over the dark ceiling from the lamps swinging in the hands of the late-shift miners as they came tramping down the road outside on the way to work, their voices rising and receding as they passed the house. And he would feel fearful of he knew not what, like a weight was pressing down on his abdomen, a sense of foreboding that would keep him awake late into the night.

Chapter Seven

The day began much like any other. Daniel was working the early shift and the house was cold and silent as Adam got dressed and gathered his books for school. He had an exam to take and he was nervous, hoping he would do well. Outside, the women in their workaday aprons were gathered on their front doorsteps gossiping. They stopped talking as he went past, looking after him as he went up the road. They weren't hostile but they weren't friendly either. Adam had lived in Scarsdale long enough to no longer be upset by their response. He wasn't one of their own and he never would be— he spoke differently to them and he didn't work in the mine. But nevertheless, the old sense of not belonging added to the free-floating anxiety that he hadn't been able to shake off since he woke up. He felt burdened by an invisible weight, the same feeling he had some- times when a sixth sense told him it was going to rain but the heavy clouds stayed hanging overhead, refusing to open. Not that that was the case today—it was a bright June morning and he increased his pace, breathing the fresh air deep into his lungs in a largely unsuc- cessful attempt to lift his spirits.

The siren sounded just as he reached the corner. The mournful inhuman cry, the signal for disaster, broke out from the pithead and reverberated through the town. Adam was shocked by the noise and yet it also felt like something he had been expecting ever since the day his father left the safety of the checkweighman's office, forced to try to earn his living underground.

All around doors were opening and people were spilling out into the street, pulling on their coats as they headed down the hill towards the mine. Everyone was talking—asking questions and getting no answers and passing out of hearing as Adam stood, rooted to the spot, looking back at the headstocks. They seemed like huge alien shapes lit up by the morning sun, hostile visitors from some other planet.

Voices rose and fell as rumours flowed up and down the hill, until suddenly Adam heard a name he recognized—*Oakwell*: the district where Edgar worked and now his father too; the district where he'd disgraced himself, fainting in front of Rawdon Dawes and his vile father. Just the other day Daniel had told Adam that he'd been sent there. He'd seemed pleased, stupidly pleased, happy that he would be working where the coal was more plentiful so that there would be more money in his pay packet come Friday evening, but what he didn't say and Adam knew from Ernest was that the Oakwell seam was deeper and narrower and less safe than the old ones—it was where the two miners had died in the winter.

Adam began to walk towards the mine, carried forward ever more quickly by the press of the crowd that was surging tide-like down the hill. At the pithead there was chaos, although the cage appeared to be operating normally and there was no smoke billowing out from the opening or other outward sign of the trouble down below. Atkins and a group of deputies were making ineffectual attempts to keep an open corridor for rescuers to get to and from the shaft, and a man with a camera was getting in everyone's way taking pictures. Some of the women were crying, desperate for news, but no one seemed to have any definite information about what had happened or who was dead or trapped.

Adam didn't hesitate. He bore no resemblance to the sweating, shaking version of himself that had climbed the pithead stairs on his last visit, feeling as though they were the steps up to the gallows. Now he waited until the cage was almost full and then rushed forward, joining the throng of rescuers inside. The banksman was too distracted by the growing hysteria of the crowd to notice the late arrival and slammed the gate shut with a clang. Forty-five seconds later Adam was released out into the mine.

As soon as the cage lifted back up, the men at the bottom went back to filling coal tubs with water from the sump at the bottom of the shaft. The full tubs were then wheeled to the stables where they were coupled up in lines to the limbers of the pit ponies whose boy drivers drove them away into the mine, passing other ponies that were coming back up the tunnels the other way pulling trains of empty tubs ready for refilling.

All around, the lights of the miners' lamps were dancing in the blackness like white dots as the men moved to and fro, but, unlike up above, their hectic activity seemed cohesive and organized as they battled against a common enemy: invisible, inaudible, but utterly real away down the black tunnels beyond the stables. And the enemy was winning—or at least that was the impression that Adam was getting from listening to the snatches of passing conversation that he was able to pick up from the out-of-the-way corner into which he had retreated while he worked out his next move.

"Fire's like a bloody dragon; it's got a thirst that canna be quenched." "Like lookin' in the mouth o' hell, it is." "I pity the poor bastards that got caught . . ."

It made Adam sick to his stomach to hear what the men were saying. He felt sure that his father was one of the poor bastards they were talking about, and he knew he had to try to reach him, even if there was nothing he could do to help when he got there; even if it was already too late. He felt no fear, just desperation because he realized that he had no chance of finding his way to the Oakwell district unaided: he'd be lucky to get round the first corner before he was trampled by one of the pit ponies. His only hope lay in hitching a ride on one of the water trains that they were pulling. But no driver would take him willingly—he had no right even to be in the mine. If he revealed himself he would be thrown back in the cage and sent back up to the surface in a second. His only chance was to stow away in one of the tubs.

His mind made up, he left his bag of books on the floor and began to edge his way carefully along the wall. Without a lamp of his own he was invisible in the darkness. Up ahead he could hear familiar voices: it was Joe the ostler talking to Rawdon Dawes. They were at the door of the stables, their faces lit up garishly by their lamps, standing next to a pony that seemed larger than the others and angrier too. It was neighing and stamping its feet, shaking its leather harness so that the shafts connecting it to the water tubs behind were creaking and clanking.

"Don't ride 'im, Rawdon, you 'ear me? I've told thee before—'e's a wild one; 'e's not like t'others," said the ostler. There was a desperate urgency in his voice, mixed with what sounded like frustration, and he was gripping Rawdon's shoulder as if to reinforce his words. But Rawdon was pulling away, anxious to be gone. The ostler was a small man, almost a foot shorter than Rawdon although three times his age, and there was something comical about the two of them, pulling each other backwards and forwards as they argued.

"I wish you didna 'ave to take 'im but t'others are all out," the ostler continued mournfully.

"I know," said Rawdon impatiently, getting on to the bumper of the first tub and taking hold of the limber chains connecting it to the pony. "You've already told me that, Joe, remember."

The ostler was about to respond but Rawdon reached forward with a stick he was carrying in his hand and tapped the pony's hind-quarters. Immediately the animal leapt forward, pulling the train of water tubs behind him. And at the last moment Adam ran out and vaulted over the side of the last tub; he landed in the water inside, which splashed over the side, soaking the astonished ostler. He shouted out but Rawdon was concentrating on trying to control the pony as it charged away down the tunnel and didn't turn round.

Adam was shoulder-deep in water, soaked to the skin. It had been cold at the maingate but now it felt as if he was being burnt in ice. And the water was foul too, drawn from the stagnant sump at the bottom of the shaft. He hadn't been able to avoid taking a mouthful as he jumped into the tub and he was still retching it up as he struggled to come to terms with the pitch-blackness all around. The tub's wheels screeched over the rails and up ahead the pony's hooves pounded through the coal dust that swirled in the air, making it hard to breathe.

Above the noise Adam could hear Rawdon shouting commands

at the pony. But they were clearly having little effect. Their speed increased on the downward slopes and Rawdon's voice rose to a scream as they reached a sharp corner and the tubs swayed hard from side to side, almost turning over. A lot of the water was spilling out over the side and at the back of the train Adam was fighting a losing battle to stay upright, using all the strength in his cold aching arms to maintain his grip on the side of the tub. He knew that he would likely drown if he allowed himself to be thrown about inside the tub, hitting his head against the iron sides until he lost consciousness and the foul water filled his lungs.

The end came just as he felt he couldn't hang on any longer. They rounded a bend and the pony smelt the smoke of the fire up ahead. Terrified, it reared up on its hind legs, and then made a violent right-angled turn to the left where a narrow side tunnel led off the main roadway. Showing remarkable presence of mind, Rawdon stood up on the limbers and jumped clear as the pony ran forward for a few yards and then came to a shuddering halt as the tubs behind left the rails and slammed into the wall at the corner of the junction.

In the darkness at the back Adam had no chance to take evasive action. He was thrown forward and then sideways as his tub crashed into the one in front and turned over, spilling its water and Adam out on to the thick dust covering the floor of the tunnel. He came to, looking up into the glare of the lamp that Rawdon was holding up over his head.

"I don't believe it. Of all the fuckin' people—" Rawdon broke off, taking a step back as he tried to absorb the double shock of discovering not only that he had been carrying a stowaway but also that that stowaway was the person he disliked most in the entire town. "What the 'ell are you doin' 'ere?" he demanded as soon as he had had time to recover at least some of his composure.

"Looking for my dad—he's down there somewhere," said Adam, pointing down the pitch-black tunnel. There was no visible sign of the fire but the smell of smoke was getting stronger and Adam coughed violently as he tried to get to his feet. Rawdon had to put out a hand to stop him falling over.

"I'm sorry to 'ear that," said Rawdon. "Well, you're welcome to go an' find 'im if you like, but I ain't givin' thee my lamp. If you helps me with the pony, I'll maybe take thee down there, but, as I say, you'll 'ave to 'elp me first." He gestured behind his head to where the pony was still standing in the side tunnel, snorting and kicking as it tried to break away from the train of overturned tubs that were now half blocking the entrance.

Adam hesitated. He desperately wanted to go on—he was frantic with worry for his father—but he knew it was suicide to venture forward without a light. The next water train that came down the tunnel would run him over even if he didn't get lost. He thought of trying to take the lamp from Rawdon by force but he couldn't bring himself to try. He couldn't in all good conscience leave Rawdon alone in the dark to cope with the maddened animal and, besides, the lamp would almost certainly get broken in any struggle. It was a miracle that Rawdon had been able to keep it intact through the crash. And if he helped Rawdon with the pony and the tubs, then they could go on together.

"What do you want me to do?" he asked.

" 'Old on to 'is collar while I take off the limmers—otherwise 'e'll run off up that side passage an' God knows where that goes," said Rawdon, smiling his trademark cold smile. He'd kept the light on Adam while he was thinking and was sure he could read what had been passing through his enemy's mind. " 'Ere, you can give 'im this," he added, handing Adam an apple that he had taken from his pocket. " 'E likes apples."

Adam had no experience of ponies and this one scared him with its neighing and whinnying and stamping feet. But he faced down his fear and edged his way into the side tunnel and along the near wall, holding his hand lightly against the pony's sweating flank as he felt for the harness straps. The water from his sodden clothes dripped down on to the dusty ground.

"What's his name?" asked Adam, thinking it might help to talk to the pony.

"Masher," said Rawdon, laughing. "Good choice, eh?"

But Adam had no stomach for laughter. His heart was beating hard as he felt the pony's hot breath on his hand and, forgetting the apple, he reached up and wrapped his hands around the collar, holding hard.

"I've got him," he shouted back. And immediately he could hear Rawdon working at the pony's back, uncoupling the shafts that connected the harness to the overturned tubs behind. But then, sensing he was free, the pony lunged forward, kicking out with his hooves. Adam just about kept his hold on the collar and he was aware of Rawdon, who was now on the other side of the pony's head, trying his best to bring the animal under control. Using all their strength, they were just about able to stop its forward momentum, but then they couldn't stop it reversing direction, kicking backwards into the timber props that held up the entrance to the passageway. There was a noise of creaking and cracking and the roof began to collapse in a roar of sound that was like a vast ocean wave crashing down on to the shore. Adam and Rawdon ran down the passage, trying to drag the pony with them but where they led it could not follow: the falling cascade of shale and rocks poured down on its hindquarters, trapping it where it stood, and cutting the boys off from the main tunnel. The pony's front half was curiously unaffected as it sank to the ground, mortally wounded.

The animal was clearly in intense pain. The thick muscles under its skin were visibly trembling and the pupils were dilated in its glassy eyes. It panted out each laboured breath through its flared nostrils but it would not or could not die.

"We can't leave him like this," said Adam.

"I know that," said Rawdon angrily. " 'Ave you still got that apple I gave thee?" he asked.

He took it from Adam and held it to the animal's mouth but it couldn't eat.

"Joe uses a spiked cap when 'e has to do it," said Rawdon. "I've seen it; 'e keeps it in the stables. Got a 'ole in the middle where the bugger's brain is and 'e bangs in the spike with a 'ammer. Me, I got to use a bloody rock."

He reached over and picked up a big jagged stone that had fallen from the ceiling, set his feet, and then brought it down with all his might on the pony's head. Again and again, until there was no possibility that the animal could still be alive. For some reason he didn't understand, Adam forced himself to watch. It felt like an obligation and, looking back on it afterwards, he wondered at the paradox that the act of terrible violence against the defenceless animal made him think so much more of Rawdon than he had before.

Rawdon's hands were shaking when he was finished and he stood for a moment with his hands on the wall, drawing deep breaths of the hot air into his lungs as he tried to steady himself before he bent down and picked up the lamp. "All right," he said, turning his back on the dead animal and setting off into the darkness of the passageway. "Let's get on our way, although I doubt we'll be much better off than Masher afore this day is done. Ain't nobody's ganna come lookin' for us—they don't know you're down 'ere and they won't be frettin' about me."

"Why?"

"Because I weren't in the fire. They'll know that. An' my father's got other things on his mind than worryin' about where I've got to."

"Like what?"

"Like startin' the bloody revolution," said Rawdon bitterly. "'E's been hopin' for a disaster like this to 'appen for as long as I can remember."

They walked in single file, soon losing all sense of direction as the passage twisted and turned this way and that. And their feet were sore and aching when they stopped to rest after what seemed like hours of wandering, although without watches they had no way of knowing how much time had elapsed. They sat with their backs to the wall and shared the apple that the pony hadn't been able to eat before it died.

"You know, if I 'ad to make a list of all the people I'd least like to spend me last day on earth with, I reckon you'd top the list," said Rawdon conversationally.

"Higher than Joe?" Adam asked.

Rawdon laughed in spite of himself. "No, maybe you're right," he said. "Joe's a pain in the backside, 'e is."

They went on in silence with Rawdon leading the way, holding the lamp aloft. Here and there, on either side, they passed old stalls where miners had once worked. There were chalk marks on the walls and sometimes a scrawled name. Adam picked up a cloth haversack from a wooden shelf and it fell apart in his hands, the stitching long since gnawed apart by rats. Each time they stopped, they could hear them scurrying away through the dust, squeaking news of the boys' arrival as they ran. The noise reminded Adam of when old Beaky had shut him up in the school cellar when he was small and the remembered sense of claustrophobia made him shudder, weakening him at the knees.

All at once the tunnel widened out and they felt a sense of space opening out around them. In the lamplight the boys made out a succession of tall black columns on all sides, supporting the roof. Adam gasped in surprise, momentarily forgetting their plight. The place was beautiful; it was like a crude version of one of the old Greek temples that were illustrated in his school textbooks.

"What is this place?" he asked.

"Old workin's—pillar an' stall, they call it," said Rawdon. "Sometimes they mine like this, leavin' pillars to support the roof, although they usually takes 'em out at the end. Lucky for us, I s'pose, that they didn't."

Whenever the path significantly divided, as it did on the other side of the pillared hall, Rawdon stopped to sniff the stale air on either side of the crossgate, trying to work out which way the oxygen was coming from. The air quality was poor, but the fact that they were able to breathe at all meant that there had to be a way back to the upcast or downcast shafts if only they could find it. Sometimes they were encouraged as they felt the ground rising beneath their weary feet but then for no apparent reason they would start going downhill again, back down into the labyrinth.

The gradient changed but the heat and the darkness remained constant. They had found no trace of the mine's ventilation system since the rock fall and they'd long ago stripped down to their underwear. Thirst was fast becoming the worst of their problems. Rawdon had a half-full water bottle and they used tiny amounts when they stopped to rest to wet their lips (despite his reminder of their declared enmity Rawdon seemed to take it for granted that everything they had should be shared equally between them), but there was not enough in the bottle to enable them to take a proper drink and the coal dust that flew up into the air as they walked got into their mouths and added to the parching of their throats. The overhead pipes dripping water that Adam remembered from his last visit to the mine were absent from this district and he looked longingly down at the puddles of black water that lay here and there on the ground, although he didn't need Rawdon to tell him that they were poisonous, impregnated with coal, and gas too probably.

Above their heads the roof sagged and Adam sensed that it was only a matter of time before some of the rotten timber props gave way and another rock fall left them buried alive, dying slowly and painfully without even the hope of the bloody euthanasia that had delivered the pony from its suffering. They were both exhausted and, although he wouldn't admit it, Rawdon's bad leg had begun to cause him intense pain. Adam could see him wince with every step they took.

Despair overtook them when the passage opened out again and they emerged into the same pillared hall that they had passed through hours before. Rawdon sank to the ground, leaning his back against one of the black columns and closed his eyes.

"I'm done," he said. "You carry on if you want to. I knew this mine'd be the death of me the first day I went down it. I'd 'ave been better off if I'd cashed in me chips when that friggin' pony kicked me. It'd 'ave saved me a lot o' grief."

Adam tried to find some words of comfort or encouragement but he could think of nothing. All that was keeping him standing was the stubborn animal refusal to be beaten that had enabled him to endure so much misfortune already in his life. It was an undying spark somewhere deep inside him that stopped him giving in even when his brain told him there was no point in continuing, and now it forced him to bend down and pick up the lamp and go on.

"I'll be back," he said, looking at Rawdon for a moment before he left him in the darkness. But there was no reply: Rawdon had slumped over on to his side and seemed to be asleep.

Once again, passing between the pillars of coal, Adam thought of the beautiful silver-white temples of Greece and Sicily, bathed in sunlight, that he now would never see. The outer columns collectively called the *peristasis* which surrounded the *pronaos*, the four-sided porch that led in turn through a beautifully carved set of double doors to the *cella*, the holy of holies at the centre of the building that housed the exquisite statue of the god which only his priests were ever allowed to see.

Except of course that there was no God or gods—of that Adam was by now quite certain. His mother and Parson Vale and the ancient Greeks were fools—poor credulous fools; at the centre of everything was nothing, just a vast emptiness in which your voice echoed back off the walls. Echoes of echoes: that was all.

At the end of the hall, Adam reached the crossgate where he had stood with Rawdon hours before. He was almost certain they had gone to the right, although the more he thought about it, the less sure he was. The darkness unsettled his memory and he hesitated, turning the lamp from side to side in a vain attempt to find something he recognized before he followed his first instinct and went left.

Almost immediately the path sloped uphill and the quality of the air seemed to improve. A few turnings later and he stumbled out into a wide open space and looked up to where the downcast shaft rose up half a mile to the surface. At the top the underside of the suspended cage blocked most of Adam's view of the sky and the dim light which did get through gave him no clue as to the time of day. He shouted for help until he was hoarse but there was no response except the mocking echo of his voice bouncing back to him off the red bricks lining the sides of the shaft. Rawdon had been right—there was nobody looking for them.

But there was still hope: from just above Adam's head an iron ladder cemented into the brickwork ran straight as a die up the side of the shaft towards the surface. In the lamplight Adam could see its rusty brown side rails and narrow treads ascending into the gloom.

———

Rawdon was asleep on the floor when Adam got back to him, and he had to shake him awake.

"Maybe we can wait," said Rawdon as he limped after Adam. "The miners'll be back down 'ere soon. When no one's working, the owner's losin' money and that matters to 'im a sight more'n respect for the dead, you mark my words."

"You're worried about the ladder?" asked Adam when they got back to the shaft.

"Of course I bloody am. It's been there forever an' no one ever uses it or keeps it repaired. We'll get 'alfway up an' then we'll come fallin' back down again an' drown in that sump down there," he said, pointing to the evil-smelling black pond at the bottom of the shaft.

Adam examined the bottom rungs of the ladder with the lamp and found it hard to disagree with Rawdon's verdict. The brick lining the shaft was damp and mouldy and the brackets holding the side rails in place gave way alarmingly when he pulled on the two that were within reach. There had to be over a thousand treads between them and the surface and what were the chances that they would all hold?

He hesitated, uncertain of what to do. His instinct was to climb but common sense told him to wait. And perhaps he would have stayed below if the changing light of the lamp hadn't taken the decision out of their hands. The flame had seemed to expand when they came out on to the landing by the shaft and now there was no mistaking its signal. There was firedamp in the air, probably spreading back from the fire, blown down the tunnels by the mine's ventilation system. They couldn't sit and wait for it to explode.

"You go first," said Rawdon. "I'll follow."

"Why?" Adam asked, surprised.

"It doesn't matter. Just do it," Rawdon said irritably.

Something in Adam always rebelled against being told what to do when he wasn't given a reason for doing it, and he was about to argue the point further—but then stopped, biting back his words, as he suddenly grasped where Rawdon was coming from. With his damaged leg Rawdon was clearly the one most likely to fall and logically that meant he should climb behind. If he went first he would bring Adam down when he fell; going second, he would fall to his death alone.

"I'll not go too fast," he said, looking Rawdon in the eye as if making a promise.

Rawdon nodded brusquely and then turned away, picking up the lamp. "Here, you're going to need this—fasten it on to your belt," he said, showing Adam how the attachment worked.

"Thanks," said Adam. He breathed deeply, wiped the sweat from off his hands, and began to climb.

To begin with, he made the mistake of looking up above his head, trying to measure the distance to the top. It quickly made him giddy and he had to hold still, waiting for the nausea to pass. And looking down was worse: below Rawdon the black water at the bottom of the shaft seemed to rise up to meet him. Slowly he trained himself to keep his eyes fixed straight ahead on the damp bricks passing slowly by as he climbed higher and higher up the rungs of the ladder.

But even if Adam wasn't looking down at Rawdon, he could still hear him, and it was obvious from his laboured breathing and half-stifled cries of pain that the climb was taxing him to the limit of his endurance. Again and again Adam had to force himself to wait so that Rawdon wouldn't get left behind in the darkness.

It quickly got colder as they neared the top so that the rusty red side rails felt icy in their sore hands, and as they gripped them harder, the iron brackets cemented into the damp wall seemed to give. Only one needs to come away, Adam thought, only one, and it will all be over. And part of him welcomed the thought—an end to the pain and the struggle and the terrible fatigue as they fell down, down, down into nothingness.

But it wasn't Adam who fell; it was Rawdon. And it wasn't a loose bracket or a broken tread that made him lose his footing; it was a rat. They'd heard them scuttling away into niches in the sides of the shaft as they climbed but this one was different. Perhaps it was sick and that was why it stayed lying on the tread as Adam went past it without noticing, but it was alive enough to react fiercely when

Rawdon's hand, following behind and reaching for the rung, came down on its back. The rat's head shot round and it bit down hard on his wrist. Rawdon screamed—a terrible gut-wrenching scream that reverberated up and down the shaft—and pulled away, throwing the rat off so that it flew back against the opposite wall and then fell, turning over and over, bouncing off the masonry until it landed with a splash in the sump at the bottom that the boys would have heard if they had been listening.

But they weren't. As the rat let go of Rawdon's wrist, Rawdon let go of the ladder. Falling back, he instinctively grabbed hold of one of the steel guides that the cage used for its descents, and after a moment he was able to loop his feet around it too. But that was the limit of his good fortune. The guide was just too far away from the ladder for him to be able to reach it with his hand. He realized immediately that there was nothing he could do to save himself and he clung to the guide with his last remaining strength only in order to prepare himself to fall.

Adam had climbed back down opposite Rawdon and now turned half to face him, keeping one hand behind him on the ladder as he tried to measure the distance between them. The light was poor and he couldn't risk trying to unfasten the lamp from his belt but he guessed that Rawdon was about five or six feet away.

"There's a chance," he said.

"No, there isn't," said Rawdon. "I'm fuckin' done for and I'm not takin' you with me if that's what you've got in mind." It cost him an effort to speak and his words came in gasps. Adam wondered how much longer he could hold on.

"Listen, I think I can get hold of your hand if you reach it out as far as you can. And if I can do that, I can swing you round on to the ladder."

"No, you can't. You're not strong enough."

"Try me," said Adam, forcing a smile. And without waiting for a response, he reached out towards Rawdon with his hand, pushing away from the ladder so that his other hand was stretched out behind him, hanging on to the rung.

He was looking straight at Rawdon, willing him to try. He could see the cold sweat on Rawdon's forehead and the tears that were forming in his eyes. "Do it," he said, making it sound like an order. And Rawdon closed his eyes and let go, reaching out across the abyss.

Adam felt Rawdon's hand close on his own in a death grip and the next moment he felt a pull on his arm and shoulder the like of which he had never known before, but somehow they didn't rupture; somehow he managed to keep hold of the ladder at his back as he swung Rawdon in and felt him stick firm as he caught hold of a rung one or two below where he was standing.

Afterwards they shook, each trembling uncontrollably one above the other as they gripped tight on to the ladder, waiting for their strength to return. And then slowly, very slowly, they climbed the remaining rungs, edging past the empty cage hanging on its steel rope, until they got to the surface and emerged out into the twilight of a day that had come so close to being their last.

"You saved my life," said Rawdon simply as they stood together at the mouth of the shaft, looking back down into the darkness. His voice was quiet and he sounded bemused, as if he was examining a strange artefact he'd just found, uncertain what to make of it.

"You'd have done the same," said Adam lightly.

"Would I?" said Rawdon, as if it was a question to which he did not have the answer.

He shook his head and turned away; and stumbled down the stairs to the standpipe at the bottom where he drank greedily before he sank to the ground, dully watching Adam as he did the same. A moment later his eyes closed and he was asleep where he sat, overcome with exhaustion.

Chapter Eight

Adam could see no sign of anyone at the pithead, but there was a light coming from the stores building. Leaving Rawdon where he was, he pushed the door open: it wasn't locked—not like the last time Adam had been inside when he'd helped to steal the dynamite for the fishing expedition. That carefree day seemed light years away now, as if it belonged to a different world.

Inside, an area had been cleared in the centre of the floor with the mine equipment pushed back against the walls, blocking the windows, and in the open space eight trestle tables had been set up in two lines facing the door. On each one a man was lying, covered up to his neck by a white sheet that smelt strongly of carbolic acid. Adam stopped in his tracks, unable for a moment to go forward as he wondered if his father was among the dead.

What light there was in this makeshift morgue came from a few oil lamps and guttering candles set up here and there, and the darkening shadows creeping in on the areas of isolated light around the bodies reminded Adam of the Rembrandt paintings of anatomical lessons in seventeenth-century Amsterdam that he had once seen in a book at school. But there was no sign of any doctor here; only Parson Vale, who was trying to console several women who were sitting on folding chairs beside the bodies of their dead husbands or sons. Some were clearly beyond the reach of comfort, crying out their pain as they rocked backwards and forwards, unable to cope with their grief, while at the opposite extreme another woman sitting closer to the door was still as a statue, making no sound at all. Taking a few steps forward, Adam recognized her with a jolt as Annie, and the body beside her on the table was Edgar's.

It was hard at first for Adam to believe he was dead. He could see that Edgar hadn't been burnt by the fire; it must have passed him by as it roared down the tunnel after the explosion, not needing to seek him out in his stall because he would have already been gone, overpowered in a moment by the firedamp gas that had suddenly swamped the seam.

Adam felt cold and nauseous. He had never seen a dead man that he knew before and he had to fight for a moment to stay upright before he forced himself to inspect the other tables. As far as he could tell, none of the other corpses was his father's, but it was hard to be sure as many of the faces were badly burnt and disfigured.

He looked up and saw that the parson was watching him from the other side of the room.

He clearly knew what was going through Adam's mind.

"Don't worry," he said. "Your father's all right. Wait for me a minute. I want to talk to you."

Adam nodded. Relief flooded through him, making him weak at the knees. But he felt guilty when he looked back at Edgar who hadn't survived but had instead been cut down in the prime of his life. Adam looked at the thick muscles in Edgar's neck and the broad set of his shoulders. He doubted he had ever seen a stronger man. And yet now this powerful body was no more than a hollow shell, a husk emptied of meaning. Soon it would fall apart and rot, food for worms in the damp ground.

Adam closed his eyes and remembered Edgar's ebullience: the way he seemed to fill a room, coming out of the scullery in his soap-suds in the evening and squatting before the hot fire to get dry; or singing snatches of old songs in a pitch-perfect baritone as he mended his boots—his voice vying for ascendancy with the hammer.

I'd shake thy hand, lad, but it needs washing first. Edgar's first words to him came floating into Adam's mind as he recalled that first morning when he and his father got off the train from London and met the miners coming home from the night shift. And then a year later he had refused to shake Edgar's hand when they left the house in Station Street. It seemed a petty gesture now.

He glanced over at Annie. She hadn't moved since he had come into the shed and she seemed completely unconscious of his presence. She was dry-eyed, staring unseeing into the middle distance behind his shoulder. Only her hands were active, pulling repetitively at the stitching of her husband's cloth cap, which she was holding in her hands. She was wearing her best black dress and a hat decked out with black imitation fruit. He wondered if she'd already known or suspected that Edgar was among the dead when she'd gone to the pit after the alarm was sounded and had dressed up for the occasion. He realized that it was a question to which he would never know the answer.

"She's in shock," said the parson, coming up to Adam and drawing him aside. "Grief can take people this way as well—they just shut down because the loss is more than their minds can accept, at least to begin with. She'll be better later, I hope."

"What about her son Thomas?" Adam asked, lowering his voice. "He was working with his father last time I was here."

"Yes, he was, but he got lucky—I think he'd gone back to fetch something when it happened. So he'll be able to support his mother. Others haven't been so fortunate. She's lost both her sons," he said, pointing over at the woman who was crying the loudest, shaking uncontrollably as the sobs were torn from her throat.

"Where is everyone?" asked Adam, looking away. "There's no one outside."

"They've gone to the Hall with Whalen Dawes. Surely you know that?"

"No, I was in the mine with Rawdon. We were lost and we just got out."

"I didn't know he was a friend of yours," said the parson, raising his eyebrows.

"He's not. Or he wasn't," said Adam, stumbling over his words. "Has my father gone too—to the Hall?"

"Yes. And I fear the worst, to be honest with you. Whalen's worked the men up to a fever pitch, saying that the accident's the owner's fault; that he doesn't care; that he thinks the miners are like the third-class passengers on the *Titanic*—not worth saving . . ."

"Well, that may be true, but that doesn't make it Sir John's fault. What's Whalen's basis for saying that?"

"He says that if they'd had reverse ventilation then they could have taken the air away from the fire, starved it of oxygen. There was a law passed last year requiring mine owners to install it but it's expensive and so they were given two years' grace, so I suppose you can argue it either way. What matters is that Whalen's been waiting for something like this to happen ever since he took over from your father—he wants to start the revolution here in Scarsdale and he thinks this is his opportunity."

"What about my father? What did he do?"

"He tried to talk the men out of going and I did too, but they wouldn't listen. They're angry and they've taken Edgar's death very hard. He was their real leader, but I expect you know that."

"How long ago did they set off?" Adam asked.

"Fifteen minutes; maybe more. I got Mr. Hardcastle to call the police in Gratton so I hope they'll get there in time. And he called Sir John as well to warn him. I don't know what more we can do."

"Well, I'm going after them. Have you got your bicycle here, Mr. Vale?"

"Yes, but . . ."

"I'd really like to borrow it. I'll look after it, I promise," said Adam, putting his hand on the parson's arm to underline the urgency of his request.

"But I don't think you should go," said the parson anxiously. "As I said, I fear the worst."

"Please, Mr. Vale. I have to. Where is it?" asked Adam, refusing to be put off.

"Outside, around the back," said the parson, bowing his head. And, reaching in his pocket, he handed Adam the key to the padlock.

"Thank you," said Adam, turning to go. But at the door he came back. "I don't like to ask, but can you make sure Rawdon's all right before you go? We had a bad time in the mine and his leg is hurting him. We almost didn't make it."

"Where is he?" asked the parson.

"He's asleep over by the pithead steps."

"You can rely on me. And I wish you luck. I think you're going to need it," said the parson, putting out his hand.

"I think I will too," said Adam with a faint smile. He shook the parson's hand and was gone.

The hours of anxious wandering, breathing in the fetid, stale air of the mine, followed by the frightening climb up the ladder had left Adam exhausted, and he cast an envious look back at Rawdon before he pushed off, pedalling hard as he began the steep climb up the road to the station with the bicycle's oil lamp flickering in its case above the back wheel. The town was quiet with a sense of foreboding in the air, and he jumped, almost losing his balance, when a stray dog ran out of a side street barking viciously at him as he rode past.

Out in front the moon hung pale and full over the eastern horizon, illuminating the church tower at the top of the hill, but down below the trees and the houses were fast disappearing into the evening shadows. Flocks of birds wheeled overhead and flew away, screeching and crying. And Adam shivered, gripping the handlebars as his mind raced, wondering what was happening up ahead.

On his left he passed Edgar's house. There were no lights on inside and he wondered where Ernest was and whether he yet knew about his father. He remembered the torment he'd suffered when his mother died and it hurt him to think that his friend would now have to undergo the same searing experience. There was no escaping the open wound of grief; only time healed or at least dulled the pain of loss.

At the top of the hill he had to stop to catch his breath, resting the bicycle against the wall of the graveyard. The moon had temporarily disappeared behind a bank of clouds, but the light on the parson's bicycle enabled him to make out the dim outline of the pitched tile roof covering the lychgate, and he remembered with a sudden intensity how he had stopped dead in his tracks when he came out of the church on that first Sunday in Scarsdale, arrested by the sight of Miriam in her simple black dress standing there beside her father. The organ had been playing in the church behind his back: a rousing fugue filling the morning with a crescendo of sound—not faint like the music he thought he could hear now, little more than a breath on the breeze, coming up soft and muffled out of the valley below.

He wiped the cold sweat from his brow with the sleeve of his jacket and rode on, accelerating as the road ran downhill into the open countryside beyond old Scarsdale village. And now he knew he was not mistaken: he could hear the music up ahead—the rich, mellow horns and cornets of the colliery's brass band playing "The Battle Hymn of the Republic," and rising up over the sound of the instruments a great swelling of men's voices singing out in unison:

"I have seen Him in the watch-fires of a hundred circling camps,
They have builded Him an altar in the evening dews and damps;
I can read His righteous sentence by the dim and flaring lamps:
His day is marching on."

Adam rounded a corner in the road and stopped, momentarily confused. The miners were close by. He could hear their marching feet, pounding the ground to the rhythm of the song's chorus:

"Glory, glory, hallelujah!
Our God is marching on."

And yet the road ahead was empty. He could see no lights in the darkness.

He rode on a little way and then braked hard as the brick wall on his left ended in a pair of high columns surmounted by stone lions with thick silver-coloured manes, staring fiercely out into the night. The wrought-iron gates between them were half pushed back, giving Adam the sense that they had been forced open, and he felt an upsurge of anxiety as he turned the handlebars and headed down a wide tarmac avenue lined on both sides with ancient elm trees.

Now there were burning lights up ahead, and as he got closer he was able to see that they were flaming torches being carried high above their shoulders by the men. They weren't singing any more and the brass band had fallen silent too, except for a single drummer beating out a monotonous tattoo. Adam slowed down, staying back just behind the marchers, not wishing to draw attention to himself until he had found out what they were going to do.

They went on at an even pace and then abruptly stopped as the line of trees came to an end and Adam caught sight of the façade of Scarsdale Hall up ahead, looming high above the miners' heads. The house looked very different now to how Adam remembered it on that summer afternoon with Ernest when it had seemed to glitter invitingly in the warm sunshine. Now, illuminated by the pale moonlight, it had a sinister appearance. Perhaps that was why the miners had come to a halt. Adam sensed their uncertainty and he could hear Whalen's voice up ahead, trying to encourage them to go on. At first it was hard for Adam to make out what he was saying, but as Whalen's voice rose and the drumbeat ceased, Adam realized that he was talking about the house and what it meant:

"Beautiful, ain't it?" Whalen's voice was thick with angry sarcasm. "But you know who paid for it?" He paused for effect before answering his own question. "You did. That's who. Ev'ry last fuckin' penny of it, with back-breakin' toil an' with yer blood." Again he stopped before going on in a louder voice so that he was almost shouting: "Yes, an' with our comrades' burnt black bodies lying under cold white sheets in the tool 'ouse back yonder. An' now Sir John, 'e must account to us for 'em; an' if 'e won't, why, we mus' make 'im. 'E canna 'ide from us, not this time."

Adam shivered, feeling the raw power of Whalen's words, and they certainly seemed to have the desired effect on his listeners, who roared their approval and resumed their march at a faster pace than before.

Soon the drive swung away to the right, curving round the side of the ornamental lake which reflected the red and yellow lights of the miners' flaring torches on the still surface of its black waters.

Adam was frightened: pushing forward, he could feel the miners' rising anger and determination. Whalen had talked of blood and he sensed that there would be more spilt before the day was done. He needed to find his father, extricate him from what was coming before it was too late. But it was too dark to see people's faces and nobody seemed to hear him when he asked about Daniel. Adam was sure his father was there somewhere but it was as if he was invisible in their midst.

A little further and they reached a fork in the drive at the front of the east wing. The parson's bicycle was an encumbrance now and Adam abandoned it in a recess, taking care to padlock the front wheel before following the marchers into the stone quadrangle facing the house. Behind them the manicured lawn ran back down from below an ornamental terrace to the shore of the lake; while in front and on both sides the house was dark, although here and there faint gleams of light were visible behind tightly drawn curtains. Mixing with the moonlight, the flickering flames of the miners' torches played up and down the pale stucco walls and across the silent windows.

The miners had fanned out, filling the quadrangle in disparate groups, all with their eyes fixed on Whalen as he strode unhesitating up the curved flight of steps leading to the entrance portico and banged the golden lion's head knocker against the ebony-black front door. Once, twice, three times but each time there was no response.

"Come out, Sir John!" Whalen shouted, bellowing out his challenge to the established order. "Eight good strong men died in your mine today an' you need to come out and tell us why. You can't hide from us an' you can't hide from them."

Adam could feel the tension among the miners all around him. They were angry, inspired by Whalen's fearlessness, but they were frightened too. No one made demands of the gentry like this; no one except Whalen. It was breaking a taboo and they sensed there would be consequences; evil consequences that might affect them all.

Whalen went back to the knocker again but harder this time—a flurry of blows that would have broken a less solid door. But still nothing happened—no sound came from the house at all and no movement except one: a curtain in a ground-floor window across from where Adam was standing was pulled back and a face looked out: only for a moment before the drapery fell back, but it was enough time for Adam to recognize the thin ascetic features of Sir John Scarsdale. And enough time for Whalen Dawes to see him as well. He'd been watching the window out of the corner of his eye because he knew it was the window of Sir John's study, having been there several years earlier when he'd come to the Hall with a union deputation, and he'd been fervently hoping that the class enemy would respond in some way to his provocation.

"I saw 'im. 'E's in there," he shouted, coming back down the steps and pointing over at the study window. "Peepin' out from behind the curtain like an ol' woman. Waitin' for the police to come an' do 'is dirty work for 'im."

It was the wrong thing to say. The lack of any response from inside the house was making the miners restive. They had started to sense that Whalen was lacking a strategy for how to proceed and his mention of the police made them think twice about what they were doing. A few of them began to back away out of the quadrangle.

And Adam could hear his father encouraging them to leave. "This isn't the right way to go about this," he said, moving from one group to the next. "Sir John'll never listen to you if you threaten him. No good will come of this—you should leave now while there is still time." For a moment Adam could see his father's strained, anxious face lit up by the torchlight but then he was lost again in the crowd, apparently unaware of Adam stepping forward and calling out his name, trying to attract his attention.

But Whalen knew what his rival was doing. "Don't listen to 'im," he shouted furiously. " 'E's not one o' us; 'e's Sir John's lackey—that's who 'e is, 'e doesn't care tuppence about any of you."

But his words had little effect. The murmuring among the miners grew louder and more and more of them began to retreat. And Whalen, sensing that he was losing them, took a stone out of his pocket and threw it hard at the study window. The glass cracked but it didn't break until he threw another. The noise stopped the men in their tracks and for an instant everything seemed to be suspended in mid-air, waiting on what would happen next. The future was hanging in the balance, and when Whalen seized a torch from the man nearest to him and threw it through the broken window it seemed to Adam like an exhalation, a moment of final decision.

Immediately the red damask curtains ignited and as they burnt away, Adam could see the fire spreading through the study. Sir John was still there, standing by a desk in the centre of the room, madly searching through the drawers, while behind him a tall bookcase was alight and flames were licking up the papered walls towards the high ceiling. And then thick black smoke began to billow out through the broken window, blotting out the interior.

It was hard for Adam to know what was happening. All around him people were shouting, screaming for water, crying for help as they ran this way and that, their stricken faces white and wild with fear as they emerged out of the swirling clouds of smoke and then disappeared back into the blackness. Suddenly the remaining glass in the study window exploded outwards, shattering in the heat, and the fire shot up the outside wall for a moment before falling back. But, as far as Adam could tell, it did still seem to be contained in the ground floor of the east wing, and he even began to feel a little encouraged when he saw a group of men, stripped to the waist, dragging a huge linen hose up from the direction of the lake.

In the midst of the cacophony he thought he could hear someone shouting his father's name from over by the front door. It was wide open now and a melee of servants was spilling down the steps, running away from the house. The chaotic scene was lit up by the blazing lights in the hall behind them. Without thinking Adam rushed towards the voice, but almost immediately he was knocked backwards. Luck was on his side and he was just able to retain his balance and so avoid being trampled underfoot, but the impact had winded him and he stayed doubled over for a moment, fighting to regain his breath.

The crowd was mostly gone when he straightened up and he could see as if through a window in the smoke a man bent almost double, staggering down the front steps, carrying another man on his back. At the bottom he slipped down on to his knees, gasping in the smoky air like a drowning man, allowing his burden to roll away on to the grey flagstones beside him. He looked as though he was praying but Adam knew he wasn't; he couldn't be: the man on his knees was his father.

Adam ran to his father's side, calling out his name. But Daniel didn't seem to hear him—he'd turned away and was bent down over the man he'd rescued, alternately holding Sir John's long aquiline nose clipped between his fingers as he blew air down into his mouth and then releasing his head to frantically massage the unconscious man's chest. Over and over again until everyone around had given up hope and Sir John faintly shook and then spluttered heavily back into life.

Daniel got to his feet, swaying slightly, allowing the Hall butler to take over from him supporting Sir John's back. Adam recognized the butler from the church where he had often seen him, sitting straight-backed at the end of one of the pews reserved for the Hall servants, singing out the hymns in an excellent baritone. Now he was dressed in immaculate evening dress and Adam noticed how alone among the servants he had made no attempt to loosen his white bow tie and high collar, even though he was obviously finding it as hard to breathe as everyone else.

"Thank you," he said. "Thank you for saving my master's life." Looking over his father's shoulder, Adam could see that the butler's gratitude was heartfelt: there were tears in the man's eyes. But Daniel didn't respond—it was as if he hadn't registered the butler's words just as he remained unaware of his son standing beside him. Instead his eyes were looking up, darting this way and that as he peered back at the east wing through the swirling smoke.

"There! There's someone up there," he shouted, pointing at the window of the room above the study. "Who is it?"

At first Adam could see nothing. But then the smoke cleared for a moment and he saw that his father was right. There was an old woman looking out, a mass of unkempt grey hair framing her small pinched face. She was clearly terrified—her mouth opened and closed like a fish pulled out of water, but they couldn't hear her. The window was closed and she seemed unable to open it. Perhaps the handles were too hot—in front of her, flames were licking the sill as the fire reached up to the second storey.

"It's the dowager—Sir John's mother. She's an invalid and she doesn't walk very well," said the butler. But Daniel was no longer listening—he'd turned away, making for the front door. At the last moment Adam reached out his hand and caught hold of his father's shirt, pulling him back.

"You can't," he said. "It's too dangerous."

"Adam," said Daniel, aware of his son's presence for the first time. He looked at him, staring into his face as if memorizing his features, and then reached out and stroked his son's cheek with the tips of his fingers.

"I have to," he said softly. "You know that." And then without warning he pulled violently away.

"No," Adam cried as his father's shirt tore away at the shoulder and he was left helplessly holding the sleeve in his trembling hands. And looking down, the white material seemed to Adam just like a flag of surrender.

Chapter Nine

Adam sat wide-eyed and sleepless beside the lake as the sun rose up from behind the gently rustling elm trees and began to sparkle on the pearl-grey surface of the water, which was lapping gently against the sloping banks of the grassy island in the centre to which generations of Scarsdales had rowed out on summer days, just like this one, to eat picnics under the flat dark green boughs of a cedar of Lebanon tree that was just now reaching the full glory of its maturity.

It was dawn at its most beautiful but Adam didn't see it, just as he didn't feel the wet dew that was soaking through his clothes.

Behind his staring eyes, his mind was repeatedly replaying the events of the night in an endless loop of tortured recollection. Once again he saw his father running up the steps to the front door while he stood there helplessly watching. Once again he saw the crazed old woman screaming soundlessly at her window and his father coming up behind her, fighting to control her arms as she lashed out in terror, before he lifted her up and put her over his shoulder as he turned away. And then once more, a moment later, he heard the thunderous explosion reverberating in his inner ear as the fire finished eating through the timber joists and the floor collapsed, crashing down into the inferno below, swallowing up the old woman and her would-be saviour in the flames.

Adam had known they were dead in that instant; he hadn't needed to stay and watch the men with the hose fight to bring the fire under control and carry out the charred bodies under a pair of white sheets while the remains of the east wing smoked and smouldered behind them.

And so he'd gone down to the lake to be alone with his grief and a succession of questions to which his dead father could provide no answers. Why hadn't he followed him into the house? Why hadn't he tried again to pull him back and save him from himself? Was it because he knew that it was hopeless; that his father wouldn't listen to reason because he was determined to atone for his wife's death? And that only the highest price would provide the redemption he so desperately craved? Was that the difference between them—that his father wanted to die, and he wanted to live? Life was terrible, never more terrible than now, but Adam knew that he didn't want it to end.

"Adam, I'm so glad I found you." Parson Vale's voice cut into his thoughts, jolting him back into consciousness of his surroundings. He looked up into his friend's kind, compassionate face, ravaged like his own by trauma and lack of sleep, and immediately turned away. He didn't want sympathy, however well intentioned. All he wanted was to be left alone.

"How long have you been here?" the parson asked.

"I don't know," Adam muttered. "I'm sorry about your bicycle. I had to leave it . . ." He stopped, unable to finish the sentence. Talking meant cutting through the numbness which was enveloping him like a protective skin, and he willed his mind not to think. He knew that grief was waiting for him around the next corner, ready to take him unawares if he relaxed even for a moment, and he was determined to keep it at bay for as long as he could.

"Don't worry about that. It doesn't matter," said the parson. "Do you know what happened—to your father?" he asked, steeling himself to ask the question.

Adam nodded without looking up. "I don't want to talk about it," he said fiercely. "I can't . . ."

"I understand," said the parson. He fell silent, looking out over Adam's head towards the trees on the other side of the lake, and when he spoke again, it was as if the words had been torn from him, forced from his lips. "Oh, God, how can you allow your children to suffer such pain?" He looked up into the empty cloudless sky as if expecting an answer to his question but there was none, just a flurry of cawing blackbirds flying up over the water, disturbed perhaps by his distant cry.

"I'm sorry," he said, wiping the clammy sweat from his brow. "It's been a long night, one of the longest I can remember."

Adam nodded, remembering the candlelit morgue at the pithead and the bodies laid out in rows on the cheap trestle tables. Edgar so alive and yet so dead.

"How's Ernest?" he asked, looking up. "Has he been told?"

"I don't know," said the parson, shaking his head. "I assume his mother has, or his brother. I don't envy them: it's a terrible thing to have to tell a boy. I'm glad that you already knew."

"Yes," said Adam, flushing. He'd felt better for a moment thinking of Ernest sharing his pain, but now he was ashamed of himself, realizing he'd been trying to derive comfort from Edgar's death.

"Have you thought about what you are going to do?" asked the parson. "There's nothing I'd like more than for you to come and live with me but I know my wife won't allow it. And with Miriam . . ."

"Please. You don't need to say it. I understand," said Adam, holding up his hand. "The truth is I can't think now. I need some time."

"Yes, of course you do," said the parson hurriedly. "But I want you to know that I'd like to help. Your father would've wanted you to finish your education. He was so proud of you—" The parson broke off, seeing that Adam was becoming distressed. He had put his hands up over his head and his body was convulsed by a series of sobs.

"Thank you," said Adam, regaining his composure with a huge effort. "Like I said, I need a little time to think, a little time on my own. And then maybe . . ."

"Of course," said the parson. "You should take all the time you need. And you can rely on me to make the arrangements, you know, for the—" He stopped, not wanting to say the word "funeral" for fear of upsetting Adam again. And when Adam nodded, he felt his meaning had been understood.

He was about to leave but then changed his mind, putting out his hand instead and placing it on Adam's shoulder. Over the last few months he had come to love the boy and the physical touch seemed to be the only way to tell him that. He stayed, standing over Adam's seated figure for a moment, looking out at the water, and then turned and went back to the house without saying anything more.

The following days passed in a blur for Adam. He walked and walked, hardly ever stopping, tramping the roads around Scarsdale in every direction, sometimes going as far as the outskirts of Gratton, until his boots were all worn through and he had to pawn his watch to buy some more. And at night he returned to the widow's house, falling into bed when he was too exhausted to walk any further. His father had already paid the rent for the month and the widow left him alone, making no reference to Daniel's absence when she passed him in the hall so that he sometimes wondered whether she even knew about the fire. He fell asleep in his clothes, sleeping dreamlessly until the sun woke him in the morning, streaming in through the open window of his bedroom. And then he hurried out, avoiding the other rooms, avoiding anything or anyone that might remind him of the life he'd shared there with his father. He knew what he was doing: he was a veteran of grief, remembering how he'd got past his mother's death eighteen months before, and he was stronger now, almost a man.

He survived on a diet of fish and chips wrapped up in local penny newspapers, reading the articles that hadn't been obliterated by the grease stains just as he used to do in London when he was a boy. Some of them were about the fire: vivid accounts embellished with purple prose from which he learnt that his father, referred to everywhere as "the hero of the hour," and Sir John's mother had been the only fatalities, and that the main house and the west wing had survived the catastrophe intact. This fortunate outcome was attributed to Sir John's foresight in installing a fire hydrant and hose beside the lake and one left-wing writer in the *Echo* dared to contrast this with the baronet's failure to install reverse ventilation in the mine. But generally there seemed to be little appetite for further conflict among the miners. Whalen had been taken into custody and his replacement as union secretary had no interest in fomenting revolution.

Parson Vale called several times but Adam was never at home and on the last occasion he left a note explaining the arrangements that he'd made for the funeral. "It's important that you are there for your father's sake as well as your own," he wrote.

Adam screwed up the letter and threw it in the fireplace: he would have given almost anything not to have to go but, as it turned out, he was glad he went. The whole town had turned out in force, cramming into the church so that there was not even standing room left at the back. The parson took St. John's Gospel for his text: "Greater love hath no man than this: that a man lay down his life for his friends." He looked down at the miners from his pulpit and told them that they had failed Daniel Raine, who had come to their town with a message of peace and reconciliation. They had listened instead to a demagogue and rabble-rouser who had manipulated their grievances for his own ends and led them into a path of error and violence. And then when the fire broke out at the Hall, Daniel had valued the lives of others more than his own and in so doing had come closer to the example of Christ than anyone that the parson had ever known. He was an inspiration to them all and they should never forget his sacrifice.

The men bowed their heads and came up one by one after the service and shook Adam's hand and he felt proud of his father, proud to be his son. He'd been angry too—for days, as he walked alone up and down the empty roads, he had raged against his father for deserting him, but now the anger receded if only temporarily, and he found that he could begin to think about him as the man he had actually been. He remembered his expression of rapt wonder, his utter stillness as he stood listening to his wife playing the piano; he remembered his reckless daring when he boxed the gypsy champion in the marketplace—his father so small and the gypsy so huge; and he remembered how on the night before the pit exploded he had glanced up from his homework and caught that look on his father's face which made him know for certain that his father loved him completely for who he was. And standing at the graveside, looking down at the coffin lying as if abandoned at the bottom of the black hole in the ground, he promised his dead father that he would try to be worthy of him; he would try to live his life to the full and be a good man.

Miriam was waiting at the lychgate, standing beside her father in just the same place that he had seen her the first time. His educated mind had been taught to think of love at first sight as a cliché, the stuff of cheap romantic novels, but he didn't know how else to describe what had happened to him that morning the previous year. He remembered with crystal clarity the sharp chill of the air; the brilliant azure blue of the sky; the smell of the recently mown grass; the moss-covered silver-grey gravestones standing at different angles as they sank down into the ground; and Miriam, so alive, so beautiful, and yet surrounded on all sides by the dead.

She had been unaware of him then—he had not yet entered her life—whereas now he knew that she was waiting for him and he could see that there were tears in her eyes.

"I'm sorry, so sorry," she said, taking his hand. And he knew that she wanted to say more but couldn't because there were people all around, people who might tell her mother if she behaved inappropriately. Perhaps even now she was watching them—Ernest had told Adam that he'd had it on good authority that Mrs. Vale had a panoramic view of the churchyard from the window of her bedroom.

He found it physically painful to release her hand after he'd felt the press of her slender, delicate fingers through her glove. He wanted to hold her, to kiss her cheek where it was rose-red with the flush of youth; and yet he could do nothing. And so he stood there tongue-tied and foolish until the parson brought him back down to earth. "Can you come to my house this evening at around six?" he asked. "There's something important I want to discuss with you."

Adam nodded, barely understanding, and began to walk away. He looked back once before turning the corner of the road and saw Miriam standing apart from her father, staring after him, and he wanted desperately to run back and take her in his arms, but instead he forced his feet forward over the crest of the hill to where the grim headstocks rose up to greet him from out of the scarred valley down below.

All that day Adam gave little or no thought to his meeting with Parson Vale. He had said he would go and so he would, but he was too raw from the events of the morning to have any room left in his mind for curiosity.

And in the parson's study, sitting in his old chair by the fire, he felt a deep melancholy settling down over him, enveloping him in a cocoon of sadness. He'd been happy here in this room, happier perhaps than he had been anywhere in his short life, and nothing in it had changed: the books with their brown leather spines and tooled golden titles gleamed in the firelight and the glass of red wine the maid had brought glimmered in his hand; but he was changed—changed forever. His father was dead, immured in a box buried in the dark earth only a few hundred yards away from where he was sitting, and he was an orphan now, alone in the world and destitute.

"Thank you for coming," said the parson. He looked anxiously at Adam, observing his pale gaunt face and air of general dishevelment. "How have you been?"

"It's been hard," said Adam, forcing himself to talk even though it was the last thing he wanted to do. The parson was now the only adult in the town who cared for him and he knew he needed his help if he was going to have any chance of making good on his promise to his father at the graveside. "It's hard being here too," he went on after a moment.

"Why?" asked the parson, surprised—it wasn't the answer he'd been expecting.

"I suppose because I used to feel guilty about being able to talk to you about things I couldn't talk to my father about," said Adam slowly. "It's like I shut him out and now he's not there any more."

"But you didn't," said the parson warmly, leaning forward in his chair to make his point. "What your father wanted most was for you to know more than him, to have a better life than he had. And I don't just mean money—he wanted your horizons to be wider, grander. He wanted you to become a man of the world."

"How do you know?"

"Because he told me. More than once. I'm sure you know he felt responsible for your mother's death. He said that she wasn't like him, that she was a reader—that was the word he used. And he thought, rightly or wrongly, that he'd robbed you of her guidance, and so he was happy when we became friends."

"Because you're a reader?" said Adam with a smile, glancing up at the bookshelves.

"Yes," said the parson, smiling too. "So the point is you have nothing to feel bad about; nothing at all."

"Thank you," said Adam, bowing his head. The parson's words helped even though part of him didn't want to admit it.

"The only guilt you should feel is in the future if you don't carry on and try to achieve what your father wanted you to achieve," said the parson, pressing his point.

"How? How can I do that? I have no money," said Adam bitterly. The parson's lack of realism annoyed him. He was going to have to find work and sooner rather than later.

"I know. And that's what I wanted to talk to you about. I—or rather someone else has a proposal to make to you and I would like you to hear it. He will be here very soon," said the parson, glancing at his watch.

"What do you mean?" asked Adam, puzzled. It wasn't like the parson to be deliberately enigmatic and he seemed nervous suddenly, ill at ease.

"Your father saved Sir John's life and he died trying to save Sir John's mother's," said the parson slowly, choosing his words carefully. "And Sir John has told me that he would like to express his gratitude by paying for you to finish your education, which would include going to university—"

"No," said Adam angrily. He wasn't going to be beholden to any man, let alone the lord of the manor.

"And he would also like you to come and live with him at the Hall until then. You would be treated as one of the family," said the parson, ignoring Adam's interruption as he hurried to finish what he had to say.

"Not treated, Frederick. He would *be* one of the family," said a voice behind Adam, who turned round and saw Sir John standing at the door, still wearing his coat and hat. As he came into the room, unbuttoning his gloves, Adam caught sight of Miriam in the doorway. Clearly she had seen Sir John through the window and had let him in before he knocked, and he had then been in time to overhear the last part of the parson's proposal, although it was unclear if he had heard Adam's vehement refusal of help which had preceded it. He certainly acted as if he hadn't, shaking Adam's hand warmly before he went to stand by the fire while waiting for Adam to resume his seat.

It was obvious that this was a man used to getting his way, standing over his listeners and talking down to them until they agreed to do what he wanted. But Adam had no intention of allowing himself to be bullied and he certainly wasn't going to let himself become an object of aristocratic charity. Pride was really all that he had left in the world and he wasn't about to sacrifice it on the altar of expediency.

"Thank you for your kind offer," he said, adopting a formal tone. "But I can't accept."

"Why not?" asked Sir John. His face was weathered and worn but his eyes were a piercing blue, demanding the truth.

"Because I want to be my own man," said Adam simply.

"Not beholden to anyone; as I am to your father?" asked Sir John with a wry smile. "No, ignore that. The point is that I want to help you so that you can become your own man, and from what Frederick here tells me, that's what your father wanted for you too."

"But this isn't about my father; it's about me," said Adam, staying firm. "I've got to learn to stand on my own two feet; I can't let somebody else do it for me."

Sir John was silent, twisting his gloves in his hands. It was as if he hadn't been expecting resistance to his offer and was now unsure how to proceed. When he spoke again it was in a softer, more considered voice.

"This isn't easy. I know that," he said. "I buried my mother yesterday and I haven't yet come to terms with my loss so it's hard for me to imagine what you must be feeling. My mother was an old woman, an invalid in the twilight of her life, but your father was in his prime and he died when you still needed him. And you've lost your mother too so this is hard, very hard for you. And perhaps I should have waited, given you time, but I didn't want you to think that you were going to have to give everything up. I didn't want you to think that you didn't have friends."

"Thank you," said Adam. He remained guarded but he had to acknowledge that there was kindness in Sir John's voice, a genuine kindness to which he could not but respond.

"And this is a strange time for me in another way," Sir John went on slowly. "I should be dead; I should be the one in the churchyard and I'm not because of your father. And that makes me think of my life differently than I did before; it leads me to want to make the years I have left valuable, worth something. And I can't think of anything more worthwhile than helping you become the man that your father wanted you to be."

He paused, and there was no sound in the room except the ticking of the clock on the mantelpiece behind Sir John's head. Adam could see how hard it was for him to talk this way when his whole training as a gentleman was to keep his feelings under wraps.

"I'm not a fool: I understand that it's hard to accept gifts when you have nothing yourself, and you certainly have a right to your pride. But what I am trying to say—not very well"—Sir John smiled—"is that you would be the one conferring the gift if you would let me help you, so I hope that you will think again."

Adam bit his lip, seized with indecision. He was moved by Sir John's words and yet he couldn't imagine living at the Hall.

"I won't fit in," he exclaimed. "It's been hard enough trying to fit in in Scarsdale; it'll be impossible at the Hall."

"The Hall is my house and when I make you welcome, everyone else will too," said Sir John, waving aside the objection.

But he was too brusque. The parson could see that Sir John's reversion to type as the lord of the manor, giving orders to his family and servants, had put Adam off, undermining the persuasiveness of his earlier appeal.

"Adam, I don't think you should worry so much about fitting in," he said quietly. "Perhaps that's something you will always find hard. This is about you—who you are; who you can become. And I think that going to the Hall will help you advance along that road. Neither Sir John nor I can ever replace your father. We wouldn't want to. But we want to help if you will allow us to."

Adam sat with his head bowed, unable to commit one way or the other, torn by conflicting thoughts and emotions. And finally it was Miriam who tipped the balance and enabled him to make up his mind. She'd been standing unnoticed in the doorway since Sir John had gone into the study and now in the moment of crisis she couldn't stay silent any more.

"Please, Adam, you can't throw this chance away." She came over to where he was sitting and took hold of his arm where it rested on the side of the chair, forcing him to look up. And, seeing her beautiful brown eyes, looking down at him so full of passionate concern, he knew he could not refuse her appeal.

"Thank you, sir," he said, standing up and holding his hand out to Sir John. "I will be glad to accept your offer."

Part Two

———•·•·•———

The Hall

The great houses stand in the parks still, the cottages cluster respectfully
on their borders, touching their eaves with their creepers . . . It is like
an early day in a fine October. The hand of change rests on it all, unfelt,
unseen; resting for awhile . . . before it grips and ends the thing for ever.

H. G. Wells, *Tono-Bungay*, 1909

Chapter Ten

It didn't take long for Adam to pack his bags, and after a night of uneasy sleep he was outside the widow's house on the stroke of eight o'clock waiting at the kerb as Sir John's Rolls-Royce loomed into view, filling up half the street as it drew to a halt beside him. He was about to get in but the uniformed chauffeur hurried round the car, opening the door for him. "Good morning, Master Adam," he said, touching his cap before he picked up the cheap bags containing Adam's meagre belongings from the pavement and stowed them away in the car's capacious truck.

It must have been a strange experience for the chauffeur to find himself helping a penniless boy half his age move to the Hall from cheap lodgings under the shadow of the headstocks, but he showed no sign of being aware of the novelty of the situation, in contrast to Adam who shifted about on his padded seat, feeling profoundly ill at ease. He had never been referred to as "Master" by anyone before and had certainly never ridden in the back of a Rolls-Royce. And he couldn't help but notice the curtains twitching in the windows of the squat grey houses as the enormous shining car went slowly by in all its glory, climbing out of the valley towards the rising sun. He knew that the news of his departure would be all over the town by the end of the morning and he wondered how his friends would view his move up in the world.

But there was little time available for reflection. Soon they were driving up the avenue between the elm trees and around the lake, and Adam was reliving the events of the night of the fire a week before. It was worse in the courtyard when he got out. Everything was quiet but to his right the wall of the east wing was black and scorched and many of the windows were boarded up: a hideous contrast to the untouched beauty of the rest of the house. And inside Adam's head he could hear once more the shouts and the screams, the shattering of glass and the fall of masonry; he could smell the thick acrid smoke and the hot sulphurous flames; and he could see his father at the door pulling away, leaving him forever. He wanted to run away, or better still get back in the car and be driven fast back through the trees and out of the gate so that he would never have to see this place again, but instead he stood rooted to the spot at the bottom of the entrance steps with his hands up over his temples, trembling from top to toe as he tried in vain to ward off the kaleidoscope of remembered sensations that were rushing through his brain.

The touch of a hand on his arm brought him back to the present and he opened his eyes, expecting to see the chauffeur. But instead it was Sir John, who was standing beside him, watching him with an expression of concern.

"I'm sorry," he said, shaking his head sadly. "I have felt overwhelmed too, standing here looking up at those empty windows, thinking of my mother—and your father too. We had several meetings in my study over there and I was always impressed by his fairness but, of course, I did not know his real quality until it was too late. All that senseless destruction—I feel sometimes that the fire has burnt some part of me away too."

Adam nodded, not yet trusting himself to speak. But he was touched not just by Sir John's sympathy but also by the way in which he had immediately understood without having to be told why Adam was swaying from side to side like a lunatic outside his front door. And as he came to know Sir John better in the coming months, Adam was often struck by the contradiction between these recurring moments of heartfelt empathy and generosity and the hidebound conservatism of his mental outlook on the world. It seemed sometimes as if he was two different people, one a product of his background and class and the other the person he might have been if he had been born outside of their confines.

"So come inside," Sir John said in a lighter tone, resting his hand on Adam's shoulder as they walked up the steps into the hall where his wife was waiting. It was a huge open area with tall portraits and Venetian mirrors in golden oval frames lining the high walls. To the left and right gilded mahogany doors led into invisible rooms and at the back a red-carpeted staircase climbed to the upper floors, lined on either side by an elaborately carved oak balustrade. It was the widest staircase Adam had ever seen: he estimated that four men could have easily gone up it side by side.

Lady Scarsdale had positioned herself by accident or design exactly in the centre of the spotlessly clean black-and-white marble floor and by way of welcome extended a silk-gloved hand in Adam's direction which he was unsure whether he was supposed to shake or kiss. After a slight hesitation he opted for touching her fingers with his own and accompanying the gesture with a low bow.

"Good morning," she said, withdrawing her hand immediately after he'd touched it. "I trust you have had a pleasant journey?" Her words were friendly but her cold voice and the firm, severe set to her mouth showed what she really felt about Adam's arrival.

"Yes, thank you. Your driver was very helpful with everything," said Adam.

"Our chauffeur, you mean?" she shot back with a thin smile. "I am glad he was able to find your lodging house. Morgan doesn't often have cause to go into the town."

"No, I'm sure he doesn't," said Adam, remembering how Ernest had told him that Sir John never went near the pit, leaving it to his managers to get their hands dirty. But then he regretted his quick riposte. He hadn't expected Lady Scarsdale to welcome him with open arms and he didn't need to give her extra cause to dislike him. "Thank you for inviting me here," he said, looking her in the eye to emphasize his gratitude. "You have been very kind."

"It's my husband you must thank," she said, smiling coldly again. "He is the master here."

"I don't think we need to be quite so pedantic, my dear," said Sir

John, clearly unhappy at the direction the conversation was heading. "When it comes to thanks, I think we need to remember that Adam's father died saving my life."

"No, trying to save your mother's life," said Lady Scarsdale quietly. "Brice and I were away in London but that is what you told me happened."

"Just so," said Sir John impatiently. "He saved my life and then went back into the fire to try to save my poor mother's and for that he and his son deserve our undying gratitude. That's my point."

Lady Scarsdale inclined her head slightly to the side but said nothing. As Adam soon came to know, it was a gesture that she often had recourse to in dealing with her husband, indicating apparent agreement with what he was saying but perfectly conveying the exact opposite. And as always the response filled Sir John with impotent frustration and he bit his lip to control his irritation.

"Where's Brice?" he asked. "He should be here to greet Adam. I thought I saw him when I came in," he added, going past his wife to look in the rooms on either side of the hall.

He came back a moment later with his hand on his younger son's shoulder. Unlike Adam Brice didn't seem to have grown much since their encounter at the churchyard eighteen months earlier so that Adam was now at least four inches taller, and his body hadn't filled out either. He'd had scarlet fever when he was a child and it had left him delicate and morbidly self-conscious about his thin and spindly frame. He was dressed in an expensive morning suit complete with a red carnation in the buttonhole and a grey silk ascot cravat around his neck, but the outfit seemed unnatural and dandified, giving the impression that he was trying to compensate for his physical shortcomings and failing in the attempt. And the wispy moustache that he'd grown since Adam had last seen him was clearly for the same purpose, but failed to conceal the drooping edges of his mouth and instead only emphasized the expression of petulance and condescension which Adam remembered from before.

"He was standing behind the door, pretending to be some kind of statue," said Sir John irritably. "Lurking! That's the word for it. And it's something you should stop doing, Brice. It's bad manners," he told his son, venting his annoyance without giving any thought to how Brice must feel about being publicly humiliated. It was a habit he had developed over many years that had long ago poisoned the relationship between father and son.

Unlike his mother, Brice had no facility for concealing his emotions and his impotent rage against his father was written all over his face. For a long time now Brice's life had been blighted with hatred born of envy. He hated his army officer brother who was brave and confident and successful; he hated his father who made no secret of his contempt for Brice's shortcomings; and now he hated Adam Raine who had been invited to live in his house without his consent. The only part of Brice's life of which he was proud was that he was a baronet's son and his father's adoption of a pauper upstart from the town had made even that attribute seem worthless.

"This is Adam, whom I've told you about," said Sir John. "He's coming to live with us and I hope you will become friends. Now shake hands."

Adam had no liking for Brice but at that moment he felt sorry for him: sorry for the way in which Sir John had treated him and sorry for how he must feel about an interloper arriving in his home. He took a step forward and put out his hand, but Brice kept his hands down by his sides and Adam could see that they were balled up into fists.

"I said: Shake hands," said Sir John, raising his voice and glowering at his son.

"I won't," said Brice. And the words were almost like a cry, as if they had been torn from him against his will. "I won't stand for it. I tell you I won't."

Sir John took a step towards his son. His face was bright red with anger and Adam could see that a blue vein was pulsing in the side of his head. But his wife put a hand on his arm and stopped him in his tracks.

"Leave the boy alone!" she said fiercely. And then continued in a more measured tone, addressing her son: "Brice, I should like to go for a walk. The fresh air will do us good. And, John, perhaps you can ask Cartwright to show Adam his room."

Brice gave Adam one last look of poisonous detestation and then went over to a small lobby-like room in the corner of the hall. He emerged a moment later with a silver lace parasol, which he opened up outside the front door, handing it to his mother when she came out to join him. She linked her other arm through his and together they walked away down the steps.

Watching this procedure unfold, Adam was struck by the intimacy between mother and son. It was an absurd notion but it felt almost as if they were the married couple and he noticed the look of intense irritation on Sir John's face as he watched them leave.

Three days later Brice had his first serious opportunity to strike a blow at his new enemy. And it was presented to him not by Adam but by Rawdon Dawes.

Adam had seen Rawdon briefly at his father's funeral and it had been clear then that Rawdon wanted to talk, but there had been no time available for conversation with a queue of remorseful miners lining up behind Rawdon's back, anxious to express their sympathy to Adam and atone a little for their ill treatment of his father, about which the parson had so forcefully reminded them in church. And then Adam had left Scarsdale without seeing any of his friends, thinking that they might try to dissuade him from a decision that he still remained unsure about. He worried now about how they were going to react. Would they accuse him of betraying them by crossing the class divide and moving to the Hall? Would they shun him for being an unscrupulous gold-digger trying to exploit his father's death by lining his own pockets? He wanted to talk to them, to Ernest especially, but he delayed going back into the town until he had worked out how he was going to explain himself to them.

But Rawdon couldn't wait. Like Adam, his life had been turned upside down by recent events. His father was now in prison awaiting trial at the next assizes. There was no doubt about his guilt and he would certainly receive a long sentence of imprisonment at the very least. And yet on the same day that Whalen had started the fire at Scarsdale Hall, Rawdon's life had been miraculously saved by the very person against whom he had carried on a vendetta ever since he had arrived in the town, largely on behalf of his father. In Rawdon's mind this turn of events was too unlikely to have been an accident; he was certain his life had been saved against all the odds for a purpose. For now that purpose was hidden from him but he sensed that while he was waiting for it to be revealed he needed to get ready to carry it out by changing his life and reassessing his outlook on the world, and he felt sure that the first step along this path required him to see Adam, express his gratitude and end the enmity between them forever. It was important, he thought, that Adam was the one who had saved him. And some instinct told him that the reason he had been saved related to Adam and that their futures were in some way tied up together.

Rawdon was impulsive by nature and once he'd decided to see Adam he couldn't brook any delay, and so on the first day he could get time off from the mine, he got on his bicycle and rode out to the Hall without even thinking about what the likely consequences would be of Whalen Dawes's son visiting the scene of his father's crime.

Adam didn't see him coming; he was up in his room lying on the bed with his eyes closed. Every day he felt more exhausted—from the emotional strain of trying to come to terms with his father's death, and from the mental strain of trying to adjust to his new life at the Hall where every social interaction was an obstacle course of dos and don'ts that he had to do his best to learn as he went along, with his every move monitored by the mocking eye of Brice Scarsdale eager to seize on his slightest mistake.

But Brice saw. He watched at the window as Rawdon rode up into the courtyard and knocked on the front door, and he listened carefully as Rawdon gave his name to Charles the footman and asked to see Adam Raine. Brice knew immediately who the visitor was. Rawdon had been with his father when Whalen staged his demonstration at the church, occupying the Scarsdale family pew, and Brice remembered how he'd had to stand impotently beside his mother, watching father and son swagger away down the hill, wishing he could drive the car at them and make them jump out of the way. He'd have liked to give them a taste of their own medicine and now, with the son at least, he thought he might have another opportunity.

It helped that it was Charles who had answered the door, not Cartwright the butler or one of the housemaids. The footman was the nearest that Brice had to a friend in the world, although he would have been appalled if anyone had dared to describe their relationship in such terms. They had a mutually beneficial arrangement—that was how he thought of it. Brice gave Charles periodic gifts in return for which Charles was prepared to run errands and listen to Brice's complaints and, when required, help Brice cover up excesses which he didn't want his father to hear about. On one occasion this had involved the footman strong-arming a thug sent by one of Brice's many creditors to collect his money, and Charles's willingness to use physical force had excited Brice, who had watched the encounter from a safe distance, concealed behind a tree.

Charles knew which side his bread was buttered. Once upon a time he had been Ben, the son of one of the impoverished farm workers on the estate. And then one lucky day Lady Scarsdale had noticed him out of the corner of her eye as she drove by in her carriage and had had a vision of what this six-foot-three labourer might look like in a white tie and tails. And from there he hadn't looked back. She had renamed him and arranged for him to have elocution lessons to erase all trace of the north country dialect from his speech; and had even gone so far as to have the brass buttons on his uniform stamped with the Scarsdale family crest. Sometimes, when she went out in the car, she had Charles drive her in preference to Morgan the chauffeur. Just looking at Charles was enough to make Lady Scarsdale forget for a moment her general dissatisfaction with her life, and she was glad that her younger son seemed to like him too.

"What is your business with Master Adam?" Rawdon heard Charles ask in his most condescending voice.

" 'E's my friend. An' I want to talk to 'im privately," said Rawdon. Brice could hear the belligerence in his voice, his cussed refusal to be cowed by the magnificence of his surroundings.

"Please wait here. I'll see if Master Adam is at home," said Charles, shutting the door. He went over to the stairs but was intercepted by Brice coming out of the same drawing room to the right of the hall where his father had caught him eavesdropping on the day of Adam's arrival.

"Do you know who that is?" asked Brice.

Charles shook his head.

"He's the son of the man who tried to burn this house down; the man who murdered my grandmother and tried to murder my father. And now he has the bald-faced temerity to come here and demand to see—" Brice broke off. He couldn't bring himself to refer to Adam as Master Adam and yet calling him simply Adam was inappropriate in front of a servant, even one he knew as well as Charles. "We need to teach him a lesson. One he won't forget in a hurry," he said, lowering his voice. "Can you help me do that? I'll make it worth your while."

The footman stared at Brice for a moment and then nodded once, listening carefully as Brice gave him his instructions.

Five minutes later Charles started up the Rolls-Royce at the back of the house. Brice was already waiting, sitting taut with excitement on the edge of the green leather seat in the back of the car, and they set off at once in pursuit of Rawdon whom they could soon see up ahead cycling slowly away down the drive. He'd not been happy when Charles had told him that Master Adam was not at home but the footman had denied him the possibility of waiting by shutting the door in his face again.

They caught up with their prey just beyond the corner of the lake where the drive entered the avenue of elm trees, so becoming invisible from the house. Charles slowed the car to a crawl, slightly turning the wheel until Rawdon was forced off the tarmac, falling sideways with the bicycle on to the verge and narrowly avoiding a collision with the trunk of one of the trees. He landed on his weak leg and winced in pain as it buckled beneath him, and then, looking up, he saw the footman getting out of the car up ahead. Charles had discarded his jacket and was pulling his shirtsleeves up above his elbows and Rawdon knew immediately what he had in mind. Using all his strength he pulled himself to his feet, picked up the bicycle and began to ride back up the drive towards the house, shouting out Adam's name at the top of his voice over and over again until he was out of breath.

Through the open window of his bedroom Adam heard the noise. He ran down the stairs and out through the courtyard on to the stone terrace from where he could see down across the lawn to where Rawdon was pedalling hard up the drive in a vain attempt to get away from the Rolls-Royce, which was coming up behind him again. Brice was leaning out of the car, laughing, obviously enjoying every minute of the terror he was inflicting, and further over to Adam's right a tall man on a grey horse was riding towards them from the direction of the house. They all came together in a flurry of movement. Rawdon swerved, riding the bicycle off the drive, and then careered down the grassy bank. Reaching the lake, he fell head first over the handlebars, and then disappeared beneath the surface of the water. And on the other side of the drive the horseman pulled up violently as the Rolls-Royce passed him by, increasing speed as it carried on up towards the house. Adam knew nothing about horses but it was obvious that the rider was highly skilled, keeping his seat and controlling the animal even as it reared up high on to its hind legs, neighing loudly in alarm.

Adam sprinted across the lawn towards the lake, shouting at the top of his voice for help, which had the unintended effect of renewing the horse's panic. He was terrified that Rawdon was going to drown. He'd seen him go under when he first fell in and then come up again as if struggling for air, and now as he reached the shore he saw Rawdon's head submerging again. The third time you drown, he remembered someone saying, or was it the second?

"Can't someone please help him?" he yelled, giving way to despair. "I can't do it; I can't swim."

"But your friend can," said a voice behind him. He knew it had to be the rider but he didn't turn round—he was too overjoyed at seeing Rawdon surfacing again beside the bank, pulling the bicycle up beside him. Adam realized he'd been wrong. Rawdon had never been in any danger: he'd chosen to go back under the water because he wanted to retrieve his bicycle. But that didn't change the shock

Adam was now feeling. His hands were shaking uncontrollably and he almost dropped the bicycle back in the lake when he reached out to take it from Rawdon. Instead he just managed to lift it away and lay it on the grass behind him before his legs gave way and he collapsed on the ground. His heart was hammering inside his chest and he was short of breath from running.

"Are you all right?" the rider asked. But he was talking to Rawdon, who was hauling himself up on to the bank. "Not broken any bones?"

"No, I don't think so," said Rawdon, spluttering a little as he spat the lake water out of his mouth. "But it ain't for want of 'em two in the car tryin' to break 'em for me."

"My brother, you mean?" said the rider. "Well, it certainly seemed that way. But why would he want to do that? Have you crossed him in some way?"

"No. I came to see 'im, not thy brother," said Rawdon, pointing towards Adam, who was now back on his feet. "The lackey at the door said 'e wasn't 'ome, but clearly 'e was. They just wanted to get me out o' sight so they could give me a good 'idin'."

"But why? That was my question," said the rider. He was smiling slightly as if he was amused by the strangeness of the situation but there was no hostility in his manner; just a detached curiosity about how it had come about.

"His name's Rawdon Dawes and his father was the one who burnt the house," said Adam. "But Rawdon had nothing to do with it. I can vouch for him."

"Which is certainly enough for me," said the rider. "Although I fear that it may not be good enough for my parents. I'm Seaton Scarsdale, by the way, and I think you must be Adam Raine. I'm sorry we weren't introduced earlier but I only just arrived here from London. I am honoured to make your acquaintance."

Seaton got down from the horse and put out his hand for Adam to shake, and he then did the same with Rawdon. It wasn't what Rawdon had been expecting and he stood, dripping water down on to the grass, looking utterly nonplussed. And Adam felt confused too: no one had ever told him that they were honoured by anything he had ever done as far as he could remember.

And he also couldn't remember ever meeting anyone who had such natural authority or ease of manner. It was strange how Seaton was the polar opposite of his brother. Up close Adam could see that they were related, but it was as if Seaton had inherited all his parents' attractive features, leaving the rest to Brice. He had the piercing blue eyes and commanding height of his father and the sensual full mouth and rich brown hair of his mother. And overall an air of calm composure that seemed incapable of being ruffled.

Now he stood thinking, stroking his chin with his forefinger in what Adam afterwards came to know was a characteristic gesture of his before he came to a decision. "I don't want to be unkind, but I think it may be best if you didn't stay," he said to Rawdon. "I apologize unreservedly for my brother's conduct but you will be the first to understand that we can't always control the actions of our near relations. And emotions are clearly running high on all sides at present."

Rawdon nodded and got on to his bicycle. He was impressed in spite of himself by the respectful way Seaton had treated him—there hadn't been a trace of condescension in his voice.

"I didn't want to cause any trouble," he said. "I came to see Adam because I wanted to thank 'im for savin' my life. That's all." Turning to Adam, he put out his hand and looked his old enemy hard in the eye, almost as if he was making a promise as Adam extended his own hand in response.

"Goodbye," said Seaton, waving to Rawdon as he got on his bicycle and rode away down the drive—a strange, bedraggled figure utterly out of place in the stately park.

"Well, I have to say I'm glad you didn't try to save him a second time," said Seaton drily, turning back to Adam. "You don't expect it but there's a sheer drop down from the bank and the lake's surprisingly deep. It's a bad place to be if you can't swim—there's nothing to cling on to. According to local tradition there's a two-headed monster lurking in there somewhere but I confess I've never seen it, even when coming home a little the worse for wear."

Smiling, Seaton took hold of the horse's reins and began to walk it back up the drive towards the stables. It was docile now, unrecognizable as the crazed animal that had tried to throw Seaton over its head minutes earlier. "I like your friend," he said. "He showed a lot of courage coming here even if it was perhaps a little foolhardy. I think he'd make a good soldier. How did you save his life?"

"We got lost in the mine on the day of the fire and we had to climb up one of the ladders. Rawdon fell and I got hold of his arm and pulled him up. We were lucky. That's all." Adam kept his answer short, uncomfortable with the idea of singing his own praises.

"And your father saved my father's life on the same day, and tried to save my grandmother's too. It seems like heroism runs in your family," said Seaton.

"It's not like that," said Adam, flushing with embarrassment. He was impressed with Seaton and the compliment pleased him but also made him feel awkward, anxious to change the subject. "How long are you here for?" he asked.

But Seaton ignored the question. "Why?" he asked, stopping to look at Adam. "Why isn't it like that?"

And Adam stopped too, feeling Seaton's blue eyes fixed on him, and told him the truth: "I did what I had to do but my father did more than that; much more. I wanted to live but I think my father wanted to die. I wish that wasn't true but I'm afraid it is."

Seaton nodded. "I'm sorry," he said. "That must be very hard."

"Yes," said Adam. "It is." He swallowed several times, fighting back the feeling that he was going to cry. He was relieved that Seaton had started walking again and they continued on in silence until they reached the corner of the house.

"We part company here. I've changed my mind about the ride. I think Caesar here has had enough excitement for one day," said Seaton, stroking the horse, which was gazing devotedly back at him. "I'm glad you're here, Adam. My father and I don't see eye to eye sometimes but I think he's got this decision absolutely right. It seems like there's hope for the old man yet." Seaton patted Adam lightly on the shoulder and walked away, leaving Adam looking after him, feeling better about his decision to come to the Hall than at any time since his arrival.

An hour later a maid knocked on Adam's door and told him that Sir John wanted to see him in his study. This room at the back of the house, looking up towards the hills, had been called into service after the burning of the east wing. Up to now it had been known as "the map room" for as long as anyone could remember, for the good reason that every available wall in it was hung with maps, and for years it had been visited by nobody except generations of servants dusting the picture frames and uncomfortable heavy brown furniture once a week. Repeated airings since the fire had failed to remove the smell of stuffiness and polish from the room and Sir John spent his time in there in a state of permanent irritation.

Now he waved Adam to one of two uncomfortable high-backed wooden chairs positioned on the other side of his desk and went back to tapping impatiently with his fingers on the green blotting pad in front of him.

"Damn the boy! Where is he?" he burst out after a moment.

"Be patient, Father. He'll be here soon," said Seaton, who was leaning back languidly in the cushioned window seat, smoking a cigarette. He'd changed out of his riding outfit into casual dress and smiled at Adam when he came in but otherwise said nothing.

Almost immediately there was a knock on the door and Brice came in, looking frightened and angry all at the same time. He looked around the room to see if there was any alternative to the chair next to Adam and then, realizing there wasn't, sat down in it with a look of disgust.

"I know why I'm here," he burst out straightaway. "And whatever he's told you"—he gestured contemptuously towards his brother—"I was totally justified. That boy's father tried to kill you and he deserved exactly what he got. He should have got more, in fact; and he would have done if *he* hadn't stopped us," he added, glancing again at his brother, who was now looking out of the window, apparently indifferent to the conversation.

"You tried to kill him, using my car as some kind of weapon," said Sir John angrily. Adam could see that the blue vein was pulsing in his temple again, just as it had before when Brice had refused to shake hands on the day of his arrival.

"No, we were making him stop, pushing him off the drive so that Charles could give him a good thrashing."

"Notice how he says Charles," said Seaton, smiling. "Not one to fight your own battles, are you, Brice?"

"Shut up, damn you!" said Brice, gripping the arms of his chair.

"No, I don't think I will," said Seaton. His tone was nonchalant and he seemed amused by his brother's rage. "Not until you get your facts right. Because I was a witness to your little escapade, remember. And you and Charles weren't just pushing young Mr. Dawes off the drive; you were pushing him into the lake where he could easily have drowned if he wasn't a good swimmer. Tell me, did you happen to know if Mr. Dawes could swim or were you hoping he couldn't?"

"Of course I didn't know," shouted Brice, turning in his chair to give his brother a look of pure hatred.

"Well, I'd say that makes you reckless at best," said Seaton coolly. "No one was going to be able to save him if he couldn't save himself. Adam here can't swim and I had my hands full trying to stay on my horse. Perhaps you were hoping I'd take a tumble and you could kill two birds with one stone. Was that it?"

"Why, you damned—" Brice got up from his chair and looked as if he was going to attack his brother until his father stopped him in his tracks by pounding on his desk with his fist.

"Enough," he shouted. "You had no right to behave as you did. You should have reported the boy's presence to me and left me to deal with it. That's what you should have done."

"It would have been too late then," said Brice.

"I said: Enough," said Sir John. "I've decided you're to stay here this month and not go to London to see your grandfather. Perhaps that will make you think twice before you do something like this again."

"You've got no right," shouted Brice. It was his turn now to become enraged.

"I have every right. I am your father."

"Then what about him?" Brice said, pointing furiously at Adam.

"None of this would have happened if you hadn't brought him here. Is this what we've got to look forward to now—entertaining cutthroats and illiterate miners at our dinner table?"

"No, of course not," said Sir John. He took a deep breath and turned to Adam. "We also need to speak," he said.

Adam nodded, wondering what was coming next.

"First let me say that I hold you blameless for what occurred today. You didn't ask this boy to come here. But I do think you need to consider whether coming to live at the Hall means that you should stop associating with young men who are now below your station in life. You may not realize this but the relationship will be uncomfortable for them as well, and I think it would be in everyone's interests if you were to cut ties. A clean break is sometimes best."

"No," said Adam bluntly. He couldn't for the moment think of anything else to say.

"No?"

"They're my friends. And I won't give them up," said Adam. "And if that's the price for living here, then I will go back to the town tomorrow and get a job down the mine working alongside them."

"Where you belong," said Brice with a sneer.

"Be quiet, Brice," said Seaton sharply. "Father, it's your decision but I have to say I think Adam is right. If it wasn't a condition of Adam coming here that he should give up his friends, then you shouldn't be asking him to do that now. Clearly they do not need to come here . . ." Seaton glanced over at Adam, who nodded, grateful for his support.

Sir John didn't answer. His brow furrowed as he tried to decide what to do. He always found it hard to change his mind but he couldn't deny the justice of what Seaton said.

"Very well," he said. "You may see your friends, if that is what they are, provided they do not come here. But I cannot permit you to associate with Whalen Dawes's son. Not after what his father did to my family. And that is my final decision."

Adam hesitated. He looked over at Seaton but he had gone back to looking out of the window and clearly there was no more support to be had from that quarter. But Brice was staring at him hopefully and perhaps it was a little his wish not to let Brice win, linked in his mind with the thought that up until very recently Rawdon had been his sworn enemy, not his friend, and a sense of what it would mean to give up school and all his prospects, that led Adam to agree to the compromise.

"I will need to see Rawdon once to explain. And when I leave here, then I must be free to see whom I want," he said.

Sir John nodded his agreement. "Good," he said. "I am glad we all understand one another."

Adam got up to leave at the same time as Brice and stepped aside to let him through the door first.

"You understand nothing," Brice hissed as he went past. "But you will," he added when they were outside. "I can promise you that."

Back in the study Seaton got up from the window seat and stretched, looking down at his father, thinking how old and worn out he suddenly looked. The fire had clearly hit him hard.

"Charles should go," he said. "But I don't suppose Mother will allow that, will she?"

Sir John shook his head and Seaton nodded. The topic of the footman had been discussed between them before.

"I like your new protégé," Seaton said in a brighter tone. "Did you notice how he never considered the option of agreeing to your proposal and seeing the Dawes boy behind your back? I don't think he could tell a lie if his life depended on it, but my dear brother, of course, finds it hard not to commit perjury every time he opens his mouth."

Seaton smiled, but his father continued to look despondent.

"Would you do one thing for me?" Sir John asked.

"It depends what it is," said Seaton.

"Don't die. If there's a war, and I think there may well be one soon, please don't die; don't let Brice inherit this estate."

Seaton laughed. "All right, Father. I promise I won't die," he said with his hand on his heart. "Now, are you satisfied?"

Chapter Eleven

Adam had been right to worry about fitting into his new life at the Hall. There were so many rules of behaviour that he had to learn: rules that everyone else in the house took for granted but which he only learnt about through the act of breaking them. The hardest tests were in the dining room. At meals, especially dinner, he often felt as if he was crossing a minefield in the dark. And it didn't help that Brice had changed his tactics since being called out for his attack on Rawdon Dawes. Now, when others were present, he pretended to have turned over a new leaf, simulating friendly concern as he went out of his way to correct each and every one of Adam's mistakes.

"No, you don't tuck your napkin into your waistcoat. I expect you learnt that from your mining friends," he told Adam at breakfast the next morning. "We do it differently here. You unfold it once and then lay it across your knees with a flourish. Like this," he said, giving Adam a demonstration and then watching with malicious satisfaction as Adam had no option but to reposition his napkin.

He seized on every opportunity: "No, we don't cool our food by blowing on it. That's bad manners." Or: "We eat jellies with a fork, not a spoon. And we never put the end of the soup spoon in our mouths; we sip from the side of it like this." Always *we*, emphasizing that Adam didn't belong at the Hall and was never going to.

Brice had been clever. The day after the incident with Rawdon Dawes he had gone to his father to apologize and had accepted his punishment with humility. And Sir John, weighed down by troubles of his own since the fire, had been delighted. He believed Brice because he wanted to believe him and he took Brice's new approach to Adam at face value, even going so far as to tell them one evening at dinner how pleased he was that they had been able to resolve their differences. And Brice knew his enemy well enough to be sure he wouldn't try to disabuse his father of his credulity. Adam was the type to fight his battles on his own.

Lady Scarsdale knew what was going on; Adam was sure of it. Each night he noticed how Brice turned to his mother and caught her eye after each sally. She said nothing but he could see from the way she watched his tribulations with detached amusement that Brice had her full support.

Brice's needling made Adam nervous and the dinners made him sick. His stomach reacted badly to the courses of rich glutinous food that followed each other in an apparently endless procession across the white damask tablecloth. Rolled ox tongue, foie gras, sauté of kidneys, truffles, guinea fowl, lobsters in aspic, multi-coloured jellies shimmering in the candlelight, all served with thick creamy sauces and decorated glazes—these dishes bore no similarity to his previous diet. And his discomfort was increased when he thought bitterly of the meagre, unnourishing food that he and his poor parents had had to eat and all the nights they had gone to bed hungry.

He tried to play with the food and not eat it, but Brice soon caught on to this and urged exotic dishes on him until a dish of Chicken Valencia sent him running from the table, overcome with sudden uncontrollable nausea.

With every day that passed Adam felt more lonely and miserable, and weary too. It was hard to have finally gained acceptance among the miners only to have to start all over again in an even more hostile environment, enduring nightly torment at the hands of Brice Scarsdale. And he had almost reached the end of his tether when help arrived from an unexpected quarter.

On the face of it Cartwright the butler was an unlikely ally. He was just as conservative as his master and couldn't have been expected to approve of Sir John's decision to overturn class barriers by bringing a working-class boy to live at the Hall as one of the family. But this was outweighed by his intense gratitude to Adam's father for saving Sir John from the fire.

He signalled his good intentions at the outset when he showed Adam up to his room after the confrontation with Brice in the hall. Hanging in the wardrobe were all the basic clothes Adam was going to need to get by at the Hall for the first few days, including white tie and tails for the evening, and, after taking his measurements, Cartwright got one of the housemaids to make the necessary alterations, and then helped Adam make the right decisions when the tailor came out from Gratton.

Cartwright felt protective towards Adam and he didn't like the way in which he was being treated. Each night, from his position behind Sir John's chair, he watched what was happening at the dinner table. Nothing escaped him. Unlike his master, Cartwright knew exactly what Brice was up to. He thought it unfair and underhanded and at the end of the first week he decided he'd seen enough and approached Adam discreetly with an offer to provide him with a rapid instruction course in the rules of etiquette.

He proved to be a patient and capable teacher, taking Adam through the endless pieces of silverware and explaining the purpose of each one, showing him what clothing was appropriate for each different occasion, and telling him how everyone in the household should be addressed. And the lessons helped: Adam stopped making so many mistakes and it was a moment to savour for both teacher and pupil when Sir John congratulated Adam one evening on his progress.

"You're almost becoming one of us," said the baronet approvingly and Brice nearly broke his wine glass as he gripped it hard in his clenched fist, striving to retain his self-control while his cheeks flared a crimson shade of red.

But there were still pitfalls for Adam because everything in this new life was so different to the one he had left behind. For instance he had been used to getting up early in the morning—Edgar and Annie would have thought him a lazy good-for-nothing if he'd lain in bed once the sun was up, but the same behaviour at the Hall got him into trouble because the early hours of the morning were when the housemaids cleaned the reception rooms downstairs. Cartwright had explained to Adam that he wasn't supposed to be in the same room as the lower echelon of servants and that he was certainly not supposed to talk to them, but Adam had failed to take the lesson to heart. The concept of servants being his social inferiors made no sense to him and he felt bewildered when the maids flushed with embarrassment and backed away when he wished them "Good morning" and asked them how they were.

One of the maids, Sarah, was less shy than the others. She was good with her needle and she was the one who had been entrusted by Cartwright with the task of making the alterations to Adam's clothes. She seemed pleased when Adam thanked her profusely for her help and didn't run away when he asked her about the new vacuum cleaner she was using to clean the carpet in the morning room.

"I've read about these machines," he said. "But I've never actually seen one before. Do you mind if I take a look?"

With Sarah's permission he compressed the bellows and then got down on the floor to examine the pipe and nozzle.

"It's so ingenious—the way it sucks up the dust," he said admiringly. The cleverness of the design delighted him. "Does it make your job a lot easier?" he asked.

"You have to get used to it, but—" She stopped in mid-sentence, turning suddenly pale. She was staring over Adam's head towards the doorway behind him and, turning round to see what was alarming her, he found himself looking up into the stern, unforgiving grey eyes of the housekeeper, Mrs. Ratton.

Her thin, pursed mouth was set in an expression of permanent disapproval, and she wore a large watch on a brass chain that she seemed to be constantly consulting. Punctuality was to her the greatest of all the virtues and she did her best to make sure that the household over which she presided ran like clockwork. She didn't like change and she didn't like Adam, feeling like most of the other servants that he had no right to be there, acting like one of the masters when he was no better than they were.

"Have you finished in here?" she asked Sarah, who nodded. "Well, then you better get on," she told her. "There's no time to be standing around idle. We have a lot to do today."

The maid took the pieces of the vacuum cleaner back from Adam without looking at him. He could see that her hands were shaking and she almost tripped as she went past the housekeeper out of the door.

"It's my fault, not hers," Adam told Mrs. Ratton as he got to his feet. "I was the one who stopped her working. I wanted to see the machine. I wish I hadn't now." He'd noticed the mean, angry look that the housekeeper had darted at the maid as she went past her out of the door and he was worried that Sarah would end up being punished in some way for talking to him.

"There can be no excuse for idleness," the housekeeper said severely, making it sound as though it was a mortal sin. And with a curt inclination of her head, she turned to leave the room.

Now Adam felt even more worried. What if Sarah was dismissed? What would happen to her? Would she be able to get another situation if she didn't have a reference?

"Please," he said, going after Mrs. Ratton and tapping her on the elbow to get her attention. She turned round violently, looking down at her arm with a shocked expression as if it had been scalded, before she raised her eyes and met his. In the face of her obvious hostility Adam took two steps back.

She clasped her hands together and breathed deeply to regain her composure. "You wished to ask me something," she said quietly.

"Yes," said Adam. "Please don't punish Sarah for what I did. Like I said, it was my fault, not hers," he finished lamely, unnerved by the housekeeper's unexplained antipathy.

"You can rely on me to do what is correct," she said with a cold smile, and Adam sensed that behind her stern exterior she was amused by his distress.

All morning Adam fretted about what would happen to Sarah. He thought of appealing to Lady Scarsdale but worried that this might just make the situation worse. Finally the decision was made for him when Charles came to his room with a summons to attend the lady of the house in her sitting room.

He found her sitting in an armchair by an open window through which there was a magnificent view over the still waters of the lake to the green countryside beyond. But she wasn't looking at the view; she was occupied instead with feeding pieces of sweet biscuit to an obese pug dog that was lying on an embroidered footstool beside her. Its paws and part of its undercarriage hung over the sides but it seemed entirely comfortable on its perch, opening its black mouth slowly to receive each morsel and then chewing contentedly until it was ready for the next one. It emitted a desultory growl when Adam entered the room but took no more notice of him when Lady Scarsdale tapped its head with a teaspoon and told it to be quiet.

On the pretty Japanese lacquer table in front of her Adam could see the menu for that evening's dinner partially obscured by the plate of biscuits, an open romantic novel and a half-drunk cup of coffee.

"Please sit down," she said, indicating a less comfortable chair on the other side of the table, no doubt placed there for servants like the cook to use when they came to see their mistress. "I wanted to see you because I have had a visit from Mrs. Ratton—"

"I can explain," said Adam, interrupting. "I wanted to see you myself in fact—"

But Lady Scarsdale had no intention of letting Adam explain. "Please," she said, holding up her hand with a pained expression. "It would be better if you let me speak."

Adam nodded, sitting back in his chair.

"As I was saying, she came to see me because she found you in conversation with one of the housemaids. And not just that, you were apparently kneeling on the carpet—"

"I was examining the vacuum cleaner. I'd never seen one before. I wanted to know how it worked."

"It is not your concern how it works. And the housemaids are not your concern either. You don't seem to understand that they have their lives and we have ours, and you are not helping them by continually crossing the barriers between us. They are there for a reason and I cannot tolerate you undermining them. Do you understand me?"

"Yes, I do. But—"

"There are no buts," said Lady Scarsdale, again holding up her hand to cut Adam off. "If you live here, you must abide by our rules. It's as simple as that. I'm sure it won't surprise you to know that I was opposed to my husband's decision to invite you here. I told him that there were other perfectly acceptable ways in which he could express his gratitude to your father, but of course he wouldn't listen to me. And incidents like the one this morning and the unseemly scene with the Dawes boy last week are exactly what I warned him about."

Lady Scarsdale paused and this time Adam had the sense not to interrupt her. "Very well," she said. "I hope we understand each other. We will keep this between ourselves but I don't want to have to speak like this to you again."

Adam got up. He felt upset and angry. He thought he'd done nothing to deserve the way he had been treated, but he also knew that it would do him no good to express his feelings. Lady Scarsdale had the power in the house and he had none. And there was nothing he wanted more now than to leave the room and exorcize his frustration with a rapid walk around the park, but he didn't feel he could do so without trying at least once more to exonerate the housemaid. He couldn't bear the idea that she should suffer when she had done nothing wrong.

"What will happen to Sarah?" he asked. "It was my fault, not her's—"

"She has been reprimanded and that's the end of the matter," said Lady Scarsdale, picking up her book from the table as if to make clear that the interview was over.

Adam breathed a sigh of relief as he went away down the stairs but he was wrong to take Lady Scarsdale at her word that the matter would stay between them, because when Brice went on the attack at dinner that evening he was primed with all the details of the incident in the drawing room. Sir John was away on business but Seaton was home for the weekend and Brice usually kept quiet when his brother was present, fearing his sharp wit, but on this occasion the information he'd got from his mother was too good for him to be able to resist using it straightaway.

"I heard a bizarre rumour that you were found down on one knee in front of one of the housemaids this morning," he said casually, looking pleasantly across the table at Adam as Charles refilled his glass of wine. "I didn't think it could be true, of course, but I thought I should mention it so you know what's being said."

"It's perfectly true," said Adam levelly. "But I think I was on both knees, not one." He still felt he'd done nothing wrong and, now that he had Cartwright on his side, he was determined not to let Brice get the better of him any more.

"How extraordinary!" said Brice, momentarily at a loss: he hadn't been expecting Adam to be so defiant. "And may we know what you were doing down on your knees?" he asked. "Proposing marriage perhaps? It does seem rather quick when you've only been here just over a week."

"No, I was examining the vacuum cleaner. I was interested to see how it worked."

"Oh, I see," said Brice, raising his eyebrows. "Well, I suppose that's one way of explaining it. But, in all seriousness, you do need to learn that we don't kneel in front of the servants. It's not good form, if you know what I mean."

"He told you what he was doing. He was looking at the machine," said Seaton sharply. He'd been watching his brother with growing irritation ever since he launched his attack on Adam. "And I have to say that I'm with Adam on this," he went on. "I think all of us should stop pretending that the maids don't exist. They have to work very long hours for very little money and the least we can do is treat them like human beings when we rely on them for everything."

"Seaton! Really!" said Lady Scarsdale, stirring in her chair. Out of the corner of his eye Adam saw her nod to Cartwright, who immediately left the room with Charles.

"Yes, really," said Seaton, warming to his theme. "Do you know that in some houses I've stayed in the maids are instructed to turn and face the wall if one of their betters happens to walk past? And yet why do we think we're better? We certainly don't set them a very good example. They get instantly dismissed without a character if they are found in the same room as one of the footmen, but in those very same houses the guests are busy fornicating with each other every time they have a weekend party. I have it on good authority that only last year the Bishop of Chester was woken up in the middle of the night by Lord Charles Beresford leaping on to his bed, believing that he was in the room of one of the female guests. And some of the society hostesses even have gongs rung in the mornings so that the guests have time to get back to their beds before the maids bring them their tea and an ironed copy of *The Times*."

"Seaton, I won't have this kind of talk here," said Lady Scarsdale, now visibly angry not just with her elder son but also with Adam, who had been unable to stop himself laughing out loud at the thought of the outraged bishop in his nightcap.

But Seaton ignored his mother. "And then sometimes the young dandies force themselves on the maids too and you can guess who carries the blame then," he went on. "Do you know what it means to be dismissed without a character, Mother? Do you?"

"I will not discuss this with you, Seaton. Your behaviour here tonight is deplorable. Absolutely deplorable! Please change the subject," said Lady Scarsdale firmly. Adam could see that she was furious but was making a supreme effort to preserve her self-control.

"Well, I'll tell you what it means whether you like it or not," said Seaton, ignoring her request. "Either destitution or prostitution—"

"That's enough," said Lady Scarsdale, interrupting. "I will not sit here and listen to this. Brice, will you come and sit with me in the drawing room?"

Brice got up and opened the door for his mother, who swept out of the dining room. Brice followed her but not before turning round to shoot a look of pure hatred at his brother, who was drinking from his wine glass, apparently entirely indifferent to the furore he had just caused.

Once the door was closed Seaton got up and fetched the decanter of wine from the sideboard and refilled Adam's glass and his own. Adam had noticed how Seaton seemed to drink almost continuously when he was at home but the alcohol never seemed to have any effect on him. He remained, as always, level-headed and detached.

"I really don't know why I take them on," he said wearily. "Nothing I say will make my mother see the world differently than she does, and Brice is indefatigable: always plotting, always nursing his own petty grievances, always with his eye on the main chance. In a way I feel sorry for him. My mother had a difficult pregnancy with him and then he was a sickly child. He almost died of scarlet fever and it's left its mark. Even though there's nothing wrong with him now, he's constantly worrying that there is, and then my mother makes it worse. I suppose she loves him so much because she risked everything to have him and he's always depended on her—unlike me. I was always independent, not wanting to be beholden to anyone, but he's forever hanging on to her petticoats. And the worse he behaves the more she wants to protect him. If no one loves him, then she needs to love him a whole lot more to make up for that, which makes him think he's right and everyone else is wrong. They're quite a pair, my mother and Brice, constantly reinforcing each other's worst character flaws."

Adam nodded, remembering how Brice and his mother had had the air of a married couple as they walked away down the steps after Brice had refused to shake his hand on the day of his arrival.

Seaton laughed. "I see people too clearly for my own good I sometimes think—and not just my mother and my ill-starred brother. My father's just as locked into his troubles as they are."

"In what way?"

"Well, as I'm sure you're aware, he's an old-world Tory, as dyed-in-the-wool a Conservative as you could hope to find anywhere in the country. But conservation costs money, especially when you own a place like Scarsdale Hall. And the sad truth is that with each passing year his income is going down."

"I know the mine is making less money," said Adam. "My father told me that."

"He was right. And it's not just the mine; it's the estate too. Twenty years ago that didn't matter so much but now it does."

"Why didn't it matter?"

"Because my father married my mother," said Seaton smiling.

"And for money, not love, which lies at the root of all their troubles. Her father, my grandfather, Sir Hubert Long, is a manufacturer of boots." Seaton pronounced the word with such relish that it made Adam laugh and then he laughed too. "Yes, believe it or not, and my father would prefer not to—boots! He supplies the army and my men swear by them. They're very good boots. He's what is known as a self-made man and like all self-made men he wanted to be accepted into society—this was before his knighthood, of course. And what better way to do that than to marry his daughter to a baronet's son? He was prepared to pay handsomely for the privilege and when my paternal grandfather got his hands on the dowry he must have thought that the family's financial troubles were over. But he was wrong. After he died most of it went on paying death duties and then quite quickly my father started getting into debt. He's never been good with money and my mother has expensive tastes. She insisted on having a house in town for the season and loved nothing more than to go over to Paris for the weekend whenever the mood took her. And then she'd come back with trunks of beautifully wrapped dresses from the House of Worth costing thousands of pounds— money they didn't have. And each time one arrived my father would become more apoplectic until he finally put his foot down and closed down the house in London and forced my mother to stay here all year round. Well, you can imagine my mother's response: she felt she was being cheated of the life to which she was entitled. She hadn't married my father and supplied him with a handsome dowry and two sons just to sit in a cold damp house in a remote corner of England and, as far as she was concerned, there was an easy solution to their financial problems. All they had to do was go to her father for help. But that of course was the one thing my father has never been prepared to do."

"Why?"

"Because he can't stand the idea of a baronet who can trace his lineage back to the Wars of the Roses going cap in hand to a boot manufacturer, who also happens to be the son of a railway porter. He prefers to borrow from moneylenders at crippling rates of interest, although I don't know how long he will be able to carry on. You know about the new taxes on land that Lloyd George has forced through, and now there's the fire."

"Surely there's insurance?"

"Yes, but I don't know if it will cover all the damage." Seaton sighed and finished his glass of wine before immediately refilling it. "Drink up!" he said with a hollow laugh, pushing the decanter across the table to Adam. "My father's Burgundy is excellent and you should enjoy it while you can. Cartwright does his best but the cellars down below are almost empty and I doubt we'll see vintages like this for much longer."

They were silent, each occupied with their own thoughts. The sun had set as they talked but the thick velvet curtains remained tied back under their box pelmets and the dining room was bathed in the soft light of the summer evening. Seaton glanced at his watch and then looked over at Adam, as if weighing a decision.

"Why are you staring at me like that?" asked Adam.

"I'm sorry," said Seaton. "It's just I'm going out. I have an appointment and I usually go alone but I was thinking that perhaps you would like to come too."

"An appointment—what kind of appointment?"

"Well, a time. There's a man not far from here who keeps balloons and when the weather is good and there's a full moon like tonight I like to go up. I know how to fly so there's every chance you'll make it back to terra firma if you're worried about the risk. But you don't have to come," he added as if he was already regretting the invitation.

"No, I want to," said Adam quickly. He felt suddenly excited. He'd read about balloons and seen pictures in the penny magazines, but he'd never imagined that he would actually get to fly in one. And he wasn't frightened—the thought of being in the air exhilarated him. It was the polar opposite of going down the mine and being confined inside the bowels of the earth.

"Good," said Seaton, getting up from the table. He seemed pleased by Adam's enthusiasm, which had had the effect of banishing his earlier doubt about extending the invitation. "You'll need to wrap up warm. It's cold above the clouds—not that there seem to be too many tonight," he observed, looking up at the sky through the window where the last golden traces of the sunset were still visible above the elm trees on the other side of the lake. "It's perfect weather for going up as long as it holds."

Seaton drove fast through the twilight, leaving a dust cloud behind the car as he switched roads repeatedly until Adam no longer had any idea where he was. He seemed to be in complete control of the car notwithstanding the copious amounts of alcohol he had drunk and they sped quickly through the sleepy villages, passing a succession of sturdy grey-stone churches and brightly illuminated public houses with their pretty painted signs creaking gently as they swayed in the light breeze, and only stopped once to allow a fox to cross the road. "Good hunting!" Seaton said softly, smiling as they watched the long brush of the fox's tail twitch several times as it disappeared into a hedgerow on the other side.

Soon afterwards he turned down a narrow track past a crude handwritten sign warning trespassers that they would be prosecuted, and parked at the corner of a large field near a long low shed-like structure that reminded Adam of the warehouse at the mine. He remembered the early-morning sense of adventure he'd felt when he and Ernest and Luke and the other boys had stolen the dynamite and cycled out through the sleeping countryside. And he felt that same sense of anticipation again now, looking out across the trampled grass to where a balloon sat tethered to the ground by a series of ropes held down with lead weights. Several men in grey overalls were moving amongst them, wheeling machinery away that Adam assumed to be the pumps they'd used to inflate the balloon. It was far bigger than he had imagined and the wicker basket in which they were to ride beneath the great silken sphere of the balloon's envelope seemed like an afterthought: impossibly small in comparison. And the balloon was beautiful too: the golden signs of the zodiac emblazoned on a sky-blue background gave it an oriental feel. It was certainly extraordinarily out of place in the centre of this barren northern field and it seemed to Adam for a moment that the balloon had come from some other planet and that they were standing waiting on the cusp of history to see what alien being would emerge from inside its vast interior.

He shook his head, dismissing the fantasy. He knew what was inside the balloon: hot air or gas heated above the temperature of the outside air to enable the balloon to rise and float. He turned, aware of Seaton watching him from the other side of the car, and experienced that sixth sense he often felt in the years to come that Seaton could see into his mind and know what he was thinking. But for some reason the sensation didn't alarm him—even though he hardly knew Seaton he felt he would trust him with his life, which was of course exactly what he was about to do.

"They have several others here but I like this one the most," said Seaton as they began to walk towards the balloon. "It's the same design as the first balloon, the one that the Montgolfier brothers built in 1783, except that there's coal gas inside this one instead of hot air. Do you know that for their first demonstration they sent a duck, a sheep and a rooster fifteen hundred feet up in the air above the palace of Versailles where King Louis and Marie Antoinette were watching from one of the balconies?"

"Did they survive?"

"Yes, without a scratch." Seaton smiled and turned away to talk to the tallest of the workmen, who was clearly the man in charge. Adam could see money changing hands and felt suddenly nervous as he contemplated the imminent ascent. Looking at the basket, it seemed like an oversized picnic hamper, and the concept of riding in it up into the vast evening sky in which the first stars were beginning to glimmer seemed an act of utter madness. But he had gone too far to turn back now and once inside he closed his eyes and gripped hard on to the sides with both his hands. Suddenly everything around him tipped on its axis and he had to fight hard to control a fit of nausea that had him gasping for breath. But fortunately Seaton didn't appear to notice: he was busy with the burners and now they were climbing with the white ropes hanging free, and down below them on the ground the mechanics waving their hands were growing smaller and smaller until they seemed no bigger than insects, and the balloon caught a current of air and was borne away over the treetops and out of sight.

To Adam's surprise his fear quickly dissipated, evaporating in the thin night air as they rose higher and higher, leaving the safety of the earth behind. And when Seaton turned off the burners the silence was intense, interrupted only by the exquisitely beautiful singing of invisible nightingales. Everything was languid and ethereal as they floated a thousand yards or more above the earth, blown this way and that on the changing currents of air, and Adam felt as though he was nothing more than "a feather on the breath of God." The phrase came unbidden into Adam's mind—he'd read it somewhere perhaps and he liked the sound of the words. It called to mind his childish image of God with his huge head and beard gazing down at London through the grey clouds. He knew better now; there was no God above the clouds, just a vast beautiful emptiness stretching out forever. Like death perhaps; he thought of his parents and felt at peace with them for the first time he could remember.

Night had fallen but it was ironically lighter now than when they had left the Hall due to the brightness of the full moon riding high in the star-studded sky. And a thousand yards below Adam could see perfectly the geometrically laid-out fields, the thick woods and the villages with their thatched roofs—a landscape unchanged in centuries. There was even the ruin of some ancient monastery beside a river; birds flying in and out through the high Gothic windows of the church were reflected below in the moonlit water.

And then they passed over a line of hills, rising like the spine of a giant buried animal, and entered the world of the new century. Below them was a panorama of massed warehouses and factories and railway yards but it was hard to see the detail through the smoke billowing out from a thousand chimneys. Here and there the orange fire from a blast furnace darted up towards them and Adam remembered the first one he'd seen with his father when they changed trains on their journey north from London. He wondered whether his father would have turned back if he had known what lay in store for him in the north or whether he would have carried on regardless. Better the way it is; better for human beings not to know, Adam thought, contemplating the unwritten slate of his own future in this new world of blast and fire.

He looked across at Seaton. They had hardly talked and yet Adam felt an intense sense of companionship with his new friend. "Thank you for this," he said. "I had no idea . . ." He stopped, at a loss for words. Those he'd spoken seemed so inadequate to describe what he felt.

"Yes, I know what you mean. I wish I could experience my first time in the sky again," said Seaton with a sigh. "I never felt more alive, which is a sensation I value more than you can imagine. Most of the time I feel like a ghost watching my life from the edge of the stage. I don't know why. I was born that way, I suppose. And I shouldn't complain—it is still different when I'm up here. The charge hasn't disappeared; it's just a little less strong each time I go up. I should like to fly one of the new aircraft. Do you know I was there when Blériot flew the Channel three years ago and won the prize for the first crossing?"

"Were you really? I saw a newsreel about it years ago in London," said Adam, remembering the grainy pictures of the little man with a handlebar moustache standing sheepishly outside Dover Castle.

"Yes, it was as if everything had changed forever. I shook his hand and I don't mean to be blasphemous but for me it was a real 'hem of his garment' moment. I was like a child asking for his first autograph. Please, Monsieur Blériot . . ." Seaton laughed at the memory. "Do you know that the King has just signed a warrant establishing the Royal Flying Corps?" he went on after a moment. "I think sometimes of resigning my commission and training to be a pilot, but of course I won't . . ."

"Why not?" Adam asked.

"Because of my men. Wellington called them the scum of the earth at Waterloo but he was wrong: they're the salt of the earth. There's the odd blackguard among them of course but most of them are like the miners who work for my father—the backbone of England. And I need to be there for them when the war comes . . ."

"You think it will?" asked Adam. Death and destruction seemed hard to imagine as they floated so peacefully in the moonlight.

"Yes. Europe is like a powder keg. Someone sooner or later is bound to light the spark."

"That's what Parson Vale told me. He talked about a spark too. And he said that once the war has begun nobody will be able to stop it."

"He's right. I've long thought that our parson is the most intelligent man hereabouts. And he thinks highly of you, but I'm sure you know that."

"He recommended me to your father. He's the reason I'm here," said Adam simply.

"And I'm glad you are," said Seaton, smiling and extending his hand. And when Adam shook it he felt as though he was entering into a compact of some kind, sealed in this strange and holy place high above the earth.

Chapter Twelve

A week later the parson came to lunch and he brought Miriam with him. Adam had seen neither of them since his father's funeral, but not a day had gone by without him remembering the touch of her hand on his arm as she urged him to accept Sir John's invitation. He treasured the moment because it had shown him how much she cared about what happened to him. She was shy by nature and the presence of the lord of the manor in her father's study would have made it doubly hard for her to intervene in the conversation, particularly at such a critical juncture. But caring wasn't the same as loving. Adam had no idea whether Miriam felt about him as he did about her and he could see no way of finding out without running the risk of losing her completely.

He wanted to tell her. So many nights he had lain awake in the darkness imagining some enchanted afternoon or evening when he opened his heart to her and she did the same and they sealed their understanding with a kiss. By a river; in a glade; beside the ruined monastery that he had seen from the balloon in the moonlight; anywhere sufficiently far removed from the long gaze of Miriam's mother, who he knew wouldn't hesitate to put a stop to his visits to the Parsonage once and for all if she thought that her daughter had become romantically involved with a penniless orphan. For now he could rely on the parson to stand up for his right to visit but he knew that Miriam's mother would soon override her husband's objections if she felt that his protégé had become a significant threat to her daughter's chances of marrying money.

He remembered Mrs. Vale's beady light grey eyes. Not much escaped her and Adam was sure that Miriam would not be able to keep it from her mother if they started to meet in secret. He loved that there was nothing false about Miriam—he sensed how much it would hurt her to tell a lie and realized that even if she did, her mother would know in an instant. Miriam was incapable of artifice—her face was a barometer of her emotions. And perhaps Miriam's mother was right. Perhaps he had no right to ask for anything when he had no money, no prospects, nothing to offer her daughter except his heart.

And all this assumed that Miriam returned his feelings. What if she thought of him only as a friend? Or what if she hadn't even considered how she felt? One of the qualities that Adam loved most about Miriam was her natural delicacy, and he sensed that she might well withdraw from him if he forced the issue. He had already lost so much in his life. The thought of never seeing Miriam again was more than he could bear. Better to remain silent and keep the little he had.

But at lunch she was changed. Adam had expected that her shyness would stop her joining in the general conversation but she was even more reserved than usual, saying almost nothing and eating very little. He sensed she was upset: on several occasions he thought he saw her lip tremble and there was a reddening around her eyes which made him think that she had been crying. He wanted to ask her what was wrong and worried that he had done something to offend her, but there was nothing he could do except wait and hope that there would be an opportunity to speak at the end of the meal.

And Brice too was quieter than usual. Adam remembered their first encounter outside the church soon after his arrival from London when they had almost come to blows over Miriam. He had no idea whether Brice retained an interest in her but he had still expected his enemy to try to show him up in front of a beautiful girl, and yet Brice didn't direct a single barbed comment at him during the meal. Instead he seemed irritable and preoccupied and Adam had the impression that he was trying hard to control some slow-burning resentment, although Adam was entirely in the dark as to its cause.

The lunch seemed to go on forever. Seaton was away with his regiment and Adam missed his lightness of conversational touch as Sir John held forth from the end of the table about his favourite topics: the warmongering Germans and the rebellious Irish and his true bête noire, the trades unions, the enemies within, who were plotting to join forces and bring the government to its knees if it did not give in to their insatiable demands.

"Have you heard about this new pamphlet called 'The Miners' Next Step?'" he asked the parson, beckoning at the same time to Charles to replenish their wine. "It's written by the same socialist rabble-rousers who organized those appalling riots in South Wales two years ago when Churchill had to send in the army to stop them looting."

"Yes, I think I saw an article about it in *The Times*," said the parson. "Don't they want workers' control of the mines; that sort of thing?"

"Yes, that sort of thing," said Sir John darkly, shaking his head. "Well, Hardcastle's told me the deputies have confiscated several copies in the mine in the last few weeks. And that means there's a lot more doing the rounds which we don't know about. I just hope they're not planning something else. They are Jacobins, these people; they will burn us all in our houses if we give them the chance, just as Dawes tried to do here."

"I can understand how you must feel after what happened but I really don't think you have cause to worry," said the parson, making an effort to sound reassuring. "My strong impression from talking to the men is that their mood has changed since the fire. They think that Whalen Dawes misled them and they wish now that they hadn't listened to him."

"Yes. A lot of them came up to me at my father's funeral and said that they regretted voting him out. They think he was right to try and negotiate with you instead of wanting to tear everything down like Whalen did," said Adam. He'd spent enough time with Sir John by now to understand that his constant preoccupation with the threats to society from without and within stemmed at least in part from the scarring experience of the fire. He might have been physically saved but he had clearly suffered a severe mental trauma and Adam welcomed the opportunity to try to help the parson allay some of his benefactor's fears. He remembered the sad silent hopelessness of the widow's house after his father's death and he felt intensely grateful to Sir John for coming to his rescue, notwithstanding Brice's vicious treatment of him since his arrival.

"And it certainly helps that you have treated Dawes's family well. That hasn't gone unnoticed," said the parson, warming to the theme. "The men expected you would evict them and stop the son working."

"Which is exactly what you should have done," said Lady Scarsdale, breaking into the conversation from the other end of the table with obvious impatience. "And not only that: you should have found out who Dawes's main supporters were and punished them too. You're too weak, John, and there's a price to be paid for that nowadays. You talk about those looters in South Wales—exactly the same will happen here unless you show some mettle."

"I read that the miners' wives in Tonypandy threw boiling water on to the heads of the police from out of their bedroom windows," said Brice, whose interest in news stories was in direct proportion to the level of their salacious content.

"That's enough, Brice," said Sir John sharply. "I apologize for my choice of subject, Miss Vale," he said, noticing that Miriam was showing signs of distress. "I didn't mean to upset you."

Miriam shook her head but didn't seem able to trust herself to speak. "Please excuse me," she muttered, getting up from the table and rushing out of the room.

Parson Vale went after her but came back almost immediately. "Miriam asks me to apologize," he said. "She felt unwell but she says she's feeling better now. She just needs a moment to compose herself."

But she hadn't rejoined the party by the time the meal ended and Adam went to look for her outside. The sun was shining and he thought she might have gone out in search of fresh air. He could see immediately that there was no sign of her at the front of the house where the wide lawn descended from the stone terrace to the shore of the lake and so he went round to the left into the ornamental gardens behind the east wing. As he approached the corner, he looked back towards the entrance courtyard and noticed Brice coming down the steps from the front door. He didn't know why but he instinctively thought that Brice was also looking for Miriam and he quickened his pace, hoping that Brice hadn't seen him.

If he'd had to choose, Adam would probably have said that the flower gardens were his favourite place at Scarsdale Hall. Some long-dead landscaper had laid out the paths and shrubberies and planted the trees and hedges when Queen Victoria was a girl and now his vision had been fulfilled in a mature harmony of shapes and colours. An elderly taciturn gardener with a grey beard and watery eyes laboured, bent double in the flower beds, from morning to night but, as far as he knew, Adam was the only one who ever came to admire the old man's handiwork. He had done a lot of his grieving here in the first days after his arrival, knowing that no one would interrupt him as he walked up and down the gravel paths trying to come to terms with the death of his father. And the contrast between the desolate scorched walls and boarded-up windows of the ruined east wing that overlooked one side of the garden and the riot of colour below echoed the contradiction in his mind between the vivid ever-present reality of his father and the terrible knowledge that Daniel Raine would never be alive in the world again.

In quieter moments there were weathered grey benches under the fruit trees where he could sit and read or just close his eyes and smell the scent of the white-starred jasmine and the freshly watered roses. His favourite place to sit was an enclosed arbour hidden away inside a circular yew hedge in the centre of the garden, where water from a stone fountain dripped down into a pond in which orange and grey fish swam leisurely through a mosaic of white water lilies. Adam hurried towards it, thinking that Miriam might have ended up there following her flight from the dining room.

He was right. She was sitting on the bench, twisting a handkerchief between her slender fingers as she rocked gently to and fro as if in the grip of some overwhelming emotion. He waited for a moment in the entrance arch cut into the hedge, uncertain what to do. He felt he was invading her privacy but he couldn't stay watching her without announcing himself and he didn't want to leave her when she was clearly so upset.

"Hello," he said, keeping his voice low so as not to alarm her. But she responded instantly, jumping up from the bench and looking round, clearly flustered. He felt for a moment that she didn't know who he was. He read fear in her face—she reminded him of an animal that had been trapped, gazing up terrified at the poacher and his gun. But then she recognized him and he could see relief flooding through her.

"What's wrong?" he asked, going forward. "Has someone hurt you?"

She shook her head but then froze. They could hear a voice somewhere in the garden calling out Miriam's name. It was Brice. And he was coming closer.

"Is he the one that's upset you?" he whispered.

Miriam nodded. And Adam took her hand, drawing her back into the shadow of the hedge so that they could feel the pointed tips of the dark green leaves brushing against the back of their necks. They were almost beside the entrance archway so that anyone standing there would be unlikely to see them unless he came into the arbour and looked around.

Across from where they were standing a blue tit was perched on the corner of the mossy green fountain, drinking. But the air was still and, apart from the drip of the water, there was no sound except the noise of Brice's approaching footsteps. They halted at the arch and Adam felt Miriam's hand gripping his as they waited to see if Brice would come through.

But he didn't. The bird flew up into the air and he turned away, walking on towards the stables. And in the distance they could hear him continuing to call out Miriam's name.

Immediately she pulled away from Adam, retreating back into the arbour so that the bench was between them. She looked frightened again now and she was breathing heavily.

"It's all right," he said, holding out his hands palms up, trying to calm her. "He didn't see us."

"But he might have done," she said frantically. "And if he had it would have been so much worse. He wouldn't have believed us. He'd have thought . . ."

"I'm sorry," said Adam. "I didn't think. You seemed so upset. I wanted to protect you."

"I know," said Miriam, beginning to breathe more easily. "It's just he pushes so hard. He won't leave me alone, and it wears me down until I don't know which way to turn."

"How long has this been going on?"

"I don't know. For most of the last year, I suppose. He gives me presents and then he's angry if I don't wear them. Like today—today was the worst. He sent me this two days ago. I don't know where he could have got the money." Miriam reached down to pick up her handbag from the bench and took out a small jewellery case. Inside was a tortoiseshell hair comb, its top in the shape of a crown inlaid with gold and tiny diamonds in a pretty scrolling leaf design that glittered against the black velvet background of the case. "There was a note with it saying that he hoped I would wear it today when I came to lunch."

"And when you didn't he got angry," said Adam, guessing at what had happened.

"Yes. He was waiting for us when we arrived. I could see all this hope in his face and then it drained away and he was crushed. I felt sorry for him but I can't make him think something that isn't true, can I?"

"No, of course not," he said. "It's not fair of Brice to put you in this position." Adam tried to sound quietly reassuring but behind his calm exterior he felt a surge of happiness coursing through him like electricity as he digested the news that Miriam had no romantic interest in Brice.

"And then when I tried to give him the comb back he wouldn't take it," she went on. "He said I was cruel and selfish and ungrateful, and all through lunch I thought he was going to make some kind of scene in front of his parents. It made me nervous and then by the end I couldn't cope any more so I came out here."

"Does anyone else know about this?" Adam asked.

Miriam nodded. She swallowed hard and he could see that tears were forming in her beautiful brown eyes, but he carried on with his questions regardless. If he was going to help her, he needed to know the full picture. "It's your mother, isn't it?" he asked, remembering Ernest's words from a year before: *The parson's hard up and Mrs. Vale wants her daughter to marry money so I suppose Brice Scarsdale would fit the bill.*

"Yes," said Miriam quietly. "She doesn't agree with me. She says I should give Brice a chance and then maybe I could learn to like him. She told me to wear the comb today but then I took it off on the way here and now when she finds out what has happened . . ." Miriam stopped, fighting back her tears.

"But why does she need to find out?" asked Adam, not under-standing.

"Because she'll ask me and I'll have to tell her," said Miriam and Adam could hear the despair in her voice. "I'm no good at deceiving people; I never have been. Which is why I can't do what she's telling me to do, but then I have to tell her when I don't. And she keeps on insisting I have to come here whenever there's an invitation, and I can't tell my father because he has so much on his mind."

"Do you want me to talk to him? I will if you want me to."

"No, it wouldn't make any difference. My mother would still get her way. She always does when she sets her mind to it."

"So what can I do?"

"I don't know."

Adam looked over at Miriam where she stood leaning against the fountain. The sun shining down over the top of the yew hedge lit up her face and burnished her hair, dark and resplendent against the bright white linen of her dress. He had never seen her more beautiful. She seemed to him rich and yet simple like a Madonna in a painting by one of the Renaissance masters and the arbour was transformed in his imagination into a sacred grove in one of the Roman poems that he had grown to love: a place such as Lucan described where the wind never blew and the branches moved of their own volition. Miriam gave meaning to the garden; she was the goddess at its centre, the source of the enchantment.

And he couldn't bear the thought that she would never come here again. The garden would be empty without her. He could protect her from Brice and then there would be more moments like this stolen out of time.

"I can be here whenever you come," he said. "Brice can't object. I live here now and he has no right to see you on his own."

"Would you?" she said. And her face lit up as she smiled for the first time that day. "I don't want to be a burden."

"You could never be that," he said, smiling himself at the absurdity of her suggestion. "Surely you know that?"

"No," she said seriously. "I don't know. I think I am one of those people who find the world hard to understand even if I do have my faith to guide me."

Adam nodded, touched by the honesty of her answer. He was glad that she believed. He knew that her life must be lonely and circumscribed with her father distracted by his commitments and her mother plotting to marry her to the richest suitor that came along regardless of Miriam's wishes. Her faith in a merciful, loving God could not but help to sustain her through dark days and he didn't need to upset her by telling her that he believed in nothing at all.

And so Adam became a chaperone, sticking to Miriam like a limpet whenever she came to the Hall. It enraged Brice but there was little he could do. Without Miriam's co-operation he could not see her on her own and given that that was not forthcoming he had to put up with the hated presence of his rival. He was jealous too: there was nothing to suggest that there was any actual intimacy between Adam and Miriam but he saw how she smiled and relaxed when she was talking to Adam and he caught the way Adam looked at her sometimes when he thought no one was watching.

Adam was stealing Miriam away from him. He was the one in the way, not Adam, bringing up the rear, carrying Miriam's parasol while they walked on ahead deep in conversation. The initial advantage that he'd enjoyed when Adam didn't know how anything worked had evaporated more quickly than he could have believed possible and now he always seemed to come out second best when he competed with Adam for Miriam's attention. Adam was taller, stronger and cleverer too: he was thriving at the grammar school in Gratton and Sir John trumpeted to anyone who would listen that Adam was destined for Oxford or Cambridge as if the boy's academic success was his success too—an endorsement of his decision to bring him to live at the Hall.

But Brice knew that the real advantage Adam had over him was that he was natural, comfortable in his skin. Brice could never escape from the prison of his own self-consciousness. He was awkward and ill at ease and he made anyone he was with feel the same. He thought of clever phrases or interesting anecdotes that might impress Miriam but there was never a right moment to fit them into the conversation. He could hear his own voice cutting in, stilted and hectoring, and he hated the sound of it.

Adam made him look bad. Against all the evidence he had convinced himself that without Adam in the way Miriam would have come to reciprocate his feelings and the frustration he felt at his missed opportunity fed his growing rage. Adam was a pauper's son who belonged with his friends down the mine or back in the London slums where he came from whereas he, Brice, was the son of a baronet. Miriam should be fainting with joy to receive his attentions instead of treating him as if he was some kind of distant acquaintance.

The injustice of his situation inflamed Brice. His father had had no right to take Adam in and treat him like a son and Adam had no right to take his place with Miriam. He hated them both in almost equal measure and his anger and resentment built up inside him, festering like a cancer. The only outlet he had was to complain to his mother but he couldn't tell her about Miriam. One of the only things that Brice's parents could agree on was that both their sons needed to marry money, and everyone knew that the parson had no independent means.

And what of Adam? He knew full well that Brice hated him but he also knew that there was nothing he could do to change how Brice felt. He couldn't leave the Hall without giving up all his future prospects and he couldn't stop seeing Miriam. And because there was nothing he could do about Brice he tried not to think about him. It wasn't difficult—he had plenty to occupy his mind. School took a great deal of his time and at home he spent hours more working at his set texts. Recently he had had a breakthrough: he was no longer always translating; instead he was reading in Latin and Greek, hearing the voices of the poets and the music in their words. He felt his mind reaching across the dead centuries to the ancient world so that, closing his eyes, he could feel the ground tremble under the legions' marching feet, hear the roar of the crowd baying for blood at the Games, and see the Emperor walking in his garden in the cool of the Roman evening, weighing matters of life and death.

And his studies had another benefit—they sustained his sense of connection to his own past. His first encounter with the Greeks and the Romans had been in the damp little house in London when his mother sat on a stool at his bedside and read to him from a big book with coloured pictures, holding the page close so she could see the words in the candlelight. *Gods and Heroes* it was called and he still had it, although its boards were beginning to come loose and the spine was cracking. Her maiden name, Lilian Grace, was written on the flyleaf and the date, 18 March 1880; she must have been given it when she was a child. Sometimes when he held the book in his hand he could see her face again, glancing up at him as she turned the page and smiling at the entranced look on his face. "Read, read," he would say, impatient to know what happened next, and her voice would begin again, transporting him to the walls of Troy or the Roman Colosseum as if he was riding on a magic carpet.

Sitting at the desk by the open window of his room, looking out at the stars while moths circled the oil lamp, Adam felt content. He missed both his parents but it felt like a dull ache, something he could bear as he went forward, secure in the knowledge that they would be happy with the direction he was going in and the person he was becoming.

Slowly but surely Adam was adapting to his new life. He was under no illusions: he knew he would never truly belong at the Hall, but he was used to not belonging. He'd been an outsider among the

miners and yet he'd ended up making friends. And there was no reason why he could not make a success of this new life too. There were
certainly pleasures to be had that he was not used to—small com-
forts like hot water in the morning instead of the icy jug that had
been his experience up to now or the wide comfortable bed warmed
with a stone bottle in which he lay reading Sherlock Holmes stories
at night after finishing his work, before turning over to sleep in the
flickering glow of the coals from his very own fire; and outside, there
was the still beauty of the estate with the swans preening their snow-
white feathers as they floated on the glassy blue surface of the lake
and the trees with their huge thick limbs like giants stretching in
the morning. Sir John told him that some of the oaks and elms were
as old as the Civil War and one magnificent specimen halfway down
the drive had a bullet mark in its trunk fired (according to legend)
by a passing Parliamentarian soldier returning home from the battle
of Marston Moor in 1644.

Adam came to understand that it was a sense of history and the
history of the estate in particular that anchored Sir John and were
the key to his personality. One day he gave Adam a guided tour of
the portrait gallery at the back of the house. To his great joy it had
escaped the fire, whose devastating effects had been entirely confined to the east wing. All the pictures seemed the same to Adam
at first: old bewigged men standing in stylized poses against pictur-
esque backgrounds, some with wives, some with dogs and some with
neither. But they came alive when Sir John began to identify them
and tell him their stories: an avaricious-looking Sir John from the
mid-sixteenth century who had profited from the dissolution of the
local monastery under Henry VIII; his grandson painted in full body
armour who had commanded one of Elizabeth's ships that sailed out
from Plymouth to meet the Armada, and further along the line an
eighteenth-century black sheep who had mortgaged the estate to pay
his gambling debts and doubtless would have lost it completely if he
hadn't been killed in a duel fought in Richmond Park over a woman
who was not his wife. And then finally at the end of the line Sir
John's father, a stern Victorian man with a furrowed brow and severe
expression, who had rescued the Scarsdale fortunes from the agricul-

tural depression by sinking the mine which was now causing his son so much anxiety and distress.

"You have to understand that I see myself as a custodian of the estate rather than its owner," said Sir John reflectively, looking at the blank space beyond his father where his own portrait would one day hang. "I mean that it is not mine to dispose of as I think fit; it's a trust requiring me to pass it on to my son in the same condition or better than I received it, which is hard, of course, when our government sees fit to tax not just our deaths but now our land too. Sometimes I wonder how much longer we can go on," he said with a sigh.

Notwithstanding its beauty, Scarsdale Hall was not a happy house. Sir John loved it but feared for its future and his wife hated it like a prison. Once, passing along a corridor, Adam heard them arguing through an open door.

"I don't care what anyone thinks. What's the point in dressing up like a lady to impress stupid miners' wives who'd like to burn us in our beds?" he heard her shout. Since the fire she had refused to accompany the family to church on Sundays.

There was some muttered response from her husband which seemed to make her even more angry: "I can't stand to see that damned mausoleum in the churchyard. Every time I go there, I imagine myself walled up inside it. Because that's how I feel: buried alive in this house in the middle of nowhere suffocated by your clean country air, while you traipse off to Parliament on the train and vote 'No,' always 'No'—anyone can do that. Dear God, what I would do if I could be in London . . ."

A door slammed and Adam could hear no more. But it was enough. He remembered Seaton's clinical analysis of his parents' marriage and wondered whether the loveless atmosphere in which he had grown up was what had made him so dry and detached, *like a ghost watching my life from the edge of the stage,* as he'd described it when they were up in the balloon. But at least Seaton was fair and just, unlike his brother who was being eaten up from within by a toxic combination of anger and hatred.

All around Adam was a sea of troubles. But it had been the same when he lived with the miners, and Adam was a survivor. He was young and strong and his spirit wanted to embrace life rather than dwell on the hardships he'd suffered. He didn't want to think about the threat of war or Brice's hatred of him when the sun was shining and he could go cycling with Ernest in the hills or steal glances at Miriam when she came and sat in the corner of her father's study when he went there to visit on Sunday afternoons.

Chapter Thirteen

Adam looked forward to Seaton's visits. He had learnt to be self-reliant and had no instinct for hero worship, but he admired Seaton. He had never met anyone with Seaton's capacity to see people for who they really were. He had a bloodhound's nose for falsehood and hypocrisy combined with an ability to express his thoughts with singular clarity and directness. In Seaton's company Adam saw the world through a different lens, one that was sometimes uncomfortable, sometimes funny, but always interesting.

Adam had noticed how the servants and the estate workers all seemed to like Seaton. He was popular because he did not court popularity and appeared to be entirely devoid of personal vanity or ambition. He was ironic and detached and yet Adam sensed that his loyalty once given would be absolute, and he was glad that Seaton was his friend.

Seaton was a mass of contradictions. He was handsome and obviously attractive to women but, as far as Adam could gather, he had never been involved in a romantic relationship; he was an army officer and yet some of the views he expressed were as radical as those of Whalen Dawes; and he was down to earth, a soldier's soldier, and yet was surprisingly well read. One day several months after his arrival at the Hall Adam had gone to find Seaton in his rooms on the other side of the house and been surprised to discover the walls lined with books and their owner seated by the window, absorbed in a volume of Dickens, although later when Adam came to read Dickens himself he understood why a writer so skilled in describing his countrymen's vices would have appealed to Seaton.

It was a fault perhaps that Seaton judged people by his own high standards and that sometimes he seemed to want to shock his audience just for the sake of shocking them. Sometimes he did this with his father but far more often it was his mother whom he targeted and she rarely failed to rise to the bait. Adam sensed that Seaton loved his father despite his prejudices, but that he felt a deep antagonism towards his mother which he was reluctant to fully acknowledge. Their values were certainly very different: Lady Scarsdale was concerned with appearances, whereas Seaton believed that the root cause of society's ills was its emphasis on the superficial. And her identification with Brice alienated Seaton, who despised his younger brother.

Every member of the family was present in the dining room on an evening in June of the following year when Adam felt that Seaton gave his most memorable performance. It began innocuously enough. The parson and Miriam and several local notables, including the mine manager, Mr. Hardcastle, had been invited to dinner and as they were sitting down Seaton complimented Miriam on her dress. It was a simple but elegant design of sheer lawn cotton in soft white with intricate lines of golden needlework sewn in a pattern around the square neckline.

"It's very pretty," Seaton said. And he was right—the dress was beautiful on her, enhancing her colouring and the dark lustre of her hair.

"Thank you," Miriam replied, flushing.

But Seaton could tell she was pleased with the compliment. "It's worthy of the Rue de la Paix," he said. "Is that where it came from?"

"No, I made it myself," she said, smiling. She knew he was teasing her but in the nicest possible way.

"Well, then you are an artist hiding your light under a bushel," said Seaton.

"Since when have you been interested in ladies' fashion?" asked Lady Scarsdale, sounding irritated. Seaton's refusal to display any enthusiasm for the opposite sex had long been a bone of contention between them and it annoyed her that he should be paying attention to the parson's daughter when he had shown no interest in any of the heiresses she'd introduced him to in the past. Part of her suspected that he was doing it deliberately just to rile her.

"I think fashion's absurd—an excuse for the rich to spend ridiculous sums of money on clothes they don't need," he said. "But it's different when something's natural and well made, unlike most of what I see women wearing every time I go out: hobble skirts so narrow that they can hardly walk—hobble's a good word for them—or laced up in corsets so tight that they can hardly breathe. What is the name of that one that's so popular these days?"

"Be quiet, Seaton. Please!" said Lady Scarsdale in a harsh whisper. She was staring at her son, looking like thunder.

But Seaton was launched now and was in no mood to stop. "I know," he said, snapping his fingers. "The S-bend corset: that's what it's called. It makes the woman wearing it jut out in front and at the back so she looks just like a kangaroo."

"That's enough. You should save this kind of talk for your officers' mess. You've no right to inflict it on us," said Lady Scarsdale, raising her voice. She was angry and embarrassed too—she'd noticed how the conversation had stopped at the other end of the table as the other guests turned to listen to Seaton's lecture on women's undergarments.

Seaton, however, welcomed the attention and carried on, paying no heed to his mother. "And then, as if not being able to breathe isn't enough, she has to fill her hair full of pins and pads and spikes like a porcupine to keep a fruit salad hat in place two and a half feet above her head. And why does the lady of fashion subject herself to this torture?" he asked, looking round the table as if in search of the answer to his question before he supplied it himself: "She does it because she's been taught to see herself as an object for men to look at. Who she is doesn't matter; it's what she looks like that counts. I must say I'm on the side of Mrs. Pankhurst and the suffragettes: women need to stand up for themselves and stop being playthings for men. What do you think, Miss Vale?"

"I agree that we are too worldly, but I don't believe in using violence to effect change," said Miriam thoughtfully. "Violence begets violence I think, not concessions."

"Well said, my dear," said Sir John. "Smashing shop windows; planting bombs—we can't tolerate that kind of thing. That woman last week throwing herself under the King's horse—it's beyond the pale."

"But without the violence who will take any notice?" asked Seaton. "Everything will go on as before. And it's not just women who are suffering. The poor live in the most appalling conditions while the rich spend money like water. At some of the houses I've been to in London they regularly spend more on a single dinner than a poor family can earn in a year."

"So what would you have us do?" asked Hardcastle. "Take money from the rich and give it to the poor? Surely, if you do that, the poor will have no incentive to work, even if the rich are left with enough to stay in business and employ them."

"The poor are poor for a reason," said Lady Scarsdale with conviction.

"And what reason is that, Mother? Please do enlighten us," said Seaton, his voice laced with sarcasm.

"Drink, idleness, dissipation—if we gave them nice homes they would turn them into slums."

"And store coal in their baths! Yes, I've heard that said before," said Seaton dismissively. "And none of it is true. The poor are poor because they have no chance to escape their condition. They earn too little and their employment is too insecure. The most they can hope for is to scratch a living and then end up in the workhouse when they get too sick or old to work any more. Don't you agree with me, Mr. Vale?"

The parson shifted awkwardly in his seat. He could sense that the disagreement between Seaton and his mother was about far more than social theory; they were engaged in a clash of wills in which he did not want to become involved. But Seaton had appealed to him and he could not remain silent. "I agree that in some ways our society has lost its way, although I don't think socialism is the answer. That is as much a false God as the pursuit of money. I believe that we need to rediscover our Christian values. We have never been as much in need of God's guidance as we are now."

"But instead we are obsessed with pleasure—an explosion of frivolity," said Seaton. "It's as though we're on some mad fairground ride. It goes faster and faster and we can't get off. Like Rome before it fell. If there's one lesson to be learnt from history, it's that decadence precedes disaster."

"I don't think our king is anything like the Emperor Nero," said the parson, trying to lighten the conversation.

"Certainly not," said Lady Scarsdale, directing a withering look at Seaton.

"No, Nero's more like the Kaiser—vain and self-important. He's an interesting character, however; like me he had a very strong-willed mother. I'm sure Adam knows all about her—Adam's our resident classical scholar, Mr. Hardcastle."

Adam cringed. Unlike everyone else at the table except Mr. Vale he knew what was coming and yet he was powerless to stop it. All he could do was sit and watch.

"Would you like me to tell you her story, Mr. Hardcastle?" Seaton asked.

Hardcastle bowed. He really had no choice but to acquiesce, although Lady Scarsdale tried to head Seaton off at the pass.

"Mr. Hardcastle doesn't want to hear it, Seaton. And neither do the rest of us," she said.

But Seaton overrode her: "I'll keep it short," he said. "Her name was Julia Agrippina and, as I've said, she was extremely strong-willed and very well connected. She was the sister of the homicidal mad Emperor Caligula, whom I'm sure you've all heard of, and the wife of the Emperor Claudius whom she poisoned with a plate of deadly mushrooms in order to secure the succession of her son. Nero, however, wasn't in the least grateful and decided to repay her with the gift of a self-sinking boat—"

"Stop this, Seaton, at once. I won't tell you again," said Lady Scarsdale, losing her temper.

But Seaton ignored her even when she got up noisily from the table and made for the door, which Charles hurried round to open for her. "Well, the boat duly sank with Agrippina aboard," he went on, "but Nero had reckoned without his mother's exceptional survival skills. She saved herself by swimming to the shore but not, I am afraid, for long. When Nero got word of what had happened he dispatched three dagger-wielding assassins who took it in turns to stab her to death. And that, as they say, was the end of that."

There was a short silence after Seaton had finished speaking and Lady Scarsdale had left the room in which you could have heard a pin drop. Adam had expected Brice to show solidarity with his mother by saying something to his brother or at least rushing out of the room after her but instead he remained in his seat, apparently lost in thought, until Sir John gave a heavy sigh and pushed back his chair.

"That was uncalled for, Seaton," he said gravely. "You will apologize to your mother." And then without waiting for a response he left the room, followed by everyone except Seaton who remained at the table, drinking from his wine glass, apparently entirely unmoved by the chaos that he'd unleashed.

Adam was the last to leave and Seaton called him back as he reached the door. "I was in rather a hurry to finish and omitted Agrippina's last words from the end of the story," he said. "I wonder if you remember them?"

"*Ventrem feri*—smite my womb," said Adam. "She wanted her murderer to destroy that part of her which had given birth to so abominable a son."

Seaton nodded. "And do you think me abominable?" he asked.

"No, quite the opposite—I hold you in the highest esteem," said Adam. "But, since you ask, I do think you went too far tonight."

"Overstepped the mark—yes, you're probably right, although there was certainly provocation. My mother's views on the poor are disgraceful, and she should think twice about expressing them, particularly when she's the granddaughter of a railway porter."

"Well, at least you didn't bring that up," said Adam with a smile. "Will you apologize?"

"Yes," said Seaton. "I shall confess my sins." And, draining his glass, he got up from the table.

———

The disastrous dinner party had important consequences but these did not involve the main protagonists. Seaton apologized to his mother and went back to his regiment and Lady Scarsdale retired to her room to nurse her grievances and pass the time sharing sweetmeats with her pug, while reading romantic novels in which damsels were rescued from a life of drudgery by dashingly handsome knights in shining armour.

For months Brice had been even more lethargic than his mother. At Easter he had been rusticated for the remainder of the year from his latest school for stealing an exam paper. Writing to Brice's parents, the headmaster had commented that if Brice had shown the same inventiveness and energy in his academic work as he had in trying to cheat then he would be at the top of his class instead of being sent home in disgrace. Sir John became apoplectic with rage but Brice didn't seem to care and immediately settled down to an intensive period of idleness from which he only seemed able to rouse himself when Miriam came to the Hall. He said very little to Adam but the occasional venomous looks that Adam caught out of the corner of his eye left him in no doubt about Brice's continuing enmity.

Now, however, Brice became suddenly energetic and began making plans for a midsummer party at the Hall. There was to be a picnic on the island in the middle of the lake and music provided by the Gratton String Quartet.

He compiled a guest list with Miriam's name at the top and spent hours closeted with his mother and Mrs. Flowerdew, the cook, working on a menu and devising methods of keeping the food and drink cold and fresh as it was transported across the lake to the island where a special marquee tent was to be set up for the occasion. Five additional rowing boats were brought over from Gratton and bedecked with red-and-white awnings to provide shade from the sun. Sir John complained about the expense but was overruled by his wife on the grounds that it was better for Brice to be doing something productive as opposed to lying on a sofa gazing at the ceiling, which is what he had been doing for the previous two months.

The Hall bustled with activity as the day of the party drew near and Adam kept to his room, working. At the end of the year he was due to sit the Oxford scholarship examination and he was under no illusions about the difficulty of the hurdle that he had set for himself, but he needed the scholarship if he wasn't going to be beholden to Sir John for the fees that he knew Sir John could ill afford. Adam would always be grateful to his benefactor but he longed to be his own man, rising or falling on his own merits. He would have liked to have started earning his living without delay but he knew that he needed a first-class honours degree from a top university to open the doors to success in life, and so he worked hard, getting up in the dawn light every morning to study.

On one such morning, the day before the party, he was sitting at his desk in his dressing gown rereading the passage from Tacitus about the death of Agrippina that he had quoted to Seaton when there was a soft knock at his door. He opened it and was surprised to see Sarah the housemaid standing on the threshold. He had had no dealings with her since the incident with the vacuum cleaner. He'd been relieved that she had escaped with a reprimand and didn't want to jeopardize her position any further by being seen talking to her, and so he was astonished now that she should have risked everything by coming to his room.

She was clearly agitated, shifting from foot to foot and repeatedly looking right and left down the corridor. "Can I come in?" she asked. "There's something I need to tell you and I don't want to be seen out here."

"Of course," he said and stood aside to allow her to enter. "Do you want to sit down?" he asked, but she shook her head and so they stood awkwardly on either side of the fireplace while he waited for her to speak. She still seemed nervous even though he had closed the door.

"I can't stay long. It's a busy morning and they'll miss me downstairs," she began but then stopped, apparently unable to continue. Adam saw that her hands were shaking even though she was trying to control them by squeezing them against the sides of her white apron. Clearly her nervousness about whatever it was she had come to say outweighed her anxiety about being away from her work station.

"You said there was something you wanted to tell me," he said gently.

Sarah nodded, breathing deeply to muster her courage. "If I tell you, you won't say it was me that warned you, will you?" she said, looking him in the eye for the first time.

"No, I won't," said Adam. "I'm very sorry I got you into trouble before and I won't let that happen again. You can trust me," he said, speaking slowly to add emphasis to his words.

"Yes, I think I can," she said, beginning to breathe more easily. "You're different. Not like the others—except Mr. Seaton maybe, although he scares me a little."

"You're not the only one," said Adam. Sarah smiled and her face suddenly lit up and Adam could see how pretty she was with her hazel eyes and the dimple in her chin.

"Yesterday, about this time, I was cleaning in the morning room downstairs," she began at a rush. "And I had to go down on my hands and knees behind the sofa because there was a stain on the carpet and so they didn't see me when they came in . . ."

"Who?"

"Master Brice and Charles—they're thick as thieves those two are."

"I know," said Adam, remembering their joint attack on Rawdon.

"Any road, they started talking straightaway and I didn't want to tell them I was there because I thought I'd get into trouble, and then when I heard what they were saying I was frightened. I got in close to the sofa and I stayed there still as a statue because I didn't want to think about what they might do to me if they found me." Sarah's voice had risen and Adam could see that her hands were shaking again as she relived what had obviously been a terrifying experience.

"I think it really would be better if you sat down," said Adam. "And let me get you a glass of water."

This time she accepted his invitation, although she wouldn't sit back in the armchair but instead stayed perched on the edge while she sipped bird-like at the water that he had poured from the pitcher on his bedside table.

"Thank you for coming to see me. I can understand how difficult this must be for you," he said, resting his hand on Sarah's arm for a moment as he gave her the water. "Can you tell me what they were saying?"

"They were talking about the party, about what they're planning to do. They're going to capsize one of the boats that are taking people over to the island for the picnic—Master Brice is going to be rowing you and Miss Vale, and then halfway across there's going to be an accident. And Master Brice is going to save Miss Vale."

"And I'll be left to drown," said Adam, aghast. "Brice knows I can't swim."

"I don't know about that," said Sarah, sounding even more frightened than before. "They didn't say what was going to happen to you."

"They didn't need to!" said Adam, still in a state of shock. "But none of this makes sense," he went on, shaking his head. "How are they going to get away with it? Rowing boats don't just capsize . . ."

"There's going to be a collision. Charles will be rowing one of the other boats. I don't know all the details."

Adam opened his mouth to ask another question but nothing came out: instead he just gasped, at a loss for words. He knew that Brice detested him but he had never suspected until now that Brice's hatred had mushroomed to the point that he was prepared to consider cold-blooded murder. Now he understood why Brice had been so unusually attentive when Seaton was entertaining the dinner-party guests with the story of Agrippina and Nero.

And he had to give Brice credit: the plan he'd come up with was simple but ingenious—he'd get rid of his rival and gain the credit for saving Miriam all at the same time. He shuddered, realizing that the conspiracy could easily have succeeded if Sarah hadn't happened to be out of sight in the morning room at just the moment when Brice and Charles were discussing their plan, and if she hadn't had the courage to come and warn him of the danger he was in.

"You've saved my life," he said. "I don't know how I can ever repay you."

"You don't have to," she said, getting up. "I'm glad I could help." She seemed calmer now, relieved that she'd done what she came to do. But she was nervous again when he opened the door for her and she darted her head out into the corridor, looking from side to side like a fox checking for hounds.

"Thank you," he said, but he didn't know whether she had heard him as she hurried away and disappeared from view around the corner.

Chapter Fourteen

Back in his room Adam paced about, trying to make sense of what he'd been told. He tried to remain calm but instead his shock and sense of panic seemed to increase as his mind absorbed the impact of the information until he was almost bouncing off the walls. He felt caged, like an animal in a trap; he had to get out into the air so he could breathe, calm his racing heart. He ran down the stairs in his bare feet and across the hall, almost knocking over a shocked housemaid—not Sarah—who was washing the floor, and pulled open the front door.

His quick steps echoed in the silent courtyard, and he looked up at the windows on all sides, feeling he was being watched. But they were empty, indifferent to him and his fate. He turned away and came to a dead halt on the threshold of the stone terrace, looking down over the balustrade to the lake below. He was frightened of it now; he could feel the weight of the dark water, imagine it filling his lungs, imagine them bursting as he struggled to breathe with Brice's distorted shadow looking down at him from above the surface—the last thing he saw before he lost consciousness and sank down into the murky depths.

He had never had such an experience—he was living his own death, feeling each moment of it until something inside him snapped and he rushed down the steps and vomited violently into the grass.

Afterwards he stood leaning his clammy sweating forehead against the stone wall of the terrace, trying to calm his breathing and regain his self-control. It was still early—the sun hadn't risen far above the horizon, and he shivered, pulling his dressing gown around his shoulders. But the cold air helped him to think. He needed to get beyond the raw emotions that were swirling around like a maelstrom inside his head; he needed advice from someone outside of the Hall, someone whose opinion he valued and whom he could trust. He needed to talk to Ernest.

Adam's mind was made up. He knew he couldn't cope with this new challenge on his own and Ernest was his oldest friend as well as being one of his only two surviving blood relatives. He also had no involvement with Brice or Miriam and he possessed that unusual quality Adam had never met in anyone else of being able to think an issue through, carefully considering all the facts, before he made up his mind. And Adam knew he would keep a secret.

Adam felt better now that he had decided what to do. And he was grateful that it was a Saturday—there was a good chance that Ernest would not be working. He went back to his room to get dressed and then set off down the drive on his bicycle just as the heavy bell in the distant tower of Scarsdale Church was striking eight, feeling his spirits rise and his head clear as he left the Hall behind and rode away down the deserted road between the summer hedgerows with the air all around him alive with the sound of birdsong.

He knocked hard on the door of the house at the end of Station Street; harder than he'd intended, and was sorry when Annie answered it looking frightened. He knew what she'd been thinking: that there'd been an accident and another of her family had been taken. She hadn't got over her husband's death—each time he saw her she seemed more withdrawn, a shadow of the vibrant, bustling person she'd been before. And the house too was quiet. There was a smell of gathering dust in the air and the grate was unswept, a mess of grey ash half spilling out on to the carpet. Adam winced, remembering the great banked-up fires that Edgar had built in the same fireplace, filling the room with smoke and red shadows while his strong baritone voice rose up, holding forth about the mine and its doings above the crackle of the burning wood.

Now he sat drinking milky tea at the table while he waited for

Ernest to get ready, trying to conceal his impatience as Annie moved about around him, ineffectually tidying up.

"It helps to keep my mind off things," she said, and rested her hand on his shoulder for a moment as she went past. "I'm sorry about your father," she told him as if offering her condolences for a recent bereavement whereas it was now a year since the fire and he'd seen her several times since.

And at the door, as Ernest and he were walking out, she put out her hand and touched his cheek when he said goodbye. "You were always such a good boy," she said. "Like Ernest," she added, looking up anxiously at her son who was now fully grown and towered above his diminutive mother when they stood side by side.

"I won't be long, Mother," he said as they set off up the path through the cornfield to the oak tree on the ridge. And at the top when they looked back they could see that Annie had come out into the side garden and was standing at the fence looking up after them. She'd tied her hair up in a thin scarf and the ends were blowing about in the breeze, and she looked small and exposed, as if a heavier gust could pick her up any moment and carry her away to where the headstocks loomed black and menacing against the distant skyline.

"Will she be all right?" asked Adam.

"I don't know," said Ernest, shaking his head. "It doesn't help that my brother's as gloomy as she is: they seem to feed off each other's misery. You remember Thomas was always a bit like that—morose and taciturn? Well, he's a lot worse now. He was closer to my father, I suppose—you know how they worked together, and then when the explosion happened he wasn't with him at the face. He'd gone back to fetch something and he seems to think that it might have made a difference if he'd been there, which is nonsense, of course. He'd just have been killed too and then there'd only have been me to support the family whereas, as it is, we're not doing too badly if you take into account the compensation. Other families have it harder than us and the community's good about supporting each other, but my mother's never been a joiner and so she stays at home and thinks about her troubles, which only makes them worse."

"And you—what about you?" asked Adam. He felt sorry for his friend whose difficulties helped to put his own into perspective.

"I'm all right. I worry about Mother and I can think of more interesting ways to earn a living than sorting coal . . ."

"Easier too!" said Adam, remembering the frenetic movement of the screen workers' hands as they picked out the stones and rubbish from off the moving belt while the fat deputy, Atkins, shouted at them from a gantry up above.

"Yes, you're right," said Ernest, nodding. "But at least the company's improved. Did you know Rawdon's working on the screens too now? He refused to go back underground after what happened."

"No, I didn't know—I've kept my promise to Sir John even though I sometimes think I was wrong to have given it. It makes me feel like a lowlife when I see him in the town and have to turn away. I just hope he understands—he seemed to when I explained it to him but that was a long time ago."

"Yes, he understands. And he's changed—for the better, unlike my brother. I don't like to say it but it's probably helped him that Whalen's been put away. Whalen wasn't like our fathers—he was always blaming everyone else for his misfortunes and he taught Rawdon to do the same. But Rawdon's not like that any more. He's convinced you saved his life for a reason, although he says he doesn't yet know what it is. Like you say, it's not easy to find salvation while that pig, Atkins, is screaming insults at you from dawn till dusk." Ernest laughed. "But it's hard to believe that the mine is real on a day like this. It's like we're in a different world, a better one than I'm used to," he said, taking a deep breath of the fresh air which was fragrant with the scent of newly mown hay.

And Adam, who had been about to tell Ernest about Brice's plot, forced a smile instead. His friend deserved to enjoy the morning a little first before Adam sullied it with the tale of his own troubles.

They walked on, leaving the path behind and cut across a wild meadow where their passage disturbed a flock of lapwings from their scraped-out nests so that they flew up into the air, making their shrill pee-wit cries as they swerved and swooped, and the boys stopped to admire the sunlight gleaming on the birds' green plumage and bright white breasts.

And then continuing on, they rejoined the climbing path and came out after a few minutes on to the high ridge where they had stopped on their first walk together two years earlier, looking down at Scarsdale Hall nestling in the morning sun among its surrounding trees. How strange it was that the Hall was now his home, Adam thought—he could never have imagined that when he was last here and Ernest had told him that *the Parsonage and the Hall are close to where we live but they might as well be on a different planet.*

The grounds had been deserted when Adam had left at eight o'clock but now workmen had arrived and were busy putting up the marquee on the island in the middle of the lake. Rowing boats were ferrying supplies across the water and servants were moving to and fro in the courtyard and on the grass where Adam had been in extremis two hours earlier.

"What are they doing down there?" asked Ernest.

"Brice is giving a party tomorrow. But it's just a front—an excuse to get people out on the lake so he can stage an accident. He's going to capsize our boat so he can save Miriam and I think he's intending to let me drown. He knows I can't swim . . ."

Ernest had turned to look at Adam as he was speaking, staring at him as if to assess whether he was serious; then, realizing he was, he let out a protracted whistle.

"Christ, Adam," he said. "What the hell have you got yourself into?"

It took a while for Adam to explain everything. Ernest knew that Adam and Brice were enemies, but Adam had not told his friend much about Miriam on the occasions that they'd met since he moved to the Hall. If he couldn't tell Miriam how he felt, then there was nothing for him to tell his friend. But now it was different. If he wanted Ernest's advice, then he needed to put him fully in the picture.

"So what do you think I should do?" he asked when he had finished describing the strange triangular dance that he and Brice and Miriam seemed to have been engaged upon for much of the last year.

"Well, it would be nice if you could tell Sir John—expose Brice, get Charles dismissed, lance the boil," said Ernest thoughtfully. "But it won't work," he added just as Adam had been about to object. "He'd have to hold an inquiry and Brice and Charles would deny it. And then it would be their word against a housemaid's and you know what the outcome of that would be."

"She'd be dismissed. And I can't let that happen. I promised her no one will find out she told me and I can't repay her by breaking my promise. She risked everything by coming to me," said Adam.

"She certainly did. And I agree with you—you can't tell Sir John so that eliminates one of your options."

"So what should I do? This party's tomorrow—I have to do something."

"Well, perhaps we should look at it another way and decide what you shouldn't do," said Ernest, unruffled by his friend's mounting anxiety.

"What do you mean?"

"I mean that you clearly can't go to this party. Not if you can't swim. It'd be suicide. And you can't let Miriam go either. Brice may be hoping to save her and act the hero but that doesn't mean he'll succeed. Do you know if she can swim?"

Adam shook his head.

"Well, it really doesn't matter. Even if she can, it's still too much of a risk so you're going to have to stop her going and that means telling her what Brice has got in mind. She needs to know who she's dealing with. Do you think you can trust her to keep it to herself?"

"Yes, I think so," said Adam uncertainly, remembering how she'd told him she couldn't keep secrets from her mother. "Maybe it'll help if I don't tell her what I think they're planning to do to me," he suggested. "There's no point in making her more frightened than she needs to be."

"Tell her as little as you can. That seems to have been your strategy for a long time now," said Ernest, shaking his head.

"It's not a strategy. It's about doing what's right. I can't ask her to have me when I've got nothing to offer her. And I don't know if she even likes me that way."

"Because you haven't asked her," said Ernest, smiling.

"And I've told you I won't until I've got my independence. For now I'm no better than a charity case."

"You could ask her to wait."

"No. She must be free to choose. I don't want to tie her down and control her. I don't want to be like Brice."

"I don't think there's much chance of that," said Ernest, getting up and stretching.

Adam stayed where he was, staring down at the Hall. "It's a beautiful house, but cursed in some way. I don't know why. It's as if the fire was just the beginning, and there's more to come," he said. He spoke meditatively, almost as if he was talking to himself.

Ernest looked at his friend curiously and then clapped him on the shoulder. "Come on," he said. "There's still some of the morning left and I don't want to spend it sitting still.

"But I do think you're right," he told Adam as they stood on the high ridge, taking one last look at the great panorama of green countryside spread out below with the house and lake gleaming jewel-like at its centre. "I think it will be better for you when you've left that place. Like I said to you before, their lives aren't like ours."

The next day Adam kept to his room, sending down a message that he wasn't well. This wasn't true but he was certainly tired. He'd been out almost all of the day before and his mind had been in a constant state of stress ever since Sarah had visited him the previous morning, making him unable to sleep for most of the night.

Now he took off his shoes and lay on top of his bed with his eyes closed, allowing the light breeze coming through the open window to play on his face as he listened idly to the sounds of the party beginning down below. Cars drove up—first a few isolated ones and then a flurry—disgorging guests; and footsteps, scores of them, crossed and recrossed the courtyard while Cartwright called out last-minute instructions to the extra servants that had been brought in for the day. And then later, at around noon, the quartet started playing Handel on the lawn, their instruments competing for ascendancy with the sound of splashing water and voices raised in excitement out on the lake.

Adam nodded off and was woken with a start by a series of loud knocks on his door. He sat up and looked at his watch—it was just past one o'clock, and he was about to respond when the door flew open and Brice rushed into the room. He was dressed even more extravagantly than usual with a gold ascot cravat set above a blazer-style piped silk waistcoat and knee breeches—all designed to impress Miriam who wasn't there to be impressed. Adam could see straightaway that Brice was in a wild rage but he felt strangely calm—perhaps the rest had done him good.

"Why didn't you come? You're not sick," Brice began, shouting at Adam from the doorway. Adam's lack of reaction to his forced entry seemed to enrage him even more and he approached the foot of the bed with his fists clenched.

"I didn't want to," said Adam, deciding on the spur of the moment not to invent some excuse. At that moment he felt nothing but contempt for Brice, dressed up in his ridiculous outfit, and he thought rightly that it would provoke Brice even more if he told him he preferred to lie on his bed than attend the party.

"Damn you, Adam. I've half a mind to . . ."

"To do what?" Adam asked. He half hoped that Brice would try to hit him, knowing he could make short work of his enemy if he did.

But Brice seemed to realize this and took a step back. "Do you know something?" he asked, giving Adam a searching look.

"What are you talking about?"

"Nothing," said Brice. "But you knew that Miriam wasn't coming, didn't you?" he went on, returning to the attack. "She sent word she was sick but I know it isn't true because Charles saw her in the town yesterday and she was fine then. She's not coming because you told her not to. Isn't that right?"

Adam looked Brice in the eye but didn't answer. He wasn't going to be bullied. Not after what Brice had planned to do to him.

"It doesn't matter—I don't need you to answer. I know you told her. You knew I was planning this party in her honour and so you decided to ruin it. Well, I've had enough of you coming between us."

"Coming between you! I don't need to. Can't you see she doesn't love you and she's never going to, however many parties you give?"

"Has she told you that?"

Again Adam refused to answer. He regretted his outburst—he didn't have the right to speak for Miriam; she was the one who should tell Brice what she felt.

"I thought so," said Brice with a sneer. "Well, I can tell you this— you won't be seeing Miriam any more. I'll see to that."

"You'll get her mother to stop her? Is that what you mean?" said Adam, finally getting angry himself. "Well, perhaps I should tell yours. I'm sure she won't be too happy when she finds out you're hell-bent on marrying a parson's daughter."

Brice looked furious. Adam could see his eyes darting round the room, as if searching for a weapon to attack him with.

"But I won't," said Adam. "I won't stoop to your level, Brice. When all is said and done, what I really want is not to be like you. And now, if you've nothing more to say, perhaps you'll leave me in peace and go back to your party."

Brice stared at Adam for a moment, biting his lip and twisting his hands. Adam could see the murderous hatred in his eyes and had no doubt at all about what would have happened if Sarah hadn't warned him and he had gone out on the lake in Brice's boat.

Finally, after giving Adam a last vicious look, he turned on his heel and walked out of the room, and Adam could hear the sound of his boots stamping on the floor as he walked away down the corridor.

Brice was true to his word. Two days after the party Parson Vale came to the Hall and asked to see Adam in private. They went into the morning room but the parson remained standing when Adam sat down, shifting his weight awkwardly from one foot to the other. Adam had always felt at ease in the parson's company but now the atmosphere was strained and the parson had the look of a man who had something to say but didn't know how to begin saying it; and so, after receiving monosyllabic responses to several attempts to make conversation, Adam fell silent, waiting for the parson to tell him the reason for his visit.

"Brice came to my house yesterday and talked to my wife," the parson began, speaking in a rush of words that underlined his obvious discomfort. "He said that you had been to see Miriam and told her to stay away from the party here to which she had been invited. Is that true?"

"Yes." There was nothing else Adam could say; he wasn't going to lie.

"And he also said that you had told Miriam to say she was sick even though she wasn't. Is that true too?"

Adam nodded. It wasn't entirely true: Miriam and he had agreed that she would have to offer some excuse and illness seemed to be the only possibility. But Adam was more than willing to take the full blame if it would help Miriam.

"May I ask why you did this?" asked the parson.

"You may but I cannot answer, except to say that it was for a good reason," said Adam firmly, looking the parson in the eye. He wished he could say more but he could not betray Sarah's confidence.

"Strange—Miriam said much the same," said the parson, shaking his head. "Brice told my wife that you are trying to stop him seeing my daughter because you have designs on her yourself. Is that true?"

"How can you ask me that?" asked Adam angrily. "Yes, I like Miriam but I don't have *designs* on her or on anybody. You should know me better than that. It's Brice you should put that question to."

"Miriam has told me about the attentions she has been receiving from Brice," said the parson quietly. "It's unfortunate that she did not tell me before as she has clearly become distressed by the pressure she has been put under, but she and I have agreed that it would be best if she stopped coming to the Hall at least for now. And I will be discouraging Brice from visiting the Parsonage."

The parson paused but Adam sensed he had more to say and thought he could guess what it was.

"You don't want me to come to the Parsonage either?" he asked.

"I think that it is best for Miriam," said the parson sadly. "She is still young and she needs time to herself." He got up to go and then held out his hand. "I am very fond of you, Adam," he said. "I hope we can still be friends."

"Of course," said Adam, shaking the parson's hand. But beneath the surface he felt angry with his old friend. The parson had a very pretty daughter and he should have been more watchful on her behalf, whereas instead he had neglected her and left it to Adam to try to protect her. And then when the situation with Brice escalated out of control he had punished Adam for his efforts because he couldn't say no to his wife. However much the parson might pretend to the contrary, Adam felt sure that the ban on him coming to the Parsonage was Mrs. Vale's doing.

And the parson wasn't just cutting him off from Miriam. He was withdrawing as well. His talk of friendship was hollow. It was a bitter pill for Adam to swallow after the parson had promised to be his protector after his father died.

All through that day and the next Adam's mood darkened. The thought of not seeing Miriam was hard to bear, but what made it even worse was that he hadn't had the chance to say goodbye. He had an acute sense of how hard and lonely her life was: he could look forward to going to university and making his way in the world but she had no such opportunities. Her sex and her class closed almost every available door to her except marriage, and so she was condemned to waiting hand and foot on her invalid mother until the day when she was married off to the highest bidder.

Adam was penniless: he could not rescue Miriam from her prison, but he could at least assure her that he was there for her if she needed him. The parson had told him he was no longer welcome at his house but Adam hadn't promised that he wouldn't try to see Miriam. At their last meeting all they had talked about was Brice and his mad plan; Adam hadn't stopped to think what the implications of thwarting it might be in the future. And now he couldn't bear to part with Miriam without seeing her one more time—he needed to tell her that she was not alone in the world; that he hadn't abandoned her. He needed her to know that.

He thought of writing to her but he suspected that Miriam's mother would intercept the letter, and that she would then redouble her guard over her daughter, making it far less likely that he would be able to find a way to see her. No, his only option was to go to the churchyard and wait. He knew that Miriam went over to the church almost every day and there was an old oak tree that he could stand behind near where his father was buried which would conceal him from the Parsonage and Mrs. Vale's searching eye, but still give him a clear view of the path leading up to the church door. And if the parson saw him, he could say that he was visiting his father's grave. The thought of using his dead father as a false excuse for his presence sat uneasily on Adam's conscience, but his determination to see Miriam drove every other consideration out of his mind.

Early the next day he took up position, hiding his bicycle out of sight in the undergrowth. The hours passed slowly and in the afternoon it started to rain. At first it was no more than a drizzle but then there was a roll of thunder and the heavens opened, sending cascades of water spouting from the gaping mouths of the grotesque gargoyles that thrust their elongated heads out at intervals from the roofline of the church. Adam was soon wet through and was about to give up and go home when he saw Miriam come hurrying up the path. He called to her but his voice was drowned out by the thunder and she went on into the church. He looked up at the top windows of the Parsonage and wondered which one was Mrs. Vale's—and then realized he didn't care if she saw him or not. He ran out from his hiding place and darted this way and that between the gravestones until he came to the porch, pulled open the heavy door, and stood panting for breath, dripping water down on to the old stone floor in front of the mediaeval font at the foot of the nave.

It took a moment for his eyes to adjust to the darkness inside the church. He was used to it being full of light, streaming in through the high leaded windows, but the black thunderclouds had turned day into night and he felt as if he was entering an unfamiliar building for the first time. The only light came from two candles that were burning up on the altar, illuminating its white cloth covering and the simple brass cross standing in the centre, and the noise of the rain beating against the windows gave him an odd sense that he had arrived at a place of sanctuary, fleeing from the terrors of the storm outside.

There was no sign of Miriam and he was about to go and look for her when she came out of a door at the other end of the church. She didn't look in his direction but instead crossed over to the altar carrying a thick bunch of flowers, which she started to arrange in a tall vase. She had taken off her coat and shaken out her hair which cascaded down over her shoulders in a mass of brown curls.

Adam stood watching her, admiring the quick practised way in which her hands moved amongst the blooms, mixing red tulips and white Queen Anne's lace with tall spikes of blue larkspur that she'd picked from the Parsonage garden to create an eye-catching effect, gleaming in the candlelight. He needed to alert her to his presence but it was hard to bring an end to the moment which seemed to contain the sacred and the domestic in equal measure, giving him a sense of peace that he had not felt in days.

He didn't want to alarm her and so called her name softly at first but, just as had happened outside, his voice was drowned out by thunder, so the next time he called louder and she turned round in shock, dropping the rest of her flowers on the ground and stumbling back on the altar steps so that she almost fell.

"I'm sorry," he said, hurrying up the aisle, full of remorse. "I didn't mean to scare you. Please. Let me help you with these." He bent down, picking up the flowers and then held them out to her as if they were a peace offering.

"You! What are you doing here?" she asked, ignoring the flowers, and her voice seemed wild, filled with pent-up emotion.

"I wanted to see you. I wanted . . ." He couldn't tell her. The words died in his mouth. He had rehearsed what he intended to say so many times before he set out, measuring out his offer of friendship without trying to claim her love, and now he was tongue-tied, looking like a fool. "You're so beautiful," he said. "It makes it very hard."

"Yes. Yes, it does," she said bitterly. It was as if his words had echoed the thought in the forefront of her mind and she was responding to it now as if she was the one who had spoken, not Adam. "If I wasn't pretty Brice and my mother would leave me alone, instead of hounding me day and night until I can't stand it any more. Sometimes I think that if I stay still, utterly still, then no one will notice me, but I can't; I can't stay still. Not for long enough . . ." She broke off and Adam saw to his distress that she had started to cry.

"Perhaps it will be better now," he said, trying to comfort her. "Your father said that he is going to protect you. But—I don't know if you know?—he has told me that I am not to see you either."

"I know," said Miriam softly and she reached out and took his hand as if he was the one who needed comfort, not her. It made his heart pound. "I can't lie to them," she whispered. "I wish I could but I can't."

"I know. I don't want you to," he said, taking her other hand in his. "But I came today because I needed to tell you that you can count on me. Not just now but always. Wherever I am; wherever you are; if you call, I will come. Do you understand?"

Miriam nodded, smiling a little through her tears.

"Because I—"

But he didn't finish. Back at the other end of the church there was the sound of a door opening and he darted back instinctively behind a pillar.

"Miriam, are you here?" It was the parson, standing just inside the entrance as he shook out his umbrella and peered up into the gloom.

"Yes, Father. I was just doing the flowers. But I've finished now," she said, drying her eyes and blowing out the candles before she went down the nave towards him.

"I was worried about you. It's a bad storm," he said. "But where's your coat?" he asked when she got closer.

"I didn't think I needed it. The rain started suddenly. I wasn't expecting it," she said. And taking his arm, they went out of the door, leaving Adam alone in the shadows, rejoicing in the lie that she'd told on his behalf.

Part Three

---•--•--

Call to Arms

Oh, we don't want to lose you but we think you ought to go . . .

Paul Rubens, "Your King and Country Want You,"
popular song, 1914

Chapter Fifteen

At the end of the first week in December 1913 Adam took the train to Oxford to sit the scholarship examination for Trinity College. He had chosen Trinity back in the spring on the recommendation of the parson, who had spent four happy years there thirty years earlier and had written a letter of recommendation on his behalf to the College President.

He was in a state of extreme anxiety. He had spent so long preparing for the exam that he had turned it in his mind into a huge, almost insurmountable barrier blocking his way forward. And it made him even more nervous when he saw the intent pale faces of his competitors: bespectacled board school boys who were equally determined to win one of the three scholarships on offer.

It didn't help that it was ferociously cold. There was some damp coal in the scuttle by the fireplace in the garret room to which he had been assigned but even his best efforts could not make them glow, and he spent the night wrapped in a blanket, kept awake by his frozen feet and the periodic clamour of bells, while an eighteenth-century prelate gazed down at him severely from a tall life-size portrait on the opposite wall.

The huge wood-panelled dining hall where he sat the papers was just as cold as his room and his hands were soon as icy as his feet. He tried to write wearing a pair of woollen gloves that he had brought with him from home but the experiment proved unsuccessful as he could not feel the pen, although it helped when he borrowed a pair of scissors from the porters' lodge and cut off the fingers.

The days passed in a blur of proses and unseens and he had little time available to explore the city. He could see that it was beautiful, magically beautiful, but he didn't want to look too hard, because he knew that he might not be coming back, and he had learnt from bitter experience that hope, like love, can hurt when it ends (as it so often does) in disappointment.

And inside its blue iron gates the college was empty and forlorn. Term had finished the week before and only a skeleton staff remained in place for the vacation. The great wide lawns were covered in a thin undisturbed layer of frost and Adam's footsteps echoed in the deserted quadrangles as he passed to and fro from his exams.

And then all at once it was over. He walked to the railway station, treading carefully to avoid the patches of black ice on the pavements, and slept on the train, lulled by the clickety-clack rhythm of the wheels and warmed at last by the steam heating in the compartment and the gas lamps burning inside their frosted glass mantles above his head. And he would have missed his stop if the kind-hearted conductor hadn't shaken him awake and handed him down his bag as the train began to move away from the platform.

Back in familiar surroundings, Oxford seemed like a dream: an unreal experience in an unreal city. Adam could not imagine his future there and, looking up at the thick granite walls and ponderous Victorian architecture of Gratton, he felt as though he was returning to reality. At home he lay on his bed rewriting the papers in his head, thinking of the answers he should have given, until he became utterly convinced that he had failed, and turned his face to the wall in despair.

But he was wrong. On the fifteenth he was awoken by a loud knocking on the door and opened it to find Cartwright standing on the threshold, holding a telegram on a silver salver. Adam tore it open immediately and stood staring at the contents.

"Is it from Oxford?" Cartwright asked.

Adam nodded.

"Please, Master Adam, tell me what it says," asked Cartwright, unable to contain his curiosity any longer and throwing etiquette to the wind—it was no part of a butler's remit to enquire into the family's private correspondence. Indeed, afterwards, reflecting on what had transpired in the privacy of his pantry, he couldn't believe he had asked such a question.

But Adam didn't mind. He looked up at Cartwright and his face broke into a wide smile. "It says they want me," he said. "They've given me the scholarship." And, committing an even more serious breach of etiquette, he put his arms around the butler and hugged him.

Later that morning Sir John instructed Cartwright to bring up a bottle of his finest vintage champagne from the cellar and insisted on the butler joining him in drinking Adam's health.

"You've made me very proud," he said, raising his glass. "And this is just the beginning. You're going to go far, Adam. I can feel it in my bones."

Adam smiled modestly, but at that moment he was sure Sir John was right. He felt a limitless sense of potential surging through his veins; he believed he could achieve anything he put his mind to; as if the whole world was his for the taking. And, remembering the moment a year later, he wondered at his naiveté for if there was one lesson that his experience should have taught him, it was that the world always confounds expectations and makes a mockery of the best laid plans.

He went up to Trinity in April of 1914. And he found the college a very different place to the cold, empty institution that he'd visited in the winter. Now the quadrangles were full of noisy young men dressed in a wild variety of outfits as they hurried to and from lectures or sports grounds or chapel. This last was a daily requirement for which his scout prepared him each morning by throwing aside the curtains and announcing: "It's half past seven, sir," in a voice loud enough to wake the dead while he prepared his bath and laid out his breakfast in front of the fire. Adam liked his scout, who had been born only a few streets away from him in Islington and had once been a regular at the Cricketers' Arms, and the scout in turn seemed to appreciate Adam's direct way of talking and his lack of condescension. At the end of the first week he told Adam that he'd never met anyone "quite like you, sir," and Adam took it as a compliment.

Adam loved his rooms—there was not just one but two of them: the bedroom looking across to the stained-glass windows of the chapel and the sitting room with an oblique view of Trinity's prized asset: the grand park-like gardens at the back of the college. In the evenings he walked slowly down the gravelled paths past the sweeping lawns, the shrubberies and the old grey walls, imagining the famous men who had been there before him. And then coming back through the garden gate in the twilight he would stop for a moment at the entrance to his staircase staring at his name painted white on the jet-black board outside, feeling a sense of pride that made his heart beat fast. He was a scholar; he had earned the right to live and work in this extraordinary place; he was beholden to no man.

But his scholarship was not a heap of gold. It paid his fees and basic board but beyond that it did not provide him with more than a basic living allowance, and Adam's insistence on taking nothing from Sir John meant that he soon began to feel the financial pinch. Trinity was a rich man's college and he quickly learnt that he couldn't reciprocate the feasts offered by the other freshmen or share their expensive lifestyle.

And it wasn't just a lack of money that kept Adam from making friends. The vast majority of his peers had come from the public schools and had no experience of the world outside of the narrow economic and social sphere in which they had grown up—and they didn't seem to have much interest in it either. Instead they passed their time in each other's rooms, drinking incredible quantities of alcohol and talking endlessly about rugby football and cricket. Sport was what mattered to them: they discussed the intricacies of leg-spin bowling and three-quarter running with an almost religious intensity, while hardly ever referring to the subject of their academic work. It was bad form to talk about your studies or to show that you cared about them and Adam soon found that his scholarship made him an object of suspicion.

He found it hard to take these gilded young men seriously. Their interests seemed to him frivolous and their mode of expression self-conscious and priggish. They went from *rollers* (chapel) to *brekker* (breakfast) and on to *leccers* (lectures), and then played their ridiculous sports for the rest of the day until it was time to dress for dinner where they got boisterously drunk, watched with apparent approval by their ageing tutors up on the high table. And sometimes after that, on particularly festive nights, they engaged in battles with the bloods of Balliol College next door—a traditional enmity maintained with enthusiasm by each new generation of undergraduates—or ventured out into the High Street or Cornmarket for town and gown fights that they talked about for days afterwards, exaggerating stories of their exploits with each retelling.

In France two summers later Adam came to think that he had in some way misjudged his Oxford contemporaries when he saw them and their like go over the top again and again, inspiring their men with a nonchalant bravery that left him open-mouthed with admiration. But for now he avoided their company, working hard at his books and walking for miles each day, driven by an insatiable desire to see every corner of the city. It was Oxford itself, not its inhabitants, that bewitched Adam in that spring and early summer of 1914.

He had an unusual understanding for his age that history whether ancient or modern was not the dry study of the dead but rather a voyage of discovery into the lives of men and women who had been alive just as much as he was alive now. This quality of appreciation had shone through in the examination papers he had written the previous winter and had been the deciding factor in earning him his scholarship. At Scarsdale Hall—under the drooping elms or in the portrait gallery—he had sensed the proximity of its past inhabitants as if they were ghosts moving on the other side of a gossamer curtain, and now in Oxford he again felt the touch of the centuries all around him. Across from the gates of Trinity in Broad Street he stood on the exact spot where Bloody Mary had burnt the three Protestant bishops; further down the thirteen Roman heads stared down at him from their high pillars at the back of the Sheldonian before he walked on into Holywell and wandered through narrow echoing stone lanes until he arrived at New College or Magdalen where he sat in the mediaeval cloisters, listening to the music of evensong spilling out from nearby chapels.

And he cycled too. Down towpaths and dusty side roads, following the winding river out into the Oxfordshire countryside or climbing up into the hills to vantage points from where he could look down on the grey towers and gleaming spires of the magical city spread out below. He thought often of Miriam, wishing that he could share his experience with her but knowing it was impossible. He had written to her once soon after his arrival, repeating the commitment he had made to her in the church and sending the letter to Ernest to pass on to her, and had received a response a week later thanking him and telling him what she had told him before—that she could not disobey her parents. And then silence; he kept her letter with him close to his heart and, remembering Ernest's example, tried to stay stoic and live for the day.

He went home in early July well pleased with his first term at Oxford. His disappointment with the people he'd met was more than outweighed by his love for the city and he had earned high praise from his tutors at the college. The newspapers in the railway stations were full of the latest news from Ireland where civil war had begun to seem inevitable, but Adam paid them little mind, preferring to while away the journey with a recently published collection of Father Brown short stories. He wasn't even aware of the developing crisis in the Balkans even though a week had already passed since the fateful assassination of the Archduke Ferdinand in Sarajevo, and it was only as the summer weeks passed that Austria–Hungary's bullying of its small neighbour, the kingdom of Serbia, slowly changed from being no more than a speck on the edge of his mental horizon to becoming a thundercloud that filled the entire sky.

Adam's lack of awareness wasn't unusual. Most people had stopped believing that a European war could actually happen. It had been predicted so many times before as one international crisis followed another and yet each time the great powers seemed to find a way to lurch back from the precipice. So why should this crisis be any different? Even Sir John, who was always the first to expect the worst, didn't seem unduly concerned.

And the unusually hot summer weather made the thought of war seem unreal. Adam was learning to swim at the municipal pool in Gratton and in the park young men in straw hats and laughing girls in light calico dresses were sharing picnics or making fools of themselves in pedal boats on the artificial lake. The fair had come to town and in the evenings the brightly painted pleasure wheel spinning high above the treetops and the tinny waltzes played by the galloping carousel reminded Adam of his childhood in Islington when the world had seemed a magical place, full of limitless possibility.

The heat increased, reaching record temperatures on the Bank Holiday weekend at the beginning of August, but by then people were talking of nothing else but war. Each newspaper edition sold out within minutes with people tearing copies out of each other's hands, but the banner headlines on the placards and the raucous cries of the paper boys told their own story: "The brink of catastrophe: Germany at war with Russia" on the Saturday; "Call to Arms" on the Monday when the order for general mobilization went out; and finally on Tuesday 4 August the dread word "ULTIMATUM" in huge black letters with "Expires at 11 o'clock" written underneath.

All that day Adam had walked about in Gratton, watching incredulously as upstanding citizens pushed and shoved each other, swearing like fishwives as they emptied the shops of staple goods and piled their purchases in cars, taxis and even dustbins. Prices rose by the hour and the poor threw stones at the car windows of the rich, venting their impotent rage that there was no bacon or sugar or butter left to buy.

In the evening the miners from Scarsdale and other local pits came into town in search of news. Adam met Rawdon going into the Picturedrome on Castle Street and shook his hand. They were seeing each other again now that Adam had gone up to Oxford and become his own master. He had told Sir John, who hadn't tried to argue, remarking only that he had weightier things to worry about than Whalen Dawes's son.

The latest news written on slides was flashed up on the screen and at the end the pianist began to play "Rule Britannia," and the audience, waving miniature Union Jacks purchased from street sellers outside, got to their feet and joined in, insisting on singing the chorus again and again until they were exhausted, before finishing up with an impassioned rendition of "God Save the King." And then they spilled out into the street, mixing with the restless crowds that were drifting this way and that through the town, waiting on the German response to the British ultimatum.

"You weren't singing," said Adam with a sideways look at his friend.

"I stood up, didn't I? An' I wasn't 'earin' too much warblin' from thee either," said Rawdon.

"I suppose I find it hard to get passionate about the King," said Adam. "I don't wish him any harm . . ."

"But 'e ain't done nothin' for us, and neither has ol' lady Britannia for that matter," said Rawdon, finishing Adam's sentence for him with a chuckle. "But that don't mean I wouldn't fight for 'er if I got the chance," he added.

"You're too young," said Adam, thinking with relief that he was too. Rawdon and he had birthdays only a week apart and they wouldn't be turning eighteen for another three months.

"Yes. An' I don't know if they'd take me wi' my leg, although I reckon those doctors'll be turnin' a blind eye once it gets a bit 'ot over there."

"But why? Why would you want to fight?" asked Adam.

"Because anythin's better than that bloody mine," said Rawdon. "An' like I told thee afore, I reckon you got to bring me up out of the pit for a reason, an' maybe that's to win this war we're goin' to 'ave."

"Maybe," said Adam, laughing. "But they've got to start it first, haven't they? And personally I'm hoping they don't. Perhaps the Kaiser'll see sense."

"'E won't," said Rawdon grimly. "Because 'e ain't got any. You know that."

And Adam, remembering his impression of the German Emperor at King Edward's funeral four years earlier, had to agree. He'd seemed half mad, capable of anything, even starting a bloodbath into which they would all sooner or later be sucked. But still Adam clung to hope. Unlike Rawdon he had everything to lose and nothing to gain from a war and he understood what it would mean far more than his friend. He'd studied war and he knew what it did to men.

And yet for the first time he sensed its probability. He'd talked about the subject often enough but he realized that that was all it had been—just talk; he'd not been able to bring himself to believe that a European war could actually happen. Not after a century of peace. And now, from one moment to the next, everything had changed and he did believe. It was a visceral sensation: he felt it like a punch to his solar plexus, making him stagger, clinging on to a railing for support.

"Are you all right?" asked Rawdon, turning round.

"Yes. I just tripped," Adam lied. He swallowed hard, forcing back the bile that had risen into his throat.

At eleven o'clock they were standing in the middle of the crowd that was now packed into the main square. Ernest was with them and Luke and the twins and they stood together in a line, staring up through the gaslight at the silhouette of the town hall as they listened to the bell in the cathedral tower behind them tolling out the hour. And then, as the reverberation of the last stroke died away, they waited in silence for the news from London to come through the telephone exchange.

It didn't take long: the door of the town hall swung open and the mayor come out on to the steps. He was a short pot-bellied man with a bald head and glasses and his heavy chain of office looked absurdly out of place around his bulging neck. And they couldn't hear what he was saying because he was too far away. But they didn't need to: everyone around them was suddenly moving, running away in different directions, shouting: "War, war, war."

Somehow they managed to stay together, walking back towards the park and the empty fairground where they had left their bicycles. The streets, usually empty this late at night, were full of people talking all at once, shouting and breaking into raucous songs. Some of them were carrying lanterns and torches and the swaying lights lit up their frenzied faces. There was an excitement in the night air that was almost tangible, building into hysteria, like a smouldering fire looking for an outlet, a chance to explode into flame.

They passed by the closed gates of Adam's school and suddenly they could hear the sound of breaking glass. The crowd had become a mob, spilling out into the road, looking for stones or other projectiles to throw through the windows of a shop a hundred yards up ahead. Even though he couldn't see the frontage from where they were standing Adam knew whose shop it was. Hoffman and Sons Butchers: he'd been in there more times than he could remember to buy sandwiches or meat pies after school. They were delicious—the shop was a gastronomic oasis amid a desert of second-rate cafés and cheap restaurants.

The owner was German: Heinrich Hoffman. He was a large, bulky man with a florid red face who spoke English with a thick guttural accent and insisted that Adam call him Heinrich, sounding out the syllables of his name until Adam pronounced them exactly right. And he loved his shop: the marble counter tops and glazed tile walls, and the big sash windows with gleaming brass handles that had his name and business stencilled in the centre of the glass complete with elaborate scrolls and flourishes; the glass that was now being smashed to smithereens.

"You need to help me! Come on," Adam called to his friends, who followed in his wake as he fought his way through the throng until they emerged out into the open area in front of the shop which the crowd had vacated when the attackers started throwing stones.

"Get out of the fuckin' way," shouted a burly man with a thick beard who seemed to have appointed himself their leader.

"No," said Adam, standing his ground. "You've got no right—"

"No right! They're fuckin' Germans," bellowed the man, advancing on Adam with his fists clenched. But instead of punching Adam, he pushed him aside and threw all his weight against the door of the shop, which caved in under the pressure.

As he picked himself up off the ground, Adam saw that the gaslight had come on inside the shop, lighting up the figure of Hoffman, who was standing at the back over by the cash register. Adam cursed him for a fool—he obviously lived in the flat above the shop and that was where he should have stayed if he'd had any sense. He was wearing a white cotton nightshirt with a ridiculous HH monogram over the breast pocket and seemed rooted to the spot as the burly man rushed towards him. But then at the last moment he dodged out of the way and the big man slipped on the broken glass and fell heavily against the side of one of the counters. But he was up again almost immediately, blocking the butcher's escape route at the back of the shop as he advanced on his prey.

Out in the street, people were shouting and Adam could make out a succession of voices: "Bring 'im out, Len!" "We'll truss him up like one of 'is fuckin' pigs!" "Teach 'im a lesson!" "One 'e won't forget in a hurry!"

"We've got to help him," Adam yelled to his friends as the crowd surged forward towards them.

"Why?" shouted Luke, hanging back.

"Because it ain't right, you bloody idiot," said Rawdon, answering for Adam, who had already gone through the open doorway and was launching himself at the back of Len, who had seized the terrified butcher in a bear hug and was now dragging him through the sawdust and broken glass towards the front of the shop.

Surprised, Len dropped Hoffman and swung round at Adam, who backed away, narrowly avoiding his fist. The big man aimed another punch which would surely have connected had Rawdon not picked up a bright red sausage machine from one of the counters and thrown it at him. Len tottered like a half-felled tree and then collapsed on the floor with an audible thud, landing on the butcher who had already fainted with fright.

Outside the shop Len's friends were screaming with rage, trying to force their way through the doorway but Luke and Ernest and the twins were standing in the breach, doing their best to hold them back. It was a losing battle but just as they gave way the mob's onward surge abruptly ceased. Blowing their whistles, two policemen on horseback had set about clearing the crowd.

Once they had discovered that no one was seriously hurt the police let the boys go on their way. Rawdon had been lucky: the burly man had a sore head but nothing more. And Hoffman soon recovered from his faint, babbling his thanks in unintelligible German and forcing bags of ready-to-eat food on them that he fetched from the cold store at the back of the shop.

"What a great way to start the war—fightin' for the wrong bloody side!" said Rawdon, laughing as they walked away down the street.

They all joined in. "But I do feel sorry for the old blighter," said Ernest. "People won't leave him alone now, you know that?"

"I expect they'll put 'im in one of 'em concentration camps like they 'ad in the Boer War," said Davy. " 'E won't be getting any sausages in there," he added with relish.

"An' then you can go an' gawp at 'im through the barbed wire on Sunday afternoons," said Rawdon. "Is that the idea?"

"No, I ain't goin' to be 'ere. I'm going to find some Germans that I can do more than gawp at, an' the sooner the better."

"What are you talking about?" said Ernest sharply. "You're too young to enlist—you're not even eighteen until next month. And no one can be sent overseas until they're nineteen. You know that."

"It don't matter. Me an' 'Arry, we've already agreed: we'll tell 'em we're nineteen an' if they don't believe us we'll find a recruitin' sergeant who does. They gets 'alf a crown for each man that signs up which is five bob wi' two of us, an' they're not goin' to say no to that in a hurry."

"Have you told your mother?" asked Ernest.

"No. What's the point? All she'll do is 'oller and shout and we're not goin' to change our minds, are we, 'Arry?"

Harry shook his head but without conviction, and Adam sensed that he was frightened but didn't want to admit to it in front of his brother. "Maybe you should tell her; hear what she has to say. She's got a right to know," he said.

"An' so she will—after we've signed on," said Davy irritably. "It's all very well for you, Adam, swannin' about wi' all 'em college boys, but the likes of us, we'd sell our grandmas to get out o' that bloody pit. I can tell thee that."

Adam bowed his head, unable to think of a response. The mine was a terrible place: he knew that from first-hand experience. And the other boys were quiet too, lost in their own thoughts.

They ate the food that the butcher had given them in the park, washing it down with bottles of beer that they had bought at a late-opening shop along the way. It was an unusually warm night and they slept on the grass under the stars, using their rolled-up jackets as makeshift pillows. Adam woke in the hour before dawn. Everything was quiet and he looked over at the peaceful sleeping faces of his friends illuminated by the pale moonlight and wondered what would become of them all. They were so young; they were only just setting out, and yet they could all be dead, blown to bits, before this war was over. "War, war, war," the crowd had shouted in the square, and the word endlessly repeated soon lost its meaning. And now, in the stillness of the night, it seemed just as unreal to Adam, except for the gnawing sensation in his gut that had woken him up and wouldn't go away, and which he had to admit was fear.

Soon after dawn the silence in the park was shattered by the sound of drums and marching feet and the boys sat up, rubbing their eyes as khaki-clad soldiers came marching up the road outside the railings with their packs on their backs and rifles over their shoulders, headed for the railway station. At the head of the column an officer, the colonel perhaps, was riding on a magnificent black stallion and the first rays of the rising sun glinted on his spurs and its polished silver harness. He sat ramrod straight, looking neither to right nor left as if his gaze was already fixed on what lay ahead on the other side of the Channel. Behind him his men were whistling an old Boer War song, "Goodbye, Dolly Gray," and as if from nowhere people started to appear on the pavements, following the soldiers and waving their hats and handkerchiefs in the air. Some of them had flowers in their hands—asters and chrysanthemums and roses— which they rushed forward and pinned on the soldiers' uniforms or stuck incongruously in the barrels of their rifles.

The boys got on their bicycles and rode fast through the park, arriving at the station before the column. The train was already waiting with the doors of the empty carriages thrown open wide to receive the men, and halfway down the platform the pot-bellied mayor, wearing the same costume as the night before, stood on an improvised dais with three of the city aldermen. Behind him the members of the municipal band dressed in identical black suits and bowler hats were lined up, holding their instruments at the ready.

A wind had got up and the Union Jack fluttered above the station roof, while several pages of the early-morning edition of the *Daily Express*, blown out of some onlooker's hand, swirled down the platform, tossing and turning in the breeze. One sheet stuck for a moment to an iron gaslight column and opened out so that the boys could see the black banner headline—"England Expects That Every Man Will Do His Duty"—before the page was seized by another gust of wind and blew away over the ticket hall and out of sight.

And from the same direction they could hear the troops arriving. As they came out on to the platform the band broke out into "Land of Hope and Glory," and the mayor came down from his dais and shook the tall colonel's hand, awkwardly bobbing up and down as he tendered him the town's best wishes for the campaign. And as the soldiers began to board the train, tearful women dashed forward out of the crowd, holding their arms up through the open windows for one last embrace of their husbands or sons. Up ahead the engine began to hiss steam and the stationmaster walked down the platform slamming the doors until he got to the end where he blew long and hard on his whistle and waved his red flag in the air high above his head. The crowd cheered as the train began to pull away, but still some of the women held on to their loved ones until the gathering speed finally forced them to let go, and they gazed down the track with haggard, grief-stricken faces as the last of the carriages rounded a curve and disappeared from view, leaving nothing behind but a cloud of smoke which soon vanished into the bright morning air.

Adam turned away. He felt like an intruder, watching the women's grief. Ernest, Rawdon and Harry were also subdued, but Luke and Davy were like men possessed.

"I ain't seen nothin' like it! Not ever," said Luke breathlessly. "Those soldiers are 'eroes. That's what they are."

"An' you know why," said Davy with equal enthusiasm. "Because they're fightin' for somethin' that really matters; riskin' their lives for their country 'stead of stayin' at 'ome lookin' after number one like the rest of us."

"But their country ain't exactly grateful, is it?" said Rawdon drily. "I bet you more'n 'alf of 'em don't have the vote."

"That's thy dad talkin'," said Luke, sounding annoyed. "You take after 'im, Rawdon—always wantin' to tear everythin' down a strip instead of lookin' for the good in anything."

Rawdon looked furious but said nothing—the attack had hit home.

And Luke hadn't finished: "I tell thee: seein' 'em leavin' like that makes me want to do my bit too," he said fervently. "Hey, Davy, are you an' 'Arry still goin' to join up?"

"O' course we are," said Davy. "The sooner the better."

Harry said nothing, just stuck his hands deep in his pockets and kept his eyes fixed on the ground.

"Well, let's do it now," said Luke. "If the two of you say you're nineteen, I will too."

"You're on. Next stop Berlin," said Davy, laughing excitedly as he got on his bicycle.

Luke and he rode on ahead, racing each other up the hill that led back to the recruiting office in the main square. The others followed more slowly. Harry was still silent. He looked white in the face and was gripping hard on to the handlebars of his bicycle which swayed from side to side. Adam worried that he might fall off and stayed back to ride beside him.

"You don't have to do this, you know," Adam told him. "You've got a choice."

"No, I don't," said Harry miserably.

"Why do you say that?"

"Because 'e's my brother. I can't let 'im go on 'is own."

"Can't you get him to change his mind?"

Harry shook his head. "Davy don't do that," he said and laughed bitterly. "It'll be better when it's done," he added after a moment. "It's the not knowin' that's the worst." And, heeding his thought, he stood up in the saddle of his bicycle and began pedalling harder, trying to catch up with his brother who was now at the top of the hill.

It was still early but a queue had already begun to form out-side the recruiting office, snaking back towards the town hall. Men from every walk of life, in cloth caps and trilbies and bowler hats, thronged the pavement, jostling each other good-naturedly as they waited impatiently for their turn to go in.

"Well, are any of the rest of you comin' or is it just me an' the twins?" asked Luke. He seemed a little less certain now, as if the enormity of the step he was about to take was finally beginning to dawn on him.

"I'll go when the time's right, but I ain't joinin' up on the back of a lie," said Rawdon.

And Ernest nodded in agreement. "I think you're all making a mistake," he told Luke. "I think you should ask your parents before you go rushing into something like this."

"An' we're not goin' to," said Luke peevishly. "So that's an end to that. What about you, Adam?"

"No," said Adam, shaking his head. "Well, at least not yet. And besides, you're going to need someone to watch your bikes for you while you're in there, aren't you?"

Luke smiled at the joke and drew a deep breath. "So, wish me luck," he said and turned on his heel, quickly crossing the road to join the twins at the back of the queue. They looked like boys, not men, Adam thought, and hoped that the doctor who examined them wouldn't believe the lies that the three of them were intending to tell.

The queue moved quickly with new recruits coming down the steps at regular intervals, holding aloft their ration books and travel warrants as though they were newly won medals, but Luke and Davy and Harry emerged empty-handed. Davy was clearly furious, aiming a kick at a lamp post which left him hobbling across the road behind his brother who had a spring in his step for the first time that day. Luke brought up the rear, looking thoughtful as if he was unsure how to react to whatever had happened inside.

"Didn't like the look of thee—was that it?" asked Rawdon, smiling.

"No, it wasn't," said Davy furiously. "The sawbones liked the look of us all right, almost 'uggin' us, 'e was. But then when we were standin' in line to take the oath, who comes in but Atkins's brother—"

"What, our Atkins? Barker from the pit?"

"Yeah. Turns out 'e's one o' the recruitin' sergeants an' o' course 'e recognizes us from when we were kids—"

"An' sent you packin' with your tails between your legs!" said Rawdon, laughing out loud as he finished Davy's sentence for him. "Oh, I'm sorry I wasn't there to see it—makes me almost wish I'd gone in meself. Well, it looks like you're goin' to have to wait a while yet to be 'eroes, don't it?"

"No," said Davy defiantly. "We're not waitin'. We'll go into York at the weekend. An' if that don't work, we'll try somewhere else. Ain't that right, lads?"

"Yeah," said Luke. But his enthusiasm had gone. He seemed deflated by what had occurred, while Harry had already got back on his bicycle and was pedalling away down the street, acting as though he hadn't heard his brother.

But it was no more than a temporary reprieve. When Adam went to see Ernest before he went back to Oxford at the beginning of October, his friend told him that they had enlisted in one of the new Pals battalions that were forming all over the north.

"We went together yesterday because it was Luke's birthday," he said. "All of us except Rawdon, and he says he's going to join up next month when he turns eighteen—if the army'll have him, of course. He seems to think his leg won't matter, although who's he to know? I'm glad we didn't lie about our ages—our parents got us to promise we wouldn't, so none of us can be sent to the front before next summer."

"Is it you who turns nineteen first?" asked Adam. He felt suddenly frightened for his friend, as if a shadow had passed across the sun, darkening the bright afternoon sky.

"Yes," said Ernest ruefully. "But everyone says the war'll be over by then so I should be OK, although it's my mother I worry about more. You've seen her—she's not been the same since my dad died. And she's worried sick now that Tom and I are in the army—he'll see action before me and I don't know how she'll cope if something happens to him."

"Why did you enlist?" asked Adam curiously. "I know you didn't want to."

"I didn't feel I had a choice. Everywhere you go there's old Kitchener pointing his finger at you or some sharp-nosed woman wanting to know why you're not in uniform. And all the going backwards and forwards about what to do was making me ill. Honestly, it's a relief not to have to think about it any more, and I shan't be sorry to see the back of the pit. None of us will. What about you—have you decided what you're going to do?"

"No," said Adam. "It's hard to give up something like university when you've worked so hard to get there. I suppose I don't feel I should have to. And I'm like Rawdon—I don't have to decide yet; I don't turn eighteen until November, so I suppose I'll think about it then."

Chapter Sixteen

Adam's hopes of leaving the war behind when he returned to Oxford proved to be ill founded. The city had been transformed in his absence. Soldiers were everywhere: new recruits dug trenches and drilled in the University Parks, wearing temporary-issue blue serge uniforms that made them look like angry postmen, while those too old to join up formed a Volunteer Training Corps and paraded through the town in suits and ties. There was a chronic shortage of rifles and almost everyone had to make do with broomsticks and lengths of piping to simulate the real thing, but this did nothing to dampen their enthusiasm.

Inside the colleges there was a strange hush. Games and entertainments had been cancelled and most of the undergraduates had left to enlist. In the evenings the windows of their empty unlit rooms loomed eerily above silent quadrangles. And outside in the streets the lights had been dimmed in response to the threat of Zeppelin attacks, which had not yet materialized but were a constant topic of conversation.

The Examination Schools building in the High Street had been turned into a hospital with a huge banner stretched across the façade demanding "QUIET FOR THE WOUNDED." Many of these were Belgian soldiers and when two of them died on the same day thousands of silent onlookers lined the streets to watch their funeral cortège go by. Belgian refugees were billeted all over the town and everywhere there was talk of the terrible crimes that the German army had committed there. Babies had been tossed on the points of bayonets; girls had been raped and mutilated; and priests had been hung upside down inside church bells and used as clappers. Adam didn't know whether to believe these stories, but he understood that the war had now become a crusade, a fight to preserve civilization from blood-thirsty Germans who would mete out the same treatment to British women and children if they weren't stopped on the continent.

There was a moral imperative to fight, to do your bit, and Adam's academic work, which had always given him a sense of pride and purpose, now felt like a hollow sham, a vain bid to escape from what really mattered. It got worse following his eighteenth birthday at the end of November, which he celebrated alone in his room with a bottle of cheap wine that did nothing to chase away his feelings of guilt. Ernest had been right about Kitchener. The War Minister's penetrating blue eyes were everywhere, glaring down from shop windows and noticeboards and the sides of buses, and Adam woke sometimes in the middle of the night in a cold sweat, feeling Kitchener was there in the room with him, pulling at his shoulder, demanding that he enlist. Not next year or next week or tomorrow but now, now, now!

Every day brought news of fresh casualties in Flanders as the Allies fought desperate battles in the sodden fields around Ypres to stop the German advance. Seaton wrote to him—amusing laconic letters that treated the horrors of war in a matter-of-fact way but left Adam in no doubt of the hell that his friend was enduring. Adam didn't want to enlist. He wasn't rosy-eyed about the war like the eager volunteers that were still joining up every day at recruiting offices up and down the country. He knew that there was a strong chance that he would die or be maimed if he went to the front and the thought of being in a trench under shellfire made him feel sick to his stomach. But the alternative—carrying on at Oxford, hurrying through the streets trying to avoid the contemptuous stares of parents whose children were dying at the front—was equally hard to bear.

At the end of term he left Oxford with a heavy heart, wrestling with his conscience as he tried to decide what to do. He'd looked forward to going back to Scarsdale so that he could talk to the parson, whose opinion he still valued, notwithstanding Mr. Vale's role in stopping him seeing Miriam. And so it had come as a heavy blow when he'd opened a letter from his old friend a week before his departure and learnt that he had left Scarsdale to become a military chaplain.

"In the end the decision was easy to make," the parson wrote. "My vows mean nothing if I do not go where I am most needed. And I pray and hope that God will spare me so that I can bring some solace and comfort to those who are crying out for it at this terrible time."

Adam had little time to wonder what the effects of her father's departure would be on Miriam because a further letter from Miriam herself was awaiting him on his return to Scarsdale Hall. He was shocked to receive it: her last letter to him had seemed like a final parting of the ways when she'd told him that she couldn't lie to her parents and communicate with him behind their backs, and his heart beat hard as he slit open the envelope and took out a single sheet of writing paper with "The Parsonage, Scarsdale" printed at the top, and began to read:

9 December, 1914

Dear Adam,

I am sorely pressed and wish for your advice. My father has left us and the trouble that was mine before has begun again.

You have always been my friend and I fear that oftentimes I have not treated you as a friend should. Can you forgive me?

You told me in the church: "Wherever I am; wherever you are; if you call, I will come." Will you come now?

I am going to Scarborough with my mother tomorrow for a week so she can take the waters. We are staying at the Grand Hotel and she always rises late. Every morning I will be in the lobby at half past seven. If you do not come I will understand.

Your friend,
Miriam Vale

Adam read the letter through twice and then pressed it hard against his heart. By not sending the letter to him in Oxford she'd run the risk that he wouldn't receive it in time to come to Scarborough before she left. He knew why: she didn't think her need should interfere with his academic studies. But didn't she know that she mattered more to him than Oxford? She didn't value herself—that was the problem. That was why she let her mother dominate her as she did.

But there was still time: it was Monday now and she wasn't leaving Scarborough until Thursday. It was too late to go today—the last train would already have left from Gratton—but he could go tomorrow, stay overnight and go to meet her in the hotel on Wednesday. He hated to think of her looking in vain for him in the lobby each morning, wondering if he had chosen to ignore her appeal, but there was nothing to be done.

He knew what had happened. Brice had renewed his attentions to Miriam as soon as her father's protection had been removed and her mother was encouraging him just as she had done before. Adam was sorely tempted to confront Brice straightaway and try to make him leave Miriam alone. But he knew he had to wait until he'd seen her first. It was for her to decide what she wanted him to do.

But she had already started to make decisions: she had changed her mind about writing to him behind her parents' backs and she'd changed her mind about seeing him too. He knew why she wanted him to come to Scarborough—there would be no spies like there were in Scarsdale to report their meeting back to her mother. She was intending to disobey and to deceive. He knew how hard that was for her. And she was doing it because she wanted to see him. It was proof that he mattered to her; mattered to her more than he had thought possible.

He knew he was being selfish to think this way. He should not want her to lie. And it grieved him that she was in distress. His first concern was how he could help her. But still he couldn't entirely stifle the surge of excited happiness that kept him awake into the small hours, watching the red coals behind the fireguard glowing in the thick darkness as the cold north wind wailed and whistled through the trees outside and rattled the windows in their frames.

———

He got to Scarborough late the following afternoon and booked into the cheapest guest house he could find. There was a light drizzle in the air and the hazy sun was setting behind him as he walked down the winding cobbled road in the gathering dusk towards the harbour. It was his first visit to the town and he knew he was not seeing it at its best. Many of the shops were closed for the winter and those that had stayed open had a forlorn feel. A few racks of saucy postcards curling at the edges and a display of cut-price buckets and spades were all that was left of the merchandise emporium that spilled out on to the busy pavements during the summer.

But Adam was strangely excited. He could hear the steady roar of the waves and smell the salty tang of the sea long before he saw it. And he was unprepared for the picturesque beauty of the harbour. The fishing boats were in for the night. Protected by the breakwater, they rocked gently against their black wooden moorings—crooked posts and pilings that creaked in the wind. Their weather-beaten owners, still dressed in their oilskins, were congregated in groups, smoking long churchwarden pipes as they repaired their nets and lobster pots. Further along the pier the orange lights of the gas lamps were reflected in the rippling murky water down below and at the end the white flashes from the lighthouse lamp lit up the angry sea beyond.

Over to his left Adam could see the waves crashing against the rocky limestone cliff of the famous headland that jutted out into the sea, dividing the South Bay of Scarborough from its northern counterpart. Columns of surf flew up into the air towards the grey stone walls of the ruined mediaeval castle surrounded by its curtain wall. Shrouded in mist, the keep seemed to Adam grand and defiant, an unbroken link to an ancient past.

Turning away, he walked a little way down Foreshore Road and bought fish and chips from a café and ate them sitting on an iron bench with a panoramic view of the bay. He remembered with a twinge of nostalgia the eel pie shops from his childhood and how the fish had come wrapped in penny newspapers with sensational stories of poisonings and stabbings that made him shudder as he ate. Now, looking out at the windswept beach, he suddenly recalled a particularly lurid account that he hadn't thought of since he'd first read it ten years earlier. It had been about a boy who had found a man drowned on a beach in suspicious circumstances. At the inquest he'd told the court how he'd put his hands in the dead man's pockets to see what he'd got and felt shrimps running over his fingers. "They were eating him, that's what they were doing, eating the flesh off his bones," the boy had said. Adam remembered his exact words.

Islington seemed impossibly far away now, wrapped in the same twilight mist that hung over the sea. The shadowy forms of several beachcombers moved about on the sand, bent almost double as they searched for driftwood and sea coal to put in their straw baskets. Nearer to the road, under a tall sign advertising donkey rides, a group of pale blue bathing machines were drawn up in a line, looking like a row of miniature houses ready to be trundled back down on their oversized wheels to the water's edge when spring returned to Scarborough.

Adam walked on, deliberately turning his face into the wet, whipping wind, enjoying its unfamiliar salty freshness on his cheeks. Up above, the skyline was dominated by the vast tawny brick façade of the Grand Hotel perched on the top of the cliff, surmounted by four bulbous grey towers like minarets around which flocks of shrieking seagulls were wheeling in a last frenzy of activity before they returned to their rooftop roosts for the night.

Miriam was in there somewhere. Perhaps she was looking out of one of the multitude of arched windows that rose in serried rows above his head, wondering if he was coming. He longed to run up the thousand steep steps of the cliff staircase and ask for her at the desk, waiting with beating heart for her to come down, careless of whether her mother knew, ready to take her in his arms. But he forced his mind back under control. He knew he couldn't afford to think this way. He had come to Scarborough as Miriam's friend, not her lover. He had to be what she wanted him to be: nothing more, nothing less.

And he had to wait to see her until morning. In the meantime he needed distraction. Most of the cinemas along the front were closed for the winter but, retracing his steps, he found one that was opening its doors for the evening. Above the entrance an illuminated marquee sign identified it as the Olympia Picture Palace offering "Variety" and "Comedy from across the Atlantic Ocean."

Inside, the Olympia was hardly a palace despite the golden arch adorned with puffy-cheeked cherubs that framed the thick red velvet curtains across the stage, and despite the chandeliers of coloured lights suspended from the domed ceiling that tinted the fug of cigarette smoke hanging in a perpetual pall over the audience. The floor was littered with orange peel and peanut shells and the seats had tears in their upholstery and sagged alarmingly, even though Adam had paid an extra sixpence to sit at the back where "extra comfort" was "guaranteed—and armrests."

The cinema was practically empty when Adam first went in but soon filled up until half the population of Scarborough seemed to be crammed inside. Fuelled with bottles of cheap beer, they shrieked with laughter as the incompetent Keystone Cops waved their ineffectual batons and chased elusive bearded villains across railway tracks and farmyards—and even in one instance a terrified lady's bedroom—to the accompaniment of a spirited ragtime played by an invisible pianist giving it his all in the orchestra pit below the stage; although even he was drowned out when words appeared on the screen and the audience as one shouted out the captioned message as if to ensure that the illiterate among them didn't miss out on any of the entertainment.

Adam relaxed for the first time in weeks. He forgot about the war and about his troubles and anxieties and laughed until his sides hurt as everyone's favourite comedian, Fatty Arbuckle, joined the Keystones and endured an escalating series of ritual humiliations at the hands of a group of street urchins, culminating in imprisonment in his own police station where he gazed out bulgy-eyed and miserable from behind the bars.

And then all at once the film part of the evening's entertainment was over. The curtains fell back across the screen and a breathtakingly beautiful woman walked out on to the stage. She had wide dark eyes matching the mass of black curls that cascaded down over the shoulders of her silver lamé tea gown, which shimmered in the lights like fish scales as she moved. She was small, dwarfed by the big stage and its ornate surround, and yet seemed entirely at ease; she had a look of wholesome innocence that was utterly out of place in the hot, bawdy, cavernous theatre that she had come to entertain.

Some rowdy members of the audience who wanted more comedy booed when they saw her but their catcalls soon ceased when she began to sing. She had a lilting soprano voice that carried effortlessly into the furthest corners of the picture palace and when she sang "I'll be your sweetheart if you'll be mine," every male member of the audience including Adam felt as if she was addressing them personally.

But then came a rude awakening. After a spirited rendition of "Tipperary" in which the entire audience joined in, she sang: "Oh! We don't want to lose you but we think you ought to go," and the curtains behind her swept back to reveal three tables each manned by a recruiting sergeant in full uniform. A gigantic poster of Kitchener beckoning with his forefinger to come up and enlist had been hung over the projection screen.

After the third refrain the gaslights in the theatre were turned up and the beautiful singer came down from off the stage, leaving the audience to carry on with the song accompanied by the invisible pianist. Slowly she began walking up and down the aisles, pointing with an outstretched finger at young men in civilian clothes or, when they were close enough, touching them gently on the shoulder. Behind her two young girls, dressed in matching silver gowns and with garlands of white roses entwined in their hair, followed, carrying baskets of freshly plucked white feathers to hand to any coward who refused the singer's invitation. But there was little need for them: either her targets had a credible excuse which they or their companions shouted out or they got up like sleepwalkers and went to the front where the recruiting sergeants were waiting for them.

Adam was enraged—for himself and for the men in front of him who had also been deceived. It was a cheap confidence trick: they had paid good money for an evening's entertainment, not to be bullied into joining the army. Enlistment was far too serious a business to be undertaken on the spur of the moment because of pressure from your peers or a pretty girl telling you that "you ought to go."

Adam could see her coming. She was close to his aisle. And something in him snapped: he had to get out into the air away from the frenzied crowd who'd now launched themselves into a raucous reprise of "Tipperary." He got up, stepping over the outstretched legs of the people sitting between him and the aisle. They made no effort to get out of the way. Quite the opposite: several of them took hold of his jacket, trying to pull him back. And when he forced his way past them, they shouted out that he was "a coward and a slacker who needed to be given a good hiding."

By the time he reached the aisle, everyone in the theatre seemed to have turned round in their seats to watch him. He had to escape: he was scared they would tear him limb from limb if they got the chance. He threw himself at the exit door, half expecting it to be locked, but instead it opened wide and he half fell out into the foyer, knocking over an old man in grey overalls who had been sweeping up ticket stubs and cigarette ends from the dirty floor. Adam picked him up, handling him as if he was a mannequin in a department store, handed him back his broom with a garbled apology, and left him scratching his head and looking bemused as Adam ran out of the main door, feeling the sudden cold hitting his face as though he was waking from a nightmare.

No one came after him and he hurried back down the road to the harbour, feeling the roar of the invisible sea crashing against the shore on his right as if it was the sound of the war summoning him angrily to its side. And as he turned up the hill towards his guest house he wondered how much longer he could continue to resist its call.

He was up early the next morning, pacing to and fro outside the entrance to the Grand Hotel, willing the time to pass more quickly. It was a still morning with no trace of the wind that had whipped through Scarborough the previous evening, but a thick clammy mist hung over the town, clinging to Adam's clothes and skin.

At half past seven he positioned himself at a spot in the lobby exactly equidistant between the lift and the grand staircase, and felt a surge of disappointment as the minutes passed and there was still no sign of Miriam. He wondered if she had already given up on him—this was after all her last day here, unless she had left already and gone back to Scarsdale. Adam had already seen enough of the town to know that it hadn't got a lot to offer the holidaymaker at this time of year and perhaps Miriam's mother had reached the same conclusion.

The thought that she was no longer in the hotel filled Adam with despair. Now he had to know one way or the other and so he went over to the front desk to enquire, drumming his fingers impatiently on its dark mahogany surface while the clerk on duty, an old man with pince-nez, began to laboriously turn the pages of the enormous guest ledger, using his index finger to check down the names of those who were currently in residence.

Adam was sure now that Miriam had left. He was absorbed in his own misery and jumped when he felt a touch on his shoulder, whirling round to find Miriam standing just a foot away from him.

"I'm sorry," she said, putting her hand on his wrist. "I didn't mean to shock you. What are you doing?"

"I was checking whether you were still here," he said awkwardly. "I thought you might have gone. It's cold . . ."

"And miserable," said Miriam, smiling. "But my mother loves it here in the winter: the worse the weather the happier she gets. She's got some theory that the spa waters are more medicinal at this time of year but I think it's more that she can get sea-view rooms for a third of the price they cost in the summer. And of course she likes it that the hotel's so *grand*"—Miriam pronounced the word with ironic emphasis and a glance over at the desk clerk who was busy putting away his ledger—"and vast. I honestly think the architect who designed this place was some kind of madman. It's all based on time: four towers for the seasons; twelve storeys for the months, fifty-two chimneys for the weeks; three hundred and sixty-five rooms . . . You get the idea?"

Adam nodded. Miriam was unlike herself, talking unnaturally quickly. He could see that she was nervous. And he was nervous too, although with him it had the opposite effect, making him tongue-tied, unable to think of anything to say. He realized he hadn't been prepared for the shock of seeing her again. He had thought of her every day during the eighteen months since their last meeting, trying to keep her image alive in his mind, but inevitably it had become faded and two-dimensional with the passage of time, no substitute for the real loveliness of her appearance. And she had changed too: she had grown from a girl into a woman. Before there had been the promise of beauty, but now that promise had been entirely fulfilled.

"Shall we go out?" she said. "I doubt my mother will come down but I'll feel easier outside." She put her arm through his and he felt just as he had on that day in the church at Scarsdale when Whalen Dawes staged his demonstration and he had felt like a prince in a fairy tale as he escorted her back down the aisle.

Outside in the square the town was slowly coming to life. Shop-keepers were taking down their shutters and a cream-and-brown tram went by with sparks flying off the top of its trolley pole as it made an acute turn across from the hotel. To their left the steam funicular was bringing its first passengers up from the Foreshore, ascending the almost vertical slope of the cliff as if by magic. Going on past its turnstiles, they paid the toll and walked out on to the Cliff Bridge where they stopped, leaning on the pale blue wrought-iron balus-trade to look out at the sweep of the South Bay down below. The fog had cleared a little so that they could make out the dim shapes of the fishing trawlers coming into the harbour where some were already unloading their catch. But the sea itself remained shrouded in mist.

Beyond the bridge, they walked a little way out on to the Espla-nade. This was the richest section of the town: elegant terraces of white stone houses each with their own name engraved in gold on their black front doors—The Laurels; The Firs; Wisteria Lodge. Opposite the houses a line of shallow trenches had been built along the edge of the cliff and barbed wire and sandbags blocked the entrances to the criss-crossing paths that led down to the Spa buildings below. But no one seemed to be taking the line of defences very seriously. A bored-looking Territorial soldier shivered in a makeshift sentry post but otherwise Adam and Miriam had the whole Esplanade to themselves.

"So do you feel better now?" Adam asked, turning to look at Miriam.

"Yes," she said. "Thank you for coming. I didn't know that you would."

"Yes, you did. I promised you that you could count on me. All you had to do was call but you never did until now." He hadn't intended to reproach her but the words spilled out before he could take them back.

"I'm sorry," she said. "I tried to do what was right. But it hurt me too—more than I can say."

He nodded, grateful to her for her admission. He didn't want her to be unhappy but he also longed to feel that he was important to her. It had made his heart beat fast at the hotel when she'd told him that she wanted to go out so that her mother wouldn't see them together because he knew that it was against her nature to lie and that she was doing so because of her need to see him.

"You've changed," he said. "You're stronger than you were."

"No, you're wrong," she said vehemently. "I'm weaker. And recently I've started to feel like I'm not myself any more; that I'm becoming a shadow of me." She spoke slowly as if she was searching for the right words and Adam remembered how Seaton had said something similar when they had been up in the balloon, describing himself as a ghost watching his life from the edge of the stage.

"It's the war," he said. "It's changed everything, made it seem insubstantial. And your father leaving must be hard. He was the one looking out for you."

"But it's more than that," said Miriam. "Yes, he was there and yes, he stopped Brice coming. But he didn't really notice me. He never has. It's like I don't exist. These last few days I've been here, when I walk on the beach I take off my shoes so that I can see my footsteps in the sand because they're me; I made them. They make me think I'm real at least while I'm down there."

"But you are real. To me you're more real than anyone I know," said Adam, taking her hand. Her words and the tone of her voice frightened him and he wanted to reassure her, make her understand how much he cared.

"I know," she said. "That's why it helps me to see you. More than you can imagine."

She looked up into his eyes and he was sure he would have bent down and kissed her if the intensity of the moment had not been broken by the sound of sudden thunder coming from off the sea. But it was different from thunder. Adam could feel the rumble as well as hear it, and immediately afterwards there was a stabbing spurt of crimson flame out beyond the castle headland and the boom was repeated, developing into a continuing roll of reverberating noise and muffled explosions. And out at sea the red gleams mixed with black smoke and the mist cleared for a moment revealing the huge grey iron sides and high masts of a warship steaming round the headland and into the bay.

"Those aren't signals; the bastards are firing at us. Where the hell is our navy?" said a gruff voice behind them. Adam turned round and saw a man on the other side of the road. He was old with a white beard that matched his flannels and a peaked yachtsman's cap, and he had obviously just come out of the house opposite. Now he was looking out past them through a pair of binoculars that he was holding with both hands.

And then all at once a faint sigh came up out of the sea, building quickly to a wild hissing shriek that seemed to be tearing at the fabric of the air around them. They froze, gripping each other's hands as the noise stopped like an intake of breath and then exploded with a terrible crash behind them. They were lucky: the force of the blast threw them forward into a wall of sandbags which cushioned the impact and stopped them falling down the side of the cliff.

For a moment Adam couldn't see anything. All around him was smoke and dust and he could hear shrapnel clattering on the road like a steel rain. Miriam was lying beside him: he could feel her body warm against his but he didn't know if she was alive or dead.

"Please, God," he said, praying for the first time since he'd been a boy in Islington asking for his father to find work.

And as if in response she opened her eyes, garnet-brown and beautiful: it was the most wondrous moment he had ever known. "What happened?" she asked.

"The ships—they're firing at us," he said, but before he could say any more a salvo of further shells came screaming towards them and burst further up the road. There were flashes of red flame and boiling columns of debris spurted up into the sky like huge black geysers. The air was full of a cacophony of sound: shattering glass, the rumble of collapsing masonry and more shrapnel singing on the cobbles. And the cloud of acrid dust and smoke filled their throats and lungs, making it hard to breathe.

"Are we going to die?" Miriam asked. He had moved his body round so that he was half covering her, protecting her as best he could. Her face, like his, was blackened with smoke and there was white plaster dust in her hair.

"No," he said, although he had no reason for thinking that they could or would survive the deadly salvoes that were raking the seafront all around them.

"Because if we do, it's my fault," she said. "I brought you here. Without me—"

"Hush," he said, reaching out with his hand to touch her lips. "There's nowhere I would rather be than here with you. Because . . ." He hesitated, feeling a rush in his ears caused not by another shell but by the intensity of his emotion. "Because I love you," he finished, looking into her bloodshot eyes.

She sighed and a look of profound peace settled over her face. "I love you too," she said. "I always have."

And taking her in his arms, amid the deafening roar of the bombardment, he kissed her.

Chapter Seventeen

There was a pause in the firing and Adam got up and looked back across the road to where the old man had been standing with his binoculars when the attack began. He was gone now and there was a huge hole in the front of his house where the first shell had passed through it. Inside a grand piano covered in white plaster dust hung suspended in mid-air, miraculously still clinging to what was left of the floor of the first storey while a metronome ticked madly to and fro on its lid. Among the rubble strewn across the entrance courtyard Adam could see the brim of the old man's yachting cap wedged between two blocks of masonry but there was no sign of its owner.

"Are you there? Are you all right?" Adam called out, approaching the house, but there was no answer.

"My mother!" said Miriam, getting to her feet behind him. "We have to help her."

Adam stood uncertainly, wondering what to do. He needed to go with Miriam, but the old man might be unconscious or dying, buried under the wreckage, and he was only spared making a decision when people began coming out of the neighbouring houses and Adam was able to tell them what had happened.

Behind him, Miriam had started running back down the road, but her progress was slow because of the temperature of the tarmac, which had started to melt in places where it had been hit with red-hot shrapnel, forcing her to go up on her tiptoes, and Adam was able to catch up with her before she reached the Cliff Bridge. Ahead of them they could see columns of black smoke rising from the Grand but the hotel was still standing, perched precariously on the top of its cliff.

And to their right, out at sea, they could see through tears in the curtain of mist that there wasn't just one ship, but two, and that they seemed to be turning round. They were close to the shore now, near enough for Adam to be able to see the sailors running to and fro like dark blue midgets on the decks. Germans! Adam hated them with a visceral intensity that twisted his gut. Scarborough was defenceless—there were no warships here or batteries of guns making it a legitimate target; only fishing boats and donkey rides and bathing huts. The bombardment was a war crime: a repeat of the barbarism they had inflicted on Belgium back in the summer. Adam had no doubts now about the terrible atrocities he had read about in the newspapers. This was a war about the survival of civilization; it was a war he was going to have to fight.

They were halfway across the bridge when the firing began again. They felt appallingly exposed, standing seventy-five feet above the valley floor below, but they made it safely to the other side and ran into the hotel. There was thick dust in the air but, as far as they could see, no structural damage in the lobby, although it was a different story in the huge dining room which ran the length of the hotel on the seafront side. Several shells had come through the walls, leaving gaping holes, and a speak-your-weight machine was hanging bizarrely out of one of them, requiring only a slight push to send it hurtling down the cliff outside. The glass in the windows had shattered, turning the blue carpet into a mass of tiny twinkling fragments that crunched under their feet like unmelted hailstones when they ventured inside. Smashed porcelain and broken furniture also littered the floor, although a table at the far end remained completely intact with two half-eaten kippers on a Royal Crown Derby plate: evidence of how guests had abandoned their breakfasts literally in mid-bite.

But where had they all gone? Adam and Miriam had seen nobody since they entered the hotel, but now, retracing their steps, they heard a low moaning coming from behind the main desk. Leaning over it, Adam saw the clerk he'd met earlier sitting on the floor, rocking backwards and forwards on his heels. He'd lost his pince-nez and was running his fingers repeatedly through his thinning hair.

"Where is everybody?" Adam asked. But the clerk didn't respond even when Adam shouted at him and it was clear that he had no awareness that they were there.

"They've run away," said Adam, answering his own question. "But maybe your mother's still here," he added, seeing the look of panic on Miriam's face. "What number is her room?"

"Fourteen," said Miriam. "It's on the first floor with a sea view. I'm opposite."

Without one, thought Adam, wondering for a moment what he was doing trying to save a woman who had always borne him nothing but ill will and had made her daughter miserable for years. But he dismissed the thought from his mind. She was Miriam's mother—of course they had to find her. "Wait here," he said. "I'll go and see."

But Miriam wouldn't let him go without her. "Don't leave me!" she said, seizing hold of his hand. "I can bear it, all of it, with you. But not on my own. Please, not on my own."

"I'm sorry," he said. He'd thought he'd be quicker on his own but he realized she was right: anything could happen. And as if to make the point, the familiar whine and screech of an approaching shell filled the air followed by the noise of a gigantic crash as it smashed into one of the floors above them. The hotel seemed to shake on its foundations and for a moment they were both quite sure that the end had come and that it would topple over the cliff, but then it settled back down, waiting for the next onslaught.

"Come on," said Adam. And hand in hand they ran up the grand staircase and turned left, following the windowless corridor as it wound past a series of doors on either side. Those on the right, the seaward side, showed signs of damage and there were cracks in several of the walls. The door of number 14 was closed and didn't open when Adam turned the handle. He knocked hard and thought he could hear someone calling from inside, but the door stayed shut.

"Does she lock it when she's inside?" he asked.

Miriam shook her head. "Not usually. Maybe it's stuck," she said.

"We'll soon see," said Adam. And standing back, he threw all his weight at the frame. The first two times he bounced back but on the third there was an audible cracking of wood and he burst through the door and into the room. And the force of his momentum took him on past the disordered bed and an overturned mahogany vanity table until he came to a juddering halt a few feet away from Miriam's mother, who was sitting in a white dressing gown and bed jacket on the floor in the corner of the room with her arms clasped around her knees in a similar pose to the desk clerk downstairs. Except that she wasn't rocking or moaning, but rather was looking at him out of a pair of shocked but keenly aware grey eyes from under the fringe of her lace nightcap.

"You!" she said. "What are you doing here?"

"We're here to help you," said Adam, holding out his hand. "If you want us to."

"So this is where you've been, Miriam," she said furiously, ignoring Adam, as she caught sight of her daughter framed in the remains of the doorway behind him.

But before Miriam could answer, her mother had put up the palm of her hand face outward as if to instruct her daughter not to respond. And then, extending her arm further, she took hold of Adam's hand and allowed him to lift her to her feet. Slivers of glass and splintered wood from the shattered window fell tinkling to the floor as she rose but her dressing gown was made of thick wool and she seemed to have escaped injury. And the damage in the room seemed to be superficial—the effect of nearby blast but not any direct hit.

"What's happening?" she asked, looking Adam in the eye, and he couldn't help but admire the way she had so quickly regained her self-control.

"German battleships are shelling the town. And the hotel too," he said as they heard the cry of another shell coming towards them. He could see it through the shattered window—a small black projectile spinning through the mist, and he pulled Miriam's mother down again as it exploded somewhere high above them.

"We have to go," he said.

"Where?"

"Away, out of the town. We can't wait here like sitting ducks."

Mrs. Vale nodded. She went to the wardrobe and got her coat and then went past her daughter in the broken doorway.

"I didn't lock it. It was stuck after the first explosion so I couldn't get out," she said, looking back at Adam, and he realized that she was trying to tell him that she wasn't a fool cowering in a corner and that she wouldn't slow them down as they tried to escape.

There was no sign of any let-up in the bombardment as they came out of the hotel. A shell had exploded in the road and the steel tramlines were twisted up into the air, looking as though they had been pulled apart by some crazed giant. They had to go slowly, clambering over fallen pieces of masonry, but Miriam's mother made surprisingly good progress for an invalid, so much so that Adam began to wonder whether her seclusion was a matter of choice rather than necessity.

"Don't dawdle!" she snapped at her daughter when Miriam started to fall behind. And she showed no sympathy, only impatience, when Miriam tripped and fell and Adam went back to help her up.

Adam may not have liked the way Mrs. Vale treated her daughter but he understood her anxiety. They needed to move a great deal more quickly if they were going to get away from the murderous shells that were still whistling overhead. Walking was going to take too long; they needed some kind of transport. And just then, as if in answer to a prayer, Adam caught sight of a horse and cart on the opposite side of the street. There was no sign of the driver and the horse was clearly terrified. Its ears were pinned back against its sweating head and it was whinnying loudly and stamping its hooves, pulling at the rope that was tethering it to a street-side lamp post and so preventing it from bolting. The two-wheeled uncovered cart behind the horse was about a quarter filled with dark grey Hessian sacks of coal as if the delivery man had abandoned his morning round near its end.

Adam had no experience of horses and approached the animal fearfully, uncertain how to bring it under control, until Miriam came up and took hold of its bridle, calling to the horse in a calm and confident voice. Almost immediately it stopped rearing up and stood still but quivering as she began stroking its withers. Adam moved forward again but she motioned to him to stand still as she waited for the horse to lower its head and then began to slowly rub between its eyes, talking to it all the time in a continuous soothing monotone. Slowly, the horse's head drooped and it became docile, unaffected by the chaos and commotion all around.

"That's unbelievable. How did you do it?" Adam asked, amazed.

"I grew up with horses. It's mostly about not showing them you're frightened even if you are," she said with a shy smile, evidently pleased by Adam's compliment. And he noticed too how she gave a sidelong look at her mother, as if satisfied that she had been able to show her that she wasn't as useless as Mrs. Vale had been trying to make her out to be since they left the hotel.

But then at the last moment she was hesitant about taking the cart: "Isn't this stealing?" she asked.

Immediately her mother came down hard on her again. "Don't be so ridiculous, Miriam!" she snapped. "Can't you see we need to get out of here? Now, before it's too late."

"Your mother's right," said Adam. "It may be stealing but we've got no choice." He helped Miriam's mother up into the back of the cart where, with his assistance, she wedged herself between two coal sacks, but then, when Miriam was about to climb in too, Adam held her arm and suggested that she take the reins. "I don't know anything about animals and I think you're going to handle that beast a whole lot better than I am," he said with a nervous sideways look at the horse as he got up on the narrow box seat beside her.

They set off up the road, weaving a path between the streams of people that were also trying to flee the town. Many of them, like Miriam's mother, were still in their nightclothes and were wearing out flimsy slippers on the hard pavements. Their faces were different shades of white, grey and black from the effects of plaster dust, soot and smoke. Most were terrified, pushing each other out of the way as they rushed forward, but a group of schoolchildren were marching along the centre of the road in an orderly procession led by their teacher, and several souvenir-hunting boys were hanging back, searching for smouldering lumps of shrapnel outside a house that had been hit minutes before. The red brick dust spattering the white fronts of the shops opposite looked to Adam just like blood.

Everyone in the crowd was talking about the trains. They were leaving all the time, people said; if you could just scramble aboard one of them you could be safe. And the station was not that far away. They were going in the right direction and they could see the leaded dome of its tower up ahead with the big black hands on the clock face approaching half past eight. The bombardment had been going on for nearly half an hour but the infernal roar of the incoming shells continued unabated. And with each minute that passed the street was becoming more clogged with refugees so that they had now slowed almost to a crawl.

"We need to find another way. We'll be here forever otherwise," Adam said to Miriam, shouting into her ear to make himself heard above the uproar. "Let's go up there," he directed her, pointing to a narrow street on their right. It climbed steeply up past brick terraces on either side and at the top Adam could see traffic actually moving on a thoroughfare running parallel to the one they were on.

Miriam turned the horse's head and succeeded in cutting through the crowd—no easy feat with the horse beginning to panic again and people shouting abuse as they were forced to get out of the way. But the horse became quieter once they'd got into the side street and Miriam leant forward, patting the animal's back and soothing it with words of encouragement.

The horse's shoes rang out on the cobbles and up ahead a woman in a flowered headscarf moved to the side to let them pass. But before they reached her a high-pitched scream broke out overhead and there was a flash of blinding light as a shell exploded at the top of the road with an ear-splitting detonation. The woman in the scarf was blown back towards them by the blast like a rag doll and the horse rose up on its hind legs and then sank down on its knees. Miriam and Adam were thrown out into the road, Adam's body taking most of the impact with Miriam landing half on top of him. But her mother, an outlandish figure in her thick black coat and white nightcap, remained tightly wedged between the heavy coal sacks in the back of the cart. None of them were injured; even the woman in the headscarf had survived the blast and was picking herself up off the ground, but their horse had not been so lucky. Its broken right front leg twisted away from its body at an obscene angle while its entrails spilled out on to the ground from where a lone piece of shrapnel had ripped open its belly. It was screaming over and over again—a wrenching inhuman cry that Adam felt like a spike drilling slowly straight into the centre of his head.

He needed the din to stop; he prayed for it to stop. And then all at once it did. All the noise stopped—not just the horse's shrieking but the shells too. And there was a moment of profound silence—a silence such as Adam had never heard before, as if it was a noise itself pressing down on his eardrums until he felt they would burst. The bombardment was over.

But the horse wasn't dead. Its sides were still heaving and its huge brown eyes gazed up into the misty sky, glazed with pain. Behind them, on the main road, they could hear people shouting: "They're coming, they're burning the town."

"We have to do something. He could take hours to die. We have to put him out of his misery," said Miriam, wringing her hands as she looked down at the horse. She had released it from the shafts, allowing it to subside to the ground, but she was at a loss about what to do next.

Adam had no idea either. He remembered Rawdon in the mine raising the big jagged stone above his shoulders and bringing it down on the pony's head. Over and over again, battering it to pulp. But there was no stone here; nothing he could see to use; until an old man came out of the house opposite carrying an antique-looking rifle over his shoulder. He was wearing a red army tunic with a row of medals above the breast pocket and he looked old enough to be a veteran of the Crimean War. It was clearly his intention to take on the invaders single-handed if need be.

"Is it loaded?" Adam asked, going straight up to the old soldier before he could leave his doorstep.

"What?" asked the old man, taken aback.

"I said: Is it loaded?" said Adam. "I need it. For the horse," he explained, pointing back behind him.

The old soldier grimaced, taking in the horse's injuries, and then took the rifle off his shoulder and handed it over. "There's a bullet in the breech," he said, looking keenly at Adam. "But mind you hold it steady; it's got a kick on it."

Adam stood looking down into the horse's eyes. It was a noble creature, and it seemed to him a crime against the natural order that it should have gone from delivering coal through the sleepy streets of Scarborough on a misty Wednesday morning to being blown apart by a German shell.

He could feel the animal's agony and he sensed rightly or wrongly that it understood what the rifle meant as Adam aimed it at its head. Out of the muzzle would come the end of everything it had ever known or would know, but also release from unbearable pain, the insensibility of extinction. But only if Adam could get it right. He had never fired a gun before, let alone a rifle, and he was terrified that he wouldn't be able to "hold it steady," but would instead succeed only in inflicting some new appalling wound on the animal which would intensify its torment, if that was possible, and prolong its agony.

At the last moment, as if sensing his doubt, the old soldier came to his rescue. "Brace the stock against your shoulder," he said. "Squeeze the trigger slowly, and then keep squeezing when it fires. Don't close your eyes and don't let go, you hear me?"

Adam didn't respond. He just did as he'd been told except that he couldn't stop himself staggering backwards as the rifle recoiled violently in his hands. And when he looked down he couldn't see the horse's eyes any more but just a mass of shattered bone and blood. He'd done what he set out to do: he'd killed for the first time and he wanted badly to be sick.

"Well done," said the old soldier shortly, taking back the rifle.

"Do you know what's happening down there?" he asked, pointing towards the sea.

Adam shook his head.

"Well, I hope the Huns have landed. There's nothing I'd like more than to give those bastards some of their own medicine," said the old soldier. He raised his hand in a gesture of farewell and turned away, marching out into the main road, and so missed the spectacle of Adam vomiting his breakfast over the kerb.

"Are you finished?" Still on his knees, Adam turned round and found himself looking up at Miriam's mother, who had got out of the cart and was now standing in the middle of the road with her arms akimbo, looking visibly impatient. He nodded, getting gingerly to his feet. "Good," she said. "Because I have no intention of letting these Germans get their hands on me or on Miriam if I can help it."

The main street was a little less crowded than before and they were able to push on towards the station. Adam glanced across at Mrs. Vale, who was once again leaving her daughter behind. Nothing that had happened that morning changed the fact that her treatment of her daughter had been cold, calculating and cruel, and he could now add mendacity to the list of her vices as no housebound invalid could possibly have set the pace she had since they left the hotel. But Adam also couldn't help but admire her courage. And there was something down to earth about her character that was also unexpected—a cynicism, perhaps, but also a willingness to talk frankly and directly that he found refreshing.

The railway station, when they reached it, was a scene of utter chaos. There were two trains waiting but there was no chance of boarding them as their carriages were filled to overflowing, with some would-be escapers being pressed back out of the windows by the crush inside the compartments. A unit of Territorial soldiers was trying to keep order on the platforms but their efforts were mostly in vain until the mayor arrived in a Ford motor car and announced from the top of a table in the waiting room that the German ships had left and that no German soldiers had landed.

The station slowly began to clear as the townspeople returned to their homes, and soon Adam was able to find a place for Miriam and her mother to sit and drink the hot tea provided by St. John's Ambulance volunteers. He took the chair beside Miriam across from her mother and held her hand under the table as he began to speak.

"There are some things we have to tell you," he said, his nervousness making him speak in a rush. "First and foremost Miriam and I—well, we love each other and we want to be together."

"You're too young," said Mrs. Vale, keeping her eyes fixed on Adam. "And you have no money."

"We know that," said Adam. "And we understand we'll have to wait, but while we do, we want you to respect our wishes."

"You said there were 'things,'" said Mrs. Vale ignoring Adam's implied question. "What else did you want to tell me?"

"I'm going to join the army. I can't not—not after today."

Beside Adam, Miriam gasped, gripping hard on to his hand under the table, and he regretted that he hadn't told her first before launching into this conversation with her mother, but he'd been desperate to have things out in the open before they left Scarborough. Back in Scarsdale he didn't think he'd have the chance to talk to Miriam's mother in the same way as he could now when the extraordinary events of the morning had temporarily blown away the normal social barriers between them.

"I understand. Your decision does you credit," said Mrs. Vale, nodding her head. "What will happen about Oxford?"

"It'll have to wait. Like Miriam and me. But in the meantime, as I said, we're asking you to respect our wishes. Will you do that?"

Mrs. Vale glanced over at Miriam, who was silently crying. A look of irritation crossed her face but she was left in no doubt about her daughter's feelings when Miriam lifted her hand and Adam's and placed them on the table still interlocked.

Mrs. Vale turned her attention back to Adam. "There will be no announcement," she said. "Not until you come back."

"You're thinking that maybe I won't," said Adam with a cold smile. He sensed how calculating she was, like a card player with a mediocre hand who still retained an ace that she thought might change the game.

"I'm saying that there needs to be no announcement. This will stay between the three of us," she said, keeping her eyes fixed on Adam.

"And Miriam's father," said Adam.

"Very well."

"And you will respect our wishes?"

Mrs. Vale nodded, and Adam sighed, picking up his cup of tea and breaking the spell. He felt exhausted suddenly, overwhelmed by all that he had gone through in such a short space of time. He closed his eyes, remembering the old man's yachting cap in the rubble, Miriam in his arms, the shells shrieking overhead, and the agonized, bewildered brown eyes of the dying horse.

He would have to try to trace the owner, he realized. And perhaps there would be compensation to pay; compensation he could not afford. And he would have to tell the university about his decision to enlist. What would they say? And what would happen to him when he went to fight? Would he come back? Mrs. Vale certainly didn't think so. The endless unanswered questions whirled around inside his head, making it ache, and he held on to Miriam's hand like a drowning man hanging on to a lifeline.

Adam waited until after Christmas and then on the last day of the year he went to Gratton with Rawdon where they both enlisted as private soldiers in the same infantry battalion as Ernest, Luke and the twins. Rawdon said nothing about the leg injury he'd suffered in the mine five years before and the army doctor didn't appear to notice it when he examined him—or if he did notice it, he chose to say nothing. The army wanted recruits and within minutes the sergeant had administered them their oaths, issued each of them with a travel warrant, a brown-covered pay book and a shilling, and told them that they couldn't be sent to France until they were nineteen.

"Eleven months!" he said brightly. "With any luck the war'll be over by then and you'll never get to see the trenches."

"No, it won't and yes, we will," said Rawdon, shaking his head as they came out on to the steps of the recruiting office and set their faces against the rain. "Luck ain't a word we knows the meanin' of, you an' I."

Adam laughed grimly in agreement and together they crossed the High Street and took shelter in the Cross Keys public house where they spent their King's shillings on enough liquor to make them forget their troubles at least for an hour or two.

Chapter Eighteen

November 1915

Brice sat in what had once been his favourite armchair in the drawing room at Scarsdale Hall, the one that commanded a view of the
terrace outside and the reception hall on his left. In bygone days
he'd liked to watch the servants, his servants, passing this way and
that, knowing he could summon them at any time with an idle tug
at the bell pull beside the chair to replenish his drink, re-iron the
newspaper or add coal to the fire. Back then he'd enjoyed the opulence of the room: the golden ormolu clock standing on the marble side table between the windows ticking out unchanging time;
the cut-glass chandelier overhead; the vast high-backed blue-velvet
Knole sofa with its plumped-up cushions opposite the Gainsborough landscape hanging over the mantelpiece. But now there was
no Gainsborough—it had been sold to service interest on his father's
debts—and there was dust on the furniture and in the air and no fire
in the fireplace before dusk: a money-saving decree of his father's that
meant Brice had to practically live in his overcoat now that autumn
was fading into winter.

And there were no servants left to minister to Brice's wants. The
Hall was being run by a skeleton staff. All the young, able-bodied
men other than Charles had left to join the army and most of the
maids had become munitionettes earning far more money making
shells than Sir John could afford to pay them, although he claimed
he was happy to see them go, and had promised them their jobs back

when the war was over. Helping the war effort and saving money had become Sir John's twin obsessions.

But it wasn't entirely one-way traffic. At the end of the summer Sarah the housemaid had come back from the Gratton munitions factory to reclaim her job less than three months after she'd left, having undergone a hideous change in the interim. She'd reacted badly to the fumes from the TNT used for the explosives, and developed jaundice. She'd recovered after three weeks in hospital but the illness had removed nearly half her hair and stained her hands and face a sickly yellow-brown. She looked nothing like the pretty girl with the dimpled chin who had irritated Brice by ignoring his attempts to flirt with her, and he had expected that she would be set to work somewhere out of sight like the scullery or the kitchen. But instead Sir John insisted on having her wait at table so that they could all be constantly reminded of her sacrifice and the example it set for them all.

The quality of the food had steadily deteriorated since the start of the war fifteen months earlier with Mrs. Flowerdew the cook taking to heart the government's urging to turn her kitchen into a section of the front line, but even when the dinner was edible, Brice found it almost impossible to swallow dishes that were served to him by "the canary" as he had taken to calling Sarah when he was talking about her with Charles, who also seemed to dislike the girl. He imagined his mother thought the same as she had switched to eating most of her meals in her room with her pug. It was the warmest place in the house as she was adamant in her refusal to comply with the ban on daytime fires, and Brice would have liked to join her there, but didn't want to pay the price of provoking one of his father's frequent rages. And so he had to sit in the cold and listen to his father conducting a monologue about the war at the other end of the table, repeating the latest claptrap news stories about heroic deeds at the front which Brice knew perfectly well were intended to highlight his own unheroic refusal to volunteer; while he kept his eyes averted from Sarah and did his best to get through Mrs. Flowerdew's latest unsavoury concoction. God knows what Cartwright made of it all, standing ramrod straight in the corner while everything went to rack and ruin all around him.

The war was everywhere—Brice couldn't get away from it. It wasn't business as usual; it was dreariness and misery wherever he went. Fashionable dress was unpatriotic; instead women wore mourning black or the utilitarian grey uniforms of the munitionettes. The golf courses and the tennis courts had been turned over to allotments and paint was peeling off the fronts of the houses. Almost all of them seemed to have notices in their windows: "A man from this house is serving in the armed forces." Or sometimes now: ". . . has died in the service of his country."

Brice sighed. He hated the war: it had come out of nowhere and drained everything of colour; it had taken all the zest out of life. The only good to be said for it was that it had removed Adam and Seaton from his life. Seaton was in France and Adam would soon be there too, and perhaps the next big battle would put an end to them both. If so, Brice would mourn neither of them. Seaton had always treated him with a supercilious condescension designed to make him feel worthless and Adam had systematically usurped his place in his home and with the girl that he loved. Brice was sure that Miriam would have learnt to love him too, given time, if Adam hadn't stolen her away from him. How could he forget those days when he had had to follow them around the gardens, holding her parasol or sketch book like some forgotten servant, while they bent closer and closer to each other, laughing at some shared joke from which he was excluded?

But everything might still change. The war had also helped his cause by removing the parson from Scarsdale. And in his absence Miriam's mother had got up from her sick bed and was now entertaining visitors at the Parsonage, although she was still not going outside its doors. Quietly, early in the spring, she had sent word that the ban on Brice's visits was at an end and since then he had started to regularly take tea with Mrs. Vale on Sunday afternoons, relishing the fact that this had been when Adam used to go there, showing off his book learning in front of Mr. Vale. Sometimes Brice saw Miriam and sometimes he did not, but he no longer tried to force his company upon her.

"We must respect their wishes," Mrs. Vale had told him before adding enigmatically: "As long as they are their wishes . . .

"Be patient, Brice," she advised him. "We live in changing times, you and I. Anything can happen." He heeded her advice and like conspirators they watched and waited and kept their powder dry.

Brice stretched in his chair, putting his unread novel aside. His joints were stiff and he needed a change of scenery. He would have liked to drive over to the Parsonage—there was always a blazing fire there and Mrs. Vale made him feel better about himself, and there was also the chance of seeing Miriam. But he had been there only two days previously and he knew that Mrs. Vale didn't like unexpected visitors.

He got up and looked out of the window. It was drawing towards evening and a steady rain was falling from the grey, overcast sky, beating a slow, incessant tattoo on the stone terrace and dimpling the dark surface of the lake. Over to the right, out from under the drooping elm trees, a car was approaching up the drive and, as Brice watched, it turned into the entrance courtyard and a man in a wide-brimmed hat, wrapped up in a thick overcoat, got out and walked up to the front door, carrying a briefcase. The light was bad and Brice didn't know who the man was until Charles had let him in and he recognized his voice as belonging to Hardcastle, the mine manager.

He was a frequent visitor. Sir John had never liked visiting the mine and the miners' march on the Hall on the night of the fire had made him even more anxious to avoid face-to-face contact with them, preferring instead to conduct all his business through Hardcastle. The manager's visit did not concern Brice and so, after nodding a perfunctory greeting through the door, he went back to his book, taking no further notice of Hardcastle as he paced up and down in the hall, waiting while Charles went to inform Sir John of his arrival.

Several minutes passed and Brice turned round in his chair, conscious of a sensation that he was being watched. He was right. Hardcastle had stopped walking and was staring at him across the hall in a way that he found quite offensive.

"Can I help you, Mr. Hardcastle?" he asked.

"I certainly hope you can," said Sir John, answering for his manager as he arrived at the bottom of the stairs just in time to hear his son's question. "I think the drawing room will work as well as anywhere else for our purposes, don't you, Hardcastle?" he went on, ushering his guest through the door without waiting for an answer.

"What's happening, Father?" asked Brice nervously. He had got up from his chair and had withdrawn to the far side of the room, putting two occasional tables and another armchair between himself and his father and Hardcastle. He had a strong sense that he had been ambushed, although he had no idea of what was coming.

"I'll tell you what's happening, young man," said Sir John, glaring at his son. "What's happening is that I for one have had enough of you lounging around this house like some damn roué, shirking your duty to your king and country. And I'm pleased to say that His Majesty's Director General of Recruiting agrees with me and has sent Mr. Hardcastle here to do something about it. He's got some things to say to you that you have a legal obligation to hear so it's no use trying to run away."

"I'm not running anywhere," said Brice defiantly. But behind his show of bravado, Brice was terrified. He felt like a cornered animal. He didn't know if there had been a policeman or a soldier with Hardcastle in the car when it drove up, ready now to come in and haul him off to France once Hardcastle had said his piece.

One thing he was sure of was that his father was lying: it wasn't the government that had told Hardcastle to come here; it was his father who had sent for him. Brice had always disliked his father but now his hatred for him reached a new level of intensity. If his father liked the war so much, then he should be the one shipped out to the trenches to be blown to pieces. Brice would have loved to see how the old man coped with that—and from a ringside seat.

"Like your father has said, I'm here in an official capacity. And I must begin by giving you this," said Hardcastle, handing Brice a letter that had Lord Derby's printed signature at the bottom. Brice read it through quickly but he was too panicked to be able to understand much of what it said.

"And now, Brice Scarsdale, I must ask you whether you will attest to join the forces. Our country is fighting for its very existence and we need every man to stand up and be counted." Hardcastle stood up straight and spoke in a nasal, rather pompous voice that Brice guessed he'd rehearsed several times in front of a mirror, but that didn't make his speech any less intimidating, and Brice's throat was so dry that he found he couldn't utter a sound when he tried to answer.

"Will you attest?" asked Hardcastle, repeating his question.

"No, he won't," said Lady Scarsdale from the doorway. Charles was standing behind her and Brice realized gratefully that the footman must have gone to fetch his mother as soon as he understood what was happening in the drawing room. Sir John had obviously reached the same conclusion and looked enraged at his wife's intervention.

But Hardcastle was unfazed. "Brice must answer for himself," he said stolidly. "It's the law, Lady Scarsdale."

"Very well," she said, looking hard at her son. "Give Mr. Hardcastle your answer, Brice, and then he can be on his way."

Brice looked at his mother and drew strength from her protective gaze. He heard the clock ticking behind him and willed himself to stand firm. "No," he said. "I will not attest. I'm a free man and I want no part of this horrible war."

"Horrible war? Damn you, boy!" shouted Sir John, advancing on his son. "You're nothing but a lily-livered coward, a good-for-nothing runt—"

"Be quiet, John," said Lady Scarsdale in a commanding voice. "I will not have you talk to our son like this and certainly not in public. Mr. Hardcastle, is your business here done? Because if it is, I think it best that you should now leave."

"No, Hardcastle's business is not done," said Sir John, turning furiously on his wife. "Charles, come in here," he called out to the footman whom he could see was still behind his wife in the hall.

"Now listen, Charles," he said once the footman was standing in front of him. "You've been out there listening and you heard what Mr. Hardcastle had to say: this country needs men, fighting men. Men just like you. And I tell you this: a man from this house is going to join the army today even if it isn't my good-for-nothing son so I am giving you a choice. Go with Mr. Hardcastle to the recruiting office and when you return from the war you can have your job back even if you're wounded. But if you don't go, I will dismiss you now without a character. I will not have any cowards working for me."

"Stop this, John," said Lady Scarsdale. "This is ridiculous. We need Charles. You know that."

The footman looked from his master to his mistress and back again, trying to make up his mind what to do. He knew the balance of power in the house as well as anyone. However much she might want to, Lady Scarsdale wouldn't be able to keep him on if Sir John was determined to dismiss him, and he wouldn't be able to find another job if he was denied a reference. Charles was not a coward like Brice but he had no wish to die in a trench for a country that wouldn't even give him the vote. And he hated Sir John for forcing him into the army like some slave to be disposed of as Sir John thought fit. If this was how he was to be repaid for years of exemplary service, Charles knew he would never forgive Sir John for the injustice, but for now he was too well trained to let his anger show.

"Will I be able to come back for my belongings, sir?" he asked Hardcastle.

And when Hardcastle nodded, he turned and went out into the hall, waiting for the mine manager to follow.

Immediately the front door closed, a furious argument broke out between Sir John and his wife.

"Would you mind telling me how you propose to run this house without Charles?" she asked. "Cartwright's too old to do any heavy lifting so are you planning to haul the coal up and down the stairs yourself?"

"We'll find a way," said Sir John defiantly. "You heard Hardcastle— our country is fighting for its very existence and the army needs able-bodied men a great deal more than we do."

"Fiddlesticks!" said Lady Scarsdale with derision.

"I beg your pardon."

"You heard me. This country isn't fighting for its existence. That's just a lie being peddled by the politicians to justify the mess they've made of everything. The truth, as you very well know, is that we didn't need to get involved in this war and we still don't. The Germans had no quarrel with us and our young men shouldn't be dying in droves because of some ridiculous old treaty with Belgium. The Germans were quite right to call it a scrap of paper because that's exactly what it was."

"You don't know what you are talking about," said Sir John loftily. "We were honour bound—"

"*Honour!*" Lady Scarsdale repeated the word with contempt. "Where's the honour in sending your sons to their deaths? Isn't it enough that Seaton's out there risking his life every day without you wanting to send Brice too? I didn't give you sons so you could throw their lives away for the sake of your vanity."

"It's not vanity; it's our duty. Brice is shirking his duty. Not like Seaton or Adam. And he should be ashamed of himself—"

"Don't you dare bring Adam into it! He's not your son; Brice is. And it's you who should be ashamed, trying to get him killed. And don't pretend that that isn't the likely result. The war's not some barnyard scrap like it says in those stupid newspapers and magazines you read. The casualty lists don't lie—it's a sausage machine. That's what it is."

Sir John opened his mouth to respond but couldn't think of anything sufficiently cutting to say and so closed it again. He hadn't anticipated the level of rage that Hardcastle's visit and the forced enlistment of Charles would provoke in his wife. Carried away by his own anger, he had forgotten that Charles was her favourite among the servants.

Lady Scarsdale looked at her husband and shook her head in weary disdain. "Do you know I can't fathom you any more, John? This stupid war of yours that you're so obsessed with is well on the way to ruining this estate that you pretend to care about so much. Look what's happened already—your taxes have doubled and your mine profits have halved because at least a third of your labour force has gone off to join the army, and yet you act as if the war's the best thing that ever happened. Like that idiotic poet that you like so much—what's his name?"

"Rupert Brooke," said Brice. He was enjoying his mother's tirade and its effect on his father and he hoped she wouldn't stop. The tongue-lashing made up a little for what his father had put him through and what he had done to Charles.

"Thank you," said Lady Scarsdale, carrying straight on. "I've read his poem—the one they printed in the paper. Making out like the war's some kind of swimming pool that's going to purge us of our sins. What nonsense! And now he's dead too, of course. It's a horrible, wasteful, evil war—that's what it is, and I won't have you push Brice into it. Do you hear me? I won't."

She looked her husband in the eye and he stared back at her. He wasn't going to admit it but he'd been taken aback by her attack and even more by her articulacy. But still he knew he was right and he was damned if he was going to let Brice ride his mother's coat-tails and evade his patriotic duty, although finding a new way to achieve his purpose would have to wait for another day.

Lady Scarsdale gave her husband a last withering look and then turned to her son. "Come, Brice," she told him. "We're finished here."

In the weeks that followed Brice came to think of Hardcastle's visit as a fork in the road. Before, he had resented the war but he hadn't seen it as a threat to his personal safety. Now he could think of nothing else. And while he was grateful to his mother for standing up for him against his father, he couldn't help but remember all that she had said about the practical certainty of death if he did end up in the trenches. His father and Hardcastle and the government were trying to kill him. It was as simple as that: they were the hunters and he was the prey and all the time he felt their nets closing around his heels.

What made it worse was seeing his name in the local newspaper near the bottom of a list of eligible men who had refused to attest, all under a named and shamed banner headline. Now, wherever he went he was conscious of eyes upon him: strangers noticing his civvy clothes, looking for a war service badge or a khaki armband to show he'd attested, and nudging each other when they saw none, pointing at him with their fingers like Kitchener as he hurried by.

He went out less and less. But inside the Hall he felt lonely and bored and claustrophobic. He missed Charles and the drives they used to take together in his father's Rolls, a flask of whisky in his hand as he sat behind Charles in his chauffeur's cap and felt the sting of the wind against his cheeks. Now he had to drive himself, although he enjoyed rushing through the country lanes at speed, letting the dirt and rain puddles fly up on either side, sometimes soaking unfortunate passers-by whom he could see in his mirrors waving their fists in impotent rage as he accelerated away, feeling the power of the engine beneath his feet.

But even this pastime soon led back to the war. He was driving through Scarsdale one late November evening, starting to head up the hill on his way home when he felt the motor begin to stutter and fail. He pulled over and stopped, cursing his luck. He would need to telephone the Hall and get Cartwright to send someone to pick him up. Over on the other side of the green he could see the lights of the Miners' Institute and the King's Head. Both should have telephones but it didn't take him long to choose the pub over the Institute. Brice feared the miners, remembering the fire which had killed his grandmother, and he drew encouragement from the lascivious, knowing face of Charles II, the Merry Monarch, lit up by the moonlight on the sign outside the pub as it swung gently to and fro, creaking in the breeze.

Inside, he laid half a crown on the counter, ordered a double whisky, and asked to use the telephone. Everything went well: the landlord was friendly and obliging, the drink revived his spirits, and he got straight through to Cartwright at the Hall. He had to talk loudly to make himself heard: Cartwright's deafness had been getting more noticeable in recent months, but he was able to make himself understood and Cartwright promised to send someone to rescue him without delay.

He paid for another whisky and went and sat down beside the roaring fire, taking off his gloves to warm his hands. And then just as he had started to relax, he heard a voice behind him saying his name, identifying him to someone else. He turned round and felt everyone's eyes upon him. There must have been nine or ten people in the bar when he came in, playing dominoes and shove ha'penny, and now they were all silent, abandoning their games to stare at him.

Brice was terrified. He'd been a fool to come in; he should have known he'd be recognized and that people would have seen his name in the newspaper. He should have braved the dark and walked home but it was too late now.

"I don't want any trouble," he said, getting up and backing away towards the bar. "I just came in to use the telephone."

But still no one said anything. It was as if they were waiting for someone or something. The minutes ticked by and finally the door opened. He'd hoped it would be Cartwright or one of the servants from the Hall come to fetch him, but instead it was a middle-aged woman whom he'd never seen before. But she knew who he was and walked right up to him, staring him in the eye. He saw that her hair was white, unnaturally white as if some shock had turned it that colour.

"Give me your hand," she said. But Brice took a step back so that his back was up against the counter. He didn't want to touch her, perhaps sensing what was coming.

"Do what she says!" said an imperious male voice from the back of the room "Do what she says or else!"

Reluctantly Brice put out his hand and the woman opened her tiny purse and took out a single white feather, which she placed on his palm, closing his fingers over it. "My boy died at Neuve Chapelle serving his country. He lost both his legs when they went over the top and he bled to death in no man's land before they could get him to a dressing station," she said, and her voice was hard, stripped of emotion. "He was nineteen years old and he was no coward. Not like you, Brice Scarsdale."

Brice couldn't face her. He had to get out. He rushed past her, sure that the men in the bar would try to stop him, but they did nothing; just watched as he pulled the door open and practically fell into the arms of the stable lad from the Hall who had been sent to bring him home.

———

In the New Year Lady Scarsdale took Brice to London to visit
her father. She knew that he liked the capital almost as much as
she did, and she hoped that the change of scenery would make him
feel better. She was worried by how listless and preoccupied he had
become since Hardcastle's visit, although he hadn't told her about the
white feather which he still retained, locked up in his desk with his
valuables. He took it out sometimes, intending to throw it away, but
each time found he couldn't, as if it had become a part of his identity
which it would hurt him to destroy. But he left it behind when he
went to London, hoping like his mother that the bustle and energy
of the city would help him forget his troubles.

Over and over again he told himself what he'd told Hardcastle:
that he was a free man who didn't have to join the army if he didn't
want to. He had the law on his side and he just needed to get better
at resisting the pressure from interfering busybodies like his father.

He liked his grandfather's tall elegant house in Belgravia. There
were no shortages and there was no dust and the uniformed servants
treated him with respect. He could see his reflection in the gleaming
silver on the dining table and enjoy the luxury of warm fires and
freshly cut greenhouse flowers arranged in vibrant displays of colour
in every room.

But outside, London had become drab and grey. On visits
before the war Brice had liked nothing more than to dress up in
his most dandified outfits and parade up and down beside the lake
in St. James's Park, swinging his gold-topped walking cane as he
admired his reflection in the water and raised his silk hat to fashion-
ably dressed ladies who caught his eye. But now the lake had been
drained because its distinctive shape and night-time glitter might
provide a guide for Zeppelins seeking to bomb Buckingham Palace,
and ugly wooden prefabricated buildings had sprouted up all over
the grass, put up in haste to house expanding government depart-
ments.

The city was quieter too. Petrol restrictions meant there were
fewer cars and buses on the streets and horse-drawn carriages and
hansom cabs had reappeared, dragged out from the recesses of cob-
webbed stables. And at night the blackout made every street seem

dark and forbidding in the dim light of the black-painted gas lamps. But there had been no Zeppelin raids on London for three months and the West End was a hive of vibrant activity that drew Brice back every night. He watched all the shows and went down into basement nightclubs where he could nurse a drink and watch girls dressed as he had never seen before in open blouses and knee-length skirts kicking up their high heels as they danced the tango and the foxtrot into the small hours. Soldiers in khaki were everywhere but the clubs were packed and no one interfered with him or asked his business as he sat in the shadows, soaking up the atmosphere.

On his last evening he went back to the Gaiety to watch his favourite show, *Tonight's the Night,* for the third time. And sitting in the stalls in his white tie and tails, singing along to the songs and laughing at the jokes, he realized with a shock that he was happy for the first time in as long as he could remember.

But the joy didn't last. Within a week of his return to the north the passing of the Military Service Act brought the war rushing back into his life like a pent-up dam breaking its banks. Sitting in the cold dining room of Scarsdale Hall on a grey January morning he read the newspaper article over and over again that his father had thoughtfully left folded up in front of his plate. On 2 March he and every other unexempted single man between the ages of nineteen and forty-one were deemed to have enlisted in the army and were to report for duty at their nearest recruiting office.

He felt faint; he thought of the casualty lists and remembered the wounded men he had seen on the streets of London: the maimed with their hideous disfigured faces and amputated limbs; the gassed with their deep rasping coughs; and the blind tap-tap-tapping along the pavements with their thin white sticks, stumbling on the kerbs. Now there was to be no escape from all of that unless . . . unless . . . Brice read the article again: yes, he was right: the Act only applied to single men. If he was married he would be exempt. And he wanted to be married to Miriam. There was nothing he wanted more in the whole world. He had always loved her. Could she not see that? See what he had to offer her? He was a baronet's son, not a penniless orphan like Adam who had left her behind to fight this stupid war and might never come back; he was here now ready to make her his wife. And if his father would not consent, they could elope. Gretna Green was just across the border. And after they were wed, they could not be unwed; he knew his mother would come round in the end and make it right . . .

Brice's mind raced so he couldn't think straight. He was in a fever: he couldn't wait; he had to know. He got up from the table and went out to the car and drove fast up the hill with his eyes fixed on the church tower ahead. And the frenzy that had gripped him since he read the newspaper announcement took him in four strides up the front path of the Parsonage and lifted his hand to pull down hard on the bell cord; but then left him abruptly and entirely when Miriam opened the door and looked so upset to see him, as if he'd broken some unwritten law in showing up unannounced.

"Hello, Brice," she said when she'd regained her composure. "My mother's not up yet. Perhaps you could come back later." Her voice was cold and he knew what she was saying—that his only business could be with her mother, not with her.

All at once he realized his foolishness. Miriam didn't love him. Wanting something didn't make it true. And it hurt him to see how beautiful she was and yet so set against him. All he had ever done was try to please her. And now he would be sent to die in some rat-infested trench in France or Belgium and everything he had hoped for in his short life would come to nothing.

Drained of energy, he put out his hand and leant against the door jamb for support. "I'm sorry," he said. "I shouldn't have come. It's just . . ."

"What?" Miriam asked. She was worried suddenly—Brice was white in the face, swaying from side to side. She could see that he was fighting back tears.

"I was frightened. I have to join the army and you know I don't want to. I've told you before about my father trying to force me, but it's not just him now. They've passed a law that says all single men must go. And I thought if you married me then I wouldn't have to. I could be with you instead."

"And that's what you came here for—to ask me to marry you?

Because you're frightened?" Miriam spoke slowly as if she couldn't quite believe what she was saying.

Brice nodded. "I've always loved you; you know that. I've always wanted you to be my wife." He spoke without passion, as if he was making a simple statement of fact.

"But I can't marry you," she said. "I'm engaged to Adam."

"I know," he said, nodding his head. "I'm sorry I came." Somehow telling the truth had liberated him at least temporarily from his fear and bitterness. And as he was about to turn away, some instinct made him extend his hand.

She looked at him curiously and then after a slight hesitation responded. Their hands touched for a moment, and then he turned and walked away while she looked after him as he got into the car, unsure what to make of what had just transpired.

Driving back to the Hall Brice felt numb and empty. But as the day wore on, his fear returned. It was a familiar pattern of mood swings between terror and despondency that was to repeat itself over and over again through the coming days.

In the afternoon he told his mother what had happened. And he could see that she was as frightened as he was, although she tried her best not to show it. His father, however, glowed triumphant, practically rubbing his hands with glee as he counted down the days to 2 March when "the stain of shame will be removed from this house once and for all" as he announced grandiloquently at dinner several days later. Brice would gladly have thrown his wine glass in his father's face in response; indeed, he might well have done so if his mother hadn't already told him that he had to keep a tight rein on his self-control.

"It's for your own sake," she said. "We're going to need your father's co-operation to get an exemption."

"An exemption!" Brice repeated the word like a drowning man grasping a lifeline. "How can I get an exemption?"

"By saying you're needed to help run the mine. It's an essential service—the country needs coal even more than it needs men."

"But I've never had anything to do with the mine!" Brice protested.

"I know. But your father has influence over the tribunal. If he tells them that he needs you here they'll give you the exemption. I'm sure of it."

"But why would he do that? You've heard him—he can't wait to see me in uniform, and the sooner the better."

"Leave him to me," she said. "He's not just your father; he's my husband and he's going to have to listen to reason."

"If you say so," said Brice. But he didn't believe it. Not for a minute. He knew his father too well to think he'd change his mind. He put in his application for exemption but felt he was doing no more than going through the motions. And as the days passed before the hearing he fell into a deep depression, smoking endless cigarettes that he allowed to burn right down to the end so they stained his fingers as he sat by the window in his room, gazing out at the steely grey sky from which the rain fell in a constant steady drizzle.

He refused to go downstairs for meals—he'd lost his appetite and he couldn't stand to be in the same room as his father. And he left the plates of food untouched that Sarah brought up from the kitchen.

Along the corridors, out on the periphery of his hearing, he could sometimes hear his parents arguing: raised voices and doors slamming and once the sound of china breaking, smashing against a wall. But he didn't try and make out what they were saying. He knew his father wouldn't bend. He couldn't even if he had wanted to—he was stubborn like a mule. Principles were more important to him than people—they always had been.

So Brice wound up his gramophone and played the songs he'd heard in London to drown out the noise of his parents' anger and the dismal patter of the rain against his window. The music pained him because it made him feel as if he was listening to the far-off sounds of a world he'd left behind and would never see again, and sometimes he even felt as if the machine's needle was playing across his skin instead of the surface of the record. But he persisted, closing his eyes and willing himself to remember and to forget.

He felt as if the house was breaking up around him. At night he imagined he could hear its hinges and joints cracking and snapping in the dark while the wind whipped around the eaves, searching for a way in. He found it hard to breathe: there was a pressure in the air building all the time, pushing for the storm to break.

But when it did, it began with a knock, a light knock on his door on a Saturday morning. He thought it was Sarah, bringing him more unwanted food and he shouted out irritably for her to go away and leave him alone. But the knocking continued and he heard his mother's voice calling to him from the other side of the door. When he opened it, he saw to his surprise that she was wearing her travelling clothes.

"What's happening?" he asked

"We're leaving," she said. "And we're not coming back—or at least I'm not. I've had enough of this house to last me a lifetime. I feel like I've been buried alive. You need to start packing. I want to get the one o'clock train." She sounded angry but resolved, certain of her decision.

"Where are we going?"

"London. We're going to live with my father. Everything's settled."

"But what about the tribunal? They've called me in, you know that."

"We don't need the tribunal. You're going to work for your grandfather and he's already got you an exemption. He wrote to me today with the confirmation. He knows people, people that matter. I should have thought about asking him before, but I wanted to change John's mind—or try to at least. God knows why! I suppose that after twenty-five years of marriage I felt I owed it to myself and to you—"

She broke off, swallowing the bitterness that she so obviously felt. But Brice was hardly listening: all he could think about was the exemption; the knowledge, unimaginable until a moment ago, that he was going to escape the war and survive. Everything was possible suddenly. As Mrs. Vale said, anything could happen. He leant forward and kissed his mother on both cheeks.

"Thank you," he said. "You've saved my life." And pulling open the doors of his wardrobe he began to pack.

They met downstairs in the hall an hour later. Sir John was there too, watching as their trunks were packed into the back of the car. He was white with anger and Brice could see the blue vein pulsing in the side of his temple.

"You can't do this," he shouted. "You're my wife. Your place is here by my side."

"So I can watch you send our son to his death?" she shot back. "No, I don't think so. The truth is you don't deserve a family. I should have left you a long time ago."

"And gone back to your tradesman father who's busy lining his pockets while our troops are laying down their lives! Yes, I suppose that is where you do belong," he ranted, advancing on his wife, who responded by turning her back on him, pulling on her gloves as she prepared to go down the steps.

But Lady Scarsdale's pug dog sensed a threat to his mistress and lunged backwards, clamping its teeth down hard on Sir John's shin, biting through his trousers. The baronet cried out in pain and lifted his leg, intending to kick the dog in retribution, but the pug jumped out of the way, displaying surprisingly quick reflexes for such an overweight creature, and Sir John's foot connected with nothing, sending him toppling forward, down on to the marble floor.

Cartwright, who had been watching the scene unfold with a look of pained distress etched across his usually impassive features, rushed forward and lifted Sir John to his feet.

"Is he all right?" asked Lady Scarsdale.

"I think so, my lady," said the butler.

"Good. I am sorry, Cartwright, that things had to end this way. There is a word for it, isn't there? *Bathos,* that's it. The Greeks knew a thing or two, didn't they?"

And with that, Lady Scarsdale, escorted by her son holding up a black umbrella, descended the steps of Scarsdale Hall to the waiting car and was driven away without giving her home of the previous twenty-five years a backwards glance.

Part Four

———◆———

The Somme

They leave their trenches, going over the top,
While time ticks blank and busy on their wrists,
And hope, with furtive eyes and grappling fists,
Flounders in mud. O Jesus, make it stop!

Siegfried Sassoon, "Attack," 1918

Chapter Nineteen

May 1916

Adam was tired. He'd been standing sentry on the wooden planks of the fire-step with his rifle loaded and extended for nearly two hours, peering out over the parapet into the darkness. It wasn't pitch-black—high in the sky the new moon shed enough light for him to be able to make out the posts holding up the British wire about fifteen yards away, but beyond that the German line on the ridge above was impossible to make out.

The front line was quiet—there had been some sporadic firing about a mile away over towards La Boisselle but it had died down in the last hour. Behind him Luke and Rawdon were asleep, curled up in their greatcoats beside a dimly glowing brazier on the other side of the trench. He felt alone, utterly alone under the stars, and yet he knew that less than three hundred yards away German soldiers were staring out into the night just like him.

Adam had been on the Somme for nearly four months now and he still hadn't seen a German. They fired their guns and sometimes he could hear them shouting or singing in their strange angry-sounding language, but they remained invisible. It had been a quiet sector of the line ever since the British took it over from the French at the end of the previous year and Adam hoped but did not believe that it would stay that way. He was sure that sooner or later there would be an attack from his side or from theirs and he would have to fight the enemy face to face, either to kill or be killed.

Perhaps it would be tonight. The longer he gazed at the crooked fence pickets the more they began to look like the silhouettes of a German patrol, crouching down on their knees ready to rush forward. The empty bully-beef tins tied to the wire were gently tinkling just as they always did. He knew it was the rats that were making the noise but it was still hard to drive away the thought that he was listening to the sheaths of bayonets clinking. The increased intensity of his hearing, compensating for the reduction in his field of vision to two earth walls seven feet apart, was a facet of trench life that Adam was only slowly getting used to. His sense of smell had however become blunted—a survival mechanism without which he wouldn't have been able to cope with the extraordinary stench of the front line: an amalgam of excrement, urine, cordite, chloride of lime and putrefaction which bore no relation to anything he had ever before experienced.

He looked at his watch. His two hours were up and it was time for Luke to take over. Carefully he climbed down from the fire-step and shook him awake. There was no risk of waking Rawdon, who slept more heavily than any other soldier in the company and always with a contented smile on his face. Adam envied him his peaceful dreams. Sleep for Adam meant entry into a nightmare world where he was endlessly chased by unseen enemies—Germans perhaps— through low-ceilinged underground chambers and tunnels similar to those he'd encountered in Scarsdale Mine. He could not outrun his pursuers: they were getting closer and closer but he always awoke in a cold sweat just as he could feel their outstretched hands touching the small of his back.

He felt stiff from standing so long. He needed to get the blood back into his legs and went for a walk, picking his way through the zigzagging bays and traverses to his right, taking care not to step on any soldiers who were sleeping on the ground. There weren't many: most of them were lying on their rubber groundsheets in funk holes scratched into the trench walls under the parados. In the shadowy moonlight they looked like effigies carved on tombs, reminding Adam of Sir John's seventeenth-century ancestors resting on their stone bed in the church at Scarsdale. He could see the church vividly in his mind's eye and remembered how he had watched Miriam arranging the flowers on the altar on that rainy afternoon three years before, but it was as if he was looking at photographs taken in another lifetime, one that bore no relation to his present existence.

The officers slept in more capacious dugouts back in the support trench, revetted with wooden posts and corrugated iron. Some of these had wire beds and shelves and were decorated with saucy pictures of chorus girls cut from the pages of *La Vie Parisienne*. But Adam didn't envy them their superior accommodation. A direct hit from a shell could bury the occupants alive and that was the trench death that Adam most feared, although the gas ran it a close second.

And they had to share their dugouts with armies of rats that watched their every move and ran over them, even bit them sometimes, while they slept. Of course there were rats outside too. They were everywhere, grown fat as guinea pigs from feasting on the French corpses that were buried inside the trench walls. But rats out in the open didn't horrify Adam quite as much as when they were in the close confined space of a dugout.

Further down the trench Adam passed the sandbagged entrance to the underground sap that ran out through no man's land to the carefully constructed hide where Thomas, Ernest's brother, spent his days gazing at the German line through the telescopic sights of his specially adapted Lee-Enfield rifle. Thomas, gloomy and morose at the best of times, had become a hero in the battalion in the last few months. Starting off as an obscure private, the marksmanship skills he'd shown during basic training had earned him a place at one of the new sniping schools and he had arrived in France with a precision-scoped rifle and an ability to remain completely motionless for hours on end watching and waiting for an enemy head to appear for a second above their parapet, which was all that was required for him to blow its owner's head to kingdom come.

In public Ernest kept his thoughts about his brother to himself but he had confided to Adam on several occasions that it didn't sit easy with him that Thomas was killing men who were going about peaceful tasks—getting through the days in their trenches as best they could, cooking and repairing duckboards and cleaning their equipment just like their British counterparts while they waited to be relieved. Adam made the obvious point that the Germans were sniping too; in fact they were the ones who had started it. But he understood how Ernest felt, and his intense hatred of the enemy which had exploded inside him that December morning in Scarborough had somewhat dissipated since he got to the front—at least as far as the common soldiers were concerned. It was hard to carry on feeling the same way when the Germans shouted, "Good morning, Tommy," over their parapets and even asked once or twice what he and his friends were having for breakfast.

But Luke and Davy kept a running total of Thomas's kills and, whenever they got the chance, bombarded him with questions for hours at a time about the various ingenious methods he'd used to notch them up. Their favourite was the carnage he'd inflicted on the enemy by working out the location of their latrines through the simple expedient of watching where the bluebottle flies were swarming. Once he knew, he would fire whenever the swarm dispersed, inferring that it could only be men going to relieve themselves who were having this effect on the insects. The Germans moved their latrines in response but they either failed to work out Thomas's strategy or couldn't get rid of the flies, and his kill total continued to rise.

Thomas hadn't grown any more talkative since his days in Scarsdale Mine and he gave the impression of being mildly irritated by Davy's and Luke's questions, but both Adam and Ernest thought that he secretly enjoyed being the focus of attention and he was certainly in no hurry to put a stop to their interrogations.

It had rained for several days when Adam's company took over this section of trench nine days earlier, weakening and undermining the walls, and several body parts of dead Frenchmen in ragged blue uniforms had half fallen out of their graves, hanging down obscenely from under the sandbag parapets. In one bay a huge half-decayed head had emerged still wearing a service cap pulled down over empty eye sockets and Davy had delighted in saluting it at every opportunity until the colonel gave orders for the corpse to be reburied. But further on at the junction with the communication trench a disembodied blackened hand had been allowed to remain, pointing back towards the reserve lines. Some wit had put up a board beside it with Amiens painted on in capitals as if it was a signpost.

Looking up at the hand, Adam felt a sense of hopelessness overcome him. They were living in a charnel house surrounded by the dead, and sooner or later they would all surely join them. Their lives were flickering like the candles that were burning here and there along the trench. Only a breath of wind was needed to blow them out.

Away down the communication trench he could hear a fatigue party approaching, bringing stores and ammunition up from the transport lines. Morning was coming and it was time to go back and try to sleep a little before stand-to. Perhaps this time he'd be tired enough not to dream . . .

But he was too restless to sleep. After an hour he fell into an uneasy doze from which he was awoken almost immediately by the sound of voices. It was still dark, but in the dim light from the brazier he could see an officer standing a few feet away from where he was lying, absently drawing patterns in the dirt beside the duckboards with the end of his cane while he talked to Luke, who was standing up on the fire-step. Even though the officer had his back to him Adam recognized the slow, easy drawl of his voice straightaway and smiled as he sat up, rubbing his eyes.

"I understand you weren't asleep, private," said Seaton. "But being awake is not the only requirement of a sentry, you know; you also have to be vigilant. Our Boche friends would like nothing better than to take us unawares."

"I wasn't expecting to be attacked from the back, sir," said Luke a little petulantly.

"By one of your own officers carrying a walking stick?" said Seaton with a smile. "No, perhaps not. But still you need to have your wits about you. You could always fix your bayonet and rest your chin on that. I'm sure that would keep you on your toes!" Luke knitted his brows, not sure whether the captain was being serious. It wasn't the first time: Captain Scarsdale was hard to read. He never seemed to raise his voice or get excited, and he had a way of making suggestions rather than giving orders. But no one tried to take advantage.

The captain had a natural authority about him and was popular with everyone in the battalion. The soldiers knew that he was one of the few front-line officers who'd been in the war from the start, choosing to transfer from his regular army battalion to this one after it had been almost wiped out in the dreadful series of battles around Ypres in the first year of the fighting. And without articulating the thought, they felt safer under his command.

It was different with the colonel, an old Boer War veteran called out of retirement to train and command this battalion of New Army Pals who had volunteered from the mining towns of the north-east in the first six months of the war. The colonel loved his men: he knew all their names and all their stories. He'd worked hard to turn them from civilians into soldiers and in the process they had given him a new lease on a life that he had thought was over. But he'd also come to value them too much. He worried constantly about what would happen when they were thrown into battle and as the months passed he allowed his burgeoning anxiety to show, not realizing the morale-sapping effect it was having on the men whom he wanted to protect.

Adam got to his feet and saluted. "It's my turn, sir," he lied. He was concerned that Luke might actually fall asleep if he remained on duty and he also hoped to have a conversation with Seaton, whom he rarely got the chance to talk to on a one-to-one basis.

Luke looked surprised. He knew his two hours weren't finished—he was supposed to be on duty until stand-to, but he wasn't going to argue. The captain had been right—he had been close to dropping off, and he welcomed the chance for a little more rest even if it wasn't his turn.

"Lance Corporal Raine to the rescue," said Seaton with an amused smile, watching as Adam took Luke's place on the fire-step. "And no more nocturnal vigils for you for several weeks, you'll be pleased to hear, Private Mason. Brigade says we're due to be relieved tonight so if everything goes according to plan—which of course it rarely does—you'll be smelling the fresh air of Picardy by this time tomorrow . . ."

"Thank you, sir," said Luke, whose slightly sour expression had been transformed in an instant into a wide grin. "That's the best news I've heard since we got here." And, lying down beside Rawdon, he fell instantly asleep.

Seaton stood, looking down at the sleeping soldiers. "I don't know if you know this, Adam, but every time I see Private Dawes, I feel a burst of joy," he said.

"*Joy!*" repeated Adam, wrinkling his brows in surprise. It was the last word he'd expected Seaton to come out with. "Why?" he asked. He was always scrupulous to salute and call Seaton "sir" when they were in the presence of others but he found it almost impossible to preserve the military relationship when they were alone, particularly as Seaton clearly had no wish to maintain it himself, talking as if they were sitting facing each other across the dinner table at Scarsdale Hall.

"Because he makes me remember our first meeting," said Seaton. "A quite marvellous moment: you sprinting across the lawn; me almost falling off my horse; Dawes riding his bicycle into the lake to evade my brother and the appalling Charles who were using my father's Rolls as a weapon of war. It was exactly like a scene from one of Mr. Chaplin's films, although I hadn't yet had the pleasure of seeing any of them then, of course. It's a memory I shall cherish to my dying day and I owe it all to Private Dawes. If he hadn't come visiting, none of it would have happened."

"I remember you said he would make a good soldier," said Adam.

"And I was right," said Seaton. "Just like I know you would make a good officer."

Adam shrugged—they had talked about this before. "My place is with them," he said, pointing down at Rawdon and Luke. But then, feeling his response was inadequate, he tried to explain: "It seems to me sometimes that all my life I have been an outsider looking in on other people's lives, as if I was marooned in some kind of no man's land all of my own. But now, here, finally, I feel like I belong."

"Except that you are a corporal now—you have already been promoted over them," said Seaton. "And you should remember that being a good officer, whether commissioned or non-commissioned, is about taking responsibility for those in your care; not just sharing their suffering. And this battalion will have need of good officers soon. The time of our trial is fast approaching, and I have seen what happens in battle. This war is not like other wars—it's worse than you can ever imagine."

"What do you mean: *fast approaching*?" Adam asked. Seaton was always so dry and detached and it unnerved him to hear his friend talking so seriously.

"I mean that we will have to attack," said Seaton, lowering his voice. "The French are dying in their thousands at Verdun. They are crying out for relief, and this is the obvious place for an offensive to take the pressure off them—here where our line joins theirs and we can try to break through together."

"*Try*," Adam repeated. "Do you think we won't succeed?"

"I don't know," said Seaton, shaking his head. "It will be very difficult."

"Why?" Adam asked

And at that moment, as if in response to his question, two white star shells burst almost simultaneously in the sky over no man's land, lighting up in a bright evanescent glow the two lines of trenches for hundreds of yards in each direction and the blasted wilderness of dank grass, broken trees and rusty barbed wire that lay between them.

"Look!" said Seaton, pointing towards the enemy positions. "See how their line follows the ridge, jutting out with the spurs and then retreating back up the valleys to the high ground. It's the same all along—they are always dominating us from above, so that when we attack they will be able to fire directly down on us with their machine guns. Six or seven hundred rounds a minute—it will be a slaughter unless we can knock them out. And that will be hard to do. The emplacements are well concealed and protected too—"

Seaton broke off, pulling Adam back from the parapet as a salvo of rifle bullets flew whining over their heads. And almost immediately, as if in fulfilment of Seaton's warning, a machine gun opened up, sending a further hail of bullets against the sandbags on the parapet as it traversed backwards and forwards along the line—until all at once the firing suddenly ceased, stopping just as it had started for no discernible reason.

And as the darkness began to blur into the soft misty grey light of the early dawn, a lark began to sing somewhere out in no man's land and Adam and Seaton fell silent, unable to comprehend how such exquisite music could exist in such a terrible place.

All at once whistles were being blown and the trenches were a hive of activity as all the soldiers stood to, manning the fire-steps. Some of them let loose with their rifles, celebrating the custom of the morning hate. Davy was the most enthusiastic participant but Ernest was convinced that it was the larks not the Germans that Davy was trying to hit. Every morning he complained about their melancholy trilling, telling anyone who would listen that they gave him "the shudders" and that he'd do anything to "make 'em stop their bloody racket."

Looking out through their box periscopes, the officers could see the Germans responding on the other side of no man's land with the red flashes from the muzzles of their guns melting into the crimson haze of the rising sun. But Ernest as always refused to join in. "I've got better things to do than spend my day cleaning my rifle for evening inspection just so I can take a few pot shots at nothing at all," he said sensibly. But his friends took no notice: they didn't feel sensible at five in the morning waking up in the trenches, and firing their rifles helped a little to relieve their tension.

After the hate came breakfast—the soldiers' happiest time of the day, at least in this quiet sector where both sides were prepared to leave each other alone while they fried bully beef and bacon rashers in their mess tin lids over small improvised stoves and brewed up tea in camp kettles, leaving a little at the end for shaving.

The bread was hard and stale and toasting had become difficult since the adjutant had come down hard on bayonets being used as toasting forks; the tea tasted of the petrol that seeped into the water as it was carried up to the front line each night in old fuel cans; and the flies were getting worse as the weather improved so that the soldiers had to constantly wave their hands over their food as they were cooking or eating it to keep them off. But Adam and his section felt a sensation almost bordering on contentment as they sat back against the trench walls after eating, wreathed in the acrid smoke of their Woodbine cigarettes and listened to Davy reading out extracts from an old copy of the *Wipers Times* that had made its way south from Belgium.

" 'Ere's a recipe," he told them. "Trench puddin': take four biscuits an' smash 'em to a pulp with your entrenchin' tool—easier said than done, that, o' course," he said, looking up with a grin. "I 'eard a bloke in C Company bit down on one of 'em t'other day an' lost 'alf 'is teeth! Any road, once you've finished with the smashin' you add a tin of Tommy Tickler's Apple Jam, stir well, 'eat over a fire an' serve with a teaspoon of Ideal Milk. Sounds tasty, don't it?"

His comrades grunted their agreement and he turned the page and began laughing out loud. "Oh, you lot 'ave got to hear this," he said. "It says 'ere there was this Tommy who got the VC so a reporter from the local rag goes round to interview 'is mum an' tells 'er 'er son's comin' 'ome cos 'e's got VD, or at least that's what the ol' bat thinks 'e's sayin'. So when our boy comes 'ome, thinkin' 'e's goin' to get a 'ero's welcome, 'e gets a box around the ears instead. Can you believe it? It says 'ere it's a true story."

As far as Adam was concerned, it didn't matter if it was true or not. All that mattered was that it was funny and it certainly had everyone laughing more than they had in weeks.

The hours passed. After rifle inspection they took off their boots and rubbed whale oil into their sore, blistered feet, and several of them unwound their puttees and took their trousers off, running lighted candles up and down the seams, relishing the sound of the lice popping, even though they knew full well that the vermin would be back in force the next day. There was no escape from the cooties and the endless itching from their bites.

They drank more tea and Davy took out his Crown and Anchor board and he and Luke and Rawdon gathered around it, throwing dice while taking it in turns to keep watch for officers. Gambling was illegal and usually punished with field punishment number two— shitwallah duties for a week. But none of them had yet been caught:

the board was made of cloth and Davy was able to get it stowed away out of sight in the blink of an eye.

Rawdon played intently. Davy always seemed to come out ahead and he was convinced that the game was fixed in some way, although it was difficult to see how Davy was doing it unless the dice were loaded and Rawdon always insisted on inspecting them before starting play, turning them over and over again in his fingers while Davy watched with amusement. Now they were playing for cigarettes as Davy had already won all their money.

Adam closed his eyes. In the next bay Harry was playing a sentimental Irish ballad on his violin and the falling cadences exactly fitted his melancholy mood. Listening to Harry's playing was one of Adam's greatest pleasures, although it never lasted long as Davy hated sad tunes almost as much as he hated the larks and as soon as he heard his twin starting in on one he would tell him to "put a sock in that tear-jerkin' muck an' play somethin' wi' a bit o' go in it!" And Harry always did as he was told: everyone knew that he had no will of his own when it came to his brother.

But today Davy was absorbed in his game and Adam could sit back and listen, allowing the nerve strings of his own emotions, deadened by the grim devastation of the trenches, to come slowly back to life, responding to the sweetness of the music, while a pair of wide-winged British biplanes circled overhead like two pterodactyl birds engaged in some esoteric mating ritual.

It didn't last long. Such moments never did. There was a bustle and commotion in the trenches as the news spread that a three-man Stokes mortar team were setting up their equipment a few bays down. The soldiers complained bitterly even though they knew it was useless. The team had been sent up by brigade HQ.

"This is a fuckin' joke," shouted Davy, charging up to the team's sergeant. He was always to the fore when it came to arguing with higher authority. "I know what you lot 'ave got in mind—you're goin' to fire that bloody thing a few times and then fuck off out of 'ere, leavin' us poor sods to get it 'ot from t'other side while you're back puttin' your feet up in your cushy billets. That's the idea, ain't it?"

"Yes, it is," said the sergeant pleasantly, but without looking up from his work as he finished assembling the mortar and began adjusting the barrel's angle of elevation while his assistant stood ready to begin loading the first of the numerous three-inch grey cylindrical shells that they had brought up with them.

"An' what's the fuckin' point? That's what we want to know," Davy ranted. "You're not supportin' an attack: we're out of 'ere tonight an' Fritz ain't doin' us any harm . . ."

"Well, I rather think that is the point," said the sergeant evenly. "We're fighting a war here in case you've forgotten and the general idea is to try and keep the Boche a bit more on their toes than you boys seem to be doing. Now, if you don't mind getting out of the way . . ."

"Don't you fuckin' talk to us like that, you smarmy bastard!" said Davy, advancing menacingly on the sergeant.

"Leave it, Davy. It's not worth it," said Adam, taking hold of Davy's arm and trying to hold him back. He was the corporal in charge of the section and it was his responsibility to keep the men under control.

But Davy wasn't listening and pulled away, balling his hands into fists as he confronted the sergeant. "You people don't 'ave a fuckin' clue what we're *doin'* up 'ere." He spat out the words practically in the sergeant's face. "An' you need to fuckin' apologize before you start firin' that thing," he added, pointing down contemptuously at the mortar.

"No, he doesn't," said a voice behind him. "Sergeant, carry on with your business and please tell us if you need any assistance. Private, I'm putting you on a charge. You'll see the colonel when we get back to billets and he can decide what to do with you. And Corporal Raine, you need to do a better job of disciplining your men."

Adam looked into Seaton's impassive face and felt as if he had been slapped across the cheek. And yet he knew Seaton was right. He ought to have stepped in quicker. Why hadn't he? Was it because he sympathized with Davy? Firing the mortar was certainly stupid—it was like stirring up a hornets' nest for no reason. But Adam knew the sergeant was right too: this was a war they were engaged in, and he needed to live up to his responsibilities and stop acting like he was just one of the men. He saluted smartly and followed his men out of the bay.

Davy had been quite right in his forecast. The German response to the unprovoked mortar attack was almost immediate. The section watched as the shells streaked steeply up into the sky like miniature footballs on sticks and then fell almost vertically down to the ground on the other side, sending geysers of earth gushing up into the air as they exploded. Then, within moments, two red rocket signal flares went shooting up from the German trenches and a minute later their artillery opened up, bombarding the British line with a barrage of high explosive.

The Jack Johnson shells tore towards them with a roar like an express train, throwing up clouds of heavy black smoke as they exploded. Most of them fell short, crashing into no man's land, but the concussion from one that burst inside the wire threw Adam back against the rear wall of the trench and half buried him under a cascade of exploding sand bags.

Spitting out the earth and sand, he got to his feet and saw that everyone in the section had curled themselves up into foetal balls except for Rawdon, who as always seemed impervious to shelling. The belief in fate that Rawdon had subscribed to since Adam saved his life in the mine had become even stronger since they arrived in France. "If it's got my name and address on it, it's goin' to find me anyway, so there's no point cowerin' in the corner, screamin' for Mama," he had told Adam on more than one occasion, referring to the reactions of some of the other soldiers in the section.

Some of them were screaming now and the sounds of their animal terror continued to fill the trench for a moment when the firing stopped, making Adam feel as if he was standing in the middle of a slaughterhouse, although no one in their bay appeared to have been hurt. But it was different further down the trench where Harry and Ernest were bent down over the supine body of Davy whose face was covered in blood.

Harry was shouting at his brother, shaking him by the lapels of his tunic, and Adam had to pull him off, leaving Ernest to drag him away to one side, crying hysterically, while he bent down to examine the injured man. Davy was breathing and seemed to be coming round and, peering closely, Adam didn't think that the substance on his face looked like blood. It was a lighter red and granular in texture and it was everywhere—all over his uniform and his haversack. No one could bleed that much. Adam dabbed his finger in the mess and raising it gingerly to his mouth he tasted not blood but strawberries. And with a gasp of relief and gut-wrenching laughter that hurt him in his rib cage, he sat back watching while Davy got blindly to his feet, spluttering and pawing at his face with red sticky hands.

"What the fuck are you laughing at?" shouted Harry, staring, like Ernest, over at Adam with enraged incomprehension.

"It's not blood; it's Tommy Tickler strawberry jam—the tin your mother sent. Davy wasn't going to let that go, whatever Fritz threw at us," said Adam, trying his best to pull himself together. But then he started laughing again and the others joined in, reluctantly at first but then wholeheartedly. Without laughter none of them would have survived the trenches.

In the evening the food that came up from the field kitchens was hot for the first time that week and everyone got their allotted allowance of rum. The earthenware jar it came in was stamped SRD for "Special Rations Department" but was better known as "Soon Runs Dry" or "Seldom Reaches Destination." But not this time— Seaton's promise of relief had come true and, on the stroke of midnight, A Company formed into a caterpillar column and began the slow march down the communication trenches to the transport lines.

Chapter Twenty

It took a long time to go back. They would stop and start and then stop again, delayed by unknown obstacles up ahead, most of the time just shuffling forward in single file down the narrow lanes with their hands resting on the shoulder of the man in front, keeping their heads tilted back to avoid being hit by the swinging water bottles and sheathed bayonets.

They were unused to marching and their feet hurt, swelling and sweating inside their thick woollen socks, and in the dark their boots slipped on unseen objects that might have been tree roots or spent shrapnel or human bones. There was no way to know except when a star shell burst in the sky behind them, creating a weird pale green glow in the communication trench that illuminated the crumbling sandbags on either side and on one occasion a painted sign at a crossroads with arrows pointing to "BERLIN" behind them and "PARIS" in front. They laughed a little at that but not much—it was too dark and too confined and they were too bloody tired to want to do anything more than keep putting one foot in front of the other. And they were worried too that the Boche might start shelling again; the thought of getting hit just when they were getting out was unendurable—unless it was a Blighty wound of course. Any one of them would have given anything for that.

Finally, after what seemed like hours, they came out into the open and were able to march four abreast along the road, passing between the silhouettes of tall thin poplar trees. They met a company coming the other way and Rawdon shouted: "You're going the wrong way, chums!" And they laughed more this time and broke out into song as the darkness began to dissolve into the misty grey light that heralded the dawn.

> "Do your balls hang low?
> Do they dangle to and fro?
> Can you tie them in a knot?
> Can you tie them in a bow?
> Do they itch when it's hot?
> Do you rest them in a pot?
> Do your balls hang low?"

They marched in tune to the song, happier now as they stamped out the beat so that the dust flew up from the road as they climbed the hill, and up above them the screens of ragged canvas fastened to the plane trees by the French to hide the road from enemy observation fluttered in the breeze like lines of listening ghosts.

They went down into Albert at sunrise, and the sound of their marching feet echoed off the walls of the empty red-brick houses standing shuttered and padlocked and here and there damaged by shellfire. The town was still within range of the German artillery and the soldiers couldn't yet fully relax.

In the market square they stopped for a rest, gazing up at the famous gilded Virgin and Child statue leaning out at a bizarre horizontal angle over the town from atop the battered cathedral tower. It hadn't been built that way. Early the previous year a German shell had hit the basilica and the statue had toppled halfway over but by some miracle hadn't fallen further so that it now hung over the marketplace like a figurehead on a sailing ship. There was a myth among the Allied soldiers that when the Virgin fell the Germans would win the war, and to guard against this happening, the French had secured the statue to the tower with strong hawsers, but from the ground it still looked as if it was hanging precariously in mid-air, ready to fall at any moment.

"So what do you make of 'er?" Rawdon asked Adam.

"I think she's sorrowing, lamenting the folly of men," said Adam, staring up into the Virgin's sad face.

"Aye, she's sorrowin' all right," said Rawdon, nodding. "But I reckon she's feelin' a bit more'n that: I think she's 'ad enough of the whole fuckin' show an' she's getting ready to throw baby Jesus face down on the cobblestones. Splat! An' then she can follow . . ."

Adam looked over at his friend and saw that he was quite serious. "Yes," he said, looking back up at the statue. "I see exactly what you mean."

Slowly, as they marched beyond Albert and out of range of the German guns, the landscape began to change. They left behind the untended fields and the shell-wrecked, abandoned villages where emaciated, ravenous dogs barked wildly at the column from the shelter of overgrown gardens, and came instead to cultivated land where teams of oxen were harrowing the fields and women in shape-less country black were bent double sowing crops. There were no young men; only old ones who sat watching the soldiers go past with weather-beaten, impassive faces; a far cry from the early days of the war when the French had welcomed the British Expeditionary Force with flowers and songs and open arms.

But the soldiers didn't care. Their mood improved with every step they took. This new unspoilt world stretching out over gentle slopes and dales to the horizon line was utterly different to the one they had been used to in the close confines of the trenches. There, one false move could mean a sniper's bullet ripping through their heads, but here there was nothing to fear and the sense of space and freedom made them giddy on their feet.

It didn't matter. Captain Scarsdale, riding down the white road at the head of the dun-coloured column, allowed the company fre-quent halts so they could rest their aching feet and smoke. White and brimstone butterflies fluttered above the daisies and buttercups and waving red poppies and the men closed their eyes, allowing the sun and the breeze to play across their upturned faces. The booming of the guns faded into the background, replaced by the chirping of crickets and the cawing of rooks in the trees, and the freshness of the

air and the hot stream of scent coming from the wild flowers intoxicated them after the nauseous stench of the trenches.

In the late morning they passed through the water meadows
abutting the River Ancre and the soldiers lay down under the weeping willow trees by the frosty-blue stream and bathed their hot faces
in the cool water, while all around frogs croaked incessantly and
water birds whistled and piped in the reeds. On the opposite bank
a heron watched them for a moment and then took flight, easing
effortlessly up into the cloudless sky on its long blue-grey wings. It
was the happiest Adam had been in months.

Finally they arrived at their billets. Adam's platoon was in a
farmhouse on the outskirts of a village which had been taken over as
brigade headquarters. The French owners were unfriendly here too,
resentful of the British who had already requisitioned their horses
and stolen their crops. They responded to the soldiers' cheerful *barn-
door* for bonjour greetings with surly nods and put up signs reading
"Napoo doolay" (no milk) and *"Napoo oofs"* (no eggs) on their gates.
But the soldiers didn't care: for the first time in as long as they could
remember they had good hot food to eat three times a day. The battalion cookers were close by and the soldiers could supplement army
food with visits to the village estaminets where they ordered plonk
and watery beer to wash down Welsh rarebit and *bombardier fritz*
(*pommes de terre frites*) served by a pretty French girl with a twinkle in
her eye who made them think of home.

They slept in barns on wooden bunk beds hung with chicken
wire, waking to the doves cooing under the eaves. But the weather
was getting warmer all the time and on the second night Adam
and his section took their greatcoats and waterproof groundsheets
into the orchard where the apple trees were in blossom and slept out
under the stars.

They could still hear the distant sound of the guns but the
trenches were far enough away that they could at least try to forget
about the war, even if the nights were punctuated by soldiers screaming out in the grip of nightmares filled with gas and bursting shells.
They slept and they ate and they played football in the sunshine and

rejoiced in being clean for the first time in months following a visit to the village brewery where they soaked for hours in vats filled with hot soapy water until their bodies turned red and the floor below was slippery like a skating rink on which one lucky Londoner fell and broke his leg—a Blighty wound which they all admired and envied.

One of the officers billeted at the farmhouse had a Decca gramophone and a small collection of sentimental songs to go with it. One in particular which he played endlessly became entwined in Adam's later recollection with those sun-soaked days:

"Give me your smile, the love-light in your eyes;
Life could not hold a fairer Paradise!"

And later in the summer in the midst of battle he remembered this time as just that—an earthly paradise.

But their freedom didn't last long. They had been brought back behind the lines not to spend their days in idleness but to train for the forthcoming "Big Push." And on the morning of the third day they were issued with new tight-fitting steel helmets and taken in a fleet of lorries to a vast, specially prepared practice area where the British and German trenches were represented by shallow indentations in the ground and the attack lines cut through the imaginary wire were marked by white tapes stretched out over the trampled corn.

Over and over again in the hot sunshine the sweating first-wave troops pretended to climb out of their trenches before forming up in lines and advancing at a precise two miles per hour across a virgin no man's land to capture and consolidate the German front line, while their comrades in the second wave followed exactly three minutes afterwards, moving steadily through them and onward to occupy the second line of German trenches.

A group of staff officers with distinctive red hatbands watched the proceedings through field glasses from a viewing platform set off to the side. Everything about them was polished: the buttons on their immaculately pressed uniforms, their Sam Browne belts, and their riding boots with silver spurs that gleamed and glittered in the sunshine. They were gathered around an older, taller man with a thick military moustache, obviously a general, who looked like the pictures of Haig that Adam had seen in the newspapers, although he was too far away to be sure. It seemed so strange to Adam that his fate depended on the decisions of this man and others like him who would never have any idea who he was. It made him feel like a very small cog in a vast untried machine that was lumbering inexorably forward towards the day of reckoning when it would be finally put to the test.

The troops were obedient but bemused by what they were being instructed to do. It was make believe. It had to be: everyone knew that standing up in no man's land, let alone walking across it, was as sure a way to commit suicide as putting a revolver to your head and pulling the trigger, and eventually Rawdon piped up and asked Captain Scarsdale what the point was of the exercise.

"Why are we walkin', sir?" he asked. "It don't make any sense—the Boche'll be mowin' us down like ripe corn with their machine guns if we don't rush 'em, an' from closer up."

"There won't be any Boche," said Seaton with a thin smile. "Or at least that's the idea."

"No Boche?" repeated Rawdon, scratching his head. "That don't make a whole lot o' sense."

"Our guns are going to blow them to kingdom come so all you're going to have to do is walk across and mop them up, just like what we're doing here."

Rawdon still looked doubtful but Seaton's bland expression discouraged further questions and, shaking his head, Rawdon went back to join in another "attack."

Not everyone was involved in the exercises on that first day. Davy had been summoned to see the colonel on the morning after their arrival at the billets and, not having any defence to offer, had been sentenced to seven days' field punishment number one for his attempt to prevent the Stokes mortar team carrying out their duty. And so, while the rest of his platoon marched past on their way to the practice ground, he was shackled to the wheel of a field gun and crucified for two hours after breakfast each morning while the flies buzzed around his head. As the days passed, he became uncharacteristically quiet, filled with pain and resentment, and the soldiers didn't like it either, so it was a relief when Seaton interceded with the colonel to have the punishment remitted at the end of the fourth day.

On Sunday at church parade, Parson Vale, now a seasoned brigade chaplain, preached that the army was involved in a just war against an enemy that was trying to destroy civilization. "Remember Belgium; remember the *Lusitania*; remember Edith Cavell," he told them, but the soldiers weren't listening. They had passes for Amiens and two weeks' pay in their pockets, and Adam sensed that the parson too was uncomfortable with his text, enumerating the Germans' sins as if by rote, and wondered if it had been dictated to him by the brigadier who sat nodding his approval in the front row.

Adam had seen little of the parson since his arrival in France at the start of the year. They had talked alone and at length only once, meeting by chance the previous month in a YMCA canteen behind the lines where the parson had bought him coffee and a roll. And, sitting listening to the sermon, Adam remembered how the parson had confided in him that he was there to minister to the individual soldiers in their time of need, not to save their souls at church parades.

"Loos was terrible," he'd said and there had been a haunted look in his eyes. "More terrible than you can imagine, Adam. And I felt a purpose there, a divine calling to minister to the men, to comfort the wounded and the dying. But justifying that slaughter from the pulpit—ah, that's a far harder task! God knows what Christ would have made of it but for me, poor sinner that I am, it makes my head ache," he'd ended with a smile and a shake of his head.

They hadn't talked of Miriam or Scarsdale except in passing. It was as if home for both of them was becoming less real by the day, a place that it did no one any good to think about.

The soldiers ended the church parade with a lusty rendition of "Onward Christian Soldiers," although Adam was quite sure that most of them were thinking about marching onward to Amiens and Madame Prudhomme's brothel rather than "the cross of Jesus going on before."

In the city Adam and his friends drank red wine and sang bawdy songs in a series of estaminets, moving from one back street to the next, waiting for six o'clock. Adam knew that they were all thinking about the brothel, picturing it in their minds. And he was too—the concept of it repelled and yet fascinated him. He thought of Miriam and her purity and goodness, waiting for him year after year, and there was some part of him that wanted to expose the contradictions between their betrothal and their separation, between his life at the front and what he had left behind in Scarsdale, and put them to the test. It was an urge to embrace ruin and degradation because they seemed like an affirmation of his life in the trenches. They were where he belonged: in the filth and horror with his comrades, sharing their trials and tribulations—not in some never-never land beyond the horizon with Miriam.

And yet when the red light came on at the end of the dirty street and the crowd of waiting soldiers stopped singing "Hinky Dinky Parlez-Vous" and surged forward towards the entrance door where fat Madame Prudhomme with her enormous bosom stood waiting, slipping their francs into her bulging fishnet stockings as she counted them in, Adam turned away in disgust and walked quickly away.

He stopped spellbound in the cathedral square gazing up past a pyramid of sandbags, which covered the statuary in the three great portals like a beehive honeycomb, to the west window and the open arches of the two high towers that rose up on either side with the blue sky behind forming a backdrop to the silver stone. Elaborate and soaring, the cathedral was a monument to the spirit of man and what he could achieve; and the sandbags a reminder of how quickly it could be torn down.

It was the same inside. The great pillars of the nave were shrouded in sandbags right up to their capitals and the stained glass had been removed for the duration of the war, but that just allowed more of the soft evening light to pour through the high wide windows of the clerestory, lighting up the soaring Gothic vaults of the nave and aisles. At the other end of the cathedral from where he was standing, evening mass was being celebrated on the high altar and Adam could see and smell the smoke from the incense thurible wafting out above the carved wooden choir stalls where the choristers were singing the Latin Creed, their voices rising and gathering with the swell of the music.

For a moment Adam was transported. His mind experienced the soaring grandeur of the poetry, the magnificent certainty of its statement of belief: *Deum de Deo, Lumen de Lumine, Deum verum de Deo vero.* And he was back at Oxford, remembering what it was like to read, even to think in Latin, experiencing the past as more real than the present. It was real here too—Caesar had camped with his legions by the Somme and the Romans had built the straight wide road that ran from Amiens through Albert up on to the German-held ridge at Pozières and to Bapaume beyond. Perhaps the Big Push would be just that; perhaps they would break through and win the war and he could go back to Oxford and to Miriam. Perhaps . . .

The touch of a hand on his shoulder broke his chain of thought and he looked round, startled, to find Seaton standing beside him.

"I hope I'm not interrupting you," said Seaton, smiling. "I wouldn't want to come between you and a religious moment."

"It wasn't a religious moment. I don't have them," said Adam a little defensively. He knew that Seaton was aware he was no church-goer.

"Nor do I," said Seaton, nodding a little sadly. "Jesus and the trenches aren't exactly a good match up, are they? Even if Parson Vale does his best to keep both balls in the air. He often talks of you, by the way; I think he's happy you're going to marry his beautiful daughter."

"I'm—" Adam began and then broke off, not knowing what to say. It was uncanny the way Seaton always seemed to be able to arrow in on his inmost thoughts as if there was a kind of one-way telepathy between them.

"It's beautiful, isn't it?" said Seaton with a wave of his hand, changing the subject. "Even with the sandbags. I'm glad they haven't covered the floor."

"The floor," repeated Adam, not understanding. Ever since he'd entered the cathedral his eyes had been drawn upwards and he hadn't really noticed the black-and-white tiling under his feet. But now, looking down, he immediately knew what Seaton was talking about. The design was almost a match for the beautiful marble floor of the entrance hall at home in Scarsdale. He remembered suddenly the day he first arrived: Sir John tall and erect walking up the steps beside him, determined to make him welcome; the cold condescension of Lady Scarsdale; and Brice, quivering with rage as he defied his father and refused to shake hands. And now the family had broken up with only Sir John left in the house, licking his wounds.

"Have you heard from my father?" asked Seaton, again reading Adam's thoughts.

"Yes," said Adam. "He told me what happened. It's all as you said. He's angry with Brice, and with your mother too, I think."

"Yes, and he's frightened as well. There's always a lot of fear in anger when you dig down under the surface. The war has changed everything for him, just as it has for us. He embraces it, waves the flag, and believes all the John Bull nonsense they print in the papers, but it's destroying him. The taxes go up and up and the moneylenders squeeze him tighter than ever, and even if he can find a way to pay them, he fears it will all be in vain because something will happen to me and he'll be left with Brice, who must hate him worse than ever after my father's ham-fisted attempts to force him into the army. I despise Brice and his cowardice but my father didn't need to drive my mother as far as he did. I don't think she'll ever go back now, and so he's left with Cartwright, shuffling through the empty corridors, listening to the echoes."

Seaton had a way with words and Adam bowed his head, saddened by the picture Seaton had painted of his benefactor. He remembered his kindness and wished that everything had turned out differently and that the war hadn't come like a slow-moving plague to eat away at them all.

"Enough," said Seaton, clapping Adam on the shoulder. "I have brought lamentation into the house of the Lord and depressed you in the process. I apologize unreservedly, lance corporal. So let me make it up to you with dinner. I know a place. You'll like it. I promise."

Seaton led the way out of the square, walking quickly down a series of side streets, each one narrower than the one before, taking them into a district of wooden houses overlooking stagnant canals until they reached the narrowest street of all, a cul-de-sac called Rue du Corps Nu sans Tête. But there was no sign of any headless body; instead, halfway down, behind a thick black door with a jingling bell and a dusty window, was Josephine's, the best oyster and fish restaurant in Amiens. It was crowded but the proprietress seemed to know Seaton well, welcoming him with a kiss on both cheeks, and found them a table in a back room with the doors open, looking out on to a magical garden hung with tangles of wild grapevines. It smelt of jasmine and was inhabited by a family of sleek white cats that could have stepped out of the pages of a children's fairy story.

They drank champagne and tipped the oysters into their mouths and shared a huge salmon which Josephine assured them had been caught in the River Somme that very morning. And they talked about the war.

"How's your section?" Seaton asked.

"Drunk, I think," said Adam, shaking his head. "And probably catching venereal disease at Madame Prudhomme's brothel."

"Actually probably not," said Seaton. "The brothels here are *maisons tolérées*—they're inspected by the State. You're much worse off going with a girl on the street, although neither option strikes me as very enticing. Still, the men need to let off steam."

"Davy does," said Adam. "He's been seething ever since he got the field punishment."

"You didn't like that?" asked Seaton, sensing an accusation in Adam's voice.

"No, since you ask. I agree he needed to be punished but not that way—it looks like a crucifixion."

"It's meant to. The idea is to set an example and Private Mac-

Kenzie needed one set. He had no business interfering with the mortar team. An army is worse than useless once soldiers start getting in each other's way, refusing to follow orders." Seaton spoke severely, without his usual detached humour, and Adam looked at him inquisitively, wondering if it was only annoyance with Davy that had sparked the outburst.

"The point is we need to follow the chain of command even when we disagree with what we're being told," Seaton went on after a moment, speaking more slowly and reflectively. "We all have to understand that it's only the generals who have the full picture. But that's not to say it isn't hard sometimes, damnably hard, not to ask questions, not to argue. If I'm not careful, I could easily be the next one on the gun wheel," he said ruefully.

"Why? What is it you disagree with?" asked Adam, leaning across the table, his curiosity inflamed.

Seaton didn't answer. He looked as though he was wrestling with himself, trying to make a decision.

"Seaton, you know you can trust me," said Adam. "Whatever you say here goes no further. It's about the Push, isn't it?"

Seaton nodded.

"You don't agree with the tactics. Is that it?"

"I think they're a gamble. They're predicated on a single article of faith: that our guns can knock the Boche out, destroy their machine-gun emplacements and smash their wire, so there's nothing left and we can walk across no man's land laden down with equipment. And I'm not sure the guns can do all that. The pillboxes are concrete and the wire is high and deep and well maintained—you know how thorough and methodical the Germans are. However many shells we fire, it's going to be damned hard to demolish their defences with shrapnel and high explosive."

"So what would you have us do instead?"

"Maybe follow Private Dawes's advice," said Seaton with a smile. "Dig saps, get closer to their wire, rush them, keep them guessing. But those tactics require initiative and variation from one sector to the next. And that's what the generals most want to avoid. They don't trust us. That's the problem: we're a new army, civilians in uniform, with no battle experience, and so they insist on everything being rigid and methodical and slow and over-planned."

Seaton sighed and filled their glasses. He had drunk far more than Adam but as always showed no sign of inebriation.

"I hope I'm wrong," he said. "I may well be. From what I can gather the artillery has more guns and shells piled up out here than any army has ever had in the history of warfare . . . And I know that the war's affecting my judgement. I sleep less and I worry a great deal more than I used to," he went on in a quieter voice, looking out into the darkening garden as if he was probing the secret corners of his mind. "It's inevitable: it does that to everyone, but I've been out here for nearly two years now and I've seen things I never thought I'd see, and each battle is harder than the last. I lost the men I used to command and I don't want to lose these ones. They're numbers to Haig and Rawlinson. They have to be. It's not their fault. They're commanding hundreds of thousands of troops, but to me, to you, they're very real. And they're like children, Adam. Don't you feel that sometimes? You saw them in the baths."

"And the brothel," said Adam.

"Yes, the brothel too. They go there like boys playing truant from school, looking for a thrill. I read their letters—they're child-like, innocent. Almost every one of them—asking for plum cakes and underpants. Laboriously written words, shaping their letters like they were taught in school. And not complaining, never saying what the war's really like. They're the salt of the earth, and we are being told to send them over the top to walk across no man's land with their packs on their backs. It breaks my heart, Adam. Or what's left of it."

Adam had never seen his friend speak so passionately. Without irony, without detachment, Seaton seemed a different person, worn down, grown old before his time.

"Is there anything we can do?" asked Adam. "Our battalion, I mean."

"Perhaps. The colonel has the same worries I do, but he's old school, likes to do things by the book. So we shall see. Thank you for listening, old man," said Seaton, putting out his hand to gently touch Adam on the shoulder. "It helps to talk sometimes. More than you can imagine. I'm glad you're here, although I also wish you weren't." He laughed and filled their glasses one last time.

Chapter Twenty-One

On their last night in the billets the platoon pulled all the chicken-wire beds out of the barn and piled them in the square close to the farm's manure pile. They hung paper streamers from the rafters and blankets on the walls and made a stage from long trestle tables pushed together, with footlights made from candles sticking up out of biscuit tins.

Davy, who seemed at least temporarily to have recovered his good spirits after his visit to the brothel, borrowed a white tie and tails from one of the officers and performed "Burlington Bertie from Bow," complete with an oversized monocle that kept falling off as he sang:

"I'm Burlington Bertie, I rise at ten thirty,
Then Buckingham Palace I view.
I stand in the yard while they're changing the guard
And the King shouts across, 'Toodle oo!'"

And then, dashing back behind a screen improvised from two army groundsheets he emerged with Luke, covered in greasepaint and dressed in wrap-around skirts with identical pink blouses filled up with quantities of newspaper to provide cleavage. They introduced themselves as two virgin sisters, Marjorie and Gracie Fewclothes, and performed a slow striptease, accompanied by Ernest on a piano that the troops had requisitioned from the enraged but powerless owners of the farm.

The entertainment was as bad as it was bawdy but that just made Adam and the rest of the platoon laugh even more, caught up in a contagious hysteria that hurt their ribs and brought tears to their eyes.

Then at the end, just when they thought it was over, Harry came out on to the stage with his violin and played "Keep the Home Fires Burning" and they all sang together as one, thinking of the homes and the families they'd left behind, and their voices carried out through the open doors of the barn and rose up into the warm Picardy night like a prayer. And afterwards they all sat silent for a minute, each lost in their own thoughts, before they got up and started clearing everything away.

They left the next afternoon, but not marching this time. The army had laid on thirty buses for the battalion and the wartime khaki paint was chipping off some of them so you could see the old red underneath. They still had some of their peacetime signs inside: "London General Omnibus Company" and "Beware of Pickpockets Male and Female," and in Adam's bus there was a working conductor's bell at the back that Davy took possession of as they were clambering on to the platform.

"All aboard," he shouted, ringing the bell like a man possessed. "Next stop Berlin!"

"I'll have a return ticket," said Adam, glancing back over his shoulder at the quiet unspoilt village that they were leaving behind.

"No chance o' that, sir," said Davy, quick with his reply. "Only one way on this bus today." He laughed but no one joined in. They all knew which way they were going.

The windows in the bottom of the bus were boarded up, making the interior dark and oppressive, and so Adam and his section went up the spiral staircase to the upper level where the wooden seats were open to the elements and they could look out over the flat countryside. Everywhere there was activity. From their high vantage point they could see pioneer battalions dotted around the flat land, laying railway track and digging wells and labouring on the roads, widening and strengthening them with heavier chalk that had been brought over from Cornwall and the Channel Islands. It was vital work: the roads were collapsing under the weight of the endless traffic: artillery limbers and ration carts and ammunition wagons and motor lorries going up to the lines and then returning to bases near the coast to pick up more supplies.

The buses had seen better days since they trundled round the streets of London before the war and they weren't made to carry this number of soldiers laden down with all their equipment. In Adam's bus the suspension was constantly threatening to give way as they jolted over the potholes and they lurched dangerously to the side every time the bus went around a corner, raising a collective sigh of relief as it righted itself again, like a drunken man pulling back at the last minute from the edge of a precipice.

At night it was even more frightening as they had to keep down low in their seats, holding their rifles across their knees to avoid getting them caught in the telephone wires that criss-crossed the road. And they shivered in the cold as the line of buses crawled along at a snail's pace and the guns flashed up ahead of them, booming out a welcome.

They reached the village that was to be their billet just as the dawn was breaking. It was very different from the virgin countryside they had left behind. The inhabitants had fled the fighting at the start of the war and the few houses that had escaped shellfire since then contained evidence of their rapid departure: drawers tumbled out on to floors; dirty discarded clothing thrown around; books pulled from shelves and now half-eaten by mice. The church in the centre of the village was a shattered ruin open to the sky and a large family tomb with pride of place in the graveyard had exploded under a direct hit, scattering the bones of the dead far and wide through the overgrown grass and weeds.

They were close to the rear guns and the noise of the firing carried on sporadically all the time, interrupted by the screech of incoming shells from the German counter-batteries which made the ground tremble with violent explosions, and at night the veil of darkness was sometimes rent aside by star shells that sent the shadows of the broken buildings moving like ghosts across the deserted roads and pavements as their lights rose and fell. But no one was there to see. From dusk to dawn the soldiers were hard at work performing a series of back-breaking tasks that left them passed out with exhaustion through most of the day. Some nights they helped to dig assembly trenches behind the front line but mostly they were carriers, hauling pickets and shovels and duckboards and rolls of barbed wire up to the front line, and even worse, although the distance was less, staggering under the weight of sixty-pound shells that needed to be piled in pits beside the waiting guns.

The work went on night after night without respite. And the soldiers complained bitterly, grumbling about the strikers back home who wanted five times the money they were getting for doing the same kind of work, and the conscientious objectors who hadn't the guts to do their share, and carping about the new tight-fitting steel helmets that pressed down on their scalps and made them want to scratch the whole time.

Everyone complained but Davy complained the most of all. He hadn't been the same since the field punishment. Sometimes his good humour returned in flashes, as at the concert party or when they boarded the bus, but such moments were few and far between and his bitterness seemed to grow with every day that passed. He hated the fatigues and when he was offered an alternative he jumped at the chance.

The staff wanted information: about gaps in the German wire, about the depth and strength of their dugouts, about the disposition of their forward guns. Most of all they wanted prisoners, preferably officers, whom they could interrogate in the orderly room, using force if necessary, to gather intelligence about what was waiting for the troops on the other side of no man's land when zero hour came.

And they were looking for enthusiastic raiders who wouldn't flinch from doing what was needed to get them what they wanted. Because they knew that the Germans wouldn't come willingly. The raiders would have to kill some of the Boche first with bayonets and clubs and daggers until there were only one or two left who could be dragged back across no man's land.

The immaculately turned-out staff officer tasked with seeking volunteers from their battalion came to the village at dusk, and explained his purpose in a hearty "up and at 'em" voice that reminded Adam of the public schoolboys he'd found so irritating at Oxford. Gesturing extravagantly with his swagger stick, he made the raid sound like a bit of sport, a chance to bowl a yorker and catch the Hun unawares, daydreaming in front of his wicket. The men heard him out in silence.

At the end he asked for volunteers and promised whoever raised their hands that they would be exempted from fatigues for a week and given a weekend pass as well. Back to the estaminets, back to Madame Prudhomme's brothel—Davy didn't even hesitate. And where Davy went, Harry had to go too. Adam saw how miserable he was and tried to talk him out of it. But it was useless, just as it had been on that morning in Gratton after war was declared when they'd cycled up the hill to the recruitment office. Harry's response was exactly the same, word for word, as it had been two years before: *'E's my brother. I can't let 'im go on 'is own.*

"What about the rest o' you?" asked Davy, looking round at his friends. "Where's your sense of adventure?"

"I left it be'ind in Blighty. In a box wi' me civvy clothes," said Rawdon. And Luke and Ernest grinned sheepishly and turned away, joining Rawdon in picking up the evening's allotment of sandbags to take up to the front line.

Davy didn't come back. His brother did, but he was the lone survivor of the ten who had set out. He was cut and confused and shaking and frightened, and he was lucky not to have been shot by the nervous sentry when he couldn't remember the password and just kept calling out his name and the fact that he was a Tommy.

They took him back behind the lines and gave him a cup of tea laced with rum, and then put him at a trestle table in a tent at battalion HQ with Seaton, his company commander, and a staff officer who had ridden over from division to ask him questions. The officer had a crown on the right sleeve of his tunic but his left sleeve was empty where the arm had been amputated below the shoulder.

To begin with, Harry told them, it had gone like a dream—they hadn't made a sound as they crept through the long grass, following a straight line from their jumping-off point. There were only two bands of wire to be cut, not three as they'd expected, and they'd achieved complete surprise when they rushed the sentries behind the parapet on the section of trench they'd targeted, which stuck out a bit into no man's land. One of them they'd stabbed but the other one was just knocked out and they could have just stopped and brought him back if the subaltern in charge hadn't got greedy and insisted on looking round.

"I suppose it wasn't 'is fault—'e said you wanted an officer," said Harry, shooting an angry look at his inquisitors across the table. "An' so we started lookin' around an' suddenly all these Jerries came chargin' out o' this dugout up ahead o' us. There was lots of 'em, a lot more'n us, and they was firing their rifles and throwin' bombs, an' we 'ad to go back; we didn't 'ave any choice. An' then they was behind us as well!"

"So you surrendered?" asked the staff officer. He spoke with an upper-class drawl and there was a hint of disdain in his voice.

"Yeah, those of us that were left. About 'alf got 'it afore we could get our 'ands up. Davy too—'e was next to me an' 'e fell. I think 'e was dyin'—I could 'ear the blood in 'is throat." Harry's voice broke and he started crying.

"They were twins," said Seaton.

"I'm sorry to hear that," said the staff officer, who didn't seem sorry at all. "What happened next?" he asked. He was becoming impatient, tapping the side of his shining black boot with his silver-tipped bamboo swagger stick.

"They shoved us down in this dugout," said Harry, making an effort to pull himself together. "An' I ain't niver seen anythin' like it. It was thirty or forty feet down these zigzaggin' stairs an' it was made o' concrete; everythin' was made of concrete. An' they 'ad everythin' you can imagine in there: bunk beds—rows of 'em, an' floorboards an' a stove an' electric lights. Yeah, I swear to you, sir: electric lights."

"You don't need to swear," said the staff officer irritably. "I believe you. You're not the first to tell me about their dugouts. But what I don't quite understand is how you got out when all the rest of your party are still over there. Can you explain that to us, private?"

"There was another way out. That's 'ow," said Harry, responding defiantly to the note of suspicion implicit in the officer's question. "There was five, maybe six o' us in there, pressed up between these bunks, an' this Jerry, 'e was shoutin' at Sergeant Blake an' slappin' 'im across the face with 'is glove. An' I was scared what 'e was goin' to do next so I backed away into this curtain behind me an' 'fore I knew it I was in this other room. It was like some kind o' command post . . ."

"How do you mean: *command post?*" asked the staff officer, leaning forward, suddenly excited. "Describe it, man. Tell us what was in it."

"I dunno. It's hard—I wasn't in there more'n a minute," said Harry, sounding nervous.

"Try!" snapped the staff officer. "You said there was electric light."

"Yeah. Well, there was maps on the walls an' a telephone an' papers—there were a ton of papers. I remember that."

"Was there anyone in there?"

"No. But I could hear the shoutin' from next door an' it was gettin' louder, so I looked round an' saw another curtain, an' behind it there was this passage an' these steps. Concrete like the first ones. An' they brought me out further down the trench. I think maybe that's where the Jerries came from afore when they 'ad us surrounded. An' there was no one there."

"No one there! No sentries—no one at all?"

Harry shook his head. "I reckon maybe they'd all gone down in the dugout to watch what was 'appenin' with the int-erro-gation." He made hard work of the unfamiliar word but he seemed determined to say it, perhaps to imply resentment at the way he was being interrogated now. "Any road, I got up on the fire-step an' through the wire where we'd cut it an' back here, an' . . ." Harry hesitated before going on.

"Yes?" said the staff officer, impatient again.

"Well, I don't know 'ow to properly say this, sir, but I want to go back."

"*Go back!* Why on earth would you want to do that?" asked the staff officer, astonished. It was the last thing he'd expected Harry to say.

"Because o' what they did to my brother, sir. Like Cap'n Scarsdale said, 'e was my twin an' I'd like to get even."

"I see. Well, that certainly does you credit, private," said the staff officer, looking at Harry with new eyes. He was impressed: it took a lot of guts to volunteer to go back across no man's land a second time, particularly after you'd come off worst in a fire-fight.

"I could find my way back, sir. An' I can get inside that command post—it looked like it 'ad stuff in there you might be interested in," said Harry. There was an eager tone to his voice that made Seaton look at him askance. He'd been so tearful and shaken up before and now he was desperate to go back. But he had lost his brother, his twin brother, Seaton told himself. That was enough to make anyone act a little strange.

"I'm prepared to go too, sir," said Seaton quietly. "I've been across before. I know what to expect."

The staff officer looked over at Seaton but didn't respond straight-away. It was as if he was appraising him, deciding which way to go.

"Very well, captain," he said finally. "You can pick your own team, but no more than five or six. Any more than that and the Boche will hear you coming. After what's happened they'll be doubly on their guard."

"Should we wait a few days?" asked Seaton. "Let them relax a little?"

"We don't have days. Time is of the essence," said the staff offi-cer testily, but then thought better of his response. "Two," he said, holding up the index and middle fingers of his only hand. "And don't worry about prisoners; just get in there, pick up everything you can find in this command post and bring it straight back. Understood?"

"Yes, sir," said Seaton.

The staff officer pushed back his chair and got up from the table and the others followed suit. "Good luck," he said, saluted smartly and, pulling back the flap of the tent, he was gone.

Harry followed, but Seaton lingered behind, drawing intricate patterns on the back of an old memorandum while stroking his chin with his left forefinger. Eventually he seemed to come to a decision and rapidly wrote down a list of names on a fresh sheet of paper. And then, going outside, he handed it to his batman and told him to go and round them up.

Adam's was the first name on the list and he was the first to arrive.

"I have something to tell you—it's not good news," said Seaton, once they had sat down.

"About Davy MacKenzie?" asked Adam. "I already know."

"How?" asked Seaton, surprised.

"Harry was telling us when I got your summons."

"That was quick. He didn't leave here much more than an hour ago."

"Yes, he was out of breath; crying too. He says he's going back over there with you to show you some kind of command post he found, but he doesn't want us to go. He says it's too dangerous. He was trying to make us promise; the others did but I refused."

"Why?"

"Because I feel responsible. The twins are in my section. I think I should have gone too the first time—"

"Which is stupid," said Seaton, sounding annoyed. "You need to start thinking more clearly. If you'd gone, you'd probably be dead; and if not dead, a prisoner, which amounts to the same thing as far as your usefulness to the army is concerned. And Private MacKenzie has no business trying to tell soldiers in this battalion what to do. He's doing just what his brother did: interfering with the chain of command. I hope you told him that?"

"No, I didn't," said Adam, upset by Seaton's angry tone. "There wasn't any time and he's just lost his twin brother, for Christ's sake."

Seaton was about to respond, but then thought better of it and took a deep breath instead. "I'm sorry, Adam," he said. "I'm worried about Private MacKenzie's emotional state and I'm taking it out on you. He's a liability we can't afford unless he can get a grip on himself, but we can't go without him because he's the only one who knows where to go. *If* he knows . . ."

"What do you mean?"

"I don't know," said Seaton uncertainly. "I suppose I'm just a little surprised that he's so keen to go back over there after what's happened. That's all. Do you trust him?"

"Yes," said Adam without hesitating. "And I want to go too. Isn't that why you called me here?"

"Yes," said Seaton. "I need men I can trust and you were the first name on my list so thank you for volunteering. It makes me feel a little better about the task ahead. We have two days before we go, so the first thing you can do is try to calm MacKenzie down. We'll need cool heads and steady hands out there if we're to have any chance of success."

Chapter Twenty-Two

They went up into the front line a few hours before they were due to go out. To complete their group Seaton had selected two privates, Neville and Earle whom Adam knew by sight—strong, resourceful men who had been on raids before, and Sergeant Duke who had played county cricket before the war and was reputed to be able to throw a Mills bomb further than anyone else in the New Army.

They'd all trained together behind the lines the night before, wriggling across a field in zigzag lines so as not to leave a straight furrow in the grass that the Germans could see if a flare went up, and watching each other's backs as they ran down steps and round corners, lighting their way with electric torches tied with black insulating tape to the barrels of their rifles.

And then Seaton had sat them down and made Harry tell them about the German trench and the concrete dugout and the command post and the two entrances and exits. Not once but over and over again until he was hoarse, and they had memorized every last detail.

Now, sitting with their backs to the wall of the front-line trench, they blackened their faces with burnt cork and made knee protectors out of old socks, and, on Seaton's instructions, removed their sleeve patches and identity tags. They were wearing black balaclavas instead of caps and Seaton had made sure they all had gloves and wire cutters to take with them.

Adam and Harry and Neville carried rifles with fixed bayonets and the sergeant and Seaton had bombs in bandoliers. Seaton also had his revolver and Earle, a taciturn man with a thin, cruel mouth who had been trained in hand-to-hand combat, was armed with a trench dagger and a knobkerrie, a frightening weapon consisting of a spiked iron ball at the end of a club lovingly fashioned from an entrenching tool handle. Each of them wore an empty sandbag around their necks in which to bring back the maps and documents that were the objectives of the raid.

"The guns are a last resort," said Seaton. "I hope we don't have to use them because as soon as we do our chances of accomplishing our mission become very slim indeed. And remember: two blasts on my whistle and we get the hell out of there."

In the gathering twilight they took it in turns to gaze through Seaton's box periscope at the German trenches and the jutting-out section opposite that was their target. They knew that the enemy would have repaired their wire after the first raid and, following instructions from the staff, the artillery had pounded the entire sector with shrapnel shells earlier in the day. Seaton hoped that the hurricane bombardment would have done at least some damage, although there was no way for them to know the full extent until they actually reached the wire and tried to find a way through.

In front, the browning summer grass and weeds in no man's land had grown tall, interspersed with splashes of red poppies and pale blue cornflowers and the stumps of blasted leafless trees. Here and there, barren grey-white craters stood out in the landscape where recent shells had exploded and there hadn't been time for the vegetation to grow back. The soldiers knew that out of sight, beneath the grass, the entire surface of the land was pockmarked like the face of the moon and covered with the debris of war: corrugated iron, rusted wire, empty tins and discarded weapons—and the remains of the dead blown out of their shallow graves by falling random shells. This was the terrain that they were going to have to cross, slithering on their stomachs like snakes, never making a sound whatever they encountered.

They were due to go at midnight and as the final hours passed, Harry became more and more tense, repeatedly visiting the latrine cut into the side of the trench several bays away from where the group was sitting. Adam asked if he could give him rum, but Seaton forbade it. "We'll never get him across if he's drunk," he said. "If he's just nervous we've got a chance."

The weather at least was on their side: it was an overcast night with the new moon hidden behind a dense bank of clouds—they couldn't have asked for better conditions. And there was little or no firing in their sector until the night was suddenly lit up for a few seconds as two green flares arrowed up into the sky over no man's land, illuminating the desolation in a sickly lurid light. They had been fired from somewhere in their trench—the waiting soldiers had heard the reports of the Very pistol close by but no one knew who was responsible. Seaton looked at his watch: it was exactly half past eleven.

Finally they moved off, crawling through the zigzag gaps that had been cut in their wire in preparation and then, once they'd got beyond the last belt, they waited for several minutes, getting used to the darkness, before Seaton set off again with Neville beside him and Harry just behind. Earle and the sergeant were over to the right and Adam was at the back. There was less than two hundred yards to the German wire but their progress was painfully slow as they picked their way laboriously through the shell holes. Halfway across, Adam felt something hard and bony under his hands and realized to his horror that he was holding the rib cage of a man, his skin picked clean by the scavenging rats that he could hear squeaking in the grass all around. He felt sick but swallowed back hard on the bile rising in his throat, remembering Seaton's injunction against making any noise.

Up ahead, Adam could hear the faint sound of cutters being used as Seaton, Neville and the sergeant began to work their way patiently through the German wire. And then all at once they stopped. In the darkness up ahead a man had coughed. Not one of their own because the cough was immediately followed by an angry German voice whispering: *"Seien Sie still! Sie werden Sie sonst hören!"* ("Be quiet! They will hear you!)." Immediately Seaton blew his whistle and began running back with his head down. He was pulling Harry along beside him, but Harry was resisting and Adam heard him yell: "Davy, are you there? Davy?" His voice was wild, an inhuman animal cry that stopped in his throat when Seaton hooked round with his right fist and punched him hard in the face.

The Germans were firing and Adam was running too. He'd thrown away his rifle. A white flare shot up into the sky, illuminating everything: the gap in the British wire a few yards away; Seaton and Neville pulling Harry along between them; and behind, from where they'd come from a voice—it sounded like Earle's—screaming: "I can't. You're caught! You're fucking caught!"

A bullet whisked past Adam's head as he turned to look back and he froze, remembering almost too late what Seaton had told him the night before—that it's movement that gets you killed in the light. If you stayed perfectly still you could be a tree or a post, but as soon as you moved you became a target. Back in front of the German trenches Sergeant Duke was throwing Mills bombs one after another in a constant precise stream into the German trench, which was being rocked by a series of explosions, while Earle pulled vainly at Duke's legs, which were enmeshed in the half-cut wire. Until suddenly the explosions ceased as first one bullet and then another ripped through the sergeant's body, throwing him sideways on to an intact section of wire which held him still elevated with his head curiously intact under the balaclava, staring at the enemy as he spilled his guts down on to the ground.

It was like a film of hell lasting only a few seconds as the flare burnt up in the sky like a magnesium flash and the darkness returned, more intense than before, and Adam ran forward, cutting himself on the broken strands of the British wire as he chased Seaton's torch beam over the parapet and down into the safety of the trench below.

He lay not moving, half-conscious and confused. Inside his head he could hear his heartbeat pounding louder than the voices of the soldiers. Everything hurt; his lungs felt as though they were going to burst and his breath came in gasps. Someone lifted him and he drank water and the people around him drifted into focus. Seaton was shouting at Harry. He had never seen Seaton lose his temper before but now he was wild with rage. And Harry was whimpering with his back to the parapet wall, and his face was a mad mix of colours blotched with the tears that were streaming down his cheeks: black from the cork, green from the grass and red with stained blood around the mouth where Seaton had punched him out in no man's land.

Seaton was threatening to punch him again. He clenched his fist and pulled back his arm but then at the last minute he turned away and walked down to the traverse, drawing deep breaths; and when he came back, he was rigidly composed and his voice was iron.

"They knew we were coming, didn't they?" he said. "That's why you fired the signal flare."

Harry shook his head, but then, looking up into Seaton's piercing blue eyes, he nodded.

"What did they tell you?"

"That they'd let Davy go," Harry whispered. It was as if he was under a spell, unable to break free of Seaton's stare.

"So he wasn't hurt?"

"No. But they said they would if I didn't—" He broke off, and Adam could see that his hands were shaking.

"Didn't what?"

"Bring you, bring others."

"But not your friends?" demanded Seaton. "You made them promise not to go, didn't you?"

Harry said nothing.

"Because they mattered, didn't they? Not like Sergeant Duke hanging on their wire riddled with bullet holes; not like Private Earle who's still out there somewhere. They didn't matter because they're nothing; nothing . . ." Seaton fired the words at Harry as if he was lashing him with a whip: sharp, harsh phrases that made Harry wince as if he'd been physically struck.

" 'E's my twin," said Harry. He looked weak, beaten. He reminded Adam of an old mongrel dog that had hung around the street in Islington when he was a child. The shopkeepers had kicked the animal whenever it got close until it slunk away,

But Harry was not going to be allowed to slink away. Two red-cap military policemen were waiting for him when they got back to the reserve line and took him away in a mud-spattered truck. And

Adam didn't see him again until he was called as a witness at the court martial.

It was held in the main classroom of a school that had been taken over by brigade as their administrative headquarters—one of the few buildings in Albert that had hitherto escaped shell damage. Adam waited, sitting on a low bench in a corridor outside while Seaton gave his evidence, turning his service cap over and over in his hands. Facing him, outside the half-open window, there was a playground with a rusty swing and a metal slide that had fallen over on to its side, but no children had played out there since the beginning of the war and the sound of their laughter had been replaced by the steady boom of the guns.

Adam fervently wished he could be anywhere else apart from where he was—even the worst places: in the front line under fire or carrying sacks of earth out of the candlelit mine shafts that the barefoot sapper companies were tunnelling under the German lines in preparation for the big day; anywhere but here, participating in the cold grim process of putting Harry MacKenzie to death. Because that was where this would end. Adam was sure of it. Harry had committed treason—Sergeant Duke's blood was on his hands and Earle's would have been too if he hadn't miraculously found his way back after a night spent lying flat on his face in a shell crater while machine-gun bullets flew over his head. Harry richly deserved the ultimate punishment for what he'd done. But Adam just didn't want to be part of it. That was all.

The door opened and he put on his service cap and went into the courtroom and took the oath. To his right, the three judges sat at school desks which had been moved up on to the teacher's dais. They were slightly too small for them, making the judges look incongruous in the setting. On the wall behind them was a clean blackboard once used for teaching algebra to the schoolchildren and above that in black Gothic letters running along the cornice the motto of the French Republic: "*Liberté, Egalité, Fraternité.*"

The judges seemed impassive, gazing out over Harry's head as he sat slumped in a chair facing them. Adam remembered the intent, entranced way that Harry would play the violin, conjuring such sadness and tenderness from its strings. But now all the light seemed to have disappeared from his eyes and he didn't look at Adam as he gave his evidence or even seem to listen. He wasn't ill, he was only nineteen, and yet he looked as if he was dying, and Adam turned away, fighting a grey sadness that was settling down on his shoulders, weighing him down.

Everyone in the courtroom seemed to be simply going through the motions. Adam's evidence lasted less than five minutes. And by the end of the afternoon Harry had been unanimously convicted and sentenced to death, and a horseback messenger had been dispatched to division headquarters so that the sentence could be confirmed up through the chain of command. In capital cases the process was expedited and the execution warrant signed by Sir Douglas Haig arrived back at Albert twenty-four hours later.

There was a hut at the back of the playground that had once housed sports and gardening equipment, but now, cleared of its contents and furnished with a chair, a makeshift bed and a candle, it had been transformed into a prison cell where Harry had been kept since his arrest and where he was to spend his last night on earth in company with the brigade chaplain, Parson Vale. Outside two redcaps kept guard in the moonlight.

Seaton had been given conduct of the execution and asked to see the parson when he arrived at the school late in the evening after the news had come through that the death sentence had been confirmed.

"This may help," said Seaton, handing the parson an earthenware jar half filled with rum.

"Thank you," said the parson. "But it'll be his choice."

"Of course. I'm just saying rum may provide rather more comfort than Holy Writ for a man in Private MacKenzie's position," said Seaton, gesturing at the worn Bible in the parson's hand.

"Men can be braver than you think," said the parson.

"And weaker," said Seaton. "It was weakness that put him where he is now."

The parson nodded and turned to go but then stopped in the doorway, looking back at Seaton who had gone back to the book he had been reading before the parson came in: Hardy's *Tess of the*

D'Urbervilles. In profile his handsome face lit by the oil lamp on the table seemed so sensitive and intelligent that the parson could not reconcile it with the role of executioner that Seaton would be performing in the morning.

"Do you think this is right?" asked the parson. "I know you, Seaton. And I can't believe you do."

Seaton looked at his old friend, considering his answer. "No," he said eventually. "I think it is vile. Just like this war. But I believe it's necessary. I don't think we have any choice. Does that answer your question?"

"Yes, I suppose it does," said the parson, shaking his head.

"Good luck," said Seaton. "I don't envy you your task."

"Nor I yours," said the parson. "Nor I yours."

Seaton looked after his friend as he left with the jar of rum in one hand and his Bible in the other and smiled ruefully, thinking how far they had both come from those long-lost summer evenings in Scarsdale to arrive at a place of such desolation.

At first light Adam and his company paraded in the town square, looking up into the sightless eyes of the fallen Virgin as they marched past her on their way to the school. Five minutes later they wheeled to the right and came to silent attention in the road across from the playground where the execution was to take place. The brigadier had decreed that they should watch the condemned man die so that his death would set an example to them all.

In the front rank Adam and Luke and Rawdon had an unimpeded view. The fence around the playground had long ago disappeared and weeds were growing up through cracks in the cement. Over to the right the eight men in the firing party were standing by the rusty swing, smoking. They were facing the company and had their backs to the two redcaps standing in front of the hut at the far end where Harry was being held.

Seaton stood alone, waiting beside an iron post with a rope hanging limply down from its top. Adam had hardly noticed the pole when he had looked out into the playground before giving evidence the day before but he was certain it had been there, and he now suddenly recognized its purpose. It was part of the playground equipment: a swinging ball had once been attached to the rope and the children had hit it to each other with outstretched hands or rackets. But now it had been given a new function. It was to be the execution post with the rope serving to secure the condemned man in place.

Seaton looked at his watch and walked over to the firing party. "All right, men. We've been over this already and you know what to do, so don't miss!" he said, and his strong precise voice carried across the still air to the watching company. "It's cruel to miss. It prolongs the agony and none of us want that, now do we?"

"No, sir," said the soldiers. They saluted and picked up the rifles that were leaning against the wall of the schoolhouse and lined up, still with their backs to the pole, facing the troops out in the road. Adam could see that several of them were white in the face and that their rifles were shaking in their hands. One of the rifles contained a blank "conscience round" but none of them knew which one it was.

Behind them Seaton signalled to the redcaps to open the door of the hut. After less than a minute Parson Vale emerged, followed by Harry. He was walking in between the redcaps but then when he saw the post his legs collapsed under him and they had to haul him forward and tie him to it using a combination of the rope and some telephone cable they had brought with them. He was panting and crying but, as far as Adam could tell, he wasn't making any intelligible sounds.

Once the redcaps were done, Seaton stepped forward and pinned a piece of white cloth on the left side of Harry's tunic, and he had just finished tying the bandage round his eyes when Harry struggled and shouted: "No, I want the parson."

Seaton hesitated and then beckoned the parson forward. "Be quick," he said.

The parson went right up to Harry and put his ear to his mouth, listening, and then, putting his hands on the condemned man's shoulders, he leant forward and whispered something in his ear and kissed him on the cheek before he stepped back.

Immediately Seaton ordered the firing party to turn. In a moment they had taken up their positions with four of them kneeling in front and the other four standing behind. "Take aim," Seaton told them before issuing the final command: "Fire!"

A ragged ear-splitting volley shattered the stillness of the morning, followed by the clatter of rifles falling on the cement as the firing party dropped them to the ground and turned away. And as the cloud of smoke from the discharge dispersed the horrified company could see Harry's body writhing against the post. He could have been dead—the movement could have been a reflex action—but Seaton wasn't taking any chances and went straight over and put a revolver bullet through his heart.

Out in the road, Luke bent over and was violently sick. He looked as if he was going to fall over but Adam and Rawdon held him on his feet and pushed him forward as the sergeant major barked out the order to march away.

Behind them, a bald-headed, bespectacled doctor checked the lifeless body and then the two redcaps came and untied it from the post and wrapped it in a blanket to take away, while a third one checked the rifles to see that they had all been fired. Failure to fire was a serious offence, and the redcaps were thorough in their work.

They were quick too. Within two minutes only Seaton and the parson remained and the pool of congealing blood at the foot of the post was the only evidence of what had occurred.

"What did he say to you?" asked Seaton as they began to walk away.

"He wanted his mother to know what had happened; he wanted her to know the truth. And he thanked me for staying with him. I told him that I would see him in paradise."

"I hope you will," said Seaton thoughtfully. "I hope you will."

It was Midsummer Day, 24 June. And as the grey morning light appeared above the German lines, the British guns opened up with an intense bombardment the like of which no one had ever heard before. It was the beginning of the Battle of the Somme.

Chapter Twenty-Three

The barrage never stopped. Day after day, night after night, it continued with a ceaseless moaning roar like the breaking of an endless succession of giant waves on a beach that was forever at high tide. The enemy trenches, white chalk lines up on the hilltops, erupted in constant climbing columns of thick black smoke as the high-explosive shells crashed down upon them. The columns rose up like ragged poplar trees and mixed in the blue summer sky with the white fleecy balls detonated above ground by the shrapnel shells that the eighteen-pounder field guns were sending over to destroy the enemy wire in a hail of molten metal.

On the afternoon of the first day Adam and his section were sent up—just as they had been before—with fresh supplies of shells to feed the heavy guns in their camouflaged emplacements, dug in under barrel roofs of sandbag and grass. They watched in awe as the vast machines recoiled violently like frightened beasts and sent six-foot flames spitting out from their thick muzzles. The noise was incredible: they felt as if their eardrums were going to burst and clapped their hands over their heads, often losing their balance as they were thrown back by the rush of hot air, ending up head over heels in the huge piles of expended shell casings that surrounded the guns.

The gunners laughed and went back to their work. Stripped to the waist with bloodshot eyes and sweating faces blackened with smoke and splashed with oil, they reminded Adam of the miners back home. And neither he nor his friends took offence at the laughter. They knew it was good-natured and they were excited by what they saw.

"I wouldn't want to be Fritz right now," said Rawdon as they stumbled back to their billet. "'E's gettin' a right pastin'."

"Yeah, a few more days o' this an' there won't be nothin' left," said Luke enthusiastically. "Maybe they're right; maybe this time it *will* be different an' we can break through the bastards, go all the way to Berlin an' bring back Kaiser Bill's moustache."

"Maybe," said Ernest doubtfully. "But it's not that easy. Remember what Harry said when he came back about their dugouts being so deep and all made out of concrete. It's hard to smash up concrete from a distance even with these guns."

"'Arry was lyin'," said Luke. "Cos 'e didn't want us to go. You're always such an ol' misery, Ern. You should try to stop worryin' an' look on the bright side for once!"

Ernest said nothing. They all knew why Luke had turned on him: none of them wanted to think about Harry. Not after what they had seen that morning. But Adam didn't think that that made Ernest wrong. Harry had lied about his brother but that didn't mean he'd lied about the dugouts, and Adam remembered what Seaton had told him about the strength of the concrete pillboxes and the thickness of the German wire when they'd talked in the oyster restaurant in Amiens.

But he kept his thoughts to himself. Luke was right—there was no point in worrying. They were tiny cogs in a vast machine and there was nothing they could do to change what was going to happen. He just hoped that the generals knew what they were doing. That was all.

The next day was Sunday. In the morning their bank books were taken in and they were paid up all that they were owed and given a day's pass, a last chance to have a good time before they went up for the attack.

"No more o' your doom 'n' gloom, you 'ear me, Ern?" said Luke, clapping Ernest on the shoulder as the four friends walked up the white chalk road together in the sunshine.

Ernest smiled. It felt good to be walking away from the war and not towards it, even if it was only a very temporary reprieve.

They passed a field in which the parson was holding an open-air service, using a Vickers machine-gun chest covered with a white cloth for an altar, decorated with a vase of wild flowers and a brass cross which trembled with the reverberations from the bombardment that was as intense as ever behind them. The soldiers in the congregation were trying to sing "Nearer, My God, to Thee," but were finding it hard to raise their voices above the noise of the gunfire.

"Bloody awful choice of a song!" said Rawdon. And they all agreed, laughing to keep their spirits up.

But it was hard. Several miles further on, they came to a newly constructed casualty clearing station, a great encampment of empty green tents ready to receive the wounded from the battle. And the dead too: in the field behind, a gang of Chinese coolies was hard at work, digging mass graves.

Even Rawdon's usually inexhaustible fund of black humour was defeated by that. And they were glad when they reached the estaminet and could begin the serious business of eating platefuls of fried food and getting drunk.

They were happy for a while, but it was a forced happiness and it took all their energy and copious amounts of alcohol to maintain it. By common unspoken agreement none of them talked about the upcoming attack, which terrified them even though it would have taken torture to get any of them to admit their fear; and they were also careful to avoid the subject of the execution, even though Harry's last moments played constantly like a slow-motion horror film inside each of their heads.

But on the way back, as they walked towards the exploding horizon with the noise of the bombardment reverberating in their sore ears, they could no longer keep up the pretence.

"I 'ate bloody Seaton Scarsdale," said Luke, breaking out with a sudden bitterness. "I'd like to stick 'is revolver up against 'is heart so 'e can see what it fuckin' feels like."

"It wouldn't beat any faster," said Rawdon. "'E's got ice in 'is veins, not blood. Just like the rest of 'em—officers an' gen'lemen talkin' out o' the back of their throats and treatin' us like we're a pack o' dirty animals."

"That's not true," said Adam passionately. "Seaton cares about us. More than any of them do. I know he does."

"No, 'e doesn't," said Rawdon "You're just sayin' that cos you're 'is friend. You ain't like us."

"Don't you dare say that," said Adam, shouting now. "Not after all we've been through together, Rawdon. Seaton's a good man, the best I know. And there's nothing he wouldn't do for us. Nothing!" he finished breathlessly, surprised by the sudden force of his anger.

"Includin' puttin' a bullet through our hearts when it suits 'is purpose," said Rawdon, sticking to his guns even though he was secretly surprised by the passionate sincerity evident in Adam's reaction. "You saw 'ow he finished 'Arry off, like 'e was a fuckin' dog 'e was puttin' out o' its misery."

Luke nodded his agreement energetically. "Bastard," he said, spitting out the word between his teeth.

"He shot Harry because he wanted to spare him any more pain," said Adam, speaking slowly and firmly as he made a visible effort to regain his self-control. "Just like he took charge of the firing squad so it would all be done properly. And because he felt he had to. He needed to take responsibility for what happened on the raid. A man died because of Harry and it could easily have been more. It could have been me. Harry betrayed us; he betrayed all of us."

"Adam's right," said Ernest, coming to Adam's support. "You want to stop talking like your dad and think about what Harry did, Rawdon. And you too, Luke. What he did—it's the worst thing you can do."

Luke grunted, his handsome face set in an ugly frown of angry disagreement. "I saw what I saw," he said obdurately. "Rawdon's right—Scarsdale shot 'im like 'e was an animal. An' it made me sick." He picked up a stone and threw it hard at a chestnut tree beside the road to emphasize his point and a flock of black birds flew up out of the thick leaves into the evening sky above their heads, cawing furiously and flapping their wings before they flew away westwards in perfect formation, following the path of the setting sun.

"Lucky bastards," said Rawdon, looking back after them. But then he was quiet, walking on in thoughtful silence until they got back to the billet.

And later that evening, after they had turned in, feeling the worse for wear following their overindulgence in the afternoon, Rawdon came over and shook Adam's shoulder, asking him to go outside where they sat side by side on the grass smoking cigarettes, watching the red glow of the ends burning in the dark. They were silent as Adam waited for Rawdon to say what he wanted to say.

"I'm sorry," Rawdon said eventually and his voice was awkward: he wasn't a person who found it easy to apologize. "Sorry about what I said about you not bein' one o' us. I don't think that any more an' I shouldn't 'ave said it."

"It's fine," said Adam, touched by the apology. It meant a great deal to him but he knew better than to embarrass Rawdon by telling him so.

"You're wrong about Seaton," he went on quietly after a moment. "He does care about us. More than you can imagine. I think it's what keeps him going, even though the war is eating him up. Just like it's eating all of us, I suppose. It's just he's been here a lot longer than we have."

"All right," said Rawdon. Just that; nothing more. But there was peace between them at last as they sat and smoked, listening to the ceaseless roar of the guns.

Two days later they were told they were going up at nightfall. All except Ernest: General Rawlinson had decreed that 10 per cent of each engaged battalion was to remain behind with the transport and Ernest had been one of the names selected.

"Well done, mate!" said Rawdon. "I suppose you been bribin' the higher-ups with those lovely fruit cakes your mother sends thee."

"It's not what I wanted," said Ernest uncomfortably. "It seems wrong after all we've been through together—" He broke off, searching for the right words.

"Don't be stupid! It's good luck. That's what it is, so don't you go complainin' about it!" said Luke. "You'll be keepin' the 'ome fires burnin' while we're up bayonetin' the Boche. An' you can stand us all drinks when we get back."

If we get back, was the thought in everyone's minds, but no one said it. And the home fires made them think of Harry again, playing his violin on that last night at the concert party before they left the training billets. And on other nights too—his music rising so sweetly into the darkness, making them feel that there was more to life than shells and rats and gas and chloride of lime. They hated that they'd had to see him die. And at their own company's hands—whether they liked it or not they all felt complicit in his death, which was of course exactly what the brigadier had intended when he'd ordered them to watch his execution.

They were in a new billet: a barn full of old straw which they thought more comfortable than four-poster beds; not that any of them except Adam had ever slept in one. A hard rain was pouring down out of a leaden sky, streaming from the gutters and creating a miniature black lake in a Jack Johnson shell hole outside the open door. The corpse of a drowned rat bobbed up and down on the surface, driven this way and that by the weight of the raindrops.

There was thunder in the air and lightning too but it was impossible to tell them apart from the boom and explosive flashes of the barrage: the natural and unnatural melded together in a *Götterdämmerung* of fire and blast.

It was late afternoon and they were about to begin moving out when two postal orderlies appeared with sacks of mail and began distributing them among the men. A great cheer went up followed by an even greater one when it turned out that Ernest had received another of his mother's famous cakes, which he immediately shared out with the group. It was a rule they had: everything edible or smokable was always divided up between them on strictly equal lines regardless of who was the actual recipient.

They sat eating and reading their letters in companionable silence. Adam had one from Miriam—it hurt him to open it, thinking of her beautiful hands that had sealed it tight. She wrote:

> *I miss you more each day, and pray constantly for your safe return. Sometimes when I am in the church arranging the flowers, I look round and think that you might be there, waiting, watching in the shadows as you were once before. Oh, what a fool I was to have pushed you away when we could have been together all that time! But I didn't know then what I know now: that every day is precious because calamity waits unseen around the corner.*
>
> *Oh, how I long to see you again and hold your hands in mine . . .*

Adam looked up from the letter, gazing out into the wet gloom. It hurt him to think of Miriam; it hurt him to read what she wrote. Because he loved her and deep down he didn't think he would ever see her again.

And he didn't know how to respond. The war was a barrier between them. He couldn't tell her about Harry writhing against the post or the sick fear they were all feeling in the pits of their stomachs but wouldn't admit to; he couldn't tell her the truth but not to do so was to lie. And so he got a field postcard from the orderly and began rapidly crossing out the sentences that didn't apply until at the end he was left with just three: "I am quite well. I have received your letter dated June 22nd. Letter follows at first opportunity. Signed: Adam Raine, Lance Corporal."

He looked down at the card, feeling sad and ashamed. But it was the best he could do and he gave it to the orderly to post.

Leaving Ernest and the chosen few behind, they formed up outside and began to march. The storm had given way at least for now to a steadier rain which dripped down heavily from the black shadowy trees beside the road. Everything was dark and sodden and smelt of wet earth, and the rainwater soaked their puttees and got into their boots as they splashed through the puddles. And it was even worse when the motor lorries passed by, sending sprays of slush flying up over the soldiers' heads as their wheels bounced through the endless

potholes in the road. The company vented their frustration by cursing the drivers and launched into new verses of "Do Your Balls Hang
Low" to keep up their spirits, yelling out the words above the gunfire
and adding a musical backing during a short rest stop by hammering
on their biscuit tins:

> "Do they rattle when you walk?
> Do they jingle when you talk?
> Can you sling them on your shoulder
> Like a lousy fucking soldier?
> Do your balls hang low?"

They halted at the divisional assembly area and formed up in squares
to listen to a general with a thick handlebar moustache bawling at
them through a megaphone.

"Listen to the guns, boys," he shouted. "And imagine what it's
like for the Hun. By the time you go over the top the only ones left
will be stark raving mad. All you'll have to do is walk over there and
take possession, just like you did in training. And the field kitchens
will follow with a good hot meal."

But within half an hour it became apparent that there was going
to be at least one significant difference from training. As they passed
the forward dumps, they were issued with more and more equipment:
extra grenades and ammunition; wire cutters and empty sandbags; a
flare; and finally either a spade or a pickaxe. They were already carrying rifles and bayonets, gas masks in satchels, a haversack with double
rations, a waterproof groundsheet and a field dressing, and now they
staggered forward with at least seventy pounds piled on their backs.

"We're not soldiers; we're bloody railway porters. That's what we
are," said Rawdon, grumbling to himself. "So I 'ope that ol' walrus
'as got it right and there aren't goin' to be any of the square 'eads left
or we'll be sittin' ducks when we go over the top. They'll pick us off
like apples in a fuckin' barrel."

"Knock it off, Rawdon. You're not helpin'," said Luke, too weary
and weighed down to argue.

They stopped for a final rest before entering the communication trenches. A field kitchen appeared as if by magic and gave them hot tea and bacon sandwiches, which they ate sitting on their waterproof groundsheets, leaning back against their packs, while the falling rain beat a monotonous tattoo on their steel helmets. And then, as they fell back in, they looked longingly after the horse-drawn wagons as they moved away down the road, wishing that they were going back too instead of carrying on into the inferno up ahead.

Once in the trenches they were forced into Indian file, groping their way forward in the darkness like blind men with their hands on the back of the packs of the man in front. They'd experienced this before but not when the rains had turned the chalk to mud. Under their feet the duckboards were slipping and sliding in all directions, while the telephone cables had come loose from the crumbling walls, creating invisible trip hazards. Soldiers were constantly falling over and when one fell, those behind him fell too, going over like nine-pins. And then it was hard for them to get back on their feet as they scrabbled about in the slippery mud and struggled to lift their massive packs back up on to their shoulders.

Several times too they lost their way and had to be sent back, only to collide with other companies coming up behind them. They vented their frustration with volleys of curses and swayed and stumbled and staggered on in a spiritless shambles for what seemed like hours until they finally arrived at their destination: a quagmire of liquid mud and collapsing parapets that had been a perfectly service-able front-line trench before the storm intervened.

The soldiers in Adam's company were set to work straightaway pumping out the rainwater. It was a thankless task and they only started to win the battle when the rain began to die away in the morning. They were exhausted but in rest periods they had to sleep standing up as they couldn't lie or even sit down on the flooded floor. And their toes were tingling and itching as they began to suffer the first stages of trench foot. The NCOs made them change their socks and grease their red swollen feet every eight hours but their orders weren't popular: it hurt the men to take off their boots and it was agony to put them back on. And then their feet were wet again as soon as they put them to the ground.

They were hungry too. The hot food they had been promised got lost somewhere in the chaos of the communication trenches and they had to make do with cold Maconochie tins—a thin stew of tasteless turnips, potatoes and carrots with a few bits of fat and grey meat floating at the top that they had to force themselves to eat, washing away the taste with cups of petrol-flavoured water.

Cold, wet, hungry, tired and facing the imminent prospect of going over the top, the soldiers' only consolation was that the Boche were having an even worse time of it on the other side of no man's land. The weather hadn't stopped the artillery from continuing the bombardment and through the bleary wet mirrors of the trench periscopes the troops looked out at a curtain of white dust floating permanently above the pulverized chalk. They told themselves that their generals had to be right: nothing could survive such an onslaught.

But their colonel was less sure. Like Seaton, he felt a passionate sense of responsibility towards his men and worried constantly that the Germans were somehow surviving the bombardment deep in their dugouts and that their wire was still intact. He wandered through the trenches, getting in everyone's way, peering out through loopholes and periscopes in a vain effort to see what was happening, and sent a runner back to brigade with a carefully worded letter expressing his anxiety. But the brigadier gave it short shrift, quoting in response a recently issued directive from General Rawlinson: "All criticism by subordinates . . . of orders received from superior authority will, in the end, recoil on the heads of the critics."

"They think I'm windy," the colonel complained to Seaton back at battalion HQ. "But I just want to know what to expect. Is that so much to ask? The staff keeps sending me endless memos. Look, these three have come through in the last hour," he said, picking the pieces of paper up from the makeshift table and reading them out loud: " 'Soldiers must keep the tin stars on their backs visible at all times to enable aeroplanes and artillery observers to identify their positions'; 'Soldiers will fire one white flare if they are stopped for any reason and three white flares when they reach their objectives.' The last one's about heliographs. You see what I mean—everything's been prepared down to the last detail; they're leaving nothing to chance. Except whether the bombardment's actually working. They never say anything about that."

But clearly the generals did have some doubts because at the beginning of the afternoon an order came through postponing the push by forty-eight hours from Thursday until Saturday, the first of July. Zero hour was fixed for seven thirty in the morning.

Chapter Twenty-Four

Daylight! We're still going in daylight," said the colonel, shaking his head in disbelief. "I hope to God they know what they're doing."

"Perhaps the delay will help," said Seaton. "If you can get the gunners to lift the barrage in our sector I can take a party across and look at the wire; and we can cut it if it needs cutting."

"Yes," said the colonel, clapping Seaton on the back. "That's the most sensible suggestion I've heard in a week. I can get the gunners to do that; I'll go back there and make them if I have to."

They went at midnight. Seaton had selected the same people who had been on the disastrous raid with Harry on the basis that they would know what they were doing, and added four more including Rawdon.

"This isn't a raid," he told them. "We're concerned with the wire; not killing Germans or taking prisoners. That can wait until Saturday."

"Pity," said Private Earle under his breath.

"Why do you say that?" Adam asked as they bent down to gather their equipment. He'd been standing next to Earle and was the only one to have heard him.

"Because I'd like to stick this into a couple of them," he said, looking down at the razor-sharp blade of his trench dagger, which he had been sharpening all evening. "We owe them that for the sergeant; and more."

Adam didn't reply. He understood Earle's desire for revenge after what had happened on the raid but there was something cold and inhuman and greedy about the way the man talked that repelled Adam and made him wish that he wasn't coming with them.

They had about three hundred yards of no man's land to cross. Silently, in single file, they passed through the narrow zigzag path marked with white tape that had already been cut in their wire in preparation for the attack, and then spread out, slithering from one shell crater to the next. The ground sloped down gently past the gaunt black arms of a blasted tree until it reached a sunken path and then rose abruptly over the last hundred yards towards the enemy wire.

As they crawled, the shells from their artillery continued to screech over their heads and it was hard to keep moving, knowing that only one of the deadly projectiles needed to fall short to kill them all, but gradually they got used to the danger and they covered the last hundred yards in the same time that it had taken to cross the first two hundred.

In the pale moonlight they could see that there were two massed belts of barbed wire each about fifteen feet deep with trip hazards in between. Here and there, the wire had been broken by the shrapnel shells but often the effect had only been to create new and thicker entanglements, rearing up into monstrous spider-web shapes, some over ten feet high. Without wasting any time, they got to work with their wire cutters, taking care not to step on the dud shells that ominously littered the ground all around.

They took it in turns to keep watch but there was no sign of anyone manning the German trench and the soldiers wondered hopefully whether what they'd been told was true and that the occupants were all dead, blown to bits by the shells that had been pouring down on them for five days and nights.

Their progress was slow and they were still cutting their way through the first belt when Seaton looked at his watch and ordered them back. They laid white tapes across no man's land as they crawled back and just as they reached their own wire, they heard the barrage moving back on to the German front line behind them.

On Thursday, Adam's company was rotated with B Company which had been in the support line for a twenty-four-hour rest, but at dusk Seaton's wiring party returned to the front-line trench and crossed no man's land to continue their work. The second belt turned out to be an even more formidable obstacle than the first and, at the end, Seaton threw caution to the winds and assembled two Bangalore torpedoes, long metal pipes screwed together and charged with explosive, that when blown almost doubled the width of the path that they had already cut.

The blast was loud but there was still no reaction from the enemy trench and the group returned to their line without having seen or heard a single German on either night.

The next day, the last before zero, the company went back into the front-line trench which was now so tightly packed with men that there was barely room to sit down.

"There are some blokes two bays down who've got pigeons in a basket," said Luke, returning from the latrine, which it had taken him ten minutes to get to and an even longer time to get back from. "Lookin' up at me wi' their eyes glitterin' they were. I reckon they knew I was thinkin' about pigeon pie."

"I seen 'em too," said Rawdon, laughing. "Fritz'll be thinkin' we're bringin' a picnic when we go over wi' those baskets."

"No, 'e won't," said Luke, suddenly serious. "Fritz's thinkin' days are over. You can't do much thinkin' when you're blown to bits." He made it sound like an article of faith.

The colonel remained less convinced, notwithstanding the good news that Seaton had brought back about the silence in the enemy's front-line trench. At a brigade conference the day before, one of the other battalion colonels had told him that a patrol he'd sent out had heard singing coming from a German dugout. "If the gunners haven't succeeded in cutting the wire, then I doubt they've succeeded in killing the Boche," he told Seaton, shaking his head. "Of course the staff doesn't want to know: they only hear what they want to hear; but I tell you, Scarsdale, I think this whole idea of strolling across no man's land with lit pipes and sloped rifles is the most tomfool idea in the history of warfare."

"So maybe we shouldn't," said Seaton quietly.

"What do you mean: we shouldn't?" asked the colonel gruffly. "I'm not going to start a mutiny if that's what you've got in mind."

"No, I'm just suggesting we use a little initiative. We've got a path cut through their wire—it's not very wide but it's wide enough, so if you let me take a platoon and go out in no man's land tonight, then we can rush their trench when the barrage lifts. And with a bit of good fortune we can take control while they're still down in their dugouts, assuming that that's where they are, of course."

"Alive and not dead, you mean," said the colonel, scratching his chin with his finger as he considered Seaton's proposal. "All right," he said eventually. "I think it's a good idea as long as we keep it between ourselves. You can go at first light. I'm going to make damn sure the men get a hot breakfast before they go, and the platoon you're taking shouldn't miss out on that. Thank you, Scarsdale. You're a good officer and a brave one too." He was about to salute but then changed his mind and put out his hand for Seaton to shake. "Good luck," he said. "I think we're all going to need it."

The colonel was true to his word when it came to the breakfast. He sent soldiers back into the reserve line to escort the orderlies up through the communication trench and the result was that the battalion had hot stew to eat and hot coffee to drink as the darkness of the night began to give way to the grey light of the early morning. And not only that: there was a generous measure of rum for each man to keep up their spirits.

A few became excited, juggling with hand grenades and making bad jokes, but the vast majority were quiet, taking advantage of the light to complete the page in their pay books which enabled them to make a will or to write letters in which they tried in halting sentences to open their hearts to parents or sweethearts back home. A light rain was falling which sometimes blotched their ink into tiny blue rivulets that the recipients of the letters often later mistook for tears.

Parson Vale had come up into the front-line trench in the early hours. He was wearing a white surplice which made him stand out from the mass of khaki uniforms like a visitor from another world. He moved slowly among the soldiers, trying to make sure he spoke to everyone, and he tried to touch each of them too, resting his hand for a moment on their shoulders or arms and looking into their eyes while he offered them words of encouragement.

His face lit up when he came to the bay in which Adam was standing with Luke and Rawdon, waiting for the order to move out. "Well met, my friends!" he said, smiling. "I didn't want to miss you before you went."

But then he stood silent for a moment, searching for the right words to communicate what he wanted to say, before he went on: "We've walked a long road, haven't we, to come from our small town to this terrible place, this valley of the shadow of death?"

They nodded, shifting uncomfortably. They weren't used to the parson's serious tone and his religious language made them feel self-conscious and awkward.

"And I know it's been a hard and bitter journey," he continued. "But somewhere along the way each of you has grown up and become a man and I want you to know that I am proud to call you my friends. May I give you my blessing?"

Rawdon and Adam were self-confessed atheists and Luke was no churchgoer but without looking at each other they all spontaneously got down on their knees. "May the blessing of the Almighty be upon you now and evermore, and keep you safe from harm," said the parson, gently laying his hand on each of them in turn.

And his words helped them. It was as if he represented everyone that they had left behind so that his blessing allowed them to feel that they had had a chance to make their peace and say goodbye, enabling them to face the morning with a new confidence.

It was time. One by one they moved down the trench to the departure bay where the colonel and Seaton were waiting, taking it in turns to go up the ladder and crawl through the gap in their wire, before they spread out in lines of six, waiting for the order to wriggle out into no man's land. With the colonel's agreement they had got rid of at least half their equipment, making it possible for them to run and not walk when the time came to attack.

The colonel saluted each man as he went past and addressed him by name, wishing him luck. He didn't get one name wrong, and Adam could see how this small detail made such a difference to each soldier. It was as if the colonel's utterance of their name made them matter, gave them value, defying the vast anonymity of the battle-field.

The rain had stopped and the sun was just beginning to rise above the horizon, suffusing with a faint yellow the curtain of flying white chalk and mist along the German line. The bombardment was continuing, although it had slackened a little in intensity during the night, and there was still no sign of any response from the German batteries. Perhaps Seaton had been wrong; perhaps the gunners really had blasted the Germans to hell; perhaps it really was going to be all right, Adam thought, straining for hope as the platoon crawled towards the sunken path, following the white tapes past the blasted tree. But its leafless branches sticking out horizontally on each side of its black trunk unnerved him as he went by: the tree seemed like a watchman at the gate of hell, telling those who passed by to "Abandon all hope, ye who enter here."

Now the platoon lay waiting, resting their stomachs on the path to avoid the wet dew. On the slope above their heads there were daisies and dandelions and clusters of poppies, standing out blood red against the chalk. Nothing moved—there was not a breath of wind in the air.

Gazing up at the German line, searching for any sign of activity, Adam was suddenly conscious of a pair of amber-brown eyes staring at him. It was a hare, perfectly camouflaged by the browning summer grass. It stayed rigid for a moment and then took off with only the black tips of its big ears visible for a moment as it bounced away up the hill.

And all at once the noise of the British guns intensified into a cannonade: drumfire the like of which none of the soldiers had ever heard before. This was a hurricane of sound, an unbroken roar, and the ground underneath their bodies quivered, vibrating their bones, as they held their hands up over their ears, feeling as though the drums inside were about to burst.

A screaming shell fell short, spraying red-hot shrapnel over the soldiers at the far end of the line. One, a boy with apple-red cheeks, had risen up in terror at the last moment and the shards tore into his abdomen, ripping him open as if with the full swing of an axe. He stayed kneeling for a moment with a strange yearning expression on his face and his hands clutching at the air and then toppled over dead. The man next to him had been struck in the side of the neck and blood was pumping from the wound. Luke was close by and was the first to react: he reached into the man's tunic and pulled out his field dressing and iodine ampoule. But then he was overcome by nerves and ended up pouring all the iodine on to the wound before slapping on the dressing. The man screamed over and over again but the noise of the gunfire was so great that the soldiers could hear nothing. His mouth opened and shut and opened again and he looked to Adam just like a fish floundering hopelessly on dry land.

Luke was shaking uncontrollably and Seaton crawled over and took hold of his hands. He looked intently into Luke's eyes and waited patiently until he was still and the trembling had stopped, and then glanced at his watch and put up five fingers to indicate the number of minutes remaining. There was no question of being able to do anything more for the wounded man: he would have to take his chances and hope that a stretcher-bearer would find him later in the morning.

Adam noticed how Luke looked after Seaton gratefully as he slithered back to his original position in the centre of their line. They had come a long way in a week, Adam thought, remembering Luke's boiling rage against Seaton on the walk back from the estaminet on the day after Harry's execution.

The minutes ticked by, slowly for some of the waiting soldiers who just wanted the waiting to be over, but too quickly, far too quickly, for others who wanted to hang on to every second they had left, convinced that they would be their last. Some fingered lucky charms in their clammy hands—coins or photographs or sprigs of heather; others prayed, repeating scraps of the Lord's Prayer over and over again like mantras. One man was turning out his pockets, dumping postcard pictures of half-naked French girls on to the path so they wouldn't be returned to his family with his personal effects if he didn't make it through the morning.

Seaton gave the order to fix bayonets. No one could hear him but enough of them had read his lips, and once the first few began to carry out the order, the rest followed suit, except for several who were shaking so hard that they couldn't attach their blades and had to rely on the man next in line to help them. The sun was now climbing above no man's land and its rays glittered on the forest of steel blades as the men waited for zero with their hearts hammering inside their chests.

Behind them, back in the still-crowded front-line trench, the rest of the battalion's first-wave troops were waiting by the three-rung ladders for the officers to blow their whistles. Their shoulders sagged under the punishing weight of their equipment as they sucked in the smoke from their final cigarettes and tried hard not to show their fear. Behind their backs, at the entrance to the communication trenches, red-capped military police stood impassively, ready to mete out summary justice to anyone who refused to go over the top or tried to run away.

Time ticked on until suddenly a new roar rent the air, rising above the noise of the cannonade as huge mines exploded under the German lines, sending mountains of earth and chalk high up into the sky where they hung like silhouettes of trees before they fell, expanding into huge cones of debris that shut out the sun. It was exactly seven twenty-eight.

And then silence; an extraordinary quiet as the barrage lifted off the German trenches and the gun layers hidden in their camouflaged emplacements adjusted their sights on to the lines behind. Silence except for the pure perfect singing of the larks, hovering and swooping through the balmy air of the first morning in July.

The world stood still, teetering on the precipice, for a minute; perhaps less. Adam had never been so close to death and because of that he had never felt more alive. With his eyes closed he watched as vivid images and sensations chased each other across his mind: the feel of his mother's soft hand holding his as they walked back from the church on the hill; the sweat on his father's chest as he danced away from the gigantic gypsy champion in the market square; the backs of the sleeping paupers' nodding heads in the sit-up by Blackfriars Bridge; Edgar's dead, muscled body laid out on the trestle table in the candlelight; the fire bursting from the upper windows of Scarsdale Hall; the stillness of the lake; Miriam in the garden; Miriam at Scarborough; Miriam . . .

He opened his eyes, abandoning his memories, and glanced over at Rawdon lying beside him with his dirty hands gripping hard on to his rifle. He thought of how he'd caught hold of one of those hands in the mine shaft, pulling Rawdon up to safety, and he was glad, utterly glad that he had been able to save Rawdon's life. For that alone everything had been worthwhile.

And he looked up at Seaton, the best man he had ever known, crouched down at the front of the line with his arm raised towards the sun, holding them back. As if sensing Adam's eyes upon him, Seaton turned round and smiled, that same warm ironic smile that Adam loved, and then with a last glance at his watch, he lowered his arm. And they charged.

Chapter Twenty-Five

They charged into fire. And far more than the soldiers had been led to expect. The colonel had been right: sheltering in their deep concrete dugouts the Germans had survived the bombardment. And the blowing of the mines had given them advance notice of the attack—enough time to man their parapets and bring out their machine guns, safe from the British artillery, which had now moved their aim off the front-line trenches in order to shell the lines behind, all in accordance with the fixed programme of lifts drawn up weeks earlier by the high command.

Adam ran. Into a hailstorm of bullets that was scything down the grass on the upward slope. Its freshly cut smell filled his nostrils and some separate part of his brain remembered England on a summer's day: the softness of the newly mown lawns; the promise of peace in the air. Men on either side of him were falling. Some had been shot; others had tripped over the ubiquitous, often invisible shell holes that pockmarked the ground. Adam fell into one, a larger crater already occupied by an injured man who was lying on his back, alternately beating the ground and clawing at it with his hands as he screamed out his agony, pulling his knees up over his wound in a vain attempt to protect himself from what had already happened. He'd been shot in the stomach—one of the most painful places to be hit and almost always fatal. Adam wished he had a morphine tablet to give him but only officers were allowed to carry them. And he couldn't stay; he couldn't give in to the fear that was turning his legs to jelly. He couldn't let his friends down; he had to go on.

Seaton was up ahead with Sergeant Harris, one of the platoon's two Lewis gunners, beckoning his men forward up the slope. It was incredible that he hadn't been hit: the air was thick with bullets and water was spouting out from his water bottle, which looked as if it had been shot through in several places. Adam picked up the wounded man's rifle and stuck the bayonet in the muddy soil in the hope that a stretcher-bearer might see it later, and then launched himself forward, looking for the path through the wire.

It was still there, marked with the white tapes. But Adam could see that some of his fellow soldiers had lost their way, rushing away to right and left where they had become enmeshed in the wire. And German riflemen up on the parapet were picking them off. One of them was smiling, clearly enjoying his work as he fired round after round into the struggling, helpless men, whose bodies jerked and jumped like puppets with each impact, just as Sergeant Duke's body had on the night of the raid. Adam hated the German. He wanted to kill him; he wanted to thrust his bayonet deep into the man's chest and watch him writhe in the same way that poor devil was writhing in the shell hole he'd just left behind. He knew how to: he'd been trained to kill with a bayonet for weeks back in England, stabbing lines of straw Germans with Kaiser Bill moustaches suspended from chains in the fields. Now he had the chance to do it for real.

He rushed towards the man. But he was too late. Showing extraordinary bravery, Sergeant Harris had stopped, slung the Lewis gun under his arm, pressed down on the trigger and sprayed hundreds of bullets up and down the parapet from close range, killing or wounding the defenders and enabling the surviving members of the platoon to storm the trench.

Adam jumped over the parapet, putting out his hands to break his fall as he landed hard on the duckboards down below. The trench was deeper than he'd anticipated—five feet or more lower than what he had been used to. His whole body hurt and he wondered if he'd broken anything. All around him was chaos—a frenzy of movement and shouting.

He got gingerly to his feet. Dead or dying grey-uniformed German soldiers were lying in contorted poses on the ground, and a few yards away a live one was jumping around with his hands in the air, pleading for his life. He was shouting: *"Nein, nein, nein,"* and Adam, disorientated still, heard the words as if they were numbers, a senseless repetition of nines. Behind Adam someone was laughing, a hyena-like sound of high-pitched guffaws.

The German was young—he couldn't have been more than eighteen or nineteen. He was clean-shaven with cheeks the colour of red apples and bare-headed with blond hair cropped close to his skull, and he was wearing a pair of cheap round-framed steel-rimmed glasses that made him look scholarly rather than soldierly. He ripped open the breast pocket of his tunic and pulled out a packet of tiny photographs, holding them out, and for a second Adam glimpsed a well-thumbed picture of a man and a woman, middle-aged and serious, sitting side by side on a bench, no doubt the young man's parents. He was crying out something else in German but Adam didn't need a translator to understand what the boy was trying to say—that he was human with parents and a girl waiting for him at home just like them. But it was useless: Earle came past Adam at a run and thrust his bayonet into the German's abdomen, expertly twisting the blade in the wound before pulling it out and then standing triumphantly over his victim as he sank to the ground and died. And the pathetic photographs released from his open hand fluttered down on to the ground where they were quickly trampled into the mud.

Something inside Adam snapped. He shoved Earle hard from behind, almost causing him to topple over the prone body of the dead German.

"Damn you, Earle," he shouted. "He was surrendering. You had no right."

Earle regained his balance and turned round, white with fury. "I had every fucking right, you little shit. Whose side are you on anyway?"

Adam backed away. Earle had his bloody bayonet aimed at Adam's chest and Adam sensed he was angry enough to use it. He was suddenly terrified: he could feel what it would be like to have the sharp steel blade turning in his guts, eviscerating him; he could imagine the terrible, terrible pain.

Seaton came to his rescue. "Put it down," he ordered, coming up to Earle from behind and aiming his drawn revolver at Earle's head.

Earle kept his eyes fixed on Adam as he slowly obeyed. "You want to watch him, captain," he said quietly. "He's like MacKenzie: batting for the other side."

"Shut up," said Seaton. "And don't kill them if they surrender, you hear me. You know damn well those aren't your orders."

Earle snorted, making his contempt obvious. "Whatever you say, captain," he said, giving an exaggerated salute.

Keeping his revolver in his hand, Seaton beckoned Adam to follow him and went further up the trench, stepping over the German dead as he counted his men. Fourteen of them had made it into the trench including the Lewis gunner, Sergeant Harris, and his number two, the corporal who carried the gun's ammunition. The second gunner and his mate were lying somewhere out in no man's land behind them, dead or wounded like the other thirty-four members of the platoon. And there was no sign of any of the rest of the battalion that had set out from the front-line trenches behind them when they rushed up the slope at zero hour.

On Seaton's instructions they set to work immediately, reversing the parapet of the section of trench that they had captured. They dragged sandbags down from one side and pushed them up on the other, creating an emplacement for the Lewis gun in the centre, and then pulled their helmets forward to try to stop the blood from the German corpses dripping back down on to their upturned faces as they pushed the dead up on to the new parapet, positioning the corpses in the best way to increase its height and provide extra protection.

As soon as the work was done, Seaton divided his force in half, leaving Harris with six others including Earle to hold what they had, while he led the other seven on a reconnoitring expedition to the left. They advanced from bay to bay, lobbing Mills bombs over each traverse and then rushing round the corners under cover of the explosions, but they encountered no one until they reached a burlap curtain hung over the concrete entrance to a dugout. Pulling it aside, Seaton threw a grenade down the stairs and then waited for the dust to settle before leading the way in, leaving Adam and Rawdon on guard at the top.

Adam shivered, looking nervously from side to side. Across from the dugout was the entrance to a communication trench, an empty square mouth in the trench wall, black and sinister. And up ahead the front-line trench continued but their view was blocked by another huge bulwark-like traverse.

Adam felt that here on the other side of no man's land he had entered another world. It wasn't just that the German trench was deeper than its British counterpart; it was stronger too, with smooth sides that looked as though they had been constructed by some kind of mechanical digger. He remembered the awed tone in which Harry had described the dugout where he had been held. *Everythin' was made of concrete*, he'd said. *An' there was another way out.* He'd lied about escaping but that didn't mean that there hadn't been another exit; just as there was probably another way out of this dugout too.

Adam thought he heard something. He could have been wrong. Perhaps it was just a sixth sense that made him grab a bomb from his sack, pull the pin and throw it over the traverse. He and Rawdon waited, counting out the four seconds before it exploded. And then, racing round the corner, they stopped dead in their tracks. Adam had been right. There was another curtain, fluttering ragged in front of an opening in the parapet. In front of it a German soldier lay dead on the ground; while another sat beside him with blood oozing out from numerous wounds all over his body. His uniform was burnt and blackened and his face was the colour of grey clay. Adam knew instinctively that the man was dying.

"Water, Tommy," he said in English and his voice was faint. Without hesitating, Adam knelt down and held his bottle to the man's lips, gently tipping the water into his mouth. The man closed his eyes and for a moment Adam thought he had gone. But then he opened them again and his hand moved up to the iron cross hanging at his neck. "Lucky souvenir, you Tommy," he whispered. And then with a faint smile on his face he died.

They were the first men that Adam had killed. And their deaths grieved him terribly. The bloodlust that he had felt charging up the slope had disappeared, replaced by an ashen desolation that he felt would never go away. Bending forward, he gently closed the German soldier's eyes. He was glad that he had given him the water.

He looked back up at Rawdon, who nodded. They understood each other very well at that moment and there was no need to speak.

Leaving Rawdon up above, Adam pulled back the curtain and began to creep down the concrete steps behind it, feeling his way in the dark as the steps zigzagged from side to side. Down below he could hear voices but they were mixed up and indistinct and he couldn't tell what language they were speaking in. He had his rifle and bayonet out in front of him with a round in the chamber and the safety catch released and he was shouting as loud as he could: "Is anyone there? Is anyone there?" He was very frightened. He knew that he might be alerting enemy soldiers down below to his presence, but he still felt certain that this entrance connected to the dugout that Seaton and the others had gone into further back down the trench and he didn't want them to open fire on him, thinking he was the enemy.

The steps stopped and he came out into a room of some kind. It was dark but there was a faint light coming from under a door at the far end and the voices were clearer now—he could tell they were talking in English. Standing to the side of the door, he pushed it open, bellowing as he did so: "It's Adam; it's me."

There was a sudden silence and then the last thing that he'd expected: the sound of raucous cheering.

"Come on in, my friend. Join the party," said Seaton in that amused ironic tone that Adam knew so well.

Adam went through the door and at first couldn't see anybody before his eyes adjusted to the artificial light and he realized that the doorway was concealed from the rest of the dugout by a double line of two-tiered bunk beds. He edged round them and came out into a large room lit by several electric light bulbs hanging down from the ceiling. He gasped with amazement: the place was unlike anything he'd ever seen before. Harry had not been exaggerating when he'd described the strength of construction of the German dugouts and the sophistication of their amenities: not only was there electric light and ventilation; there was also a stove and an enamel sink with a tap dripping water over on the far wall where six terrified German prisoners were sitting in a line, staring up at their captors.

Seaton smiled. "It's impressive, isn't it? But disgusting too, which I suppose isn't too surprising, given what these poor Fritzes have had to endure down here for the past week while our guns have been trying to blast them off the face of the earth."

Adam saw what he meant: there were flies everywhere, swarming and droning around their heads and forming black lattices in the air as they clustered around the naked light bulbs, and the dugout stank of urine and stale sweat and excrement. The floor was covered with a layer of filth: broken bottles and scraps of uneaten food and dirty clothes and bloodstained Deutschmarks. And over by the staircase a dead German lay in a pool of blood, killed by the bomb that Seaton had thrown down the steps before he went in.

Several of the soldiers had found souvenirs: medals and epaulettes and even a leaf-shaped bayonet, but Luke had secured the best prize—an officer's black spiked Pickelhaube helmet. It didn't fit him properly and he looked so ridiculous with it perched on his head above his filthy uniform that the other privates burst out laughing.

"You're just jealous," he said, flushing with embarrassment as he took it off and turned it round in his hands. *"GOTT MIT UNS"*: he read aloud the inscription emblazoned in the centre of the helmet, puzzling over the words. "What the fuck does that mean?"

"God's with us," said Seaton. "Which he isn't, I'm afraid, Private Mason. If there's anything that the events of today have shown me it's that God's with nobody at all."

He turned to Adam: "We need to get back," he said. "And ceremonial helmets aren't going to help our cause. Was there anything useful out there?" he asked, pointing to the door through which Adam had come in.

"I don't know," said Adam. "It was dark."

"Well, let's see."

They were in luck. The room that Adam had walked through turned out to be a capacious storeroom. There were bottles of mineral water and tins of dried fruit and sausage and Argentine bully beef, and boxes of bombs that looked like condensed-milk cans on sticks with toggles at the bottom instead of pins. And at the far end, stacked up against the wall, were rolls of barbed wire, which they dragged up the steps to create a thick barricade across the next traverse in the trench up above.

But when they were done Seaton wouldn't let them rest. They dragged the rolls that they hadn't used back up to where Sergeant Harris was waiting with the rest of the men and created an equally strong barricade at that end of the trench.

And then, to complete their defences, they threw Mills bombs over the traverses beyond the barricades in an attempt to destroy the walls of the fire bays and make them impassable, and with the same purpose in mind rolled the grenades into the communication trench. The resulting explosions were loud and satisfying, shaking the ground beneath their feet, but they weren't going to go exploring to find out the extent of the damage.

The hard work left them pouring with sweat. It was a hot day without a breath of wind in the air—a complete contrast to the unseasonable weather of the previous week, and the visibility was perfect as, horrified, they gazed back past the remains of their friends hanging on the German wire, across no man's land to the trenches they'd left behind six hours earlier.

The German shelling had moved off the British front line to concentrate on the support lines behind. Columns of earth and smoke rose up like black trees in evenly spaced rows, but there was no sign of anyone trying to get through them. The attacks had stopped at least for now and no man's land was strangely still, as if in the aftermath of a gigantic storm that had left the broken ground strewn with khaki corpses, some clearly visible, others half concealed with knees or arms sticking up at strange contorted angles out of the grass or shell holes into which they had fallen. There were so many of them that a separate, detached part of Adam's brain, which wanted to deny the reality of what he was seeing, thought that they looked like crowds of people in a city park or on a beach sunbathing on a balmy July day without a care in the world.

It was worst inside the British wire where the corpses were literally piled one on top of the other—hills of dead that made Adam think of paintings by Hieronymus Bosch that he'd seen in a book in Oxford and dismissed at the time as the absurd offshoots of a mad imagination, although now they didn't seem like that at all.

Days earlier the German gunners had registered their sights on the narrow white-taped attack paths that they had observed being cut through the British wire and at zero hour they had directed a murderous fire at the troops advancing up these funnels, turning them into monstrous killing corridors.

A hundred yards away Adam could see the sunken white chalk path from which the platoon had begun their attack gleaming in the sunlight. It was empty of bodies, indicating that none of those attacking from the British front line had even got that far. Behind it, on the gentle slope, the survivors, many of them wounded, sheltered in shell holes or behind the dead bodies of their friends, but the tin triangles on their backs flashed in the sunlight whenever they moved, giving away their position to enemy snipers who were quick to take advantage. And, further back, rifles stuck in the ground to attract the attention of stretcher-bearers to the wounded also often proved fatal to those they had been placed there to help as the German snipers and machine gunners knew what they signified and peppered the area around them with bullets.

In the foreground, between the sunken path and the German trench, the few wounded survivors of the platoon's charge were in the same situation, except they knew that their comrades were only yards away from them on the other side of the wire. They cried out to be saved or for water but Seaton would not allow them to be rescued. For now the trench was entirely free from shellfire. The British guns were firing uselessly over the platoon's heads, providing cover for non-existent troops that were supposed to be attacking the German third line. And the German artillery appeared unaware or at least uncertain that the trench had been captured, so Seaton wasn't prepared to risk anything that would give their position away.

He knew they were in an impossible situation. They could not hold the trench without reinforcements and yet they could not risk firing red flares to signal their position without alerting the enemy as well. Without carrier pigeons, the only alternative was to send back a runner but the chances of one getting through were very slim indeed, judging from the deadly sniper fire that followed any movement at all out in no man's land. And even if the runner did by some miracle get across, what chance was there of troops being able to reach them, given what had already happened that morning? And yet they could not retreat or they would face the same fate.

There were no good choices. All that they could do was stay where they were, hoping against hope that the Germans would continue to leave them alone until nightfall when the cover of darkness would allow at least the chance of getting back across no man's land.

And so they waited while the sun reached its zenith expecting an attack every minute. Seaton was always in motion, trying to maintain the men's fraying morale. He rotated them frequently between the defensive positions they had constructed at the two ends of the trench, although he was careful to keep Earle away from the dugout. He wished that he did not have the prisoners on his hands as the two soldiers needed to guard them meant two soldiers fewer to defend the trench, but he could not send them back across no man's land. It would have been the same as putting his revolver to their heads and dispatching them one by one and he wasn't going to do that. The war had besmirched so much and he sometimes felt that his conscience was the only decent possession he had left after two years at the front.

At noon they fetched food and bottled water from the storeroom and were halfway through eating when bombs started exploding at the dugout end of the trench. They didn't reach the guards sheltering behind the huge traverse and responding in kind, but Seaton quickly realized that this wasn't the Germans' intention. Looking round the corner, he could see that they were aiming instead at the barbed-wire barricade, degrading it with shrapnel bursts. And at that moment, clearly concluding that they had done enough damage, two Germans appeared at the other end of the bay carrying a duckboard to lay across what was left of the entanglement. But reacting with extraordinary coolness, Rawdon shot them both down, quickly working his bolt between each round.

Seaton hadn't even known he was there. "Good shooting, Private Dawes," he said. "I didn't know you were a marksman."

"I been practisin' on the rats," said Rawdon succinctly. But Seaton could see that he was pleased with the compliment.

They did their best to repair the barricade, fetching more wire from the storeroom, and then piled up the corpses of the dead Germans to create a further barrier behind it. Between trips Adam looked into the dead face of the German to whom he'd given the water and saw how in death he'd become no more than a sandbag. Hour by hour, the experiences of the day were stripping depth and meaning from Adam's perception of the world and he wondered dejectedly whether these qualities would ever return.

And back in the dugout fetching more supplies, he passed a grimy mirror hanging on the wall and did a double take. He hadn't expected it to be there and when he first looked at his reflection he didn't recognize himself. He saw that he was changing, becoming old before his time with sunken cheeks and dulled eyes; just like his companions the war had robbed him of his youth and it wasn't done with him yet.

The German counter-attacks at the dugout end of the trench continued sporadically through the afternoon and the mound of dead grew higher. But there was no breakthrough and Seaton and his men were beginning to hope that they had got through the worst when a German in a gas mask appeared on top of the heap of bodies with a tank of oil on his back and jumped down towards them, spraying twenty feet of liquid fire from the nozzle of a hose that he was gripping in his gloved hand.

The effect was devastating. The first two defenders were killed instantly. In the next bay another one managed to fire a round into the man's chest before the flames engulfed him, but the bullet had no effect beyond knocking the German back for a moment. Almost immediately he regained his balance and rushed forward, burning up everything and everyone that stood in his way. And he would surely have wiped out the entire platoon if Seaton had not jumped out from the entrance to the dugout into which he'd instinctively retreated as the German approached and shot him in the back of the head with his revolver just after he'd gone by.

The German crashed to the ground and the fire sprayed up into the air for a moment like a red-and-yellow geyser before falling back to the ground as his dead hand gave up its grip on the machine's nozzle.

"Stand back!" Seaton yelled out just in time as the cylinder on the dead man's back exploded, immolating his body in a ball of fire. The air was black with thick choking smoke, which only slowly cleared, revealing no trace of the German's body except a few chunks of charred flesh splattered on the walls of the trench and a puddle of steaming blood on the ground mixed with the half-melted remains of an armour-plated waistcoat. Involuntarily Adam turned away and vomited up the dried figs and German sausage that he'd eaten for lunch, requisitioned from the dugout stores.

They had lost five men. They gritted their teeth, swatted the flies away with their hands, and dragged the dead over to join the barricade of corpses at the far end of the trench: German and English bodies thrown indiscriminately together one on top of the other, united in death, with Luke and Rawdon standing guard behind them like sentries at the gates of hell.

All along the trench the exhausted survivors stared out through box periscopes or across barricades as they counted down the hours and minutes to the end of the day. Slowly, infinitely slowly, the sun descended towards the British line, throwing out a blaze of blood-red-and-gold glory as it set. As one they willed it to sink but their shout of joy when its disc finally disappeared below the horizon was premature. The Germans had also been waiting for dusk and as the twilight deepened they attacked again. This time, however, they came across the open land that divided the front-line trench from their second line behind. The British bombardment had pitted the ground between with shell holes and the grey soldiers came on in short rushes, leaping from one crater to the next. Up on the parapet, behind his improvised cover of sandbags, Sergeant Harris swung the Lewis gun from side to side, spraying bullets in a continuous arc that held the attackers at bay. Tack-tack-tack: the chatter of the gun was the platoon's heartbeat. It was keeping them alive. But then inevitably it jammed. The men could hear the mechanism catching uselessly as the loader, a young, nervous-looking corporal called Bennett, tried in vain to reposition the belt, which kept slipping through his sweating hands, and the noise felt like a death rattle in their throats.

"Bring it down," Seaton ordered. And as he and Bennett examined the gun on the floor of the trench by the light of an electric torch, the others stood on the parapet among the corpses that they had hoisted up there at the beginning of the day and threw the German stick grenades that they had brought up from the dugout, until their arms were so sore that they could hardly lift the bombs above their heads and had to toss them out underhand. The attackers were close now and there was no wire to protect the trench. And they were responding in kind: bombs came hurtling through the air and several of the defenders fell back into the trench, mortally wounded.

But the defenders' tactics were working: judging from the guttural cries and shouts out beyond the parapet some of the bombs were finding their target and the red flashes of the explosions lit up the Germans' retreating figures in silhouette as they withdrew beyond the range of the grenades. But they had not given up: it was as if they knew that the supply of bombs would soon be exhausted and that the Tommies would then be at their mercy.

Unless the Lewis gun could be repaired—Seaton knew that everything turned on that. He could feel the belt was wet. That had to be the problem. Bennett pulled it out and pushed a new one into the feed block and held it up for Sergeant Harris to take. But the sergeant didn't respond. Perhaps he couldn't hear. Bennett reached up and tapped him on the shoulder to get his attention, but the sergeant didn't turn; he just fell back from his sandbag emplacement, landing with a thud at their feet. There was a small, neat hole in the centre of his forehead and a larger, scruffier one at the back of his head where the rifle bullet had exited after blasting through his brain.

Bennett's teeth were chattering and the Lewis gun was shaking in his hands. It was a miracle he hadn't dropped it on the ground. Seaton went up close to him and held his shoulders, looking hard into his eyes.

"This is your moment, corporal. This is what you've trained for. You can do this; I know you can," he said and his voice was clear and calm amidst the maelstrom. Up above, there were almost no grenades left and the Germans had resumed their advance. Soon they would be in the trench.

Bennett swallowed and nodded. Gripping the ladder, he climbed up into the sergeant's sandbag emplacement and took the gun from Seaton's upstretched hands. He set it in place and immediately began firing. The new belt ran freely through the block and the bullets flew out, mowing down the enemy just as they reached the trench. It was enough: the Germans had no answer to the machine gun's deadly fire and those that remained crept away into the dusk. The attack was over.

Chapter Twenty-Six

Leaving Bennett in charge of the gun, Seaton walked the length of the trench, counting the living and the dead. Luke and Rawdon were still at their posts but someone was missing. It was Earle, and Seaton suddenly knew where he was. He ran towards the dugout with Adam following, wondering what on earth had gone wrong.

Seaton stopped at the first entrance and took out his revolver, releasing the safety catch as he stood listening inside the doorway. The sound of raised voices was coming up from down below— German and English mixing together, high-pitched, angry, terrified. Seaton put his finger to his lips and began to slowly descend the dark stairs with Adam following behind. Some of the steps were damaged from the grenade that Seaton had thrown in the morning and they had to be careful with their footing. Halfway down they stopped, clapping their hands over their ears in a vain attempt to protect them from the piercing boom of a rifle being fired in the enclosed space down below. The concussion left Adam disorientated and he stumbled forward, knocking into Seaton who lost his balance and fell down the remaining steps, landing with a thud on the corpse of the German that was still lying at the bottom covered with a blanket. Behind him Adam was able to arrest his own fall by throwing himself against the wall of the staircase before it turned at a diagonal to descend into the dugout below.

Somehow Seaton had kept the revolver in his hand without either firing it or letting go. He pulled himself back behind the corpse, keeping his head down low, and then raised himself up an inch to look over, turning the barrel of the gun with his eyes as he tried to take in the chaos of the scene in front of him. Two yards away Taylor, the private he'd left in charge of the prisoners, was lying on his side. He was breathing and the absence of any visible wound or blood made Seaton think that he had been knocked out rather than shot or stabbed. Over to the right, by the far wall, five of the six German prisoners lay dead, their eyes staring vacantly up at the naked light bulb that was swinging gently from side to side above their heads. They had each been stabbed in the chest and their blood was pooling out on to the dirty floor. Their hands were still tied with the cable that Seaton had used to secure them when they were captured and he realized with a shudder of remorse that by doing so he had effectively signed their death warrants, rendering them powerless to resist when Earle attacked them with his bayonet.

Seaton knew what had happened—it didn't require a detective to put together the sequence of events. All day Earle had waited patiently for his opportunity and had then seized it in the chaos that accompanied the Germans' twilight assault when shortage of men meant Seaton had been able to leave only one soldier in the dugout to guard the prisoners. He'd crept down the stairs and taken Taylor unawares, knocking him out with the butt of his rifle, and then set about butchering the prisoners. One had escaped and Earle had fired his rifle at him as he fled, but it was unclear whether the bullet had found its target. He could see no body and there was no sign of Earle either.

But one or other of them was still in the room. Seaton could hear movement over among the bunk beds and, looking down, he saw a pair of British ammunition boots and the beginnings of muddy puttees. It was Earle. There was no sign of any German jackboots so perhaps the prisoner had got away out into the storeroom behind. Seaton hoped for his sake that he had.

"Stay back, Adam," he hissed under his breath, sensing Adam beginning to come down the stairs behind him. And then raising his voice, he called out: "Come out now, Earle! I don't want to shoot but I will if I have to."

On the other side of the room there was the sound of a rifle bolt being drawn back, but apart from his boots Earle remained invisible. He must have pulled the blanket down from one of the top bunks to give himself cover, Seaton realized.

"You're not the only one with a gun," Earle called back, and there was a sneering leer in his voice: contempt in the face of danger. "And you want to know something? I doubt you'll use it. You're too fuck-ing good for this war—that's your problem, captain. Anybody with any sense would have killed those Huns when we got down here. They'd have done the same to us."

"Perhaps," said Seaton evenly. "But you're wrong about my will-ingness to use my gun. You need to put down your rifle and come out now or I will shoot. I can assure you of that, Private Earle."

There was a moment's silence and then a crash as Earle threw his rifle out into the centre of the floor where it landed beside Taylor, who was groaning and beginning to show signs of coming round.

Immediately Earle stepped out from behind the bunks. Seaton looked up and saw that one of his arms was behind his back. He was raising it now and Seaton suddenly saw what was coming. The bay-onet knife was in Earle's hand and he was aiming it, ready to throw. Instinctively Seaton lurched to the left and pressed the trigger of the revolver. The recoil threw him back and the knife buried itself in his upper shoulder, while the bullet missed Earle altogether and embed-ded itself in the concrete wall.

Earle rushed forward, ready to pull out the blade and finish Sea-ton off. But Adam, dashing down the last three steps of the staircase, swung his rifle round and fired directly into Earle's body, blowing a large hole in the middle of his chest and killing him instantly. He fell backwards exactly as if he had been poleaxed with his last expression, a look of utter astonishment, etched upon his face.

Seaton was still alive, although his breathing was laboured and the colour had drained from his face. Adam's first instinct was to pull the blade out of the wound, but Seaton reached up and took hold of his hand just as he was about to do so.

"Don't," he whispered. "It'll make it worse—if that's possible." His grip, like his voice, was extraordinarily weak and his hand fell back by his side as he closed his eyes.

Adam took off his tunic and bundled it up under Seaton's head to act as a pillow and then took out his field dressing; he crumbled the iodine ampoule over the gauze pads and bandaged them around the wound. He could tell Seaton was in intense pain: his whole body was rigid and the muscles were stretched tight across his face, so he reached down into Seaton's pockets and found his morphine bottle. But Seaton shook his head when Adam tried to put a tablet in his mouth.

Over on the other side of the dugout there was a crash. The noise sounded as though it was coming from the storeroom.

"What's happening?" asked Taylor, who was now sitting up, rubbing a swelling, purple bruise on the side of his temple.

"Earle knocked you out so he could do that," said Adam, pointing over at the dead prisoners. He grimaced as he looked at Earle's handiwork, swallowing down the bile that had risen in his throat.

"I thought there were six of them," said Taylor uncertainly.

"There were. One of them got away. I think he's in there," said Adam, pointing over towards the storeroom. "Come on," he said. "We'd better try and flush him out."

He began to walk over to the other side of the dugout but Seaton's faint voice called him back.

"Don't kill him," he said, raising his head. "We need to be different; we need to try . . ."

"It's all right. I understand," said Adam, meeting his friend's eye and then glancing over at Earle's body.

"Good," said Seaton. And his head fell back—the effort to speak had obviously cost him a great deal.

Adam stood to the side of the storeroom door with Taylor behind him and pushed it slowly open. "Come out," he called into the darkness. "We're not going to hurt you, I promise."

There was no response. But Adam sensed the German's presence. Only a few feet away he could hear a sharp intake of breath.

"The bad man—he's dead," said Adam, wishing he knew some German. He racked his brain, trying to think of a word that would help but all he could think of was *"Nein"* and the German in the trench at the start of the day shouting it out over and over again as if it was the number *nine*, holding out his pathetic photographs. Another of Earle's victims.

It was Taylor who came to his rescue. *"Kamerad,"* he shouted. *"Kamerad!"*

And it was enough: perhaps the German recognized Taylor's voice from earlier, but for whatever reason he called back in a faint, strangled voice the same word: *"Kamerad,"* and a moment later appeared in the doorway. He had his tied hands raised above his head and he was shaking uncontrollably so that he could hardly stand.

Somehow Adam and Taylor succeeded in getting Seaton up the broken stairs and out into the trench where they propped him up with his back to the wall. They left the prisoner down below with a bottle of water, having thrown blankets over the bodies of his friends.

Leaving Taylor with Seaton, Adam walked through the fire bays, shining his torch down on the duckboards as he picked his way past the dead. It was dark now and he called out in a low voice but only Luke and Rawdon answered, following him back down the trench like sleepwalkers with their heads bowed, listening while he told them what had happened. Bennett, the Lewis gun loader, remained at his post, crouched down over the gun, staring out into the night.

Out beyond the parapet a white flare sailed up into the black sky like a comet, lighting up the tiny group of survivors sitting around Seaton at the dugout entrance in an eerie pale light, before it reached its zenith and fell back to earth. Behind and in front, the battlefields remained quiet, interrupted only by the occasional brief rattle of a machine gun and the boom of a distant gun. But there was an ominous quality to the silence: they all knew that it was only a matter of time before the Germans resumed their attack.

"I'll 'elp thee with the cap'n," Rawdon told Adam. "But we'll need somethin' to carry 'im in. 'E ain't goin' to be able to walk."

"No," said Seaton, raising himself up. "I'm staying. That's an order." Even though they could hardly hear him, they could sense the urgency in his voice, his desperation to impose his will upon them even as it flickered on the brink of death.

He breathed deeply, gathering his strength before he went on: "You'll have a much better chance without me. I can fire the Lewis gun if they come again." He was barely able to finish his sentence before his head fell back and he seemed to drift out of consciousness.

"I'm not leaving him," said Adam quietly. He wasn't arguing; he said it as though he was making a bald statement of fact.

"Me neither," said Rawdon, nodding. "But Luke, you an' Taylor need to go first an' take Bennett wi' thee. You've got a far better chance if you can get down on your 'ands and knees, an' if they see us, we'll jus' bring their fire down on thee."

"He's right," said Adam, shooting a look of gratitude at Rawdon. He wanted desperately to try and save Seaton and he knew that he had no chance of getting him across no man's land on his own. "You should get Bennett and go now," he told Luke and Taylor. "We'll wait ten minutes before we follow."

"What about the prisoner?" asked Taylor, pointing towards the dugout.

"We'll leave him down there," said Adam. "He's got his hands tied and he's too scared to do anything even if he wanted to. I've never seen a man shaking like he was when we got him out of that storeroom. Poor bastard—I doubt he'll ever stop!"

They shook hands. And then Luke, just as he was about to follow Taylor down the trench, turned back and, kneeling down, put his arms around first Adam and then Rawdon.

"What the fuck!" said Rawdon who was notorious for hating to be touched.

But Luke ignored him. "Good luck," he said and they could hear his voice was choking. "I'll see you at breakfast." And then he walked quickly away and was gone.

"Bloody idiot!" said Rawdon. But Adam could tell he was moved as he reached up and brushed his hand across his face. He looked as if he was wiping away the dirt and sweat but Adam guessed that there were tears in his eyes.

They spent most of the waiting time working out what to use as a stretcher. They considered laying Seaton on one of the fire-step ladders but settled at last on wrapping him in Rawdon's waterproof groundsheet on the basis that he would be less likely to fall out of that as they stumbled in and out of the shell holes that pock-marked the entire surface of no man's land.

They picked him up gingerly, trying to avoid moving the bayonet that was still sticking up out of his shoulder, but it was impossible not to stretch the wound as they hoisted him up the ladder and over the new parados. Seaton cried out as they laid him down, applying more bandages to his shoulder in an attempt to staunch the seeping blood.

"Leave me," he said as his eyes briefly focused on Adam and Rawdon bending down over him. But it was as if he knew it was pointless to insist and he closed his eyes, furrowing his brow as he carried on an inner communion with his pain. Again Adam tried to give him morphine but again he shook his head when he felt Adam's fingers at his lips. And a minute later Adam heard him whispering as if to himself: "I want to know; I want to know what it's like."

They went along beside the wire, not crossing until they found the white tapes that they'd charged through in the morning when they captured the trench. It seemed so long ago now, like an event they could only dimly remember.

Here and there, as they passed, they could see the grotesque remains of their comrades silhouetted in the moonlight, hanging on the barbs, riddled with bullets. They weren't human any more; rather they seemed like the straw Guys dressed in throw-away clothes that Adam remembered the neighbourhood children wheeling through the gas-lit Islington streets in half-broken perambulators on Guy Fawkes nights when he was a boy. "Penny for the Guy, penny for the Guy," they had chorused every time a door opened in response to their repeated knocks.

Adam and Rawdon moved slowly out into no man's land, picking their way carefully through the shell holes as they went down the slope towards the white chalk line of the sunken path. Seaton groaned as they went but otherwise said nothing. It was a terrible place: they had to watch each step they took to avoid tripping in the muddy shell holes or stepping on the wounded or the dead and it was worse, much worse once they reached the path and began to go up again towards the British line. Bodies were everywhere and rats too, screaming as they approached. They felt hands groping weakly at their puttees and demented voices calling out pitifully for help or for water or for their mothers—such a strange cry, Adam thought, in this blighted landscape where no woman had ever been.

The moaning and the howling and the groaning and the crying synthesized in their ears into one single unearthly wail. This was Golgotha, the hill of the skull, the field of bones at the end of the world.

Seaton was heavy and they had to stop to rest. A man with half his face shot away was lying wedged between two dead comrades, a tall thin one and a short fat one with a handlebar moustache who looked like characters from a slapstick comedy. "Shoot me," the man begged them. "Shoot me." Over and over again the same two words in the same monotonous voice until Adam wanted to join in the wailing too and surrender to a mad despair.

Rawdon was watching him and seemed to sense what he was feeling. "We need to go on," he said, getting to his feet. "Remember the mine, Adam. Remember how you got us out."

And Adam did remember. But in the mine they had been alone. There had been no dead, no wounded, no guns or bayonets or wire. He felt suddenly as if he had no strength left and sank down on to the ground, laying his head on the cool grass and closing his hot eyes. "Shoot me," said the voice, but there was another voice too, competing for his attention—Seaton's, telling him to give the man morphine and a drink of water. "He needs it," said Seaton. "He needs it more than me."

Slowly, as if he was coming up through water, Adam pulled himself together and did as he was told. It took no time: once he'd swallowed Seaton's morphine the man was quiet as his eyes misted over and he drifted away. And Adam looked over at Rawdon and nodded his head. Together they bent down and lifted up the groundsheet and went on up the hill, gazing at the evening star that seemed to be beckoning them forward as it rose glittering in the western sky like a beacon. Ahead in the moonlight they could see a path through the wire opening up like a funnel.

"Halt! Password!" shouted a nervous British voice, and their hearts stopped as they heard a rifle bolt snapping into place.

"We don't know it," said Rawdon. "We've been over the other side since this mornin' an' we're only just now comin' back. Come on, mate. Do I sound like a fuckin' square 'ead?"

There was the sound of whispered conversation and a bright light was shone in their faces that blinded them for a moment, making them stagger back and almost drop the groundsheet.

"What you got in there?" demanded the sentry.

"Our captain," shouted Adam. "He's been hit. We need a doctor."

"Good luck with that," said the sentry, beckoning them in. "There's none of 'em left up here. You'll have to go back to the field ambulance to find one."

"Where's that?" asked Adam.

"Albert. In the church," said the sentry. "All this—it's a fucking mess. That's what it is." He waved his hand at the sea of bodies all around him: soldiers who had failed to even get over the top, blown back into the trench by the hail of machine-gun bullets and shellfire that had scorched the parapet at zero.

They soon discovered that trying to find a way back through the narrow communication trench was harder than crossing no man's land where they could at least move freely, picking their way between shell holes. Here the ground was choked with men killed or wounded while waiting to go over. It was impossible not to walk on them with their hobnail boots and the piteous cries that followed Adam and Rawdon as they edged their way forward soon became unbearable so they gave up and climbed up out of the trench, taking their chances out in the open. The German artillery was largely quiet now and the British guns had also fallen silent. Further back, they passed gunners lying asleep on the ground. It was a warm night and they were stripped down to their filthy vests, palely illuminated by the moonlight. One group was awake, leaning back against the wheels of a howitzer with its huge muzzle pointing hungrily up into the sky. They were drinking tea and offered some to Rawdon and Adam, who couldn't resist stopping for a moment to rest their aching arms and legs.

"How bad is it?" asked one of the gunners, pointing back the way they'd come.

"Bad," said Rawdon. "Worse than you can imagine." And he went back to drinking the hot sugary tea, concentrating his entire attention on each sip and swallow.

Inside the groundsheet Seaton had lost consciousness and his face was white, drained of blood. It was hard to tell whether he was still breathing and Adam checked his pulse to see if he was still alive. The beat was faint, almost undetectable. They were running out of time.

But it was hard to stand up, hard to lift Seaton again, and even harder to find the will to put one foot in front of the other and keep going with their backs bent over like old men broken by years of labour.

Eventually they came out on to the road and joined the throng of wounded going down the hill into Albert, all with luggage labels tied to their tunics on which medics at the front had scrawled their injuries and the drugs administered. Many were on foot, either alone, using their rifles as crutches, or in pairs, hanging on to each other for support as they swayed precariously from side to side like inept three-legged racers at a fair. Others were being carried, whether on stretchers or in carts and wheelbarrows or inside horse-drawn wagons from which a chorus of agonized groans went up, rising above the jingle of the harness and the clop of the horses' hooves each time the wheels lurched over one of the innumerable shell holes in the road.

They were all headed for the basilica whose shell-splintered brick bell tower pointed up towards the moon like a gnarled finger with the golden Virgin hanging off the top, ready to fall.

Out in the square the line of wounded queued up to be seen by a receiving doctor standing outside the open doors of the church, while an orderly went up and down the line, giving each of them a tetanus shot and marking a T on their foreheads with an indelible pencil as soon as he had pulled out the needle. Looking up ahead, Adam could see that the line was splitting in three directions: some of those on foot were being directed to board the motor ambulances that were ferrying them to the casualty clearing station ten miles up the road; while other wounded were being admitted into the church; and a further group, none of them walking, were being sent to the right where they joined hundreds of other soldiers laid out on the paving stones in tightly packed rows with a narrow space left between each row to allow orderlies to walk up and down.

As far as Adam could see, these men were receiving water but no medical attention. Many of them were quiet having been given morphine at the door but those that were crying out in pain were ignored. And it was only when they were still and lifeless that orderlies would come and pick them up in the blankets on which they were lying and carry them to GS wagons waiting round the corner, opening up a new space on the ground for another mortally wounded soldier to occupy while his life ebbed away in turn.

They were being sent to the right to die. And any doubts that Adam had on that score vanished as he and Rawdon and Seaton neared the top of the line where they could hear the doctor arguing angrily with two stretcher-bearers.

"Don't bring them in when they're like this!" he shouted, pointing down at the hideously mutilated mess of a man that had been a fit and healthy soldier at the beginning of the day. "Can't you see that he's too far gone? Or perhaps you're too stupid? Is that the problem? Is it?"

The stretcher-bearers backed away as the doctor's voice rose in exasperation. They had reached the limit of their endurance performing a task that they were now being told was useless, and they looked hopeless and miserable, like beaten animals. But the doctor wasn't watching them any more. He'd pointed to the right and now he was bent down, examining Seaton where he lay, apparently unconscious, in the groundsheet. Over the doctor's head Rawdon and Adam could see into the shell-blasted church where guttering candles, reeking kerosene lamps and shards of moonlight shining down through the holes in the roof illuminated the shattered stained glass, the broken mosaic tiles, and the other doctors in this RAMC unit, who were operating at makeshift tables up and down the nave, their arms deep in blood and guts, while wounded men lay like sandbags at their feet waiting their turn under the knife.

"What the hell happened here?" asked the doctor who'd been examining Seaton. "This bayonet looks like one of ours."

"It is," said Rawdon. "A bastard called Earle threw it—I knew 'e was trouble from the start; I should've dealt with 'im then."

"Well, it's too late now," said the doctor, getting back to his feet. "Take him over there," he told them, pointing again to his right. "The orderly'll make him comfortable."

"No, he fucking won't," said Adam, losing his temper and seizing hold of the doctor's wrist, gripping the three braid bands denoting the doctor's military rank while his other hand clenched into a fist.

"Let go, soldier," said the doctor. And his voice was quiet now as he looked Adam hard in the eye. "It sounds to me as if there's been enough mutiny in your company for one day."

The doctor's measured tone brought Adam to his senses. He saw suddenly that the man wasn't cruel or callous; he was simply trying to do his job under appalling circumstances—in the same way they were.

"I'm sorry," he said. "It's just you have to save him because . . . because . . ."

"Because he's special," said the doctor. "I know. But they're all special," he said, waving his hand in an expansive arc that included the wounded in the queue, the wounded on the right, everyone. "And, God knows, I wish we could save them all. But we can't. Some of them are going to die. And I'm afraid your captain is one of them. He's bleeding inside, has been ever since whoever it was stuck that blade in him. It's a miracle he's still alive."

Adam was about to argue but Seaton, who'd clearly been listening, opened his eyes and stopped him: "The doctor's right, Adam," he said with that faint smile that was so uniquely his own. "And really I would prefer to be outside under the stars rather than inside a church: it seems more sacred somehow."

It was the doctor's turn to smile. "Do you want morphine?" he asked.

"No," said Seaton. "The pain is better and this is really not an event I want to miss."

"Very well," said the doctor, nodding. "I can see you were right about your friend," he added, turning to Adam with a sigh. "He does seem special. I wish there'd been something we could do. But . . ." He opened his arms in a gesture of weary impotence and then raised his right hand in a farewell salute before turning to the next case, a Glaswegian who had lost an arm and a leg and was babbling incoherently about Blighty. But soon he was following Seaton to the right, although quieter now as he *had* been given the morphia.

Seaton's wish to be present at his own death looked destined for disappointment. He'd lost consciousness again as soon as they'd picked him up and remained comatose when they put him down. And Adam wondered whether it would be for the best: there was nothing sacred about the men around them writhing in fevered pain, assaulted by clouds of buzzing flies. For a moment he thought that the soldier lying next to Seaton had died. His jaw had fallen open, but then his head moved slightly as he exhaled and a swarm of disturbed bluebottles poured out of his open mouth only to return a moment later.

Over to the side the orderlies were carrying used dressings over to paraffin stoves. The dirty white cotton gauze bandages splashed with bloody red shone for a moment before the flames took them and, looking back down at Seaton, Adam saw that his eyes were open again as he watched the fires.

"Like lanterns," he whispered. And his voice was so faint that Adam had to lean down very close to hear him. "They put them up at Christmas last year." His voice trailed off and he closed his eyes.

"Who?" asked Adam, not so much because he wanted to know the answer, but because he wanted to keep Seaton talking: words, any words meant that Seaton was still alive; and Adam didn't want Seaton to die. More than anything else in the world he didn't want that.

"Who put them up?" he asked again.

"The Boche. Up on the parapets. We thought it was an attack, at first. But it was for Christmas. Chinese lanterns. And they were sing-ing: '*Stille Nacht, heilige Nacht.*' It was beautiful. And we sang too. All of us. We couldn't come out. We had orders. But we could sing . . ."

Again Seaton closed his eyes and his head sank to the side.

"I think 'e's goin'," said Rawdon.

But he was mistaken. Rousing himself for one final effort, Sea-ton looked up at Adam. "Tell my father I'm sorry. It's a bad habit: making promises you can't keep," he said. And again he smiled: that slight ironical smile that Adam had always loved.

Seaton sighed. "The men were marvellous steady," he said. "Mar-vellous—I couldn't have asked for more." And he looked at them intently, as if memorizing their faces—every feature, every detail; and kept looking until they realized with a start that he wasn't seeing them any more, because he was no longer there; because he'd gone from behind his eyes.

Chapter Twenty-Seven

They found their way back to battalion HQ just before dawn. There was no one in the billets and so they walked out beyond the farm buildings to where the ground sloped down into a natural glade, surrounded by hawthorn trees whose outlines were picked out in the early-morning light as if by a draughtsman's pencil.

Looking down, they could see the colonel and the adjutant sitting behind a table set up on the grass at the far end. In front of them the men who had come back, pitifully few in number, were sitting on the ground. They had taken off their helmets and beneath their matted, tangled hair their bloodless, unshaved cheeks were the colour of dirty parchment. They looked like a gathering of ghosts.

Adam and Rawdon searched the faces, looking for Luke, and breathed a sigh of relief when they saw him up near the front with Taylor and Bennett, the Lewis gun corporal.

Over to the right those who had stayed behind during the attack were standing awkwardly, shifting from one foot to the other. Their clean uniforms and polished boots contrasted sharply with the torn, mud-spattered, chalk-daubed outfits of the survivors. There was an empty space on the grass between the two groups; it was as if they belonged to different armies.

The adjutant was calling out names, reading from a list by the light of a flickering lamp. He paused after each name. Sometimes a hand went up and a weary voice answered, but usually there was silence; just the early-morning breeze rustling the leaves in the trees.

And then the adjutant would ask if anyone knew anything of the man and sometimes a mate would call out that he had seen him fall when they went over. But often there was no response. And the adjutant would mark an "M" for missing against the name and move on down the roll.

The colonel sat beside him red-eyed and stony-faced, flinching slightly in response to each unanswered name. He looked out at the utter ruin of the battalion that he had worked so hard to mould and train and he despaired. He bitterly regretted that he hadn't gone over the top with the men and shared their fate, ignoring the orders from division to remain behind. He felt he'd lived too long and seen too much and he wished that he was dead.

At the end of the roll call the survivors were given rum and then lay down where they were on the grass while those that had been left behind in the attack shuffled back to the billets to begin the day. Rawdon had gone over to join Luke but Adam remained where he was. The sun was coming up over the trees. He could feel the first stirrings of its warmth on his face, and the dew in the grass was glistening silver, interwoven here and there with cornflowers whose exquisite blue matched the pale colour of the sky and the wings of a chalkhill blue butterfly fluttering just above their upturned petals. How could such beauty exist in the world? Adam thought with a dull, uncomprehending wonder.

Behind him he felt a hand on his shoulder and, turning round, he came face to face with Ernest.

"I'm sorry," said Ernest. "I wish I could have been there with you; helped—"

"No, you don't," interrupted Adam harshly. "You're a fool if you think that."

Unprepared for Adam's anger, Ernest took a step back. "I didn't choose not to go," he said. "You know that."

"Yes. And so be grateful you didn't," said Adam, refusing to be appeased. He didn't want to talk to Ernest: he was like a stranger; someone he didn't know any more.

"Was it that bad?" asked Ernest.

Adam nodded.

"And the captain?"

Dead, Adam tried to say, but he found he couldn't. His throat was dry and his head was throbbing and there was a sound of rushing in his ears mixed up with distant gunfire, and he couldn't see Ernest any more, just a swirling kaleidoscope of dead glassy-eyed faces: Seaton and Earle and the German who'd called him Tommy and the bodies in the blankets piled up in the back of the GS wagons behind the basilica. He was crying: hot, salt tears in his eyes and on his cheeks; and Ernest reached out just in time and caught him, arresting his fall as he fainted, his legs buckling beneath him like dead wood.

He came round with his head in Ernest's lap, gazing up through a blur into his friend's kind, anxious face. Ernest had his water bottle in his hand and raised Adam's head with his other one to enable him to drink. The petrol-flavoured liquid had never tasted so good and Adam drank greedily and then reached out, tipping more of the water up over his face.

"I'm sorry," he said, sitting up and rubbing his eyes. He felt incredibly weak but at least the world had righted itself and the rushing had disappeared from his ears.

"I'm glad I was here," said Ernest. "To catch you, I mean."

"So am I," said Adam, smiling. And Ernest smiled too and spontaneously they both laughed, dissolving the tension between them. Down below some of the men were moving, gathering enthusiastically around a khaki figure with a Vest Pocket Kodak camera in his hands.

"Come on," they shouted, rousing those who were still asleep. "Come an' 'ave your picture took."

Adam and Ernest went down the hill. And the soldiers pulled Adam to the front to join the rest of the group that had come back from the German trench in the place of honour at the centre of the photograph. Next to Adam sat Luke, self-consciously staring at the camera with the ill-fitting German Pickelhaube helmet perched on his head—all that the battalion had to show for their participation in the Big Push.

———

Life went on. The sun rose and the sun set and the mail orderly brought parcels from home. Many of them were for the dead and missing, but the soldiers opened them just the same and shared out the chocolate and cake sent by mothers who did not yet know the fate of their sons, raising mugs of lukewarm tea to toast the memory of their departed comrades.

They were angry. Angry and disillusioned. They had lost faith in the generals who had promised them victory only to deliver disaster, and they mocked the staff officers who rode by on tours of inspection with their pressed breeches and shining silver spurs, calling them plush-arsed buggers and geraniums after the red bands they wore in their hats.

Stories abounded of how out of touch they were: according to Rawdon, who had it on good authority from a corporal he'd met on fatigue duty, one staff captain had gone up to the front line, looked out over the parapet, and exclaimed: "Good God, I didn't know we were using colonial troops!" Rawdon was a good mimic and gave a perfect imitation of the officer's strangled upper-class voice before reverting back to his own north-country dialect: "So 'e wanders off pokin' the duckboards wi' 'is swagger stick like 'e owns the place, an' the sentries are laughin' at 'im behind 'is back, laughin' fit to burst. 'Ain't the bastard seen a dead man afore?' they go. 'Cos the poor bugger's turned black i' the sun o' course; black as the fuckin' ace of spades.' "

Everyone laughed. They might have lost their innocence but they hadn't lost their sense of humour and laughter helped keep their fear at bay: the fear that it was taboo to admit to, but which haunted each and every one of them as soon as they were alone, gnawing constantly at their minds, now that they knew what going over the top really meant.

Up ahead, other battalions were taking their turn and having more success too. The generals—or at least some of them—seemed to have learnt their lesson from the first of July: the troops attacked now in the misty grey light just before dawn after short hurricane bombardments that kept the Germans in their dugouts until they were nearly across, following an exact one hundred yards behind a creeping barrage of high-explosive shellfire that rolled forward at a precise fifty yards per minute. This new clockwork warfare enabled the British to edge slowly up the hills, advancing from one enemy line to the next, but there was no breakthrough, no cavalry charge into open country, and the casualty figures mounted steadily as the weeks passed and the Germans fought over every inch of the land, constantly counter-attacking in an effort to take back what they had lost.

Between each attack there were pauses while the generals conferred in their châteaux behind the lines and the vast British war machine laboriously readied itself to throw another lumbering punch. Adam's company went back into the front line in the middle of one such pause, occupying German trenches that had been viciously fought over during the previous week. The British had also for a time established a foothold in the next line but had been driven back across a new no man's land that was now as full of corpses as the land behind.

These men required Christian burial or so at least Parson Vale believed. He had changed since the Push, although Adam was sure that the seeds of the transformation had been germinating inside his old friend for months. The war changed everyone except perhaps the staff, and the parson had been at the front almost since the beginning—an unimaginably long time. Adam remembered him talking in the YMCA canteen about his divine mission to minister to the men, but now he seemed to have abandoned that vocation to focus on the dead instead. Perhaps it had just got too hard to keep telling soldiers living in terror and misery that God loved them, whereas the dead asked no questions. All he had to do was say the words of committal, make the sign of the cross over their bodies, cover them up with mud, and he could send them to paradise on the wings of a prayer.

In his new incarnation the parson had become hard and obsessed, forever looking impatiently over the shoulders of whoever he was with, anxious that he wouldn't be able to reach the burial target that he had set himself for the day. Gone was the wise, sophisticated, learned intellectual that Adam had grown to love almost as a second father during the long afternoons and evenings they'd spent together in the parson's book-lined study, talking about Greece and Rome and God and the future back in those days when Adam thought that he had one, while the sun set over the trees and the shadows lengthened across the carefully tended lawn and the flower borders outside the window.

In consultation with the colonel, the parson had fixed the twilight hours before dawn and after dusk as the safest times to carry out his chosen work, and he would arrive in the front-line trench precisely on time wearing a white surplice over his uniform and then stand, looking impatiently at his watch, while the burial detail formed up—usually a corporal and two privates. Rawdon, Luke and Ernest did everything they could to avoid involvement even though volunteers were excused other fatigues and rewarded with tots of rum before and after the work to wash away the germs and give them courage. But Adam frequently agreed to go out of a sense of loyalty to his old friend, even though the parson never referred to the past any more and eschewed any kind of small talk. One morning when Adam asked after Miriam, the parson didn't seem to know whom he was talking about.

The burial party divided into two groups. Parson Vale and Adam, out in front, would search the body and drag it over to the nearest shell hole, position it facing the enemy, and then the parson would say the words of committal before they each shovelled twelve spadefuls of earth down on to the corpse and moved on, leaving the two privates, following behind, to add twenty more and plant the dead man's helmet on top of a bayonet to mark his grave.

Sometimes, if they stayed out too long in the morning, the enemy would catch sight of their shadowy figures and start firing at them as they worked, forcing them to get down on their stomachs, but this didn't stop the parson; in fact the bullets only served to increase his determination. Lying flat on the torn-up ground at the lip of a shell hole, holding out the cross around his neck above the mangled remains of a soldier, looking like a scarecrow in his filthy surplice, he would shout out the words of committal: ". . . in sure and certain hope of the resurrection to eternal life through our Lord Jesus Christ," so loudly and fervently that for a moment Adam almost believed in them too.

Sometimes resurrection arrived quicker than anticipated when a shell came crashing down, blasting the newly buried corpse back out of his grave, but the parson paid no heed to this. He took care never to look back over his shoulder, as if he knew that that was where doubt was waiting, and every day his wide-open blue eyes obsessively seeking out the next corpse seemed to Adam to have become more fixed and staring than the day before.

The smell of the bodies was appalling: a foul sweet stink of putrefaction that rose up in nauseous waves as soon as they were moved. Soon the soldiers took to wearing gas masks as they worked. But the parson refused to wear even a handkerchief over his face: God needed to hear his prayers as he sent the dead to Jesus.

And it wasn't just the smell; the corpses were dreadful to look at even in the semi-darkness and were almost unbearable to touch. The rats screamed and ran as the burial party approached, but the flies, clustered so thickly on the rotting flesh that they looked like black fur, were so drunk from feasting that they crawled rather than flew away, leaving their white maggot progeny behind, rustling like silk as they wriggled against each other inside the wounds, and the soldiers had to remove their gas masks to vomit their disgust before they could carry on with their work.

Some of the bodies had no legs or arms and some had even lost their heads, and with these the parson drew the line. Dismembered corpses had no prospect of eternal life; without a head there could apparently be no hope of resurrection. The worst were the cadavers that had lain in shell holes filled with rainwater. Fat and bloated but apparently whole, the bodies came apart in the buriers' hands. But still they had to keep searching through the slimy decomposing flesh, feeling to find the two identity discs that every British soldier wore around his neck.

They removed the red disc but left the green one. And where the uniform was still intact, they took the pay books from the right-hand breast pockets of the dead men's tunics and their wallets from the left, and gave them to the parson who saved them in small canvas bags of which he kept an endless supply in his pockets.

The pay books had details of the man's religion so that he could be buried with the correct rite, but Parson Vale paid no attention to that. All the dead were his flock and he was sure he could save them all: Catholic, Protestant, Baptist, even the agnostics and atheists. And besides, he knew that he was the only chance they had: none of the other padres were crazy enough to walk up and down the front line twice a day, risking their lives for the dead.

Their wallets often had sad and useless lucky charms inside— sprigs of purple heather or St. Christopher medals—and there were tiny photographs too of mothers and sweethearts who were probably pacing the halls of their houses somewhere on the other side of the Channel at that very moment, waiting for news of Joe or Henry or Bob, hoping for the best, unaware of the carrion that their loved ones had become. And the parson made it his business to make sure that they didn't. Back behind the lines, in the breaks between burying, he wrote letters to the next of kin named in the pay books, telling them that their sons had met heroic and instant deaths in the service of their country. "I lie to them," the parson told Adam, looking triumphantly defiant. "And I glory in the lies."

It couldn't go on. The parson was going mad and the soldiers speculated on whether it would be an enemy bullet or the final unhinging of his mind that would put a stop to his activities. But as it turned out, it was a combination of the two. One morning, just after he'd climbed up the fire-step ladder into no man's land to begin work, a star shell lit up his surplice in a brilliant white light and a sniper's bullet tore into his shoulder. He was luckier than Seaton: his wound was less deep, and the RAMC surgeon was able to extract the bullet and send him back to the base hospital to recover. But he got off the train at the first stop and made his way back to the front, covered in bandages, determined to resume work. And when the redcaps tried to stop him, he became violent, lashing out in all directions and reopening his wound in his process. Bloody and raving, he was carried away and taken under guard to a different kind of hospital in Rouen where there were bars on the windows and locks on the doors and a new sort of electric shock treatment to be had in a soundproofed room at the end of the corridor.

The late June rains that had delayed the Big Push returned now with a vengeance, falling steadily out of leaden skies in which the guns lit up the heavy rain clouds hanging low over the battlefield in blackened red and gold. In the dripping gloom the trenches turned to mud and the duckboards sank away into glutinous depths. The soldiers tried to improvise shelters by stretching out their waterproof groundsheets and hanging them over their heads, but all too often these makeshift tents collapsed under the weight of the rain, treating those underneath to a sudden and unexpected cold bath.

The Germans had built the trenches they were now occupying and this meant that their artillery was able to exactly register their field guns on the new targets and send over an irregular but accurate barrage that took a heavy toll on the company's numbers and their morale.

It was a terrible existence. During artillery attacks the company stood with their numbed feet and calves covered in filthy water, cowering against the shaking sides of the trench as they listened to the invisible coal-box shells roaring through the air towards them. The crescendo of noise became a wild shriek as they approached, only to pause silent for a moment before they crashed into the parapet or parados, sending a torrent of displaced earth down on to the defenders' heads as they staggered backwards under the impact of the concussion, coughing in the black acrid smoke, choking on the vile smell of the cordite, and counting their luck if they escaped being hit and burnt by the exploding shrapnel that sizzled in the wet earth all around them like white-hot cinders scattered from a fire.

The whizz-bang shells were even worse: flying faster than the speed of sound, they gave no warning of their approach. And it was one of these that buried Adam at the end of the company's first week in the front line. Suddenly, without warning, the trench wall against which he was standing collapsed and he was in the pitch-black dark.

He couldn't hear anything or see anything but he could taste the sticky, cloying mud on his lips and he could feel it pressing down on his body. He tensed his muscles hard against its weight but the effort was useless: he couldn't move at all—and he was only able to breathe because his steel helmet had slipped down an inch over his face as he fell, protecting his eyes and nose and creating a tiny air pocket.

He could hear his heart hammering in his ears like a piston and he desperately wanted to scream, but he gritted his teeth instead and forced his mouth to stay shut so he wouldn't swallow the mud. The oxygen was fast disappearing and his lungs were bursting when he felt the earth moving above his body, and he pushed up madly in response because he suddenly could, and Rawdon was pulling him by his hands upright into the light, and he opened his mouth and half choked, gulping and gagging on the air as though it was water.

He'd been buried for no more than a few seconds but afterwards he could never forget the experience and his dreams became strings of nightmares in which different events always led to him being immured in pressing blackness either alone or with the cold bodies of the dead for company—his father, his mother, Edgar, Seaton, the men he'd killed—piled up around him like in the barricade they had made at the end of the German trench. He struggled for breath, he began to suffocate, but he never quite died; he just awoke screaming beside his friends who were shouting at him to shut the fuck up because they were desperate for sleep just like him.

Like them, like the parson before, Adam was slowly but surely coming to the end of his tether. He longed for an end, any end, even death if it was quick and easy and not a stomach wound like the one that had got the poor devil he'd left behind in the shell hole, clawing at his spilling guts, when they'd charged the German trench, or one of those mutilations that kept you screaming out in agony for days like the maimed men he and Rawdon had passed when they carried Seaton back across no man's land in the moonlight.

But death wouldn't come. Instead Adam seemed to lead a charmed life. The very day after he was buried alive another shell came howling straight towards him and embedded itself in the earth a yard away from where he was standing with a box periscope keeping watch, but it failed to explode. He stared blinking at the dud and thought that his survival couldn't be explained by chance; there had to be some higher power that was watching over him, engaged in a diabolical experiment to measure his suffering and capacity to endure.

He remembered the Devil-God that he'd half believed in for a time after his mother died: more cruel and vengeful than even the version of Jehovah propagated by old Father Paul, the red-faced hell-fire preacher who had terrified his captive congregation every Sunday from the pulpit of the Church of the Holy Martyr. And this vision of a malevolent fate controlling the world returned to him now, rein-forced by his reading of *Tess of the D'Urbervilles*. Seaton had given him the book in late June, inscribing a dedication to "my dear friend, Adam" on the flyleaf, but he had only started reading it now, snatch-ing opportunities between shelling and fatigues, often at night when he strained to make out the print by the light of a guttering candle that he held up to the side to prevent the hot wax dripping down on to the page.

The book was precious to him because it was Seaton's gift but he also felt an instinctive understanding of Hardy's vision. Like Tess he and his friends were playthings, puppets in the hands of a cruel fate, waiting for the President of the Immortals to grow tired of his sport.

They were all gripped by fatalism, each of them waiting for the shell that had their name on it to arrive, packed by some bored girl in a faraway Krupps factory, loaded by some anonymous Hun artil-leryman, but destined for them and them only. And as they waited, they sang resounding choruses of the old music hall song:

"Just break the news to Mother,
She knows how dear I love her,
And tell her not to wait for me,
For I'm not coming home . . ."

. . . to the accompaniment of a tuneless maudlin whine extracted by Rawdon from his penny mouth-organ, which made them laugh.

They were worn out; growing old; and it seemed sometimes that all they had left was laughter. They laughed at Rawdon's jokes and at the rats they clubbed and bayoneted and hung up in rows off the parapet like trophies from a game shoot; they laughed at each other making raspberry farting noises through the coagulated saliva in the rubber flippers that extended outside their crazy-looking gas helmets, while they waited for the gas shells the Germans had sent over to dissipate in the Vermorel spray; and they even laughed at the exploding shells that sent the mutilated corpses bursting up from Parson Vale's graves out in no man's land, performing mad head-over-heels somersaults before they crashed back to the ground, even bouncing sometimes before they broke up into a hideous mess of decomposing flesh and bone. They laughed because there was nothing else they could do, trapped impotently in the smashed-up trench as the shells poured down, unable to raise their heads above the parapet for fear of the German snipers awaiting their opportunity to take a pot shot at their heads.

Just as before the Big Push, Ernest's brother, Thomas, came into his own. Sniping, like football, was a focus of competition between battalions and Thomas was claimed to have more kills than any other sniper in the division. The difficulty of confirming any of these hits was conveniently overlooked by his comrades, just as they ignored the fact that his contribution only served to attract more enemy fire down on to their heads as the Germans tried to eliminate him. The soldiers wanted some form of payback for their suffering and Thomas provided an outlet for their frustration, in addition to serving as a distraction from their misery. They enjoyed his ingenuity: one day Ernest and Adam were on sentry duty when he came round the corner of the traverse, holding a huge turnip in a helmet high up above his head, spiked on the end of a bayonet. They burst out laughing; they couldn't help it: Thomas looked so solemn, as if he was carrying the cross at the front of a religious procession.

"Shut the fuck up," he said, giving Ernest an angry look. The brothers had never been close and the war had pushed them further apart. Thomas thought that Ernest was unmanly with his insistence on looking at both sides of every question and Ernest thought that his brother was a homicidal maniac.

"Sorry," said Ernest. "It's just you should see yourself: you look like such an idiot."

Thomas stopped for a moment, as if considering whether to take down the turnip and use the bayonet on his brother instead, but then turned away. "You're the one who's an idiot, Ernest," he said slowly, measuring out his words. "Dad thought that too, in case you didn't know."

Now it was Ernest's turn to look enraged, but Thomas had gone and all they could see was the helmeted turnip continuing on its way down the trench until moments later it exploded as a German sniper "got his man," and Thomas got his first bearing on the sniper's position.

After a reasonable interval Thomas did it again, going back down the trench the other way, hoping that the enemy sniper wouldn't suspect this double carelessness and see through his ruse. He didn't: the second turnip was duly blown to smithereens and Thomas had a cross bearing from which he could deduce the sniper's position behind an iron loophole in the German parapet, artfully concealed among the sandbags.

And then it was just a question of watching through his telescopic sights, waiting hour after hour until his inexhaustible patience was rewarded and the slot in the loophole slowly opened. The muzzle of the sniper's rifle emerged like a snail's head protruding from its shell, and Thomas fired the perfect shot, allowing himself a small cold smile of satisfaction as the enemy's rifle fell forward uselessly out of his dead hands.

That night everyone except Ernest drank Thomas's health from a double rum ration, and everyone except Ernest agreed with Luke's proposal that dispatching an enemy sniper should be worth at least five other kills, if not ten.

Chapter Twenty-Eight

Their mood of celebration didn't last. They had been more than a week in the trenches: much longer than they had been used to before the Big Push, but the new normal now that the army was having to cope with escalating casualties; and they had assumed that they would be due for at least the same period of rest behind the lines. But they had only been back in their billets for three days when they were sent forward again. And this time they had orders to attack. The generals were impatient for progress: the army's advance had slowed almost to a halt and they were desperate to drive the Germans out of the strategically positioned woods to the right of Pozières. Without control of them the British could not get over the ridge and into the open country beyond.

One of the generals—a junior one, "nowt much more than a brigadier" in Rawdon's estimation, stood on top of an empty water cart to address them through a megaphone while they stopped to rest and drink tea. It was a dark night with the new moon hidden behind low-lying clouds, and the general couldn't see his audience. But they could see him: flaring paraffin lamps burning at each corner of the improvised platform lit up his corpulent stomach, red, choleric face and walrus-like moustache.

"Don't stop—not if you're wounded; not if your best friend's wounded. Stopping is cowardice in the face of the enemy. That's what it is. And you're not cowards, you're soldiers. Bloody good ones too,"

395 | NO MAN'S LAND

he told them, emphasizing his words by striking the wooden planks with his swagger stick at the end of each sentence.

"Do you hear me?" he demanded and then paused, waiting for a response, but there was none—just a sullen murmuring and shuffling of feet in the invisible ranks down below.

And so he carried on, warming to his theme: "Don't stop, and when you get to the enemy don't hesitate. Because they won't: they'll bayonet you in the blink of an eye if you give the bastards a chance. And remember: the more prisoners you take the less chow there'll be afterwards, because we'll have to feed them out of your rations."

He chuckled so they would know he was joking, but no one laughed in response. Instead a voice somewhere at the back shouted out: "Why don't you fuck off back up the road, you fat pig?" And *that* made the men laugh: a rising tide of hysterics that swept through their ranks, enraging the general up on his platform.

"Who was that man?" he shouted. "Sergeant major, find out who the hell that was." he demanded of the RSM who was standing in front of the cart facing the men. But the general was wasting his time and he knew it. He'd have liked to punish the whole battalion but he knew just as well as they did that there was no worse punishment he could inflict on them than sending them over the top, which is where they were going anyway in just a few hours.

"Your battalion's a disgrace," he told the colonel as he climbed down the ladder, making for his staff car that was indeed going to take him back up the road to his château headquarters.

"No, it isn't," said the colonel. "It's the best damn battalion in the whole army. Or what's left of it," he added sadly. He wasn't sure whether the general had heard him as the rear door of the car closed with a bang just as he finished speaking, but he saluted anyway before turning back to his men.

There's only one thing I want to know," he shouted to them. "Are we downhearted?"

"No," they shouted back.

"I didn't hear you," he told them, cupping his hand to his ear. "Are we downhearted?"

"No," they roared. They loved their colonel just as much as they hated the generals and the sleek, self-satisfied staff.

"Good," he said. "Rum ration all round, sergeant major. The men deserve it."

They hoisted their rifles and packs and marched on silently along the broken, shell-cratered road with stony, expressionless faces. It was different to when they had gone up for the Big Push: now they knew what to expect and fear gnawed like a rat in the pits of their stomachs and at the back of their dry throats, trying but never quite able to extinguish the flickering flame of hope that each of them kept burning in their hearts right up to the last moment.

They were within range of the enemy's guns and it was hard to keep putting one aching foot in front of the other when shells were landing all around. After one explosion lit up the sky, two wild, terrified horses came charging down the road towards them, forcing the men to jump aside into an overgrown cornfield to avoid being trampled underfoot. The horses had broken free of their shafts when the wagon they'd been pulling overturned and shattered under the impact of a blast that had also killed their driver, whose sightless eyes stared up at the troops from behind a wheel as they passed him by minutes later. They tried to ignore what had happened. Everyone knew that wagon drivers were getting killed all the time, but they still felt that what they had seen was an omen, auguring the worst for the attack.

Adam could feel Ernest shivering beside him as the column thinned to two abreast in order to pass through the narrow communication trench that led up to the front line. "I'm glad you're here. I missed you last time," he said, putting a hand on Ernest's shoulder during one of the frequent stops caused by a soldier in front of them tripping or becoming entangled in the festoons of telephone wire that had come loose from its staples on both sides of the trench.

"Thanks," said Ernest. He knew perfectly well that Adam hadn't missed him on the first of July, but he also understood that his friend was trying to tell him that he wasn't alone, and the knowledge helped.

Up ahead two green star shells rose slowly up into the night sky, temporarily illuminating the densely forested wood which they had now entered. And as the lights reached their zeniths and dropped back down to earth, the birches and oaks seemed to elongate, reaching their tangled branches out towards the soldiers as if they were tentacles trying to pull them into the undergrowth. Some of the trees had already been damaged or uprooted by shellfire and their leaves hung yellow and limp, poisoned by cordite. The wood was a sinister, baleful place and the soldiers' courage failed them at the sight of it.

The front-line trench when they reached it turned out to be a trench only in name. The diggers' spades had been defeated by the thick tree roots, and the soldiers had to crouch down in what was no more than a shallow ditch in order to find any shelter. But at least they didn't have to wait long. Just as the darkness began to give way to the grey mist that prefaced the dawn, the guns behind them opened up a deafening fusillade, supplemented by the rapid firing of several Stokes mortar batteries that had accompanied them up into the front line. Adam remembered how Davy had argued so bitterly with the mortar sergeant when he started firing from their trench and how he had been tied to the gun wheel for his pains when they went back behind the lines. All those events seemed so long ago now, as if they had taken place in some other lifetime. And Davy wouldn't be complaining now, Adam thought: they were going to need all the firepower they could muster to keep the Boche quiet when they went over.

He reached out again to calm Ernest's shaking arm, but realized his was shaking too. And he needed to keep his hands over his ears: the noise of the gunfire was terrible, building inexorably towards a mad climax. On the other side of Ernest, he could see the white, ashen faces of Luke and Rawdon. He stared at them, nodding his head. And beyond them the lieutenant, a new officer fresh out from England, looked at his watch and rose unsteadily to his feet, sending them all forward with an inaudible whistle and a wave of his arm that reminded Adam utterly irrelevantly of a referee starting one of the football matches he'd played in on the muddy Scarsdale pitch years before.

Ernest wasn't moving and so he pulled him up and together, gripping hands, they went forward. It was hard to see. Ahead there was an expanding cloud of smoke, but it wasn't the grey smog-smoke that billowed up out of Yorkshire chimneys poisoning the sky; this was a curtain of different colours intermingling in the cool early-morning breeze to create beautiful tints that coalesced and vanished, only to be immediately replaced by new tapestries, all lit from inside by the explosions of the barrage that was advancing too, at a steady fifty yards per minute, towards the German line. It was a vision of heaven, and hell too: there were bullets in the smoke and all around them the wood was crackling under their impact as though it was on fire.

It was hard to keep going behind the shells, trying to believe that none of them would fall short. And hard also to stay in touch with the other men: the tall trees rose up out of the smoky mist one after the other like gaunt sentinels blocking their path and the ground between them was uneven, covered with thick undergrowth that concealed invisible roots. Adam couldn't keep his hold on Ernest and when he called out to him there was no response. He blundered forward. Up ahead there was a break in the trees: one of the rides or paths through the wood that they'd been told about before they went up. On the other side of it was the German trench and Adam was sure he could see shadows charging across the open ground. He started to run. It was like the first of July, except that this time they had the barrage and the smoke for cover and they were going to succeed. Adam was sure of it. He was determined not to be left behind.

He tripped, banging his knees hard and knocking his chin. He could taste blood in his mouth where his teeth had bitten into his lip, but it didn't matter. He was about to get up, readying his legs for the final surge across the ride, when a vast scream tore into his ears, followed by a sledgehammer crash close by that threw him back on to the ground. He could hardly breathe: he felt as if he'd been punched by a boxer hard in the solar plexus. Inside his helmet his head was pounding, while up above, the smoky sky was filled with stars, shaking like the inside of a child's kaleidoscope.

And into this wild vision came a great shadow, blocking out

everything else. But it was real. He knew it was because he could feel the tree roots ripping in the ground under his body; he could hear the fatal rupture of the old trunk; and with all his senses he was aware of the huge tree plunging down towards him. Instinctively he lifted himself on to his palms, thrusting backwards on his hands and feet like an upturned insect in a frantic effort to get away. Everything around him was tearing and breaking and he closed his eyes as his body went rigid, awaiting the shock and the pain, readying itself for death.

But he didn't die. The ground quaked, shuddering under the impact of the falling tree, but Adam was unhurt. His final despairing backwards lurch had precipitated him into a slight declivity in the ground, a small shell hole perhaps, and the uprooted tree had come to rest just above his thighs. He lay still for a moment, unable to comprehend this latest proof of his charmed life. But then, when he went to withdraw his legs, he found that there was another side to his luck, and that he hadn't in fact escaped scot-free. His lower body was trapped beneath the tree trunk. Wriggling and squirming made no difference. He could raise himself on his elbows but he couldn't properly sit up to the point where he could even start to try and dig down underneath his thighs.

He lay back with his head on the ground, exhausted. Now he cursed his luck. He'd been saved for nothing. Sooner or later he'd die here alone of thirst and heat exposure if a stray bullet or shell didn't finish him off first.

But he wasn't alone. Someone was cursing too, swearing and crying out in pain, and he was sure he recognized the voice. He looked round and there on the higher ground behind his head was a soldier, lying on his side so that Adam couldn't see his face. But he knew it was Thomas. And he also knew at the same moment that Thomas was dying even if Thomas didn't know it himself. He was missing an arm, probably severed by shrapnel from the shell blast that had trapped Adam under the tree; blood was spouting from the wound. And there were probably other injuries too that Adam couldn't see.

"Thomas," he shouted. "It's me, Adam." Then he stopped, at a loss for what to say next because it wasn't right to ask a dying man questions, even though he wanted to know what the hell Thomas was doing out in no man's land when everyone knew that trained snipers were under strict orders to stay behind in the trenches during attacks. He was far too valuable to the army to be used as cannon fodder sent over the top like his brother or Adam.

But Thomas answered Adam's question for him anyway. Because that was what he was cursing about in between his anguished cries: he yelled that he'd been forced over the top by the fucking stupid redcaps who wouldn't listen when he told them he was a sniper. No, he wasn't, they'd told him: they'd heard that one before. He was a shirker, swinging the lead, and when zero came they'd shoved their revolvers up against his head and pushed him out kicking and screaming into no man's land.

"They've killed me; tell my ma the army's been and murdered me," he screamed. "And after all I've fuckin' done for 'em."

And he started to cry: great, heaving sobs brought up from his lungs as if by a bellows.

"I'll tell her," Adam called. "And I'll make sure they don't get away with it; I'll make sure everyone knows. I promise."

But he didn't know if Thomas had heard him. Although Thomas's lungs continued to labour, he said nothing else and after a moment Adam heard the death rattle and Thomas's body twitched and was still.

Adam's mind reeled as he thought of the madness of it all. The redcaps had been criminal idiots. But their idiocy was no greater than the generals', sending thousands and thousands of men to die for the sake of at most a few miles of ground, or the governments' who wouldn't agree to a compromise peace because the sacrifice of those men would then have been in vain. He remembered Seaton talking about the politicians one night under the stars in some billet back behind the lines—"pounds and pennies men" he called them. And closing his eyes, Adam could almost hear his friend's voice, rich with irony, telling him about how eventually the two sides would run out of money and men and the war would come to an end and grass and crops would grow back over the trenches and everyone would forget. "Oxen and the plough instead of guns; farmers and woodcutters instead of soldiers; all just as it was before; all just as if the war never happened, except that we won't be here any more to see it," Seaton had said and Adam remembered how he'd smiled that slow, amused smile that Adam had loved so much but now would never see again.

He lay back, trying to clear his head. There was fighting all around him. He could hear the chatter of machine guns, the screech and roar of bursting shells, the tearing of shrapnel through the leaves and branches, but despite all this mayhem he continued to remain unscathed. It was as if he was in sanctuary, alone on an island atoll in the midst of a tormented, tempestuous sea, in the still eye at the heart of a hurricane.

Sometimes he could hear men running in the undergrowth; he could hear their shouts and yells. But he couldn't make out what was happening in the battle and he couldn't risk crying out for help. Some voices were English, but others were German, and he remembered all too clearly how they had shot at the soldiers caught on their wire on the first of July, laughing as they riddled them with bullets.

The hours passed and the sun rose high in the sky, beating down on him mercilessly. He had covered his face with his tunic but the heat was still driving him crazy with thirst. Early on, he had succeeded in reaching back far enough behind his head to get hold of Thomas's water bottle but then he had drunk it too quickly, and now he wouldn't permit himself more than the occasional sip from his own one. Over to his right there was a deeper shell hole half-filled with stagnant water but he could see the green scum of gas spread out over its surface and he knew that it would be fatal to drink from it.

In the afternoon he fell into a half-delirious sleep, dreaming of water. He walked once again through wet meadows to the banks of the River Ancre and knelt to drink, gazing down at the intricate reflections of weeping willow trees in the glassy surface of the stream. But he leant too close and the trees rose up suddenly to seize him, pulling him down into the river's black depths where their branches wrapped themselves around his legs and arms, holding him under as his lungs filled up with water. They were bursting and he had no breath and he was drowning until his brain suddenly pulled away from the edge and he was coughing his way back up to the surface of consciousness. He felt the rasp of the cough like the tip of a knife in his parched throat and sipped a little more of his fast-diminishing water to try and stave off some of the pain and dehydration.

Overhead a British aeroplane swooped and soared above the wood, graceful as a kite bird, while the pilot tried to make sense of what was happening down below. Eventually the aircraft dipped down low and Adam could see the pilot in his helmet and goggles leaning out as he repeatedly pressed the klaxon horn on the plane's pale cream undercarriage. It was a signal to troops down below to fire flares to indicate their position but there was no sign of any such response, just the sound of machine guns opening up, forcing the plane to climb steeply away, leaving only a trail of white smoke in the sky as it disappeared from view.

The episode led Adam to think that the attack through the wood had been unsuccessful. And his worst fears were confirmed when he looked out through the trees and saw grey-uniformed German soldiers walking in the ride. They had rifles with fixed bayonets in their hands and, as he watched, Adam could see the soldiers thrusting down with them. From where he was he couldn't see the floor of the ride but he knew full well what the Germans were doing. They were murdering the wounded, and every so often Adam could hear a shout or a scream as one of the victims cried out a last, vain protest.

The bile rose in Adam's throat and he vomited. Any one of those voices could be Rawdon's or Ernest's or Luke's, and he knew it would be his turn soon if the bastards crossed over into the trees to carry on their cruel work. Innumerable times in the last weeks he'd thought of death, imagining it as a release from all his suffering. But this abstract concept was a world removed from the agony of dying on the point of a bayonet, transfixed while the blade twisted inside his poor body until the end came.

He remembered the terror on the dead faces of the prisoners that Earle had murdered in the German dugout and their blood and guts seeping out on to the floor. He had to try and save himself. Lying flat on the ground, he stretched back behind his head, feeling for a hold on Thomas's tunic. But instead he was touching the soft, gluey stump of Thomas's arm where it had been severed from the shoulder. He recoiled violently, swallowing hard in order not to retch, and forced himself to try again.

Now he had hold of the webbing around Thomas's midriff and, using all his strength, he pulled Thomas's body towards him. It came more easily than he had anticipated, turning over as it rolled down the slight slope before coming to rest against his head. Thomas's face was now inches from his own. The cheeks were blotched purple and the mouth was set in a ghastly grimace exposing Thomas's chipped yellow teeth, and it took all Adam's powers of self-control to stop him from pushing the head away, letting the body roll further down the slope and out of reach. Over beyond the trees he could hear German voices and the sound of gunshots and they seemed to be coming nearer.

Hastily, he pulled any undergrowth he could get hold of towards him for cover and then hoisted Thomas's body face-up over his own, turning his head hard to the side so that he could breathe. But at the last moment, just as he heard footsteps in the undergrowth, he remembered his feet. He thought there was a chance that his khaki puttees might blend in with the surrounding undergrowth but his boots were a different matter, sticking up like sore thumbs on the other side of the uprooted tree trunk. He just had to hope that whoever was approaching wouldn't look that way.

And they didn't. The footsteps paused for a moment and Adam held his breath and tensed his body so that it was as rigid in that moment as the one covering him, stiffened by rigor mortis. It took less than a second: enough time for the German officer to glance down at Thomas's livid, utterly dead face and move on. No point in wasting a bullet on a corpse, and certainly not a corpse as dead as that one, thought the young lieutenant from Nuremberg, softly whistling as he walked away.

Adam waited, counting the minutes. The footsteps had gone but he stayed where he was, terrified that they would return, until he could stand the weight of Thomas's body no longer and pushed it away, taking deep draughts of air down into his aching lungs.

It was cooler now and he felt hungry, so he ate the cheese and meat from his iron ration, but then regretted it immediately as digesting the food increased his thirst and he had very little water left in his bottle. He fought hard against the impulse to drink until suddenly some barrier in his mind broke and he reached out and tipped the bottle up on its end, taking all the remaining water into his mouth. He held it there as long as he could and then swallowed it in tiny bird-like gulps, delighting in the softness of the liquid as it passed across his raw, parchment-textured throat. But it wasn't enough: soon the dry craving returned, rasping and burning his tortured mind.

He lost touch with the world around him. Everything was jumbled and confused. Someone was calling to him, calling his name, but he couldn't answer. He wanted to. He opened his mouth to speak but no sounds came out, however hard he tried. He was crying but there were no tears; just a dry shaking that went on and on until he opened his eyes and saw a shape looming over him: a human shape. And water: someone was giving him water, and as he drank he could see that the shape was Rawdon. And Rawdon was digging and pulling and half supporting, half carrying him back through the stricken twilight wood.

"We were all lookin'," he said. "All of us. But I found you. I dunno why but I knew I would."

Adam nodded. It made sense and no sense all at the same time, and so he closed his eyes and slept.

Part Five

———◆———

The Parting of the Ways

He who fights with monsters should look to it that he himself
does not become a monster. If you gaze long into an abyss,
the abyss also gazes into you.

Friedrich Nietzsche, *Beyond Good and Evil*, 1886

Chapter Twenty-Nine

Adam slept for hours, oblivious to the gunfire. But when he woke up his hands were shaking so hard that he could hardly hold his mess tin to eat, let alone fire his rifle. The battalion's medical officer tapped his knees and elbows with a small hammer and listened to his heart and lungs and sent him out on the next ambulance train to a convalescent camp on the coast to "recharge his batteries." He was a kindly man whom Adam had always liked but he had a way of talking about the men as if they were machines, which was perhaps the only way in which he could cope with the nightmare that his job had become since the first of July.

But in this case the prescription proved effective. Every day at low tide Adam and the other camp inmates were marched down to the beach and arranged on the hard sand in a series of six-man circles, and as the white waves crashed in on the shore behind them, a no-nonsense Scottish sergeant in a kilt taught them to dance the Dashing White Sergeant and the Sir Roger de Coverley, shouting his instructions through a megaphone as he walked up and down beside the surf, observing their progress.

The soldiers were self-conscious at first but soon forgot their embarrassment as they became absorbed in learning the steps, bowing and turning and forming arches for the others to pass under. To their surprise, they found that within a few days they had become quite competent: the dances were like elaborate extensions of the parade ground drills that they had learnt while training back in

England. But they had to concentrate. The steps were complicated and there was no time for them to think about the war.

At the end of the week there was a performance inside, with a musical accompaniment supplied by a severe-looking local spinster with pince-nez playing the hospital's upright piano and the sergeant beating time in the centre of the floor with his walking stick. And at a break between dances halfway through the evening Adam glanced down at his hands and saw that they were quite still, resting on his knees.

Next morning he was packed and ready to return to the front when he was summoned to the office of the French doctor in charge of the camp and told that he had been given a week's immediate leave.

"Have you arranged this?" Adam asked.

"Arranged? I do not understand," said the doctor, looking puzzled. He spoke English fluently but slowly as if he was choosing his words.

"I mean: have you arranged for me to go on leave because you don't think I'm ready to go back to my battalion?" Adam's tone was almost angry. He was shocked by the doctor's announcement, as he knew that almost all leave had been cancelled since the start of the Big Push, but he was also surprised by his own negative reaction to the news. The thought of going back to England filled him not with joy as he might have expected but rather a sense of sudden dread that gripped him in the pit of his stomach.

"No, I assure you I have arranged nothing," said the doctor, smiling and opening his hands palms up as if to emphasize that he was telling the truth. "The leave warrant coming today—it is a coincidence. They do happen, you know." The doctor paused, looking quizzically at Adam, who was still frowning. "I hope you will pardon me asking but is there a reason you don't want to go back to your country?" he asked. "You don't seem to be very excited at the prospect."

"No, no reason." Adam shook his head and looked over towards the door, impatient to be on his way. But the doctor didn't take the hint. Instead he pointed to the chair opposite him across the desk and lit a cigarette while he waited for Adam to sit down.

"Going home is hard," he said reflectively. "The war stops. We leave it behind and the silence is intense. We understand that it is possible for it not to be. And yet we know we must return."

He was quiet for a moment, blowing smoke up towards the ceiling, watching its colour change from white to blue in the shafts of sunlight coming in through the tall window. Adam shifted uneasily in his chair, unsure whether he was being asked to respond, but then the doctor went on: "It is hard, too, going home because the soldier's family has no idea what he has gone through. And he cannot explain it to them because the war is outside the scope of their imagination. It is too terrible, too awful; it is beyond words. Do you agree?"

"I suppose so. I have never been on leave," said Adam.

"Yes, I know," said the doctor, looking Adam in the eye. "My point is that perhaps it is better not to try to explain or to describe. Rather be quiet and sleep for a few more days. The rest here has already helped you." He gestured towards Adam's hands.

Adam understood what the doctor was saying and felt grateful to him for his concern, but he also knew that his advice was impractical. Going home meant that he would have to talk about the war—to Sir John about the loss of his son and to Thomas's mother about the loss of hers, and, worst of all, to Miriam. He was changed, utterly changed from the boy that she had known before, and how could they remain pledged to each other if she had no knowledge of the person he now was? But who was he? What did he have left to offer her? And if he couldn't answer these questions himself, how could he answer them for her?

The journey home was slow and uneventful. Adam's stomach rose and fell with the troop ship as it ploughed its way through rain and choppy seas to Dover. His spirits briefly lifted when he saw the white cliffs rising up out of the gloom, but sank again as he walked with the other soldiers in their grimy, mud-stained uniforms through the town's shabby streets to the railway station. He hadn't expected that there would be flag-waving crowds to welcome them as he remembered seeing in Gratton in the first year of the war, but he also hadn't been prepared for the weary indifference of the people they passed in the street, hurrying by in shapeless raincoats turned up at the collar without even a sideways glance at the men who had been fighting to save the country from the Hun.

Old tattered advertisements lauding the charms of Brighton and Bexhill-on-Sea hung on the walls of the dirty waiting room and the windswept platforms alongside newer recruiting posters that included several reminding travellers to "REMEMBER SCARBOROUGH!" which made Adam smile sardonically. How could he possibly forget the place? he thought, thinking anxiously ahead to the reunion with Miriam that awaited him at the end of his journey.

Inside the crowded gas-lit carriages it was hot and hard to breathe in the fug of stale cigarette smoke. But when Adam made the mistake of pulling down the leather strap to open the window and get some air somewhere south of Doncaster, the ash and soot from the train's smoke stack blew straight back into his face, leaving him half-blinded and black in the face. He laughed as soon as he had finished coughing the ash out of his lungs, but no one else in his compartment even smiled. They just looked irritated at his stupidity. He felt like a fish out of water. This was a new kind of England that he had never seen before: a dreary, humourless country where everyone was hunched over, minding their own business, just trying to get through their days in a grim struggle for survival.

And Scarsdale was the same when he finally arrived there the next morning. The town had always been poor and dirty but there had also been life in the streets. Now they were mostly deserted. Blinds were drawn behind the peeling paint façades of the box-like terraced houses, and the only sign of real activity that he witnessed was a group of filthy, barefoot children running quickly and intently past him in pursuit of a horse-drawn coal cart that was shedding bits of coke for them to retrieve as it juddered its way along the cobble-stones.

Half way up Station Street he stopped to look at a makeshift shrine. Some wilting carnations in a brass vase stood in front of a sepia photograph of a young uniformed soldier propped up against the brick wall beside a cardboard-mounted picture of the King and

Queen Mary, which had clearly been cut out of a magazine. With a start Adam recognized the man in the picture as Harry, remembering suddenly that the corner where he was standing was only a few doors down from where the twins used to live in a dark, squalid alley known as Paradise Row. Opinion in the town had always been equally divided on whether the name was a simple joke or a reference to the fact that the row's residents were already halfway to the afterlife, given the unhealthy conditions in which they had to live.

He'd remembered just in time. Out of the corner of his eye he could see the twins' mother, Mrs. MacKenzie, a prematurely aged woman in faded black widow's weeds, shuffling along the pavement towards him, and he took off up the hill at a run, hoping that she hadn't seen him. He doubted whether she would have had the courage to mourn her son publicly if she'd known of his execution and he wanted neither to support the army's lie nor tell her the truth about his fate.

He came to a sudden stop, forcing his brain to block out a crystal-clear vision that it had conjured up while he was running of Harry's bullet-riddled body writhing against the execution post in the playground in Albert. Scarsdale was a minefield, he realized—a mental no man's land in which ghosts and nightmares awaited him around every corner. Only a little way up ahead was Edgar's house where Adam had lived with his father, and he knew that sooner or later that was a door on which he would have to knock. But for now, Annie, like Miriam, would have to wait.

He broke into a run again, surging past the house at the end of Station Street and then left the road, heading out into the open country in order to bypass the Parsonage and the watchful eyes of Miriam's mother. He walked through fields overgrown with tall grasses and weeds—white nettles and burdock and Queen Anne's lace—breathing their fresh wet smell deep down into his lungs, and his khaki uniform blended in with their colours so that he looked and felt like a part of the landscape.

He was hungry and picked fruit from the trees and bushes as he passed and in one hedgerow he touched a warm bird's nest by mistake, withdrawing his hand quickly as the mother thrush rose squawking into the air. Carefully parting the branches, he could see the minute open beaks of the fledglings peeking out from above the sides of the nest and he stood there for a moment motionless, lost in admiration for its perfect construction—the tiny twigs woven and glued together into a cup-like shape rounded to perfection by the pressing breast of the mother. And yet he knew that all around there were predators who would seize the first opportunity to kill and destroy this intricate creation in the blink of an eye. He could make no sense of it, and he turned away, gripping his hands against his sides to stop them from starting to shake.

Over to his left, above the tops of the tall trees, he could see the golden weathervane on the roof of the Hall, and he clambered down the steep slope towards the road, holding on to overhanging branches covered with moss and lichens to stop himself slipping on the drifts of wet leaves that covered the ground. Everything was damp and loamy and the ferns growing under the trees were emerald green, their fronds arching out into fantastical fans.

He reached the bottom at a run, surprising a pair of rabbits that hopped rapidly away down the road before disappearing into the undergrowth. Adam followed them more slowly, glad to feel the firm surface of the tarmac beneath his boots, and, rounding the corner, he stopped in front of the familiar wrought-iron gates. On both sides the stone lions looked out just as before from atop their tall columns, but the crusted white bird droppings spattered across their heads and manes had the effect of diminishing their ferocity. And walking up the drive, Adam couldn't help but notice other signs of neglect. Here and there he could see potholes in the surface of the tarmac and several elms that had fallen close to the verge had been left where they were to rot. Beyond the trees, the white swans still floated regally on the lake but the water beneath them was choked with algae and its colour had turned from dark blue to a sickly shade of green. The lawns were overgrown and some stray grass was even growing up out of the tiny cracks between the flagstones in the entrance courtyard.

He went up the steps and was about to ring the doorbell but changed his mind at the last moment and turned round instead, looking out towards the lake. He had a strange sense that he could see himself as if in a mirror, a misfit standing there in his muddy uniform framed by the black door, alone in the silent courtyard surrounded by the lines of empty windows. He stayed quite still, waiting, as though his mind was a camera taking a photograph, and jumped, pirouetting around when the door unexpectedly opened behind him and Cartwright, shocked in turn, called out his name.

"Master Adam! We had no idea. You should have told us and we could have sent a taxi to pick you up from the station, although they're difficult to get these days—" The butler broke off, sensing that he was chattering in a way quite unbecoming to a butler.

But Adam wasn't listening. What mattered to him was the spontaneous, uncomplicated joy he could see on Cartwright's face and, feeling the same, he reached out, putting both his muddy hands on the back of the butler's immaculately pressed morning coat and hugged him close, just as he had on that winter morning nearly three years earlier when Cartwright had brought him the telegram from Oxford announcing his scholarship.

"Cartwright! I am so pleased to see you," he said and he meant it, although he was sorry about the dirt he'd got on his friend and was about to make it worse by trying to brush it off before Cartwright stopped him, horrified that Sir John might witness these multiple breaches of etiquette.

"How are you?" he asked, turning to look at Cartwright as he followed him through the door. After the changes he had seen in the grounds, he was nervous about what he would find inside the Hall and it reassured him that Cartwright looked the same as ever, straight-backed and perfectly dressed.

"I'm well, Master Adam. Thank you for asking. My hearing's not quite what it was, but I can't complain," Cartwright replied, consciously trying to introduce a little formality into their conversation after the unbutlerlike debacle on the front step.

In the hall he insisted on taking Adam's coat and boots and even his rifle, which he handled extremely gingerly as if anxious that it might spontaneously fire a bullet at any moment, even though Adam assured him that it was unloaded. He propped it upright in the umbrella stand beside the door and, turning round, he saw that

Adam, an utterly incongruous scarecrow-like figure standing on the ornamental black-and-white marble floor in his filthy puttees, was swaying from side to side.

Exhaustion had finally caught up with Adam. He'd hardly slept since he'd left France and he needed Cartwright's help to get up the stairs and down the corridor to his old room where he fell straight to sleep on the bed, deaf to Cartwright's pleas that he should take a bath or at least change into his pyjamas.

Charles woke him at six o'clock, bringing up hot water for the bath. Adam was surprised to see the footman. Sir John had written to him early in the year, sounding pleased that he had at least been able to force Charles to "do his patriotic duty" even though "that weasel, Brice," as his father called his younger son, was still refusing to join up, and so it made no sense that Charles was now back at Scarsdale Hall, hauling water up and down the stairs.

"What happened, Charles?" he asked curiously.

"I got shot in the leg," said the footman.

"I'm sorry to hear that," said Adam. "Were you at the Somme?"

"No, it happened over here while we were training. One of the other soldiers had left his safety catch off. Bad luck, I suppose."

Or good if it meant not being sent to France, Adam thought, wondering if Charles was telling the truth about how he'd come by his injury. He'd heard of too many examples of self-inflicted Blighty wounds since he joined the army not to be suspicious, and he'd noticed how Charles was studious about avoiding his eye when he spoke, although, that being said, the footman always seemed wary whenever their paths crossed, and Adam wondered not for the first time whether Charles suspected that he knew about his involvement in Brice's drowning plot three years earlier. Adam had never been able to confront Charles because that would have meant exposing Sarah, but he heartily disliked him and he was sorry to see him back at the Hall.

"You must be pleased that Sir John was able to take you back," said Adam.

"Yes, I was lucky," said Charles, not looking as though he meant it. "I limp a little but I can get around pretty well. If that's all for now, sir, I'll be back with more hot water."

"Yes, thank you," said Adam, looking curiously after the footman as the door closed. He wondered what Charles really thought about coming back to the Hall. He'd noticed how he hadn't taken the opportunity he'd been given to express gratitude to Sir John for taking him back, but then it didn't seem likely that he would be brimming over with thankfulness towards an employer who had rewarded his years of service by forcing him into the army. But there was no way of knowing. Charles had not been Lady Scarsdale's favourite servant for nothing: he was a past master at keeping his face a closed book.

The solitude and warmth of the bath was a luxury that Adam hadn't enjoyed since before he went to France. His pores opened in the steam and he scrubbed his skin until it was red and raw, exorcizing the trenches. But afterwards, looking in the mirror as he combed his hair, he could hardly recognize himself in his white tie and tails. The exorcism could only be skin-deep and he felt like an actor in fancy dress, about to step out on stage without a script.

Sir John was waiting for him when he came down the stairs. And, as with Cartwright before, Adam was touched by the warmth of his benefactor's welcome.

"Come and eat," said Sir John, putting his arm around Adam's shoulder and leading him into the dining room. "You look like skin and bones; they've clearly not been feeding you properly in those trenches!"

But it turned out that the Scarsdale Hall dinner was not much better than what the battalion field kitchen had to offer: a soup of watery vegetables was followed by a chop which contained more bone than meat, accompanied by a few overcooked turnips. The days of Mrs. Flowerdew's feasts had clearly long since come to an end, but Sir John didn't seem to notice. He drank heavily and Adam noticed how Cartwright's attempts to limit his master's consumption by not refilling his glass proved ineffective because Sir John kept pointing to it, demanding more wine. At one point when Cartwright was absent from the room, fetching another bottle, Sir John leant over and apologized for the butler: "He's getting old, you know; slowing down. It happens to all of us," he told Adam, nodding sagely.

At first sight Adam thought that Sir John was doing himself a disservice. His hair was slightly greyer and there were a few more wrinkles around his eyes than before, but the pupils had the same bright blue intensity, and he spoke with the same restless energy that Adam remembered from before. And it was only as the evening wore on that Adam came to realize the extent to which Sir John's recent troubles had affected his mental equilibrium.

As Adam had expected, Sir John was full of questions about the war and he did his best to answer them, even though he would much rather have talked about any other subject. But he soon discovered that Sir John wasn't really listening to his responses.

"We need to drive the Hun out of Beaumont-Hamel. That's the key to the whole battle, isn't it?" he asked, lining up the salt and pepper pots in front of him in a crude simulation of the Hawthorn Ridge.

"I'm not really sure," said Adam. "I'm only an insignificant lance corporal, you know. We don't get told much about the overall strategy."

Sir John nodded, but then five minutes later he asked virtually the same question again: "Tell me about Beaumont-Hamel. It sounds like quite a fortress!"

"Like I said before, I don't really know. I've not been in that sector, although I've heard of course about how hard it went with the Newfoundlanders on the first day," Adam said patiently, trying to come up with a variation on his first answer in order to keep the conversation moving.

But it was useless. After an even shorter interval Sir John was back on the same old hobby horse, asking Adam whether he thought the cavalry could be used to break the stalemate around Beaumont-Hamel.

Adam didn't know how to respond. The absurdity of Sir John's suggestion that the cavalry could be sent charging across no man's land was proof of how little he understood the nature of trench warfare and his constantly repeated questions about Beaumont-Hamel indicated that his brain wasn't functioning properly. Adam hoped that the wine was responsible but feared that the cause was more profound. Looking up, he caught a pained expression on Cartwright's face for a moment and also thought he detected a gloating look on Charles's, although it was too quick for him to be sure as the footman dropped his eyes as soon as he became aware of Adam's scrutiny.

It was strange too, Adam thought, how Sir John didn't mention his eldest son or ask about the circumstances of his death. It was the first question Adam had expected him to ask, and he had spent time on the journey north mentally preparing his response both because he found the subject painful and thought it would be easier to deal with if he knew what he was going to say, and because he believed that he owed it to Seaton to tell his father the true facts.

And so when dinner ended without Seaton being mentioned, Adam felt he could no longer remain silent. He waited until Cartwright had served the port and had left the dining room with Charles, and then launched into his prepared speech.

At first he thought it was going well. Sir John nodded vigorously, expressing his appreciation, as he described Seaton's bravery in leading raids across no man's land before the Big Push and his heroism in heading the charge on the German trench on the first of July. But problems arose when he tried to explain what happened in the dugout with Earle.

"You're saying Seaton was killed by one of his own men?" asked Sir John, looking bewildered.

"I'm afraid so. This man Earle had murdered all but one of the prisoners—"

"And what's wrong with that?" demanded Sir John, banging his fist on the table. "'The only good Hun is a dead Hun!' That's what Horatio Bottomley says and he's quite right."

"Not when they've surrendered," said Adam, standing his ground. "We have to try and stay civilized. It's hard; I can't tell you how hard it is out there sometimes, but we have to try. There's no point otherwise. That's what your son believed. And he was right."

"Well, I don't know about that," said Sir John, scratching his head. "This is war, you know."

"I do know," said Adam hotly. But then stopped, biting back angry words. He had been determined to stay calm, not just for Sir John's sake but also for his own. Even thinking about Seaton distressed him and it was unbearable that Sir John should not appreciate his son's true worth.

"Seaton wanted to stay in the trench with the Lewis gun," he went on after a moment, once he'd composed himself. "On his own, perched up on the parapet, so he could keep the Germans at bay while we got back—"

"Got back?" Sir John interrupted, looking puzzled. "So you didn't win . . . ?"

"No, we won nothing," said Adam, finally losing patience. "You can't *win*. That's the whole point. The generals and the politicians say you can, but the truth is you can't."

"Why?" asked Sir John, looking shocked. What Adam was saying contradicted everything he'd read in the newspapers since the beginning of the war, and yet there was something about the way the boy was talking—a vehemence and a sincerity, that broke through his certainties and opened him to doubt.

"You can't win because of the guns," said Adam with a sigh. "Machine guns, mortars, field guns, howitzers: it doesn't matter how much courage soldiers have, how much will; flesh and blood can't pass through bullets and shells, or at least not in sufficient numbers to have any effect. The guns win in the end and they always will. Not us, not the Germans—the guns."

He sat back, suddenly exhausted. Delivering a prepared speech was one thing, but to actually think about the war, to try to explain it, was almost beyond his capacities. And yet he had to finish; he had to tell Sir John about Seaton: not just part of what happened but all of it, right up until the end.

"We carried him back across no man's land. Me and Rawdon Dawes—you remember? The boy you didn't want me to see after my father died. Well, he's a man now. Only a few days ago he saved my life—" Adam broke off again, collecting his thoughts. He needed to stop being angry, he realized. It wasn't Sir John's fault that he didn't understand the war—it was impossible to understand it unless you went there and saw it and heard it and smelt it for yourself, and even that might not be enough if you were just a visitor, a tourist able to return home when you felt you'd had enough . . .

"We brought him back to Albert," he went on quietly. "Do you know where that is?"

"I think so," said Sir John. He was listening now—Adam could see that.

"Good. So there's a church there. It's been knocked about quite a bit, but it's still standing. And the RAMC had set up a hospital inside, but they wouldn't let Seaton in."

"Why?"

"Because there was nothing they could do for him. He was dying. And he understood that. And at the end, lying there on the hard ground under the stars, surrounded by all that . . . *mess*, he remembered you. He told me to tell you that he was sorry he couldn't keep his promise. He said that it was a bad habit making promises you can't keep. I don't know what he meant but those were his exact words."

Adam looked up and saw that Sir John had understood the message. He rocked back in his seat, as if he was absorbing a blow, but Adam carried on regardless, determined to get to the end of his account.

"Afterwards, in his last moments, he was talking about the Germans; about how they put up lights and sang carols last Christmas. That was what he remembered at the end," Adam said. "And I'll never forget that."

They were silent. Sir John looked at Adam across the dinner table for perhaps a minute. Several times he seemed as if he was about to speak before he thought better of it, until finally he got up from his chair and came round to where Adam was sitting and rested his hand on Adam's shoulder.

"Thank you," he said. "Thank you for telling me. I can understand how difficult it must have been."

He smiled sadly and then turned and walked away through the door, leaving Adam alone in the candlelit dining room with his memories for company.

———

Later, Adam found it hard to sleep. He tossed and turned, beset by night visions: a diffusion of dreams and mixed-up memories that gave him no rest. He thought he could hear voices—Seaton's infused with cool irony; Brice's hissing with pent-up rage—but when he sat up, listening intently, the sounds resolved into the creaking of floorboards and the noise of the wind in the chimney.

He was unused to the softness of the bed and halfway through the night he took his blankets down on to the floor. It felt better, but now there was the noise of distant thunder reverberating in his troubled mind like gunfire, and the sudden rattle of rain against the window panes as the storm broke felt like bullets. His thoughts reached out fearfully towards his comrades in France. He knew perfectly well that his absence had no effect on their safety. Survival in the trenches depended almost entirely on luck, and there was nothing he could do even if he was there to stop a shell blowing one or more of them to smithereens if it had their names on it. But unconsciously he was convinced that he had endangered them by coming home. He had tempted Providence and Providence would find a way of punishing him for his offence.

He remembered the cries of the men waiting to be butchered by the Germans in the wood; he remembered how he'd thought some of them were his friends out there in the ride, and he prayed over and over again to a God that he had no faith in whatsoever to "keep them safe until I get back; keep them safe, keep them safe, keep them safe . . ."

Muttering the words like a mantra, he got up, wrapped in his blanket, and pulled back the curtains, and sat in his chair watching the grey dawn breaking over the rain-spattered lake and the thick-leaved elm trees beyond. Until after a while his head nodded and he slept.

There was no sign of Sir John at breakfast, which was served to him by Sarah the housemaid. She had heard him coming down the corridor and, facing the door, had steeled herself to wait for his arrival. And it wasn't that she was surprised when she saw his look of instinctive revulsion. She'd been expecting it: she hadn't seen Adam since her illness and she knew full well how the yellow stain of the jaundice had ravaged her face. But she still felt hurt by his reaction; grievously hurt, in fact. She couldn't help it: she'd always liked Adam and hadn't slept most of the night herself after Charles had given her the news of his unexpected return the previous afternoon.

"You're not wanted at dinner," Charles had told her with a smirk. "Sir John thinks that Master Adam deserves a pass on looking at your pretty face his first night and I have to say that for once I agree with the old man."

Sarah hadn't responded. She'd long ago learnt that there was no point. Charles had a cruel tongue and had always hated her, and there would have been nothing he would have liked more than an excuse to treat her to some more of his vicious barbs. But she knew that with Adam staying in the house their paths would be certain to cross sooner or later, and she couldn't help her heart beating fast as her mood swung back and forth between dread and nervous excitement. She knew how he would react to seeing her but she couldn't help hoping that he wouldn't.

And so she felt crushed as she turned away from his horrified stare, going over to the sideboard to fetch his coffee when she longed instead to run past him through the door and up the back stairs to her tiny garret room where she could bury her face in her cold pillow and cry away her grief.

Her hands were shaking and she willed them to stop because she didn't want him to see. She was so upset that at first she didn't really take in that he was talking to her.

"Sarah, I didn't know you had come back. It's good to see you," he said. And, as she turned round, she could see from the open, almost eager look on his face that he meant it, although she didn't understand why or that there was no way he could ever explain it to her, not without telling her that she was ugly, which of course he couldn't do.

Because it was the ugliness that drew him to her: it told him that she had suffered and been ruined by the war just like him. For her the damage was visible, whereas for him it was hidden beneath the surface. But they were still the same—casualties, walking wounded, carrying on without hope of recovery, separated from the rest of the population by an experience that they could neither share nor explain.

He got up and held out his hand for her to shake and they talked while he ate his breakfast and she waited on him. In answer to his questions, she told him about the munitions factory and her illness and about the changes at the Hall since she had come back, although she was careful with her answers because she didn't want to sound as if she was complaining about her lot. She remained genuinely grateful to Sir John for taking her back after her illness even though the work had become steadily harder as the other servants left to join the war effort.

"How do you cope?" asked Adam. "This place is huge."

"We don't. There are whole sections of the house that we can't keep open any more so Mr. Cartwright has us put sheets over the furniture and seal up the doors. I suppose we're like an army on the retreat, except our enemies are dust and mice, not guns." Sarah smiled anxiously, regretting her fanciful choice of analogy. She'd been trying to avoid any mention of the war, instinctively understanding that that was the last subject Adam would want to talk about.

But he liked her image: "So Cartwright's your general," he said. "And a pretty good one, I should think; I'd wager he'd do a better job than Haig if he was given half a chance!"

Sarah laughed but then looked uncomfortable. Through the open doorway she could hear the old grandfather clock in the hall striking ten. The butler would be beginning his rounds and he could come into the dining room at any moment. She blanched, thinking how awful it would be if he was to overhear her discussing his merits with Master Adam, although she had to admit that that was unlikely, given his growing deafness. It had been getting worse recently and Charles enjoyed making fun of him behind his back, drawing cartoons of him holding up a speaking trumpet bigger than his head on the back of Sir John's copy of *The Times*, which came downstairs to the servants' quarters after the Master had finished reading it so that Cartwright could peruse it in turn before it was thrown away.

"Will that be all, sir?" she asked, anxious now to get away before the butler arrived.

"Yes, thank you, Sarah. Except . . ." Adam paused, looking nervous himself now. And then he got up from the table, taking a couple of steps towards her before he went on: "I want you to know that I haven't forgotten what you did for me. It took a lot of courage, and if there's ever anything I can do for you, you've only to tell me. I hope you know that?"

"Yes, sir; yes, I do," said Sarah, looking flustered. She turned, desperate now to get away, but Adam, apparently oblivious to her discomfort, stopped her by holding out his hand, just as he had done when she first came in. She had no choice but to take it, and Cartwright, coming into the dining room at that precise moment, stopped dead in his tracks, shocked by the impropriety.

"Thank you, Sarah," he said severely, drawing himself up to his full height and meaning quite the opposite. "That'll be all." And pulling her hand from Adam's grasp, Sarah scuttled past the butler and out of the door.

"Really, Master Adam! Don't you remember anything of what I taught you?" Cartwright shook his head, looking positively funereal.

"Not much," said Adam, smiling sheepishly. "But at least we weren't down on the floor examining the vacuum cleaner so I suppose there's been some improvement."

"A very minor one," said Cartwright, refusing to be appeased.

"Oh, get off your high horse," said Adam, laughing. "It was my idea to shake hands. I wanted to thank her, and don't think I'm going to tell you what for!"

"I'm glad to hear it," said Cartwright.

"But that doesn't mean I don't want you to answer me a question," Adam went on, suddenly serious. "It's about Sir John. You saw how he was last night, repeating himself, not really knowing what he was talking about some of the time, although he was better at the end. Is that normal?"

"I can't really say. He is not often in company. We are very quiet here now, Master Adam," said Cartwright, looking uncomfortable.

"Come on, Cartwright," said Adam. "Don't fence with me. You know that we both want the best for him and if I'm to help I need to know what's really going on."

"Sir John has had a great deal to contend with in the last twelve months," said Cartwright, choosing his words carefully. He was anxious himself about Sir John's mental state but it went against his grain to talk about it, even to someone he liked and trusted as much as Adam. "There are the financial anxieties and then he has had to cope with Lady Scarsdale leaving and Mr. Seaton's death. It's not surprising that these events have had an effect on him."

"What kind of effect?"

"He is distressed."

"And so he drinks?"

Adam apologized for his question almost as soon as it was out of his mouth, realizing that he had overstepped the mark—it was entirely inappropriate to expect Cartwright to discuss whether his employer was an alcoholic. But Adam also didn't need Cartwright to respond. He could picture clearly enough what was happening. Sir John tried not to think about "the events" as Cartwright called them, perhaps in part because he felt responsible for his money troubles and for driving his wife away. And so the anxiety and the guilt bubbled away underneath the surface, unhinging the operation of his mind that was also being damaged by his excessive drinking. He vividly remembered Seaton in Amiens Cathedral painting that word portrait of his father *shuffling through the empty corridors, listening to the echoes.* And it seemed as if those echoes were now driving the old man mad.

Sir John's demeanour at lunch underlined Adam's concerns. He talked in the same hurried, obsessive way that he had on the previous evening, although his chosen subject had now switched from Beaumont-Hamel to conscientious objectors. In a monologue that lasted through both the soup and meat courses, he described with obvious satisfaction the harsh treatment meted out to them by the

Military Service Tribunal in Gratton of which he remained an enthusiastic member.

"We ask them what they'd do if a Hun got hold of one of their sisters. Would they stand aside and watch or would they do something about it? And you can bet they haven't got a decent answer for that. Damned pasty-faced cowards—we give them three months in solitary picking oakum if they won't stop their conchie nonsense."

"They're not all cowards, you know," Adam said. "Some of them are, I grant you, but there are others who believe in what they're saying."

"Believe what?" demanded Sir John angrily. "That we should let the Hun come over here and ravage our women? Burn us in our homes?"

"No, they believe that you shouldn't kill other human beings—not for any reason; that that's God's law, which I suppose in a way it is—Christ's anyway."

"You sound like you're one of them."

"No, I'm not brave enough to have those kinds of principles!" said Adam, smiling. "Some of the conscientious objectors really are brave, you know. The Quakers run trains and ambulances to evacuate the wounded from the front. I saw them in Albert that night when Seaton was dying—good, brave men, trying their best to help. They deserve our thanks, not our contempt."

For the first time since he sat down Sir John was silent, although Adam had no idea at first whether it was the forcefulness of his words or his mention of Seaton's deathbed or a combination of the two that had had this effect. But it alarmed him that Sir John's face had become so pale and that the muscles around his mouth were working unnaturally as if he was biting his lip. He looked as though he was fighting some strong, overwhelming emotion.

"I hope I haven't upset you, sir," said Adam anxiously. "That wasn't my intention."

"No, you haven't upset me," said Sir John, putting out his hand to cover Adam's for a moment. "It's Seaton. No one has talked to me before about what happened to him out there, and last night and today you've made it seem real. That he's dead; that he won't come here again; that he was a good soldier. And I'm grateful to you for helping me see all that, but that doesn't mean it's not hard, very hard—" Sir John broke off, looking away towards the window while he fought to master his emotions.

"I suppose I hate the conchies so much because they remind me of Brice and of what the future will be for this house now that Seaton is gone," he went on in a stronger and yet still reflective voice. "That was the promise my son was talking about when he died; the meaning of the message that he asked you to give to me. Years ago I asked him to promise me that he would stay alive so that Brice wouldn't become my heir and now everything that I feared has come to pass. And there's not a damn thing I can do about it. The estate is entailed and it will be Brice's to fritter away when I am gone." He gestured with his hand. "And my only comfort is that I won't be here to see it happen."

Sir John beckoned to Cartwright to fill their glasses and then raised his to Adam in a toast: "Let's drink," he said. "To the last of the Scarsdales!"

Chapter Thirty

Throughout the afternoon Adam was about to go to see Miriam, but found excuse after excuse not to leave. He put on clean clothes and then changed into his dirty military uniform because he was a soldier, and then changed out of it again because it was so dirty, and finally got off his bicycle when he was halfway down the drive because there didn't seem to be enough air in the tyres. Delay after delay after delay until it was evening and he had no choice but to call off the visit for the day.

He felt ashamed of himself. Gossip spread quickly in a town as small as Scarsdale and Miriam would probably know by now that he was back, but he didn't have any idea how he would explain that he hadn't come straight to see her.

He already carried the burden of having to justify the brevity and infrequency of his letters. He could try to blame this on the war, which was true in a way, although it wasn't lack of time that had rendered him such a bad correspondent; it was rather that he hadn't the power of expression to communicate his experience to her, even if he wanted to, which he didn't.

He loved Miriam just as much as he always had. Even more perhaps, if that was possible; in France he had guarded his memories of her, taking them out one by one in quiet moments behind the lines, holding them up like a miser taking jewels from a treasure box.

He remembered, as if it was a vision, seeing her for the first time as he came out of the church on that winter morning, standing next to her father at the lychgate utterly unaware of him as he stared at her transfixed; he remembered the delicate, extraordinary softness of her hand when he held it for the first time in the arbour; and he remembered how he'd looked down at her lying on the Esplanade at Scarborough after the explosion not knowing if she was dead, and the wonder of the moment when she opened her eyes and he kissed her. That moment, that defining moment—perhaps the best moment in his life, when everything in the world had seemed charged with possibility despite the danger of the falling shells. And yet it was also the moment when his war really began; the war which had infected him like a cancer, taking him to a place where she could not follow.

Couldn't follow because he couldn't tell her what the war was really like without exposing her to its filth and corruption. It was different talking to Sir John—perhaps because he was a man— although even that was hard, but telling Miriam would be a sin which it was beyond his power to commit. And yet he also knew that if he didn't try to describe it, to convey it to her in some way, the gulf that had already opened up between them would soon grow too wide to bridge. Because the war had changed him; he was no longer the callow idealistic youth that had left England fit and ready for action nine months earlier. He had seen too much, heard too much, smelt too much: he had lost his innocence.

And so, fenced in on all sides, Adam had resorted to postcards and brief letters: platitudes that communicated nothing of his real experience. But now that wasn't enough. Unless perhaps they could pretend that everything was the same, he thought despairingly as he finally fell asleep in the small hours: put off explanations at least for now; paper over the cracks.

And so the next morning he dressed in a suit of clothes that he hadn't worn since he joined the army, as if to deny the reality of everything that had happened since, and set off on his bicycle, pedalling hard up the hill to the Parsonage, enjoying the feel of the wind blowing back through his hair. He was inspired by a sense of recklessness, almost optimism as he filled his lungs with the fresh, clean country air. He was ready to see Miriam, he told himself. In fact he was longing to see her. He loved her and everything was going to be all right.

And yet, just as he was approaching the Parsonage, he allowed himself to be delayed again. Glancing over the dry-stone wall of the graveyard, he saw a woman dressed in an old ill-fitting beige mackintosh kneeling down beside one of the newer graves. She had her back to him but he was immediately sure that it was Annie, Ernest's mother. He remembered the thin cotton scarf she was wearing over her head—faded roses intertwining on an off-white background. It had blown about in the breeze just as it was doing now on that day before the war when he went walking with Ernest and she came out into the side garden of her house to watch them go up the hill.

It was obviously Edgar's grave that she was tending. This was the newest section of the cemetery, containing the graves of the miners who had died in the 1912 explosion, and further back, in the shadow of the oak tree where he had waited in the rain to see Miriam three years before, Adam could see his father's grave with its carved white headstone, giving his name and dates. Parson Vale had seen to that, collecting the money from the contrite miners to pay for its erection. Adam remembered the funeral and how they had all come up to shake his hand as he stood looking down at the simple pine coffin sitting incongruously at the bottom of the black hole as if it had fallen in there by mistake. "Dust to dust, ashes to ashes": he'd seen enough burials now to last him a lifetime, although that one at least had not been accompanied by the sound of roaring gunfire and Jack Johnson shells flying overhead.

Annie had flowers in her hand: chrysanthemums and marigolds and a large red dahlia, which she was trying unsuccessfully to stand up in a thin glass vase at the head of the grave. He could see the problem: the bunch was too big for the vase, and the wind kept blowing it over on to the grass. But still she kept persisting, picking up the flowers and standing the vase up again and again. It was painful to watch and Adam felt compelled to intervene, although the thought also crossed his mind that he would prefer to have the talk with Annie about Thomas out here in the open rather than inside her house from which it might be more difficult to make an escape.

She didn't seem to hear him coming up behind her, and he had to say her name several times before she turned round and looked up. And immediately he took an involuntary step back, startled by the radical change in her appearance. He was sure, given Ernest's age, that she had to still be in her forties, and yet in the year since he had last seen her she had become an old woman. The change was so marked that he wasn't sure he would have recognized her if it had not been for the headscarf. Some of the stray hair peeping out from under it was bright white without a trace of the brunette that he remembered, and her small watery green eyes, recessed behind her thin cheekbones, peered up at him nervously as she took in who he was.

"Adam! Why are you here?" she asked in a querulous, fearful voice. "Has something happened?"

"To Ernest? No. He was fine when I left. I'm back on leave. That's all. Can I help you with that?" he asked, pointing to the flowers that she had dropped on the ground when she saw him.

"With what?" she asked, not seeming to understand.

"With the flowers: it may help if we embed the vase in the ground a little," he said, getting down on his knees beside her and digging down into the soil with his hands.

She watched approvingly while he fixed the vase in place and arranged half the flowers in a spray, giving the remainder back to Annie. "They're beautiful," he said. "Where did you get them?"

"From the garden. Edgar planted them," she said, pointing to the headstone as if her husband was standing there beside them. "And now there are lots of them . . ." Her voice trailed away as she let her eyes wander over the graves all around, contemplating the universality of death. "I wish my boy was here," she said. "I wish they'd bring him home."

It was an opening. *Tell my ma . . .* Adam could hear Thomas's anguished voice crying in the wood, demanding she be told the truth, and his own voice answering, promising that he would. Now was the time, except it was hard; harder than he could have imagined. She was so desolate: how could he bear to add to her suffering?

But she had a right to know and he had a duty to tell her. It was the soldiers' code: promises made to the dying on the battlefield were sacred, not to be broken.

"Can we sit down? There's something I need to tell you," he asked, putting out his hand to help her to her feet.

"What? You said everything was all right." The fear was back in her voice and he could feel the tension in her arm, fragile and rigid against his as he guided her over to an old wooden bench near the wall of the church.

"It is," he said. "It's just I have to tell you about Thomas . . ." He hesitated, searching for the right words.

"What? Do you know something, Adam?" she asked eagerly, gripping his hand; hope replacing terror in the blink of an eye. "They can get things wrong. I've heard that."

"No! I don't mean that at all. It's the opposite: I was with him when he died." Adam was practically shouting at her, horrified that his verbal stumbling had caused her to jump to the wrong conclusion. He cursed himself for not having prepared what he was going to say in advance, but then he hadn't expected to see her when he did.

"Oh!" The tiny word escaped from Annie like the air leaving a pinpricked balloon. Adam felt her hand grow limp and release him as the sudden charge of energy left her body. "What do you want to tell me?" she asked.

"That you should be proud of your son: he was an exceptional soldier," he said. He needed to tell Annie something positive about Thomas before he told her about the circumstances of his death, and this statement at least had the merit of being true, as far as it went. He hadn't liked Thomas but he had certainly respected him. "He was a marksman," he went on, "one of the best in our division, perhaps even the very best."

"A sniper, you mean. Yes, I know what he did. He killed people. He told me," said Annie. Her voice was flat, strangely lacking in curiosity.

"He killed them to stop them killing us," said Adam. He knew that this assertion was more dubious as it was hard to think of a German crouching over a latrine as a threat, although it was true, of course, that later he might become so. But Adam knew he needed to stay positive. "Thomas was special," he continued, choosing his words carefully. "And so he shouldn't have been sent into battle with the rest of us, but there was a mistake. And he wanted you to know that. I told our colonel about it before I left and he said he would make a report so I hope the men responsible will be punished," Adam finished lamely, sensing that Annie was no longer listening.

" 'A mistake,' " Annie echoed his words, staring out over the graves. "He should never have gone. That was the mistake."

"He died quickly," said Adam, lying now with reckless desperation as he tried to mitigate the hurt that he felt he'd inflicted. He was sick with guilt for having told her the truth, even though he knew he would have felt just as guilty if he hadn't.

"And then later, even though he was dead, he helped me," Adam told her. "A German officer was shooting the wounded with his revolver and I hid behind Thomas's body so he wouldn't see me, and he didn't. Without that, without Thomas, I wouldn't be here; I wouldn't have survived."

Adam spoke passionately, needing to insert something affirmative into the desolation and convince Annie and himself too that Thomas's death hadn't been all in vain. But she didn't seem to understand.

"Where is it?" she asked, staring at him out of her empty eyes. "Where is my son's body?"

He hesitated, not knowing how to answer. And in the silence, over to his right he heard a woman's voice calling his name. He looked up and saw Miriam running towards him. She was dressed in white, holding a straw hat with a red ribbon in her hand and the wind was blowing her rich brown hair behind her in a stream as she ran. She was beautiful. But she didn't belong. Not here; not now. He put up his hand and she stopped like a bird arrested in mid-flight.

"I don't know," he said, turning back to Annie, steadfast now in meeting her gaze. "Rawdon saved me, but your son was dead. There was nothing we could do—nothing! You have to understand that."

Annie was silent, lost in her thoughts. Out of the corner of his eye Adam could see Miriam waiting at the door of the church.

"I'm sorry," he said, getting up. "I told you the truth; perhaps I shouldn't have done, but I promised Thomas I would and so I felt I had to."

"No, you did right." Reaching up with her hand, Annie touched his cheek for a moment with her fingers just as she had once before. "Thank you," she said and, picking up her flowers from the bench, she turned and walked away.

For a moment or two he kept his back to Miriam, watching Annie as she approached the gate at the bottom of the churchyard, a diminutive grey figure not much taller than the long grass growing on either side of the path. She was receding from him but he was also pushing her away in his mind, because she represented the war and he knew he had to put it behind him to be with Miriam; he knew he had to try.

Drawing a deep breath, he turned and walked quickly over to Miriam where she was standing just inside the porch. And immediately, without thinking, he took her in his arms and kissed her, looking deep into her garnet-brown eyes as though he was drinking from a fountain to give himself strength. She was beautiful, more beautiful even than he remembered, but she was pure too, innocent and unblemished. And he was not. He was bloody with dead men's blood; he was filthy like a pig. He wasn't worthy of her; he should run away and hide before he infected her with his sickness . . .

He closed his eyes, fighting back his thoughts, determined to try and make it work between them. It was only for a few days. Surely he could find a way to muddle through.

"What is it?" she asked, drawing back. She'd seen the furrowing of his brow as he kissed her, the look of what seemed like pain on his face.

"It's nothing. I've missed you. That's all. And I didn't know when I would see you again. Happiness hurts sometimes," he said.

"Yes. Yes, it does," she said passionately. "I missed you too. Here." She put her hand on her heart. "And I've been so frightened. Every day the newspaper is full of pictures of dead soldiers' faces, lines and lines of them with their names underneath, and I kept thinking I was going to see you and it would all be over. I can't let my mother see what I'm feeling because she gets impatient"—Miriam glanced up towards the upper windows of the Parsonage—"but that doesn't mean I don't feel it because I do; I do!" She broke off, wiping tears from her eyes.

Adam took a step back, battered by the force of her outburst. It made him panic, made him want to run away. Because he knew what giving way to emotion meant; he'd seen it in the trenches: men curled up on the ground, crying like babies, fit for nothing.

"I'm sorry," she said, seeing the look of alarm on his face and making an effort in response to rein in her emotions. "I'm happy too. Really I am. I've been worried about you. That's all. But you're here now so it's all right."

She took his hand as if to reassure him and he raised it to his lips, wondering where they could go. Not to the Parsonage: he knew he would have to call on Mrs. Vale before he returned to France, but he didn't want to see her now and Miriam's glance back over her shoulder had told him that her mother was probably watching them from her window. They could go for a walk except that he felt suddenly exhausted. He'd slept badly ever since he got to England and the interview with Annie had been far more of an ordeal than he had expected. And so, keeping hold of Miriam's hand, he led her over to the bench where he had sat with Annie. It was out of view of the Parsonage and he needed to sit down.

"Was that Ernest's mother you were talking to?" Miriam asked. "I thought I recognized her."

"Yes."

"I know she lost her son just the other day. Not the one you're friends with; the other one. What was his name?"

"Thomas. He was in my battalion. Like Ernest."

"And her husband died too in that explosion. It's terrible. I can't imagine what she must be feeling."

"No."

He shifted uneasily: he knew that he had become monosyllabic in his responses, but to answer more fully would open him up to telling her about Thomas, bleeding to death from his severed arm in the hot merciless sun, cursing the army and God and France and anything else that came into his head. And he couldn't go down that path.

"Have you been all right?" he asked. "Apart from the worrying, I mean?"

"Yes, although I wish I could do something," she said. "Make some kind of contribution. I feel so useless staying here, arranging flowers in the church, knitting socks . . ."

"Why don't you?" he asked.

"My mother—she makes it impossible. When I talk about becoming a nurse or working on the land or anything like that, she has a funny turn and says she can't manage. But then when I stop she gets better. It's like magic!" Miriam smiled and he smiled back. This was better: if they talked about Miriam and her life here in Scarsdale then he could join in without reserve, and it could be like it had been before with no barrier in between them. But it was a vain hope. Almost immediately Miriam led the conversation back to the war: "Have you seen my father?" she asked anxiously. "We haven't heard anything since he went into the hospital in Rouen and he doesn't write."

"Well, you'll know he was wounded then, but I don't think it was too serious. He should make a good recovery. What he really needs to do is rest because he's been under a lot of strain," said Adam guardedly. "I'm sure he'll write when he's better."

"What kind of strain?" asked Miriam, looking into his eyes in the hope that she might find an answer to her question there. Already she'd sensed that he was holding back on her, limiting his answers in a way she didn't remember. The Adam that she loved and had agreed to marry was honest and open, not watchful and wary as he seemed now. The change in him alarmed her, making her want to understand its cause, which was of course precisely what he wanted to avoid.

"Please, you have to tell me," she said, pressing him when he didn't answer straightaway. "He's my father—I have a right to know."

Adam nodded, giving way. "Your father took his responsibilities seriously; too seriously perhaps," he said, weighing his words as if assessing the exact minimum of information that would be required to satisfy Miriam and stop her asking more questions. "He was braver than the other padres who stayed out of the front line; he went up there every morning and evening and in the end it had a bad effect on him. That happens sometimes."

"What kind of effect?"

"He became agitated; too agitated to be able to do his work."

"What work? What was he trying to do?"

"Bury soldiers. There were too many of them; far too many—" Adam's voice broke and he got up from the bench and walked away to the other side of the oak tree, standing with his back to Miriam. In his mind he was back in no man's land in the hour before dawn with the HE shells exploding in his ears and the rotting mutilated dead lying all around and Miriam's father, mad in his white surplice, dragging their corpses into shallow muddy graves and shouting about Jesus. He couldn't tell Miriam that; of course he couldn't, so why did she keep on asking questions? Why couldn't she be quiet and leave him alone?

"I can't talk about this," he said, returning to the bench but not sitting down. "I know you want to but I can't. I'm all in. I think that if your father rests he may get better; there are plenty of other men that have got over his kind of trouble. But I'm not a doctor. I'm sorry I'm like this but that's the way it is. I'll come back tomorrow I promise—I hope I'll be better then."

He bent down and kissed her, muttered again that he was sorry, and fled the churchyard without a backward glance.

Chapter Thirty-One

Despite another sleepless night, Adam returned to the Parsonage the next morning, even more determined to try and make it work with Miriam. And it helped too that she seemed calmer, more willing to avoid difficult subjects. He didn't go inside: she had come out of the door when she saw him coming up the path and so there was no encounter with her mother for Adam to negotiate.

They crossed the stile on the other side of the road and, holding hands, followed the winding path through the meadows until they came to a beech wood where they sat down beside a stream that was racing busily through a bed of white rocks and fallen branches. Adam took off his shoes and lay down with his head propped up against the side of Miriam's lap, looking up to where a red-headed woodpecker was tapping busily away at its chosen tree and the noonday sun was peeping down through the leaf canopy in patches, creating plays of dappled light and shadow. There were purple foxgloves growing wild on the bank near where they were sitting and Miriam picked a few, twisting them into the band around her hat. It was so far removed from the Somme that Adam could hardly credit that two such different places could exist in the same world.

"I'm sorry about yesterday," he said. "I got overwrought. Annie was upset, and it's not been easy up at the Hall. Sir John's taken Seaton's death hard, and his wife leaving hasn't helped."

"Perhaps he brought that on himself," said Miriam quietly.

"By trying to force Brice into the army, you mean?"

"Not everyone is brave like you," she said. "Brice was terrified and his father wouldn't let up."

"How do you know?"

"He told me he wouldn't."

"When?" Adam asked, looking up, surprised. It wasn't the answer he'd expected.

"He visited the Parsonage a few times last year, and he was quiet and respectful; not like he was before. He's changed. The war does that to everyone, not just those who are fighting, you know." Miriam gave Adam a sideways look from under her lashes. "I think he was lonely and he was frightened about the war. I felt sorry for him."

"I thought you hated him."

"No. I've never been very good at hating people—you know that. I'm better at forgiveness, I think, or at least I hope I am."

"Why didn't you tell me about this?" Adam felt irritated. He didn't like the idea of Brice seeing Miriam when he was gone, and he didn't believe that his old enemy had changed. Not for a moment. Miriam was gullible and Christian, always believing the best of people, and Brice knew that.

"It didn't seem important," she said. "He spent most of his time with my mother. She was the one who invited him. And when he did see me, he left me alone. My mother told him about us when he first came, and he seemed to accept it. Well, not at the end, but that was different." Miriam flushed: she was like a person who has gone down a road without realizing where it is leading, and is horrified when she turns a corner and sees where she's arrived.

"What do you mean— 'not at the end'?" Adam demanded. He was sitting up straight now, staring at Miriam.

"It was after they brought in conscription—you remember? To start with there was an exemption for married men and so Brice came over to the Parsonage and . . . well, he said why he'd come." Miriam finished her sentence awkwardly, nervously picking apart the flower she still had in her hand.

"He asked you to marry him?"

"No, he could see there was no point. He said he was sorry he'd come and we shook hands. That's all. I haven't seen him since then, except that he wrote to me from London to apologize. He said he was enjoying his new job and that his life was better."

"I bet it is, living in the lap of luxury while we poor sods suffer in the damn trenches," said Adam bitterly. He got to his feet and began pacing about among the trees. "You should've told me," he said. "You had no right to keep this from me."

"I didn't want to upset you. Nothing happened. He was just in a panic about being called up and so he did the first thing that came into his head. That's all."

"You should still have told me."

"I'm sorry," said Miriam. "You're right. But, like I said, you were in France and I didn't want to make it into something it wasn't. And you don't tell me anything of what's happening over there, do you?"

"That's different," said Adam angrily. "I'm not seeing other girls, am I?"

"You've got no right to say that to me. I've done nothing wrong," said Miriam, getting to her feet. He could see that she was crying and he felt suddenly contrite, and desolate too, sensing that his anger had spoiled the day.

"I'm sorry," he said, taking her hand. "I didn't mean it; really I didn't."

"It's all right," she said, wiping the tears from her eyes and allowing him to kiss her. But it wasn't all right. The mood of the day had changed and they couldn't recapture their earlier carefree happiness. They walked on, leaving the babbling brook behind and the trees closed in densely on either side, shutting out the light so that it was a relief when they came out into the open air.

But now Miriam had a headache and so they turned for home. They both regretted their quarrel and wanted to put it behind them, but there was an awkwardness between them that they couldn't shake off. And, as they came in sight of the Parsonage, Adam felt overcome by that same mind-numbing exhaustion that he had experienced in the churchyard the day before. It was as if the months of sleepless, anxious nights in the trenches were all suddenly catching up on him now that his body had understood it finally had the chance to rest. And, although neither of them wanted to admit it, they both felt relieved to say goodbye, hoping that the trouble between them would have disappeared by the time they met for lunch the next day.

But things didn't turn out as they had anticipated. The following morning the telephone rang just as Adam was getting ready to cycle over to the Parsonage for lunch. Coming down the stairs, he heard Cartwright shouting for the caller to speak louder. The butler hated the telephone as his growing deafness made it almost impossible for him to hear what was being said, but he steadfastly refused to cede his answering responsibilities to Charles as he feared that this would undermine his authority in the house. The result was that messages often didn't get through or, if they did, Cartwright transcribed them in such a garbled manner that they were rendered incomprehensible. On this occasion, however, the caller was persistent and Adam was surprised to hear Cartwright calling out his name as he went past.

"Master Adam, it's somebody called Pleace asking for you. I should warn you it's a very bad connection," he said, handing Adam the earpiece.

Adam was mystified. He knew no one called Pleace and was in the middle of telling the caller that he didn't when an exasperated crystal-clear voice at the other end of the line loudly interrupted him: "This is the police, Mr. Raine: Constable Fletcher. There's been an unfortunate incident at number sixty-seven Station Street and we need your help."

Adam felt suddenly numb; 67 Station Street was Ernest's house. And he knew without needing to ask what had happened. He was numb but he wasn't shocked: it was almost as if he had been expecting this news.

"Are you there?" asked the policeman.

"Yes," said Adam. "It's Annie, isn't it? She's dead."

"I'm afraid so," said the policeman. "We'd like you to identify the body. It's a formality but it needs doing."

"Why me?"

"Because with her son being in France, you're the next of kin. Your father was her husband's cousin, I believe?"

"Yes, that's right. I'm on my way now. I'll meet you at the house," said Adam, thinking how strange it was that he should be Annie's next of kin when he had never once thought of her that way.

He replaced the earpiece and then unhooked it again to call the switchboard operator who connected him to the Parsonage. He told the maidservant when she answered that something urgent had come up so he couldn't come to lunch and that he would call again later to rearrange, and was surprised and ashamed to realize as he finished speaking that he was feeling relieved that Annie's death had given him an excuse not to have to go. He loved Miriam but the fact was that each meeting with her since he'd arrived had been like crossing an emotional minefield, leaving him drained and exhausted and longing to get away.

He cycled up the hill, pedalling hard so as not to have to think. He knew that sooner or later he was going to have to confront the question of his own responsibility for Annie's suicide but for now he needed to get to the house. The policeman was waiting for him in the road outside, wiping the sweat from his brow with a blue-and-white checked handkerchief. Adam didn't recognize him: he was an older man brought out of retirement to replace the town bobby who had joined up at the same time as Adam and had lost his life at the Battle of Loos.

"It's a hot day," said Constable Fletcher, shaking Adam's hand. "And a sad one too," he added, glancing up at the house.

"Yes, it is," Adam agreed. He couldn't think of anything else to say.

"Well, shall we get it over with?" the policeman asked. "There's still a little bit of a gas smell in the house, I'm afraid, but we've had the windows open so it's nothing to worry about."

Adam nodded. He followed the policeman up the path to the door, noticing the riot of colour in the garden to his right. Annie's flower-picking had made no visible dent in the display and the air was alive with bees and butterflies feasting on the nectar.

But inside it was dark and silent except for the rhythmical tapping of the low-hanging branches of a sycamore tree against one of the open windows. The tree must have been fast-growing because

Adam hardly remembered it from the days when he'd lived in the house, but now it was blocking out most of the light from entering the room.

Adam coughed but not because of any smell of gas. It was the thick dust in the air mixed with a strong odour of damp and mustiness that made it hard to breathe.

"I don't think the old girl's opened the windows since the war started," said the policeman, shaking his head. "And look over there," he told Adam, pointing to two small piles of old towels lying on the floor under each of the window casements. "We found those stuffed behind the panes to stop any air coming in through the cracks, and it was the same upstairs. It looks like she was intending to do the deed in here and then changed her mind and went upstairs. God knows why!"

"Did she leave a note?" Adam asked.

"Just a line on the back of a pawn ticket. It was on that table over there," the constable said, pointing to the rectangular deal table at the back of the room on which Adam had eaten so many meals. "'Please tell Ernest I'm sorry.' That's all. Ernest's her son, I think. Yes?"

"Yes."

"Bloody awful for him. But people don't think about that, do they?"

Adam didn't respond, still looking around the room, jarred by the acute contrast between the present and the past. He remembered Edgar's booming voice; the red glow of the fire lighting up the walls; the smell of bacon cooking. And now this thin emptiness—it was almost impossible to credit that it was the same place.

"All right then. Best get on with it, I suppose," said the policeman, going over to the foot of the stairs and then pausing for a moment to check whether Adam was following before he began to climb.

"I expect you're used to this kind of thing from being over there," he said, talking back over his shoulder.

"What kind of thing?"

"Gas: it's horrible stuff. They shouldn't be using it out there if you ask me. There should be a law against it or something."

"There is," said Adam quietly. "They still use it though."

At a turn in the landing they went past the bedroom which Adam had shared with Ernest and where he'd worked through the long evenings at his Latin and Greek. Two beds, side by side, but no desk any more; not a trace of the past. And then up again to the top of the house where a faint smell of gas did still hang in the air like rotten eggs, even though all the windows were wide open.

"She's in here," said the policeman, pausing on the threshold of the bedroom to take off his helmet. Adam was touched by this unexpected sign of respect for the dead and decided he liked Constable Fletcher.

He paused too. Despite living in the house for over a year he'd never been up to the top floor before and he felt guilty for a moment, as though he was breaking the rules, which was stupid, of course. He knew that.

Annie was lying on her back on the near side of the double bed that took up most of the room. It was made up and hadn't been slept in.

Her thin cheeks were cherry-pink—a sign of the gas poisoning—but her face wasn't otherwise disfigured. Her eyes were closed and Adam was relieved to see that her expression was peaceful, almost as if she had gone to sleep.

Beside her on the bed was a man's suit of clothes, which Adam recognized as Edgar's, and she was holding the sleeve of the jacket tight in her hand. Against the far wall the door of a mahogany wardrobe stood half open and Adam could see more of Edgar's clothes hanging inside. Clearly, she hadn't pawned them.

She was wearing the same black dress that she'd worn on that evening long ago when she'd gone up to the pit to sit beside Edgar's body. The hat with the imitation fruit was missing, revealing her white hair, but the dress was the same: Adam was sure of it. Just as she had all those years before, Annie had dressed up for death.

And through the open windows the sun, high now in the sky, shone down on to the worn carpet and bathed the room in a warm golden glow. Adam had expected to feel guilt. It was obviously no coincidence that Annie had chosen to end her life just two days after he had told her about Thomas in the graveyard, but to his surprise he felt instead a sense of quiet peace. He understood that she had travelled a long journey to reach this destination and that their meeting had been no more than the last stop on her way.

The policeman coughed to gain his attention. "If you wouldn't mind, Mr. Raine, could you identify the deceased for me?" he asked apologetically. "It's just a formality but it needs doing."

"Yes, of course. She's Anne Tillett," said Adam.

"Thank you," said the constable, making a note in his book. "And have you any idea why she might have done this? No need to tell me if you don't know, but any information you do have helps with the report."

"Her husband died a few years back and recently she lost her eldest son too. He was in my battalion. I think she'd just had enough."

"Yes, I can understand that. The war affects people in different ways, doesn't it? There's some bereaved folk as goes in for this spiritualism business. It's a lot of nonsense, I think. But there's a big market for it since this new battle kicked off. We had an old woman over in Gratton last month who was holding these séances and chattering away to the dead, and it turned out that it was her husband behind a screen putting on the voices and operating some kind of smoke machine. They're in the gaol now where they belong." The policeman shook his head, contemplating the magnitude of human folly. "Would you be wanting some time alone with the deceased?" he asked.

"Just a moment. That's all," said Adam.

"Of course, sir. You take your time," said the policeman, going out on to the landing where he busied himself putting on his helmet.

Adam went over to the bed, looking down at the dead woman for a few moments before he bent down and gently touched her cheek, imitating her farewell gesture to him in the churchyard. And then he turned away and followed the policeman down the stairs.

Chapter Thirty-Two

Adam's immediate anxiety after leaving Annie's house was to see what could be done to enable Ernest to return to Scarsdale for his mother's funeral. As a lowly lance corporal he could do no more than send telegrams to Ernest and to the colonel and hope for the best, and it turned out to be Sir John who was able to make that hope a reality.

Adam was surprised and touched by his benefactor's concern when he told him what had happened. He knew that Sir John had cordially disliked Edgar whom he associated with Whalen Dawes and the militancy in the colliery that had led to the attack on the Hall. But there was not a trace of that old animosity in his reaction to the death of Edgar's widow, and he went straight to the telephone as soon as he understood what Adam wanted.

Adam was pessimistic that Sir John would be able to achieve anything: he never went to London any more and the government's only interest in the baronet appeared to be to ensure that he was paying his ever-increasing taxes on time. But to his surprise it turned out that Sir John knew someone influential in the War Office who knew someone else, and by the end of the afternoon Ernest's leave was confirmed and a date had been set for the funeral. Adam would be gone by then: he was due to report back for duty in France on the day after Ernest had left and he thought how strange it would be if their trains were to pass each other in the night.

There was now no time to go back to the Parsonage but Adam called again as he'd promised and explained what had happened to

Miriam who had seized the telephone from the housemaid as soon as she heard it was him.

"I'm sorry," she said. "That's terrible. It must have been awful for you having to see her like that."

"Yes, but I'm glad I did."

"Why?"

"Because I owed it to her, I suppose. It's complicated."

Miriam was silent. "Are you there?" he asked.

"Yes."

"What's wrong?" The line was good and he could sense from her voice that she was upset, and he felt his stomach muscles clenching tightly in response.

"Nothing. It's just . . ."

"What?"

"Well, I don't understand why you didn't come here to tell me. Don't you think it's something we should be sharing together? I don't know—sometimes it seems like you're avoiding me, like you don't want to be with me." Miriam's voice rose as she spoke and Adam sensed that her emotions were about to flood over the ramparts of her self-control.

"That's not true," he told her urgently. "I had things I had to do. I've been busy all day, trying to make sure Ernest can come back in time. Surely you can understand that?"

"I suppose so," she said, sounding unconvinced. "It's just you've been home five days now and I've hardly seen you and it seems so cruel—" She broke off and now he could hear that she was crying. As before on the first day in the churchyard it made him panic. He couldn't think straight; he just wanted the conversation to be over so that he could escape somewhere quiet; quiet like it had been in Annie's house . . .

"I don't mean to be cruel," he said, speaking slowly and deliberately, determined to keep control of his own emotions. "I didn't ask for this to happen today. It just did. But tomorrow will be different, I promise you. We can have the whole day together. I'll come at the same time. Is that all right?"

"Yes," she said. And although she'd stopped crying he could still hear the sadness in her voice. "Goodbye."

"I love you," he told her. But a moment too late as she'd already hung up and his endearment fell on deaf ears like a stone dropping into an empty well.

Mrs. Vale was downstairs with Miriam when Adam got to the Parsonage. He'd not seen her since he'd been back and he was unsure of how she would receive him, given her disapproval of his engagement to her daughter. But she welcomed him with apparent enthusiasm, kissing him on both cheeks and giving him the place of honour between her and Miriam at the head of the table.

She was as much the invalid as ever, leaning heavily on her stick as she walked, and producing two bottles of pills and a pair of thick-lensed reading glasses from her handbag as soon as she'd sat down. She studied the directions and then carefully extracted a green tablet from one bottle and a blue one from the other and swallowed them with a grimace, accompanied by a glass of water. But Adam felt the same sense he had in the past that this was all a show and that Mrs. Vale could abandon her illness without a backwards glance if it suited her purpose, just as she had in Scarborough when the Germans attacked.

Miriam's nervousness around her mother seemed to have intensified while Adam had been away, and the atmosphere of tension in the Parsonage's small, intimate dining room soon became strained to breaking point when Mrs. Vale began asking Adam a series of apparently innocent questions which exposed and aggravated the simmering discord between him and Miriam.

"When will you be going back?" was her opening sally after swallowing the pills.

"Tomorrow evening," he said. And to his right he could see Miriam blanch, twisting her napkin between her fingers. Up to now both of them had avoided any direct reference to his upcoming return to the front. As Adam was well aware, the prospect terrified Miriam and she had striven hard to avoid thinking about it, but now here was her mother bringing it up almost as soon as they had sat down.

"That must be very hard," Mrs. Vale went on, blithely ignoring her daughter's distress. "You've been unlucky with having this unfortunate business with your friend's mother foisted upon you, but even without that there's barely enough time to start to relax before you're back on the train."

"It is hard," Adam agreed. "Leave is disorientating: it's like you're half here and half there. Torn between the two, I suppose." Just as in Scarborough, he had the sense when talking to Miriam's mother that he was playing chess with an enemy who respected his skill but intended to win. It put him on his mettle and he rose instinctively to the challenge.

"And is it very bad over there?" Mrs. Vale asked. "We read about the fighting in the newspapers, but I doubt that tells the half of it, does it?"

"Mother, please. Adam doesn't want to talk about the war," said Miriam.

She was right: it was the subject Adam most wanted to avoid, and he was grateful to Miriam for her protest, which he knew it must have cost her a good deal to make, given her fear of her mother. But he had no intention of showing weakness by admitting his reluctance to Mrs. Vale. "It's all right. I don't mind talking about it," he lied. "And yes, it is bad. A lot of young men are dying and we don't seem to be making much progress."

"Well, we're very glad that you're not one of them," said Mrs. Vale, reaching out her hand to gently pat Adam's. She sipped her wine, preparing her next salvo: "I suppose the worst part is all these shells flying about. There's really not much you can do about them, is there, except hope for the best? I remember that in Scarborough."

"No. If your name's written on one of them, it's going to find you. A lot of the soldiers think that way."

Adam was about to say more, but stopped as Miriam pushed back her chair, muttered something about not feeling well, and ran from the room.

Adam was stricken, realizing too late the effect this kind of talk would have on her. He got up, intending to go and see whether she was all right, but Mrs. Vale gestured for him to sit down. "Don't worry, she'll be down again soon," she said. "Miriam gets upset far too easily: that's her problem. I've noticed how she came back here distressed after seeing you the day before yesterday and it was the same the day before that. It can't be easy for you having to cope with her being so emotional when your leave is so short."

This was perfectly true but Adam wasn't going to admit it. "I understand how she feels," he said. "It's hard for her not knowing whether I'm all right or not."

"And yet you write so seldom. Why is that?" asked Mrs. Vale, quick to seize on the contradiction between Adam's words and his actions.

"Our letters are our affair," said Adam, bridling. Verbal sparring was one thing, but he felt that Mrs. Vale had crossed the line when she started talking about their private correspondence.

"Yes, of course they are," Mrs. Vale responded unperturbed as she moved seamlessly on to the attack. "But I am Miriam's mother and I have her best interests at heart, so naturally I am concerned when she is unhappy. And she seems to be unhappy most of the time."

Adam was stymied for a response. Mrs. Vale was quite right that Miriam was unhappy about how little he wrote to her, but how would she feel if he told her what the war was really like? Ignorance certainly wasn't bliss but it was surely better than knowledge for someone as sensitive and highly strung as she was. He could explain all this to Mrs. Vale, but it wouldn't change Miriam's state of mind. She was right: her daughter was unhappy and there was nothing he could do about it.

And he felt irritated with Miriam too. He was sorry that he had upset her, but that didn't mean she should have rushed out of the room and left him alone with her mother, who wanted nothing more than to be given free ammunition with which to attack their relationship.

He could feel her beady grey eyes fixed on him now, coolly appraising him as she drank her wine and waited patiently for his response. And suddenly he felt he'd had enough. No one in Scarsdale had any idea what he had had to endure. The doctor in France had said he needed rest and quiet, but instead every day seemed to bring more trouble. His leave was nearly over and he didn't want to spend any more of the time he had left hemmed in by the walls of this tiny dining room while Miriam's mother put him through the third degree.

"I'm very sorry," he said, getting up. "But I think I am going to have to go home. I don't want to be rude but I find it hard to cope with any kind of stress nowadays. It's the war, I think. It's changed me."

Mrs. Vale looked at him and then to his surprise got up herself from the table and extended her hand. "I'm sorry too," she said. "I am concerned about Miriam but I had no wish to upset you. I know how difficult your life must be at present."

Adam shook Mrs. Vale's hand and nodded. He realized that her gracious friendliness was probably just another tactical move in her longstanding campaign to separate him from her daughter but, if so, the ploy was a success because he couldn't think of a response. And as he left the room he had the sense of having come off second best in their encounter.

Outside the gate he was just getting on his bicycle when Miriam came running down the front path. She was red in the face and looked as if she'd been crying.

"Please don't go," she said, leaning against one side of the honeysuckle arch over the gateway to catch her breath. "I'm sorry I left. It's my mother—she stirs everything up deliberately. We should have gone out."

"But we didn't," he said flatly. "And every day it's the same. There's too much pressure."

"But it won't always be like this," she said pleadingly. "One day the war will end; it has to—"

"No, it won't," he interrupted fiercely. "For you maybe, but not for me. It's got me; it's taken me over."

"What are you talking about?" Miriam was frightened: there was a tone of finality in Adam's voice that she hadn't heard before.

"I've seen things, terrible things," he told her.

"What kind of things?"

"Things you can't imagine; things it's better you shouldn't know."

"But I want to know," she said defiantly. "I'm not some milksop that has to be mollycoddled and protected. I want to help you. But I can't do that if you keep shutting me out of your life. You have to tell me what you've seen; you have to share it with me."

"You don't understand," he said sadly, shaking his head. "This isn't about the horrors; it's the effect they've had on me that I'm talking about. It's like I looked at the sun too long, and what I've seen has burnt away the meaning from everything. It's left me hollow inside, like a shell."

"You can't say that."

"Why not?"

"Because we are God's creatures: we don't have to be in the hell you're describing if we don't want to. God's there for us if you'll just let him in."

"God!" Adam spat out the word so scornfully that Miriam flinched. "If God's in his heaven, which I very much doubt, then he certainly doesn't care about what's happening down here on earth," he told her.

"All right then, even if you don't believe in God, you should still believe in my love for you. I can help you with this. I know I can. Please, Adam." There was desperation in her voice. She could feel him slipping away and she grasped hold of his hand as if to try and pull him back. "Talk to me. Don't leave me out in the cold," she implored him.

"I can't," said Adam sadly. "I just can't. I'm sorry, Miriam." He held her hand up to his lips for a moment, and then, letting it go, he got back on his bicycle and rode away.

Back at the Hall, Adam paced the grounds, barely conscious of his surroundings as he tried to cope with a maelstrom of conflicting emotions. He felt guilty for having pushed Miriam away, but he also felt angry with her for spoiling his leave with her displays of uncontrolled emotion. Time and again he'd told her that he needed to be steady and quiet but she wouldn't listen. She'd had to keep pressurizing him until he couldn't stand it any more.

But the guilt hurt him and so he tried to keep it at bay by finding justifications for the way in which he had treated her. He remembered how she had been prepared to break with him three years before just because her father told her to, and he thought about how she had been seeing Brice behind his back, even though he knew full well that he was being unjust. Miriam was the most truthful person he knew. She was incapable of deceit or subterfuge.

And so the next moment he was thinking of her beauty and goodness and using her qualities to justify his conduct. Here he was on stronger ground: he did truly believe that he wasn't worthy of her, that he was foul with the filth of the war, and that he had a duty to protect her from its contagion.

But the guilt still remained, needling him despite all his excuses. He knew she had a just claim upon him: they were engaged; he had pledged himself to her. But he belonged too to his friends, trembling with fear in the trenches, waiting for the next attack. Every day that he was away he missed them more. He was terrified of going back, but he was even more frightened that one of them might have been killed while he was away.

And he felt acutely that she was asking him to choose her over them, even though he knew there was no rational basis for this idea. To talk with Miriam about when the war was over, to make plans for their future, to try to be happy, was to deny their suffering and their shared experience and he couldn't do that.

Couldn't—the thought had a finality that brought him to an abrupt halt, and, looking up, he saw that he had entered the flower gardens behind the east wing of the house. He remembered how he used to come here and walk the gravel paths when he had first come to live at the Hall and was grieving for his dead father. He had only had the old taciturn gardener for company and the peace and beauty of the place had poured balm on his tortured soul, helping him find the strength to begin again.

And he remembered too how he had found Miriam here in the arbour that summer afternoon when she had run from the lunch table. He was close to the arbour now and he sensed suddenly, just as he had then, that he wasn't alone. Looking through the entrance arch cut in the yew hedge he saw that he was right: a woman was sitting on the bench by the stone fountain, and when she turned her head he saw that it was the housemaid, Sarah.

"I'm sorry," she said, getting up in consternation and spilling some of the food that she had been eating down on to the grass. "I know I shouldn't be here. I'll—"

"Let me!" he said, running forward and bending down to pick up what she had dropped. But he was too late: the second piece of her sandwich had escaped its wrapper and was now being airlifted away by a triumphant starling that had been watching for just such an opportunity from the branch of an overhanging chestnut tree.

They both laughed, dissolving the tension for a moment, but almost immediately Sarah became flustered again, brushing the crumbs from her dress and adjusting her uniform.

"Oh dear, if Mr. Cartwright knew about this he'd have me on my way in five minutes," she said anxiously.

"Chasing you down the drive with one of Sir John's umbrellas," said Adam, smiling.

And again she had to laugh. "He's kind really," she said. "But he has his standards . . ."

"He certainly does," said Adam. "Cartwright expects every man to do his duty. And woman," he added, looking at Sarah. And suddenly the light-heartedness left him and he felt awkward and self-conscious. Just like that morning at breakfast, he wanted to put up his hand and stroke her blotched, yellow face.

But she was preoccupied with her own situation and didn't seem to notice. "I only started coming here because no one else does except the gardener and he never says anything . . ."

"Yes, I remember that. A grunt was the most I ever got," said Adam, smiling again. "I'm glad he's keeping this garden going though, even if the rest of the grounds are getting overgrown. I used to come here often, and I think of it sometimes when I am over there. It's so peaceful, a place where time has stopped."

"When are you going back?" she asked, and he could hear the anxiety in her voice. But for some reason it did not upset him as it did when Miriam asked.

"Tomorrow," he told her.

"I wish you weren't." She spoke without thinking, and immediately flushed, stammering a confused apology: "I'm sorry. It isn't my place . . . I shouldn't . . ."

He could see she was upset and he wanted to make her feel better, and so without thinking he took hold of her hands. And immediately he felt a charge run through him, a surge of physical longing to which he could feel her responding as her body arced in towards him. It was dark, like a tidal wave that was going to submerge him and carry him away, powerless to resist, unless he stopped.

He stood suspended in the moment, torn. He thought of Miriam, Miriam here in this same place, and he wanted to punish her. He didn't know why. Perhaps it was himself he wanted to punish. And he realized suddenly that that was wrong, that he couldn't do this. Not to her; not to himself. Not this way. Not now. And, responding impulsively to this new understanding, he pulled away from Sarah, who stumbled back, shocked by his unexpected withdrawal.

"I'm sorry," he said. "It's not you; it's me." The words were inadequate and anyway she wasn't listening. She was crying and he felt bitter remorse. Sarah had saved him from drowning; she'd been his friend, and this was how he had rewarded her. He reached out his hand but she'd already turned away and, standing quite still, he could hear the sound of her running away down the path. Soon the noise died away and he was left alone in a silence broken only by the steady drip of the water from the fountain into the green pond below.

He sat on the bench for over an hour before he went inside. He was shocked by what had happened. Looking back, he realized his whole leave had been punctuated by these violent eruptions of emotion: Annie lying dead by her own hand; Miriam distraught at the gate; and now Sarah . . . He had brought the war back with him into this peaceful backwater of England and it was time he was gone. Back to where he belonged.

There was no sign of Sarah at breakfast the next morning. And when Adam asked Cartwright where she was, the butler told him that it was her day off. He was dismayed by the news. He felt ashamed of how he had treated her and he had hoped that he would have an opportunity to properly apologize before he left.

"She told me about her illness. She's had a hard time, hasn't she?" he said, making conversation. After what had happened between them, he found it strange that he knew so little about her, and the one-way nature of their relationship added to his sense that he had taken an unfair advantage of her.

"Yes, it was very sad what happened," Cartwright agreed. "And she has other troubles too. But she's not let them get her down. She's a hard worker and I've no complaints."

"What other troubles?"

"Her mother's not well. She lives on the other side of Gratton. That's where she goes on her days off. As far as I know," Cartwright added, as if sensing that he'd said too much and that the private life of the housemaid was not a subject he should be discussing with the family, even if he had always been on rather more relaxed terms with Adam than with the rest of them.

Outside in the hall the telephone rang and Cartwright left the dining room in almost unseemly haste in order to get to it before Charles. Through the open door Adam winced as he listened to the usual conversational debacle getting under way: intense silent pauses interspersed with Cartwright asking whoever was on the other end of the line to "speak more clearly please!" and then repeating his request louder and louder until he was practically shouting into the mouthpiece.

Cartwright's deafness was clearly getting worse, at least as far as the telephone was concerned, and Adam couldn't see how the call was ever going to end. He had got up from his chair intending to go and offer assistance, even though he knew that this would cause Cartwright grave offence, when a breakthrough in the conversation finally seemed to occur. "Please hold the line, madam. I will go and ask Master Adam," Cartwright told the caller, and Adam dashed back into the dining room to resume his place so that Cartwright wouldn't see that he had gone out into the corridor.

"Mrs. Vale is on the line. She would like to come here and see you at eleven o'clock," Cartwright announced when he had come back in.

"Here?" repeated Adam incredulously. "That can't be right. She's an invalid. She never leaves her house."

"No, Master Adam, it is right. She was very clear that she wished to come to the Hall. I was surprised myself and that's why I asked her to repeat her request. What shall I tell her?"

"Tell her yes, I suppose," said Adam with a sinking feeling. Mrs. Vale was the last person he wanted to see that morning.

She arrived in a horse-drawn carriage just as the grandfather clock in the hall had finished striking eleven. Where the horse had come from Adam couldn't imagine: the Hall stables had long ago been emptied by the army's requisitioning sergeants with every healthy animal in the kingdom seemingly sent out to France where most of them were suffering an even worse fate than the country's men.

Charles showed her into the drawing room and served her coffee, and when Adam joined her he found her looking curiously around with the air of an antique dealer taking an inventory of contents before an estate sale.

"Have you been here before?" he asked her as they sat down.

"Yes, some years ago. Things appear to have changed somewhat since then," she said, without making clear whether she was referring to the general air of neglect or the sale of pictures and heirlooms to pay taxes that had been going on for a long time but had accelerated since the start of the war.

"I am glad to see you out visiting," said Adam.

"Glad or surprised?" she asked with an ironical smile.

"Well, both," Adam admitted. "I would have been happy to come over to the Parsonage if you had asked me. I hope you know that."

"Yes, I do. Thank you. But I really didn't want Miriam to be present for what I want to say and so I thought it better to come here. And I have to say I have enjoyed the drive. It was very . . ." She stopped, searching for the right word. ". . . bracing. Yes, bracing. I must do it more often."

She sat back in her armchair, drinking her coffee, apparently in no hurry to explain the purpose of her visit until Adam lost patience and pressed her: "What is it you want, Mrs. Vale?" he asked. "Please tell me."

"Well, as I'm sure you've guessed, I want to talk to you about Miriam. And yes, I know it's a difficult subject and one you don't like to talk about," she said, holding up her hand when she saw him shifting uneasily in his chair. "But this time I want you to hear me out. I am worried about my daughter, Adam; very worried. As I told you yesterday, she is constantly unhappy and the main cause of the trouble seems to be her anxiety about you. That is understandable, of course, when you are at the front, but the last week while you have been home, I have noticed that she has become even more distressed. Yesterday she was hysterical after you left and I had to give her some of my own medicine to get her to calm down. And, speaking frankly, I am concerned that this turmoil and misery may be affecting her health. As you know, she is an unusually sensitive girl and sooner or later her unbalanced mental state will affect her physical wellbeing."

"So what are you suggesting?" asked Adam, twisting in his chair. All his guilt of the day before had come rushing back as Mrs. Vale described her daughter's state of mind, and it was compounded now by what had happened with Sarah.

"I am suggesting that the time has come to reconsider your relationship if all it is doing is making you both so unhappy."

"Well, that's rather what I expected you to say. But there's more, isn't there?" Adam had been watching Mrs. Vale and he sensed that she hadn't as yet put all her cards on the table.

"Yes, since you ask," she said. "I don't want to talk about money—"

"But you're going to," Adam interrupted with a thin smile.

"Yes, I must. I'm sure you recall that I was concerned about your lack of means when you first announced your engagement to me in Scarborough, and I imagine that you are in the same financial position now as you were then?"

"Exactly the same," said Adam. "Serving my king and country is not a pathway to riches, I am afraid."

"And nor has it been for my husband. As you may be aware, he is currently in a hospital in France, suffering from what his doctors call a "paralysis of the nerves." They are unable to say when or even if he will get better and the most that we are told to hope for at present is that he will be able to come back to England and be cared for in a sanatorium somewhere in the north where we will be able to visit him. As you can imagine, this leaves us for the foreseeable future in a parlous financial situation. We are currently receiving an allowance tied to Frederick's work as a military chaplain but I don't know how long that will continue, and we are also likely to lose our home if he is unable to return to being the parson here when the war is over. And then there may be medical bills to pay. Our prospects are bleak. Do you follow me so far?"

"Yes." Adam wasn't going to admit it but he was shocked by the picture that Mrs. Vale had drawn. He wondered why he had never thought through the implications for Miriam of her father's illness.

"However, Miriam does have an opportunity to change this situation—"

"By marrying Brice, you mean?" Adam interrupted angrily.

"Yes. He wishes to marry her. And, unlike you, he has very good prospects. His mother's family is wealthy and he is now the heir to all this . . ."

"Because his brother was brave and he is a coward."

"That may well be true, but facts are facts," said Mrs. Vale, unperturbed by Adam's vehemence. "And I'm asking you to look at them for what they are. Is it right for you to stand in Miriam's way?"

"In your way, you mean?" said Adam acidly. "It's not just Miriam who will be impoverished if she doesn't marry Brice; it's you too. Perhaps you should be less disingenuous and acknowledge your own interest in all this?"

Mrs. Vale paused, but not because she had taken offence. She was considering her response. "You are right," she said eventually, inclining her head. "It is in my interest for Brice to marry my daughter, but that doesn't mean that it isn't in her interest as well. Money is important in this world however much idealists like my husband may wish to deny it. And I assure you I wouldn't be saying any of this if her engagement to you was making her happy, but you know just as well as me that it isn't."

Adam said nothing. He didn't like Mrs. Vale but he couldn't argue with anything she said. He loved Miriam but her mother was entirely right that he was making her unhappy. He was unable to share anything of his life with her and he had nothing to offer her as a future. She deserved better. He hated the thought of her being with Brice but what right did he have to stand in her way? Like a screw turning in his soul, he remembered how she had told him in the wood that Brice had changed. Perhaps he had; perhaps he would make her happy.

"Miriam must be able to choose," he said, looking Mrs. Vale in the eye, as though he was laying down a challenge.

"Yes," she said, meeting his gaze. "But she can't choose unless you release her. You must do that first."

"Very well," he said, getting to his feet. "I will write to her before I leave. I hope to hell that I'm doing the right thing."

He was committed. It was like a door had crashed shut in his mind, blocking out his dreams, although he couldn't yet feel the pain.

Chapter Thirty-Three

Brice drove fast, kicking up white dust from under the silver wheels of his Straker-Squire open tourer. He had always enjoyed the sense of power that motor cars gave him, compensating for the weakness he felt in his own body, but he loved this car with an almost physical passion. It was the same model as the fifteen horsepower that had won races at Brooklands before the war, and when he was depressed he could cheer himself up in an instant by just walking round to the garages in the mews behind his grandfather's house and stroking his hands along its sleek metallic red sides; although now he was worried about keeping it there for fear that one of his army of creditors might try and levy distress by seizing it at an opportune moment.

He hated their sneaky way of accosting him as he left the house. Sooner or later he would have to go to his mother and confess his sins and hope that she would ask her father to bail him out a second time. God knows, the old man could afford it, but he seemed to take pleasure in keeping Brice on a tight leash, trumpeting that it would help him learn to "stand on his own two feet." And he had got quite shirty when he found out about Brice's money troubles the first time, summoning his grandson for a "friendly chat" in his enormous office overlooking Pall Mall. The chat hadn't been friendly at all, and Brice hoped to postpone a repeat visit for as long as possible.

But for now he didn't need to think about any of that. He was driving towards a new dawn in his life, one that he had never thought would come. Twenty-four hours earlier he had been slouched over the desk in his hot stuffy office responding to yet another letter from yet another government department about boots (the fact that everything in his grandfather's business revolved around the subject of footwear was driving Brice slowly mad) when a long-distance telephone call had come through from Scarsdale. Not from his father, whom he hadn't spoken to in more than six months since the day he swept out of Scarsdale Hall in his mother's imperious wake, but from the Parsonage. And as he listened to Mrs. Vale's voice coming down the crackly line his spirits began to soar. That fool Adam had released Miriam from their engagement and Miriam was passive, pliable. Now was the time to ask her if Brice could find the time to come . . .

He didn't need to be asked twice. He made an excuse to get off work the next day and, dressed in his most elegant outfit of dove-grey trousers, matching silk waistcoat and morning coat protected by a huge Burberry dustcoat, he went out and purchased a ring from Asprey's on credit that he couldn't afford, and set off for the north. Petrol shortages meant that the roads were largely empty and Brice made good progress, arriving in Scarsdale in the early evening.

He slowed to a crawl, staring at the squat grey houses and the King's Head pub where the awful crazed woman had forced the white feather into his hand the previous winter. The memory of the encounter was burnt into Brice's mind and in London he never went out without fastening his prized "ON WAR SERVICE 1916" badge to his lapel to ensure there would be no repeat of his humiliation. He hated this place; hated its meanness and drabness and monochrome misery, and as he accelerated away up the hill towards the Parsonage he felt with a sudden sense of exultation that he was Miriam's knight in shining armour, come to rescue her from a life of drudgery and despair.

He passed the last houses on Station Street and, rounding a corner, he had to brake hard and swerve to avoid running down a young man in khaki uniform who was walking down the hill almost in the centre of the road, apparently oblivious to his surroundings.

"Watch where you're going, you idiot! You're damn lucky I didn't run you down!" he shouted angrily back at the soldier whom he vaguely recognized, although he couldn't for the moment put a name to his face.

"I wish you had, Brice Scarsdale! I wish you had," said the soldier with a hollow laugh.

The unexpected way he had addressed him by name disconcerted Brice, and all at once he felt an intense need to escape the long empty stare of the soldier's eyes, and so without saying anything more he turned his head and drove away. Although he didn't want to admit it, the incident had unnerved him, dissolving the euphoria he'd felt a minute before, and he drove slowly and carefully now, peering ahead into the shadows, possessed by a sense of creeping unease.

At the crest of the hill he passed the graveyard where Tyler, the town sexton, stripped down to his vest, was busy with his spade heaving earth back into a newly dug grave. It was past sunset and there was a weight of melancholy in the humid evening air. A bunch of carnations lay discarded on the grass to the side of the diminishing mound of soil, and Brice intuitively made the connection between the soldier in the road and the grave. He'd been burying someone, his mother perhaps. Home on leave for that! No wonder he didn't care if Brice ran him down and put an end to his misery when he had nothing left at home and nothing to look forward to in the future except a return to the slaughter on the other side of the Channel. Brice remembered the cold terror he'd felt during those awful weeks at the beginning of the year when he thought he would be forced into the army. This new world was truly a city of dreadful night if you were young and male and able-bodied, unless you got lucky of course and escaped the recruiting sergeant's beckoning finger as he had been able to, handed a reprieve at the very last moment.

Brice felt sorry. He wished now that he'd apologized to the soldier even though he hadn't been the one in the wrong. Maybe he had been driving too fast but the man had been walking almost in the middle of the road.

Suddenly something clicked in Brice's mind and he remembered who the soldier was: Ernest something, the son of one of those Red miners who had fought his father before the war; one of Adam's friends from the pit. He'd seen them together when he'd been out driving with Charles, who'd told him who he was.

Adam! Always there in his way, taking what should be rightfully his. But no longer! Brice remembered the purpose of his journey and felt his energy returning as he parked outside the Parsonage gate.

Going up the path, he remembered how he had slumped against the door jamb the last time he had been here, overcome by a bitter sense of futility when he had realized the pointlessness of his marriage proposal before he had even made it. But now it was different: he'd learnt from his mistakes and listened to Miriam's mother when she'd told him to bide his time instead of trying to force the issue as he had in the past. He was older now and wiser and, if she was right, his patience was about to be rewarded.

The housemaid answered the door and, after taking his coat, showed him straight into the parson's study where Mrs. Vale was waiting for him. There was no sign of Miriam.

"Welcome!" she said, her face lit up by a rare smile as she got up from her chair and shook his hand. "I'm glad you've come. And so quickly too! Did you have a good journey?"

"Yes," he said, his spirits now fully restored. "It was excellent."

"Excellent!" she repeated, raising her eyebrows. "Now that's the kind of word I like to hear—positive and energetic: qualities sadly missing from our backwards little town. Close the door, Betty," she told the maid. "We're not to be disturbed."

As soon as they were alone, she went over to a side table and poured two glasses of sherry from a cut-glass decanter. She handed one to Brice and clinked her glass to his before she stepped back, looking him up and down. It was strange how she was so clearly the one controlling the dynamic of their relationship even though she was nearly a foot shorter than Brice.

"Well, do I pass muster?" he asked a little uneasily.

"Yes, you certainly look the part, but now you're going to have to act it as well, which isn't quite so easy," she said, waving him to the seat opposite her as she sat back down.

"What do you mean?"

"I mean that you must take into account not just your own feelings but my daughter's as well. Miriam is suffering from grief. Whether you like it or not, she still loves Adam and it will take time for her to get over what has happened."

"So then I should wait?" asked Brice, not understanding.

"No, hear me out. Like any emotion, grief is a process. It goes through different stages. First there is shock, then a passionate out-pouring of sorrow, and then a period of passivity. That is the stage my daughter has now reached and I believe it provides you with your best opportunity, which is why I asked you to come. But you must try to keep her passive. So be gentle, not passionate. Don't pull the apple from the tree but rather let it fall into your hand. And accept that she may agree to your proposal because for now she does not care what happens to her or even that she may see it as a way of validating her misery. Are you ready for that?"

"Yes," he said, answering without hesitation. "She will learn to love me. I am sure of it." It was what he had always believed. Adam had come between them, poisoning Miriam against him. Without Adam, Miriam and he would have been together a long time ago.

"I agree. That is what I believe too," said Mrs. Vale, nodding as she got back up. "Wait here now and I will send her to you."

As the door closed, Brice felt suddenly nervous, fingering the engagement ring in his pocket. Miriam's mother might believe that this was his best opportunity but there was no guarantee of success. He loved Miriam and felt he couldn't bear for her to reject him again. His heart was beating fast and he felt pinpricks of sweat beading on his scalp.

He got up from his chair and looked anxiously at his reflection in the mirror over the fireplace. He straightened his tie and combed his hair and breathed in, lifting his shoulders, but it didn't make him look any manlier and so he turned away and began to pace the floor. The carriage clock on the mantelpiece ticked softly but otherwise the only sound in the room was his footfalls.

He was hot and went over to open the window. But he pulled too hard on the sash causing it to stick and so he knelt down on the carpet, trying in vain to loosen the side that had wedged. And that was how Miriam found him when she came in.

"What are you doing?" she asked.

"It's stuck," he said, feeling like a fool. And he was about to get to his feet when some instinct made him stay where he was while she came over and expertly tapped the window back into place, sliding it up its runnels.

"Miriam," he said, looking up at her. "Please. Will you marry me?"

"Why?" she asked, saying the first thing that came into her head. Her mother had prepared her for Brice's visit, listing all the reasons in favour of accepting his proposal, but she had still not decided how to respond, and she had also not expected him to ask her so suddenly without giving her any warning.

"Because I love you," he said, reaching up and taking hold of her hand. "I always have. You know that, don't you?"

"Yes." It was true. He had always loved her—or at least he said he had, even if she had often felt it wasn't love he was feeling but just an insatiable desire to possess her even against her will, although she had to admit that that had changed in the last year. *He was not like he was before,* she had told Adam in the wood. Adam! Her heart lurched as she thought of his final letter to her, lying on her table upstairs, bathed in a thousand tears.

"So will you?" Brice asked again, getting to his feet and taking hold of both her hands. He wanted to kiss her, to sweep her off her feet, but he remembered her mother's advice to be gentle, not to force the issue.

"I don't know," she said. And there were tears in her eyes again now. "I don't love you, Brice. You know that. Doesn't that make it wrong?" She looked at him as if she was a prisoner at the bar appealing for mercy.

"No. You can learn to love me. We're young; we have all the time in the world. Please, Miriam. Say you will?"

And something inside Miriam gave way. Adam had abandoned her and she had nothing left to hope for. And life was too exhausting:

her father was gone and she didn't have the will to stand up against the pressure—from her mother, from Brice. It was easier to make them happy if this was what they wanted.

"Will you?" he asked. And she nodded, surprised that surrender was as easy as that: not even a word, just an incline of the head being all that was required to give herself away forever.

He took her in his arms and kissed her and she didn't resist and she didn't respond. It was as if she had abandoned her will to his and now it was for him to do with her as he would. And she said nothing when he took the ring out of his pocket and put it on her finger. It fit well and, looking down at it, Brice felt a rush of excitement. The ring meant that she was his. It was there for everyone to see, witness to a fact that no one could deny.

But Miriam's passivity disconcerted him. He wanted her to be happy like him, to start making plans and talk about their future together, but instead she was silent or answered in monosyllables, and soon he was asking her to find her mother so that they could tell her the good news.

"So how soon will you be married?" Mrs. Vale asked as they sat down to dinner after she had finished toasting the happy couple from a bottle of champagne that she had had put on ice before Brice's arrival, so confident had she been of his success.

"I don't know," said Brice, who had given no thought to the practical issues involved in actually getting married. He was still in shock that he had in a moment achieved what had seemed impossible for so many years,

"Personally, I am against long engagements," said Mrs. Vale, who had given a great deal of thought to the subject and knew almost by heart the salient provisions of the Marriage Act of 1753. "There's many a slip twixt cup and lip, as the old saying goes, and I see no reason to wait, do you?"

"No," said Brice, agreeing wholeheartedly. He thought he knew what slip Mrs. Vale was referring to: Miriam could change her mind, particularly if Adam started interfering, as he had in the past. She was certainly not showing any enthusiasm for the wedding, be it delayed or immediate, and since her mother had joined them had remained as quiet as before.

"What do you think, Miriam?" asked Mrs. Vale, turning to her daughter.

"I don't mind," said Miriam, staring at her plate. She spoke so softly that her mother had to ask her to repeat what she'd said.

"Good. I'm glad we're all in agreement," said Mrs. Vale, who began to tuck into her dinner with a healthy appetite, in marked contrast to her daughter who desultorily pushed the food around her plate but showed no sign of eating any of it.

"How is your father?" Mrs. Vale asked Brice at a pause between courses.

"I don't know," he said. "As you know, we are not on good terms."

"Yes, it is unfortunate. So will you be asking for his consent?"

"Do I need it?"

"No, not if you publish banns, and it may be best, if I may suggest, for you to do that down in London, which is, after all, where you will be living once you are married. There will be less likelihood then of any outside interference, particularly if you keep everything quiet until after the wedding. I am assuming your mother will not object?"

"No," said Brice. He was quite sure that she would not be happy at the prospect of him marrying a penniless girl, but he was confident that he could win her round. He'd always been able to in the past.

"Excellent! Well, we have everything settled then," said Mrs. Vale briskly. "It's all very exciting, isn't it?"

"Yes," said Brice, who wanted to be excited but was finding it hard to maintain his exuberance when his fiancée looked so forlorn, in contrast to Mrs. Vale, who seemed to be blissfully unaware that there was anything wrong with her daughter.

The atmosphere was heavy and forced and it was almost with a sense of relief that Brice got up to go at the end of dinner. He had only been able to take one day off from work and he didn't want to incur his grandfather's wrath by being late back into the office the next morning. His plan was to drive back to London unless he became too tired on the way, in which case he would put up at a roadside inn and complete the journey early the next morning.

He stood with Miriam outside the open door of the Parsonage, wrapped up in his dustcoat. There was a smell of evening jasmine in the air and a nightingale was singing in a tree on the other side of the road. And Miriam was beautiful, bathed in the moonlight. It was the perfect romantic setting but she remained detached, engaged to him but disengaged, and he almost resented her for spoiling the moment. For years he had wanted to marry Miriam, but now, less than two hours after taking the first step towards realizing his dream, he was discontented, wanting more from her than she was able to offer.

"Will you try to love me?" he asked Miriam, self-consciously irritated by the note of pleading he could hear creeping into his voice.

"Yes," she said softly. She was telling the truth. She knew it was her Christian duty to try to love her husband, but she also felt weary; all she wanted to do now was to lie down and sleep.

And, sensing that a commitment to try was the most he could hope for, Brice pulled her close and kissed her and then walked rapidly away, ashamed and yet excited by the rush of longing that he had felt running through his body when he held her in his arms. He was glad that Mrs. Vale had suggested an early marriage; it was what he wanted too.

Chapter Thirty-Four

Brice started the car and set off back down the hill, intending to link up with the main road where it came into the town just below the station. But after less than a minute he pulled over, needing to think. The sexual charge he had felt when he held Miriam had renewed his earlier sense of excitement when he had put the ring on her finger.

The girl he loved was going to marry him! It was a life-changing moment and he felt it should be the catalyst for further transformation. If Miriam could learn to love him, then surely his father could too.

His father had wronged him but Brice felt a surge of generosity. He could be magnanimous; he could forgive even if he could not forget. Now that Seaton was dead he was his father's heir and it was in both their interests that they should turn a new page and begin again.

Turning the wheel, he drove back up the hill and slowed to a crawl as he passed the Parsonage. A light was on in an upstairs window, burning yellow behind the thin curtains. He sensed it was Miriam's room and he imagined her sitting there in a white lace nightgown, brushing out her long brown hair in front of the mirror with the gold ring on her finger glittering in the gaslight. When they were married, she would be waiting for his footsteps on the stair. The thought entranced him and he accelerated away down the hill, entering the dark woods that enshrouded the road all the way to the Hall.

Coming out of the avenue of elms, Brice slowed to a crawl, gazing past the lake up towards the stone terrace and the rows of rectangular sash windows running along the façade of the house, all palely illuminated by the baleful light of the full moon. The lines of dark glass gave the whole place a quality of foreboding, accentuated by the stillness of the night. Above the purr of the car's engine he could hear an owl hooting in the gardens behind the east wing, but there was otherwise no sign or sound of life.

But Brice refused to be daunted. He was seeing his old home through new eyes. Growing up, he had enjoyed the social prestige of being the baronet's son but it was not the same as being his heir. And even though he had enjoyed the opulence of the house before the war, he had also felt imprisoned there, shut out from life, whereas now, living in London and liberated from his confinement, he felt unexpectedly exhilarated by the beauty and grandeur of the estate. He was glad he had come. The Hall wasn't quite a mansion but it was a great deal more than just another country house and it had been in his family for generations; it was a home to be proud of; a home commanding respect. He began to understand why his father cared about it so much, and he unconsciously puffed out his chest as he contemplated his inheritance.

He parked by the stables at the back of the house and, as he was getting out of the car, he became aware of a figure standing smoking outside the tradesman's entrance behind the kitchens. The moonlight didn't penetrate there and Brice only recognized the person as Charles when he threw away his cigarette and came forward out of the shadows.

"Charles, what are you doing here?" Brice asked. The footman was the last person he'd expected to see standing at the back of the Hall. Brice hadn't seen Charles since he went away with Hardcastle to join the army the previous November. He'd sent a five-pound note borrowed from his mother shortly after Charles left and had received a short letter thanking him for the gift several days later, but he had had no news of him since and had assumed that he had gone to join the carnage in France.

"I work here," said Charles. "I got shot in the leg and your father took me back."

"He should never have sent you away in the first place. When did this happen?"

"A few months ago, and then I was in hospital for a while."

"Are you all right?"

"Yes, better than I expected actually. I limp a bit but I can still get around pretty well. How are you, Master Brice?"

"*Mister* Brice," said Brice, correcting him. "I'm the heir now, remember. No, don't take it like that," he went on straightaway, seeing Charles step back in the face of the admonishment. "I'm fine, better than I've ever been in fact, and I'm pleased to see you," he added, putting out his hand for the footman to shake.

"Have you come to see your father?" asked Charles, looking mollified.

"Yes, but he's not expecting me. He's here, isn't he?"

"Yes, he's in his study," said Charles, pointing up at the back of the house where lights were burning in two of the upper-storey windows in contrast to the pervasive darkness round at the front. "Shall I go and tell him you're here?"

"Yes. Tell him that I've got good news; tell him it's a friendly visit. And let me have one of your cigarettes, would you? I'll smoke it while I'm waiting. They're good for the nerves."

Brice's mood of excitement, which had sustained him since he left the Parsonage, had started to evaporate, replaced now by an anxious fretfulness about his forthcoming interview with his father that had him shifting from one foot to the other as he drew the acrid smoke deep down into his lungs. He wished that the owl would stop its damn hooting out in the gardens.

Charles was back quicker than he'd expected and he followed the footman down the long gallery hung with the family portraits. The gaslights set in mantles between the windows were all extinguished and Charles was carrying a lantern to guide them through the dark. Its light flashed across the faces of Brice's forebears and he found it hard not to be unnerved by their expressions: resolute, severe, some almost sneering as if mocking his pretensions to follow in their foot-steps. Until at the end of the line they came to Brice's grandfather, who had died when Brice was still a child but whom he vividly remembered bellowing abuse at him from his bath chair whenever he made any noise playing in the old man's vicinity. He looked stern and unforgiving in his portrait too—character traits that he had passed on to his son, Brice thought, remembering his own father's implacable antagonism towards him over the years, which had cul-minated in Sir John's failed attempt to send him to the front to be killed with the rest of his generation.

Why should his father change his attitude now when he had always been against him? Brice wondered. And, having no answer to his question, he started to wish that he had never come. It was a fool's errand he was on, doomed to end in disappointment. But it was too late now to change his mind. His father knew he was here and he wasn't going to let the old man think he had run away with his tail between his legs.

"How is he?" he asked Charles as they began climbing the stair-case that led up to the door of Sir John's study. "Don't worry. You can speak freely. We used to be allies, remember? And we can be again."

Charles nodded. He had enjoyed his illicit adventures in Brice's company in years gone by although he was under no illusions that Brice was trustworthy. He remembered only too well how Brice would switch from treating him like a friend to treating him like a servant in the blink of an eye whenever the mood took him, and he had no intention of becoming a hostage to fortune by revealing the depth of his own grudge against his employer.

"He's not in the best of moods," he told Brice in answer to his question. "But he rarely is these days. I suppose he has a lot on his mind."

"What did he say when you told him I was here?"

"Not much," Charles lied, thinking there was nothing to be gained by telling Brice what Sir John had actually said, which had consisted of a few sentences spoken in quick succession: "I won't see him"; "What does that wastrel want?"; and, "Oh, very well! Bring him up. We might as well get it over with."

Like Brice, Charles didn't think that this encounter was going to go well, although he hoped to be surprised. A return of the prodigal son to Scarsdale Hall would at least relieve the monotony of evenings spent with only deaf old Cartwright, even deafer Mrs. Flowerdew and Sarah for company after the other servants had gone home. Tonight even the canary was gone, off visiting her sick mother in Gratton.

They had reached the door of the study. Charles knocked, waited for Sir John to shout a surly "Come" from inside, and then went in, holding the door back for Brice to follow as he announced: "Mr. Brice, Sir John," in his most formal footman's voice, before immediately performing an almost military about-turn that took him in one stride back out of the door which he pulled firmly shut behind him, leaving father and son to fight it out alone.

The room was lit by a curious combination of gaslight blended with the moonlight shining in through the half-open window, and Sir John also had an oil lamp on his desk to help him see to write. He was finishing a letter as Brice came in and, without looking up, waved his son to one of the two uncomfortable high-backed wooden chairs facing him across the desk.

Brice felt annoyed by his father's casual rudeness: he hadn't seen him in six months and yet his father wasn't prepared to give him a word or even a glance of welcome; just a wave of the hand as if he was some tradesman required to wait his turn while the master of the house dealt with more important business. But Brice refused to let his anger get the better of him. It had been hard to come back and he wasn't going to waste the effort he had made before he had even tried talking to his father.

As a distraction, he looked around the room, taking inventory of the familiar objects: the window seat with its faded green cushion; the mahogany bookshelves filled with rows of boring books with uncut pages; the bust of his father's hero, the Duke of Wellington, occupying pride of place in the centre of the mantelpiece over the empty marble fireplace (Brice had always preferred the upstart Napoleon to Wellington and had often wished that the Prussians had not arrived in the nick of time at Waterloo); and the dusty old maps hanging on the walls just as they always had, except behind Sir John's head where two of them had been taken down to make way for a large unframed contemporary map of the Western Front covered with coloured pins. Brice didn't need to ask to know that it was his father who had put them there and who moved them around in response to the news he read in *The Times* each morning, staring at the unfamiliar French names through the half-moon glasses that he was wearing now as he tried to make sense of the incomprehensible.

The image he'd conjured up of his father fussing with his pins like some aristocratic washerwoman touched and irritated Brice in equal measure, and he looked away from the map to the desk where his father had finished reading through his letter and was now writing out the address on the envelope. Brice noticed with surprise the laborious effort of concentration he was clearly making for what should have been a mundane task. His father was slowing down. That much was obvious.

Sir John had his arm across his green blotting pad so Brice couldn't see what he was writing, but there was a stack of sealed letters at the front of the desk and by craning his neck a little he was able to read the upside-down address of the one on top: "Ephraim Hardcastle, Manager, Scarsdale Colliery." The name made him shiver, reminding him yet again of his father's abortive attempt to force him into the army. And he looked away, trying to keep his temper, which it would have been far harder for him to control if he had instead read Adam's name on the envelope that his father was now in the process of sealing.

Finally Sir John looked up and bestowed on his son a glare of such dislike and derision that Brice actually flinched.

"Why are you here?" he asked, turning to refill his glass of wine from a half-finished decanter on a side table beside his desk without offering any to Brice.

"I wanted to see you—"

"Evidently," interrupted Sir John, his voice laced with sarcasm. "But that doesn't mean that you should show up here in the middle of the night without any warning. Why not behave like a civilized person and write and say you're coming, or at least give me the courtesy of a telephone call?"

"I don't need an appointment," said Brice defensively. "This is my home."

"Which you walked out of six months ago without a backwards glance! God knows what you've been doing since! Running up more debt probably—is that why you're here?"

"No, it isn't. I've been working," said Brice, drawing a deep breath. He was damned if he was going to stoop to his father's level. He'd come here to talk, not exchange insults, and he wasn't going to be deflected from his purpose by his father's irrational irascibility. "You should be happy," he told him. "You always wanted me to stand on my own two feet and that's what I'm doing."

"I wanted you to get a real job," Sir John shot back. "Something worthwhile—not helping profiteers make dirty money out of our soldiers' suffering."

"My grandfather's helping ease their suffering actually. Without our boots the soldiers would be a lot worse off. They'd tell you that themselves," said Brice, sitting back in his chair and adopting a deliberately cool tone. There really was something different about his father, Brice thought. He knew that his father disliked him but he'd done nothing to provoke the level of rudeness and anger with which he'd been treated ever since he sat down. His father had clearly been drinking, but Brice remembered the way he'd toiled over addressing the envelope and wondered whether there was something else wrong with him.

"Don't you dare come in here, talking about soldiers!" said Sir John, almost spitting out the words. "The only reason that you're doing your so-called job is because you're too much of a coward to go and fight. Look at you! Dressed up like a turkey, but that won't hide your white feathers!"

Sir John smiled as he saw his son recoil. It was a lucky shot. He knew nothing of the trauma Brice had suffered in the King's Head the previous winter, but he wanted to hurt his son whom he had made the scapegoat in his mind for almost all his misfortunes.

"Listen, Father," said Brice. "You can abuse me all you like but you need to start being realistic. Now that Seaton's gone, I'm your heir—"

"You can never replace Seaton," said Sir John. "He was a hero, worth a hundred of you . . ."

"Maybe so, but he's dead and you need to start getting used to it," said Brice brutally. Now it was Sir John's turn to flinch and Brice rejoiced inside—his father deserved to feel a little pain after the things he'd said. "And you don't need me to tell you that you can't break the entail," he went on, "so if you care about the estate, which I know you do, perhaps you should start thinking about working with me, not against me."

Brice paused, waiting for a response, but none came, and he had no idea whether his father was listening or just thinking up another bitter jibe to throw at him across the desk. "Listen," he said, leaning forward in his chair, "I came here tonight without telling you in advance because I just got some good news and I wanted to share it with you because . . . well, because you're my father. I'm going to be married."

"Married!" Sir John repeated the word in amazement. "To whom?"

"Miriam Vale."

"The parson's daughter?"

"Yes. She accepted me this evening," said Brice. He felt happy again for a moment—each time he told someone it made the incredible real: that he had won the beautiful girl; that she was going to be his wife.

"I thought she was engaged to Adam," said Sir John and then went straight on to the attack without giving Brice the chance to answer. "Have you no shame?" he demanded. "There's nothing more despicable than some dandy coming along and stealing a soldier's girl while he's away fighting for his country."

"I didn't steal her. He gave her up."

"And so you stepped in to take his leavings! I suppose there is some justice in that!" said Sir John contemptuously.

"What do you mean by that?"

"I mean that Adam's a man and you're not. If he was my son, I could die in peace."

"Damn you! Damn you to hell," said Brice, clenching the arms

477 | NO MAN'S LAND

of his chair with his fists as a red mist descended over his brain. As always it was the mention of Adam that sent him over the edge: he could stand the animosity and derision; he was even beginning to find a way to get over his rage against his father for trying to force him into the army; but he could not stay calm when he thought about his father's ham-fisted attempts to set Adam over him in his own home. And it was as if Sir John knew this, deliberately provoking his son past endurance.

"Yes," he said. "Damn me to hell! And the estate too, which you suddenly claim to care about so much! You know this girl's penniless, I suppose? But you didn't think about that, did you, when you went down on your bended knee? You know as well as I do that the only hope for this estate is for the heir to marry money, just like I did, but you're too special for that so you're going to do the opposite. Well, here's some news for you, young man: you're not twenty-one yet and until you are, I can stop you. And I promise you I will. Wherever you try to read the banns I'll be there to object. Or Hardcastle will: he's capable of being very thorough, I can assure you."

Brice spluttered with impotent fury. Not just against his father but against himself too. What a fool he'd been! Why hadn't he listened to Mrs. Vale, who'd told him to keep everything quiet until after the wedding? Instead he'd told the one person who could put a stop to his plans. And why? Because of some pipe dream that his father would undergo a miraculous transformation and start treating him like a son instead of an enemy. He was never going to do that. Leopards don't change their spots; old dogs don't learn new tricks.

His father watched Brice across the desk and enjoyed his victory. Once Brice was twenty-one there would be nothing he could do about the marriage but that was over a year away—more than enough time for passions to cool and Brice to learn some sense.

But Brice wasn't cool now. He shook with anger. Old dogs don't learn new tricks! That was what his father was—an old dog who should be put out of his misery once and for all.

"You should go now," said Sir John. "I'm tired and I need to go to bed. Charles will show you out." He got up from his chair and pushed a bell on the wall over by the fireplace.

"I'm not going anywhere," said Brice, white with rage. He hated his father; hated his contempt and his meanness and his refusal to love him. Years of anger and resentment coalesced into a blood frenzy that was filling up his brain like a haemorrhage so that there was no room left for thought or conscious decision-making. All he wanted to do was hurt the man who had hurt him; make him understand what it felt like. Just for a moment. That would be enough.

And now finally the fever possessed him completely, launching him forward out of his chair, charging at his father, who had no time to react as he was thrown back against the marble pillar supporting the left side of the fireplace surround. From there he sank down on to the hearth with his son on top of him, locked in an embrace that they had never experienced in life.

Brice let go of his father's jacket and got slowly to his feet. He felt winded and all the anger had gone out of him, replaced by a surge of paralysing fear as he stared down into his father's glassy blue eyes, uncovered now by the half-moon spectacles which had some-how fallen without breaking into the coal scuttle. His hands were shaking and his heart was pounding and he felt a clammy nausea rising up out of the pit of his stomach. He wanted to cry out but he could hardly breathe; he wanted to run away but his legs were too weak to move; and most of all he wanted to undo what he had done. Because he knew with utter certainty that his father was dead and that his life had changed forever.

He had no idea how long he stood there, gazing transfixed at the thick viscous blood seeping out from under his father's head on to the hearth tiles, before he became aware he wasn't alone and turned round to find Charles standing behind him in the doorway.

He was smiling! For the rest of his life Brice would always remember that wolfish expression on Charles's face, partly because it was so utterly unexpected, but also because Charles never let his true feelings show. He had been trained too well to ever let his mask slip except in the most extreme circumstances.

"I didn't mean to," said Brice stupidly. What did it matter what he'd meant? Murderers killed for a wide variety of motives but most of them still ended up on the gallows.

"Are you sure he's dead?" Charles asked, coming forward.

Brice nodded, keeping his eyes turned away from the corpse, staring instead at the full moon hanging like a pale white watcher outside the window. "Can you help me?" he whispered, unaware of how he was twisting his hands together in front of his chest as though trying in vain to wash them clean of filth.

"With what?" Charles asked, deliberately obtuse.

"With this. With making it look . . ."

"Like an accident?"

Brice nodded.

"Like he fell down the stairs and hit his head?"

"Yes."

"Because it was late and he'd been drinking," said Charles, glancing over at the empty glass on the desk.

"Yes, exactly," said Brice eagerly. "And you found him because I was never here. Who else is in the house?"

"Cartwright and Mrs. Flowerdew. I was the only one up when you arrived and, even if they were awake, I doubt they'd have heard you when you came in—they're both deaf as posts."

"What about yellow-face?"

"Not here. She's with her mother over in Gratton. Comes back tomorrow."

"So it can work," said Brice, unable now to control his excitement. He felt able to breathe again, as if an imaginary noose had been pulled away from around his neck.

"*Could* work," said Charles, making the correction with a thin smile.

"What do you mean?"

"I think you know," said Charles, watching with amusement as the light of understanding dawned on Brice's face, followed by a look of quick anger.

"What do you want?" he asked through gritted teeth. He understood now what the price of escaping justice would be. He would be in thrall to a servant, a dirty blackmailing footman. Until the end of his days.

"I want to be your right-hand man, Sir Brice," said Charles in his most deferential voice; he even made a slight bow. "Someone indispensable to you, sharing in your success."

"You want to be butler instead of Cartwright?"

"That would be a beginning, certainly. The rest can follow. Eventually I might wish to step into Mr. Hardcastle's shoes."

"Yes, all right. You can have whatever you want," said Brice, throwing up his hands. There was no point in arguing: he knew he had no choice in the matter.

"You give me your word?"

"Yes, I give you my word," Brice said impatiently. "Now what do we need to do?" he demanded. "I have to get out of here and the sooner the better."

"First we have to deal with the blood. There'll be no time later," said Charles, looking carefully over at the corpse. "Here, give me your coat," he said, snapping his fingers when Brice didn't immediately co-operate.

Charles lifted up the dead man's head, wrapped Brice's morning coat underneath it, and moved the body across the fireplace so that the bloodstain spreading over the tiles was fully exposed.

"Wait here," he told Brice. "I'll be back soon."

Charles was true to his word, returning almost straightaway equipped with a bucket full of soap and water, cloths, a scrubbing brush and a sack, and immediately set to work on his hands and knees cleaning up the blood.

"Is it coming out?" asked Brice anxiously.

"Yes. You're lucky he fell where he did. It's a lot easier to get blood off porcelain tiles than it is out of a carpet. But I think he's still bleeding and we're going to have to be careful when we're taking him downstairs."

"*We?* Do I have to?" Brice asked desperately. He found it hard to even look at his father; the thought of actually touching his body horrified him.

"Yes, of course you have to, unless you've got a way of explaining why he's bled on the stairs before he's hit the bottom. I can't carry him on my own and keep the wound covered," said Charles, getting to his feet. He had put everything he'd brought with him into the rubbish sack except the bucket, which he now took over to the open window, kneeling on the alcove seat to tip away the remainder of the soapy water into the bushes below.

"All right, let's get on with it. I've turned on the gaslights outside now he's not here to object, so that should help," he said, nodding towards the corpse. "If you take his legs I'll take his top end like I said."

"I don't think I can," said Brice. His hands were shaking and he thought he was going to faint.

"Well, then don't," said Charles contemptuously. "You can explain to the police what happened in here if that's what you prefer. It's up to you."

Brice shivered. Just the mention of the police had made him feel again that he couldn't breathe, as if the invisible noose was tightening once more around his throat. He had to help Charles with the body; he had no choice.

And, to his surprise, once he had forced himself to take hold of his father's thin legs and lift them up the task suddenly became easier. The horror left him as he had to concentrate all his attention on working with Charles to manoeuvre the body through the door and down the stairs.

At the bottom Charles arranged the dead man's limbs in what he considered the most convincing position for someone who had died falling down the stairs, and then went back over every inch of the ground that they'd covered to check that no blood had been spilt, while Brice watched impatiently from down below.

"Well, did you see any?" Brice asked nervously as soon as Charles had come back down the stairs, carrying the rubbish sack.

"No. I think this may actually work," said Charles, sounding a little smug, like a craftsman admiring his own handiwork. "One last touch and we're done," he added, taking Sir John's spectacles out of his pocket and laying them on the ground beside the corpse before casually lifting his foot and stamping on them.

"Now take this with you and get rid of it once you're out of York-shire," he told Brice, handing him the sack of soiled cloths to which he now added Brice's morning coat covered with his father's blood. "I'll wait ten minutes before I sound the alarm."

Charles looked at the coat almost fondly as Brice stuffed it into the sack. He was truly delighted that Brice had murdered his father. He had quietly hated Sir John ever since he had forced him into the army against his will, and he had been sorely tempted to push him down the stairs himself on more than one occasion. But now Brice had not only saved him the trouble but had also delivered himself permanently into his power. Already in the last half-hour Charles had been beginning to savour the reversal of roles between them, giving Brice orders instead of receiving them. It was the shape of things to come and he inwardly rejoiced, looking forward to his life under the new baronet.

But Brice felt no joy as he drove away into the night. He remembered the happiness and excitement he'd felt as he sped down the same stretch of road through the woods an hour earlier. He'd felt so alive: the world had seemed charged with possibility, whereas it had now become a place of fear and shadow. Everything was changed: if he was lucky enough to escape punishment for his crime he would have years of guilt to look forward to with Charles beside him turning the screw.

Beyond Scarsdale Brice accelerated, driving as if he was trying to escape, even though he knew it was a waste of time.

Chapter Thirty-Five

Adam arrived back at battalion headquarters on Tuesday evening, exactly twenty-four hours before the murder of his benefactor.

His company was encamped in bell tents set up in a muddy field. Whatever crop had once grown there had long since been trampled into oblivion by the soldiers' boots. But now they were all lying on their groundsheets, propped up on their packs, watching a screen set up under a poplar tree.

These open-air cinema shows were popular with the men and Adam had enjoyed them too, laughing at the antics of Fatty Arbuckle and the Little Tramp. But no one was laughing at this film. Instead the soldiers were uncharacteristically silent and absorbed and several of them shouted abuse at Adam as he obstructed their view for a moment while he looked for a place to sit down.

It was dark and the moon was invisible, hidden behind heavy low-hanging clouds that promised rain, although for now it remained dry. On the eastern horizon up ahead, lights flickered on the hilltops where the Germans were being subjected to a half-hearted bombardment. But the camp was over ten miles behind the lines and the noise of the guns was a dull boom rather than the ear-splitting roar that the soldiers had to endure when they were in the trenches.

Up on the screen the film they were watching was called *The Battle of the Somme,* but it was an entirely different battle to the one they had been fighting since the first of July. In this version everything was silent. There was no roar of guns, no screech of shells, no rattle of machine guns; there were no screams or shouts; just silence as lines and lines of grey, grainy soldiers marched up dusty roads towards the Big Push. They seemed happy, waving their hands and their hats in the air as they passed, apparently entirely ignorant of the fate awaiting them out in no man's land. Lambs to the slaughter: many of these jaunty-faced Tommies would be dead now, Adam realized. They were an army of ghosts and it seemed to him entirely fitting that they should be silent.

Perhaps it was a trick of the camera but the soldiers on the screen seemed to march faster than in real life and their synchronized step had a metronomic quality as if their legs were automated, obeying a higher will. And the artillerymen too had the same slavish quality as they stood in lines transferring endless shells from hand to hand until they reached the loader. The howitzers and the mortars with their mean, cruel mouths were like animals and the shells were their food and it was never enough. Adam remembered what he had told Sir John: *You can't win because of the guns.* But watching the film, seeing the slow panoramic shots of the smoking inhuman ruins of what had once been peaceful villages like Fricourt and Mametz, Adam realized he'd only understood half the truth. The machines had mastered their inventors. This was their war: *Deus ex machina.*

Afterwards Adam heard familiar voices shouting his name and, turning round, he discovered that he'd been sitting only a few yards from Luke and Rawdon in the darkness. Ernest wasn't there: he was back in Scarsdale, keeping vigil with his own ghosts in the empty house in Station Street while the branches of the sycamore tree tapped against the window.

" 'Ow's Blighty?" asked Luke.

"It was all right," said Adam.

"No, it weren't *all right*," said Rawdon. "We want to know what it was really like. We deserve to: we ain't been there in nigh on a year. You've got the gift of the gab more'n we 'ave, Adam. So tell us!"

"All right," said Adam, laughing. Despite the difficult question, he already felt more at ease back in the mud with his friends than he'd felt at any time since he left France. "The countryside's beautiful," he told them. "It's a green summer, full of fruit and flowers and blossom, and the air is fresh, deep down in your lungs fresh, so that cycling in the lanes is wonderful; better than I can describe. And it's quiet; quiet like it hurts your ears quiet."

"Yes, I can understand that," said Rawdon with a faraway look in his eye, as if he was trying to make pictures out of Adam's words. "Go on."

"The people are quiet too. But not in a good way. They walk bent and they don't laugh or smile or wave flags. Not any more. It's as if . . ." Adam paused, searching for the right word. ". . . as if they're enduring—without knowing why; they're just enduring for the sake of enduring. And it's hard to talk to them. It's awkward, like we don't speak the same language any more."

"Well, seein' this ought to 'elp," said Luke, pointing up at the screen that several of the soldiers were now busy dismantling. "I dunno if you heard what the adjutant said at the beginning—about 'em showin' the film in the cinemas all over Blighty so people can see what we're 'avin' to put up with over 'ere. Seein' it'll make 'em understand, I reckon."

"Maybe," said Rawdon, sounding unconvinced.

"Why only maybe?" Adam asked Rawdon curiously.

"Because the film won't be enough to make 'em understand. That's why. It showed the war but not the battle; the back but not the front," said Rawdon slowly, searching like Adam for the right words. "There weren't no fighting—just some Tommy shovin' one of the prisoners. That's the nearest it got to anger or hatred! And there weren't any of the pain and the blood and the stench and the fuckin' bloody noise . . . You know what I'm sayin': the film ain't real; it never could be—not unless the camera blokes were going to get 'emselves killed makin' it which they never were. The truth is you can't know what it's like bein' in the trenches unless you're in 'em. And once you're in 'em, then you can't get out of 'em," he finished with a rueful laugh.

Adam was surprised and also impressed. Rawdon wasn't given to making long speeches, but he'd explained the unbridgeable gap between the experience of trench warfare and the attempt to portray it better than Adam could have done. And he was right: endless shots of men marching and loading guns and carrying stretchers couldn't convey what the war was really like. The camera wasn't in the places that mattered and most of the time it had stayed too far away from its subjects, panning indiscriminately over distant, indistinct faces. Except that every so often, for a few seconds here and there, it had closed in and lingered: on a bemused black-haired private sitting in a sunken road in no man's land on that fateful first morning, staring open-eyed into the lens as he waited to go on, perhaps to his death; or on an exhausted soldier staggering under the weight of a dying man whom he was carrying on his back down a trench. Even in the silence you could sense the inhuman extremity of their experience. The images were fleeting but they were true: enough if you were watching closely to understand a little of what the war really meant for those caught in its web; enough perhaps for Miriam to understand why he'd been unable to put it into words.

But it was too late. Three days later he received a short undated letter from her, acknowledging the one he had sent before he left England, releasing her from their engagement. "You have broken my heart and taken away my purpose," she wrote. "My mother has sent for Brice and he is coming. Without you, how can I resist their pressure? I am a sheep among wolves."

Adam buried his head in his hands, fighting back tears. He was filled with bitter regret and he couldn't understand now why he had broken with Miriam. He felt as if he had been possessed by a self-destructive urge that had taken him over as soon as his train had arrived in Scarsdale, driving him on to the point where he had almost welcomed Mrs. Vale's intervention, only for the impulse to vanish without trace as soon as it had accomplished its goal of terminating his engagement. And now, in the aftermath, he felt empty and mystified by his actions, looking back on them as if they had been the work of someone else, someone he didn't know.

But regret was useless: he couldn't turn back the clock. He had done his work too well: whatever had transpired between Brice and Miriam had long since occurred for better or worse, and there was nothing he could do to stop it. *For better for worse . . . Till death us do part . . .* Adam knew without needing to be told what had happened:

the wedding vows that he and Miriam had intended for each other would now be spoken by her and Brice. And he would be separated from Miriam forever: *Those whom God hath joined together let no man put asunder.* She had been the promise of a future in his life and now there was nothing but the present; nothing except the war. And death—let death part them now; let death put them asunder.

And as if in answer to Adam's prayer, the bugler sounded an assembly call, gathering the company together out in the field where the colonel, sitting astride his horse, announced in a quavering voice that they would be going back up to the front line the next morning, with orders to participate in a further attack: yet another attempt dreamed up by the high command to attain the longed-for but ever-elusive breakthrough.

As the colonel finished speaking it began to rain: a hard downpour that continued throughout the night, beating down on the tents and transforming the road that led back to the trenches into a quagmire. It was the same all over the Somme. Since June the thin crust of metal on the road surfaces had been cut through and eroded by the constant passage of gun limbers and heavily laden wagons and trucks; and now the torrential rain penetrated down into the road's chalk substratum, turning it to viscous mud.

At dawn the company struck camp and began to march. The soldiers wore their waterproof groundsheets as improvised capes over their uniforms and kept their faces down both to avoid being lashed by the driving rain and to watch their footing. They stumbled and slid their way forward, venting their frustration in a chorus of obscene oaths shouted out above the noise of the rain. If they fell, the resulting mud bath left them shivering with cold, while their rain-drenched packs became heavier on their backs with every hour that passed.

Adam, Luke and Rawdon were near the back of the column, marching just in front of the traveling field cooker, a long-limbered vehicle drawn by two horses whose driver had got down from his box seat to lead his charges by hand along the treacherous road. It was a good position, putting them at the front of the queue for hot tea and food whenever the company halted to rest. But it also meant that they were the first to be called upon to help when one of the horses lurched forward and fell into one of the mud-filled shell craters that were becoming a more frequent hazard as they got closer to the trenches.

The cooker tipped alarmingly over on to one side and the soldiers had to rush round and push up against it to stop it from keeling over, while the driver somehow succeeded in detaching the trapped horse from the vehicle's shafts. The mud sucked at the horse's withers and its frantic efforts to extricate itself from the mire only made it sink further in. Adam and Luke got down beside the driver, trying to push the horse's backside up and forward while Rawdon stood at the front, pulling on the reins. They groaned and swore and coaxed, but all to no avail; and they were just about to give up when the horse found some kind of unexpected purchase in the crater and rose up on its hind legs, leaping clear of the mud and straight at Rawdon whose hands were momentarily caught in the reins. He fell over but miraculously escaped being trampled. Instead the horse's hooves passed on either side of his prone body and dragged him head first off the road where he collided with the trunk of a tree. The reins tore out of his hands and the horse galloped on into the field, pursued by the corpulent driver who was yelling out: "Stop, Baby" (apparently the horse's name) at the top of his lungs, while the soldiers fell about laughing as they watched him run and fall flat on his face and get up and run again like one of the Keystone Cops, until he finally caught up with the horse that had stopped in the middle of the field and was busy chewing on the grass as if nothing had happened.

But Rawdon wasn't laughing. At first he thought he was all right. He was sore and shaken and he had scratches on his face and hands. Some of them were bleeding but the cuts all seemed to be superficial and none of his limbs looked or felt broken. But then when he tried to stand up, he collapsed in a heap, feeling a sharp pain in his right foot. Something had happened which meant he couldn't put any weight on it. It was the same leg that he had injured before in the mine. And he winced with pain, clenching his teeth to stop crying out as he took off his boot, sock and puttee to enable the MO to assess the damage.

It didn't take him long. "You've been lucky," he said, getting up. "I don't think it's much more than a badly sprained ankle. You'll be right as rain in a week or two provided you stay off it and there isn't a fracture."

"Stay off it! I can't stay off it! I've got to go with them," said Rawdon wildly.

"With who? What are you talking about?" asked the MO, perplexed.

"I 'ave to be with my friends. They need me tomorrow."

"Well, that's very laudable, Private Dawes," said the MO, patting Rawdon on the shoulder. "Most of your colleagues would be jumping for joy getting an injury like this just before an attack. But facts are facts. You're unfit for duty and the only place you're going to is hospital. You can ride in one of the wagons until we get to the new HQ and then there'll be transport to take you back."

Adam and Luke had been standing to one side while the MO was examining Rawdon's injury and now they lifted him to his feet, each taking one of his arms over their shoulders. But he shook them off, forcing his right foot down on to the ground in an effort to walk. Immediately his leg buckled and he fell over, screaming out with pain.

"Don't you dare do that again," shouted the MO. He was angry now and his earlier friendliness had disappeared. "I've got no time for idiots and neither has the army. Next time you'll be on a charge. Do you hear me?"

White in the face, Rawdon nodded, and this time he allowed Adam and Luke to carry him over to the wagon.

"Why are you so upset? What's so important about you coming with us tomorrow?" asked Adam, standing looking down at his friend over the backboard. Rawdon cut a sorry and rather comical figure, lying wedged among the spare wheels and gun parts, wearing an enraged look on his face.

"Because we 'ave to stick together," said Rawdon furiously. "I dunno why—if I did, I'd tell thee. I just know we 'ave to, that's all."

"Well, we can't," said Adam harshly. "You can't stand, let alone walk, so there's no point crying about it." He didn't want to admit it but he found Rawdon's desperation upsetting. He was worried enough about the attack without Rawdon making it worse.

Late in the afternoon the company reached the new battalion headquarters—a group of dilapidated farm buildings with dark windowless interiors and dirt floors strewn with old rubbish. The rain had slowed to a drizzle and the soldiers looked out through the open double doors towards the grey windswept slopes scarred by the white chalk of the old front lines. It was a barren landscape littered with burnt-out vehicles, some of them overturned, and the bloated bodies of mules, lying in the grotesque, contorted postures in which they had met their deaths. The ground, the trees, the buildings—nothing had escaped the German shells, except by some miracle the roofs of the cowsheds and barns in which the soldiers now sat trying to get dry, drawing comfort from hot tea and stew.

Rawdon lay morose in the corner, darting murderous looks at his injured foot. And his misery turned to rage when several of the soldiers congratulated him on his good fortune. He threw his mug of tea at them, narrowly missing their heads, and they were all relieved when the MO appeared in the doorway, calling out Adam and Luke to carry Rawdon to the truck that was waiting outside.

As they settled him in the back under the tarpaulin cover, Rawdon reached out and took hold of the collar of Adam's tunic, pulling him close. "Be careful," he said. "Don't let them . . ." He didn't finish his sentence but his voice was urgent and he was staring up into Adam's eyes as if trying to convey his meaning without expressing it in words.

"What?" asked Adam. "Don't let them what, Rawdon? Kill us? Is that what you mean?"

"Yes," said Rawdon. He still had hold of Adam's tunic.

Adam shook his head, staring down at his friend. "This isn't like you, Rawdon," he said.

"What isn't?"

"Being so stupid and superstitious. You know as well as I do that this whole damn war's a game of chance and that the odds are getting worse each time we attack. Remember what you used to say: if a bullet's got your name on it it's going to find you and there's fuck all you can do about it. Well, you were right. That's the truth. And you not being there and us keeping our heads down isn't going to make a blind bit of difference once we go over the top and you know it."

"I found thee before, didn't I? Out in the wood. No one else did," Rawdon shot back.

"You got lucky," said Adam. "Just like you're lucky to have hurt your foot. I don't care what you say, Rawdon: I'm glad you're out of it. And I wish Luke was too, and everyone else in our section. And yes, if it makes you happy, I'll sure as hell try not to let the bastards kill us. Are you satisfied now?"

Rawdon sighed and gave an almost imperceptible nod, and Adam reached across to where Rawdon was still holding on to his tunic and gripped his hand hard for a moment, looking into his eyes, before he let go and turned to walk away.

Luke caught up with Adam when he'd got halfway back to the barn and they stopped to watch as the truck drove bumpily away down the rutted road, sending a spray of filthy brown water up on to the verges on either side, until it turned the corner and disappeared.

"Well, looks like it's just you and me now," said Adam, putting his arm around his old friend's shoulder. "Last Scarsdale men standing: that's what we are. I'm glad you're here, Luke."

"Yeah," said Luke. "An' I'm glad you're 'ere too. We'll give 'em 'ell tomorrow, won't we, Adam?" He'd meant to be assertive but fear had got into his voice and he ended up sounding as if he was asking a question.

"Yes, we will. Fire and brimstone," said Adam, saying it as though it was a cast-iron fact, not to be denied. He'd never felt less sure of anything but he knew he needed to reassure Luke who, despite his brave words, appeared to be nearing the end of his tether.

He paused at the door of the barn, looking up at the sky. The rain had stopped now and the wind had chased away some of the clouds, allowing the pale sun to peer weakly through the remainder as it sank down towards the western horizon. And the artillery had taken advantage of the temporary improvement in visibility to winch up an observation balloon that was now hanging in the air about a mile behind where Adam was standing. It was an ugly contraption: an oblong grey gas bag tethered to the ground by steel cables, with the observer's tiny basket hanging impossibly vulnerable underneath; it bore no relation to the beautiful sky-blue and gold sphere beneath which he had floated with Seaton across the sky of northern England before the war, tasting an ethereal freedom that he had never experienced before or since. The flight seemed unimaginable now: a vision of heaven entirely out of place amid the hell he was experiencing down below.

Later, another truck drew up outside in the dark and the soldiers gave a ragged cheer as the mail orderly appeared in the doorway, weighed down with a sack of post. And there were more parcels back in his van filled with cake and chocolate and cigarettes: gifts from home to distract them from what lay ahead.

Adam had a letter from his benefactor; the same letter that Brice had watched his father finishing and addressing in his study minutes before he murdered him. Charles had had the presence of mind to go back and retrieve Sir John's spectacles from the coal scuttle, but he hadn't had any way of knowing that the stack of letters on the desk contained anything incriminating. And so he had left them where they were and Cartwright had given them to the postman the next morning.

Adam read the letter through twice. Sir John thanked him for telling him about Seaton. "Your task wasn't easy, yet you stuck to it admirably," he wrote, "so that now I can grieve for my son, knowing his true worth." And then, showing a remarkable willingness to write from the heart, he told Adam that he was proud of him. "You know I think of you as my son," he wrote. "And now that Seaton is gone I wish that I could make you the heir to my estate. But I cannot. I may have been unwise in my life but I have strived to be a good man, and

I do not know what I have done to deserve Brice." Here there was a pause in the letter before Sir John resumed with a final paragraph:

> *Speak of the devil. Charles has just been in to tell me that Brice is here with good news. Good news! After an absence of six months I am sure that the only news he has to impart is that he is up to his ears in debt. Well, I shall have news for him. I have no money to give him. Lloyd George and his cronies have taken it all. I wish he would leave me alone but I suppose I shall have to see him even though it's nearly nine o'clock and I would far rather go to bed. Write to me when you can: your letters mean a great deal. I think of you often and I pray for you, with the love of a father.*
> *John*

Adam was grateful for Sir John's heartfelt words. They made him feel that something good had come out of his disastrous leave. He had discharged his duty to Seaton and he had renewed his bond with his benefactor. *Benefactor:* not for the first time Adam sensed that the word was wrong, although he was unable to come up with a better alternative. It was too formal and businesslike and it did nothing to convey the depth of affection he felt for Sir John, who had more than honoured the promise he'd made him in Parson Vale's study all those years ago *to help you so that you can become your own man . . . the man that your father wanted you to be.*

Adam thought of Sir John on the day he left the Hall, shaking his hand and pressing a ten-pound note into it as a parting gift. And he smiled as he thought of him, glass in hand, holding forth at the end of the dining-room table, or taking his afternoon constitutional down the drive, straight-backed, tapping out time with his walking stick on the tarmac. But all the time he had no idea that Sir John was lying on an undertaker's embalming table in Gratton and that Brice was the new master of Scarsdale Hall. And his ignorance meant he couldn't know that the letter he was holding in his hand was the only evidence which now existed that Brice had been at the Hall on the night his father died.

Adam folded the letter up into a small square and put it in his wallet, determined to keep it because of what it meant: that he was loved and that he had a home to go to somewhere in this Godforsaken world.

The company left at midnight. Tallow-faced, unshaven and exhausted, the soldiers marched with stony, expressionless faces along the moonlit road and then fell into single file when they reached the communication trench, picking their way slowly through the mud. Their uniforms were still wet and they shivered, grimacing with pain as the blisters on their swollen feet rubbed against the inside of their hard hobnailed boots.

Frequently they had to stop, flattening themselves against the crumbling walls of the trench as stretcher-bearers came stumbling past with their burdens hidden under dirty blankets. And sometimes they fell, slipping on the unstable duckboards, but they didn't have the energy now for more than a few muttered oaths as they picked themselves up and went on.

The guns had been largely quiet as they passed, but a stray shell hit a dump of Very lights and set off a mad firework display that illuminated their surroundings in a blaze of fantastic colours just as they came to a break in the communication trench where it crossed a cart track used by supply vehicles.

They could see that they were standing at the entrance to a wood or rather the remains of a wood. It had undergone such terrible destruction that there was no way for Adam to know whether it was the same wood where he had lain trapped beneath the huge tree trunk three weeks earlier. All the oaks and birches had been either uprooted or blasted down into jagged leafless stumps, allowing the soldiers to see past them into the interior. There were dead men out there: from where he was standing Adam could make out fragments of ragged uniform and rifles and distended limbs sticking up above the tangled undergrowth and broken timber. Perhaps it was a trick of the lights but Adam fancied he could see dead hands waving gently in the breeze.

Here and there the impact of larger shells had created sizeable craters that were now filled to overflowing with rusty water that was the colour of dried blood, and above one of these ponds Adam could see the bald head of a soldier staring back at him out of empty eye sockets, wreathed in a lurid green haze that Adam recognized as gas.

This was more wasteland than wood. Ghastly and ghostly in equal measure, it appeared to Adam like an angry storm-tossed sea frozen at the height of its turmoil.

The lights fizzled out and a spectral moonlit calm returned to the wood as Adam's company made their way up to the new front line through recently captured German trenches. In the aftermath of the attack the British had been too preoccupied with dealing with their own casualties to find time to remove the bodies of the dead German defenders and in some places there was no choice but to walk on them. Holding their noses against the sweet stench of putrefaction, the soldiers felt they were balancing on top of a series of air cushions with the soft bodies wobbling and yielding under their feet.

Luke made the mistake of looking down and started to shake. The rain had hastened the process of decomposition and some of the Germans' faces were turning inky black around the white teeth which they had exposed in the agony of their deaths. It was too much. "I can't," he moaned, coming to a halt. "I can't do this."

"Can't what?" demanded the company sergeant major, who had been two men back from Luke in the line and had now pushed his way forward past Adam to find out what was causing the delay.

"I can't walk on 'em. Not on their faces," said Luke with tears in his eyes.

"Well, then fucking jump," said the sergeant major brutally, and he pushed Luke hard in the back so that he almost fell. "We ain't got no time to dawdle, Mason, you hear me? We have to go before dawn or the Jerries'll see us coming. I'm going to be right behind you from now on and if you stop again I'll put a bullet in your head. I swear to Jesus I will."

Luke kept going after that. But it was still dark when they got to the front-line trench and they had to wait twenty minutes before the hurricane bombardment began. And then it was all just as it had been before: bullets flying in the smoke and the creeping exploding barrage up ahead and the troops creeping along behind it or at least those that were able to stay upright as they tried to pick their way through the treacherous undergrowth.

There was one change: Adam saw the colonel over to his right and wondered what the hell he was doing. It was against orders for field commanders to join in the attacks. Perhaps he'd had enough, Adam thought. Perhaps he couldn't stand to take another roll call of the dead and wanted to share their fate instead. If so, he soon got his wish, blown to pieces by a high-explosive shell almost as soon as they had gone over the top.

Adam kept close to Luke just as he'd promised Rawdon he would. They followed the barrage through the trees and came out into a ride across from the German trenches and that was where their luck ran out.

Shells were falling everywhere. Adam thought they had to be British; there was no way the Germans would shell so close to their own trench line. And, just as on the first of July, Adam could see the German defenders firing from the top of their trenches. In the pre-dawn light he could make out their faces, some with glasses, some with moustaches, and each and every one of them taut with a fear and agitation that mirrored his own. Until suddenly they were gone, and he was flying up into the air, and everything was blue and then black by the time he fell back to the ground.

He came to in the sunlight. He was lying on his back and he knew he was wounded because it hurt terribly when he tried to move. Pushing himself up with his arms, he could see a mess of blood on both his legs. He was weak, terribly weak, and it took all the strength he had left to reach round and get his water bottle. He drank deeply: he sensed he was going to die so there was no point in stinting himself.

And then he lay back exhausted on his left side: for some reason he felt more comfortable in that position and as long as he stayed still he felt no pain. After a few moments he opened his eyes and saw Luke, lying on his side too, facing him. It was as though they were engaged in some secret conversation except that Luke was dead. Adam knew that straightaway. His green eyes were glazed over and opaque and Adam felt a vast sadness engulf him. He remembered oh so much: a flash of visions tumbling through his mind: Luke flying down the hill on his bicycle; Luke dripping and laughing as he waded out of the hidden lake laden with the silver fish for their picnic; Luke grinning sheepishly for the camera with the ill-fitting Pickelhaube helmet perched ridiculously on top of his head; Luke so alive and yet now so dead! How was it possible? How could something as miraculously multifarious as a human personality end in a moment, snuffed out by an explosion and a shard or two of scrap-iron shrapnel?

The bitter grief exhausted Adam. He didn't have the energy to think any more; he was just seeing. Images passed across his eyes: the blasted, splintered trees; the azure blue of the sky, the emerald wings of a green hairstreak butterfly fluttering above the arid broken ground a yard or two away. It settled on the lapel of Luke's jacket, half camouflaged by the khaki. Perhaps it knew that he was dead. And Adam watched as its wings quivered in the sunlight. Dull brown and nondescript when open but iridescent green when closed. So delicate, so beautiful, so unexpected: the green matched the colour of Luke's eyes. Life and death side by side: the wonder of it; the inexplicable wonder!

He could hear shots: revolver shots. And voices: German voices. They were coming closer. And there was nowhere to hide; no body to lie beneath. Not this time. Adam reached out and took hold of Luke's hand, and then he sighed and closed his eyes. He didn't want to see his own death.

Part Six

———

Ghosts

GHOST: If thou didst ever thy dear father love . . . Revenge his foul
and most unnatural murder.

William Shakespeare, *Hamlet,* Act 1, Scene 5

Chapter Thirty-Six

February 1919

So satisfy my curiosity, Sir Brice! Why do you stay in here when you could move that desk to anywhere else in the house?"

Charles spoke in a bantering tone that he knew from past experience infuriated Brice, particularly when it was spiced with the faintly mocking use of Brice's title that Charles had perfected over the past two and a half years. And it didn't fail this time either.

"Mind your own business," said Brice irritably. He was sitting in the study that had once been his father's, behind the desk where his father used to sit, drumming his fingers on a glass paperweight containing a brightly coloured image of the Scarsdale coat of arms. It was almost the only object in the room that he'd inherited from his father that he actually liked. "What I do or don't do in my own house is my affair," he announced, laying down the law.

"Indeed it is," said Charles, nodding his agreement, "provided of course that it doesn't lead to you spilling our little secret to one of these newfangled London head doctors that I've been reading about in the newspaper." Charles had stationed himself beside the fireplace in exactly the position where Sir John had been standing when Brice attacked him, and now he tapped the side of the mantelpiece to give added effect to his words.

"I'm not *spilling* anything," said Brice, banging the paperweight down on the desk. "And I'm not seeing any doctors, so what the hell are you talking about?"

"I'm talking about you sitting in here night after night thinking about your father; driving yourself mad with guilt about something you can't do anything about . . ."

"I don't feel guilty. He provoked me. It was an accident—"

Charles smiled, sensing that Brice had stopped in mid-sentence because he couldn't get past the absurdity of using the word *accident* to describe smashing his father's head against a marble fireplace. "You're lying," he said scornfully. "And you know it. You feel guilty all the time and you carry it around with you like a sack of Scarsdale coal on your back. And then you come in here and sit staring over at this fireplace going over what happened because you're trying to fight the guilt and justify what you did. But you can't because you're weak and you feel sorry for yourself and still wish that your father had loved you just a little bit, which he was never going to do even if he'd lived to be a hundred. Oh yes, I can read you like a book, Sir Brice, and I just hope no one else learns to do the same."

"Damn you, Charles," said Brice, half getting up from his chair. It enraged him that his father's ex-footman should talk to him with such contempt. But it frightened him too. He wasn't going to admit it but Charles had got his measure: he was weighed down by his guilty secret almost beyond enduring and he longed to share it with someone. Countless times he had found himself about to confess all to his mother or to Miriam, only to bite back on his words at the last moment.

"If you must know I sit in here because I have to; because you're making such a damn mess of everything," he said, trying to change the subject. "I should never have agreed to get rid of Hardcastle, or Cartwright for that matter. I hated them just as much as you did, but at least they knew what they were doing, which is a damn sight more than you do. And they weren't lining their pockets like you are either."

Brice didn't know for sure whether Charles was embezzling the mine's profits. Figures gave him a headache at the best of times and he had no idea how to read accounts. But he strongly suspected Charles of some form of serious malfeasance, and he wanted to turn the tables on him and put an end to his bullying. But the strategy didn't work. Charles was entirely undaunted by the accusation.

"If I choose to put my hand in the till from time to time to supplement the woefully inadequate salary that you're paying me, then there's nothing you can do about it and you know it," he said contemptuously. "You've sold your soul to the devil, Sir Brice, and there's no use crying about it now. If you ask me, your father was a mean-spirited bigot who treated you badly from start to finish and deserved exactly what he got, so stop being miserable and enjoy life a bit like I do. Live for the day. That's my advice to you."

Charles stretched his arms above his head, conveying a sense of lazy power. Lady Scarsdale had chosen him to be her prize footman because of his tall athlete's body and he remained strong and thickly muscled, notwithstanding his wartime injury. Only a slight fattening around the waist and a faint red tinge to his cheeks gave a clue to the dissolute lifestyle he had been leading since the lucky day when Brice killed his father and delivered the estate into his clutches.

"It's been a long day," he said. "Time for bed, I think. You're going to London in the morning, aren't you?"

Brice nodded.

"Well, give my regards to your mother, won't you? She's a fine woman. And let's hope you can tap the old man for a bit more of a loan than you managed last time. The estate's coffers are in sore need of a fresh injection of funds, I can tell you that."

"I wonder why," said Brice caustically. He had no intention of mentioning Charles's name to his mother, although he knew that she and her father were likely to bring it up. His inability to explain her ex-footman's rapid promotion first to butler and then mine manager had already set alarm bells ringing down in London and he knew that his desperate need for money would mean more questions about Charles's role that he wouldn't be able to answer.

Charles opened the door and paused on his way out. "Remember, no head doctors!" he said, and then with a wave of his hand he was gone.

Brice picked up the paperweight again and aimed it at the door, miming the deadly throw at Charles's head that he would have liked to execute a moment before. He hated being in thrall to a man who had probably been born in a cowshed, and he sat back in his chair for a moment, thinking how wonderful it would be if Charles was magically removed from his life. He briefly imagined him losing control of the car and spinning off the road into a tree trunk or falling out of one of the Hall's top-storey windows and smashing his head to pulp on the stone courtyard down below. And then, with a sharp intake of breath, he pictured another scene in which his tormentor lay stretched out by the fireplace where he'd just been standing with a bullet hole in the centre of his forehead and his brains leaking out on to the carpet. This vision was more real than the others because Brice had the means to accomplish it. On a visit to London soon after the Armistice he had bought a service revolver from a demobbed down-on-his-luck officer whom he'd met in a Soho bar and ever since then he'd kept it loaded, under lock and key in the bottom drawer of his desk.

He took it out sometimes, turning it over and weighing it in his hand. Like the motor car, it made him feel powerful, but he was frightened of it too. He'd never fired a gun and he was too nervous to take it out to practise. And he understood his own character well enough to suspect that when the moment of crisis came he wouldn't be able to pull the trigger. He could talk about murder as when he'd toyed with the idea of leaving Adam to drown in the lake before the war, but he didn't have the stomach or the will power to turn talk into action. He'd killed his father in a moment of sudden madness and he'd bitterly regretted it ever since.

Nor did he have the money to pay someone else to do the deed for him—that was if he could find such a person—and he knew that this too was a fantasy. Even if successful it would be a pointless exercise: he would simply be replacing one blackmailer with another, and it was far more likely that Charles would find out about any plot long before it came to fruition. And then all he would have to do is go to the police and tell them what had happened to Brice's father. And they would offer him immunity from prosecution in return for his testimony and Brice would be tried and . . .

Brice gripped the desk, straining every sinew in his mind and body to stop his accelerating train of thought from running out of control, because he knew full well where it was leading: he could feel again the tightening of the imaginary noose around his neck; the vain struggle for breath and life; the knowledge of the fall before he fell; the dangling death.

Ever since his father's death he had been tortured by recurring nightmares populated by these visions from which he would come violently awake, crying out for mercy, and their frequency seemed to increase whenever he felt under threat from Charles. Soon after his wedding he had had to stop sleeping with Miriam for fear that he would blurt out his secret to her, and Brice recalled with shame that it was Charles who had advised him to leave the marital bed. There was nothing that he didn't feel able to poke his nose into, and the worst part was that in this instance he'd been right.

Brice fought to regain his composure. Gradually his breathing grew more regular and his heartbeat returned to normal, and he took out his handkerchief and wiped away the clammy sweat that had formed on his brow. Over on the mantelpiece the pretty French clock with which he'd replaced his father's bust of the Duke of Wellington struck ten. He sighed, pushing away the mound of letters that covered the desk (all of them variations on the same common theme: demands for money that he didn't have the means to pay), and got to his feet. He *would* move out of this room, he decided. It would be the first thing he'd put his mind to when he got back from London, hopefully with some money in his pocket so he could create a richly furnished study-library in his own image, fitting to his position. He wished he'd made the change before Charles suggested it as he hated giving the ex-footman the impression that he was controlling Brice's actions like some kind of puppet master, but it was better late than never: he'd spent enough time wrestling fruitlessly with his father's ghost. He needed to make a fresh start.

He walked down the corridor towards his bedroom and stopped at the open door of his wife's dressing room. She was sitting at her table with her back to him, brushing out her long burnished-brown hair so that it cascaded down the back and arms of the white lace chemise she was wearing in lustrous rivulets. He stood utterly still and slightly to the side so she wouldn't see him unless she turned right around, greedily watching the quick graceful movements of her hands and studying the perfect sculpted profile of her face. She was so natural, so easy and free, but he knew that that would cease in an instant if she knew he was there.

This was how she would be if she loved him. This was how she could be. But she never was. Instead she remained forever passive, submitting to his embraces but never returning them, filling him with an equal mixture of longing and frustration. And sometimes these emotions boiled over into anger. Once or twice he had raised his hand to her, although he had never struck her. But still she didn't react.

Instead she apologized. "I should never have married you," she'd told him quietly after he'd lost his temper a few weeks previously. "I was weak and there was a lot of pressure from you and from my mother. But it's no excuse. I knew how it would turn out for us both and yet I let it happen. Can you forgive me, Brice?"

"No, I don't want to forgive you," he'd shouted. "I want to be married to you. Can't you see that? I want you to be my wife and not just in name; I want you to try. Don't I deserve that?"

But she had shaken her head, smiling sadly. "That's not the way it works, Brice," she'd said. "Human beings can't try to love that way; we do or we don't. That's the way it is. I can't help it."

But he didn't believe her. Or at least he believed that everything would have been different if Adam Raine hadn't come between them all those years ago. And remained between them ever since, even though he was now dead, rotting in the mud of the Somme. Miriam never referred to Adam but he could sense that she was constantly thinking about him, setting up an altar to his memory in her heart which she was forever tending. It was intolerable: he had been unable to compete with his rival when he was alive and now he couldn't displace him when he was dead.

Brice had been careful not to openly rejoice when the news came through soon after his father's death that Adam was missing in action, and he hadn't interfered or commented when Miriam retired to her room to cry for days on end. But when the magical words "presumed dead" were added to Adam's Red Cross status a year later he had dared to hope that Miriam might start to move on. Instead, however, she had remained as cold and distant as ever, nursing her silent grief, and it was only her son that seemed to excite her interest.

Brandon Scarsdale was the one real bond connecting Brice and Miriam. They both loved their child, who had recently celebrated his second Christmas with a fanfare of exotic presents that Brice had brought back from the London toy shops. But the family's joy had quickly turned sour when Brandon came down the next day with a fever, cough and sore throat. Brice and Miriam were terrified, fearing that their son was succumbing to a new wave of the deadly Spanish flu pandemic that had already extended its bony hand several times into Scarsdale, indiscriminately carrying off men, women and children for whom Tyler the sexton had had to open up a new section in the overcrowded graveyard.

Brice and Miriam had taken it in turns to sit by their son through the long nights and Brice had trembled, remembering how scarlet fever had come so close to putting him in the churchyard too when he was a child. But, despite their worst fears, Brandon's illness never became severe and he was now well on the road to recovery, although Miriam still had him sleeping in a cot in her bedroom so she could keep an eye on him during the night.

Brice was intending to leave early the next day for London and wanted to see his son before he left, and so he tapped gently on the door and entered the room, noticing with a pang how Miriam's face set into a tight watchful mask as soon as she looked up and saw him. The change in her hurt him just as it always did; it didn't seem to matter that he'd been expecting it. But he made an effort to stifle his resentment. He didn't want to part on bad terms.

"How's Brandon?" he asked.

"He's better, I think. He went to sleep as soon as I put him to bed. He needs his rest after all he's been through."

"Can I see him? I won't wake him up," Brice asked, thinking how strange it was that he should need to ask permission to enter his own wife's bedroom.

Miriam nodded and Brice walked past her into the dimly lit

room. Brandon was lying fast asleep with his arms encircling a bright white teddy bear with shiny shoe-button eyes. His tiny fingers met at the base of the bear's back, locked together in a tight embrace that continued throughout Brandon's waking hours. The child loved the bear with a rare intensity: its name had been the first word he spoke. Brice remembered the moment vividly: his son pointing intently at the bear sitting opposite him, perched on a chair in the corner of the nursery, and saying "Bob" very clearly when he'd never said anything meaningful before.

Later, there had been a terrible day when Bob had gone missing and Brandon had screamed out his grief until he was literally blue in the face, and Brice had felt agonized by his impotence to help until the nursemaid came to the rescue and found the bear lying hidden under a cushion.

He had been amazed by the love he felt for his child. Up to now his emotions had been essentially selfish. He wanted to possess or to be avenged or to be loved or esteemed, but this was different. His son was small and helpless and needed his protection. No one had needed Brice before like Brandon did. He'd always been in the way: the second son; the second best; the third wheel when he would follow Miriam and Adam across the lawns, holding her parasol. But he was at the centre of his son's universe. He was rightfully there; he could not be displaced. He was Brandon's father.

The child stirred in his sleep, throwing back his covers, and Brice stared down mesmerized at his son's hand. It was so small and wrinkled and perfect; so delicate and fragile. And he was suddenly frightened. The world into which Brandon had been born was unsafe and dangerous. To live in it was like walking on a thin layer of ice that could crack and break in an instant, sucking you down into the black waters underneath. Nothing was secure. The war had taught Brice that lesson as it came hurtling down like an unexpected meteor out of the clear blue summer skies of 1914: first a distant speck, and then a black thundercloud shutting out the sun, and finally a roaring cataclysm that had devoured his generation. It had almost caught him too in its red maw: he had escaped by a whisker, clutching on to his grandfather's coat-tails. And the influenza that had begun last year was the same, stalking the shuttered streets of Europe like the Angel of Death, entering here and there at random to claim those that the war had left behind. People who felt under the weather at breakfast would often be dead by nightfall, drowning in the thick, clotted fluid that had filled up their lungs.

Where would it end? What plague would come next? How could he protect his son against the slings and arrows of outrageous fortune when he was so weak himself? Brice thought of the white feather that he still kept in an envelope locked up with the gun in the bottom drawer of his desk. He was a coward and a murderer, dependent for survival on the goodwill of a reckless blackmailer. So how could he also be a father to his son?

He leant over the side of the cot and felt a wave of tenderness pass through him as he pulled the blanket up over the boy's body. It hurt with a sharp pain, unfamiliar because it was so foreign to his nature, and he found himself uttering a silent spontaneous prayer addressed to the Angel whom he imagined hovering outside the window in the impenetrable darkness: "Whatever happens, please let me die first. That way I can pretend he'll live forever." It was the best, most selfless moment in Brice's life.

"He's beautiful, isn't he?" said a soft voice just behind him. He'd been too absorbed in his thoughts to hear Miriam come in.

"Yes," he said. "He's perfect." But then something bitter and contrary rose up inside his chest and made him spoil the moment: "Have you ever stopped to think he wouldn't exist if you hadn't made the mistake of marrying me?" he asked her. "Maybe you should consider that sometimes when you give me the cold shoulder."

He leant over and kissed his wife chastely on her cheek, perhaps regretting his harsh words, and then went past her out of the door, leaving the room without waiting for her response.

London. Over the past three years Brice had come to love and hate the city in equal measure. At the end of 1916 he had succeeded with his grandfather's help in obtaining an extension of his exemption from military service to enable him to return to

Scarsdale to administer his estate, but the noise and bustle of the capital continued to attract him like a magnet, and he remained a regular visitor.

He went there eager to forget about his troubles, diving into the brightly lit West End nightclubs where the bartenders knew him well and were quick to serve him the bourbon highballs that were his favoured method of becoming quickly and efficiently drunk. The tinny ragtime and the raucous jazz reverberated in his head as painted girls with made-up French names like Claudine and Colette hung on his neck, offering him a good time in some seedy attic room rented by the night. And a few times he had gone with them because at least they had to pretend they cared, unlike Miriam who was incapable of pretence. But that hadn't been for a long time now: the hollow sordid show left him depressed and guilty, and frightened that he might have caught a venereal disease or the flu.

The epidemic wouldn't go away; if anything it seemed to be getting worse. People wore gauze muslin masks across their noses and mouths. And the children skipping rope in the playgrounds sang:

"I had a little bird,
Its name was Enza.
I opened the window
And in-flew-Enza."

Everywhere the black horses trotted through the deserted streets pulling hearses to the burial grounds. The buses and the trains and the cinemas all stank of cheap disinfectant.

At night the gas-lit streets were crowded with impoverished demobbed soldiers in ragged khaki. Some slept curled up on benches or on church steps wrapped up in old newspapers, while others tramped the pavements for hours at a time, trying to escape their dreams. And some of them wore masks too, but not because of the flu. They were there to conceal the horror of missing noses and mouths and jaws that had turned the men into living gargoyles from whom their wives and children had fled in terror when they came back from the war.

By day the veterans begged or sold bootlaces and books of

matches from off pathetic wooden trays hanging down from around their necks, scrabbling to stay alive.

London was dying. On Brice's previous visits the music halls and nightclubs had remained defiant in the face of the epidemic but now many of them were closed and those that remained open were depressing places offering no escape from the prevailing mood of fear and misery. And so Brice stayed home with his mother at the house in Belgravia drinking sherry and playing gin rummy in her pretty sitting room overlooking the gardens of Eaton Square.

Lady Scarsdale was happier now. Before her husband's death she had worried that people were whispering about her when she left the room, speculating on the reasons for their separation, but widowhood had restored her respectability, and she had even had several outfits of black weeds specially made for her, which she had worn for a few weeks in the autumn of 1916 until she grew tired of their monochrome colour.

She cared a little less about her figure, indulging her love of the sweetmeats that she shared with her beloved pug dog, which had now become so rotund that it could hardly move, and she enjoyed the lack of responsibility and financial constriction that came with living under her wealthy father's protection.

Her one source of anxiety was her son. His ascent to the baronetcy had not made him happy and, as the years passed, he had grown gloomy and distracted. She knew he had financial difficulties but she sensed there was more weighing him down than that. And on this visit he had been worse than ever, constantly getting up and pacing the room like some kind of caged animal.

"What is it?" she asked solicitously. "There's something you're not telling me."

"It's nothing," he lied, looking out of the window in order to avoid her eye.

"It's Miriam, isn't it?" she probed. "I told you she wouldn't make you a good wife. How could she when she was in love with someone else?"

"Adam's dead," said Brice wearily. They'd had this conversation many times before.

"It doesn't matter. She's the type of girl that loves the dead even more than the living. What else can you expect when she's spent her whole life down on her knees in church, mooning over crucifixes? You should have listened to your own mother instead of hers before you went ahead and married her in such a rush. They're gold-diggers, both of them. I told you that," she said bitterly.

"No, you're wrong about Miriam, Mother. She cares less about money than anyone I've ever known," he said angrily. It was one thing for him to rail against his wife, but quite another to have to listen to his mother attacking her. And what she said made no sense: if Miriam was such a pious Christian then she was hardly likely to be a fortune-hunter as well.

"Well, she's a fool if that's her attitude," said Lady Scarsdale, refusing to be put off. "And so are you: even your idiotic father understood that heirs to titles have to marry money. That's why he married me, for God's sake. But you were too good for that, weren't you? You had to go off and marry a penniless parson's daughter!"

Brice stirred uneasily in his seat. He was tired of his mother's hounding but the turn of the conversation did suit his purpose. He desperately needed financial help from his grandfather if he was to keep the estate from going under and his only chance of success depended on his mother advocating his case for him. Sir Hubert had always had a soft spot for his only daughter but the trouble was that she had already prevailed upon him to bail Brice out twice before.

Brice's grandfather was as rich as Croesus but as tight-fisted as Ebenezer Scrooge. It was in Brice's favour that Sir Hubert was a snob and liked to be able to tell his cronies at the Carlton Club that his grandson was now Sir Brice Scarsdale of Scarsdale Hall, but there was a limit to the monetary value that he placed on the connection, and he had made it quite clear that that limit had been reached when he'd reluctantly agreed after his son-in-law's death to clear Sir John's mountainous debts as well as his grandson's (for a second time) and to pay the huge estate duties due to the government.

"Now, I've given you a clean start so let's see if you can make a better fist of getting the Hall to pay its way—and the mine too," the old man had told Brice as he wrote out the final cheque in his big office at the top of Pall Mall. "Your father made an almighty mess of his affairs before he chose to fall down those stairs, but you've got some of my blood in your veins so maybe you can do better. But if you can't don't come running back to me! It's time for you to stand on your own two feet, young man, and show us what you're made of!" Brice had tried to stand. But he was like King Canute facing the ocean waves and he was soon toppled over. The estate was run down and the mine's productivity was in decline, and any realistic chance he had of staying afloat disappeared when Charles forced him to dismiss Hardcastle and appoint him in his place. Brice had tried to resist, knowing where this would lead, but Charles had been adamant and, feeling the noose tightening around his neck, he had given in just as he always did. And so for nearly two years now Charles had been sitting in the manager's office beside the mine behaving like a tin-pot Napoleon while he lined his pockets and ran the business into the ground.

As his debts mounted Brice had had recourse to the moneylenders that had battened on his father, borrowing larger and larger sums just to service their extortionate demands for interest. But recently they had begun to realize that he had no funds left to back up his promissory notes and they had started to demand repayments of principal. Brice knew he had run out of options and that his grandfather was his only hope of survival.

Slowly, stumbling over his words, Brice outlined for his mother a picture of his debts. It was far worse than she'd expected. And it continued to make no sense to her that he had promoted a footman to run the mine.

"There's something you're not telling me," she said. "Does Charles have some kind of hold over you?"

"No, of course not," said Brice. But he remained evasive in response to her questions and Sir Hubert was quick to seize on the issue when she broached the subject of Brice's money troubles with him that evening.

"He won't even talk about helping you until you've got rid of Charles," Lady Scarsdale told her son.

"I can't do that."

"Well, then there's nothing I can do. Unless you're prepared to tell me what's really going on. Remember I'm your mother: you can trust me."

She looked him hard in the eye, searching for an answer. And he longed more than ever to take her into his confidence. She would understand that it wasn't his fault what had happened—he had gone to see his father with the best intentions only to be rebuffed and pushed beyond endurance. Anyone would have snapped after all those years of ill treatment. His mother, more than anyone, knew what he had been subjected to. She would ease his conscience and tell him what to do about Charles.

But something held him back. He had kept his secret close to his chest for so long that he couldn't bring himself to surrender it. The words of confession stopped in his throat as he felt the hangman's rope slipping over his head and tightening around his neck, and he turned and left the room with a few muttered words of apology and ran down the stairs and out of the house, joining the soldiers pounding the pavements through the small hours as they tried to keep their nightmares at bay.

And in the morning he was gone, driving back north with nothing accomplished. It struck him as he picked up speed on the open road that these long solitary journeys in his beloved Straker-Squire motor car were the only times when he could relax and be happy: either headed down to London, hoping that his grandfather would pay his debts and looking forward like a drug addict to losing himself amid the mad noise and glare of the West End; or returning home, imagining that everything would be different with Miriam and that Charles would suddenly become reasonable. Sitting behind the wheel with the countryside flashing past and the cold wind whipping around his ears, he was neither in one place nor the other but suspended between the two in a no man's land of his own creation where anything was possible and he could spin daydreams into reality.

Chapter Thirty-Seven

Earlier that Sunday, just as Brice was leaving London behind, Miriam arrived at Scarsdale Church for the morning service. She found these weekly journeys up the hill from the Hall bittersweet. They were voyages back into her childhood when the church had been at the centre of her life and her father had been God's holy minister, the shepherd guiding his flock with a sure hand through the hard, thorny passage of their lives. She had admired him so much—for his learning and his goodness and his leadership—and it hadn't upset her, at least not then, that he talked to her so little because she'd known that he had far more important matters to attend to: visiting the sick and the poor; helping the miners with their troubles; and preaching the wonderful sermons that she listened to so avidly on Sunday mornings. Sometimes she sat in his study in the evening with her embroidery while he was writing them and he would occasionally look up and smile at her or kiss her on the head distractedly as he passed her chair to fetch a book, but he never talked to her about what was on his mind. And she never spoke because she didn't want to disturb his concentration. She might as well have been a cat or an old dog: a comfortable presence in the background of his life.

But she never complained: she was happy just to be with him and she rejoiced when he complimented her on the flower arrangements that she spent hours creating in the silent church. She had set her father up on a pedestal and she wouldn't allow herself to criticize him when he took no notice as his wife and Brice harassed her, or when he unjustly stopped her from seeing Adam, who had been the only one to protect her from the harassment, or when he left her behind to go to the war with another distracted kiss and a wave of his hand.

And now he was a wreck of the man he had once been, shut up in a sanatorium in York, raving about the unburied dead and their thwarted hopes of eternal resurrection. Seeing him in such a state and not being able to help him get better caused her such distress that she had recently started to visit him less frequently, which meant adding guilt to her other afflictions.

Her mother, who had a far more practical nature than her daughter, never went at all. But that didn't mean that her husband's illness didn't affect her. Up until now the Church had taken account of Parson Vale's exemplary service as a military chaplain and had kept open the possibility of him resuming his duties in Scarsdale by assigning a curate based in Gratton to look after the parish. But the end of the war and the absence of any improvement in the parson's condition meant that they were now looking to fill the vacancy, and it seemed inevitable that sooner rather than later Mrs. Vale would be asked to pack her bags and leave the Parsonage. And she had made it quite clear to Miriam that when that day came she would be coming to live at the Hall, whether her daughter liked it or not.

The prospect of a renewed intimacy with her mother filled Miriam with dread. Life was already hard enough: she had to cope with Brice's demands and his increasingly erratic behaviour. She knew they were in debt, although he wouldn't discuss the subject in detail, and that it had something to do with Charles, who sometimes joined them at dinner, leering at her in a way that made her squirm in her seat. Brice had to see what was happening but he did nothing to stop it. And he wouldn't explain why he had given Charles so much power: it was clear he didn't like him and the tension in the room when they were together was palpable, with Brice continually on the brink of an explosion, while Charles made snide comments and looked on amused.

Sometimes, even though she knew it was a sin, she wished that she could go to bed and snuggle down under the blankets and sleep and sleep and never wake up. She had lost faith. Not in God—the

Creator had always been too much at the centre of her life for her to be able to doubt his existence—but in the benevolence of his creation. And she came to church on Sundays not just to remember the past but also to search for a way back to being the person she'd left behind. She knew that once upon a time she had sat in the same pew where she was now and had found solace in the quiet timelessness of the weathered mediaeval architecture, sensing the invisible presence all around her of the generations of good Christian men and women who had come here to be baptized and married and laid to rest: an endlessly repeated cycle of birth and death and regeneration in harmony with the natural world outside. But the war stood between her and that other life like an impassable barrier. It had changed everything, ushering in a new dispensation, and the church seemed empty now and desolate. In the pews a few women in mourning black murmured prayers for their dead sons and husbands lying buried far away in France—or worse, unburied: gone from the earth as if they had never been. Like Adam. How many times had she knelt here since the news came that he was missing, pleading with God for a word to say that he was still alive, out there somewhere! And still she kept the flame of her hope alive, although with each month that had passed since the Armistice it burnt a little lower until it now resembled a guttering candle about to be extinguished by the next breath of wind. "All Our Brave Prisoners Are Home" had been the headline in the *Gratton Echo* the previous Sunday. But not Adam: from him not a word or a whisper; just silence.

She was the last to leave the church at the end of the service. As she was passing through the wooden porch she heard someone say her name and, turning, saw a young man sitting on the side bench whom she recognized as Ernest Tillett, Adam's second cousin.

She knew him very little. The Tillett family had not been churchgoers and their paths had only crossed a few times after she had become engaged to Adam and he had come back to Scarsdale with Ernest and his other friends on occasional weekend furloughs before they were sent over to France. But she remembered with a twinge of guilt and shame how impatient she had been with Adam when Ernest's mother committed suicide, grudging the time that he had spent identifying her body and making arrangements for the funeral because she wanted him to be with her in the last days of his precious leave.

Oh, how she regretted that accursed time when some invisible power had come between them, twisting their words and thoughts until the bond between them had ruptured under the strain, leaving her without even the comfort of their commitment to each other to fall back upon when he had gone missing!

"I'm sorry," said Ernest, noticing the look of pain on her face. "I didn't mean to startle you."

"You didn't," she said. "It's just seeing you reminded me . . ."

"Of Adam?"

"Yes." She winced: it was a long time since she'd heard Adam's name spoken aloud. He was constantly in her mind's eye and yet she never talked about him to anyone. Perhaps that had been a mistake, she thought. Perhaps she should have written to Ernest and Adam's other friends and asked them about the horrors that they had shared together; the horrors that Adam had kept from her when he came home. Except that she knew why she hadn't: it would have been too painful for her to read about Adam in the past tense, and she couldn't have taken the risk of her husband finding out about her enquiries. Any reference to his hated rival was guaranteed to send Brice into a rage that made life unbearable for everyone around him.

"How are you?" she asked, reaching out and touching Ernest's shoulder. She was aware suddenly of how selfish she was being, thinking only about herself and her own grief when Ernest had lost his entire family: his brother and his mother, and his father too in the mine explosion before the war.

"I'm well. Thank you," he said, sounding a little awkward. He had been affected by her gesture but didn't know how to respond. It occurred to him that he had never spoken to a Lady before.

"Won't you sit down?" he asked. "I've something to tell you—"

"About Adam?" she interrupted. "He's dead, isn't he?"

She'd been dreading the news for so long and was so sure that this was what Ernest had come to say that she didn't hear his answer. Instead she felt her legs giving way underneath her and she would have fallen and perhaps hurt herself if he hadn't reached out and caught her in his arms.

He could see that she was very pale but had not lost consciousness so he deposited her gently down on to the bench where he had just been sitting.

"Oh, God, I've made such a mess of this," he said, half to himself, as he stood looking down at her, impotently fanning her face with both his hands. "I told him he should come himself but he insisted it would be better this way . . ."

"Who insisted?" asked Miriam.

"Adam. He wanted to break it to you gently and that's why he sent me—"

"You mean he's alive? Here? Now?" Miriam's voice rose up a register with each question as she passed in quick succession from astonishment through incredulity to exaltation.

"Yes, that's what I said. I thought you heard me."

"No, but I do now. And you haven't made a mess of anything; you did wonderfully," she said. And, reaching up her hands, she took hold of Ernest's shoulders, pulled him down towards her and kissed him on both his cheeks.

"Is he all right?" she asked as they walked quickly together down the hill towards the town. Even though Ernest had the longer stride he was finding it hard to keep up with her.

"Yes. He's been through a lot though. That kind of experience changes you."

"What do you mean?"

"He's more controlled; more watchful. The trenches changed all of us: made us older, and drier—like we're trees that have lost their sap. It's hard to put it into words. And then Adam didn't just have to deal with that. He's been a prisoner too for a long time and I think it was hard for him, very hard. He'll tell you . . ."

"No, he won't," said Miriam with a shake of her head. "That was the trouble before: that he couldn't tell me anything. But it doesn't matter, Ernest. He's survived; he's come home. That's what's important. And I'm happy; happier than I can ever remember." And unconsciously her feet skipped along the pavement as if she was beginning to dance.

"Don't worry," she said, looking back over her shoulder and noticing with a smile that Ernest had taken a step to the side. "I'm not going to kiss you again. Twice is enough for one day!"

And they both laughed. But then when they got to Ernest's house she was nervous again, running her hands through her hair and straightening her dress.

"Do I look all right?" she asked, sounding just like a coquettish young girl rather than the wife and mother that she was.

"You look beautiful," said Ernest, making it sound like a simple statement of fact rather than a compliment. And she smiled, feeling reassured, as he opened the door.

Adam was sitting eating breakfast at the table at the other end of the room and got up straightaway when he saw her come in. Rawdon Dawes was there too but Miriam only had eyes for Adam. She ran to him with her hands outstretched, clasping his arms and burying her face against his shoulder. And then held on to him tightly, racked by the thick, harsh sobs that were shaking her body.

She felt his hand gently patting her back but he wasn't embracing her as she was him. Instead he stood ramrod straight, waiting for the violence of her emotion to subside.

She pulled back and looked at him, hesitantly putting up her hand to touch his cheek and his ear and his hair. He was thinner and paler and more weather-beaten than she remembered and she could see the bones in his face. The wrinkles in his brow and around his eyes could have easily belonged to a man twice his age. But he wasn't disfigured or maimed. The wounds that he was carrying were all inside.

"I thought you were dead," she said. And there was wonder in her voice as if, like Thomas the Apostle, she doubted the evidence of her senses.

"So did I on quite a few occasions," said Adam with a smile. "I've been buried alive, blown up and half starved to death by our old friend, Kaiser Bill, but I never quite got past the finishing line. I lead a charmed life, as my friends here will testify—Rawdon in particular. He's twice saved me from extinction, haven't you, Rawdon?"

Adam beckoned to Rawdon and he came out a little awkwardly from behind the table and shook Miriam's hand.

" 'Ow are you, Lady Scarsdale?" he said, and then stopped, seeing how she had flinched almost as if she had been struck when he called her by her name. "I'm sorry," he said, looking crestfallen. "I was just bein' polite; I didn't mean to offend thee."

"Of course you didn't," said Adam, who, alone among those present, seemed entirely unaffected by the awkwardness of the moment. "I'm sure Miriam has got used to her title by now. Come and sit with us, Miriam, and have some breakfast. I hope that Ernest didn't give you too much of a shock. I thought it would be easier on you if you didn't just suddenly catch sight of me standing like a ghost in the middle of the churchyard, but perhaps I was wrong. There's no real guidebook for how to best manage your own resurrection, is there?"

Adam's easy conversation as he settled everyone around the table surprised Miriam. His manner was in marked contrast to the tongue-tied awkwardness that he'd suffered from when she had last seen him; but her intuition told her that it was like a suit of clothes tailor-made to protect the man inside from outside scrutiny. And his guarded response to her embrace and evident wish for his friends to stay with them in the room seemed to support her theory.

She wanted to hold him and to touch him and to cry on his shoulder, but she understood instinctively that she needed to respect the boundaries that he was setting. And yet she couldn't help feeling hurt by his reserve and suffered a stab of jealousy as she saw the easy way he interacted with his two friends, bringing out fresh food from the kitchen and making more tea. There was an unconscious harmony between the three of them that she had never encountered in a group of people before. It was as if they knew each other better than they knew themselves.

"Ernest did wonderfully," she said, raising her cup of tea in his direction. "He even caught me when I started to keel over in the church porch."

"Did you, Ernest?" said Adam, looking fondly at his friend, who had flushed crimson with embarrassment. "Well, congratulations! I wish I'd been there to see it."

"No, you don't!" said Rawdon. "The 'ole idea of Ernest goin' instead of thee was to give . . . Miriam"—he hesitated over her name and she smiled—"a chance to get used to thee bein' back, so it wouldn't 'ave made much sense if you'd been standin' there gawkin' at 'em, now would it?"

"No, I suppose it wouldn't," said Adam. They all laughed and he nodded appreciatively at Miriam, and she sensed that he was thanking her for following his lead in keeping the conversation light.

"How long have you been back?" she asked.

"Only a few days. I was late returning because I got sick."

"With what?"

"Typhus. It was touch and go for a while but I pulled through. I'm damned lucky it wasn't the influenza as I doubt I'd have had the strength to fight that. There was a German doctor who helped me. They're not all bad, you know," he said with a glance across at his friends. Miriam sensed that this was an often-discussed subject among them.

"And you've been staying here?"

"Yes, Ernest has made me very welcome."

"You don't need to say that," said Ernest. "This is your home too. I've told you that."

"I know," said Adam smiling warmly at his cousin. "And it does feel like it; really it does. It's as if I've come full circle. I remember my father in this room, and Ernest's—and yours too, Miriam," he added, as if this last was something he'd just remembered.

"Mine?" she repeated, surprised.

"Yes. I don't know if I ever told you but he came here to see me on his bicycle. It was a rainy evening at about this time of year and I was sitting where I am now, working on my Tacitus, and we talked about Rome. I was excited because I was only—what?—fifteen and I hadn't had that kind of conversation before."

"What do you mean?" asked Miriam.

"I was young and I knew next to nothing about anything whereas he seemed to know everything, and yet he was genuinely interested in what I had to say. He made me feel like my opinion mattered; that it was worth something. It was the beginning of our friendship."

"Yes, he was good with people like that," said Miriam sadly, thinking of how he had worked so hard to connect with other people, and yet never with her.

But Adam misinterpreted her reaction: "I'm sorry," he said. "I was being thoughtless. His illness must be terrible for you. Is he any better? I hope there has been some progress?"

"No, very little. It's like he's trapped somewhere horrible back in the war, forever reliving whatever it was that unhinged him, and I don't know how to reach across and pull him out of the rut he's fallen into. And the hospital doesn't seem to know either: they just give him pills to make him sleep and say to be patient. But I've been patient for years now and nothing seems to change so it's hard, very hard," said Miriam, shaking her head to express her frustration.

"'E was a good man," said Rawdon, who had been clearing up the breakfast plates from the table but had stopped to listen when Miriam began talking about her father, giving her his full attention. "Do you remember 'ow 'e came up into the front line an' gave us 'is blessin' when we went out on the first mornin', Adam?" he asked, looking over at his friend. "I ain't no Christian, but it 'elped somehow, 'avin that send-off, an' we was grateful. I remember that."

"Yes, we were," said Adam, bowing his head.

"An' it was a damn shame what 'appened to 'im afterwards," Rawdon went on, turning back to Miriam. "The war went to 'is 'ead, like it did to a lot o' people. An' I'm sorry for it."

"Thank you," said Miriam, struck by the heartfelt sympathy she could hear in Rawdon's voice. She liked him, she decided. He was nothing like his father.

Soon the table was cleared and Rawdon put on his coat and beckoned to Ernest. "Come on," he said. "I'll buy thee a drink down at the King's Head. These two 'ave got a lot to talk about."

Adam smiled, looking after his friends as the door closed behind them. "Can you stay?" he asked.

Miriam nodded. There was nothing in the world that would have induced her to leave Ernest's house at that moment.

"What about your husband?"

"He's been down in London. He telephoned this morning. He's driving back now but he won't be home until this evening."

Adam nodded. "And your son . . . Ernest says you have a son. What is his name?"

"Brandon."

"Brandon," Adam repeated, sounding out the name as if to see what he thought of it. "It's a brave name," he said. "Is he a brave boy?" he asked with another smile.

"It's too early to say," said Miriam, laughing. "I love him. He's beautiful. That's enough for now."

"Of course it is," said Adam. "He's yours so how could he not be a prodigy?"

He went over to the fireplace and used the poker to stir the coals into life. "Edgar, Ernest's father, made the best fires in this hearth I have ever seen," he said, staring meditatively into the glow. "This is a pale imitation. It's strange being in this house without him. He was larger than life. I think I can hear his voice sometimes as I come down the stairs. But it's the same everywhere, isn't it? We're surrounded by the ghosts of the dead. Up at the Hall would be no different with Seaton and Sir John." He gave Miriam a narrow look as he mentioned the name of his benefactor but she didn't seem to notice.

"Why didn't you write to me, Adam?" she asked quietly. "All those years I spent hoping and fearing the worst! One line would have made such a difference."

She hadn't meant her question to sound like a reproach but it came out that way, expressing all the pent-up bewilderment she had been feeling ever since she'd first found out that he was alive.

"I couldn't," he said. "At the start I was wounded with shrapnel in both my legs, and I tried to escape from the hospital they sent me to, which was stupid as I couldn't walk very well and was never going to get very far. And then, when I'd recovered, the Germans punished me by keeping me in France, building trenches for when they retreated to the Hindenburg Line. And after that it was railway lines and roads, so I was never registered as a prisoner of war, which meant that the Red Cross didn't know about me. I didn't exist. Not like our friend, Davy, and the others who were sent off to Germany and received their parcels and letters every month. I had nothing: just codfish soup and stewed acorns and something which looked like bread but wasn't; and time, time to write letters in my head to those I'd left behind. Mostly to you: I wrote to you many times."

"What about?"

"Apologizing; finding a hundred different ways to say I was sorry. I treated you badly when I came home on leave. I found it hard to talk about what I'd seen and I didn't want you to know that there was such ugliness in the world. But really I wasn't protecting you; I was protecting myself. I was shut up as tight as an oyster in its shell and I didn't want to let anyone inside; but I hurt you by not trying. And then at the end when your mother came to see me, I pretended I was breaking off our engagement because I was holding you back, but in fact it was because I felt unclean and unworthy of you. And so I failed you—"

"My mother talked to you?" asked Miriam, interrupting. She'd stopped listening when Adam mentioned her mother's visit to him. She was shocked as this was the first she'd ever heard of it.

"Yes, she came to the Hall," said Adam. "I was surprised to see her, knowing she never left her house—"

"I hate her." The utterly uncharacteristic words escaped Miriam like a cry torn from her throat. "She forced you away and then she forced me into marrying Brice! She's ruined my life and yours and his too! And for what? A title and a bag of silver! I swear I won't forgive her. Why did I have to be so weak?"

"Don't blame yourself. I was weak too," said Adam. "Your mother was just the catalyst for what happened between us. The war had mastered me by the time I came home, made me its plaything. And afterwards I hated that. All my life I'd wanted to be my own man, to stand on my own two feet and make my own choices. And now I feel I've got that power back and I mean to use it—"

He stopped, reining himself in. But Miriam looked at him quizzically. It had only been for a moment but she thought she'd glimpsed something new and fierce under the surface of Adam's controlled exterior and it disturbed her.

"What do you mean by 'use it?' " she asked.

"I told you I've led a charmed life," he said slowly, choosing his words carefully now. "And it's true: I've been saved so many times. By Rawdon; by hiding under the body of Ernest's brother; by a German officer deciding on a whim not to shoot me but to save me when I was lying wounded and helpless out in no man's land; by the doctor when I got sick. And I think it all has to be for a reason."

"What reason?"

"To bear witness; to tell the truth about those who haven't been as lucky as me. The dead deserve not to be buried under lies."

"What lies?"

Adam looked away into the fire and there was a faraway look in his eyes. And when he finally answered it was with a question of his own: "Do you remember the last letter you sent me before I was captured?"

"Yes, I think so. I didn't know you received it."

"Yes, I did. I have it here," he said. And taking out a battered army-issue wallet from his pocket, he extracted from it a worn sheet of writing paper that had been folded up into a square. He carefully opened it out and read it aloud: " 'You have broken my heart and taken away my purpose. My mother has sent for Brice and he is coming. Without you, how can I resist their pressure? I am a sheep among wolves.' "

"You kept that all this time?" she asked.

"Yes. I had nothing else of yours," he said. "I left everything else behind when we went up for the attack that last time."

"I wish I'd never written it," she said. There were tears in her eyes. "It hurts to think that that was what you had to remember me by when you were so alone."

"You were right to write the letter. It was the least that I deserved. And to have something of yours was much better than having nothing at all," said Adam with a smile. "But I read it to you because there is something I want to ask you. You wrote that 'Brice is coming' and I would like to know what happened when he came. Did he propose marriage to you?"

Miriam nodded. She was crying now.

"And you accepted him?"

"Yes. It was like I said in the letter: I was weak; I couldn't resist their pressure."

"And then he left?"

"Yes. He said he had to work the next day."

"Did you see him leave?"

"Yes, we said goodbye at the door."

"But did you see which way he went?"

"No. I mean I don't remember. I may have gone back inside. He said he was going back to London. I already told you that. What are all these questions about, Adam? Please tell me."

"It's just something I need to know," he said. "And I've only got one or two more, I promise. Was Brice happy when he left? I imagine he must have been after you'd accepted him."

"Yes, I suppose so. I don't want to think about it. I don't understand why you can't see that."

"One more," he said. "Just one: when Brice came, was it the same evening that Sir John died?"

"Yes, I think so," said Miriam. "In fact I'm sure of it: I remember we heard the news the next day. But Brice didn't have anything to do with that if that's what you're getting at. Sir John fell down the stairs. And Charles found him straightaway. There was no one else there. It was in all the newspapers."

"Yes, so I've heard," said Adam. But he didn't sound convinced. Quite the opposite in fact.

"You think he did have something to do with it, don't you?" she asked and there was a note of panic in her voice as she remembered the strange phrase Adam had used earlier: *the dead deserve not to be buried under lies.*

"I don't know what to think," he said. "Not without talking to Brice. I need to see him when he comes back. And I was wondering whether it might not be better for you to remain here until we've finished our business. I remember that Brice has a quick temper and our conversation could become heated, particularly if you are present."

"No," said Miriam and she practically shouted the word. "My son's been sick. I can't leave him. And I don't want you to go there. Please, Adam. No good will come of it. I know it won't."

"I must," said Adam.

Again she felt that new iron will in him that she had not known before, forged in an adversity that she couldn't even begin to imagine. Her intuition told her that it was pointless to argue and she got up to go. The chauffeur would still be waiting at the church and she needed to talk to Brice when he got back, and then perhaps she could persuade him to leave again before Adam came. She felt an overwhelming need to keep the two of them apart.

But Adam had read her thoughts. "I won't ask you not to tell your husband," he said. "I remember how you always hated to tell lies."

She went over to the door but paused with her hand on the knob, looking back at Adam where he was standing by the fireplace. It wasn't fair, she thought. None of it was fair: that they had met and fallen in love and lost each other but survived against all the odds to be forever separated, aware of each other across a gulf that neither of them could ever hope to bridge.

"I love you," she said, looking at him hard as if she was committing his face to her memory.

"I know. I love you too," he replied.

But they made no move towards each other, as if acknowledging their separation, and after a moment she walked out of the door.

Chapter Thirty-Eight

As he drove through Scarsdale in the early evening Brice's anxiety returned. A steady rain had been falling since before sunset and on the hill beyond the railway station he passed Adam's friend Ernest, standing just outside the open door of his house, the last one on the street. Ernest's face was illuminated by the lights in the room behind him and Brice recognized him straightaway, even though he was in civilian clothes, as the soldier whom he'd almost run over on that fateful night when he had killed his father. And then, as Brice slowed down, he saw Rawdon Dawes come out of the house and join Ernest on the step, peering out into the rain. What were they doing together and who were they waiting for so expectantly? Brice wondered uneasily as he put his foot down on the accelerator and drove past them.

There were lights burning too in the windows of the Parsonage at the top of the hill. He rarely saw Mrs. Vale any more, but he was careful to ensure that the estate continued to pay her the generous allowance that he had settled on her after his marriage. He had no evidence that she knew he had gone to the Hall after leaving the Parsonage on the night Miriam accepted him, but he sensed that she suspected it and that she would start making trouble for him if he did not keep her happy.

The sense of freedom that Brice had felt in the car earlier had now entirely disappeared and his nervousness increased as he turned through the Hall gates and drove up between the elms. The wind had intensified and he could hear the wet trees creaking and groaning as they swayed against each other on either side of the drive. In the twilight he felt them pressing in on him, constricting his ability to breathe. And he didn't feel any relief when he came out into the open and caught sight of his house wrapped in clouds and shadows. It seemed sinister somehow, even threatening, and he remembered how he'd imagined the Angel of Death hovering above it when his son was sick. Some instinct made him want to turn around and drive back the way he'd come, but he dismissed the thought as stupid and irrational. Instead he carried on past the black lake dimpled by the rain and into the silent entrance courtyard where he took off his muffler and gloves and hurried up the steps to the front door.

Inside, he was met by a flurry of activity. Briggs, the new butler—an inadequate replacement for Cartwright—was scraping his heels on the diamond-shaped black-and-white marble floor tiles, announcing that there was a visitor waiting to see Sir Brice in the drawing room, and Miriam was running down the grand staircase, talking to him even before she reached the bottom: "I need to speak to you, Brice. It can't wait," she told him breathlessly, talking over the butler, who was saying something about the rain.

"He gave his name as Mr. Raine," said Briggs for the second time. And Brice finally understood whom the butler was talking about when Adam appeared in the doorway of the drawing room.

"Hello, Brice," he said, staying where he was. It was as if he understood that there was no point offering to shake Brice's hand.

Brice felt a deep sense of shock and for a moment he was unsteady on his feet. He was bowled over by Adam's return from the dead and yet it also seemed like a fulfilment of the free-floating feeling of apprehension that had been growing inside him ever since he arrived back in Scarsdale and saw Adam's friends standing together like conspirators in the doorway of the house in Station Street.

"What do you want?" he demanded. His astonishment was giving way now to raw anger. There was something infuriating to him about Adam's nonchalance; about the way he was standing there with his hands in his pockets as though he owned the place when he had no right to be in the house at all.

"I want to talk to you. It should only take a few minutes," said Adam blandly. Brice's rudeness seemed to have no effect on him at all.

"Please, Adam!" said Miriam. "You don't have to do this!"

"Do what?" asked Brice, looking at his wife in surprise. It wasn't like her to be so wild.

"I don't know," she said, suddenly wary. "I just don't think this is a good idea. That's all. I've got a bad feeling."

Brice had a bad feeling too. "I want you to go," he said, turning back to their visitor. "This isn't my father's house any more, it's mine, and you're not welcome here. Briggs, please see Mr. Raine out."

"It's about your father that I wanted to speak to you," said Adam, ignoring the butler's ineffectual attempt to show him the door. "And I honestly don't think it's in your interests that I should leave. I have some things to say that you should hear, but if you refuse to listen, then I will have no option but to tell them to other people and that could be to your disadvantage. But of course it's your decision."

"What things?"

"It's better that we should talk in private," said Adam. He remained serenely calm and unruffled, in contrast to Brice, who was growing more and more agitated.

Brice knitted his brows, trying to think. His instinct was still to throw Adam out, but the veiled threat Adam had made scared him, and he didn't think that Adam was the type of person to play a game of bluff. It surely couldn't hurt him to hear what Adam had to say and then he would be in a better position to decide what to do.

"Very well, I'll see you in my study," he said grudgingly. "But I need to change first. I've been driving all day. I'll ring down to tell you when I'm ready and then Briggs can show you up. And, Miriam, you said you wish to speak to me. Now would be a good time."

Miriam started to follow her husband but then turned to look back at Adam with her hand on the newel post of the balustrade. "Please go," she pleaded. "Can't you do something for me, just this once?"

But Brice didn't give Adam a chance to answer. "Miriam!" he said angrily, turning round and beckoning her to come on. And he waited where he was, looking like thunder, until she bowed her head, accepting his reprimand, and came past him up the stairs. At the top he led the way down the corridor and ushered her into his dressing room and closed the door.

"What the hell was all that about downstairs? Why don't you want me to talk to him?" he asked, staring hard into her eyes.

"Because I think he wants to hurt you," she said softly.

"And why would you think that? It's because you know something, isn't it? Have you been seeing him behind my back?"

"No, I've only seen him once and that was after church this morning. Before today I was just like you: I didn't know he was alive."

"But you were hoping he was, weren't you? Down on your knees, praying for it, I expect," he said viciously. But then he immediately stepped back and took a hold of himself, remembering Adam's threat. He needed Miriam on his side; he needed to know what she knew. "I'm sorry," he said. "I'm upset: I didn't mean any of that. But you must tell me what he said. I'm your husband and I have a right to know."

"He was asking about the night your father died. Where you were, what you said. He didn't tell me anything."

"But he made you think I had something to do with it, didn't he?"

"No. I don't know," said Miriam, sounding flustered.

"Well, I couldn't have done because I wasn't here that night. I was with you at the Parsonage and then I drove back to London just like I said I was going to do. You believe me, don't you?"

Miriam nodded, but she looked doubtful, and he wanted to keep talking to her until he had chased all her doubts away once and for all, but he knew that now wasn't the time.

"I'll come to your room after he's gone," he said. "I want to see Brandon too. Has he been all right?"

"Yes," said Miriam. "He misses you when you're not here."

And it was better between them for a moment so he leant forward and kissed her and refused to get upset when she didn't respond in the way he wanted her to.

———

Brice pushed the bell by the fireplace and went back to sit behind his desk. And then, taking out his keychain, he unlocked and opened the bottom drawer and looked down at the gun resting in the open box in which he'd bought it. He reached down and ran his finger up and down the revolver's silver barrel. He'd told nobody about buying it and there was nothing to connect it to him. If he had to use it he could tell the police without risk of contradiction that Adam had tried to attack him with it and they'd wrestled and . . .

Brice's head spun. He didn't want to use the gun. It scared him. Just looking at it made his hands shake. But he was glad it was there, and when Briggs knocked at the door he left the drawer open.

He didn't get up when Adam came in but instead gestured off-handedly for him to sit in one of the two hard-backed wooden chairs positioned on the other side of the desk. They were the same chairs that had been there when his father was alive and he had kept them in place not for their aesthetic value—they were singularly ugly— but because he enjoyed putting people at a disadvantage when they came to talk to him about business, watching them squirm in discomfort while he sat back in his own comfortable armchair. He had never forgotten how his father had kept him waiting on one of the chairs as if he was some kind of inferior tradesman on the fateful night he came to tell him about his engagement. And he would have liked to do the same to Adam now but quickly realized that he would be wasting his time: Adam seemed entirely at ease and he was the one who was unable to sit still.

"What do you want to tell me?" he asked. "Please be brief. I'm tired and I should warn you that I don't take kindly to threats."

"I'm sure you don't," said Adam. "And I'll be as quick as I can, but first, if you don't mind, I have a question. Where were you on the night your father died?"

"It's none of your business. But I wasn't here if that's what you're getting at."

"You're certain about that?"

"Of course I'm certain," said Brice angrily. "If you've come here to make baseless allegations—"

"Not baseless," said Adam, interrupting. "I have evidence to back this one up."

"What evidence?"

"A letter," said Adam, reaching into his pocket and producing a folded-over sheet of paper with a red seal on the back that he carefully opened up on his lap. "It's from your father to me and is dated on the day of his death, and he appears to have been writing it just at the moment when you came to see him. Here, let me read you what he said:

> "Charles has just been in to tell me that Brice is here with good news. Good news! After an absence of six months I am sure that the only news he has to impart is that he is up to his ears in debt. Well, I shall have news for him. I have no money to give him. Lloyd George and his cronies have taken it all. I wish he would leave me alone but I suppose I shall have to see him even though it's nearly nine o'clock and I would far rather go to bed."

Adam looked up. "He did see you, didn't he?" he asked.

"Let me look at that!" demanded Brice, not answering the question. He was enraged and frightened all at the same time and his hand was shaking again as he reached out across the desk.

"By all means," said Adam, handing the document over. "But I wouldn't waste your time trying to destroy it if that's what you've got in mind. It's a certified copy. I've deposited the original in a lawyer's safe in Gratton."

Brice was aghast at his own stupidity. The letter had to be the one that his father had been reading through and addressing and sealing while he was sitting where Adam was now, waiting like a tradesman. How easy it would have been to pick it up from the pile on the desk afterwards and throw it on the fire, but instead it had sat there until morning and been given to the postman to send to France! Why hadn't he looked at the envelopes? Why had he relied on Charles to go back up the stairs and check the room for evidence? Why had he been such a fool? He'd read somewhere that there was always some small apparently insignificant detail that a murderer overlooked and this letter was his detail—and likely to be his undoing.

"I keep thinking how strange it is that I hung on to it all those years when I had no idea of its true significance," said Adam. He spoke pensively and it was almost as if he was talking to himself while Brice was busy reading the letter. "I only found out that your father was dead when I came back here a few days ago. And then when I heard about the circumstances and compared the dates it felt like he was communicating with me from beyond the grave, asking for my help. Like Hamlet's father, I suppose," he added with a smile.

Brice wasn't listening. Each sentence in his father's letter felt like a stab to his heart: "You know I think of you as my son . . . I wish that I could make you the heir to my estate. But I cannot . . . I do not know what I have done to deserve Brice." He read and reread them and with each reading his rage grew.

It was all so monstrously unfair. His father had never given him a chance. He'd always despised him and made no secret of his contempt even when he was a child. Brice was weak and sickly and stupid and lazy and—later when the war came—cowardly: the worst sin of all. Not like his brother who was manly and clever and brave. And after Seaton had left to go and play soldiers, his father had brought in a pauper from the back streets of London to set up over him. Adam was the son his father wished he'd had; not Brice; never Brice. He hated them: his dead father and his dead brother and Adam most of all, sitting there so smugly, enjoying the power that this stupid disgusting letter had given him. He threw it down on the desk and sat back in his chair with his face twisted into a livid, snarling expression.

"I am sorry if it makes unpleasant reading, but you did ask to see it," said Adam, picking up the letter and replacing it in his pocket. "And, now that you have, are you prepared to admit that you were here on the night your father died? Here in this room?"

Brice stared at Adam without saying anything and Adam met his gaze, waiting patiently for an answer. Finally Brice nodded and then dropped his eyes, glancing down at the gun in the open drawer beside him. "What do you want?" he hissed.

"I want you to tell me exactly what occurred on that night from start to finish," said Adam. "I want to know whether your father fell down the stairs or whether he was pushed; or whether something else happened—in here perhaps?"

Brice swallowed hard several times and his mouth worked but he said nothing.

"Maybe I can help you get started," said Adam pleasantly. "I already know from Miriam that you had been to see her at the Parsonage before you came here and that she had accepted your marriage proposal, so I think we can safely infer that that must have been the 'good news' that Charles told your father about when he came in to announce your arrival. And I think we can also deduce from that that you didn't come here intending to kill Sir John, which is certainly a point in your favour. But what happened after that? That's what I want to know."

"Why? Why should I tell you? You'll go to the police anyway," said Brice furiously.

"No, I won't," said Adam. "Not if you tell me it was an accident and I believe you, although I will obviously have to speak to Charles too and see if your accounts match before I make a final decision. And I wanted to talk to you first."

"So you're to be judge and jury, and prosecutor too, all rolled into one?" said Brice sarcastically. "Who gave you that right?"

"Sir John did. I am here for him, not me. Because I believe the dead have a right to be heard. They have a right to the truth," said Adam, and there was passion in his voice for the first time—a hint of the iron determination that lay behind his cool reserve.

Brice breathed heavily. His brain was a chaos of conflicting thoughts. He didn't trust Adam, but he also knew it didn't matter if he did or he didn't because any lie he told him would soon be exposed by Charles, who would waste no time throwing Brice to the wolves as soon as he was shown the letter and had a chance to realize that he was now under suspicion. There was no way out, no escape. Unless—unless he stopped Adam now before he could talk to Charles or go to the police. If Adam was dead, then it wouldn't matter about the letter in the lawyer's safe in Gratton because no one would ever come to claim it. And he deserved to be dead for what he had done: usurping Brice's place with his father and with Miriam; spoiling everything he touched. He deserved to be dead just like everyone had thought he was, until he came back out of the past like some unwanted ghost with his letter and his threats . . .

"So are you going to tell me or are you not?" asked Adam. "It seems to me that I'm being remarkably generous."

It wasn't enough; Brice's anger wasn't enough, however much he stoked it. His hand hung down over the open drawer but he couldn't bring himself to pick up the revolver. He thought of the white feather in its envelope lying underneath the box. It told the truth: he was frightened of the gun, just as he was frightened of what would become of him if he didn't use it.

He thought of the dank, dark execution chamber and this time he didn't run away from the pictures in his mind. He forced himself to watch his hands being tied tight behind his back, the blindfold being pressed down over his eyes, the noose slipping down around his neck, the hangman forcing him out on to the trapdoor; he could hear the strangled cry in his throat; he could feel everything giving way. He would do anything to stop that. Anything. Even fire the gun. And, reaching down, he took it in his hand and pulled it up, aiming it at Adam's head, his hateful handsome head. He tried to pull the trigger but he couldn't. His hand was shaking and he needed the other one on the grip too. And then he could fire.

The gun exploded violently in his hand. He'd never felt anything like it before. The recoil threw him back violently in the chair and he almost dropped the weapon. And when he looked back up Adam wasn't where he'd been before; he'd dived away to his left, rolling across the carpet towards the door. He'd got it half open but he was still in the room. There was still time for one more shot. He aimed, he fired, and Adam wasn't there. He'd gone, disappeared somewhere, and Brice was alone with the gun.

Completely alone, with nothing to look forward to except the blindfold and the noose and the drop. He'd struggled so hard for so long, and the deck had always been stacked against him, however hard he'd tried to get ahead. And now his race was run. It was over. He was finished. He felt like an animal pursued into a corner, a rabbit or a fox crying out its pain into the night before its death. It was intolerable. He'd had enough. He took the gun and put it to his head and pulled the trigger.

The shots reverberated through the house, bringing everyone trembling to their feet. And they were silent, holding themselves rigid, expecting more until none came and they got up and looked cautiously out through their doors, peeping into deserted corridors with frightened, bewildered eyes.

Miriam looked out and saw Adam. He was down on the floor but he was getting to his feet and edging back towards the study. She was frightened but she needed to know what had happened and she ran down the corridor and stopped face to face with him in the doorway where he stood, trying and failing to block her view of her dead husband who was sitting slumped over the desk with the pool of his crimson blood seeping out on to the green blotting pad, turning it a sickly shade of yellow.

She beat on Adam's chest with her fists. She wanted to hurt him and she wanted him to hold her; she wanted him to go and she wanted him to stay. She hated him and she loved him in precisely equal measure.

Chapter Thirty-Nine

Two days later, on a bright but cold morning, Adam cycled out to the Hall, riding fast along the deserted road in order to try and keep at bay the confused and anxious thoughts that had replaced the sense of confidence and certainty he had felt when he last came this way, intent on holding Brice to account.

In the immediate aftermath of the shooting Adam's reaction had been primarily physical as his body reacted to its close shave with death. Again and again through that first night he had relived the deafening explosions of the gun and felt the deadly rush of the bullets flying beside and over his head as he somehow scrambled his way to safety and, trembling, heard that final shot with which Brice had taken his own life.

But then with the new day the shock and relief gave way to guilt. He hadn't killed Brice but he had set in motion the events that led to his suicide as surely as if he had put the revolver in his enemy's shaking hand. And he had refused to listen to Miriam when she'd pleaded with him to think again both at Ernest's house and then later at the Hall.

He worried now about how she would receive him or indeed whether she would receive him at all. He'd never seen her so upset as she had been on that night and he couldn't get her last words out of his mind. "What about my son? What am I going to tell him?" she'd shouted at him from the doorway as he got on his bicycle after Constable Fletcher had finished with them for the evening.

And when he could think of no response, she'd added bitterly as she turned to go back inside: "Why did you bother coming back if this is what you were going to do?"

Why indeed! He'd been like a man possessed when he returned from his captivity and realized from the date on Sir John's last letter that Brice had to have been involved in some way in his father's death. Just as he'd told Brice in the study, he had felt as though Sir John was calling to him from beyond the grave, demanding justice, and he'd been determined not to allow anything or anyone to stand in his way of delivering it. He had been blind, wilfully blind to the possible consequences if he forced Brice into a corner and he had been deaf to Miriam's pleading, just as he had been deaf to her suffering when he'd turned his back on her at the end of his leave, abandoning her to Brice and her mother. He had enough insight now to recognize the same pattern of behaviour repeating itself: an impetuous rush to act followed by a descent into useless regret as he looked back uncomprehending on the destruction and misery that he'd wrought.

He remembered how he had told Miriam at Ernest's house that he was no longer mastered by the war and that he had regained power over his actions so that he was his own man capable of making his own decisions. Grand talk! But now he doubted himself again and, looking in the mirror, he wondered about the true identity of the person that lay behind his hard staring eyes.

He parked his bicycle in the courtyard and knocked on the front door, keeping the lion's head knocker in his hand for a moment when he was finished, almost as if it was an old friend. Standing there waiting on the top step with his fast breath turning to white smoke in the cold winter air, he had a sudden flash of recollection taking him back to the day when he had arrived here from the widow's house with his cheap bags so out of place in the back of the Rolls-Royce, and Sir John had come down the steps to welcome him to his new home, resting his hand on his shoulder as he led him inside. And, in spite of Brice's best efforts, this house had become his home. It had been a solace to him to think of it awaiting his return when he was in France both before and after his capture. But then when he came back and learnt of Sir John's death that feeling of home had evaporated like water in the hot sun. Was that why he had been so eager to call Brice to account? he wondered. Because he believed that Brice had robbed him of his home as well as his adopted father? He didn't know the answer. Everything which had seemed so clear to him two days before was now shrouded in a fog of uncertainty and confusion.

Briggs opened the door but didn't have time to do more than usher him inside before Miriam came out into the entrance hall. She was dressed formally in a black dress and gloves with a matching embroidered shawl covering her shoulders and she looked beautiful but in a remote way, as if her widowhood, even more than her marriage, had taken her out of his reach.

She seemed surprised to see him, which he had anticipated as he hadn't telephoned ahead to say he was coming, but then to his great relief she came forward and took his hand for a moment before dismissing Briggs with a quick word as she led the way into the drawing room. There was an air of purposeful self-possession about her as she gestured for him to sit down in an armchair opposite her own that was unfamiliar to Adam and combined with his sense of his own wrongdoing to make him ill at ease.

"I wanted to say sorry," he said, feeling immediately the inadequacy of the hackneyed word to express his sense of responsibility for Brice's death. "And to see how you were and to explain—"

"I'm afraid there isn't time for that, or at least not now," she said, cutting him off. "My mother is coming here to see me. In fact I thought it was her when you knocked at the door."

"Do you want me to go?" asked Adam.

"No. I am glad you are here," she said, putting out her hand to stop him getting up. "If the purpose of her visit is what I suspect, then I shall be glad of your support."

"What is it you suspect?"

The sound of a brougham pulling up in the courtyard outside the window stopped Miriam from answering. Instead she got up from her chair and smoothed out her dress, and Adam noticed with a stirring of sympathy how she had balled up her hands into fists as she stood waiting for her mother to come in.

"Thank you, Briggs," he heard Mrs. Vale say out in the hall and the familiarity of her greeting struck him as odd. Perhaps nowadays she left the Parsonage more than she used to, but Adam somehow doubted it, and, remembering the reputation that she had had in the town for maintaining a network of paid informers, he wondered whether Briggs was performing that function on her behalf at the Hall.

The sound of Mrs. Vale's voice took him back to the last time he had heard it in this same room when she had persuaded him to release Miriam from her engagement. The memory increased his sense of unease and he got up and went over to stand by the fire, trying to dismiss it from his mind as he warmed his hands over the slow-burning coals.

"Good morning, Mother," said Miriam coolly as Mrs. Vale swept into the room. "Adam's here. I think you know he's back."

"Yes," said Mrs. Vale and the terse single-word acknowledgement amply conveyed her lack of enthusiasm for his return from the dead even without the look of hostility that she bestowed on him over her daughter's shoulder as she submitted her cold cheek for Miriam to kiss. It was unlike her to reveal her feelings unnecessarily but she had not expected to find Adam at the Hall and she had her own reasons for having hoped to find her daughter alone.

But she quickly recovered her composure and shook Adam's hand firmly when he came forward. "I understand you were in the room with my son-in-law when he took his life," she said, making the statement sound exactly like an accusation.

"No. Not at that moment," he corrected her. "He had twice tried to shoot me and I had been lucky enough to escape out into the corridor by the time he turned the gun on himself."

"I wonder why," said Mrs. Vale caustically. And she was about to say more when Miriam unexpectedly interrupted her.

"Please can we not discuss this, Mother," she said impatiently. "I explained to you what happened when we talked on the telephone and the subject's still painful for me and I imagine for Adam too. And I don't think that's why you're here, is it?"

Mrs. Vale looked as surprised as Adam at Miriam's intervention and remained silent for a moment deciding how to respond. "I would prefer to talk to you alone," she said eventually.

"No," said Miriam. "Whatever you wish to say I would like Adam to hear as well."

This time Mrs. Vale looked even more surprised. Something had changed in her daughter. But she had come with a purpose and she was not going to be deflected from carrying it out, so she nodded briefly, as if the defeat was of no consequence, and then sat down opposite Miriam in the chair that Adam had been sitting in before she came in. She kept her beady grey eyes fixed all the time on her daughter, as if to make it clear that Adam was to be no part of their conversation even if he remained in the room. And finally, when she was ready, she began to speak. "I understand you may not wish to talk about Brice," she said, "but I think you will agree that his death changes things."

"Yes," said Miriam. "It does."

"Good, I'm glad you see that. You are clearly going to need help bringing up Brandon and administering this estate. These are heavy responsibilities that you cannot undertake on your own—"

"No, Mother, as a matter of fact I can," said Miriam, interrupting. "The law empowers me to do precisely that. Mr. Sowerby, the estate's lawyer, was here yesterday and he told me that I am now Brandon's sole guardian, given that Brice did not appoint anyone to act jointly with me. I am not obliged to consult with anyone."

"Really," said Mrs. Vale, snorting to conceal her surprise. Miriam was the last person she would have expected to know her legal rights. "Well, even if that is true, you would be a fool not to seek help," she went on, recovering her composure. "You are young and entirely lacking in worldly experience and you need all the support you can get. And as your mother and Brandon's grandmother I am clearly the right person to give it to you, so it seems to me nothing short of providential that I should be leaving the Parsonage just at the time when you have most need of me here at the Hall."

"No," said Miriam simply. "You're not coming here."

"No?" repeated her mother angrily. "What do you mean: *No*? Is there something wrong with you that you should see fit to talk to me in this way? Have you taken leave of your senses?"

"Actually I think I have finally taken possession of them," said Miriam with a thin smile. There was no break in her voice but Adam could see that her hands were still balled up into fists and the rigidity of her posture left him in no doubt of the superhuman effort she was making to defy her mother and change the submissive habit of a lifetime.

"Adam has told me all about how you came here behind my back when he was home on leave and persuaded him to break with me," she went on. "You took advantage of him when he was at his most vulnerable, scarred like my father by the war, and then you turned your attention on to me, sending for Brice to press his suit when I had lost my will to resist and felt I had nothing to live for any more because of what you had done. You have been scheming and cruel and I don't forgive you for it. Do you hear me? I don't forgive you. I won't, I can't—"

Miriam's voice trembled and broke—it was incredible to Adam that she had kept it under control for so long—and the tears that had formed in her eyes began to roll down her cheeks. But they were tears of anger, not sadness, and she did not try to brush them away.

"Everyone has always treated me like a child, you most of all. And it's been my fault that I've let them. I allowed you to manipulate me and we have all paid the price—not just me but Adam and Brice too. Years of unhappiness you have caused, but now it's over. I can't be weak any more; I have to be strong for my son. And that means keeping you away from here. Where you go is your affair: I will ensure that the estate continues to pay you your allowance as long as you don't make trouble, but you will have to make your own arrangements."

Miriam stood up. Adam could see that she was shaking and he was worried that she was going to fall over. He took a step forward to offer her support but she steadied herself by leaning on the back of her chair.

Mrs. Vale stared up at her daughter with an expression that fused rage and incredulity in equal measure. Miriam's utterly unexpected defiance had left her momentarily at a loss for words, and it was Miriam who spoke first.

"I want you to leave now, Mother," she said quietly but firmly as she went over to the side of the fireplace and pressed the bell. "I am sorry you have had a wasted journey but this is a difficult time for me and there is other business I need to attend to."

The butler appeared at the door as she finished speaking, carrying a tray containing coffee and biscuits, and looked completely nonplussed when he saw his mistress and her mother glowering at each other across the room.

"My mother is leaving, Briggs," said Miriam. "Please would you see her out?"

At first it seemed as if Mrs. Vale was going to defy her daughter and remain where she was but then she slowly got to her feet.

"You're making a serious mistake, my dear. And I hope that when you have had a chance to reflect, you will come to see how wrong you are to reject my help," she said, adopting a regal more-in-sorrow-than-anger tone. "I have always had your interests at heart whereas this young man"—she gestured contemptuously in Adam's direction—"is unstable and untrustworthy. He spreads ruin wherever he goes. He'll ruin you too and then it'll be too late for you to come running back to me."

Miriam said nothing but just watched her mother's slow progress across the room and past Briggs through the door. And when it had finally shut behind them she ran back to her chair and, leaning over the arm, gave way to a storm of wrenching sobs.

It hurt Adam to see her in such distress and he went over and gently laid his hand on her arm while offering her a handkerchief that he had taken from his pocket. "You were magnificent," he said. "Absolutely magnificent."

"No, I wasn't," she said, looking up at him angrily. "This isn't some kind of theatre show. I did what I had to do. I have to learn to stand on my own two feet and not depend on people whom I can't trust. And that means you as well, Adam. My mother was right: you are untrustworthy—and selfish too. You deserted me; you broke your promise; and how does it help me that you feel sorry about it now?" She paused for breath but then went on, without giving him the chance to respond: "You say you've changed but you haven't; your demons are still controlling you, however much you like to pretend they're not. That's why you wouldn't listen to me when I told you not to come here. That's why Brice is dead and my son has no father."

"I'm sorry," said Adam, taken aback by the venom of her attack. "I didn't know he had the gun; I swear I didn't. And if I had, I would have done things differently. But I still think he should have had to explain what happened to Sir John—if not to me, then to the police—because he was here that night. I know he was. Don't you think that matters?"

"No," she shouted, practically spitting the word in his face. "I don't care about any of that. The dead are dead; it's the living you should be concerning yourself with. Like me! But instead you come back out of the blue and treat me like I'm some kind of acquaintance when I've been praying for you every day, long after everyone else had given up on you. You're cold, cold as ice; and shut up just as tight in that oyster shell of yours as you were before. You've grown a thicker skin over it. That's the only difference."

She closed her eyes and laid her head back against the cushion and he wanted to bend down and kiss her like he had kissed her on the promenade at Scarborough and chase all their troubles away. But he couldn't. He had wronged her and betrayed her trust and he didn't know if he could ever win it back.

"You're right," he said quietly. "It was foolish of me to think I could explain myself to you when you know me better than I do myself. But I am sorry for what I have done. Truly I am. And I want to help if you'll give me the chance to prove myself."

"I don't need your help," she sighed.

But her voice was no more than a whisper and carried no conviction. Emboldened, he carried on: "I think you do. Charles has been running the estate and the mine into the ground. And after what has happened with Brice there's no telling what he'll do next. You have to stop him now before it's too late, and I think I know a way to do it if you'll let me."

Miriam opened her eyes and looked up at Adam. She was angry

with him—angrier than she had been able to put into words. But she loved him too. Already that morning, she had returned again to the study and reached up to touch the gunshot holes in the walls. Embedded inside them were the bullets that had been intended to kill him. He had survived by a miracle. She thanked God for his deliverance, thanked him down on her knees, even as she remained determined not to let Adam see how she felt. And she knew that he was right. He was her only friend and she did need his help, if she could just receive it on her terms and not his. The battle with her mother had left her emotionally drained and other battles lay ahead. The funeral was fixed for two days' time and Brice's mother was coming from London: she had sent a coldly worded letter in response to Miriam's telegram, confirming her attendance and expressing the wish that Brice should not be buried in the family mausoleum with his father. And then, beyond the funeral, there were the debts that the lawyer had talked about when he came: frightening sums that made her head spin . . .

"Can't I just dismiss Charles?" she asked wearily. "I've got the power, so won't that work?"

"It's better not to give him any warning. Once he knows what you have in mind he'll try and take everything that's left. And I don't want you to have to confront him yourself."

"Why? Because you think he's dangerous? You do, don't you?" said Miriam, becoming agitated again. "I won't let you get hurt. What happened with Brice was enough. Do you hear me, Adam?"

She had risen from her chair, causing him to take a step back. And he was sorry she was upset but happy too because her outburst told him that she cared.

"I promise I won't go in there myself," he said. "I'm hoping the police are going to help us."

"How?"

"Leave it to me, Miriam. You've got enough to cope with. I want to support you, and this is something I can do if you'll let me."

She gave him a long searching look and then slowly nodded her head. "Be careful," she said.

"I will. He'll be gone by the end of the day. But—I know you haven't thought about this—you're going to need to appoint a replacement."

"Whom do you suggest?"

"I'd recommend Mr. Hardcastle if he'll agree to come back. He was a hard taskmaster but he was honest and had the miners' respect. I can ask him if you like."

"Yes, please do. Is there anything else?" She felt exhausted now and longed to lie down and close her eyes.

"Just this," said Adam hesitantly. "And it's only a suggestion. I think you should get rid of Briggs too. It's just a feeling I got today but I think he's your mother's eyes and ears in this house."

Miriam was surprised at first. But then it made sense. There was that slight familiarity between them that she had half noticed, and in recent months her mother had always seemed to know more about what was happening in her life than she would have expected.

"You need to have someone in charge here whose loyalty is to you," Adam went on. "And you can rely on Cartwright for that. He is one of the best men I know: I would trust him with my life. And there is nothing he wants more than to return to the Hall. The house and the Scarsdale family are his life; he is bereft without them."

"How do you know?"

"Because he's told me so. He's one of the first people I went to see when I came back."

"Before me?"

Adam bowed his head, accepting the rebuke. "I was nervous of seeing you, Miriam. Because of what I'd done; because you were married to Brice. Like I said before, I'm sorry I've made such a mess of things."

"We've said what we needed to say about that," she said, getting up from her chair and holding out her hand. "Now we must try to look forward, not back."

He took her hand and unexpectedly leant forward and kissed it. "I won't fail you. Not this time," he said, and then turned and quickly left the room without waiting for a response.

Chapter Forty

Adam knocked at the door of the Scarsdale Police House, which happened by coincidence to be at the end of the terrace where he had once lived with his father. He had no idea whether the widow was still in residence but nothing on the outside seemed to have changed in the years since he had last been here. The squat box-like houses were just as begrimed with soot and smoke as they had been before the war and the women in their coarse aprons were still out on their doorsteps gossiping, although they fell silent to look him up and down as he stood waiting under Constable Fletcher's blue lamp. He wondered how many of them recognized him from when he had been their neighbour, going to school every day with his satchel and leaving that last time in Sir John's Rolls-Royce, giving them a story which they'd discussed up and down the street for weeks afterwards.

He was in luck. The constable was home, sitting down to a late breakfast, and he invited Adam through the front police section of the house into the homely kitchen at the back where he poured him a cup of tea from a pot covered with an enormous dark blue cosy, complete with a bobble on the top.

"Navy blue to match my uniform," said the constable with a smile. "And hand-knitted too: I got it as a gift from a grateful Scarsdale spinster after I reunited her with her marmalade cat last September. Policing doesn't tend to be that exciting round here most of the time—unless you're honouring us with your company, of course, when our quiet little town seems to become like an outpost of the

Wild West. So what is it this time, may I ask? High treason or just a common-or-garden murder?"

"Maybe a murder," said Adam. "Although I think we may have trouble proving that. Perjury seems a likelier possibility."

"Perjury?" repeated the constable, suddenly serious. "What's this about, Mr. Raine?"

"Sir John Scarsdale's death: you told me when you came out to the Hall two nights ago that you were the officer who attended after his death as well."

"That's right."

"And so you would have been a witness at the inquest?"

"Yes. But I didn't have any evidence of foul play if that's what you're getting at. There was a half-drunk decanter of wine in the study and everyone in the house admitted that Sir John had been drinking to excess for some time. There was nothing to say he hadn't fallen down the stairs."

"But you had doubts?" asked Adam, picking up on an undertone of uncertainty in the constable's voice.

"Yes, since you ask. He had no history of falling and the footman, Charles, was just a little too quick with his answers. But you can't build a case on hunches and the inquest wasn't much more than a formality. A verdict of accidental death and it was all over in less than an hour as I recall."

"Who gave evidence?"

"Myself and Charles."

"What did he say?"

"That he heard a crash and came running, found Sir John dead at the bottom of the stairs, and called the police."

"He didn't say there were any visitors?"

"No, he said he was alone. The butler and the cook had gone to bed and there were no other servants sleeping in the house."

"Well, he was lying. And I can prove it. Sir John was writing me a letter that evening and in it he says that Charles was about to show Brice up to the study. I have a certified copy here for you to look at. The original's at a lawyer's office in Gratton," he said, handing the policeman the document he'd shown Brice.

The constable read the letter through and looked up. "Did Sir Brice see this?"

Adam nodded.

"Well, now I understand why he wanted to kill you," he said. "May I ask why you didn't show me this document two nights ago, Mr. Raine?"

"Because it was late and I'd just escaped death by a whisker and I suppose I didn't want to blacken Brice's name just after he'd killed himself. I needed time to think," said Adam. "That's not a crime, is it?"

"So why are you showing it to me now?" asked the constable, not answering the question.

"Because Charles needs to account for what he did. It's not just the lie at the inquest, although maybe that's all we can prove. He's been blackmailing Brice for years. That's how he got to be manager of the mine."

The policeman put down his cup of tea and looked at Adam severely. "You would have done better to bring me this letter three days ago instead of confronting Sir Brice with it," he told him. "That way he would still be alive and we might have been able to get to the bottom of what actually happened in the Hall that night. You've been a damned fool, if you don't mind me saying so, Mr. Raine."

"I know I have," said Adam ruefully. "But at least I've learnt from my mistake, which is why I've come to you now."

"Instead of rushing off to confront Charles, you mean?"

Adam nodded. "He's at the mine now," he said. "I went there on my way here. I saw him. He was standing outside his office."

"Did he see you?"

"No, he couldn't have done. I was behind one of the sheds and he wasn't looking in my direction."

The policeman stroked his chin, thinking. "I'll make a call," he said. "I'm going to need authority from higher up, and support too. I've got a feeling our friend won't come quietly."

"I don't think you should delay," said Adam. "He may have got the wind up after what happened with Brice."

"I understand that, but you need to let me get on and do my job.

I'll go today if I can. But you're to stay out of it. Do you hear me, Mr. Raine? No more meddling!"

Adam had no intention of meddling but that didn't mean he didn't want to be present when justice finally caught up with Charles. And so, after cycling back to Ernest's house to make a packed lunch, he set off for the mine with a snap tin in one coat pocket and a Dudley flask of tea in the other, feeling like a collier on his way to work.

Down below in the valley bottom the timber headstocks towered up into the blue sky with the spokes of their huge wheels spinning backwards and forwards in the winter sunlight as they raised and lowered the cages up and down the deep shafts of the mine. Adam remembered how awed he had been when he saw them for the first time from the window of the train on that distant morning eight years before when he had arrived in Scarsdale with his father, full of hope and ignorant of all that lay ahead. That awe had quickly developed into fear as he lay awake at nights picturing the cages free-falling through the darkness, and he remembered even more vividly that moment when he had forced himself up the wooden stairs leading to the platform, feeling exactly as if he was mounting the steps of a monstrous gallows. And then a year later when the scream of the emergency siren sent him and the whole population of the town surging down the hill towards the mine on the morning of the disaster he had imagined the headstocks as merciless alien creatures newly arrived from another planet, ready to rain down destruction on the ant-like humans at their feet. Their black shapes were now forever embedded in his unconscious mind, archetypes of power and danger that often formed the backdrop to his troubled dreams.

At the bottom of the hill Adam padlocked his bicycle to a railing and left the road, picking his way instead through the narrow corridors between the pithead buildings until he came up the side of the stores shed and stopped at the end, crouching behind a pile of broken coal tubs from where he had oblique views across the open waste ground to Charles's office at one end and the screens at the other.

He hadn't been back to the mine since his return from France and he felt overwhelmed by a host of unfamiliar sensations. He could feel the ground beneath his feet vibrating with the pulse of the nearby steam engine. Its roar filled his ears and he could smell its oil and tar and acrid smoke tingling in his nostrils. He closed his eyes for a moment, turning away from the coal dust that was swirling in the breeze, and was assailed by memories too.

Here, right here, was where he'd stood waiting, shivering in the cold with Ernest and the twins while Luke opened up the stores with the deputy's keys on that March morning when they had stolen the dynamite. He could hear Luke's voice somewhere in the recesses of his mind saying: *I hope you can keep a secret, Adam Raine?* And he could see his face aglow with a sense of adventure as they lit their candles and went inside. He'd loved Luke: the least complicated and yet the sweetest of all his friends. He remembered his fear on that last night when they had gone up into the wood; his horror of walking on the bloated German bodies; and he saw again the glassy opal of his dead eyes and felt the warm palm of his dead hand in his own as they lay together side by side on the battlefield. They had been like brothers and Adam loved him still even though he was gone. Luke's death and Seaton's too felt like amputations and Adam imagined his blood still flowing out to the missing limbs.

He kept his eyes closed, screwed up against the pain of the recollection, and forced his brain to replace the image of Luke dead with another picture of him smiling self-consciously in his ridiculously ill-fitting Pickelhaube helmet as they sat together on the grass, posing for the group photograph on the morning after the first day of the Big Push. It was a technique he'd mastered during the long lonely years of his captivity: training his mind to replace the bad with the good; refusing to be swamped by the devastation of the past as he struggled to survive into the future.

He opened his eyes and scanned the pithead, looking for Charles, and caught sight of him in the distance standing with Barker Atkins up on the gantry above the screens. He was a distinctive figure, dressed like an owner in a black tailcoat and striped grey trousers and wearing a tall black top hat, which accentuated his height advantage over Atkins, who appeared fatter and angrier than ever, bellowing threats at the workers down below, whose fingers darted lightning quick among the coal, removing the slate and stones as it passed by them on the constantly moving belts.

Ernest was in there amongst them. Stoical as ever, he had gone back without complaint to his old job on the screens, unlike Rawdon who had refused to even contemplate a return to the mine, preferring to commute to Gratton every day where he drove a delivery van for a firm that sold furniture on the High Street. Adam had been luckier, receiving a small government pension based on the pay he'd missed when he was a prisoner which bought him time to consider his options. He knew that he could return to Oxford but something held him back: a wish to live life rather than study it perhaps; and after the years of isolation he did not want to be parted from his friends. Or from Miriam.

Now, as he watched, Charles descended from the gantry and began stalking up and down the lines of sorters, peering over their shoulders to watch their work. One of them became even more nervous than the others under this scrutiny and started to make mistakes, and suddenly Charles reached forward and pulled him back by the shoulders so that he toppled over on to the hard ground.

"This man's an idiot," he called up to Atkins. "He's throwing away perfectly good coal. Pay him out and send him on his way. And keep a better watch, Mr. Atkins. These screens are your responsibility."

"Please, sir. I'll do better. I promise I will. I've got kids at home," implored the man, getting to his feet with difficulty and reaching out to touch Charles's sleeve. Adam could see that he was lame. Screen work was an option for miners crippled by the war, who hadn't the mobility needed to go back underground.

But Charles took no notice, brushing away the man's hand and walking back to his office without a backwards glance. Looking out from behind the coal tubs, Adam could see the self-satisfied smirk on his face as he went past. And he longed to rush out and pull him to the ground too and teach him not to bully soldiers who had fought for their country when Adam was sure Charles had taken the coward's way out and shot himself in the leg to avoid going to France.

But he restrained himself, remembering his promise to Miriam, and stayed where he was, watching as Charles went inside and closed the door.

The hours ticked by and at four o'clock the pit siren sounded, signalling a change of shifts. Miners came out of the cage with tired, blackened faces and tramped away across the waste ground in their clogs, passing by their replacements who stood around beneath the headstocks in small groups, waiting their turn to go down into the mine. They were blocking Adam's view of Charles's office and he might easily have missed the arrival of Constable Fletcher and two other uniformed policemen if he hadn't taken the chance of coming out from behind the coal tubs and approaching closer.

Fletcher didn't see him, but Ernest did. His shift had finished too and he came over to Adam, clapping him on the shoulder. "What brings you here?" he asked.

"Charles," said Adam, gesturing in the direction of the office door that was just now closing behind the three policemen. "Don't say anything yet but they're here to arrest him."

Ernest's face lit up and he couldn't restrain himself from uttering a muffled screech of pleasure that had several of the nearby miners turning round to look at him. Some of them had also seen the police arrive and, as word spread, the groups around the headstocks began to move back towards the office, curious to find out why they were here.

"That's the best news I've heard since the Armistice," said Ernest excitedly, bending close to whisper in Adam's ear. "Or rather since you came back," he added, correcting himself. "Can they take Atkins too while they're about it? I'd like to see him doing hard labour."

"I'm afraid not," said Adam, smiling. "But I'll make sure Hardcastle gives you a better job when he comes back. I deserve something for getting Charles out of here."

But Charles didn't come out in the way Adam expected. Suddenly the door of the office flew open and Charles appeared, this time without his hat and almost immediately without half the sleeve of his tailcoat as well, which Constable Fletcher was left impotently holding in his flailing hand as Charles took off, running diagonally across the open ground.

The astonished miners gave way as he rushed towards them and in a moment he had passed through the crowd and disappeared from view behind the blacksmith's forge, chased by the police officers. Dodging between the buildings, Charles picked up several discarded horseshoes and threw them back at his pursuers, hitting one of the younger policemen a glancing blow on the head which sent him crashing to the ground.

"Quick," Ernest shouted to Adam. "I know where he's going. We can cut him off." And, leading the way, he began running up the hill towards the levelled-off area of tarmac where Charles kept his Wolseley tourer motor car, his pride and joy and the symbol of his success and power. He would have preferred to park it outside his office but the lower section of the road that led down to the pithead buildings was no better than a bumpy potholed track and so he had had to settle for the construction of the parking area several hundred yards up the hill. He paid two of the pit-pony boys a few extra pennies to wash and polish the car every other day and its sparkling green bodywork infuriated the filthy miners as they walked past it on their way back from the pit, which was precisely Charles's intention. They muttered to each other about 'chuckin' a big lump o' coal through the bugger's back winder,' but none of them had dared to follow through on their threats. Times had changed since Whalen Dawes's day and Charles was feared as well as hated by everyone at Scarsdale Mine.

Adam rounded a bend in the path slightly ahead of Ernest and came out on to the road where he caught sight of Charles, who had emerged from behind the pit buildings and was approaching the parking area from the side. But the wound in his leg was slowing him down now and he was running with a strange half-skipping motion. He glanced back and let out a grunt of rage as he caught sight of Adam gaining on him. And, making a last desperate effort, he reached the tarmac and was within touching distance of his car when Adam threw himself forward and tackled him to the ground.

Adam pulled himself up into a kneeling position but kept his hands on Charles's arms, pinning them to the ground, even though Charles was too bruised and exhausted to make any further effort to escape. Behind him he could hear Ernest's panting breath echoing his own and in the background the noise of shouting and pounding feet.

"What happened?" he demanded of Charles between gasps. "Was it an accident or did Brice kill him?"

Charles's shoulders heaved and after a moment Adam realized he was laughing. "I might have told you if you'd asked politely," he said. "But, as it is, I think I'll exercise my right to silence. You think you're so much better than me, don't you? But you're nothing but a dirty slum kid underneath all your airs and graces. Brice was right about that much."

"Yes, he was," agreed Adam. "And I'm proud of where I came from and what I've become. Being poor doesn't mean people have to turn out like you, Charles. A monster is what you've become."

Adam stood up, letting the younger policeman, the one who had escaped injury, take custody of Charles. He pulled him to his feet and handcuffed his wrists. Constable Fletcher, who was too old for running, was still yards away, a solitary dark blue figure among the crowd of miners who were surging towards them up the hill. They stopped when they saw their hated enemy in handcuffs and erupted as one into a cacophony of wild cheering. And the darkening afternoon sky was suddenly filled with a sea of cloth caps thrown up above their heads in spontaneous celebration.

Chapter Forty-One

The weather broke on the morning of Brice's funeral two days later. A great storm battered the church, and the crash of thunder and the beating of hail on the leaded window panes half drowned out the words of the curate from Gratton, who sensed in the downpour God's displeasure with the dead man, who had sinned by taking his own life and was entitled as a result to only an abbreviated form of the usual funeral service.

And the curate was distracted not just by the rain but also by his anxiety over the application he had recently made to make the church his own. He fervently hoped that the bishop would look kindly on his years of service but feared that a more highly qualified outsider might appear at the last and steal the preferment away from under his nose.

Miriam sat self-consciously alone in the Scarsdale family pew at the front of the church, almost within touching distance of her husband's dark oak coffin. Her mother-in-law had chosen to sit two rows behind her and Miriam could feel her eyes glaring at her back in the gloom. Otherwise the church was almost empty apart from the Hall servants who sat in a line at the back. It was a forlorn contrast to Sir John's funeral when there had been so many mourners that they had spilled out beyond the porch on to the path leading back to the lychgate.

Cartwright sat at the end of the row of servants. Miriam was intensely grateful to Adam for suggesting the restoration of the butler to his rightful place at the Hall. She had felt an immediate sense of support personal to herself from the moment he had stepped out of his taxi the previous afternoon, dressed immaculately in his black tailcoat and tie. He had taken immediate charge and by dinnertime that evening she had felt a new stability in the house as if it was a storm-battered ship that had reached safe harbour.

She gazed at the coffin through her widow's black veil and was racked by conflicting emotions. She was sorry that Brice was so little mourned. He had not inspired love except in his mother and in his infant son, who remained back at the Hall with his nursemaid, blissfully ignorant of his father's departure from the world. Brice had always been selfish, driven by cancerous resentments over which he had no control, but with Brandon he had been different and, watching the two of them together, she had sometimes glimpsed the person Brice might have been if his life had turned out differently. She felt relieved that the child was too young to understand what had happened but she felt sad too, desperately sad, that he had been deprived of his father's love.

She wished for Brice's sake that he had not reached a point where he had become so unhappy that he wanted to kill himself. But she also knew that she was glad he was dead. The knowledge shamed her to the core of her being. It made her feel unclean and she prayed to God for forgiveness, but she couldn't deny that from the moment she knew he was gone she had felt a great weight lifted from off her chest. The sensation was physical: she was able to breathe properly for the first time in as long as she could remember and her determination to keep breathing was what had given her the courage to take on her mother.

Outside in the churchyard Cartwright stood beside her on the wet grass, holding an enormous black umbrella over her head and his as they stood facing Lady Scarsdale, and her manservant, who was performing the same function for his mistress on the other side of the newly dug grave. Miriam felt her mother-in-law's hatred beating against her across the black hole. It was like a physical force, as strong as the rain that was pounding a relentless tattoo on the taut fabric of the umbrellas, and it took all Miriam's strength to stand her ground as the curate hurried to finish reciting the committal prayer and the casket was lowered into its final resting place.

The mourners began to disperse but Lady Scarsdale remained where she was. All her life she had valued the virtues of steadiness and self-restraint. She knew that the maintenance of her rank in society depended on observing a complex set of rules of behaviour which had as their bedrock an avoidance of all public displays of emotion. But now she wanted to throw etiquette to the winds and get down on her hands and knees and beat the muddy ground with her head and tear her hair and yell and scream her grief over her poor dead son's coffin lying down there in the dirt and pooling water. It was agony for her to remember how unhappy he had been all his life and to acknowledge her own inability to help him overcome his troubles. She remembered how she had stayed up through the long watches of the night when he was a child racked by scarlet fever, holding cold compresses to his fevered brow until he recovered, but later she could do nothing to exorcise the demons that had taken possession of his mind. She had not been able to save him, and on that last evening in London he had run away from her down the stairs and she had not seen him in the morning when he left . . .

She couldn't bear to blame herself and so she had to blame others for her son's death: the upstart Adam Raine whom her loathsome husband had set up in Brice's place and Parson Vale's penniless daughter who had married her son for his money and had never given him the love he deserved. Lady Scarsdale knew what they had done. The facts spoke for themselves. Brice had tried to kill Adam before he turned the gun on himself. Why? Because Miriam had betrayed him and Adam had come to taunt Brice with their adultery. She hated them both and, looking down at the coffin for the last time, she swore to her dead son that she would avenge his untimely death.

Miriam had forced herself to remain at the lychgate, sheltering under the narrow timber roof. Lady Scarsdale had not responded to her written invitation to return to the Hall for lunch or to stay the night and she felt duty bound to ask her again now. But she trembled inwardly as her mother-in-law approached and wished that she could take flight in the Rolls-Royce that was waiting for her at the roadside only a few yards away.

"Would you like to come back—" she began awkwardly.

"I have no intention of ever returning to the Hall," said Lady Scarsdale, interrupting. "And I may say that I had hoped never to see this church again either, but you and Mr. Raine have put paid to that aspiration."

"What do you mean?" asked Miriam, taken aback. Even with the hostility that she had encountered at the graveside she had still not been prepared for this level of vitriol.

"I mean that I hold you responsible—" Lady Scarsdale began angrily but then stopped. "I will not bandy words with you here. Not today," she went on after a moment, speaking in a cold, controlled voice. "But you will be hearing from me—or rather from my lawyers. I need to consider the interests of my grandson."

"What interests?" asked Miriam, becoming upset. "I know the law. I am Brandon's legal guardian. Mr. Sowerby has told me—" She broke off, conscious of the rising desperation in her voice, and Cartwright, who had been standing waiting beside the Rolls-Royce, saw her distress and began to move towards her.

Lady Scarsdale had already walked out into the road. "I'd start making plans for your retirement, old man," she told the butler acidly as she passed him on the way to her car in which, moments later, she was driven away from Scarsdale for the last time.

Miriam heard nothing more from her mother-in-law for two months but then, just as she had been lulled into a false sense of security, Cartwright brought her a large official-looking envelope under the seal of the High Court of Justice. She opened it in the drawing room with shaking hands and saw that it was a writ requiring her to appear in London on a date three weeks later for an initial hearing of an application for her to be replaced as custodian and guardian of the child Sir Brandon Scarsdale by Anne Lady Scarsdale, his grandmother and the applicant in the suit. It was worse than she had thought; far worse: not only was her mother-in-law seeking to take over the administration of the estate and the mine on behalf of her grandson, she was also applying to take Brandon away from her.

Miriam felt faint. The thought of her precious son, so small and vulnerable and utterly dependent upon her love, being taken away from her and transported into the cold care of her mother-in-law was more than she could bear, but the ornate document and its flowery legal language intimidated her and made her feel impotent to resist, and she buried her head in the sofa cushions and gave way to a wild grief. Cartwright, who had been passing by the door, heard her crying, connected it with the envelope, and immediately dispatched the stable boy to cycle to Adam's house in Station Street with a message asking him to come to the Hall without delay.

Luckily Adam was at home and came at once.

"What is it, Miriam? What's the trouble?" he asked, remaining in the doorway. It hurt him to see her in such distress and part of him longed to take her in his arms and comfort her, but there had been an invisible physical barrier between them ever since his return from France that he didn't feel able to cross.

They were divided by their past. He had broken their engagement and she had married Brice and had a child. They had not been true to each other. These were facts that could not be denied and made them distrust not just each other but also the possibility that they could have any joint future together. They had not discussed their relationship since the day when Miriam had faced down her mother, but they both felt that it was brittle and could easily break if it was put under strain. And so they kept their distance, seeing each other no more than once or twice a week, believing it was better to keep hold of what they had than to risk losing everything again.

Miriam sat up and dried her eyes, wishing that Adam had not seen her looking so weak. But she was glad he had come. Catching sight of the writ, she felt panic sweeping over her again. She couldn't fight the clever silver-tongued lawyers in their wigs and gowns; she knew she couldn't; she needed help.

"It's Lady Scarsdale. She wants to take Brandon away from me," she said, holding out the writ for Adam to read and beginning to cry again. "I don't know what I am going to do!"

"We'll think of something," said Adam, but his voice was distracted as he was concentrating all his attention on the document, which he read through twice before setting it carefully back down on the table.

"She's not going to change her mind. She blames me for Brice's death," said Miriam despairingly.

"How do you know?"

"Because she told me so at the funeral. She said she was going to her lawyers too but I thought that maybe she was just lashing out and didn't mean it. And then when nothing happened I started to hope—" She broke off, trying and failing to keep control of her emotions. "Oh, what a fool I am, always hoping that life is going to get better!" she cried. "I should have learnt my lesson by now."

"But the point is it has got better! You have made progress. The mine is doing better and the estate too," said Adam, looking suddenly excited. "And maybe that can help us."

"How?" asked Miriam, puzzled. "She doesn't care about any of that; she just wants to hurt me. That's why she's doing this."

"I understand she doesn't care," said Adam. "But her father may and it's his opinion that matters. He's going to be the one paying for the lawsuit and if we can persuade him to withdraw his support, then she won't be able to continue with it."

"But why would he do that?"

"Because he's a businessman and he's put a lot of money into this estate, even if Brice did his level best to fritter it all away. We need to get him to understand what really happened to Brice: that it was Charles and not you who drove him to commit suicide; and that with Charles gone and Hardcastle back in place, there's a real chance that you can turn things around up here. And if he believes that, then maybe, just maybe, he'll lose faith in the litigation and will want to protect his investment by supporting you—or at least holding off on trying to sabotage our efforts. I know it's a long shot, but I think it's worth trying. And we have nothing to lose. I can help you draft a letter asking for an interview."

"Would you come too?" she asked nervously.

"Yes, of course, although I don't think you need to tell him that in the letter. You can count on me. I've already told you that. So, are we agreed?"

"Yes," she said, drying her eyes. "Thank you. I don't know what I would do without you, Adam. Really I don't."

Miriam's simple words went straight to Adam's heart. He looked into her dark brown eyes and longed to reach over and stroke the trouble from her brow, but he knew that he could not make it go away. He hadn't wanted to tell Miriam but the writ frightened him too. He knew that there wasn't the money in the estate to fight a legal case in the High Court and it was obvious that Lady Scarsdale's father would be far more likely to listen to his daughter than to them, even if he agreed to see them. But they had to try. Right and truth were on their side and that had to count for something.

Miriam heard back more quickly than she had expected. A short two-line letter arrived at the Hall at the beginning of the following week stating that Sir Hubert Long would be pleased to see her at half past eleven on the Tuesday following at his office in Pall Mall. It was signed by Sir Hubert's private secretary with a postscript asking her to make sure she was on time as "Sir Hubert has a very busy schedule that day."

"Well, I agree it's not the warmest of invitations," said Adam with a wry smile as he read the letter when he came over to the Hall later that day. "But he was never going to welcome you with open arms, was he? Not after what his daughter must have been telling him. And the main point is that we've piqued his interest enough for him to see you. The rest is up to us."

They took the train on the Monday and stayed at an inexpensive hotel situated conveniently close to their terminus, the King's Cross railway station. It was Miriam's first visit to London and she felt unnerved but excited by the grandeur of the tall buildings and the crowds of people and vehicles thronging the wide streets. It was as if she was glimpsing for the first time that the world which she had known all her life was just a tiny, insignificant corner of the real world, whose immensity dwarfed anything she had been able to imagine. Her eyes darted this way and that, taking in the unfamiliar sights, and Adam had to reach out more than once to stop her tripping on the kerbs.

In the evening he insisted on taking her to dinner in the iconic Great Northern Hotel beside King's Cross. They drank dry white wine under the chandeliers and Adam told her about how he had worked outside the station when he was a boy, earning coppers helping the cabbies load and unload their passengers' bags. He'd spoken little about his childhood in the past but now he opened up under her questioning and described the street where he grew up: the mournful cries of the street sellers calling out their wares; the barefoot children dancing around the standpipe to the music of the barrel organ; the sunlight refracted in the thick cut-glass windows of the Cricketers' Arms; all the poverty and the richness of that vanished life wound together in a vivid tapestry of his recollection.

"I feel like I can see it," said Miriam, leaning forward with enthusiasm. "You have a gift for making people and places come alive, Adam. Do you know that?"

"Perhaps," said Adam, looking pleased but also unexpectedly serious. "At least I hope I do. I haven't told you this but since I came back I've been trying to write about the war. It's hard work a lot of the time but I keep going because I want people to understand what our soldiers went through. Not why we won or whether the generals were right or wrong, but just what it was like: how frightened and hungry and wretched the men were but also how brave and loyal and uncomplaining. I don't want them to be forgotten. I remember Seaton telling me that that is what would happen—that the grass would grow back over the trenches and it would all be as if nothing happened. But I won't accept that. I can't. I still feel certain that there was a reason I had all those narrow escapes, surviving when I should have died. When I first came back I thought it was to deliver justice to Sir John. I suppose I was struck by the improbability of receiving his letter on the last day before I was captured and keeping it all those years without knowing its true significance, and of course

I owed him so much: he was the one who stepped in and saved me when my father died. But then when Constable Fletcher took Charles away I found I wasn't satisfied; I felt instead a great restlessness; a need to make something of the writing. And that's what I've been trying to do ever since."

Adam paused and gave a rueful grin. "Sorry," he said. "That was quite a speech. And I don't want to get ahead of myself. I'm not an experienced writer and I know that there's no guarantee of success."

"It doesn't matter about experience," said Miriam passionately. "I know you can do this. You just have to believe in yourself."

"Thank you," said Adam. "That means a great deal, coming from you. You've always believed in me, even though I've done so little to deserve it. Perhaps the writing is also a way of making amends," he added thoughtfully, looking at Miriam with a shy smile.

"What do you mean?"

"I know I hurt us both by refusing to talk to you about what the war was like when I came back on leave, so if I can find a way to tell you now, then maybe it will help us heal."

"Yes," said Miriam. "I think it will." The wine and the excitement of her new surroundings had intoxicated her and she felt for a moment a boundless sense of future possibility. It made her face glow in the candlelight and Adam thought he had never seen her look more beautiful.

But her sense of elation didn't last. She was unused to the alcohol and she slept badly, afflicted by troubled dreams in which Brandon was torn repeatedly from her arms by men in hoods and masks and his cries were drowned out by the noise of her father dressed in pyjamas prophesying doom from the pulpit of Scarsdale Church.

And in the morning her anxiety about the interview with Sir Hubert, which had receded amid the distractions of the previous day, returned with a redoubled intensity so that she could hardly eat any breakfast. It didn't help that Adam was absent, seeing a publisher who had expressed an interest in his writing, and when he was late getting back Miriam became so agitated that she didn't think she was going to be able to go through with the meeting.

But she knew she didn't have any choice: not if she was to have any chance of keeping her son. In the taxi she took deep breaths, nodding without comprehension as Adam pointed out the London sights. The meeting with the publisher had gone well and he was excited, but for her it was all a blur: the Opera House and the West End theatres and Lord Nelson standing 169 feet in the air astride his column flashed by the window, and as if in no time they were riding the lift up to the top floor of the imposing building in Pall Mall that had been the headquarters of Sir Hubert Long, self-made millionaire boot manufacturer, for longer than either of them had been walking the earth.

The commissionaire in his resplendent green frock coat pulled back the brass grille of the lift and they walked out into a large foyer lit by a vaulted skylight. A severe-looking lady with her white hair drawn into the tightest bun that either Miriam or Adam had ever seen sat behind a desk positioned at a precise right angle to the closed mahogany door of Sir Hubert's office. And her expression became even more severe, developing through puzzlement into outright disapproval, when Miriam and Adam gave her their names.

"The appointment is for Lady Miriam alone," she said, glancing down at the diary in front of her. She was about to say more but the telephone on her desk rang. Adam could hear that it was Sir Hubert, punctual to the minute, asking for Lady Miriam to be sent in, and he immediately took her arm and steered her through the door. Behind him the flustered secretary had got up from her desk and was telling him to come back, but he took no notice, closing the door on her protests.

"Who the hell are you?" demanded Sir Hubert, a surprisingly small wiry man with a bristly grey moustache, a pair of bushy eyebrows and a prominent forehead that was so wrinkled it looked as if it had been furrowed by a miniature plough. He was obviously well past retirement age but his eyes were bright and Adam sensed that very little got past him.

"Adam Raine," said Adam cheerfully, approaching Sir Hubert's enormous desk with his hand outstretched. "I'm a friend of Miriam's."

"No, he's not. He's her lover," said Lady Scarsdale, who was standing to the side of her father. "He and that woman"—she pointed derisively over at Miriam who had remained near the door—"were carrying on behind Brice's back which is why Brice tried to kill him before he turned the gun on himself. My son's blood is on their hands and yet they have the bald-faced effrontery to waltz in here as if they've done nothing wrong. I told you not to see her; I told you!" she shouted down at her father, stamping her foot.

"Well, I certainly didn't agree to see *you*," said Sir Hubert, who had remained staring up at Adam but ignoring his hand during his daughter's tirade. "So please leave."

Adam took an involuntary step back. He felt as if he had been physically pushed. He had not been prepared for the old man's power. Even though Sir Hubert was seated and everyone else was standing, he had a natural authority and power of command developed over decades that enabled him to dominate the room without any apparent effort. It was hard to resist.

"Certainly I'll go if you want me to," said Adam, trying to keep his voice calm and measured. "But before I do, you need to think about whether you want to know what really happened to your grandson, because I'm the only person who knows. I was there in the room with him. No one else was. And it had nothing to do with Miriam."

"You're lying," said Lady Scarsdale.

"I'm not," said Adam. "And I can prove it if I have to. My friends in Scarsdale know that I had had no contact with Miriam in over two years until earlier that day so there was no time for any 'carrying on,' as you put it. And what you're saying makes no sense: why would I go to the Hall to talk to Brice if I'd been seeing his wife? Surely he'd be the last person I'd want to run into! And why would he shoot himself if he'd done nothing wrong?"

"I won't listen to this," said Lady Scarsdale furiously. "You need to leave: you heard my father."

"So why did he? Tell us if you know the answer," demanded Sir Hubert, overruling his daughter.

"Because I'd shown him evidence he was in the study on the night his father died," said Adam.

"What evidence?"

"A letter Sir John was writing to me when he arrived. It was posted the next day. Brice tried to kill me because he thought I would expose him, and when that failed he turned the gun on himself because he couldn't face the truth coming out about what he'd done—"

"What truth? You can only prove he was there; you don't know what he did," interrupted Sir Hubert.

"No, but Charles does. And he knew Charles would talk to save his skin once my letter proved he lied at the inquest about being on his own that night. Charles had stayed quiet up to then because he thought no one else knew what had happened, but he'd extracted a high price for his silence. He'd been blackmailing Brice for years; he was the one who drove him to suicide."

"How do you know this?"

"Why else would he have made him manager of the mine? Didn't that strike you as odd when Charles had no qualifications for such a position?" Adam asked. And the searching look that Sir Hubert darted up towards his daughter made him think that the subject of the ex-footman's rapid promotion had already been a topic of discussion between the two of them.

"Look, the point is Miriam's done nothing wrong," he went on forcefully when Sir Hubert didn't respond to his question. "There's no truth in any of these allegations that your daughter is making about her. And Brandon needs her: your great-grandson has just lost his father; please don't try and take away his mother too."

"Father—" Lady Scarsdale began, but Sir Hubert held up his hand for quiet. And there was no sound in the room except for the pendulum wall clock ticking above the mantelpiece as he continued to look up at Adam and Miriam over his hands, which he held steepled in front of his lower face. He occasionally stroked his chin with his thumbs but he was otherwise entirely still.

"Lady Miriam may be an excellent mother," he said eventually. "But that does not mean that she will be a good guardian for the child. She is a parson's daughter and has no experience of worldly matters."

"No, but I am learning," said Miriam, speaking for the first time.

She'd been grateful to Adam for standing up to Sir Hubert but she knew that she had to be the one to speak now. She would be admitting her own weakness if she remained silent.

"From whom?" asked Sir Hubert.

"Mr. Hardcastle. He managed the mine for Sir John."

"I know who he is."

"Yes. Well, he's back in charge again and I see him almost every day. And Mr. Cartwright has got the Hall running properly again. And then Adam is helping me too."

"Adam has no experience either," said Sir Hubert.

"He's clever and he has common sense—unlike Brice," said Miriam spiritedly. "And the mine's doing a whole lot better now that Charles isn't embezzling the profits. He's in prison awaiting trial at the next assizes and Constable Fletcher says he's sure to be convicted. And Mr. Hardcastle says the demand for coal is growing and he's started a new scheme allowing the miners to buy their houses on instalments. Sir John wouldn't agree to it but I think it's a good idea," she went on breathlessly. "And he even thinks there may be a new seam—"

"Father, this is ridiculous," interrupted her mother-in-law. "How long are you going to allow this farce to continue? It's obvious she doesn't know what she's talking about. How could she? She's been arranging flowers in the church all her life; she knows nothing about the mine."

"I know the miners," said Miriam, standing her ground. "I've been visiting their homes with my father since I was a girl. They're good men and hard workers if they're treated well."

Sir Hubert looked at Miriam and allowed himself a rare smile. She wasn't at all what he had expected. He liked her spirit, which surprised him after all the negative propaganda that had been poured into his ear by his daughter ever since Brice married her. And he shared Miriam's opinion of Brice's capabilities. The boy had always been a fool and a good-for-nothing and his daughter's judgement, which he usually admired, had always failed her when it came to her favourite son.

"What about you?" he asked, turning to Adam. "What is your interest in all this?"

"I want to make things right with Sir John, who took me in when I had nothing," said Adam, speaking slowly and thoughtfully, as if he was searching for the correct answer to the question as he spoke: he'd picked up on the value Sir Hubert put on straight talk. "I remember how passionate he was about the estate; he felt it was a sacred trust, so I want to try and help save it for his sake. And I also want to help Miriam because I abandoned her before when she needed me and I'm determined not to do that again. And, yes," he added hesitantly, "I suppose I want to make it up to Brice too because I pushed him over the edge and I regret doing that now. Brandon is his son and I'm sure he would have wanted him to have his inheritance."

Adam looked over at Lady Scarsdale and he could see surprise and pain and anger written across her face. But Sir Hubert took no notice of his daughter's distress.

"What is it you want from me?" he asked.

"A chance to show you that the mine and the estate can pay their way," said Adam. "We can't do that and fight a court case so we're asking you to suspend the litigation."

"And what about Brice's debts?" asked Sir Hubert. "What are you going to do about them?"

"I won't lie to you," said Adam, looking the old man in the eye. "In the long run I think the estate is going to need your help. Charles did a lot of damage. But we're proposing that for, say, the next six months it will pay the interest on the debts and Mr. Hardcastle will send you copies of the quarterly accounts so you can see for yourself whether you think there's a future worth investing in on Brandon's behalf."

Sir Hubert nodded briskly and got up from his chair, indicating that the interview was at an end. But then, quite unexpectedly, he came round his desk and went up to Miriam. "Thank you for coming to see me," he said, making her a short bow. "I understand that it can't have been easy. I will consider your proposal and you will hear back from me in the next few days."

He didn't wait for her to respond but instead went past her and opened the door, standing back to allow Adam and Miriam to pass through.

"No calls for the next fifteen minutes, Miss Preston," he said to the secretary.

The door closed and as they waited for the lift on the other side of the foyer Adam and Miriam could hear the muffled sound of Lady Scarsdale's angry voice coming through the mahogany.

Back in Scarsdale Sir Hubert's answer arrived sooner than they had expected. This time he wrote in person: a short letter agreeing to Miriam's proposal. And when Adam came to dinner that evening Cartwright brought up one of the last bottles of Sir John's vintage champagne from the cellar to celebrate, and at Miriam's insistence he was prevailed upon to drink a glass himself in honour of Brandon's great-grandfather.

Chapter Forty-Two

10–11 November 1919

Six months after their first visit Adam and Miriam returned to London to see Sir Hubert and take Adam's manuscript to the publisher's office in Museum Street. Perhaps because they thought it would bring them luck they stayed at the same hotel behind King's Cross and ate at the same restaurant and even drank the same wine as before. But this time they talked of the present and not the past, and Miriam told Adam about Rawdon and her father.

"He's been visiting him every weekend since the spring. Did you know that?" she asked.

"You've told me he went and so has he, but I didn't know it was that often," said Adam, looking surprised. He'd been to see Parson Vale several times himself but his visits had never coincided with Rawdon's and he'd been unable to face going more regularly as it grieved him terribly to see his old friend and mentor so changed and broken.

"Yes," said Miriam. "He never misses even when he has to work overtime in Gratton. And my father responds well to him. He recognizes Rawdon and he's calmer when he's there."

"Yes, I can understand that," said Adam. "Rawdon always had the coolest head of all of us when we were in the line. We used to laugh about how he could sleep through bombardments while we were trembling like bunny rabbits, but we were also helped by his example. It gave us courage."

Miriam laughed at the image and then looked away in confusion, feeling ashamed. "I'm sorry," she said. "I shouldn't laugh. It's not funny."

"No, of course it is," said Adam, smiling. "I'd never have survived the war without laughing. Or without Rawdon," he added. "Tell me about him and your father. I'm sorry I interrupted you."

Miriam nodded. "We were both there on Saturday and Rawdon told me he'd had this idea for . . ." She paused, looking for the right word. "For a funeral."

"A *funeral?*" Adam repeated, looking mystified. "I don't understand."

"Nor did I to begin with," said Miriam. "But he explained it to me and I agreed, so we got my father ready and took him out into the sanatorium garden, walking in a crazy kind of procession with Rawdon at the front carrying a spade and a canvas bag and then me and my father and two of the nurses at the back. I suppose they were there to see he wasn't going to dig up the roses, although he must have got permission from the authorities because he'd dug a hole in advance over by the fence. So we all stood around it in a circle while Rawdon squatted down beside the bag and took out my father's uniform and an old dirty surplice that came back with him from France and his Bible and the Book of Common Prayer he used out there too."

"I remember them," said Adam with a shudder. How could he forget the parson's surplice and the parson's books? The memory of those burials of the rotting dead under enemy gunfire in the dirty grey pre-dawn light still gave him nightmares which he was never going to tell Miriam about.

"Do you?" said Miriam. "So anyway, Rawdon held each of them up for my father to see and then he put them in the hole one by one. We stood there in silence for a moment before he filled the earth back in and then we went back inside. And I don't want to get my hopes up, Adam, but I think it made a difference." Miriam stopped, trying to control her emotions.

"What kind of difference?" he asked

"My father was talking about silly things like the tea we were drinking and the dress I was wearing. He's never really done that before. And then the doctor telephoned me yesterday to say he has seen an improvement too. He says that if it continues my father could start coming home for short visits. I know he's never going to be the person he was, but if he could enjoy life a little, it would mean so much to me . . ."

"I'm glad," said Adam. "Truly I am. I loved your father and I hated what happened to him. And Rawdon—do you know I think he's the best of us now? Which is strange when I think of how angry and bitter he was when I first came to Scarsdale all those years ago, trying to knock me down on the green before we'd even said hello! But we've all changed, those of us that survived—except Ernest maybe. He's a stoic, made of a different set of atoms to the rest of us. He's Hardcastle's assistant now but it hasn't gone to his head. He's just the same person as he was when he was working on the screens before the war." Adam smiled.

"What about us? Have we changed for the better or for the worse?" asked Miriam, leaning forward. Adam's willingness to talk about the war and its effects was new to her and gave her hope for the future.

"I'd say the jury's still out on me, considering their verdict," said Adam thoughtfully. "But you're definitely better than you were. Suffering has made you stronger and taught you to be your own person—I admire you for that. But there are others who are worse, much worse than before. Like your father, or Davy MacKenzie, who sits in the Miners' Institute all day drinking his way to oblivion. He used to make us laugh all the time in the trenches. He had a gift for comedy that was in his bones, but now it's gone: vanished without trace as if it was never there. I've tried to talk to him; tried to help, but there's nothing left. The war took it."

"I'm sorry," said Miriam, sensing Adam's sadness.

"I think it's because he ended up alone," said Adam sadly. "It started to happen to me too when I was a prisoner, but I thought of you and Rawdon and Ernest and that helped me survive. And now, since I came back among you, it's like I've come in out of the cold. Like one of Shackleton's men, I suppose. The numbness has gone and it feels for the first time as if we could live; as if—"

Adam stopped, looking at Miriam, and she knew intuitively

that he was thinking of their future and of whether they could be together again. It had remained a subject they never discussed, even more taboo than before since their last visit to London when Lady Scarsdale had accused them of carrying on together. It was as if they had to remain apart in order to remain innocent of the charge she had laid against them. But for how long? It was a question to which neither of them seemed to have an answer.

The interview with Sir Hubert was very different from their first encounter. The secretary, Miss Preston, didn't welcome them with open arms but nor did she object to Adam's presence. And on the other side of the mahogany door they were relieved to find there was no sign of Lady Scarsdale. Sir Hubert was as businesslike as before but there was no inquisition. This time he had made his decision already. He professed himself more than satisfied with Hardcastle's accounts and said he was prepared to take over Brice's debts and pay the death duties in return for a minority stake in the mine. Miriam agreed with alacrity but there was a sting in the tail.

"I should like to see the boy," said Sir Hubert. "Christmas is the best time for children so I am inviting you to spend it with me at Eaton Square."

He looked at Miriam, fixing her with a searching look until she reluctantly nodded her head.

"You're thinking about my daughter, aren't you?"

Again Miriam nodded. She couldn't trust herself to speak: she looked as if the earth had just opened up under her feet.

"Well, don't," said Sir Hubert, getting up from his chair. "I can assure you of a warm welcome."

"I can't do it," said Miriam as they went down in the lift. "She'll eat me alive."

"No, she won't. Sir Hubert's a man of his word," said Adam, smiling. "And I don't think there's anything you can't do if you put your mind to it. You're a match for anyone."

Out in the street Adam glanced at his watch.

"Do we have time?" asked Miriam.

"Yes, I told you we would. I telephoned the publisher's office and put back the appointment to twelve. We'll be fine as long as I don't lose the manuscript," said Adam, glancing down a little anxiously at the kit bag that hadn't been out of his sight since he left Scarsdale the previous morning.

They set off quickly, turning down Cockspur Street and past Admiralty Arch, heading towards the top of Whitehall. But there they could go no further. People thronged the pavements and the road too. In the distance, over the heads of the crowd, they could see the empty tomb on the top of the wood and plaster cenotaph that had been put up for the Peace Day Parade in July, and beyond that, high in the sky, the black-and-white face of Big Ben whose hands were fast approaching eleven o'clock. Flags hung down from all the buildings, fluttering at half-mast.

Somewhere out towards the river a maroon rocket fired and all around them everything and everyone came to a halt. The only sound suddenly was the noise of men taking off their hats until they were all bareheaded as the clock's quarter bells sounded out the chimes and seconds later the great bell struck the eleventh hour of the eleventh day of the eleventh month and the two-minute silence ordered by the King to commemorate the first anniversary of the signing of the Armistice began.

Here and there people were kneeling on the ground but most just stood with their heads bowed. The silence was complete and awful, filling the city. It was the language of the dead that the living were trying now to speak, reaching out across the great divide towards those whom they had lost.

Adam felt it like a noise rushing through his mind and within it, whispering at first but then louder, he heard the war: the whine of the shells flying overhead and the dull roar of the guns and, beyond them, almost out of range, the other sounds that he'd half forgotten: the larks singing in the morning as they soared up into the white clouds impervious to the carnage down below; the sad, sweet lilt of Harry's violin; the rich amused irony in Seaton's voice. It was real:

more real than the silent crowd all around him. The sun was on his face and he was back in the wood on that last day, holding Luke's hand, waiting to die.

But, just as before, he didn't die. The crowd sighed and the men replaced their hats and the traffic in Trafalgar Square behind them began to move again and he looked down and found he was holding Miriam's hand tightly in his own.

He looked at her and she smiled and, keeping her hand in his, he reached down to pick up the bag containing his manuscript. He didn't know how good it was, but it was a start: an attempt at least to fill the silence.

Acknowledgements

First and foremost I wish to thank my publishers: Nan Talese in the United States and David Brawn in the UK. I have been inspired by their belief in my writing, and they have both worked tirelessly to make *No Man's Land* as good as it can be.

My wife, Tracy Tolkien, has been a rock of support. On countless occasions she has helped me when I have become stuck both down the mine and on the battlefield!

John Garth was thorough and painstaking in his vetting of the manuscript. His Great War expertise has—I hope—kept me clear of technical mistakes.

Richenda Todd and Rachel Winterbottom helped me with editing the novel, and Daniel Meyer did an excellent job of overseeing all aspects of the American publication process.

I am grateful to my agent, Marly Rusoff, who has been a passionate advocate for *No Man's Land,* and I appreciate the work of Claire Ward and Michael Windsor, who designed the cover, and Michael Goldsmith, who has been in charge of the publicity campaign. Andy Phipps helped me with my website, and Lauren Weber promoted the book online.

Many people have encouraged me while I have been researching and writing this novel, but I would like to express particular thanks in this regard to my children, Nicholas and Anna; my aunt, Priscilla Tolkien; my father, Christopher Tolkien; and my friends Tom Johnson, Fiona Taylor, Robert Cutter, and Margaret Reason.

SIMON TOLKIEN
Santa Barbara, California
June 2016

A Note About the Author

Simon Tolkien is the author of *Orders from Berlin, The King of Diamonds, The Inheritance,* and *Final Witness.* The grandson of J. R. R. Tolkien, he was a successful criminal law barrister in London before moving to California with his wife and two children to take up writing full-time.